MW01202062

CORRUPTION

Rogue | Ruin | Rule

CD REISS

Corruption - CD Reiss

cdreiss.com

Cover Art designed by the author
Previously released as Complete Corruption

ROGUE

Foreword

The mafia. The mob. Cosa nostra. Camorra. 'Ndrangehta. Organized crime.

You'd think you could nail down a little consistency with organizations that are behind so much modern-crime folklore.

Alas, organized crime in 2014 bears no resemblance to versions from the '70s, '80s, or '90s. The illusion of constancy arises from the mythologies of the men of tradition running them, not from historical fact.

But tradition is not the same as uniformity. And the authorities think they know shit. They don't. Wikipedia is a joke. I've got books. Each tells a different story, and all the stories are true. The facts are not neat and tidy, and the anecdotes are often confused with universal truth.

So, let's do this instead.

Let's have some fun.

You've met my broken billionaire. My submissive musician. My shattered celebutante. My painful dichotomies. I've introduced you to my family traditions, my honorable pledges, my versions of ambition and art.

Let me introduce you to *my* mob.

This is my Neapolitan camorra. These are my rituals, my sold souls, my men of honor.

This is my Los Angeles.

Chapter One

Oh, Jonathan. I thought, keeping my eyes focused on the singer. She had a lovely voice that snuck up on you. It wasn't quite like a bird, but more like a dozen of them layered one on top of the other. The effect was hypnotic.

I glanced at my brother again. "Jonathan?"

"Yeah?"

"You just agreed that the Angels were superior to the Dodgers."

He looked away from her, and I sensed the air between them rip. I hadn't felt anything but annoyance with his lack of attentiveness until he looked at me again, and his entire face changed from voracious and single-minded to the usual bemused and arrogant.

"This season?"

"Are you even paying attention?" I asked.

"You were saying?"

"Daniel. I don't know if I should forgive him. I should. But—"

"Look, you have six sisters and me. All your sisters will tell you to forget your ex completely. I'm telling you to forgive him if you have to, but if you're going to, just do it and drop it."

He was in love with his ex-wife, who had left him for another man. Of course he'd be the most forgiving, and of course he was the one whose ear I chose to bend.

"Every time I look at him," I said, turning back to the singer. "I can't stop seeing him having sex with that girl."

"Don't look at him."

I folded my hands on the table. I shouldn't see my ex. Ever. But he'd called, and I had lunch with him, like a damned fool. He'd said it was business, and in a way, it was. We had a mortgage together, and bills, and I knew the intimacies of his campaign for mayor about as well as I'd known the intimacies of his body. But with so much dead weight between us, I had trouble eating. In the end, of course, he'd asked for me back, and I'd held back tears and declined.

"He keeps asking to see me," I said.

"He's stringing you along." Jonathan tipped his drink to his lips and watched the woman standing by the piano like a hawk observing a mouse. "I thought I had it bad."

I felt a sudden ball of tension wrap up in my chest. I couldn't exactly place it, but it irritated me. "Do you know her? The singer."

"We have a thing later tonight."

"Good, because I was going to say you might want to introduce yourself before you slobber on her. Maybe dinner and a show."

He smiled a big, wide Jonathan grin. After his wife left, he'd turned into a womanizing prick, but he rarely let us see that side of him. He was always a gentleman, until I saw him look at that singer. It made me uncomfortable. Not because he was my brother, which should have been enough, but because of an uneasy, empty feeling I chased away.

"Go to Tahoe or something for a few weeks," he said. "Slap some skis on. You're giving yourself an ulcer."

The musicians stopped, and people clapped. She *was* good. My brother just applauded with his eyes and tipped his glass to her. When she saw him, her jaw tightened with anger. Apparently, he knew her well enough to piss her off.

He leaned over and whispered in my ear, "I know damn well how not fine you are."

I looked him square in the eyes, and I knew his hurt matched mine. He healed himself by seducing whoever he fancied. I didn't think the same strategy would work for me. I didn't fancy much of anyone.

The singer made a beeline for our table.

"Hi, Jonathan," she said, a big, fake smile draped across her face.

"Monica," he said. "This is Theresa."

"That was beautiful," I said.

"Thanks."

"You were incredible," Jonathan said. "I've never heard anything like that."

"I've never heard of a man trying to sandwich another woman between fingering me and fucking me in the same day."

I almost spit out my Cosmo. Jonathan laughed. I felt sorry for the girl. She looked as if she was going to cry. I hated my brother just then. Hated him with a dogged vehemence because he being careless with her feelings—yet he still looked at her as if he wanted to eat her alive. And he would. He would have her and a dozen others. She wouldn't even know what was happening.

"I'm going to the ladies'." I slid out of the booth and down the hall. I didn't look back, sure I'd see blood and pretty black feathers as my brother destroyed that poor girl.

I leaned against the back of the stall, staring at the single strip of toilet paper dangling off the roll. I had a few squares in my bag, just in case my brother brought me to yet another dump, but I didn't want to use them. I wanted to dig into that feeling of emptiness and find the bottom of it.

Daniel looked at me with pride, as if he'd found the most suitable partner for who he wanted to be. He was as pleased as a king opening a pie and finding the miracle of four-and-twenty blackbirds.

He'd never looked at me the way Jonathan looked at that singer. Never. I was Tink, short for Tinkerbell, because of my curvy, petite frame. A sprightly, delicate fairy. Not someone you looked at hungrily. That was why Daniel had sex with his speechwriter. He didn't respect her. He wasn't charmed by her nor did he find her to be a proper match.

He fucked her.

I saw the singer in the hall, looking distant and resolute at the same time, as if she was convincing herself of something. She stopped short when she saw me.

"I'm so sorry," she said. "I was rude and unbecoming."

I was going to deny it, but I was struck by a distraction that cut me to the core. I smelled pine trees, deep in the forest, damp in the morning after a night of campfires and singing. The burning char and dew mingled in the song-like trails of cigarette smoke, rising and disappearing. And then it was gone.

"My brother's an asshole, so I don't blame you." I regretted that almost immediately. I didn't talk like that, especially not about family. I took her hand and squeezed it. "We both loved your voice."

"Thank you. I have to go. I'll try to see you on the way out." She slipped her hand away and walked toward the dressing room.

I caught the scent again and looked for its source. It could have come from anyone. It could have been the gorgeous black lady with the sweet smile. It could have been the plate of saucy meat that crossed my path. Could have been the waft of parking lot that came through the door before it snapped closed.

But it wasn't.

The man in the dark suit and thin pink tie, the full lips and two-day beard. His eyes were black as a felony, and they stayed on me as his body swung into the booth.

The smell had come from him, not the man sitting with him. It was in his gaze, which was locked on me, disarming me. He was beautiful to me. Not my type, not at all. But the slight cleft in his chin, the powerful jaw, the swoop of dark hair falling over his forehead seemed right. Just *right*. I swallowed. My mouth had started watering, and my throat had gotten dry.

He turned to say something to the hostess, and I took a gulp of air. I'd forgotten to breathe. I put my hands to my shirt buttons to make sure they were fastened, because I felt as if he'd undressed me.

I had two ways to return to Jonathan: behind the piano, which was the crowded, shorter way, or in front, right past the man in the pink tie.

I wanted him to look at me but he spent the entire length of our proximity talking earnestly to the baby-faced, bow-lipped man next to him. As I passed I caught the burned, dewy pine scent that made no sense and kept walking.

I felt a tug on my wrist, a warm sensation that tingled. His hand was on me, gentle but resolved. I stopped, looking at him as his hand brought me to his face. He drew me down until he was whisper close. A sudden rush of potential went from the back of my neck to the space between my legs, waking me where I thought I'd died.

I couldn't breathe.

I couldn't speak.

If he kissed me, I would have opened my mouth for him. That, I knew for sure.

"Your shoe," he said with an accent I couldn't place.

"What?" I couldn't stop looking at his eyes: brown, wide, with longer eyelashes than should be legal, hooded under arched brows proportioned for expression.

Was I wearing shoes? Was I standing? Did I need to take in air? Eat? Or could I just live off the energy between us?

He pointed at my heel.

"You brought yourself a souvenir from the ladies' room."

He was beautiful, even as he smirked with those full lips. Did I have to turn away to see what he was talking about? It was that or put my tongue down his throat.

I looked down.

I had a trail of toilet paper on my stiletto.

"Thank you," I said.

"My pleasure." He let go of my hand.

The space where he'd touched felt like a missed opportunity, and I went to the bathroom to return my souvenir.

Chapter Two

I walked under a viaduct downtown at six a.m. The food truck was set up, and the gaffers and grips were just arriving. In an hour it would look more like a movie set than an empty parking lot.

My roommate, Katerina, was already at the coffee station. She'd left at an hour before the first crack of dawn. This movie was her last chance. She'd sued the the studio that had funded her Oscar-nominated movie for profits she was entitled to share; they insisted the production operated at a loss. Fancy, indefensible, and legal accounting proved them right, leaving her bank account empty and her production underfinanced.

Now her name was proverbial mud, but she put this thing together with spit and chewing gum.

Her script supervisor, the person responsible for the continuity of the shots, had two other jobs and couldn't work nights or weekends. Katrina's long pitch about my attention to detail, my love of consistency and order, and my eagle eye for continuity led to her begging for me to step in for those hours.

On set, we hovered over the coffee and fruit. It was still dark, the ambient hiss of the freeway above as low as it would ever be.

"Let's face it, Tee Dray," she said, pointing the straw of her coffee at me, "it's not like I have enough money to pay union for weekend calls." She wore a baseball cap over a tight black pixie cut that only she could pull off. A Vietnamese Mexican with an athletic build, she carried herself as if she owned the joint. Every joint. When we were at Carlton Prep together, she was a dominant outcast and the most interesting person at school.

"You're paying me on the back end," I said.

"Sure," she said with a smile. "But I keep the books."

"You know I'd fund the whole thing," I said. The project was financed through a tiny holding in Qatar that was happy to have Katerina Ip write, direct, and produce—but the budget was tight.

"Would you, now?"

"I haven't made a dent in my trust fund."

"I'd feel obligated to fuck you."

"I think I'm getting to the point I'd take you up on it."

"You need a man," she said. "A rebound cock to fuck the sad right out of you."

"Nice way to talk."

"The truth isn't always nice. Let me set you up with my brother, and you can set me up with yours."

"You don't have a brother."

"Can't blame a girl for trying. What about Michael?" She raised an eyebrow, tilting her head to the man getting into his trailer. The lead actor in the production had made it clear he was interested in me and a couple of other attractive women on set. He was a man whore, but a nice one.

"I'm not ready," I said.

"I know, sweetheart. It'll come back. Some time."

I pressed my lips together, and though the sun was just peeking over the skyline, it was light enough for her to see the prickly heat brush my cheeks.

"Theresa," she said, head tilted. "What just happened to your face?"

"Nothing. Call is in four minutes.

"Exactly. I'm not going to have time to talk. So tell me now. And fast."

It was a miracle we'd even had time to talk already. Directing a movie was like having a wedding every day for four months. You threw the party but couldn't enjoy it.

"I went out with Jonathan last night, and there was a guy. A man. I had toilet paper on my shoe and—"

"You? Miss Perfect?"

"Yes. I was so embarrassed." I lowered my voice to a near whisper. "He was breathtaking."

She leaned on one hip. "Los Angeles is wall-to-wall breathtaking."

"He was different. When he touched me—"

"He touched you?"

"Just my wrist. But it was like sex. I swear I've never felt anything like that."

"You tell me this *now*?"

Edgar, her assistant got within earshot, and I dropped my eyes. Even thinking about that man in range of a stranger made me feel vulnerable.

"Kat," Edgar spoke fast, "the LAPD—"

"Can wait five minutes," Katerina shot back, pulling me behind a trailer. The hum of the generator almost drowned her out.

"You should work," I said. "I'm fine. Nothing happened."

"You cried on my lap for hours over Danny Dickhead. Now you have a hundred-twenty seconds to tell me about this new one."

"There's nothing to tell."

"I will cut you." She didn't mean it, of course. Even coming from the wrong side of Pico Boulevard, her threats were all affect.

"Brown eyes. Black hair."

"You must be off blonds since Dickerino Boy."

"Six feet. Built. My god, his hands. They weren't narrow or soft. They were wide, and strong and... I'm not making any sense. But when he looked at me, my skin went hot. All I could think about was… you know."

"You got a number?"

"Not even a name."

Her phone dinged, and three people approached at once. Her day had begun. She turned away but called over her shoulder.

"You look like you just got woken up."

She was right.

Chapter Three

Daniel and I had bought a loft in an old corset and girdle factory that had been abandoned in the sixties, used as a warehouse by a stonecutter and cabinet maker, then expanded and converted into luxury lofts just before the Great Recession. The units had gone at fire sale prices, which didn't matter to me—I was from a wealthy family—but it was a dealmaker for Daniel.

Now he was gone and I was stuck with it. He'd moved to Mar Vista after I kicked him out, and I commuted across town to Beverly Hills to run client accounting at WDE—the biggest agency in Hollywood, attracting the world's best actors, directors, writers and swaggering, toxic assholes.

"Hey, Fly Girl." Gene stood over my desk. "Rolf Wente's business manager needs you to follow up with Warner's."

I tapped my phone log. "We have calls out to them."

"You look tired. How was the weekend? Do the whole party thing?"

If I didn't answer, and if I wasn't specific, he'd spend fifteen minutes telling me about his party habits. "Went to this little dump the other night. Frontage. You been?"

"Yeah. Of course."

"My brother and I saw this lounge act. The singer was terrific. Faulkner. Something Faulkner. Like the writer."

"Never heard of her," he said.

"Nice voice. Original."

"Whyncha send me the deets? Maybe we'll get out there on the WDE dime. Bring the assistants. Make them feel loved."

"Okay." I turned back to my work, hoping he'd leave.

"And get on Warner's, okay? We lose old Rolf, and we're up the ass on the bone dry freeway. Let me know about the singer by the end of day."

I didn't realize that by suggesting a musician, I was obligated to ride the company dime to yet another show at Frontage. I was exhausted even thinking about it, until I remembered the man with the pink tie.

What if he was there again?

After checking the schedule at Frontage, I grabbed my phone and went outside.

"Deirdre?" I said when I heard her pick up. "You there?"

"What time is it?"

"Ten. What are you doing next Thursday night?"

Sheets rustled. "I have to be at the shelter late."

"Wanna go out?"

"I can't do anything fancy, Tee. It makes me sick." My sister Deirdre despised the consumptions of the rich. She lived in a studio the size of a postage stamp and put every penny of her trust fund interest toward feeding the hungry. It was noble to the point of self-destruction.

"It's not fancy. Kind of dumpy. I don't want to go with just work people. They all look at me like they're sorry for me about Daniel. I hate it."

"I'm not a good buffer."

"You're perfect. You keep me on my toes."

She sighed. "All right. You're buying, though. I'm broke."

"No problem."

We hung up. Deirdre would give me a reason to escape the WDE crowd, especially if the breathtaking man was there.

Chapter Four

"How many have you had?" I asked Deirdre as she nearly fell forward over the Frontage bar.

"My second." She took her hand off her mop of curly red hair to hold up two fingers. All eight of us shared the red hair, but only she had the curls. "Not that it matters."

"It matters," I said.

"No." Deirdre put down her glass. "It doesn't. Do you know what matters?"

"Let me guess. The poor and hungry?"

Deirdre huffed. I'd caught her before she could make her speech. She hated that. "You've got more money than the Vatican. You're cute as a button and you think you have problems."

"Looks and money aren't the whole of a person."

"Don't pretend they don't matter. They do. If you saw what I saw every day."

My sister was sweet and compassionate, but she was a belligerent drunk. If I let her, she'd tell me my sadness came from material idolatry and that it was time for me to give all my money to charity and live in service to the poor. I'd often considered the possibility that she was right.

The lights dimmed and we applauded. The singer—Monica Falkner—appeared by the piano for "Stormy Weather" as if she wanted to rip the clouds from the sky but couldn't reach high enough. A nobody singer in a town of somebodies, stood in front of the piano crooning other people's songs in a room built for other purposes. She moved from "Stormy Weather" to something more plaintive. My God, she was fully committed to every word, every note.

There was no halfway with that woman. She had control over me. She sang in the tempo of keys clacking and printers humming. There was an open place inside me, past where the professionalism cracked and the weariness fissured and the sadness throbbed. She caressed that place then jabbed it.

I missed Daniel. I missed the hardness of his body and the touch of his hands. I missed his laughter, and the way he cupped my breast in his sleep, and the weight of his arm on my shoulder, and the way he brushed his light brown hair off his face. I missed calling him to tell him where I was. I was an independent woman. I could function fine without him or anyone. But I missed him, and I missed being loved. Once he'd cheated on me, all my delight in his love drowned in bitterness. I was wistful for something dead.

"You all right?" Gene asked. He'd left the table to come talk to me at the bar. He was my "type": dark blonde, straight-laced, ambitious, easy smile, confident. But he was awful. Just the most awful Hollywood douchebag.

"Yeah, thanks."

"She's good. The singer. "

"Great." I felt an absence to my right, where Deirdre had been standing.

"I think we could do something with her. Little spit and polish, shorter skirt. Use the body. Sammy's got Geraldine Stark under contract. She's trying to move into fashion. Could be a tight package." He winked as if I might miss his double entendre.

"I hope it works out," I said. "I'm off to the ladies'."

"See you back at the table." He picked up his glass. "Don't be a stranger."

Deirdre wasn't in the bathroom. I ended up looking at the same roll of toilet paper from two weeks ago. Still one square hanging. A different roll, obviously, but the same amount. Not enough.

Just not enough.

The hall outside the bathroom led outside, where a little seating area with ashtrays was blocked off from the parking lot. I heard yelling and repeated calls of "bitch." Though I normally avoided disagreeable behavior, I went to look.

A red Porsche Boxster was parked in the handicapped spot, and on the hood, all five-eleven, hundred-and-fifty pounds of her, Deirdre sprawled on her back. The man yelling was six inches shorter and twenty pounds lighter—if I didn't count the weight of the petroleum in his hair products. He wore head-to-toe leather and had a voice like a car screeching to a halt.

"Get. Off. The. Porsche." He pushed her as he yelled, but she was dead weight.

"Excuse me," I said.

He may have heard me. I had no time to think about that; the rest happened so fast. He pulled at Deirdre's lapels, yanking her forward. Like a baby with a bellyful of milk, she projectile vomited. It splashed on his jacket, the ground, and the car. He squealed and let her go. She rolled off the hood, puking as she went, and landed on the ground.

"Fuck!" he yelled as I tried to sit my sister up against the wheel. "Shit. God. Puke? Puke is acid! Do you know what that's going to do to the paint? And my fucking jacket?"

"We'll pay for the damage."

I was too busy with Deirdre to bother looking at the creep. She was unconscious. I squeezed her cheeks and looked into her mouth to see if she was choking. She wasn't, because she threw up right down my shirt. I leaned back and said something like *ugh,* but it was drowned out by the man in leather.

"This is a custom paint job. Fuck! Bitch, the *whole car's* gotta be redone. And I got a thing tomorrow."

"Sorry," I mumbled, tapping Deirdre's cheek.

If he hadn't been blinded by his rage and stupidity, Leather Guy probably wouldn't have done what he did in front of me. Holding his arms so they didn't touch the puke on his chest, he came around the car and kicked Deirdre in the hip.

"Hey!" was all I got to say.

I didn't even have a chance to stand and challenge him before he fell back as if an airplane door had opened mid-flight. Then I heard a bang. I looked back at Deirdre, because in my panic, I thought she'd fallen or gotten hit by a car.

A voice, gentle yet sharp, said, "Does she drink like this often?" A blue-eyed man with a young face and bow lips crouched beside me. He didn't look at me but at Deirdre. "I think she's got alcohol poisoning."

Another bang. I jumped. A splash of vomit landed on my cheek, and I looked up at the hood of the car. Leather's cheek was pressed against the hood of the Porsche.

"Spin," Bow Lips said, "take it easy, would you?"

Above him, with his arm pinning down Leather's face, was the breathtaking man, with those eyelashes and his jaw twisted so tight the muscles popped.

"Tell this lady you're sorry." He pushed Leather's cheek into the puke. "*Adesso, stronzo.*"

"He should apologize to my sister," I said. "Not me."

"Fuck you!" The douchebag wiggled. He got thumped against the hood for his trouble. "I ain't saying shit."

Spin pulled Leather up by his collar and slammed his face on the hood with a sickening thump.

"I'll call 9-1-1," said Bow Lips.

"But I—" *I thought you were this guy's friend.* I stopped myself, realizing he was going to call about Deirdre, not his breathtaking friend or the creep getting his face slammed against a car.

"Say." *Slam.* "You're." *Slam.* "Sorry," the guy called Spin said through his teeth.

Leather's face slid to the edge of the hood, wiping puke until, from my crouching position I could see the blood and paint-shredding stomach acid mixing on his cheeks.

He was a douchebag and he'd kicked my sister, but I felt bad for him. "It's okay, really, I—"

"Yeah, we have an emergency." Bow Lips, into the phone completely unflustered. "Alcohol poisoning."

Bang.

"I'm sorry!" he cried.

"Do you believe him, *Contessa*?" Beautiful. Even beating the hell out of some guy on the hood of a Porsche, his lips were pure sex. "Do you think he's sorry?"

It took a moment for me to realize he was speaking to me, one eyebrow arched like a parabola, his face closed with resolve, impassioned with purpose, yet calm, as if he was so good at what he did he didn't need to break a sweat.

"Yes," I said, "I believe him."

"I believe he regrets it," he said. "But I don't believe he's remorseful." He leaned toward me on the owner of the Porsche, who was crying through a bloody nose. "What do you think?"

I don't know what came over me. The need to be truthful turned me and that gorgeous man into cohorts. It was intimate in a safe way, and the creep in leather needed to suffer.

"No, I don't think he is remorseful."

His smirk lit up the night. I feared a full-on smile might put me over the edge.

"Show her you mean it," he said in Leather's ear but looked at me. "Get the puke off this ugly fucking car." He wouldn't let the guy move. "Get it off."

"Female," Bow Lips said, all business. "Mid thirties. Built like a brick shithouse."

"Lick that shit up, or you're kissing the hood again."

Leather choked and sobbed, blood pouring from his nose. I stood up and looked at the guy who had kicked my sister. I felt something pouring off the two men locked together on the car. Heat. Energy. Something that crawled under my skin and made it tingle. And when the creep stuck his tongue out and licked the vomit off the hood, the tingle turned to a release from anxiety I hadn't realized I carried.

"That's right," Spin said. "You believe him now, Contessa?"

"Yes."

Spin yanked the man up, and I knew from the look on his face that he was going to make the guy kiss the hood again. The distance and force applied would not just break, but smash bones.

I stood. "I think you've made your point."

Spin's face, so implacable, breached into something gentler, more open, as if an understanding reached not his intelligence, but his adrenal glands.

He smiled. "I thought you'd enjoy a big ending."

"My sister will be bruised. His face is cracked open. Justice is served."

"*Come volevi tu,*" he said, yanking Leather Jacket back again. "Keys." He held out his hand as the man cried, tears streaking the mass of blood.

"No, man, don't take my car."

"This car?" He pulled the keys out of Leather's pocket and hit a button. The doors unlocked and the lights flashed. "You're taking this low-class piece-of-shit entry-level tin can out of my sight."

He opened the door and pushed the man in, throwing the keys in after him before slamming the door shut. In a few seconds, the car started and screeched away.

"Ambulance coming," Bow Lips said from behind me, his voice strained.

He had stood Deirdre up and was about to fall under her dead weight. His friend intervened and helped carry her to the smokers' benches. From inside, I heard clapping. The singer was done. People would come out for their cigarettes soon. The breathtaking man pulled the sleeves of his jacket straight and touched his tie. It was blue.

"You okay?" I asked.

"Yes. You?" He took a pack of cigarettes from his pocket and offered me one.

I refused with a tilt of my head and glanced at Deirdre, who leaned against Bow Lips. He'd need to be rescued.

"I'm fine. Covered in throw up, but fine," I said.

"You didn't get upset, seeing that. I'm impressed." He poked out a smoke and bit the end, sliding it out of its sardine-tight box while absently fingering a silver lighter.

"Oh, I'm upset."

He smiled as he lit up, looking at me over the flame. He snapped the lighter shut with a loud click, taking his time. I had a second to run and sit next to my sister—take a step back. But I didn't.

"You don't look upset," he said. "You're flushed. Your heart is racing. I can see it." He stepped forward. "Your breath, you're trying to control it. But it's not working. If I saw you like this in a different time or place, I'd think you were ready to fuck."

Just watching me, he let the smoke rise in a white miasma. My lungs took in more air than they ever had in such a short period of time. Foul language usually put the taste of tar and bile on my tongue, but from him, it sent a line of heat from my knees to my lower back.

"I don't like that kind of talk." It was out of my mouth before I realized I didn't mean it.

"Maybe." He reached into his pocket and pulled out a white business card. "Maybe not."

I took the card. Antonio Spinelli, Esq., A number in 213. I glanced up to ask him what kind of lawyer made douchebags lick puke off a car, but he was already walking toward a black Maserati. Bow Lips gently leaned Deirdre against me.

"You got her?"

"I got her," I said, keeping my sister erect. "Thank you."

"Take care of her." He indicated that I should sit next to Deirdre before one of the many smokers exiting the club did. "She's dangerous."

I smiled at him and watched as he got in the passenger side and they drove away. I sat next to my sister and waited for the ambulance.

Chapter Five

I put the card in my pocket and rode in the ambulance with Deirdre. My sister was chronically depressed, and she medicated with alcohol. We all knew the drill. She got wheeled in. People shouted. They took her vitals. A nurse gave me scrubs so I could get out of my puke-covered clothes. The V-neck top had wide sleeves and teddy bears in a cloudy sky. My dressy heels were absurd with the pink pants that were four sizes too big.

They gave Deirdre B vitamins, and once they'd determined that she hadn't done any damage to her brain she couldn't afford, they left me in the room with her. My stink-soaked clothes were in a plastic bag under my chair. Before, I'd call Daniel. But my new roommate and I had agreed that she'd be the person I checked in with, since checking in was what I missed most.

—I'm at the hospital with my sister.
Everything ok. Won't be home.—

THE TEXT CAME IMMEDIATELY.

—Breaking down the set in three hours.
Need me to come?—

—Sure. Sequoia—

MY JACKET WAS CRUMPLED in the plastic bag. I'd moved the lawyer's card to the pocket of the scrubs for reasons I couldn't articulate. It weighed forty pounds in my pocket. It had gotten warmer when the paramedics asked for my sister's stats, her insurance, her age, how many drinks she'd had. It vibrated and buzzed as I waited for her to regain consciousness.

—Ok. Which sister?—

—Deirdre. She's been in sri lanka. You never met her.—

—Boozy left-wing freedom fighter?—

—LOL yes—

I went out to the ER waiting room. Sequoia was a nice hospital, but the next few hours were going on the "really bad times not interesting enough to even talk about" list. The waiting room was active late at night, but slower, as if the horrors of Los Angeles took a break for a few hours. Babies fussed, and the TVs screamed joyful network news. I went to the vending machine and stared at the library of packages, unable to decide what I didn't want the least.

A kid of about seven jostled me out of the way and jammed a dollar into the slot, punched buttons as if it was his job, and stood in front of me while the machine hummed. But nothing happened. No goodie was forthcoming.

I ran through the next day in my head. Katrina would have to drive me back to Frontage. I'd get my car, make it home, and—

There was a loud bang, as if a bullet had hit fiberglass, and I jumped, not realizing I'd spaced out. Antonio Spinelli, still in his black suit, touched the machine and, finding the spot he needed, banged again. Two bags of chips fell, and the kid jumped at them. The lawyer smirked at me and shrugged. He was more gorgeous in the dead, flat fluorescents than he'd been in the dark parking lot.

"You want something?" he asked.

He kept his eyes on my face, but I felt self-conscious about my scrub-clad body and dress shoes. "What are you doing here?" I sounded small and insignificant, probably because I was trying to speak while holding my breath.

He shrugged. "Getting you a late dinner." He indicated the array inside the machine like a tall blonde turning letters. "Cheese chips? Ring Pop?"

I felt alone on a Serengeti plain with a cheetah circling. "You waited for me all this time?"

"I noticed you might need a ride home, so I followed the ambulance."

"A lawyer. Chasing an ambulance."

He smirked, and I wasn't sure if he got the joke or if it was outside of his cultural matrix. "What kind of gentleman would I be?"

"Again. What are you doing here?" My mouth tasted as if a piece of week-old roast beef had been folded into it. I was wearing scrubs that wouldn't have fit even if they were the right size, and my spiked heels felt like torture devices. My head hurt, my sister was in the hospital for alcohol poisoning, and a beautiful god of a man wanted to share a Ring Pop with me.

Antonio took out a bill and fed the machine. "I think I made a bad impression in the parking lot." He punched more buttons than any one item required.

"Your intentions were good. Thank you for that."

"My methods, however?"

Things dropped into the opening. Chips, candy, crackers, cookies, *plop, plop, plop, plop*. He must have put a twenty in there.

"I'm trying not to think too hard about it."

"You were very composed." He crouched to retrieve his pile of packages. "I've never met a woman like that."

"Except for looking aroused?" I crossed my arms, feeling exposed.

"That, I've met." He handed me an apple, the one piece of real food available in the hospital vending machine. He looked at me in a way I didn't like. Not one bit.

Except I did like it. I took the apple. I became too aware of the teddy bears on my shirt and my hair falling all over the place. My lips were chapped, and my eyes were heavy from too many hours awake. Maybe that was for the best. Looking early-morning fresh would have made his gaze seem sexual rather than intense.

He stepped back next to an uncomfortable-looking plastic chair, indicating I should sit. Holding my apple to my chest, I sat. He dumped our meal into the seat next to me and sat on the other side of it.

"How's your sister?" he asked.

I sighed. "She'll be fine. I mean, she won't, because she'll do it again. But she'll be up and running by afternoon."

He looked pensive, plucking a bag of nuts from the chair and putting it back. "It's impossible to change what you are. You drink like that when you fight yourself."

"How did you get so educated on the matter?"

"I had an uncle."

He opened a granola bar, and I watched his finger slipping into the fold of cellophane, exerting enough pressure to weaken and split the bond between the layers. It took exactly no effort. A child could do it. But the grace of that simple thing was exquisite. I pressed my legs together because I kept imagining those hands flat on the insides of my thighs.

"It was my job to collect him in the mornings," he continued. "He supported my mother, so he had to go make money. Every morning, I had to look for him. I found him in the street, in the piazza, wherever. Passed out with wine all over his shirt. I splashed water on his face and sent him to work at the dock. I mean, he called me a *stronzo* first, but I got the job done."

His story opened doors and corridors to further questions. The possibility of spending hours in that waiting room with him was a little too appealing. I'd seen what he'd done to the man who'd kicked my sister, and I had the feeling he wasn't a normal lawyer. Something was up, and finding out was akin to stroking a snake to feel the click of the scales.

"What are you doing here?" I asked. "In Los Angeles?"

He shrugged. "The California bar is easy. And the weather's nice."

"My name is Theresa."

"I know." He smiled at my shocked expression, looking about as concerned as a cat on a windowsill. "I used to see you on TV during Daniel Brower's campaign for mayor. Part of it, at least. I think he might win."

I must have turned purple, though my face didn't shift and my shoulders stayed straight.

He cast his eyes down as if he'd said too much. "It's not my business, of course."

"It's Los Angeles's business, apparently, that my fiancé was having sex with his speechwriter. Any details in the paper you missed and want me to fill in?" I was having a complete emotional shut down. Not even his full lips or the arch of his eyebrows could pierce my veil of defensiveness. "That's why you were watching me at Frontage that first night. Trying to put the face with the story."

"No."

"I'm not interested in your pity, or in you proving yourself, or anything for that matter." I stood. I'd talked myself into a deep enough hole, and the shame of the entire incident swelled inside me. "Thanks for dinner."

I spun on my heel and walked to the nearest door that led outside. I should have headed back to Deirdre. I should have gone to the ladies' room. I should have gone to the desk. But outside looked so appealingly anonymous, as if I could walk into the darkness and disappear. Once I got there though, I had nowhere to go, and the cars speeding down LaCienega didn't slow enough for me to cross. In any case, I couldn't go far. Deirdre needed me.

I walked down the block as if I had a destination. I'd been foolish. I'd wanted him, spine to core, but he knew who I was. I couldn't run away from what had happened with Daniel. Everyone knew, and any relationship I had would be painted with the brush of my humiliation. I felt that beautiful hand on my elbow, and part of my body continued forward despite his best effort.

"Wait," he said, "you never let me finish."

"I don't want you to," I said, letting him hold my elbow while I caught my balance.

"I was watching you because yes, I wanted to place the face." I started to object, but he put his fingers to my lips and said, "And when I did, I was... how do you say?" He squinted as if trying to squeeze the word out of his brain. "Awestruck." I pulled away and he let go of me. "Don't go. It's not what you think. Yes, I saw you on TV with Brower. You always stood so straight, even when they attacked you. Reporters, the other side, even your own people. And you never cracked. Then tonight, you stand up and tell me to stop hurting that man, like it's your right under God to do it. You could run the world. Do you realize?"

I said nothing. I hated that he had observed my shame with Daniel so closely in such one-sided intimacy.

"Let me take you out," he said. "My attention isn't going to hurt you."

"Look, I'm sorry. You're nice enough. And I have to be honest, you're handsome. Very handsome." I couldn't look at him when I said that. "But I'm a curiosity to you. To me, it's still very real." I folded my arms so he had to release my elbow. A bus blew by us with a shattering roar, sending a warm breeze through our hair. "I'm just not ready."

"Let me take you out anyway."

"Tee Dray!"

I spun around. Katrina jogged toward me from the parking lot, carrying a huge satchel and wearing Uggs with her leggings. She was early, and not a minute too soon.

"I'm sorry," I said, backing away toward Katrina. "I can't." I felt her at my back, panting.

"Hi," she said.

I turned around and realized she wasn't saying hello to me. "Katrina, this is Antonio."

"*Ciao*," he said with a nod before he directed his gaze back at me. "You have my card, Contessa."

"I do."

"*Ciao* then." He smiled, nodded, and walked toward the parking lot entrance.

Katrina spun around to watch him as he turned and waved. "Holy fucking hot fire."

"Yes. Holy hot fire."

"That's not the same guy, is it?" she asked.

"It is."

"Is he an actor? I could use him. Fuck, I could write feature films about the way he walks."

"Lawyer. Italian. Which is nice if you're into that sort of thing. You're early, by the way."

"We actually got shit done." We started back toward the hospital. "Michael was a bruiser. He asked about you," she said.

"Not interested."

"How's your sister?"

"Should be awake by now. Can you wait for me?"

"An hour. Then you drive yourself home," she said as if she meant it. She put her arm around my shoulder and walked me in.

Chapter Six

"They'll send a priest if you want to see one," I said, sitting by Deirdre's bed.

"I don't need counseling." My sister looked flush and healthy and energetic, despite being waist-deep in sheets. Nothing like a mainline of B vitamins to bring a woman to the peak of health.

"They can't release you without it. And I'm sorry, but I agree with the policy. You could have died."

"I'm a grown woman." She threw off her sheets, exposing a blue hospital gown that matched my scrubs.

I put my hand on her shoulder. "Dee, please. I've got your vomit all over my clothes. We can get Dr. Weinstein back if you want."

She tucked one curly red lock behind her ear, where it would stay for three seconds before bouncing in front of her eyes again. "I want to go to work."

"You need a break from that job. It's turning you into a grouch."

"I can't do anything else," she said. "I don't know how."

One of the downsides of being incredibly wealthy was the ease with which one could go through life without marketable skills. The only ability she'd developed was compassion for people who didn't have what she had and contempt for those who did. Self-loathing went deep, a trademark Drazen trait.

"There's a trade school around the corner," I said. "You could learn to fix cars."

"You think Daddy would buy me a shop in Beverly Hills?"

"Anything to get you out of social work. Heck, I'd buy you a shop."

She put her face in her hands. "I want to do God's work."

I held her wrists. "God didn't build you to see what you see every day. You're too sensitive."

She took her hands away from her face. "Can you go to that thing with Jon tonight? At the museum? I don't think I can take it."

Jonathan was only seen in public with his sisters in the hope of drawing back his ex-wife.

"If you give the counselor one hundred percent, I'll go."

She leaned back in the bed. "Fine."

"Thank you."

"You smell like a puke factory."

I kissed her head and put my arms around my crazy, delicate sister.

Chapter Seven

Katrina was in the waiting room, sleeping on her binder and drooling on the breakdown script for the next day.

I sat by her head and put my hand on her shoulder. I felt guilty for calling her while she was in production, and I felt lonely for needing her so badly. "Come on, Directrix. I'm driving."

"Five minutes, Mom," she whispered.

By the time Katrina dropped me at Frontage, my little BMW was the only car in the lot, and condensation left a polka dot pattern on my windshield. It was a 1967 GT Cabrio with chrome detailing that wasn't happy about water drying on it. I shouldn't have bought it. The car was a death trap. But Daniel had gone to the automotive museum's auction to show his face, and I'd walked out with what he called LBT, the Little Blue Tink. He'd been annoyed, but I'd fallen in love.

I wasn't ready to end the night. Though the rising sun would end it for me, I wasn't ready to process it. It was almost six in the morning, and my brother never slept, so I called him.

"Hey, Jon," I said. "I saw your singer last night."

"I heard."

I could tell by his sotto voice and cryptic words that he wasn't alone. "You want the good news or the bad news?"

"Bad."

"Everything's fine, before you panic."

"Okay, I'm not panicked."

"Deirdre again."

"Ah," he said.

"And I didn't just pour her into bed. She had to be hospitalized. Nothing a few B vitamins couldn't fix, but honestly, I think she has a real problem. I saw her have two drinks, but she had a flask and she went to the bathroom, I don't know, fourteen times."

"You're exaggerating."

"Not by much. So I'm coming with you tonight."

"Fine."

"Can I be honest?" I didn't wait for his answer. "I think your perpetual availability isn't helping draw Jessica back."

"Very mature, Theresa. Very mature."

"Take a real woman, Jon. Stop being a patsy."

I never spoke like that to my brother or anyone. I rarely gave advice or told anyone to change, but I was tired, physically and emotionally. I hung up without saying good-bye. I had to get Katrina home and get ready for work.

Chapter Eight

I got to my office, where Pam waited for me. My assistant had neon pink hair in a 1940's style chignon, pierced nose and brow, and smart suit; a story of contradictions she called psychabilly. I hadn't heard of it before or since, but when her boyfriend showed up looking like Buddy Holly with tattoos, I got the aesthetic.

"You look wrung out," she said, as if wrung out was a compliment.

I'd cleaned up as much as I could, but make up could only achieve so much. "Thanks. I was sober for the whole thing. Did the late list come through?"

"It's printing. Arnie wants to see you," Pam said as she tapped on her keyboard. She chronically tapped out beats on the table and her knees.

"Did you get a new piercing?" I touched my forehead.

"Like it?" She waggled her brows and handed me a folder with the day's check reports. "Bobby got one on his... you know." She pointed downward.

I couldn't imagine what kind of face I made. Something broadcasting distaste and empathy, probably.

"It's hot," she whispered. "And for my pleasure."

"Grotesque, thank you."

"The DA's been calling you." Pam had started calling Daniel "The DA," since he was the district attorney, when we broke up. She said uttering his name made her sick, and though I told her I could fight my own battles, she'd never said his name again.

"What's he want?" I said around the lump in my throat.

"Lunch. I said you were busy."

"Set it up."

She looked at me over her rhinestone frames.

"I can handle it. Get us into the commissary," I said.

No one in the WDE commissary even bothered glancing at a mayoral candidate, or the mayor, or anyone for that matter. Everyone there worked in the business, so everyone had an important job. To approach someone in the commissary meant you didn't have access to them elsewhere. No one would admit they weren't cool enough to get a meeting with Brad Pitt. Too bad the food there tasted like cheap wedding fare.

"Your Monday three o'clock's been cancelled," Pam said.

"What? Frances?"

"Frances doesn't have the clearance to cancel a meeting for you." She pointed at a little double red flag on the time block. "Only Arnie's girl does."

I checked my watch. "I'm going to see him. Hold down the fort."

"Held. I'll set up the lunch."

I left her wrinkling her nose while she dialed Daniel's number.

IN LOS ANGELES, windows separated the dogs from the bitches.

Not my saying. My sister Margie said it, and when I told Pam, she believed it so ardently she repeated it regularly. When I was moved to the only office in accounting with a window, she called me a newly minted dog.

Once.

"Oh, Ms. Drazen, you know it's a compliment."

"No one should ever repeat anything my sister says. She's out of her mind."

That one window, which took up only half the room—while all the other executives had full walls of Los Angeles behind them—could have meant the world to so many. To me, it didn't change a thing. I'd been born into four generations' worth of money. I had a job because I wanted one, which meant I could leave at any time. My value wasn't in my loyalty, but in my skill, which I'd take with me if I left.

The two walls of windows in Arnie Sanderson's office sat at right angles. Across from the north window was a twelve-foot-high mahogany shelving unit that housed antique tools of the agent's trade. Typewriter.

Approval stamp. Cufflinks. Crystal decanter and glasses. Photos of agents gladhanding household names. The only things missing were a collection of super-white dental caps and rolled up hundred-dollar bills coated with cocaine residue.

"Theresa," he said when I came in. His jacket pulled at the gut, even though it was custom made, and his tie was held by a gold bar so out of style, it would be back in style in six months. "You all right?"

I assumed he was referring to the dark circles that screamed late night out. "Gene took some of us to see an act last night."

"Ah, Gene. I'm sure the bill will be of magnificent proportions. Sit." His smile, which sparkled from his white teeth to his eyes, was the product of decades of asking for things and getting them.

I sat on the leather couch. "It's nice to see you."

Actually, it wasn't. Being invited to his office meant something was wrong, especially in light of my three o'clock Monday meeting's cancellation.

"Can I get you something? Water? A drink? Hair of the dog?"

Only half the staff came in half sober on Fridays. It was the life. As if proving my unmade point, he poured himself a drink as amber as a pill bottle.

"I'm fine."

"I hear you're on Katrina's set. Michael's movie," he said.

Agents and producers called talent by their first name whether they'd ever pressed flesh with them or not. Arnie, of course, was one of the few who'd actually earned the right that everyone else took for granted.

"Script supervising in off hours. It's fun."

"I imagine you'd be good at continuity. And you picked the one director we represent who's a walking time bomb."

"She's my friend." I was suddenly, inexplicably, unusually nervous, as if he could see right through me.

He sat across from me and crossed his legs, an odd gesture for a man. "She's dangerous. She has entitlement issues. After that lawsuit with Overland, she's poison, to be honest. Be careful."

"Have you ever known me to be anything but careful?"

"You are famously vigilant." He smiled, but it was reserved. He really didn't want me working with Katrina; it was all over his face. "I wanted to thank you for getting so many of our clients off paper. Saves man hours and money. They love us for it."

"It's what you hired me to do."

"Everything's running so smoothly, I thought you might have a little time on your hands?"

"I still have to run the department," I said. "But if you had something in mind, I'm open to it."

"Well, it's irregular, if you will."

"I'm not much of a pole dancer."

He laughed gently. "Well, as that wasn't on your resume, I'm sure we can overlook it." He sipped his drink. "We rep a kid right out of USC. Matt Conway. You may have heard of him?"

"Oscar for best short last year."

"Nice kid. Shooting a little movie on the Apogee lot. They have some nice European sets over there. Mountains in the back, the whole thing."

"I've seen it," I said.

"He rented a dozen or so vintage cars. The little stupid boxy things with the long license plates. Well, the company that owns the cars has audit privileges, in case anything going wrong. It's irregular, like I said, but they're exercising the right, and they insisted the head of our accounting department do it. I thought they meant our internal accounting, but they meant you."

"Me?"

"Normally, I'd tell them to go pound sand, but this isn't some prop company. There are powerful people involved, and if I say no, the phone's going to start ringing."

"What am I looking for?"

"He'll tell you," he said.

"I have a department to run."

"Is that a no?"

"It's just a statement of fact."

"Good. We have a gentleman from the fleet rental and a representative from the studio coming at three, Monday."

Three o'clock. Of course. Arnie hadn't taken no for an answer in thirty years.

DANIEL HAD BEEN to the commissary before, on bank holidays when he had off and everyone in Hollywood worked. So when I got there, he was comfortably tapping on his phone, left alone for an hour during a tight campaign. Seeing him work the device tightened my chest. I'd thrown his last phone in the toilet.

"Hi," I said, sitting down and putting the linen napkin on my lap.

He pocketed his phone and smiled at me. "Thanks for seeing me."

I nodded, casting my eyes down. When would I stop playing the injured party? Why did I fall into victimhood so easily?

And why did he fall into the role of evildoer without so much as a blink? His hunched pose, something his handlers had trained out of him a year ago, returned. That lock of light hair, the one he used to brush away in a move the cameras hated, dropped in front of his forehead. I saw the effort he expended to not move it. I saw the extra tightness in his fingers as they wove together in front of him. I saw everything, and when I would have made an effort to relax him before, I just felt a thread of satisfaction.

I hated our dance. It made me sick. But I didn't know how to stop the music because I still loved him. The man who let me arrange the house any way I wanted, who laughed at my stupid jokes, who rubbed lube on me when I wasn't working right. The man who made such good but failed efforts to get me to orgasm with his fingers or his dick in me.

"How's Deirdre?" he asked then continued when I tilted my head. "One of the admins saw a Drazen admitted and called me. She thought it was you."

"Is that even legal?"

He shrugged. "I know people. It's my job. Is she okay or not?"

"She's fine."

I'd ordered our food ahead of time, and it came to our table in wide-rimmed white dishes that would go out of style at the turn of the next century.

"How have you been?" He shuffled his food around with the heavy silver fork. Because of his childhood impoverishment, he ate as quickly and cleanly as a steamshovel on amphetamines, so he only ate when his company was distracted by conversation.

"Fine, thank you. I'm script supervising for Katrina when I can, so I'm a little tired. But it's fun. She got Michael Greenwich for the lead, and he's been incredible. On the strength of his performance alone, she's hoping to get distribution."

He huffed. "I'm surprised anyone wants to deal with her after the lawsuit."

"Yes, she's just another uppity woman asking for what she's due."

"You know I don't mean it like that, Tink."

I stopped chewing. He wasn't supposed to call me that anymore. I looked out the window. "One day, we're going to get over this," I said, looking again at the man I loved. "Until then, let's avoid the small talk."

He cleared his throat. "The thing with us, it hurt me. My numbers. Especially on the east side, where they're really conservative."

"Yes, I know." God, the ice in my voice. It felt like someone else was talking. I could will myself quiet. I could will myself honest. But I couldn't will myself warm.

"I don't want you to think I'm just talking about what happened like it's all about me and the campaign, okay? But that's the business of the lunch. If you want to talk about it on a more personal level, I'm happy to."

"You're fine. I get it. Go on."

"I have a Catholic Charities thing Thursday," he said.

"Okay."

"They're supporting me because I'm not sitting still on income inequality, but the thing with us—"

"And Clarice."

"And Clarice—who is gone—was a sticking point. They almost pulled out. So I'm here to ask for a symbolic gesture from you."

"Of?" I asked, but I knew what it was.

"Of forgiveness. Christian forgiveness that'll play with the San Gabriel Valley. Your family is a big diocesan donor. It won't go unnoticed."

"What does this symbolic gesture of Christian forgiveness entail?"

"If you could attend the fundraiser and stand by me." He held up his hand as if warding off an objection I hadn't yet made. "Not as my fiancée, obviously, but as a supporter. As someone whose priorities are my own."

I chewed. Swallowed. Sipped water. I knew I'd agree, but I didn't want to throw myself at his feet. He didn't deserve it. Or I didn't.

I'd heard a lot about what Daniel deserved. I'd heard that he was a worthless scumbag, and I'd heard promises to make his life in the mayor's mansion a living hell. Those promises meant nothing to me. No one would hurt Daniel over infidelity. In five years, it would be forgotten. So I'd kept my venom to myself in public, and I released it around my family and Katrina.

But something came into my mind—a vision of Antonio beating Daniel's head against a car. I smelled the blood and heard the crack of his nose as it broke from the impact. I imagined a tooth clacking across the metal, his contorted face as he said he was sorry, and Antonio and I partnering over the difference between his regret and his remorse.

"Why are you smiling?" he asked.

I changed the subject. "We decided the public appearances weren't working."

"And normally, I'd think it would just remind everyone of my weakness. But in this case, if people see you forgiving, they might follow. I can't win unless I do something."

I leaned back, appetite gone. "I can see the op ed pieces now. Another political wife forgives her overambitious man's failings with other women. Judge her. Don't judge her. She's a feminist. She's the anti-feminist. She's a symbol for all of us. None of that falls on you. It's all on me."

"I know."

"You are so lucky I don't want Bruce Drummond in office."

The air went out of him. He didn't move, but I saw the slight shift of his shoulders and the release of tension in his jaw. "I can't thank you enough."

"We'll figure something out."

"I'd still marry you if you'd have me back."

"Daniel, really—"

He leaned forward as if propelled. "Hear me out. Not as the maybe mayor. As me. Dan. The guy you taught how to walk straight. The guy who bit his nails. That guy's going to be seventy years old one day, and he's going to regret what he did. I want you back. After this campaign, win or lose, let me love you again."

Joy, terror, shock, sadness all fought for my next words. None of them won the race to get from my brain to my mouth.

"I swore I wouldn't do what I just did," he said. "But I miss you. I can't hold it in anymore."

My words came out with no emotion in them. "I'm not ready."

"I'll wait for you, Tink. I'll wait forever."

I didn't respond because I couldn't imagine myself being ready, and I couldn't imagine committing myself to anyone else.

Chapter Nine

On Monday, I had twenty minutes before my meeting with the fleet guy and the studio rep, exactly enough time to get briefed by Pam.

"Studio's sending a courier," she said, leaning into the screen. "They said you could handle it."

"Wow," I interjected, "they don't even pretend to care."

Pam dropped her voice to nearly inaudible. "Rumor is Matt got the cash for his short from a Hollywood loan shark, and Overland covered the note to the tune of way too much. So if there's a bus coming, he might get thrown under it."

"They need to get their own accountants to do their dirty work. They have the best of the best."

She slipped her rhinestone horn-rimmed glasses halfway down her nose and looked at me over them. "What do you think you are?"

"Adequate, since you asked."

She shook her head and went back to work. I cleared my desk of a few million in incidentals before going to the conference room to do Arnie his favor.

THE CONFERENCE ROOM WAS HUGE, set into the office's bottom floor. Two sides were glass, looking over the reception area, and the other two walls were glass, looking out onto Wilshire Boulevard. It was designed for big faces to be seen together by the rest of the agency and by whomever was waiting in reception. Appointments might be based around making sure Mr. Twenty-Million-Dollar-A-Picture Actor was seen shaking hands with Mr. Academy-Award-Winning-Director in front of Ms. Top-Agent just as Ms. Actress-Who-Refused-The-Nude-Scene waited for an appointment. Like everything in the entertainment industry, it was maximum drama, maximum visibility.

Every time I went into that particular conference room, I checked the smoothness of my stockings, the lay of my hair, the seams between my teeth, even when I was just meeting a messenger to pass over audit materials. What used to arrive in a banker's box of paper and ledgers and folders now came in the form of a flash drive and a manila envelope with a few summary sheets, which were useless. They were delivered by a short man in shorts, sneakers, and a flat cap. Matt's line producer.

"I'm Ed, nice to meet you," he said as he shook my hand and slid the hard drive and envelope onto the table.

"Nice to meet you too. What do we have here?"

"Everything up to the minute for the whole production. Hope you can help with this. It was kind of unexpected."

I was about to respond and open the summary schedules so I could ask intelligent questions. Then I was going to finish my work and pick up dinner. I was feeling a turkey sandwich, salad, and bottle of water.

But that got shot out the window in a storm of hormone shrapnel when I saw Arnie coming through reception with a man in a dark suit named Antonio Spinelli. They were talking, but through the window, I saw Antonio's eyes flick up at me and a smile stretch across his face. I frowned when Arnie opened the door to the conference room.

"Ms. Drazen," he said cheerfully, "how is the handoff going?"

I slid the papers from the envelope just to distract myself, but my hands shook with rage or nerves. Possibly both.

"Just got here," said Ed.

"This is Mr. Spinelli," Arnie said in full agent-smarm. "He rents exotic cars to the business."

"I know," I said, cutting off my boss in a way I never would. I immediately caught my faux pas and held out my hand. "We've met."

"Ms. Drazen." He took my hand, and I felt tingling heat between my legs. "I wanted to say hello before you started."

"Hello," I said flatly, releasing his hand but not his gaze, which seemed just as physical.

"Great," Arnie said. "I'm heading into a meeting." He shook Ed's hand, nodded to Antonio, and left.

When the glass door clicked behind him, I spoke. "We've got it from here, Ed." I shot him a look. We were on the same side. I was watching out for him.

As if he understood, he nodded. "Later." Ed tipped his cap and left.

Only the pull of the air between Antonio and me remained.

"This is flattering," I said, "but it's not going to work."

"You can't prove they didn't take care of the cars?"

"Oh, you name it, I can prove it."

"Good, I wanted the best."

"You got me instead, but that doesn't mean you've got me."

"So you say."

I tried not to smile. That would only encourage him. The last thing the arrogant ass needed was encouragement. "I won't deny I'm attracted to you. I'm sure I'm not the first. But I'm not a conquest. I don't like being chased, especially not through the offices of WDE. This is my job, Mr. Spinelli, not a mousehole. You can't stick your paw in and hope to catch me. I don't care to mix business with displeasure. Now if you'll excuse me."

I reached for the flash drive and envelope, and he stood in my way, getting close enough for me to catch the forested smell of his cologne.

"I could kiss you right now," he said.

"You wouldn't dare."

The windows suddenly felt like cameras. I felt the presence of everyone's eyes as if they were pressure on my skin.

"I will. And you might push me away, but not before you kiss me back. You know it. I know it. And everyone else in this office is going to know it," he said.

"Don't."

"See me then. Let me take you out Thursday night."

I was relieved. That was the perfect out. "I have plans on Thursday."

"Cancel them."

"I can't. It's a fundraiser."

"Catholic Charities?" He raised an eyebrow. If it was at all possible for him to look sexier, he did.

"Yes." I stood straight. I didn't want to have to explain it, but I had a compulsion to excuse myself I had to quell.

"Good." He stood straight. "I was invited to that. We'll go together."

"No!"

"So we should see each other another time, then?"

Of course not. We should be together some other never. But I hesitated, and that was my mistake.

"I think I should see you before the fundraiser," he said, "because I want to go with you and show Daniel Brower what he's missing."

"You going to take him out to the parking lot and beat him up for me?"

"He deserves far worse."

Knowing better than to encourage him, I held up my chin. "I'll decide what he deserves. Thank you, though."

"Good. I'll pick you up Wednesday at eight."

"I'm busy."

"I'll have to kiss you now then." He stepped forward.

I swallowed because his lips, a step closer to mine, were full and satiny, and more than anything, my mouth wanted to feel them.

"Follow me please," I said like an automaton.

I brushed past him without waiting for a response, walking out the door and down the hall with the manila envelope in my arm. I nodded to my associates and knew he was behind me from the sense of movement and heat at my back. I slipped into a windowless, empty conference room and closed the door when he entered.

"Mister Spinelli—"

On the way to the closed office, I'd prepared a short speech about respecting my boundaries, but I swallowed every word when those satin lips fell on mine. His kiss was a study in paying attention, reacting to me as I reacted to him with increasing intensity. When his tongue touched mine, I lost myself in desire. His hands stayed on my neck, and I became aware of their power and gentleness.

When I put my hands on him, he moved closer, and with a brush on my thigh, I felt his erection. Oh, to be anywhere else. To explore that rigid dick, to feel it in me while those lips hovered over mine. My legs could barely hold me up when he kissed my neck.

"Wednesday," he whispered, the warmth of his breath and timbre of his voice as arousing as the touch of his lips.

"You don't really care about the cars."

"No, I don't."

"I'm not making it up. I told my friend I'd be on her set after work Wednesday. I can't ditch her. Friday. We can do Friday."

"I accept the spirit of your agreement."

He reached behind me and turned the doorknob. I put my hair in place and thought cold thoughts. He left, and I watched him stride down the carpeted hall. I didn't move until he was out the office door. I couldn't believe he left it like that, without setting up a definite time and place for me to be flat on my back. I felt ill at ease as I scooped up the audit materials and headed back to my little window in my little office in my little corner of the Hollywood system.

Chapter Ten

"You want to fuck her."

Michael nodded. He and Katrina sat on stools at the counter of a tiny coffee shop she'd rented for the scene with staff all around. I held my clipboard and waited, having been told to stay within Michael's eyesight.

"Right," he said.

"You know if you fuck her once, she's yours."

This conversation happened as if no one was around. As if there weren't three gaffers playing with the lights and keys with clothes hangers clipping wires and aligning scrims. As if the assistant camera person wasn't holding up his little light meter to every color of everything and calling out numbers.

"You have to fuck her," Katrina said with real urgency. "You're not getting it."

"I'm getting it."

Katrina hauled off and slapped Michael in the face. The sound echoed in the halls and rooms of my brain. I flinched and looked at them. I wasn't supposed to. That was very personal actor/director business, and everyone else had the good sense to ignore it.

Michael made eye contact with me as it happened.

"That," she said. "That feeling. Right now."

"I have it," he said, putting his hand to his lips as if he wanted to hide his face.

"Good. Get to makeup." She winked at me as Michael strode off, then she called to the cameraman, "We're shooting him from the right. Have the stand in mark it." She walked off, barking more orders, and I marked the change in angle on my clipboard.

We would be filming late, and I girded myself with coffee and the knowledge that helping Katrina, even in the tiny role as part-time script supervisor, would right a great wrong that had been done her.

Michael played the scene, which did not include the woman in question, but her best friend. His character was about to bed her out of spite, like a man on a mission to save his testicles. He was riveting. He seized the scene, the set, the crew, and the mousy character who had no idea what she was getting embroiled in. He put his hands up her skirt as if he owned what was under it, but his character didn't take an ounce of responsibility for what he was doing.

"Cut!" shouted Katrina.

I noted the shot and take, but only after the scene was fully broken. "There's your Oscar," I mumbled to Katrina.

"I just want someone to touch this thing with a ten-footer." She took my clipboard and flipped through the pages on it. "We never got that last line on page thirty. I think we can ADR it."

"I think WDE will get behind you. Honestly. As long as you promise not to sue anyone again."

She made a *pfft* sound that promised nothing. "Dinner break, everyone!"

A production assistant ran up to me as I tucked my papers away. "There's a man here asking for you."

It took me about half a second to figure out who he was. "Dark hair and brown eyes?"

"Yeah. He brought dinner."

"Of course he brought me dinner." I had to process that while fixing my hair and straightening my sleeves.

"No," he said. "He brought *everyone* dinner. He brought *you* wine."

MOVIE SETS that weren't dependent on sunlight stayed up all day. So though I'd shown up at six p.m. to relieve the other script supervisor, the set had already been up for twelve hours. Because no one left when there was work to be done, meals and snacks were provided to the entire crew. Bigger productions got more services, with above the line crew (actors, director, producers) getting gourmet catering, and below the line crew (camera, grips, gaffe, PA, AD, on and on and on) getting something good but less noteworthy. On Katrina's set, everyone got the same mediocre food from a truck wedged into the corner of the parking lot. A few long tables with folding chairs took up parking spaces. The day Antonio showed up for dinner, our French fry and burger habit was broken.

He had a bottle of red wine tucked under his arm and wore a grey sports coat with blood red polo. A woman in her sixties stood under his arm as he talked to Katrina. In front of them were four chafing dishes, plates, utensils, and a line of people.

"You do not get to invade my set," Katrina said, but I saw her eye the food ravenously. It was peasant food—meaty, saucy deliciousness that would satiate everyone for another four or five hours.

"*Mea culpa,*" he said. "Your script supervisor accepted a dinner invitation, and Zia Giovana thought it would be rude to bring only for us."

"It's my fault," I said. "I forgot to tell you."

She spun and gave a smirk just for me. "You lie."

"If it means you can just eat, I'm guilty as charged." I pointed at Antonio. "You, sir, are pushy."

"As charged," he said. "Let me make it up to you."

"I think you just did." A plate of lasagna was pushed into my hands, but Antonio took it from me and passed it to the person behind me.

"Come on. I'm not feeding you outside a trailer."

He pulled me, but I yanked back. "I have to work."

Katrina didn't even look up from her food. "We have to set up the next shot. I'll text you when I need you. Get out of here."

I let Antonio put his arm around me and lead me onto the sidewalk. He held the wine bottle by the neck with his free hand. The neighborhood was light-industrial hip, with factories being converted into lofts and warehouses housing upscale restaurants.

"There's a place around the corner," he said. "No liquor license yet, so you bring your own."

"Let me see." I held my hand out for the bottle and inspected the label. "Napa? You brought a California wine?"

"It's not good?"

"It's a great wine, but I figured, you know, Italian?"

He laughed. "I was trying to not be pushy. Meet you halfway."

"This is how you say 'not pushy'?"

"You can run. I won't chase you."

"You won't?" I handed him the bottle.

He smiled. "Yeah. I will."

"Has it occurred to you that the chasing might be what you like about me, and that if I stop running, you might get bored?"

"I don't get bored. There's too much to do."

"It's funny," I said. "That's kind of what I find most boring. Everything to do."

"You're doing the wrong things, no? What do you love?"

We crossed onto a block of restaurants. The cobblestone streets were crowded. Tables were set on the sidewalks. Heat lamps kept the chill at bay.

"I don't love anything, really."

"Come on. The last thing you enjoyed, that made you feel alive."

I stopped walking, feeling disproportional frustration with his questions.

He turned to face me and walk backward. "Kissing me doesn't count."

"Funny guy."

A parking valet in a white shirt and black bowtie nearly ran into me, dodged, and opened a car door.

"Think hard," Antonio said. "The last thing that made you love life."

"Saying it would be inappropriate."

He raised an eyebrow. "I could learn to love this thing too, I think."

My annoyance turned into cruelty. "The last thing I loved doing? Working with Daniel on his campaign. I miss it."

Still walking backward, arms out to express complete surrender, he said, "Then, to make you happy, I announce that I will run for mayor."

I laughed. I couldn't help it. He laughed with me, and I noticed how reserved it was for a man who claimed to enjoy life.

He was on me before I could take in another second of his smile. He pushed his mouth on mine, his arms enveloping me, his hands in my hair. My world revolved around the sensations of him, his powerful body and sweet tongue, his crisp smell, the scratch of the scruff on his chin, and the way he paid attention to his kiss.

I matched his attention so carefully that when we got knocked into by a valet, I gasped. Antonio pulled me close, holding me up and protecting me at the same time.

The valet held up his hands. "I'm so sorry." He backed away toward a waiting car, reaching for the handle.

"You're sorry?" Antonio asked. "You don't look sorry."

I'd be the first to admit he didn't look sorry. He looked interested in opening the car door.

"It's okay, Antonio. He didn't do it on purpose."

He looked down at me for a second before looking back at the valet. "He could have knocked you over."

"But he didn't."

The valet opened the door with one hand and with the other, in a slight movement that could be denied later, flicked his hand, as if dismissing Antonio. Quick as a predator, Antonio took two steps toward the valet and pushed him against the car. I stepped into the street, heel bending on the cobblestone, and got between them. The valet's face was awash in fear, and Antonio's had an intensity that scared me.

"Antonio. Let's go, before I have to go back to work," I said.

He held his finger up to the valet's face. "You're going to be careful. Right?"

"Yeah, yeah." The man looked as though he wanted to be anywhere else.

He stepped back, and I put my hand on his arm. He looked at me with an unexpected tenderness, as if grateful I'd pulled him from oncoming traffic.

"Is there a problem here?"

The authoritative voice cut our moment short. Antonio and I looked to its source.

A short man in a zip-up black jacket and black tie, with a moustache and comb-over, appeared to recognize Antonio when we turned toward him. "Spin."

"Vito." Antonio looked the man up and down, pausing on his tag for *Veetah Valet Service – Proprietor*. He touched it. "Really?"

"I can explain."

"Yes, you can. After I bring the lady to our table. You'll be here."

"Yes, boss."

Antonio put his arm around me and walked toward an Italian restaurant with tables outside.

"What was that about?" I asked.

"He works for me. I'm going to have to talk to him for a minute."

"It wasn't a big deal about the valet."

"It's not about the valet."

I dropped my arm from his waist. He'd closed himself off so suddenly that touching him seemed out of place.

A young man with menus approached. "Outside or inside?"

"In," Antonio answered, giving the waiter his bottle.

He brought us to a table inside. Antonio held my chair for me and sat across the table, looking a million miles away.

"What happened?" I asked. "You look really annoyed."

He took my hand. "Trust me, it's not you."

"I know it's not me. What did that guy do?"

"He's not supposed to run other businesses while he works for me. That's the rule."

"That's a weird rule."

He smiled but looked distracted. "Let me go talk to him. Then you'll have my full attention."

I tapped my watch. "Quickly. I could turn into a pumpkin at any moment."

After Antonio walked away, the waiter returned with two glasses and our bottle of Napa wine. He poured a touch in my glass, made small talk, filled both glasses, and left.

I waited dutifully, tapping on my phone and watching people. I was walking distance from home and a few blocks from the set, but I wanted to be at that table. I was hungry, and I liked the Antonio I'd walked there with.

The wall facing the street was all windows. Past the rows of outdoor tables, I saw the lights change and cars roll by. Valets ran back and forth with keys and tickets. Antonio came into view, pinching a cigarette to his mouth and letting the smoke drift from out casually. What a stunning man he was. Maybe not in the same affable mood as he had been on the walk to the restaurant, but the intensity that condensed around him made me unable to look away.

He took a last drag and flicked his cigarette into the street. Then he walked in, smoke still drifting from his mouth. "Sorry about that," he said when he sat.

"Everything okay?"

"Yeah. Just a little talk."

The waiter came, we heard the specials, and ordered.

Antonio picked up his wine. "*Salute*."

I held up my glass and looked at his when they clinked. His hand was firm and powerful, all muscle and vein, and his knuckles were scraped raw. I brushed the backs of my fingers against them.

"Antonio? Were you just talking? Or do they drag when you walk?"

He smiled. He'd gone out tense and returned relaxed. "One of the valets pushed me into a wall. I tried to break my fall, and this is what happened. These guys, they're paid per car, so they all jump to open doors a little too quick. How is the wine?" His smile was deadly.

"Good. What part of Italy are you from?"

"Napoli. The armpit of Italy, my mother used to say."

"And you came here for the weather and the easy access to litigator privileges?"

He smirked. "Do I have to answer everything right away?"

"Chasing me around won't go well if you don't."

He leaned over and touched my upper lip. Having him that close, I wanted to let those fingers explore my body. "You tell me where you got this scar. Then I'll tell you why I came here."

"I got the scar from a boy."

"Ah. And I came here because of a girl."

Appetizers came, filling little dumplings drenched in red sauce. He slipped a couple on my plate then a couple on his.

"You followed a woman here?" I watched him eat with clean efficiency.

"I followed men." He moved on to the next subject as if his life wasn't worth lingering on, brushing it off with a practiced, charming facility. "And this boy? His cutting wit, perhaps?"

"His high school ring. This girl. Was she chasing you?" I looked at him over my wine glass.

"No. She's back home."

"The girl is home, and you chased a man here because of her?"

"Close enough. What happened to the boy?" he asked.

"He's dead."

"Note to self. Don't scar Theresa Drazen."

I raised my wine glass to my lips to hide my expression. He'd gotten closer to a truth than he realized.

"So you own a hell of a lot of cars, a restaurant, and you're a lawyer," I said. "You contribute enough to the charity of your choice to get invited to the fundraisers. Oh, and you don't like Porsches. You can beat a guy nearly unconscious with your bare hands. You're a very interesting guy, Mister Spinelli."

He touched my hand with the tips of his fingers, finding a curve and tracing it. "Running an accounting department for the biggest agency in Hollywood. Working on the mayoral candidate's campaign. Helping your friend with her movie in your spare time. And the most poised, graceful woman I ever met. I'm not half as interesting as you."

I formulated an answer, maybe something clever or maybe I'd continue to ask uncomfortable questions, but my phone dinged. It was Katrina's new AD.

—We're starting in ten—

"This has been fun," I said. "I have to go."

He stood, reaching into his pocket. "I'll walk you."

He tossed a few twenties down and went to the door with me, putting his hand on my back as we exited. I pressed my lips together, avoiding a silly smile. I liked his hand there.

I didn't see Vito around. The valets were still working the block quickly, if less exuberantly.

"Tell me something," I said. "Why weren't you afraid that someone would call the cops that night with the Porsche? I mean, if you didn't break that guy's nose, I'll eat my shoe."

"Tell me what you think. Why would that be the case?" He put his hands in his pockets as he walked.

"That's a common debate team switch. Putting the speculation on me."

"Speculate." He smiled like a movie star, and I couldn't help but smile back.

"I'd rather you told me."

"Maybe I've met enough cops in my profession to know how to talk to them, should it come to that."

"Which profession is that?"

"I'm a lawyer."

I hadn't thought much of our harmless back and forth, but when he reminded me he was a lawyer, I caught a tightness in his voice. He glanced away. Most people were puzzles one had to simply collect enough pieces to figure out. My questioning had merely been fact-harvesting until he subtly evaded something so simple.

"If I look up criminal cases you've filed, what would I find? I mean, cases where you've dealt with the LAPD."

He looked down at the curb as we crossed the street, holding me back when a car came even though I'd stopped.

"I'm a lawyer for my business. I've only had a couple of clients, and mostly they need my help talking to the police. Anything else you feel like you need to know?" He said it with good humor, but there was a wariness to his tone.

"Yes." We got to the outer edge of the set, where the street was closed off to keep it silent.

"What?"

I knew I shouldn't ask, but I was tired and still hungry, and the wine had sanded away my barriers. "Is Vito still outside the restaurant running his business?"

The look on his face melted me, as if a fissure had opened and he was trying desperately to keep the lava from pouring out. Then he smiled as if just having decided to let it all go. "Contessa, you are trouble."

"Is that good or bad?"

"Both."

My phone dinged again. I didn't look at it. I knew what it was about. "I have to go."

"*Come vuoi tu.*" He cupped my cheek in his hand and kissed me quickly before walking away, the picture of masculine grace. He didn't look back.

Chapter Eleven

I strapped up my stockings with the TV on. I saw it behind me in the mirror. Daniel wore his pale grey suit and tie, ice in the sun. He'd done well at the debate that afternoon, keeping himself poised, still, and focused. He was the perfect Future Mister Mayor.

BRUCE DRUMMOND: My opponent hasn't opened a serious case against any crime organization in over a year. Just because it's peacetime, do we sit on our laurels?

I hadn't heard from Antonio since he'd left me at the set. I'd been tempted to reach out to him, but to what end? As I watched Daniel, I knew I still had feelings for him. How could I get involved with someone else? How could I take Daniel back? How could I use another man to break my holding pattern?

DANIEL BROWER: Believe me, my office has been gathering information and evidence against a number of organizations. We won't open a case unless we're sure we have the evidence we need. Please, let the people know if your administration will recklessly accuse citizens, so they can start looking for an independent prosecutor.

Antonio would be at the fundraiser. Though I was excited to see him, despite the fact that I had to avoid him, he'd become tight and unreadable. He'd avoided telling me about his business, and his story about being pushed by a valet was absurd. Vito hadn't gone home whistling Dixie. Antonio was Italian. From Naples. Was he a lawyer or criminal? Or both?

BRUCE DRUMMOND: In closing, I love my wife. She's the only woman for me, and that's why I married her. As your mayor, I'd never distract—

I liked nice men. Lawful men. Men with a future, a career, who could safely support children. I wasn't the type to look for the dangerous, exciting guys.

The dress went over my head in one movement. I twisted, struggled, and got the zipper up by myself.

IT WAS eighty degrees and humid as hell, the wettest, nastiest, buggiest fall in L.A. history. Totally unexpected. Nothing anyone from the Catholic Charitable Trust could have foreseen when they'd planned an outdoor event ten months before. A string quartet played in the background, and wait staff carried silver trays of endive crab and champagne flutes. I made my way through the crowd alone, smiling and sharing air kisses. The house was a Hancock Park Tudor, kept and restored to the standards of a hotel as if the taste had been wrapped, boxed, and shipped in from a decorator's mind.

I was standing by the pool with Ute Yanix, talking about Species—the only raw foods place in L.A. that served meat—when Daniel crept up behind me. Ute's eyes lit up like a Christmas tree, and she brushed back her long straight hair like a silk curtain. Daniel did have a certain something. That thing had made him a frontrunner before the race even started.

"Ute, I'm glad you could make it," he said.

"You know I support you. All Hollywood does, whether we say it in public or not."

"I appreciate you being here publicly then." His hand found mine. "It's even more important than the donation."

She laughed a few decibels louder than necessary. "Now more than ever, huh?"

And with a look at me, the heiress in the candidate's corner, she implied the ugliest things. The first and most dangerous was that Daniel had been running the campaign on my money and now couldn't.

"I assure you, donations have always been appreciated." My smile could have lit the Hollywood sign.

The sexting incident was never mentioned on the fundraising floor, but in the bathroom, whispered voices, offered words of support, empathy, understanding, and others were clearly derisive. I had stopped fielding both sentiments.

I didn't hear the rest of the conversation. Over Ute's shoulder, I saw a man in a dark suit. Lots of men in dark suits milled around, but they had jeans, open collars, ties optional. He wore a suit like a woman wore lingerie, to accentuate the sexual. To highlight the slopes and lines. To give masculinity a definition. He held his wine glass to me, tearing my clothes off and running his hands over my skin from across the room.

"...but what you're going to do about the traffic—"

"I'll be Mayor, not God." They both laughed.

I'd lost most of the conversation during my locked gaze with Antonio Spinelli. "Excuse me," I said to my ex and the actress. "Duty calls."

I walked into the house. The unwritten rule was if the party was in the backyard, guests stayed in the backyard. Wandering off into the personal spaces was bad manners, but I couldn't help it. I went to the back of the kitchen, to a back hall with a wool Persian carpet and mahogany doors.

"Contessa."

I didn't have a second to answer before he put his hands on my cheeks and his mouth on mine. I didn't move. I didn't kiss him back. I just took in his scent of dew-soaked pine, wet earth, and smoldering fires. He pulled back, unkissed but not unwanted, his hands still cupping my face.

He brushed his thumb over my lower lip, just grazing the moist part inside. "I want you. I haven't stopped thinking about you."

"What happened then?" All my resolve to not use him as a rebound went out the window. "You froze me out yesterday."

"I don't like answering questions about myself."

"I can't be with you if I don't know you."

"Do you want me?"

His breath made patterns on my face. I could have pushed him away, but his attention was an angle, a point of reference, and I was but a line defined by it.

"Yes," I whispered, putting my head against the wall.

"Let's have each other then. My body and your body. No expectations. No questions."

Before I could get offended, he kissed me hard, hurting me. His tongue probed my lips, my teeth, pushing my head against the wall. I was aware of every inch of his body, its warmth, its supple curves, the hair on his face, and I yielded. My insides melted, pooling between my legs. I moved with him like a wave, tongues dancing, jaws aligning. I fell into that kiss, its taste of wine and sweet water, the hum vibrating from the back of his throat. I thought I would burst from my hips outward.

He pulled away with a gasp, still close to me, his eyes darting across my features. "You're blushing. And you're panting, just a little."

I couldn't speak. I wanted him to kiss me again. My body wanted it. The hairs on my arms stood up when I thought about it.

He put his hand to my chest, between my breasts, and pressed a little. "Your heart is beating hard. This is what it takes."

He moved his hand slightly, brushing my hard nipple through my dress. I wanted him to stop, but I didn't want it to end. If I spoke, the spell would be broken. I'd have to go back to the other me, that spurned, unwanted woman. I opened my mouth but just shook my head. What had I become? What was wrong with me?

"Since the minute I saw you," he said into my neck, "I've wanted to open your legs and take you."

His words had fingers, and as he spoke, they drifted down my body, fondling me and arousing me. No one had ever spoken like that to me, because I would have laughed with discomfort. But when Antonio said it, I forgot everything but his voice and the image of him moving over me.

"I'm not good at casual sex," I said in a breath.

"I never said it would be casual."

I didn't know what he meant. I didn't know how sex could be just two bodies meeting without being classified as meaningless. I couldn't wrap my head around it because he was near me, his hands on my hips, the scruff of his face brushing my neck.

"Take me," I said before I thought about it.

Like a cat leaping into action, he pulled me through an ajar door, clicking it behind us. We were in a bathroom with marble tiles and double sinks. White curtains. A thousand details I couldn't absorb because his lips were on mine.

When I heard him lock the door, I surrendered to what was happening. I stopped worrying about where I was or what the future might bring. I tangled my hands in his hair and kissed him for all I was worth. He pulled my knee up over his hip, stroking the back of my thigh. I tried to remember to breathe, but when he leaned into me and I felt the hardness between his legs against the softness between mine, I forgot.

"I'm going to fuck you right here," he growled. "Are you ready?"

"Yes." The word came out in a hiss.

"Yes, what?" He pushed against me. "What do you want me to do to you?" He took my hands from his hair and put them above me, pinning me to the wall as he kissed my neck.

"Fuck me." I said it so softly a butterfly wouldn't have heard me.

"Say it again. But this time, own it."

"Fuck me." A little louder.

He let go of my hands. His fingers brushed past my breasts to my waist, where they pushed me down against his erection.

"You are so sweet," he whispered, wrapping my other knee around him, pinning me with his hips. "*Dolce*. The way you don't like to say the word fuck, and you say it to me anyway. I know how bad you want me to make you come."

With that, he hitched me up and carried me to the vanity. He balanced me on it as he kissed me, grinding between my legs and driving me crazy. I yanked up my skirt.

"Antonio," I said, "protection."

"I have it."

I spent a little time worrying about having sex with a man who carried condoms around. Just a second. Just a stab of my real self, the one who was going to walk out of that bathroom when we were done. He took half a step back and pulled my knees apart. I leaned back as he slipped his fingers under my garter belt, finding the crotch of my panties.

"I like these," he said.

"Thank you."

He poked his finger through the lace and yanked with his other hand. The lace gave way with a bark of a rip, leaving my underwear with a gaping hole. He stroked me. I didn't know if I'd ever been that wet.

"I can't help it. I have to taste you." He put his face at the inside of my thigh and brushed his tongue on the sensitive skin. His hands stroked, tongue flicking, lips a soft center to the roughness of his face. When he made it to my pussy with a soft suck at my clit, I moaned. "Do you like it?" he asked before he circled my opening with his tongue.

"Yes."

"Yes what?"

"Yes, suck it. Eat me. Take me with your mouth."

The string quartet purred outside, and the party hummed along while I begged for a man's tongue on me. His tongue flicked, finding every want, every emptiness, and filling it with sensation. He sucked just a little then ran the flat of his tongue over my clit until my pussy felt like a bursting balloon.

"Antonio." My voice squeaked. I was on the edge.

"Come," he said, looking up at me. "I'm still going to fuck you."

When he put his lips on me again, his eyes watching me over the horizon of my gathered skirt, I let him fill me. I came hard, lifting my hips as he grabbed my thighs to keep me from falling over. I was beyond cries, beyond words. I was just a receptacle for the pleasure of a tiny percentage of my body.

I didn't have a second to breathe before he positioned himself above me. His pants were open, and his dick lay against my engorged clit. I reached down. He'd gotten it out and wrapped while he was eating me.

"You're very skilled," I said. "And you're huge."

He put his fingers in me. I was sensitive and swollen, soaked in desire.

"You're tight. So tight. Fuck." His eyes went to half-mast, and he sucked in a breath. "Spread your legs all the way."

I did, and he guided the head of his dick into me. I stretched when he thrust, a little sting of pain drowned by pleasure.

"You okay?" he asked.

I nodded. I felt as if I had a telephone pole in me, but I wouldn't complain about it. Maybe I should have asked him to go slow, because he shoved himself in until my expression told him he couldn't go any farther. He shifted my hips then pushed forward. He found space to fill and drove into me up to the base, pushing his body into me. I put my hands on his face, and he leaned down. We were eye to eye, nose to nose, bodies moving together, the swell of tension returning.

"You're beautiful," I said, my thumb on his lips.

He kissed my thumb, running his tongue along the length as he fucked me. We were dressed up but joined in our most vulnerable places. My back hurt where it was pushed against the stone vanity, and my shoulder was jammed into a cabinet. I heard the sounds of the party, and one of my shoes was about to fall off. I felt ripped apart by the size of him.

But I was going to come again, and I couldn't come with anything inside me. I knew that. It was an indelible fact.

"I'm coming inside you," he gasped. "I'm going to come so fucking hard in you."

"Me too." I didn't even believe it. "You're making me come."

The swirl of feeling dropped away then coalesced, increasing until my limbs stiffened and I put my face in his neck to stifle my cries. The impossible happened. I came just from a man inside me. I pulsed around him, drowning in the power of it.

He thrust hard with a grunt then a moan. I felt the pulse at the base of his dick on my stretched pussy. He was coming. Making that beautiful man lose himself in me felt like a gift. I pushed into him until he slowed, stopped, and kissed my neck.

"*Grazie,*" he said.

"You're welcome."

Slowly, he slipped his dick out of me. It was still rigid, and I felt every inch of it against my raw skin. He tied off the condom and wrapped it in toilet paper as I sat up.

"Stay there," he said, pressing my legs open.

Was he going to have me again? I didn't think I could take it. Though I was already feeling twinges of shame and guilt, I wouldn't have turned him down. He balled up a wad of tissue and pressed it between my legs, cleaning me. The gesture was so much more intimate than the actual sex that I blushed.

"I can't send you back outside with sex dripping down your leg, now can I?"

Despite the sounds from the party, I'd forgotten that there would be a "back outside." I'd forgotten about Daniel, his meek request that I come back to him, and the air of forgiveness my attendance was supposed to provide. I closed my legs and sat up.

"I have to get back out there." I put my left shoe on all the way and popped off the vanity. "Thank you."

"My pleasure."

The shreds of my underwear tickled my inner thighs, bunching as only ripped lace could. I straightened my skirt and smoothed my stockings, knowing he was watching me. I didn't look at him as I went for the door.

He slipped between me and the knob. "Contessa."

"Yes?"

"Don't leave like this."

"How should I leave?"

He kissed my forehead, and I let myself enjoy the tenderness. I didn't want to rush out, but I couldn't delude myself into thinking I was fully present, either.

"It doesn't have to be meaningless," he said.

"You won't answer questions about your life, and I'm still in love with my ex. I don't know how it can be meaningful."

"I'll answer one question right now if you kiss me back like you mean it."

"Why are you doing this? You're the one who wanted two bodies meeting and no more."

"Because I can't walk out of this room like this. You're like a stranger all of a sudden. One question."

"The girl. Who was she? To you, I mean? Why did you come here for her?"

"That's three questions."

"Pick one."

"My sister. She's my sister. Her name is Nella."

"And?"

He bit his lip and looked down at my face. After a second, I realized he wasn't going to answer me.

"Excuse me." I pushed him away, but he shoved me against the door.

"I want my kiss," he said.

"That was no kind of answer."

"I answered two of the three. If you only cared about the last one, you should have said so."

"Lawyer." I said it like an indictment, and he smirked. I elbowed him, but he caught my forearms and pinned me to the door.

"Your underwear's already ripped, and if I checked, I bet you're wet again."

"Get off me," I said.

"I should fuck you right now."

"Go to hell."

I twisted, but his hands were bruising, and the growing hardness of his dick was enough to weaken my knees and my resolve. "Take your kiss then."

He did, without hesitation or gentleness, prying my mouth open with his tongue, thick with the taste of my pussy. He pulled away when we had to breathe, and we stared at each other, panting.

"I hope you enjoyed that," I said. "Now excuse me."

He backed away from the door, and I went through it before he and his beautiful dick could stop me. The air outside the bathroom felt fresher and thinner. I smoothed my dress again and pulled the pins out of my hair, letting it fall down in a red cascade. It was easier to keep that way.

I felt a weight between my legs. I could easily get my appearance together for the rest of the party. But I couldn't hide the fact that my cheeks were pink with arousal and my nipples stood on end. My arms still had goose bumps, and I was so wet I felt the moisture inside my thighs. But I walked outside as if it were my house, my party, my world, because that's what I did. It was easier than math.

Dinner had started. Daniel was at his table with an empty seat next to him. He hadn't mentioned the seating arrangements, but they shouldn't have surprised me. Forgiveness didn't sit across the room. He stood as I took my seat.

"Thank you," I said. When our eyes met, I was sure he knew what I'd just done.

Chapter Twelve

The next morning, two things happened simultaneously. One. A dozen red roses on Pam's desk.

"Wow, these from Bobby?" I asked.

"They're for you." She tapped a pen to the desk blotter, as if writing a song in her head.

Before I could open the paper flap of the card, the second thing happened. I caught the image on my assistant's screen of Antonio and me in the hallway. It had been shot through the window the moment before we kissed. Next to that image was one of Daniel and me sitting together at dinner.

I'd feared looking weak. I'd feared the op ed pieces about my neediness and desperation, about Daniel's ambition and mindless drive for power. The inevitable comparisons to greater women's choices about cheating political mates. Maybe I should have worried about looking like a whore.

"Who's that?" Pam asked.

Who was he? I ran the question over and over in my mind, and I didn't have an acceptable answer. He was a man I'd met the other day. He was a magnet for my sexual hunger.

"He's being investigated for fraud," Pam said, as if he was just a guy on the screen and not someone I had been standing so close to I could feel his heat. "Is he the same guy with the cars?"

"Same," I choked. "What's the article say?" I opened the envelope so I wouldn't have to look at the screen. I figured the flowers were from Daniel, asking for another reprieve.

"Says you and Antonio Spinelli are friends through WDE. And you're reconciling with Daniel Brower."

"They used that word? Reconciling?" I looked at the card.

ONE MORE QUESTION.

NO NAME. An arrogant avoidance of redundancy. I folded it back into the envelope.

"Yeppers," Pam said. "Right next to that picture with the hot Italian guy. Sneaky."

"Journalist. In Latin it means 'to say everything while saying nothing.'"

"Really?"

"No. But if the ancients had known anything at all, it would."

I'D GOTTEN up and dressed like any other morning, expecting nothing more than the usual inconveniences. Traffic. Runny stockings. Coffee too hot/cold. Daniel and I had parted amicably the previous night, with him whispering "think about it," in my ear. I promised to, and I would, but it was hard to think of Daniel when I woke up with a soaked, sore pussy courtesy of Antonio.

I relieved myself, fingers stroking the soreness. I loved the pain of remembrance. He'd been so good, so hard, and talking during sex was something new. I whispered to myself *fuck me fuck me fuck me hard* until I came, ass tightening, hips twisting, balancing my whole body on the top of my head and the balls of my feet.

Only when I took my first panting breaths, cupping myself in my palm, did I consider how poorly we'd parted. I couldn't be with someone so closed off. Later at work, when Pam told me he was under investigation, I knew why he didn't like being interrogated. I had her hold my calls for an hour.

ONE MORE QUESTION.

WHAT WOULD IT BE? More about Nella? Another reason to land in Los Angeles besides easy Bar exams? No. All that was too facile and obviously loaded for him.

I locked my office door. I had a million things to do, but none would happen while those pictures sat in my mind. I needed to solve all of it immediately with an internet search.

If I could have bottled the next hour in a fragrance, it would have been called frustration. If the size of the bottle contained the amount of information I found on Antonio Spinelli, it would be one ounce, not a drop more, and the contents would be worth less than the vessel.

In other words, one sidebar article in *Fortune* had not one undigested word. I found one professional photograph in which he looked gorgeous, an unsubstantiated complaint in the comment section of a real estate blog bitching about how many cars he had and how much property he owned, a short fluff piece about Zia Giovana in the *San Pedro Sun,* and an investigative piece in the same paper from two years later.

The investigative piece was recent enough to matter. Antonio Spinelli, owner and proprietor of Zia's restaurant, was under investigation for laundering millions through the establishment. The claim was absolutely impossible to prove, and apparently the money trail died before the reporter's deadline.

Pam texted me.

—Mister Brower is on the line—

—I have another twenty minutes—

—He's pretty insistent—

Pam knew me, and she knew my ex-fiancé. She wouldn't interrupt for nonsense. I picked up the phone.

"Hi," I said.

He started before I had the chance to take another breath. "What are you doing?"

"What?"

"With a known criminal. What are you doing with him?"

I was shocked into speechlessness.

"Tink? Answer me. It was in the *LA Times.*"

"I'm not *with* anyone. Not that it's your business."

"Your safety is my business. I'm sorry. That's not negotiable now or ever."

His voice seemed physically present, coming through not just the phone but the walls, and I realized he was right outside my locked door.

"Let me in," he said.

I hung up and opened the door. "You have to relax." It was barely out of my mouth before he slammed the door and shut out his bodyguards, who seemed to be holding back Pam.

"Daniel, really—"

"Really? Really, Theresa? Where did you pick him up?"

I put my hands on my hips. I had to bite my lips to keep in all the pointless recrimination. We didn't need more of it. Daniel knew things.

"Do you want to take it easy and talk to me?" I said.

"No," he said, taking my shoulders. "I don't." He kissed me, pushing me back against my desk.

I kept my mouth closed not out of anger, but confusion. By the time he pulled back, we'd both calmed down.

"I'm sorry," he said.

"Sit down." I indicated the chair across from my desk, and I sat next to it.

He pulled his chair close to mine as if he was still entitled to breathe my air, as if I'd agreed to the newspaper's reconciliation in real life. "I need you to tell me everything," he said, gathering my hands.

"There's nothing to tell."

"How did he approach you?"

I pulled my hands away. "This is not fair. You're not exactly entitled to any information about me or my love life anymore. If I tell you it's nothing, you're going to think I'm lying. If I tell you it's something, it's like I'm trying to hurt you. I'm just trying to live my life, okay? I'm just trying to get through my days and nights."

"You're stumbling into a place where you can get hurt."

"All roads lead to hurt, trust me."

"I deserved that."

"It wasn't directed at you." I threw his hands off me. "Can I just talk to you without all the baggage?"

"No, because you've forgotten who you are."

"I'm not yours anymore."

"You're an heiress. A socialite. You run one of the biggest accounting departments in Hollywood. You funnel millions of dollars a day. You have access to the district attorney."

"This is about *you*?"

"No! Fuck!" The curse was pure exclamation. Not a lead in or a modifier.

He paused for half of a microsecond, but I caught it. When he and I were together, I hadn't liked cursing. I thought he didn't do it until I found his texts to Clarice, and I found out just how well he used the word fuck.

He put his elbows on his knees and put his face in his hands. "He's the capo of the Giraldi crime family, Tinkerbell."

If I'd had a muscle in my body that wasn't tensed to pain, they caught up. Even my toes curled. "You're making that up."

His face was red and sweaty. He looked more like a man and less like a mayor than he had since the morning I discovered his infidelity. "I wish I was. I wish I was only jealous."

My ex-fiancé didn't get jealous often, but when he did, he burned white hot. I'd never betrayed him or any of my boyfriends. My relationships had ended because of educational choices (Randolph went to Berkeley, and I went to MIT) or because the other party strayed or because there was nothing worth bothering with, as was the case with Sam Traulich. He was a nice guy, just completely incompatible with me.

Sam and I stayed friends, and when he'd called to ask if I had any contacts at Northwestern Films, I agreed to a lunch. It had gone long. At three thirty p.m., Sam and I were laughing over some crumb of nostalgia when Daniel stormed into the little diner. At first, he was thrilled to see me alive. He'd apparently been calling the office for hours about our dinner plans, and no one knew where I was. My cell battery had died, so he tracked me down by having his friends on First Street look into my credit card transactions for the previous two hours.

For some reason, that didn't bother me.

Once he'd gotten over his initial delight, he got a good look at Sam, who was burnished brown from the sun, joyful as always, laid-back, and in good humor. Daniel put on his politician game, apologized, and appeared to forget about it. We made it to dinner on time. Life moved on.

But not for Daniel. I was shocked to find out years later, through a mutual friend, what had followed. As an extraordinarily popular young prosecutor, Daniel had arranged for Sam to be picked up by the police, brought in, roughed up, and detained. Daniel visited the detainee and mentioned that if he ever kept his girlfriend too long again, Sam would be joined in his cell by at least three gang members who owed him favors.

I had been livid. I slept on the couch for three weeks and barely spoke to him. That was the last intolerably stupid thing Daniel ever did on my behalf.

"Okay," I said. "I'm listening. Antonio is what... in the mafia?"

"Yes."

"You mean there's still a mafia?"

"Yes, Virginia, there is a mafia."

I paused for a long time. On the one hand, he might as well have told me Antonio was a leprechaun. On the other, I couldn't say I was surprised.

Chapter Thirteen

I texted Antonio.

—I have my one question—

—I want you to ask it in person—

—Agreed—

The address was in Hollywood Heights, overlooking the Bowl, on a hairpin turn that looked like a sheer drop on the right and a fortress wall on the left. A thirty-foot long, fifteen-foot high dumpster was visible over the hedge, and crashing and banging drowned out the scrape of cricket wings. I edged past a pickup truck that looked as though it had survived a demolition derby and parked next to a low sports car covered by a grey tarp.

The house was Spanish with a red tile roof, leaded stained glass accents, and thick adobe walls. Tarps swung from rafters, and every wall's plaster had been cracked down to the lathe. I followed the banging and crashing, nodding at the rough men pushing a wheelbarrow of broken house detritus.

"Is Antonio here?" I asked.

I couldn't imagine him hanging around a scraped-to-the-beams structure, but one of the guys thumbed toward the back of the house. I thanked him and headed in that direction. The pounding, thumping sounds were followed by the tickle of pebbles hitting the floor. The air got dusty, and the smell of pine hit me as I saw him.

I'd always been attracted to clean cut, educated men, men who had people to change their flat tires, drive them around, break down their walls. They exerted themselves mightily in gyms and squash courts. But none of them had ever looked like Antonio. He hoisted a sledgehammer and brought it down. The wall crumbled under the weight, and he wedged the head behind the wall and yanked it out, sending a shot of plaster and shredded lathe toward him. He didn't stop, though. Didn't even pause. His wiry muscles shifted and pulsed. The satin sheen of sweat on his olive skin brought out every muscle and tendon.

I knew women who liked that sort of thing: a sweaty man doing physical labor. I had never understood the appeal until that moment. He brought the sledgehammer down with a coil of force, like a righteous god smiting an errant creation off the face of his earth. The movement was so dramatic the gold pendant around his neck swung around to his shoulder.

"I know you're there, Contessa." He brought the hammer down again.

"Don't you have people to do this for you?"

He tossed the hammer down as if he was done with the day's violence. "It's my house, and demo's too much fun to delegate." His face was covered in dust, sweat, and a smile.

"You should hire yourself," I said.

"Like it?"

"It'll be nice once you mop. Dust. You know, maybe a few pictures on the wall." I swept my hand to the view of the city, the busted everything, the sheer potential.

"Let me show you." He headed out an archway, indicating I should follow.

He led me onto a balcony on the west side of the house. The terra-cotta floor looked to be in good shape, and the cast-iron railing curled in on itself, making a floral design I'd never seen.

"I love this view," I said, understating the grandeur of the ocean of lights. "I could look out on this all night."

He pulled a pack of cigarettes from his back pocket and poked one out. I refused his offer, and he took out a big metal lighter.

"Sit here at night, have a glass of wine. Or in the morning, a cup of coffee, just look over the city." He lit his cigarette with a *click* clack, his profile something out of an art history class. He put his fingertips to the back of my neck, his stroke so delicate I didn't lean into it, just stayed as still as I could.

"You had a question?" he asked, tracing the line where my shirt met my skin.

"Are you a leprechaun?" I asked.

"Only when St. Patrick's Day lands on a full moon." He was smiling, but I could see the question had confused him.

"I'm sorry. I had a real question, but I forgot which one I picked."

Because they were all ridiculous, of course. If he was some cartoon capo, he'd have a dozen guys around him all the time. He'd wear pinstripes and a fedora. He'd carry a gun. He'd say *capisce* a lot.

"Do I get any questions?" he asked, interrupting my thoughts.

"I'm an open book."

He laughed softly, smoke trailing behind him. "Right. Open, but in a different language."

He gave me an idea.

"I'm not going to ask you a question," I said. "I'm going to tell you what happened to me today."

"Let me make you coffee."

THE KITCHEN WAS in bad but useable shape. The beige marbled tiles with little mirrored squares every few feet, dark wood cabinets, and avocado appliances told me the place hadn't been redone since the seventies.

Antonio sat me in a folding chair at a beat up pine table. "Best I have for now."

"You living here during all this mess?"

"No. I have another place." He gave no more information. "Do you like espresso? I have some hot still."

"Sure."

He poured from a chrome double brewer into two small blue cups. "Does it keep you up?"

"Nope."

"Good. A real woman." He brought the cups and a lemon to the table and set a cup before me. I reached for the handle, but he made a little *tch tch* noise. "Not yet." He cradled the lemon in one palm and a little knife in the other. "What happened to you today?"

"Today, my assistant found a picture of us in the paper."

"Saw that," he said, cutting a strip of lemon peel. "You looked sexy as hell. I wanted to fuck you all over again."

If he was trying to get my body to turn into a puddle of desire, it was working. "Everyone saw it."

"Everyone want to fuck you as bad as I did?"

"My ex-fiancé showed up."

"The Candidate…" He dropped a yellow curlicue into my saucer. "Bet he regrets what he did, no?"

"You'll have to ask him."

I reached for the espresso, but he stopped me again, plucking the rind from my saucer and rubbing it on the edge of my cup.

"Do you want Sambuca?" he asked.

"Sure."

He reached back, plucked a bottle from a line of them, and unscrewed the top. "In Napoli, the men point their pinkies up when they drink espresso to show their refinement. Once they've been here long enough, they drink like Americans." He poured a little Sambuca into our cups.

"How do the women drink?"

"Quickly, before the children pull on their skirts."

I sipped the drink. It was good, thick, rich. I took a bigger mouthful but didn't gulp.

"So there's a picture in the paper of us, and let's not play tricks with each other," he said. "It looked like we're intimate."

"It did."

"Next to a picture of you and him." He picked up his cup.

I followed suit. "Yes."

"And he runs to your office, how many hours later? One? A half? Or are we measuring in minutes?"

We looked at each other over our cups.

"I don't see that it matters." I blew on the black liquid, the ripples releasing the licorice scent of the Sambuca.

He smirked. "Maybe it doesn't. What did it take him one to sixty minutes to tell you?"

"That you run an organized crime empire."

He said nothing at first, just put his espresso to his lips and drank. He kept his pinky down, holding the demitasse with his curled fist. "I'm very impressed with me." He clicked the cup to saucer. "Less so with him. I might have to vote Drummond."

"I looked into it after he left, once I knew what I was looking for. You're being investigated for all kinds of fraud. Insurance. Real estate. And you don't want me to ask questions, so what am I supposed to think?"

"Is that your question?" he asked. "What are you supposed to think? I have an answer for that one."

"I don't have an actual question. I know you haven't been convicted of anything, and I know what we had was just a casual screw."

"It wasn't casual."

"We can't make any commitments to each other. And that's fine. But I don't sleep with strangers. If you're going to continue to be a stranger, then I can't do this."

He closed his eyes and cocked his head left, then right, as if stretching before a boxing match. "I have a history, and it followed me here."

I sat back. "Go on."

"My father didn't exist to me. My mother shooed off the idea of him. Like she made me herself, out of nothing. I didn't know who my father was until I was eleven. I had some business, and he was the man one went to with business."

"At eleven? What business did you have at that age?"

"It's a different world over there. Things need to be taken care of. If the trash wasn't getting picked up, you went to Benito Racossi. If the delivery boy was stealing from your mother, you went to Racossi. My mother rarely left the apartment, and my sister… Well, I'd never send her to a man like that. But once I met him, I saw it." He made a quick oval around his face. "Like looking in a mirror, but older."

"He was your father?"

"He didn't deny it. Took me under his wing. Gave me work. Legal work. Anything he had to keep me out of trouble. My mother? It nearly killed her. She didn't want me in the life. She never believed I didn't do anything illegal. Neither did the *polizia*. Neither did Interpol. Neither does Daniel Brower, who's going to make my life hell if he's mayor. But as God is my witness, every business I have runs because I watched how my father did it, but I've never imitated what he did. So I'll tell you this once and swear to it, I've beaten every charge against me and I'll beat everything they put on my back because I'm clean."

"I believe you."

"Don't put me in a position where I have to defend myself against this again."

He was so definite, so stern, so parental that I didn't think I could spend another second in his presence. I stood. "If asking you questions urns you into an ass, I'll be sure to only make declarative statements on he infinitely small chance I ever see you again. Thanks for the coffee."

I spun on my heel and walked out of the kitchen, winding up in a room hadn't come through. Then I found another with a broken stone staircase. didn't feel him following me until a second before he grabbed me and ushed me toward a leaded glass window.

"Let go of me."

"No."

I clawed at his hands as they fondled me, going under my shirt and bra vithout prelude or hesitation. The flood of arousal was painful.

"Stop," I said, trying to get his arms off me.

"Next time you say stop will be the last." He placed my hands on ither side of the window. The stone was cold, and the pressure of him on ny back was harder than the wall. "What do you want to say?" He shifted ehind me, unmistakably getting his dick out. I heard the tick of a condom vrapper hitting the tiles. Was he wrapping it up again? God, I hoped so.

I wanted to say stop. No. Don't. But I needed him to relieve my ache, nd I knew he meant that my next objection would send him away.

'Do it."

He yanked down my pants. I saw his reflection in the window, broken y curved strips of lead, looking at my ass. He put one hand on my throat, is thumb resting behind my ear, while his other hand yanked down my nderwear and drove into where I was wettest.

"I'm going to fuck you so fucking hard." He tightened the grip of oth hands.

I'd made him angry. That was clear in every vowel. I shouldn't like hat. It shouldn't turn me on. But as I stood with my ass jutting out, my bra nd shirt pulled up until my breasts swung, and a man's dick at my opening, I could only wonder how to make him angrier.

"You'd better make it worthwhile," I said. "I have no time for weet talk."

"You're such a rich little princess." He pressed my neck down and ulled my hips toward him with the fingers he had inserted in me.

"Fuck you," I whispered. "You're a worthless street punk."

I thought he would put his dick back in his pants and walk away. nstead, he jammed it in me with animal brutality. I cried out not because it urt, but because the way he did it, plus the raw physical pleasure it reated, pushed the wind out of me.

"You like this?" he said, thrusting with every word. "You like this. Vorthless. Street. Punk. Fucking. You?"

His arms constricted around me. His right squeezed a breast, his left had four fingers on my clit, shifting like tectonic plates with every thrust. I grunted. I didn't think I'd ever grunted during sex, but that wasn't sex. That was two animals mating under a bush.

He pulled out and yanked me up. I saw us in the reflection in the window.

"Look at you. That face. I want to see you when you come." He growled it. "Since the minute I saw you, I've wanted you. I've wanted to open your legs and take you." As if his words were fingers, they drifted down my body, fondling me, arousing me. "I've seen women come. They forget to look beautiful. They forget who they are. I want to see you when you lose yourself and all you know is my name."

He sat on the windowsill, holding his hand out for me. I straddled him, lowering myself onto him. He guided me by the hips.

"This is good?" he asked as if he already knew the answer.

"So good. Fucking you is so good."

"Look at me."

He pressed me down, pressing my clit against his root. I gasped, trying to keep my eyes on him.

"Let me see," he whispered over and over. "Let me see you come."

He fucked harder and faster, and I lost myself.

"Oh God," I gasped. "Coming. Coming."

"Give it to me, Contessa. Show me."

He put his hand under my chin, pushing it up until my vision was filled with him. I opened my mouth, but nothing came out. My lungs constricted around my heart, and my joints stiffened. I felt held up by his dick, but his arms and hands bound me to him as I came, watching him.

I pressed my forehead to his shoulder and put my hands on his biceps, and without an ounce of tenderness, he pulled my hair back and down until I was on my knees with the slick head of his cock against my cheek, and he stood over me.

"Take it. Now."

He pulled the condom off. I opened my mouth, and he guided himself in. I choked, and he pulled out. I prepared myself, holding down my reflex and pressing the back of my tongue down. I put my hands at the base of his shaft and put his cock in my mouth, sliding the bottom of it against my flattened tongue. As he slid it out, I sucked, tasting my fluids on him.

"Yes, Contessa, that's it. Suck my cock. All the way."

I took him into my throat as far as I could, making up the rest with my hands, and sucked as he pulled out.

"Look at me," he said.

We made eye contact, and he pushed forward. I opened my throat, but he was a lot of man for one mouth. I paused and, again, took him far down. His lips parted, and I knew I'd done it right. He thrust into me. He felt good, tasted good. I wanted him to come hard, and my desire to please him rattled the back of my throat.

"I'm coming in your mouth." He grunted. "Take it. Take it all in your throat."

His eyes closed tight, and I watched him as he thrust and came, flooding my tongue and throat with bitter, sticky lava. He muttered something in Italian, spitting curses through his teeth. I'd never seen anything so hot, and I swallowed every drop of him.

When he opened his eyes and saw me beneath him, he took a sharp breath. "So sweet." He brushed my hair away from my face then pulled my head to him.

I didn't even understand my reactions. "Not casual. I know what you mean."

"But no questions. It means I have to defend myself. I don't like it."

"Okay. No more questions." I didn't know if I could keep that promise, but I could definitely put it on hold to have sex like that again.

I turned, wrapping my arms around his legs, and I turned to watch the image of us, me on my knees before him, with his hands at my back, in the window.

I screamed. Like a glowing mask floating in the night, a woman's face sat framed in the window.

Chapter Fourteen

Antonio had me behind him so quickly and smoothly I didn't even realize he was protecting me until I tried to stand. My pants restricted my thighs, and I nearly fell.

He held me up. "Marina!" he shouted.

I straightened my shirt and pants. Antonio zipped himself up and ran for the door.

He turned and held up a finger to me. "Don't go anywhere."

And he was gone. I still had the sting of his spunk in the back of my throat.

I straightened, breathed, and went outside. His admonition to stay put had fallen on Teflon ears. I didn't know who Marina was or what she was doing outside his window. She could be a sister or cousin or the local convent rep, but she was young and attractive, and my blood went a familiar shade of green. I didn't like feeling that way, especially about a man I had no claim to.

I intended to get in my car and drive away. Around the bend, I found the balcony. I knew how to get back to my car from there, but I heard voices. A Mercedes was parked in the rear drive, lights on and engine running. The woman stood by the open driver's door. She was upset, hands flailing, voice squeaking. Antonio shouted recriminations in the spaces between hers.

That wasn't a fight between cousins. I stepped back, and my foot shifted a loose tile. The scrape was louder than I would have imagined.

They looked up at me. I backed away then turned and ran to my car. I managed to get in my car and get it started before he got to the window. He knocked on the glass. I waved good-bye.

He got in front of the car. "Open up."

I cranked down the window. "That only works during, not after."

"It's not what you think."

"Is she a blood relation?"

He came around to my side of the car.

"Yes? No? What is it, Antonio? Oh, I'm sorry. Did I phrase that as a question?"

I put the car in gear, and he threw himself through my open window. I screamed from the shock of having him between me and the windshield. He yanked the emergency brake.

"Don't make me drag you out of this car," he said.

"If you have something to tell me, just tell me. I'm not asking anything."

"Come inside."

"No."

Still leaning through the door, he held the bottom of my face. "I want you. First, I want you."

"Thanks. I'm glad I'm not a second. You know what? I'm tired of playing in an orchestra. I want to go solo. Now." I pulled the brake down. "Get out of my car, or half of you is getting torn off when I drive away."

"It's not what you think."

I put the car in drive. "You have no idea what I think."

I let go of the brake, and even though I couldn't see through Antonio's gorgeous body, I drove. He cursed and pulled out of the window. I turned onto the street and left him behind.

Chapter Fifteen

"What's your problem?" Katrina asked three days later.

We were on set in Elysian Park from seven a.m. to three p.m. on a weekend, and the light had been consistently softened by clouds. I shrugged. I had no idea what she was talking about. I still had to go through the other script supervisor's notes.

She put her knee on the park bench where I had set up my files. "You got a frown." She formed her hand into a claw and pivoted her wrist as if turning a knob on my face. "It needs an inversion."

Pam had called it a sourpuss, and I'd given her the same answer. "I'm fine. Just a cold."

"Bullshit." She was fatigued. The days were very long, and she had confided that she was losing faith that it would ever be a movie. It was a common malady at the seventy-five percent mark. "I don't have time to needle it out of you because in two minutes, someone is going to come here asking me which shirt Michael should wear, and I'll have to convince them I care. So tell me."

I slapped the clipboard on the table. "The Italian guy. He gave every indication he didn't want me close. I slept with him twice, neither time in an actual bed, and I'm an idiot for being shocked that I wasn't the only one he was with. So no, I expected nothing from him. But maybe once, for kicks, I'd like someone to be exclusive for fifteen minutes."

"Ah."

"Fuck it. I don't care."

She stood still for a second then said, "Did you just say what I think you said?"

I flipped through my pages without looking at her. "Go direct a movie. You make me crazy."

She stepped away from the table, walking backward to the camera. When she was far enough away, I checked my phone. That text was the first I'd heard from Antonio since I almost tore him in half with my car.

—I'd like to speak with you—

—I'm all out of questions—

—I'll do the talking—

What was he promising? More non-answers? That game was old. Either he would be forthcoming or he wouldn't, and the more he promised to reveal who he really was, the less appealing he became. I needed overall sincerity. I needed intimacy. I didn't need a sex doll, no matter how good the sex was.

—No. I'm sorry. I'm done with this—

—But I'm not—

I shuddered and pocketed the phone. I wasn't going to encourage him.

Michael threw himself into the chair next to me, his lithe, tight body encased in a henley and grey jeans. "Heard that conversation back there."

"And you have the answer?"

"I have *an* answer. Wanna hear it?" He raised his eyebrows as if he was offering candy. He was a handsome guy, and twice as fine on camera.

"Sure."

"It's not you, it's him."

I laughed.

Michael leaned forward. "I mean it. Look, I'm… let's say active. It's not the girls. Some are real nice. Good people. Make someone a great wife. But I'm on set until the wee hours. I can't do the maintenance a guy's gotta do. So we're clear on that in the beginning."

"You're a charmer, you know that?"

"Any time. And if you want to be clear about something, some time, we can be maintenance-free. You and I."

"I'm this close to taking my pants off and jumping on you. I mean, you can really sell a girl."

He laughed, shaking his head. "All right. But friend to friend, it's not you. You're very cool, very beautiful, very smart. Just unlucky so far." He bounced up and gave me a salute. "Remember all that. And if you're ever looking, let me know."

"Thanks. I mean it."

He strode off to makeup. I checked my phone. Antonio didn't send a follow-up, and I didn't answer. Michael had cheered me up somewhat. He was all right, and maybe if I wanted something forgettable sometime, I'd call him.

The park shoot bled into Sunday, and I collapsed on my couch with a duffel bag full of binders and notebooks at my feet. Katrina dropped her head on the kitchen table with the TV on.

Chapter Sixteen

Our Monday meeting had been a drone of problems and the same processes to manage them. Then we talked about implementing new processes to manage the same issues. Then we had new discussion points that were just shades of the old ones. The agency collected money on behalf of clients, deducted ten percent, and sent the rest. Anytime money moved, there were the twin matters of how much and how fast it moved. Nothing else really counted.

When I came back, Pam tapped her fingers like a drum machine, hitting the stapler on fourths. "Danny Dickinsonian."

"Is he here?" I asked.

"Nope. Wanted you to meet him at his office downtown. Said it was important and apologies for the imposition et cetera. New polls show he's getting beaten on the east side. Badly. Might be about that." Tap tap tappa.

Running for mayor was an eighty-hour-a-week job. I'd known that from the beginning. "What do I have this afternoon?"

"Staff meeting at one. Procedure and protocols touchbase with Wanda's team at two."

Taking an afternoon jaunt downtown was undoubtedly ten times more appealing than either of those events. "Tell him I'll be there."

THE DA'S office was in a 1920s stone-carved edifice a few blocks from my loft, so I parked at home and walked. The heat weighed on me. The streets, though not crowded, were populated.

The DA's building was set back from the street with an expanse of lawn utilized by birds, squirrels, and urban picnickers. The tweedy grey brickwork matched the flat city sky, and as I got closer, I saw the stonework from a lost era. Like Roman reliefs, granite men carried logs, fished in a pebble sea, built houses from petrified wood, all immortalized with the toil of a sculptor's sweat.

The lady at the front desk knew me, but I still needed to sign in and get a sticker. I was spared the thumbprint. I saw Gerry, Daniel's top strategist, in the hall.

He stopped short and put out his hand. "Theresa, thank you for going to Catholic Charities." When he shook my hand, he also kissed my cheek and patted my back.

"I was afraid I did more harm than good," I said.

"No. Even a failed tactic can serve an overall strategy. Don't forget that."

"So I'm a failed tactic now?" I said with a smile and a lilt. "I thought I meant more to you than that."

He pressed his lips together. "You're perfect. You have politics in your blood. If I could, in good conscience, ask you to take that stupid bastard back, I would. He can't lose with you by him."

I had a few answers, none of them politic or kind. I chose the most bland. "He can win just fine without me."

"Maybe, but it'll be close."

"Any idea why I'm here?"

"Come," he said.

I let him lead me down the hall to Daniel's office. A married couple he used for promotion was just leaving. They greeted me, then suddenly I was alone with my ex-fiancé.

He had a biggish office by 1920s standards. The windows slid up and down with rackety tick*tick*s, and the walls were molded in every place molding could be placed. Over the last ninety years, it had been painted bi-annually, rounding out the edges until the room looked like the inside of a wedding cake.

"Found her wandering the halls," Gerry said before ducking out.

Daniel had on a thin blue tie and white shirt with the cuffs rolled to the elbows. His wooden chair was dressed in his jacket, and he was every bit the good-looking, hardworking crusader for justice. "Theresa, thank you for coming."

"After the election, this beck-and-call thing is over," I said.

He approached a chestnut table that must have come with the building and pulled out a chair for me. I sat. He leaned on his desk and crossed his arms instead of sitting with me. I crossed my legs and faced him.

"It's been a tough few days here," he said.

"I have a protocol review I can still make if you don't have something to say to me."

"I know how much you love those." He smiled his big, natural white smile.

"There were threats something would actually get done at this one."

"Then it's not really a protocol review."

I sighed. "This is about Antonio again? Just say it."

"I need to know what he is to you."

"Oh, God. Really?" I stood. "Dan, honey, you're so far out of line."

"It matters. It matters to my campaign, and it matters to me. I need your help, and in order for me to even ask, I need to know the nature of your relationship with him."

"It's nothing."

"Have you had sex with him?"

"Daniel!"

"I need to know."

"Is this a deposition? Are you taking notes? Where's the court reporter?"

He sighed and dropped his arms. "We've reached a wonderful pause in a war that's been going on for a few decades. We have the Carlonis for all manner of shit, and I'll file charges when everything's in order. But the other side? The Giraldi family? I have nothing. I have accounting files we got from the NSA, but everything looks clean. I need them looked at by someone with your eye."

"And you don't have a team of people?"

"They have skill. You have talent."

"I think this is about more than my talent." I couldn't hold to that line for long because he'd asked me to look at the Carloni files months ago. He'd switched to their rivals, but his ideals about my talents were well known.

"We got Donna Maria Carloni on embezzlement thanks to a mole. Good mole. I got nothing with Spinelli," he said.

"Who you can't even prove is the head of any kind of crime organization, much less the Giraldis."

"He's committed a few murders to get to where he is, Tink. Just because I can't prove it doesn't make it any less true. And yes, I'm terrified of you being anywhere near him, and yes, this is two birds with one stone. I get your eyes on his books, and I get *you* to tell *me* where his malfeasance is. But if you're sleeping with him, I can't use you. I'll have to fly a guy in from Quantico, and that'll alert everyone that I have the NSA docs. They'll be questioned and possibly yanked."

"This is a hot mess."

"I know."

"The only way for me to avoid drama is to walk out right now," I said. "But you have me curious. And you know I think you're the best man for the mayor's mansion."

"So will you?"

"I had sex with him twice. But it's over."

He looked down to hide his expression, but I saw his fingers tighten. My first reaction was to tell him tough crap. He threw me away. It was my right to sleep with anyone I wanted. My second reaction was subtler.

"Do you have time for a personal question?" I asked.

He looked at me. I'd hurt him. I loved him, and I'd hurt him. I knew how he felt when he did it to me.

"I need it answered completely and honestly," I said. "I have no energy for beating around the bush or confidence boosts right now."

"Okay."

"Is something about me just not enough? I mean, is there something inherently unsatisfying?"

He took a long time answering. "I always wondered if you really enjoyed it."

I picked up my bag and slung it over my shoulder. "I did. A lot."

He rushed to open the door for me. "I'm avoiding asking for another chance."

"Well done, Mister Mayor."

I GOT BACK to WDE in time for the protocol review, which was marginally productive. When I got back to my office, another vase of red roses stood on Pam's desk.

I DON'T GIVE up so easy

YEAH. He'd chase me, catch me, and continue with Marina or whoever else made him feel good. An inaccessible little heiress would quickly become boring.

After seven years, Daniel didn't know if I'd enjoyed sex. What was wrong with me? Was I empty inside? I'd thought I'd imagined every horrifying answer he could have given me, but I hadn't even scratched the surface.

At least I knew what the problem was. Maybe if I went back to Daniel with the assurance that I did like sex, he wouldn't look elsewhere. Maybe. But the thought of going back to him just depressed me.

Chapter Seventeen

I woke to the smell of bacon. I'd somehow crawled into bed during the middle of the night. Katrina had been known to put breakfast together when she felt chipper, and I was very grateful for her mood and her hospitality, especially on a work day. I showered and put up my hair, masking the circles under my eyes with some very expensive stage makeup. I was mid-stairwell when I heard a man's voice coming from the open kitchen. Katrina said something I couldn't hear above the crackle of pork belly. Then the man laughed.

"Antonio?" I bent around the iron bannister.

"He said I have to call him Spin," Katrina called.

"*Buongiorno*! I brought you breakfast."

I stepped into the kitchen. "I smelled the bacon."

"It's pancetta," Katrina said, picking a few squares out of the pan and putting them on toast. "He's corrected me, like, seven times already. He's cute but annoying."

"Mostly annoying," he said, shifting scrambled eggs across the pan.

"Annoy me any time." She folded up her sandwich and slipped it into a bag.

"This is a little presumptuous considering the way we left it last time," I said.

"Gotta go!" Katrina gave Antonio the one-kiss-per-cheek exit and bounced out with a wink to me.

I crossed my arms, but I was hungry. The pancetta smelled delicious.

Antonio pointed the fork at me. "This suit? It's nice for a funeral."

I sucked in my cheeks. I'd chosen a black below-the-knee wool skirt and matching jacket, and he was trying to throw me off in my own house. He looked perfect in a light blue sweater and collar shirt.

"Insulting me?" I stood next to him and bumped him with my hip. "This is how you seduce me?" I snapped a wooden spoon from the canister and poked at the eggs.

"If I wanted to seduce you, the suit would be on the floor already."

"You don't want to seduce me?"

He took a piece of egg on a fork and blew on it. "I do, but as you know, we left on poor terms last time." He held the fork to my lips, holding his palm under it to catch if it dripped.

"And tell me, Mister Spinelli, how do you intend to improve the terms?" I let him feed me.

"By explaining." He divided the eggs onto two plates.

"What? I can't hear you over this explosion of delicious."

He looked genuinely pleased that I liked his cooking, and he counted the ingredients on his fingers. "Salt, milk, *parmesano*, rosemary, and pancetta, of course. You have all my secrets now." He put the plates on the center island and pulled a stool out for me. He'd already set out coffee, juice, and toast.

"You've buttered me up quite thoroughly."

He sat and poured me coffee. "A compliment for a job well done?"

"Yes."

"I appreciate that. But I want to give you the explanation part now, if the taste of the eggs won't interfere with your hearing?"

"Okay, go ahead."

He cleared his throat and sipped his juice. "Marina and I were a regular thing until a few weeks ago. She claimed I was distracted, and she was right. So we ended it. Or I thought we did. The other night, I found out that I'd ended it and she'd paused it." He took a couple of bites of his breakfast then continued. "She comes from the same place I do. A little town outside Napoli. This was a connection between us. She's a nice girl. I won't speak evil of her. She took our thing more seriously than I did, and it didn't break as easily as I'd expected. I've spent the past few days making sure she understands. I don't want any crossover, or however you call it."

I sighed and put down my fork. "I'm going to be honest. I like you. And I love this breakfast. But if I end up believing you're telling me the whole truth, it'll be a conscious decision I'm making. And with my history, that decision takes some effort. I don't expect or want a commitment, but I don't like crossover, as you say."

"I don't either."

"And the questions thing? It bothers me."

"I can't negotiate that."

"Then what are we doing?"

"We are enjoying ourselves. Do you object to that?"

"I guess I can live with it for now. It'll come to bite us, though."

"Maybe." He leaned in to kiss me, much of his hardness and cocky arrogance gone. His lips looked soft and sweet as opposed to inaccessibly beautiful. His tongue was warm, slick, moving in harmony with his tender mouth. The smell of a pine forest in the morning, all dew and smoldering campfires, swelling my senses.

I wanted him. His neck, his jaw, his legs between mine. I wanted to suck on his fingers and thumbs. I reached between his legs, and he stopped me.

"This was only breakfast."

I groaned. "Please?"

"Tempting, Contessa. But it's been twice, and too hurried both times. The next time we fuck, it's going to be for a few hours, and you're going to need to be wheeled out. I'm not cheating you again." He reached for the dishes. "I'll clean up. Go get ready for work."

By the time I'd brushed my teeth and put my hair and makeup in order, he'd finished clearing the island. We walked out the door kissing. I didn't think I'd ever been so happy. Then I remembered what I'd promised Daniel, and by the time Antonio closed my car door and stepped away, my happiness had been worn away by the friction of reality.

I'd told Daniel it was over, and that had just changed, and I didn't even know how. I was curious about Antonio's alleged corruption. I couldn't be with a criminal, much less a murderer. Not since my first experience at thirteen, which left me scarred and the boy dead, had I encountered a dangerous man. I'd kept clear of all manner of worthless street punk—until Antonio, who could still back off any question he didn't feel like answering.

We were together. We weren't. It didn't matter. I was looking at those books.

Chapter Eighteen

My expertise was in accounting, but really, it was in the movement and flow of money. I looked at ledgers with a broad eye, finding patterns and flow. Like rivers on a map that fell into lakes, disappeared into mountains, and got spit into the ocean, the shifts of money were seen best from far away, with the finer details removed.

Bill and Phyllis, the core of the DA's financial analysts, were a married couple who had met in the Los Angeles district attorney's office forty-three years previous. They were detail people, in all their Midwestern glory—she was from Cadillac, Michigan and he was from Collett, Indiana. They reveled in getting it right, in not one shred of a detail falling through their fingers.

Thus, they missed everything.

If they'd understood the first law of fiscal dynamics—that money cannot be gained or lost, only moved—they'd understand that it all went somewhere. It was most important to follow a flow of cash downriver, and let the creeks taper into mysterious blue points. The answer was in the streams' and the rivers' undercurrents.

"Hi," I said.

"Hello, dear," Phyllis said, gracing me with a brilliant smile. "How are you?"

"Fine." I put my bag on the table.

Bill sat at the old banker's desk, tapping on a loud keyboard, his face a few inches too close to the screen. "Got mail from the boss." His chin pointed at his screen, eyes squinted. "Miss Drazen's looking at the Giraldi files. That right, Miss Drazen?"

"Theresa. Yes. If you don't mind?"

"We looked at them already. There's nothing there. We had the guys from downstairs working with us."

"Probably," I said. I didn't want to step on his toes, or the toes of the hundreds who had pored over the documents. "Just a new set of eyes."

"Have at it." He felt abused, if his expression was any indication. He dragged four document boxes from a shelf, one at a time, with the scratch of heavy cardboard sliding on wood.

"Anything digital?" I asked.

"Some," said Phyllis, opening the boxes. "I'll get it for you."

Bill wiped his nose with a cotton handkerchief, fidgeted, and sat. Poor guy. I'd flattened his toes, and it wasn't even lunchtime. I slid folders out, and with them came a scent. Not the musty odor of dust bunnies and paper residue. It was cologne, spicy and sweet with an undercurrent of pine trees after a rain. I caught a hint of something that I couldn't identify until I'd unloaded the whole box.

I inhaled again, trying to catch it, but it was gone. Only the dewy forest morning remained.

I hadn't spent more than an hour with the ledgers before I caught something. Just a few million in property tax payments. Legal payments from legal accounts containing legally obtained money.

One house in particular, in the center of the lots, had been purchased three years earlier with money from an international trust. The rest had been snapped up in the previous six months. It was a lot of property, tight together in the hills of Mount Washington, and it rankled.

Chapter Nineteen

Margie's red hair was tied back in a low ponytail, but strands had found their way free to drape over her cheeks. She was on her second chardonnay, and lunch hadn't even arrived. She could have had seven more and still litigated a murder trial.

"Mob lawyers are consigliore," she said. "They learn the law to get around it. But they don't get to be boss."

"Why not?"

"They're not made. Before you ask, made means protected. And other things. It's a whole freemason ceremonial shindig. They have to kill someone. Contract killing, not a vendetta. Now do I get to know why you're asking?"

"Because you'd know."

"Oh, shifty sister. Very shifty. You know what I meant." She waved as if swatting away murder. Then she nodded and sat up a little.

I followed her gaze to Jonathan, who sauntered toward us after shaking hands with the owner. He kissed Margie first, then me. A waiter put a scotch in front of him.

"Sorry, I'm late," he said.

"How was San Francisco?" Margie asked.

"Wet, cold, and amusingly liberal. I saw your picture in the paper," he said to me. "You're taking him back?"

"No."

"She has other things on her mind," Margie said.

"Such as?" He looked at me over the rim of his glass.

"Nothing."

"She's either writing a book or dating a mafia don," Margie said.

I went cold and hot at the same time. I set my face so it betrayed nothing. If Margie or Jonathan had suspected anything, they would have noticed the two percent change in my demeanor, but they only knew what I'd told them.

"Top secret," I said. "This doesn't leave the table. Drazen pledge."

"Pledge open," Margie said.

"Pledged," Jonathan agreed, holding up his hand lazily.

I dropped my voice. "Dan got some files on a certain crime organization from the NSA, and he's having me look at them."

Their reaction was immediate and definitive. Margie dropped her fork as if it was white hot. Jonathan picked up his whiskey glass, shaking his head.

"Is he trying to get you killed?" Jonathan asked.

"He needs to grow a set of fucking balls," Margie added.

She tilted her head a little, as if checking to see if I was going to make a fuss about her language. She'd once verbally cornered me at Thanksgiving dinner, bullying me into describing *why,* which I couldn't. Mom had begged her to stop, and Daddy had broken out laughing at my tears.

"Marge, really." Jonathan tapped his phone. "It's not that big a deal. He's the DA. If he can't protect her—"

But Margie continued undaunted. "Please, let me be the one to explain the obvious. If the mafia doesn't come after you for looking into their books, whoever's running against him will use you to undermine him. Think Hillary Clinton doing healthcare. Giving your disgraced ex-fiancé—"

"Thanks. I appreciate you defining me."

"The press will do a fine job without me," she said.

"Leave it to them then."

I glanced at my brother. He was fully engaged with his phone, smiling as if the Dodgers had won the Series. I knew he'd heard everything but had no intention of stepping into rescue me.

"Is he trying to get you back?" Margie asked. "This is his plan?"

"This was fun." Jonathan glanced up from his phone while still texting. "No, wait, we're in pledge. This wasn't fun at all."

Part of being "in pledge" was secrecy partnered with honesty, no matter how hurtful.

Jonathan put down his phone and leaned into me. "Most things, Dad can save you from, and he will."

"For a price," Margie muttered into her glass.

"Right," Jonathan continued. "But this? The mob? I don't know. That's big fish."

Our food arrived: sour lemon salads and more wine than anyone should drink at noon on a workday. We leaned back and let the waiter serve us, laying down oversized white plates and offering ground black pepper. Margie and Jonathan started eating, and I smoothed a crease in the tablecloth. Everything looked washed out by the sun and fill lights, every corner and curve of my body visible.

"We don't know if it's organized crime," I said. "Everything looks clean. Dan's looking for something illegal."

"I don't like it," Margie said.

"That's because you hate Daniel," I said.

"I was there. I saw what he did to you." Margie speared salad and glanced at me, head not moving, expression bland and open. Her lawyer look.

"I think I found something," I said. "But I'm not sure."

"Proceed quietly."

"I noticed some transactions. Real estate taxes. I followed the addresses to Mount Washington. The lots are grouped together in a really bad area. Fire sale prices."

Jonathan plopped his phone down and leaned back in his chair.

"You look like you just ate a canary," Margie said to him.

"I'm about to," he said. "Now, Margaret, stop bullying her. You're being bitter."

"Fuck you."

He turned to me. "Theresa, tell me about those buildings. Open permits? Zoning changes?"

"I don't know."

"Calls to the police about squatters? Still water?"

"I don't know."

"Complaints to Building and Safety?"

"Should I be making a list?"

He pushed his plate aside and put his elbows on the table. "If they're warehousing property, they'd raze the structures to get rid of the reporting problems. Then they'd just build an ugly apartment building when they had the land they needed. But they're keeping fire and liability traps standing. And that neighborhood... there's no way some kids won't use those buildings for business and burn the places down cooking meth."

"Who the fuck cares?" Margie moaned.

"Real estate fraud isn't covered under RICO, so they won't be federally prosecuted if they get caught doing whatever they're doing. You'd have mentioned that if you weren't busy giving her a hard fucking time."

"I'm trying to discourage her."

"Something's going on with those buildings, Theresa," he said. "Get your man to figure out what it is."

"Great idea." Margie put her napkin on the table and stood. "Encourage her. I'm going to the ladies'. By the time I get back, I expect bullets through the window."

We watched her stride across the room.

I sighed. "She thinks I'm made of sugar." I pushed my salad around my plate. Jonathan didn't say anything, and I didn't realize he was staring at me until I looked up.

"What's going on?" he asked as if he expected an answer. As if "nothing" wouldn't cut it.

We knew each other too well. As kids, the eight of us had had the option of banding together or falling apart. As a result, the youngest and the oldest had wound into two cliques, held together on the spool of Margie.

"Is this your way of getting him back?" Jonathan said. "Keeping an eye on him?"

The silence between us became long and tense, but he wouldn't give an inch. I thought Margie had gone to the bathroom in Peru.

"It's not that simple," I said.

"Go on."

"There's someone else. I won't talk about it more."

"Ah." He leaned back. "Use someone else as a threat, and then he tries to get you back with these books as an excuse? You're a tactician. I forgot to thank you for your suggestion to bring a woman I wasn't related to. Worked."

"Really? Jessica came back? That's amazing."

"Yes, but I don't want her. I'm keeping the new one. Unexpected upside."

I was stunned into silence. He'd let go of something he'd been holding onto for a long time. "What happened to change your mind?"

"It was just gone. Whatever was there. Poof, gone. And for a while, too.

Which is great, but neither of them is going to get me killed. You? You're getting deep in shit."

I didn't want to say another word about it because I didn't want to spin out of control. I just wanted to find out about Antonio without asking him questions.

"You speak Italian, right?" I said.

"Yes."

He spoke everything. It was his gift.

"*Come vuoi tu.* What does that mean?"

"Kind of 'as you wish,' more or less. Why?"

"Pledge closed," I said.

"Fine. Pledge closed."

Margie came up behind us. "Closing pledge. Who wants coffee?"

Chapter Twenty

Like every other part of central and eastern Los Angeles, Mount Washington was facing a real estate renaissance. Yet that particular hill seemed to have been passed over. The commercial district was a row of empty storefronts with gates pulled shut, broken glass, some burned out, and most graffitied over. Five blocks of third-world devastation stretched in either direction. I turned left up the hill, cracked asphalt bouncing my little car. The sidewalks ended under deep, thorny underbrush. Even at nine in the morning, I heard the beats of someone's music on the other side of the hill.

A right, then another left, and I found an eight-foot high chain-link fence stretched around a hairpin turn and up the hill. Across the street, another fence. The buildings were overgrown, unkempt, with peeling stucco and beams warped under the passion flower vines. When I opened my car door, an avocado with the squirrel-sized bite rolled down the hill with a *skit skit skoot*, popping up on a crack in the pavement and landing on the asphalt. I looked up. A cloud-high avocado tree shaded the block, spitting its bounty onto the sidewalk.

I shut the door. My car made a familiar chirp that alerted the neighborhood that something expensive was nearby. I glanced back at it then forward.

The late Frankie Giraldi had bought everything behind those fences, from what I could tell, but one house he'd bought first. He'd purchased it as an individual. Years later, his estate had moved it into trust and bought up everything around it.

The executor of the trust was the law firm of Mansiatti, Rowenstein, and Karo. Antonio Spinelli, Esq., LLP had bought them when they went belly up. They had one client: the Frank Giraldi estate. A snake eating itself. The estate's trust owned the property, and Antonio managed the trust. Did he actually own it outright? I couldn't tell from the papers I'd had in front of me.

The overgrowth detonated my allergies. I felt my sinuses swell and press against the bones of my face. A drip tickled the back of my nose. I checked my bag. Advil, tampons, wet wipes, and an empty tissue packet. Great. The tickle worked its way to the back of my throat. I put my hand in front of my mouth, checked to see if anyone was around, and made a very unladylike noise to scratch my throat as I walked down the block.

I found the house. I was allergic to just about everything growing around it.

I didn't know what I'd expected, but there was nothing but a run down, bright yellow house with a fifty-foot front yard. An old Fiat was parked on top of rosebush stumps. Stacks of faded children's toys pressed against the fence. Bars on the windows. A porch stacked with bags of leaves. The driveway had been kept clear though, which meant someone came in and out often enough to need a path. A few steps to the right, I saw muddy tire tracks from something bigger than a car.

The entrance to the drive had been chained shut. Though a hole had been cut in the fence at the next dilapidated house, it had been repaired with sharp twists of wire. I walked on a few feet and found a new opening.

I crawled through it. A thorny strand of brush found my stocking and gave it a good yank. I had an extra pair in the car, but I was still anxious about the drooping egg shape at my calf. Pushing past bamboo, bushes with sticky burrs, and tall weeds with yellow flowers that I knew tasted like broccoli, I came out into the end of the driveway, at the front end of the backyard.

The house had been built into a hill, so the backyard was at a slant, the square footage taken up by a slope that got more vertical as it bent away from the house. The structure itself was no surprise, with its beaten yellow paint and bent eaves. But the fence surprised me. Though the barriers from the street were old, hand-repaired chain link, the fences between the properties were new.

A loud crack echoed off the mountain. It could have been anything. A car backfiring. A piece of lumber snapping. Even a shotgun.

A smack of fear in my lower back sent me rushing through the bamboo and mustard weeds and through the hole in the fence, leaving behind strands of nylon for the thorns. I ran down the block and hurled myself at my car, almost twisting my ankle. The car blooped and I got in, turning the key before buckling. A drip of snot freed itself from my left sinus.

The car didn't start.

Daniel's voice bounced around my head, complaining that the car was unreliable, maintenance-heavy. He was right, and I was stuck on Mount Washington, turning my key repeatedly while nothing happened and a line of clear snot dropped down my lip.

My box of tissues was wedged under the passenger seat. Since I was stuck, and uncomfortable, and frustrated, I let go of the key and reached under the seat, rooting around for the feel of flat cardboard. I touched it and pushed, but a heavy iron pole got in the way. It was a security device called the Club that had been a big thing in the eighties, when the last owner had bought the car. Though I'd never used it, I kept it, even when it got in my damn way. I got the iron bar out and unbuckled my seatbelt. Leaning over, I curled my arm under the seat. The snot that had been sitting uncomfortably on my upper lip followed gravity. I shifted to get a look at what the box was caught on and yanked it free.

Clackclackclack

The sound of a ring rapping on the window. Too late to notice my skirt was hiked up, and I was showing full-on black garter belt to the world. I twisted to get a look at the guy standing over my car. He wore a neat striped shirt under a light windbreaker.

"You all right?" His voice was muffled through the glass.

I pulled my skirt down and sat up. "I'm fine." I snapped the last tissue out of the box and wiped my nose quickly. I cranked down the window.

"This is a nice car."

"Yeah, it won't move." I got a good look at him and recognized him by the bow lips. I held up a pointer finger and squinted, the universal sign for unreliable recognition.

"I thought I knew you," he said. "How's your sister?"

"Never better. Can you give me a push?"

"Sure. I know a garage down the street. They're honest."

There seemed to be red zones everywhere, so the garage was probably a good idea. "All right. I never got your name," I said.

"Paulie. Paulie Patalano."

"Nice to meet you again, Paulie."

Another man got out of a car behind me. He had a low forehead and moustache.

"This is Lorenzo. He's harmless," Paulie said.

"Hey, Paulie."

"Zo, this is Theresa. We're giving her a push to East Side. Yeah?"

Zo agreed. They pushed, joking the entire time about horsepower, the division of thrust between them, and who got to direct traffic when we crossed Marmion Way onto Figueroa. I steered and wondered at the odds of meeting the bow-lipped man again. When one considered the actual mathematical odds, chance meetings were nearly impossible, yet they happened all the time.

And then, I wondered, what were the odds that Antonio was somewhere near his friend? Was he somehow behind any of this?

East Side Motors appeared a block away. A typical car repair dump, with a dirty yellow and black sign advertising that every car brand in the universe was a specialty, it looked no better than any other shop around. As we got closer, it became apparent that business was brisk. The lot was packed, and men in grey jumpsuits hustled around bumpers and grilles, moving cars, shouting, and laughing.

I turned in and was greeted by a balding guy with a chambray shirt and moustache. He opened the door as soon as I stopped.

"Ma'am," he said, "we don't do German cars."

I looked up at the sign. What had looked like every brand in the universe was actually every brand in Italy. A quick glance around the lot revealed Maseratis, Ferraris, Alpha Romeos, but no German, Japanese, or American cars.

"It won't turn over," I said. "Could you hold it until I get a tow? I'll pay for the storage."

"You got it." He turned to Paulie. "Sir? Are we charging?"

"No fucking way. She keeps it here as long as she needs to." He held his hand to me. "Come on to the back."

His manner was so friendly and professional, I thought nothing of following him. I thought I'd find coffee, a seat, a stale donut perhaps. But as I walked through the hustle of the lot into the dim garage, where everything looked dusted with grime, a man in a clean, dark yellow sweater and grey jacket looked up into the underbelly of an old Ducati, exposing the tautness of his throat. Such a vulnerable position, yet he held it with supreme confidence. Antonio. Another chance meeting that I was beginning to think had little to do with the natural laws of probability.

"Spin," called Paulie from behind me.

When Antonio pulled his arms down from the Ducati, he saw me and seemed as surprised at my presence. I kept doing probabilities in my head, switching the numbers between him knowing and not knowing.

"Contessa?" he said, glancing at me then his friend.

"Up by *l'uovo,*" Paulie said.

A concerned look crossed Antonio's face, but then it was gone with a nod and a smile. He snapped a handkerchief from his pocket and carefully wiped the engine grease off his fingers. Having erased reactions from my face my whole life, I knew exactly what he was doing. He was collecting himself from surprise.

"I got this, Pauls."

"Oh yeah?"

"Yeah. We'll be in the office," Antonio said.

They stared at each other for a moment, then Paulie held out his hand. They shook on it.

"Benny!" Antonio called to a stocky man tapping at a smudged keyboard. "Friction plates, rubber, and rings, okay?"

"You got it, boss."

Boss? Okay. Lawyer. Restaurateur. Mechanic.

"Come on." He held out his hand for me.

I didn't take it. I trusted him less and less as the minutes wore on. Antonio just turned and walked through a door, holding it open as he passed into a clean, sundrenched room with industrial grey carpet and car posters.

I followed him. Coffee had been set up for the people waiting and reading magazines. Behind a counter with phone banks and more magazines sat a woman in her fifties.

"Spin," she said in a thick Italian accent, handing him a clipboard. "Sign please. I want to order the paint."

He signed without looking and walked to another door marked "Private."

I stopped. "I'm surprised to see you."

"I have the same feeling."

The middle-aged woman went about her business as if nothing was happening.

"You could have called if you wanted to see me," he continued.

"I didn't come to see you." With those words, I realized the trouble I was in. I'd been asking questions behind his back. Investigating. I couldn't imagine how angry he would be. I had no reason to be in that neighborhood except to stare at a bunch of innocently acquired property that was just a cluster of buildings with zero illegal activity surrounding them. Maybe that was my secret weapon.

"Really?" he said with a raised brow.

I smiled coyly. "I'm here now."

He opened the door and smiled back, but I couldn't tell if he'd fallen for my act or not. The office was walled in glass and striped with shadows from natural wood blinds. The décor was warmer than the rest of the business, with a dark wood desk with clawfoot legs, shelves with car manuals, and a buffed matte wood floor. Antonio closed the blinds, and my eyes adjusted. The diffused light was still more than enough to see by.

"So," he said, "up by the yellow house?"

"There was a yellow house. Needs a paint job."

He nodded. "It's not for sale."

"I hoped the owner would be in. Maybe I could talk him into selling."

"You couldn't afford it." He took two steps forward and was right in front of me.

"I have lots of money," I whispered.

"He isn't interested in your money."

His lips were on mine before he'd even completed the last vowel. His tongue found my tongue, and his hands were under my shirt, caressing my ribs, slipping under my bra. He believed it. He believed I'd come to the neighborhood hoping to see him. Maybe there was a sliver of truth to that. My legs wrapped around him, and he put his hand up my skirt unceremoniously.

He pressed his hips into the thin lace of my underwear. Would he rip another pair? I hoped so. From the bottom of my pelvis, I hoped he would.

"I don't have hours to fuck you like you deserve." He slipped a finger under my panties, finding where I was wettest. "I have a few minutes to make you hold back a scream."

He found my engorged clit, and I stiffened. He pushed me onto the arm of a chair. My arms braced me as his hand stroked.

"How did you come here, Theresa?" he said as his fingertips blinded me with sensations, making me vulnerable.

I couldn't think. "The one ten freeway."

He pulled away, moving his hand so his thumb rotated on my clit as he stood over me. I felt intimidated and powerless, and I was as afraid as I was aroused.

"Look at me," he whispered tenderly. "Spread your legs."

I did it, looking and spreading until both hurt.

He was perfectly put together, with one hand in me the way it had just been inside a transmission. "What were you doing by the yellow house?"

"I wanted to see where you lived."

"That's not my legal address."

"I hope not. It was a mess."

He answered my sarcasm by sliding two fingers into my soaking hole. "I didn't get a call about anyone trespassing at my house."

"Oh God, Antonio, I'm so close."

I noticed, as I got closer, that he wasn't telling me what he was going to do to me. Where was the dirty talk? Something was wrong, but I was too close to the incoming tide of my sexual pleasure to think clearly about what that meant.

He put his hand on the back of the chair and leaned down, his strokes getting lighter and softer, keeping me on the edge. "I want to like you, Contessa. I want to. But I can't trust you."

His words didn't sink in soon enough. My wet, engorged sex was still in his hand. On the third stroke, I exploded in an orgasm that was supposed to be a release, but instead was humiliating. The emotional disconnect cut the pleasure short, and I twisted away from him, breathing heavily with my bra half pulled over my breasts and my skirt bunched at my waist.

"What was that?" I said.

"I wondered how you just show up in my neighborhood." He took the grease-smeared hankie from his pocket and wiped the fingers that had been inside me. "You weren't looking for my house. You were looking for *something*. The district attorney sent you. You've been working for him the whole time, haven't you? It's on the side of a barn, like you say."

"You think my ex sent me to fuck you?" I straightened my clothes, seething so hard I didn't even care what I said or how I said it. But the more I wanted to say what was on my mind, the more crowded my mind became. "You think he's whoring me out? What kind of world do you live in? And let me assure you, the lack of trust is mutual. Talk about what's on the side of a barn. You react to questions like I'm spraying acid on you. You have no real law practice. A hundred different businesses. You can bust a guy's face on the hood of a car. Maybe the police questioned you so many times because you're a criminal lowlife." I brushed past him, but he caught my upper arm. "Let go of me," I growled from deep in my throat.

"I run legitimate businesses."

"What better way to do the laundry?"

His tongue pressed between his lips, and his eyes drifted to my mouth in a nanosecond of weakness. "Be careful."

"Good advice. I'm staying away from the dirtbags from now on."

He tightened his grip on my arm, and we stood like that, breathing each other's air, until a light rap came from the other side of the door.

"Spin?"

He waited a second and kept his eyes on mine as he answered. "Yeah, Zo?"

"Tow's here, and they don't know where to take the Beemer."

Silence hung between us. His jaw moved as if he was grinding his teeth. I held his gaze. He could go straight to hell, and I still wanted him. The knock came again.

Antonio whipped his head around and shouted, "What!"

Zo's voice was timid. "The tow guy has another call."

Antonio pulled me to him so hard I knew I would walk out of there with a nice bruise. He pressed his lips together as if he had something to say but didn't know how to say it.

I answered as if he'd spoken. "I know what's between us. I know it's real, as real as anything I've ever felt for a man. And I know you don't really believe Daniel whored me out to get information. Even if you think he'd do something like that, you know in your heart I wouldn't. But none of that matters. Even though you don't believe I have ulterior motives, you're scared of it." He loosened his grip just a little, and I took that as my cue to continue. "That's not the way to be together. It's too long a bridge to cross. Let's both be grown-ups and walk away before this gets uglier."

It took a few seconds, or forever, for him to remove his hand, his fingers slipping over my sleeve as if magnetized. I took a long breath, memorizing his scent, the thickness of his hair, the cleft in his jaw, the angle I held my head to look into his deep brown eyes.

"I'll have someone drive you home," he said.

"I can get a cab."

"I know. But someone from here will drive you." He opened the door. Zo was right behind it, hunched and tense.

"Make sure she gets home," Antonio said.

"Sure, boss."

I followed Lorenzo and looked back for the briefest second, enough to catch Antonio closing the office door.

On the way out, I saw a man with a comb-over I would have sworn I recognized. He wasn't wearing a mechanic's jumpsuit, but a zipper jacket. His left eye was badly bruised, almost swelled shut, and a bandage held a cut together at his brow. It was Vito, and when he saw me, he turned and walked in the other direction.

After some discussion, some signed papers, a few minutes spent waiting for something I couldn't remember because I was distracted by Antonio's presence in his office and the distance between us, I let Paulie Patalano drive me home. Apparently, my house was on his way.

Chapter Twenty-One

"You ever been in a Ferrari?" Paulie asked.

"You're joking," I said as I got into the flashy yellow car.

"Gotta ask." He slid into the driver's side and shifted his shoulder a little, touching something behind him before he got his seatbelt on.

I'd dated a detective in college, and he made the same exact move when he got into a car. When he'd caught me watching, I got a lecture about how he had to wear his gun even when off-duty and how he didn't want to take it off for a short drive. We had a long drive ahead of us, and poor Paulie was going to be very uncomfortable. He put the top down, and we got onto the freeway.

"Thanks for driving," I said once we hit traffic and the wind didn't whip as much.

"I was heading out this way." He drove with the seat pushed all the way back and his wrist on the top of the wheel.

I had my bag in my lap and my knees pressed together. "I'm glad you found me at the bottom of that hill."

"Yeah."

"You work at the car shop?"

He smiled. Changed lanes. Adjusted the hunk of metal at his back. "I own it with Spin."

"Oh, partners?"

"In everything. He's like my brother. Pisses off my real brothers, but they're douchebags. A cop and a lawyer."

"And you?"

"Businessman."

I put on my most political comportment because it was obvious what kind of business he did from the back of a body shop, with loose hours, carrying a firearm. I'd never seen one on Antonio though, which seemed strange.

I didn't care. No, I shouldn't care. It should all be meaningless small talk in a yellow Ferrari going twenty miles per hour on the 10 freeway.

"You weren't really heading west, were you?" I said more as a statement than a question.

"Zo is the only other guy I'd trust to not speed, and he'd bore the paint off the car." He glanced at me. "We just fixed it. He'd return it with primer, shrugging like, 'dunno what happened, boss, I was just talking.'"

I laughed. "Sure."

"And, you know, I want to get to know you. See what your deal is."

Did he think I was working for the DA as well? I couldn't easily ask. "My deal?"

"Spin likes you. Ain't no secret."

The road opened up for absolutely no reason, and the wind whipped my hair like cotton candy.

"I'm sure he likes plenty of girls." I pulled out my bun and let my hair fly.

"Not like this," Paulie said.

"Like what?"

He shook his head and put his eyes on the road.

"No, really," I said. "I'm not asking you to tell stories about your friend."

"Oh no? You women, you're all alike."

"Like what?"

"Like you don't want a guy to like you. You have to know how much. How high. How deep. Never simple. So before you ask again, he's never looked at a woman who's not from home."

"Pretty small dating pool."

"He don't date. You ain't getting another word outta me." He raised his index finger and put it to his lips. "Just know I'll protect him with my life."

"He's a lucky guy."

"Right about that."

Nothing he said should have hurt me, because my thing with Antonio was done, but as I watched the city blow by me, it did.

ROGUE

KATRINA WAS on set when I got home. The loft had never seemed so big, so modern, so clean. Everything had a place, and everything was in it. The surfaces were wiped sterile, and dust bunnies were eradicated.

I threw my bag on the couch. It didn't belong there, but I left it.

I missed something. I felt a longing and a regret for something I'd lost. I couldn't pin it down. In a way, it was Daniel. I missed his constant talking on the phone, the hum of his ambition, the steady foursquare geometry of his dependence. I missed his presence spreading over me even when he traveled, covering me in a way Katrina's couldn't.

"Fuck you, Daniel," I whispered. I threw my jacket over a chair and left it.

Dad had always said all we'd ever need was our family, and I'd never doubted him. But he was wrong. Dead wrong. I couldn't mold my life into any of my sisters'. I couldn't take joy in breathing their air, or feel the electricity of physical connection. I couldn't look at my house and see them coexisting with me as anything but an imposition.

The refrigerator. Vegetables in the crisper. Proteins on the bottom shelf. Leftovers above that, and on the top, condiments. I pulled out a tub of hummus. Crackers on the bottom shelf two over from the sink. I stood at the island, dipping, eating, dipping, eating. Double-dipping, even.

A blob of hummus plopped onto the counter. I swiped it up and ate it. The residual paste was the only disruption of the pristine surface.

What the hell had happened with Antonio? What was I thinking? Had I been trying to get away from Daniel in the most violent way possible? Was I trying to reject not just my comfort zone, but my lawfulness? Wasn't there an easier way to do that than by getting involved with someone I had nothing in common with? No matter how my body reacted to him. No matter how excited or how free he made me feel. No matter how alive I felt around him.

But I couldn't shake the sense of profound regret. I'd dodged a bullet but fallen onto a knife.

I let the paper towel roll drop from my hand. It rolled from the kitchen island to the front door. I needed something in my life besides a job and a man. I needed a purpose. I had nothing to care about besides myself. No wonder Daniel's infidelity had thrown me so far off the deep end.

I whipped the stepstool around to the refrigerator and reached into the cabinet above it. As a kid, I'd collected porcelain swans. I didn't know why, but I loved swans. Their grace, their delicacy. But when we moved to the loft, the mismatched animals didn't make sense, so I hid them in the highest cabinet, where they wouldn't get broken.

I took the first one out. It had a blue ribbon that flew in the wind as it raised its wings to take flight. It had cost a shameful amount. I put it on the counter. The next one was Lladro. Cheap, with a little cupid. There was a black one. An ugly duckling. One with an apron. Laughing. Swimming. Necks twisted together. I put them all on the counter until I came to the little white one in the back.

It was made of Legos. It had a red collar in flattish bricks and a bright yellow beak. My nephew David had made it for me some random Christmas. Hyper and brilliant David. How old had he been? Four? Aunt Theresa loved swans, and he'd made her a bird with such care. And she'd put it in the back of a cabinet she couldn't even reach because it didn't go with the décor.

"Fuck you, Aunt Theresa." I got down from the stepstool and put the Lego swan in the center of the island.

I opened my dish cabinet. I loved my dishes. They had blue stars with gold flourishes. Why were they in a cabinet? I took them out and laid them on the counter in piles that specifically made no sense. My flatware had been chosen with utmost care. With no room on the counter, I threw the silver on the floor like pick-up sticks.

All of it came out. Everything in the cabinets I'd ever chosen. Everything I liked. Everything beautiful and worthy. The glass jelly jars and inherited Depression glass. The gold-leaf embellished glass rack from my great-grandmother. I didn't break anything, but the frosted glass tray we got as an engagement gift almost slipped off the sink. I caught it and continued. Out of style napkin holders. Stained plastic containers. A red sippy cup Sheila had left behind on some visit. Out out out.

When I got to the last cabinet and found the dust and dirt in the back of it, I stepped into the living room where I could see the open kitchen. It was a wreck. I'd left all the cabinet doors open, and nothing was neatly or safely placed.

I reached over the island and moved some stacks until I found the little Lego swan. I had a date with my empty bed. I could figure out what to do with my life in the morning.

The bed still seemed too big. The mess downstairs offered a momentary peace then irked me into wakefulness. But I refused to go down and clean it. I had put my Lego swan on the nightstand, and when I wondered if I should just go put my life back in the cabinets, the swan clearly said no. Go to sleep. Think about the mess tomorrow.

Katrina came in. Lights went on. The TV went on. The toilet flushed. The water ran. The TV went off. The lights went off. I slept.

Chapter Twenty-Two

"What happened?" Katrina asked as she pulled a swan-shaped coffee cup from the pile. Its neck was a handle, and its wings wrapped around the bowl. "I can't find the spoons."

I picked one up from the floor. "Here. I'll wash it."

She snatched it and blew on it. "Sanitizing pixie dust. Knife too, please."

I picked one of my best silver butter knives off the floor and handed it to her without offering to wash it. The sink was full of china cruets anyway.

"I'll put it all away later."

"Whatever." She cleared a space in front of the coffee pot and poured herself some.

"But we have to be on set today, then I have work on Monday. I'll get Manuela on it when she comes Tuesday," I said.

"Whatever."

"Are you mad?"

"Mad? No. I almost broke all these damned dishes last night in a rage, but not because of them. Only because they were in front of me."

I handed her a dish. "Go ahead. Break it."

She took it and waved it up and down, balancing it on her fingertips like half a seesaw. Then she put it on top of its stack. "It's pointless." She put the heels of her hands to her eyes and growled in a tantrum.

"What?"

"Apogee fell through," she shouted, as if yelling at the entire Hollywood system.

"What? They won't distribute it?"

"No, they backed out of post-production."

"Why?"

"Because." She shook her hands as if she was at a loss for words. "Lenny Garsh moved to Ultimate, and the new guy's only backing projects he believes in. Completed projects." She stamped her feet. Full-on tantrum. "Fuck fuck fuck fuck. I have the editing bay and ADR place booked, and I can't pay."

"Okay, we can work this out."

"There's nothing to work out. I'm screwed. I tapped everyone I know to do production. Now there's no point in even finishing." Her face collapsed. It took seconds for the muscles to go slack and the tears to gather. She sniffed, hard and wet. "Fuck, what am I going to tell Michael? He was depending on this. He's a star, you know? In his gut. And I told him... I told him we'd get this done."

"You will get this done," I said, taking her shoulders.

"Ernie shot it free because he believed in me."

"Katrina—"

"It's my job to get the money, and I let everyone down." She was full-on blubbering and trying to talk through hitching gasps.

I put my arms around her. "Directrix?"

I was answered with sobs.

"You have another week of production. Do you have the money to finish it?"

She nodded into my shoulder. "But—"

"No buts. Get it together."

"I don't have enough. I missed a wide on the dinner scene."

"You won't be the first. Now we have twenty minutes to get out of here and get to set. People are waiting."

She pulled away and wiped her eyes. "I have to tell them."

"No." I put up my hands. "What is wrong with you? That'll kill the momentum."

She put her head in her hands. "I don't know what I'm thinking."

"Go take a shower, and let's go. Come on. I took a week off work to finish this with you. We have to get this thing in the can by Friday. Reschedule your ADR. It's a phone call, right?"

"If they have space. They book months in advance."

"Fast, cheap, or good," I said, quoting the old filmmaking motto that no one can get more than two of the three. "Fast isn't happening."

"I have to eat. I can't mooch off you forever."

"Whatever. Let's deal with today. Okay? We're shooting at the café again?"

"Yes."

"If you start freaking out, you come to me, right?"

"I love you, Tee Dray. You're so together."

Chapter Twenty-Three

I checked my phone after the thirty-fifth take. It was a long shot of Michael watching the woman in question over the food counter, and with so many moving parts, it was difficult to get. But the shot was meant to show infinite hours of longing for a woman who didn't want him, and on the thirty-sixth try, it was stunning.

I didn't expect Antonio to try to reach me, but I was surprised by my burning hope. Did I want him? Or did I want him to want me? He was toxic, and I shouldn't touch him even if I was operating on all emotional cylinders, which I wasn't. I had to keep in the front of my mind the fact that I couldn't trust any man with my body or heart. No matter how intense. No matter how strong. No matter how much the sex was unlike anything I'd ever experienced.

Even thinking about Antonio, I felt a familiar throb between my legs. Even as I noted the placement of every extra's arms and legs, I ached for that treacherous man, his pine scent, his rock of a dick.

"Cut!"

Katrina was barely finished her encouragements to the actors before I had my phone out. Nothing from Antonio. Three from Gerry, Daniel's strategist. I got back to business making my notes. I needed to arrange my finances so I could get Katrina half a million dollars in such a way that she would accept it.

I didn't know how I'd get it done in time. I had a week before she lost her mind. I was incorporated, but not as an investor. I couldn't decide if I wanted her to know it was me who was fronting the money. It was two in the morning, and I was tired. Hardly ready for Gerry to show up in a three-piece suit looking as though he'd just woken up, showered, shaved, and taken his vitamins.

"Almost the first lady of the city," he said with a jovial tone, "packing binders in a parking lot."

"What are you doing here?" I stuffed the last of the day's work into a duffel.

"Los Angeles never sleeps."

"Daniel Brower does. A good five hours between midnight and dawn."

"That's when I get to work. Can we talk?"

I slung the bag over my shoulder. Katrina would get home on her own. "Sure. You're driving though. My car's busted."

THE FRONT SEAT of Gerry's Caddy SUV was bigger than the couch in my first apartment. The bag was in the back like a dead body.

"He's not performing," Gerry said, turning onto the 110. "Every time he flubs or goes back to some old habit, it's like a snowball. It hasn't affected his polling yet, but soon, it's gonna get obvious."

"After the election, he'll get it together again."

"He started biting his nails."

"The ring finger?"

"Yeah. In a meeting with Harold Genter. I think I bruised his calf."

I sighed. Years, I'd spent years in media skills sessions. We'd discussed that every movement, every breath, was ten times bigger on camera, and those moves flowed into real life. People wanted their leaders polished. Policy was secondary, and politics took third rung. If he was seen biting his nails, flipping his hair, or slouching, he'd be a laughingstock.

"He needs you," Gerry said.

"He should have thought of that."

"Okay, lady, yes. You can be bitter and aggrieved. You earned it. You happy? Are you going to hold your bag of self-righteousness into your dotage? It gets heavy when you get old. Believe me."

"I can't trust him ever again. How am I supposed to carry that around? And for how long? Into the presidency?"

"As long as you want." He drove on the surface streets—stop start stop start—obeying the lights even though no one was around.

I knew I'd let it go eventually. I'd learn to trust another man. He wouldn't be Daniel, of course. I would have to invest in someone else all over again. Get hurt, move on. Hurt someone, move on. Antonio had proven how easy that was. One day, I'd fall in love. Maybe. I was thirty-four. I'd never felt too late until Gerry asked about my dotage.

"I hurt all over," I said. "All the time. I don't know what I feel any more. I don't know what I want. I feel separate from my own thoughts. The fact that I'm telling this to a political strategist is enough of a red flag that I need to be medicated or institutionalized."

I didn't say that I think about hurting but not killing myself. I couldn't cry. I felt unanchored. I loved Daniel still. The last time I'd felt marginally alive was with Antonio. I'd always depended on men for my happiness.

"*Big Girls* is opening Friday," Gerry said as he pulled up in front of my building.

"Yeah."

"It's about domestic violence. We pitched that as your hot button during the campaign. I've seen the picture. It's good."

"You're making a movie recommendation?" I asked.

"Daniel is making it a point to see it and release a statement after."

"You're trying to set me up on a date? Are you serious?"

"This is a high stakes date, Theresa. Please."

I opened the car door and stepped out, slamming it shut and opening the back for my bag. "You're a crappy Cupid."

I should have taken a cab.

FUCKING GERRY. I walked in the door cursing him, flinging my bag into a corner.

Fucking fucking Gerry. The man was made of the finest, most indestructible plastic in the universe. He didn't have a feeling in him.

Or maybe he did. Maybe he just didn't have a feeling for me.

Or maybe he did. Maybe I didn't have a feeling for me.

Or maybe it wasn't about me. Maybe it was about Daniel and the city of Los Angeles. Maybe it was about a campaign I'd invested my heart and soul in, and when Daniel fell through, what I'd wanted for myself fell through.

Or maybe it didn't matter what Gerry thought was important. Maybe something was bothering me. Something that had excited me, given me something to look forward to, made me forget how much I despised my fucking life.

Antonio had made me feel alive, as if I'd been asleep for months. He shook me, slapped me. I was finally ready, and I'd thrown it away. It had been a casual nothing, a little dirty talk, something to fill the hours while I waited to get over Daniel. I wasn't allowed to get upset over such a little nothing, but I was desperately upset, and I couldn't admit it to myself until I was asked to be Daniel's beard yet again.

I picked up a porcelain swan by the neck. I knew what I was going to do before I did, and once decided, the tension released.

I smacked it against the edge of the table. It bounced. I smacked it harder. The body broke off, clacking to the ground, and I was left holding the tiny head. In seconds, the tension came back. It was only relieved when I looked at all of my swans and stopped caring whether they ever went back into the cabinet.

I didn't feel rage when I smashed the swans. I must have looked angry and emotional, but I wasn't. I was dead, empty, frozen, doing a job I'd contracted myself to do. I bashed them against the marble countertop, leaving millions of plaster, porcelain, and glass shards everywhere.

It took about seven minutes to destroy years' worth of swans and a few dishes. I stood over the puddle of sharp dust and said what I'd been too upset to consider.

"I want you."

I pushed a china blue swan wing to the right. It had separated from the rest of the swan but hadn't broken completely. Not nearly enough.

"I want you, you criminal punk."

I picked up my foot and smashed the wing under my heel.

"And I'm going to have you."

Chapter Twenty-Four

I paid my cleaning lady extra to make sense of the mess, sweep up the porcelain swan guts, and put everything back. I dressed for work before I called Antonio. No answer.

I texted.

—Call me, please. I want to discuss something with you—

I read it over. It seemed very businesslike. I was a well-mannered person, but that didn't mean I had to evade everything, did it?

—Specifically, your cock—

I smiled. That should do it.

I PRACTICALLY JUMPED out of bed the next morning. I layered slacks and a tight button-down shirt over a satin demi and lace panties. Rippable lace, because I was going to find that fucker and tell him what I thought, what I wanted, and how I wanted it. He would learn to trust me if I had to give him a signed affidavit and a blood sample.

I heard Katrina downstairs just as I was deciding to leave my hair down. No, I didn't hear Katrina—I heard a dish clatter along the concrete floor as if it had been kicked.

"Sorry!" I called as I ran down.

She blew on a dish and returned it to the pile. "What the fuck?" She pointed to my broken swans.

"You don't like the mess? I spent eight minutes making it."

She waved and pulled the coffee down then dropped it. "I don't care about the mess. It's you breaking things. You're Tee Dray. You don't break things."

As she scooped the coffee, I saw her hand shaking.

"Directrix," I said, "have some chamomile, please. You're jacked up."

"We're almost done. I'm excited. You coming to the wrap party?"

"I'm springing for an open bar."

Katrina flicked on the TV. The talking heads talked, and the news ticker ticked.

"You should bring the hot Italian," she said, reminding me of my text.

I checked my pocket. No response. "I might. The last time I saw him, it was weird."

"You didn't tell me."

"You're busy."

"So what happened?"

My lips stayed closed. I focused on the way they touched, because I had to shut up. It was just that kind of casual sharing and speculation that worried Antonio, and with good reason. I wanted to earn his trust behind his back.

"I think it's over," I said to deflect further questioning.

"Probably for the best. You know southern Europeans. They have a Madonna- whore complex. They either debase you and kick you to the curb, or revere you and never fuck you."

Again, I pressed my lips together to keep from speaking. He'd fucked me, and fucked me dirty. I felt a familiar tingle between my legs just remembering it. But he didn't want me to know about his life. It seemed as though he had disappeared long enough to get horny and then relentlessly pursue me when he wanted a whore. I hadn't noticed the pattern because I'd been so close to it.

I shook it off. I didn't have time to worry about how I was seen or wonder what he thought. I had to do what I wanted, and I wanted to feel alive again. He was like my drug, and I would either get a hit or go into withdrawal, but I wouldn't abdicate my right to chase him.

I checked my phone again. Nothing. Just a traffic alert. The 10 was jammed up because of a car-to-car shootout that had resulted in a five-car pileup and police actions across a mile-long stretch. Venice Boulevard was in the red from the overflow.

"Fuck," Katrina said.

"Yeah, the 10," I replied, but Katrina was looking at the TV.

"This has been going on for days already."

I looked over her shoulder. I recognized LaBrea Ave. The shot was daytime, and the tag said yesterday.

Two days of gang violence across the west side. Two shootings, one death in a seemingly unmotivated spree.

Daniel's face filled the screen. The signage in the background told me the news crew had caught him at a campaign rally. "We're working closely with the police to make sure justice is served."

They cut him off there. God help him if that was the meat of the interview.

Could this be Antonio? Somehow? If he was what Daniel said he was, then he certainly could be involved, but there were hundreds of gangs in the city. The victims didn't seem related, and the violence wasn't all deadly. There was speculation about Compton gangs, the SGV Angels, and an Armenian outfit in East Hollywood.

"Good thing we're downtown," Katrina said, turning away from the TV. "But everyone on the west side's going to miss call time."

Daniel appeared again, mouthing the same promises. His hand appeared on the screen. The right ring fingernail was bitten down.

Chapter Twenty-Five

I'd learned when a script supervisor was needed and when she'd spend hours waiting around, so I knew when I could split for an hour or two. My first stop was the garage in Mount Washington.

I got in my car, which had been quickly repaired once the ignition coil had been reconnected. My mechanic had shrugged. Old car. Things bend and tighten. It happens, apparently. I asked if someone could have done it on purpose, and he said something noncommittal, like "Anyone can do anything on purpose."

Especially when they wonder if you're snooping around.

I got to Antonio's repair shop in record time. A chest-constricting worry nearly kept me from driving in. The hum of activity I'd noticed last time was gone. The lot held half as many cars, and I didn't see as many guys in jumpsuits. When I got past the gate, no one greeted me. I parked and went into the office.

"Hi," I said to the woman behind the desk. "I'm looking for Antonio."

"He's out. You can just pull into the garage." She was new, her black hair down and gum cracking against her molars. She had an accent. Italian, again. She was older, but I couldn't help wonder if he'd fucked her.

"I was hoping to see him."

"Not in." She shuffled some papers.

"Any idea where he is?"

She regarded me seriously for the first time. "No. You can leave a message."

I thought about it for a second then declined. I texted him again.

—I still want to talk to you—

I didn't expect to hear back, and I didn't. I shot back downtown to finish the day's work.

EVERY TIME my phone dinged and buzzed, I hoped it was Antonio. But it was always Pam with some new meeting or appointment. I started seeing the world through the hopeful window of my device.

"Hey."

I spun around to find the source of the voice.

Michael stood behind me in costume: Dirty jeans. Grey T-shirt. A filthy apron and hair net. "We got a place from ReVal for the wrap party on Saturday. Some corporate loft they haven't staged yet."

"Wow. Nice work. Are we starting filming?"

"Nah, they're still getting the lights up."

I stepped deeper into the parking lot. "That getup really works for you."

Anything would work for him. He was a celebrity waiting to happen.

"Like it?" He pointed to a particularly egregious brown smear. "I had this chocolate streak put on just so people would think it was shit."

"Bold."

"That's my middle name. Speaking of—well, no, not speaking of. This is actually a major non sequitur."

We walked through the lot, ignored in the busy hustle of the camera crew testing every corner for the right light, adjusting scrims and lamps.

"I like a good non sequitur as much as the next person."

He stopped and turned toward me. "I heard we lost our post funding."

"You know Hollywood gossip is cheap."

"My agent told me."

"And agent gossip is the cheapest. Seriously, Michael, consider the source. Pilot season's happening when you'll be doing scene pickups for Katrina. He can't like that."

"You're not denying it."

"You assume I know in the first place."

"Still not denying it. You're an artist at that, you know." His smile seemed genuine, but it could have been acting. "Now, Ms. Ip? Not such an artist."

He took out a pack of cigarettes and poked one out. I was reminded of Antonio Spinelli's fluid motions, his clacking lighter, the smoke framing his face. Michael was less intense. My observations could have been colored by my sexual indifference. Sometimes, between two people who shared so little heat, a cigarette was just a cigarette.

"I'm glad you brought it up with Katrina first," I said. "She needs to know if something like this is going around town."

"I've done some of my best work in the past couple of weeks. Pilot season's not my future. This movie is."

"I'm glad you—"

"I do feel that way. Let me finish. If this film gets shelved, I'm shelved. I'm home in Park Forest, Illinois, working in the pizza shop on Blackhawk Way. I have no money to put up, but I would, and she knows that."

"Stop." When he tried to blow through me again, I held up my hand. "She won't take money from me."

"I know."

"You think you know a little too much."

"We haven't even scratched the surface." He took a scrap of paper from his apron pocket just as Ricky, the new AD, called talent to the set. "This guy funds low-budget, non-union gigs that run out of money."

I looked at the paper, though I suspected I knew the name already. Scott Mabat, Hollywood loan shark and part-time pornography producer. "This guy's a career-killer."

"He made Thomas Brandy who he is."

"A statistical anomaly. The rest couldn't pay him back and wound up in a ditch."

He stepped back toward set, where I also belonged. "I believe in this picture."

With that, he spun around and trotted inside, leaving behind the implication that I didn't. As I followed, I counted the days I had left to get Katrina her money.

WHEN THE SET BROKE, I hopped over to the Spanish house in the hills. The gate was locked, and the driveway was empty. I got out and listened. No banging or hammering. No sledgehammer demolition on an ill-placed wall. Nothing but the screech of crickets.

I got back in the car. *Where to, Contessa?*

It had been four days. Was the trail getting cold, or was I just getting really crappy at this? I still had no idea where he lived. The car place was probably closed for the day. Where else had I seen him? Frontage. The offices of WDE. A Catholic Charities fundraiser. Katrina's set downtown, where he'd brought dinner and wine.

Zia.

I tapped my phone a few times and came up with a restaurant in Rancho Palos Verdes. A thirty-minute drive if the freeways had cleared from the spate of violence that had something or nothing at all to do with Antonio.

Chapter Twenty-Six

Zia's didn't look authentic. It looked like what authentic was supposed to look like. If you went to Italy, you'd expect every café and restaurant to have a supply of red checked tablecloths, containers of parmesan, and baskets of bread with saucers of butter. Considering the quality of the neighborhood and the sophistication of the residents, the cheesy décor was bound to be a turnoff.

I parked in the little lot and went around to the front, where two tables sat on the sidewalk. At one sat two men in their sixties, hunched over a game of dominoes. The one farthest, with the white moustache and huge belly, glanced at me, nodded, and rolled the dice. The other, in a fedora and open-necked shirt, didn't acknowledge me. A sense of apprehension came over me. I was stepping into Antonio's territory. Wasn't that exactly what he didn't want?

A wood bar stretched over one side of the restaurant, and the rest of the floor was taken up by small round tables and booths decorated with gingham and little oil and vinegar carts. A mural of Mount Vesuvius took up all available wall space.

Half of the four booths had little "reserved" tags on them, and at the other two sat clusters of men. One of them, a short guy with a brown shirt and goatee, stood between the two tables, speaking Italian as if he was regaling them with a story. He checked me out when I entered then went back to waving his arms and making everyone laugh.

"Can I help you?"

I turned and saw Zia, doughy fingers clasped in front of her.

"Hi," I said. "How are you?"

She pointed at me. "I recognize you."

"Yeah. I remember you."

Her expression went from warm to suspicious, as if she saw right through me. "You're here to eat?"

The jocularity of the booths went dead. Some signal must have been given, because I felt their eyes on me.

"No."

"Something else?"

Best to just get to it. "I'm looking for Antonio."

"He's not here."

"I..." What did I want to say? This was my last ditch effort, wasn't it? After this, I had nowhere else to look. "I mean him no harm. I'm here on my own."

She smiled. In that smile, I didn't see delight or kindness, but an emotion I'd inspired many times before. Pity.

I stood up straight. "I'm going to find him now or later, Zia. So, best now."

A man's voice came from behind me. "You want me to walk her out?"

I turned and saw the potbellied dominoes player. But I didn't move or offer to leave.

"It's woman stuff," Zia said, waving as if my appearance was just an inconvenience, not something heavy. She indicated the doors to the kitchen. "Come."

My phone vibrated in my pocket. I knew I needed to get back to the set. I would have to go in the kitchen, tell Antonio what I wanted and that I wasn't taking no for an answer, then hustle back. Zia walked me through the tiny commercial kitchen, past stock pots simmering on the stove and a man in a white baseball cap scrubbing a pan. I thought she was taking me to Antonio, but she opened a door to the parking lot.

"Zia," I said, "I don't understand."

"He's not here."

"Can I leave him a message?" I asked as I walked into the parking lot.

"If you think I'll deliver it."

"Why wouldn't you?"

She looked into the bright sun then back into the kitchen. "I have to go."

She tried to close the door, but I held it open. "Why?" I demanded.

"Just tell me why. Is it a trust thing? You all think I'm running back to my ex with details?"

Zia took the doorknob so firmly that I knew I didn't have the strength to hold her back if she decided to close it for once and for all.

"Please," I said, taking my hand off the door, "I mean no harm. I swear."

"I believe you," she said. "What you mean, I know. But meaning harm and doing it? Not always the same."

"Is he okay?"

"Is he okay? *Si*. Until I kill him. Until I shake him out with my hands." She opened them and hooked her sausage fingers, shiny with years in the kitchen. "*Quel figlio di buona donna* asks me to cater a movie set. Doesn't tell me he's seducing you." She moved her hand up and down, tracing the vertical line of my body as if I was a monument to every girl he shouldn't be with. "*Stronzo*. That's what he is."

Her insults were affectionate, but she was very angry. I could pretend I didn't know what about me was so offensive, but I knew damn well it was my relationships, my culture, everything I was.

"Can you just tell him I was here?"

She shook her head as if I was an idiot. "No. If you chase him into our world, we will chase you out." She closed the door.

I THOUGHT of every worst-case scenario on the way to the set. Antonio was dead, in trouble, shipped back to Naples. He was responsible for the violence that had taken over the news channels, or he was the as-yet-undiscovered victim of it.

And I had nowhere else to look. I had no proof that anything was anything, and if I chased him, his world would chase me out.

On set that night, as I pondered the worst, I wasn't much more optimistic about Katrina. By the wide radius she kept around me, I could tell she sensed my discomfort. I kept my eyes on who was where, what buttons were unbuttoned, where arms and legs were placed, what lines dropped. It was the last day in the café. They were tearing it down. Nothing could be missed.

Then it broke like a fever. Katrina practically whispered "cut," and everyone cheered. It was over. We packed up for the umpteenth time, put everything back in the trucks. The affairs that had started during shooting would either amount to something or not. The friendships would be tested. If the movie would get to theaters depended on the next few weeks, and no one but me, Katrina, Michael, and the deepest Hollywood insiders knew how unlikely that was.

I got in the car, thinking I'd just take a midnight drive up Alameda and crawl into bed. I texted Antonio, even though it felt more and more like screaming down an empty alley.

—I know I'm harassing you and I don't care. If everything's okay just text me anything back. A fuck you would be sufficient—

I waited ten minutes, watching the last of the PAs pack up. I was distracted by the silence of my phone. Tired of waiting for something that wasn't going to happen, I left.

Chapter Twenty-Seven

Our final shoot had been in the West Valley, a straight shot down the 101. The freeway was relatively empty, and I went into auto pilot, listening to the news that the shootings and violence were unrelated, random. A southside gang shooting had hit the wrong man. A shooting during a robbery attempt. A beating in Griffith Park.

"The lady doth protest too much," I mumbled.

A Lexus cut me off as I was complaining to myself. I slammed the brakes, screeching and swerving as adrenaline dumped into my bloodstream. The Club slid out from under the passenger seat.

"Fuck!"

The Lexus picked up speed, and I did too. I was filled with a blinding hot anger. The Lexus swerved around, and I saw the man in driver seat. Young. Goatee. Flashing me his middle finger. He sped ahead, and I had no choice whatsoever.

I chased the car. I had no idea what I would do when I caught it, but I would catch it. It sped up even as it pulled off without a blinker. I rode his ass in my little blue car. Twenty-four, then twelve inches away at eighty. I was insane, not thinking like Theresa.

He didn't know who was in my car. I could have been a gangbanger, and he ran. Oh, if I caught him, what would I do… Choke. Kill. I couldn't imagine it any more than I could control it.

We landed on Mulholland, the most dangerous, twisted street to speed down, but we did. He would get an ass full of vintage BMW if he slammed to a stop, and I didn't know how to care. The Lexus turned so fast I almost missed it. We stopped on a private street with only our headlights illuminating the trees on either side of the road.

A bloated bag of unreleased rage, I grabbed the Club from the floor and got out of the car. "What the fuck is wrong with you?" I yelled from deep in my diaphragm.

His driver side door opened. I didn't have time to hope there was only one of them. I swung the Club at the nearest taillight.

Smash.

That felt good. I went for the brake light.

"What the fuck?" shouted Goatee.

As the light smashed, I recognized him from Zia's. He'd been in a booth. I went at him with the Club, and he stepped back.

"Lady, you're fucking crazy."

He reached into his jacket just as the street flooded with light. Cars. I felt caught in the act and rescued at the same time. Goatee got his hand out of his jacket. He had a gun in it, but instead of shooting me, he shot at the cars pulling up behind me. A *ping* and a *clunk*. Another shot, and Goatee spun, screaming and clutching his bloody hand. His gun had been shot out of it.

Three car doors slammed behind me. I couldn't see the three men due to the backlighting, but I recognized the shape of a Maserati.

"Bruno, you dumb shit." It was Paulie.

When I felt strong hands on me, pulling on the Club, I knew it was Antonio. I felt like falling apart, but I didn't, even when I saw his dark eyes, their joy and charm gone. He had the face of a mafia capo.

I yanked the weapon away from Antonio and stepped forward, nailing the side of the Lexus on the foreswing. I aimed for Bruno's screaming head on the backswing. He ducked, and I swung again.

Everything happened at once. I was pulled back. Bruno's screaming stopped. Doors slammed. Road dirt sprayed my face. Antonio shouted in Italian, and Paulie shouted back in English. A few *fucks* were the only words I understood.

I was in the passenger side of my car, and the car was moving. Fast. Antonio was driving. I held the Club up, and he grabbed it from me while driving with his other hand.

"You're fucking crazy, you know that?" he said.

He hit the gas, slipping the seat back to accommodate his height. In front of us, the Lexus took off, and Antonio chased it.

"Where were you?"

"Put your seatbelt on." He threw the Club into the back seat. "What did you think you were doing?"

"Breaking things!" Why was I screaming while I was obeying? "Not like it's your business, but I was going to crack his head open."

"Do you know who that was?"

Our car swung around a corner. Behind us, the Maserati followed, with Paulie at the wheel, I assumed.

"Bruno Uvoli," he said. "*Cazzo!* He's a made man. He'd sell his sister for a dollar. And you're like a fucking beacon, asking about me everywhere. What the fuck, Theresa? I'm trying to protect you, and you step in it. Deliberately."

"Answer a text next time."

We blasted into the Valley on the Lexus's tail, onto flat, wide boulevards and poorly lit side streets.

"Hold on." With one hand, he held me to the seat while he followed the car under a viaduct and out into a twisty service road, clipping the concrete wall in a shower of sparks. We were going seventy-five, and though I thought I should care about what my car would look like at the end of this, I didn't.

"I want you," I said, breathless. "I want you, and I'm going to have you. That's it."

"I'm death to you." He accelerated. The BMW kicked awake as if that was its shining moment.

"No. You're like mainlining life. I want it. I need it. I don't care what I have to do to earn your trust, I'll do it."

He pushed me down, swung the car right, then left, bumping the Lexus onto a turn up the foothills. The Maserati shot around us and in front of the Lexus, taking it in the side with a crunch.

"*Cazzo,*" he growled again, but not to me. He screeched the BMW to a halt inches from the Lexus.

Paulie and Zo were already out of the Mas with their guns drawn.

Antonio unbuckled me with one hand and pulled my head onto his lap with the other. "Stay there."

I glanced up at him, his rock of an erection at my cheek.

He looked out the windshield. "I need you to drive away."

"You're not getting rid of me." I heard a scuffle outside.

"I don't want you seeing this. I don't want you near it."

"I'm not going back to Daniel with any of it."

"It doesn't matter. Look at you, ready to kill a man with a club. I've contaminated you enough." He slipped out from under me, opening the door and getting out.

I sat up. In my headlights, I saw how desolate the area Antonio had pushed the Lexus into was. Bruno was pinned to the ground by Paulie's foot on his busted hand. Zo knelt on him with one knee on his unbusted arm and the other on his thigh. Bruno's sneaker had been stuffed in his mouth to muffle his screams.

It all sunk in, what I'd gotten into and how. I froze, becoming myself again for a second.

Antonio leaned in the door. "Contessa. Drive."

"I want you."

"I heard you."

"You don't believe me." My eyes were locked on the pinned man.

"You want a man you imagine. If you knew who you were talking to, if you knew what I could turn you into, you'd run back to your DA." In my peripheral vision, I saw him take a pack of cigarettes from his pocket.

I turned to him. "Walk away. Don't do this. Not over a little road rage."

He lit the smoke with a clack of his silver lighter. "This wasn't road rage. He is stupid and dangerous. And he was after you. Now I have to make sure he never touches you, and that I never touch you." He closed the door and spoke through the open window. "Make no mistake, I will hurt you to protect you. Now go." He turned to the three men. "Zo, get off him, I got it. Drive her if she won't go."

"Yes, boss."

Antonio turned his back on me, and Zo approached. My beautiful capo didn't look back, only down at the man who had gotten me to chase him into a desolate area for a purpose I could only imagine, with the smoke and fire of hell winding around his fingertips.

Before Zo could reach me, I backed out and into the street. I didn't get far before I had to pull the car over. I covered my mouth with my hands and cried, muffling myself as tears fell down the cracks between my fingers.

What had I done?

Of all the things I could do from the front of my dented BMW, I had not one I *would* do. I could call 9-1-1. I could call Daniel. I could reveal the whole thing to the press. But I wouldn't, and I knew it.

And Antonio knew it. On some level, he trusted me.

Chapter Twenty-Eight

I thought Katrina would come home and collapse, but when I walked in and found the house empty, I was the one who collapsed, throwing myself on the couch with my forearm over my eyes. They hurt from crying and would continue to hurt because the tears came again. I didn't even know what I was crying about exactly. Was it stress? Or the man I knew was going to die? Or the fact that I was responsible? Was it because I was pretty sure I had been about to kill him myself?

I don't know how long I laid there like that, but I fell asleep. I woke to a knock on the door. I looked out the peephole and felt so much relief that I whispered his name when I saw him. I opened the door.

"Contessa." His voice was rough.

"Capo." I leaned on the door, looking up at his eyes, sunken and tired and a little bloodshot. They flinched when I called him that then warmed.

"Send me away," he said. "Slam this door in my face."

I stepped aside and let him in.

"I tried to stay away," he said. "I've never wanted a woman this much in my life. I'd burn cities to have you. I'd fight armies. I'd commit murder to take you right now."

I grabbed his lapels and pulled off his jacket. He let me slide it down his arms. I didn't ask him any questions as I unbuttoned his cuffs. I didn't ask how he was when I undid the front of his shirt. I must have been a sight with my swollen eyes and stained cheeks.

He touched his thumb to the hollow of my eye. "You were crying."

I put my fingers on his lips, shushing him, and he kissed the tips.

"I can't keep away from you," he rasped.

"Don't. Don't ever." I took his hand. "Come. Let's wash tonight off."

I pulled him upstairs, walking backward. Halfway up, he lifted me. I hooked my legs around his waist and my arms around his shoulders, letting him carry me to my bedroom. We didn't kiss but kept our eyes open and our faces close, sharing breath and space.

He set me on my dresser. I finished unbuttoning his shirt and slid it off. I got his undershirt off so fast his gold charm clinked and dropped. That's when I noticed the yellow hospital wristband.

"What happened?" I asked.

"I'm fine."

"You were admitted."

"Somebody had to be. For the records. Otherwise they have to report a gunshot wound, even in the hand. Nobody wants that."

I inspected his face for a second.

"What is it, Contessa?"

"You took him to the hospital?"

"To a doctor I know at the hospital. We have people for emergencies."

My face got hot again. I felt my nose tingle and my eyes moisten. "You didn't kill him?"

"No."

A breath whooshed out of my mouth, and I cried with a smile. "I'm sorry. I'm so sorry. I just wanted to see you again. I didn't mean—" I was lost in tears.

"He's ambitious, and he saw an opening. What he did is past forgiving, but I kept seeing your face." He looked away and set his jaw. "If he comes near you again, I will kill him."

He held my chin in those powerful hands and tilted my face up. Our mouths crashed together. Our arms twined around each other, seeking purchase, finding it, and moving again.

He brought his lips to my ear and whispered, "When you left my office, I thought I'd never see you again, and it made me crazy. I was so angry at myself, I did stupid things it'll take years to fix. God forgive me."

I held him, kissing his neck and cheek with all the tenderness and forgiveness I could manage. It wasn't enough, not by a lot, but it was all I had. I wanted his skin against mine. I pulled my shirt off and twisted out of my bra.

Looking down, he touched my nipples with the backs of his fingers. "This is wrong. We're wrong. You and I. One of us is going to get the other one killed."

"I think about you all the time."

"I can't let you into my world. It won't work. They'll rip you to shreds."

"I touch myself thinking of you."

"I've done things I can never talk about. Even knowing what they are could hurt you."

I slid off the dresser and took his hands. "Come with me." I led him to the bathroom and turned on the shower. I wiggled out of my pants then reached for his waistband.

"This doesn't fix anything," he said.

"There's nothing to fix." I unfastened his trousers, and they dropped to the floor. I reached into his underwear and got out his cock. "This works."

"It's for fucking you."

I snapped the shower door open. "Never stop putting that cock in me."

He kissed me hard, pushing my head against the wall. "God help me. You make me crazy. We can't be together, but you're all I think about. Making you mine completely."

"I'll be yours. Let me be," I said.

"You'll be destroyed, Contessa. Peacetime is over. If anything happened to you—"

"We won't tell anyone. I'll be your secret, and you'll be mine. We'll meet in the night, when no one can see."

"It's too late for that."

"No, we'll say it's over. It's that, or nothing. If never seeing me again works for you, then go. I won't chase you again."

"Promise?" he asked.

His body relaxed, and I thought he was really going to go. It seemed impossible that his body wouldn't be pressed on mine, but it was his choice to make.

"I promise. I have the will to do it."

He put his nose to mine, his eyes scanning my face, then dropped his gaze. "I believe you." He kissed me, and the rigid pressure of his body returned. "You have the will, but I don't. I have to have you. Tonight and after, you're mine. Your first loyalty is to me. Every moan on your lips. Every wet drop from your cunt. When the thought of fucking crosses your mind, it's mine. Say it."

"I'm yours, Capo."

"No more halfway bullshit."

I swallowed nervously, because I didn't want to test our resolve or find out his desire truly was halfway, but I wanted to surrender completely to our pledge.

"I want your skin on my skin." I hated to bring it up, but it was my last chance. "After I found out Daniel cheated on me, I got tested for everything. I'm clean. And I left the IUD in."

He smiled, and my heart opened. "I'm a condom guy."

"Every time?"

"Of course."

"No halfway bullshit, then."

I got into the shower. He peeled off his underwear and joined me.

The water was hot and powerful. He leaned his head back and let it fall over his face in rivulets. The water darkened his lashes, making them stick together. I rolled the rectangle of soap in my hands then put them on his neck, running soap over the curves of his body. Shoulders, biceps, forearms, the space of his chest under the gold chain with the circle charm. He enfolded my hands in his, transferring the soap.

"What's this?" I asked, touching the gold medal.

"Saint Christopher. Patron saint of protection."

"Does it work?" I kissed it and the skin around it.

"Am I dead?"

I took his cock in my hand. "Apparently not."

Turning me, he put his hands between my shoulders, my ass, the backs of my thighs, then up the crack, massaging my pussy with his finger and my ass with his thumb. I picked up my leg and rested it on the ledge so he could get his fingers farther into me.

"Oh God, Antonio. I've wanted you for days."

"I'm going to fuck you so hard, little princess. I'm going to break you in two."

I twisted to face him. "Do it. Take me hard."

He looped his arm under my knee, pulling it up. The skin of his dick was so smooth on my pussy, he stretched and slid into me. He had to thrust twice more to get all the way in, hitching up my leg. He was so rough that I had no choice but to be a doll in his hands.

"You're so fucking hot," he said, pressing his thumb to my ass.

"Hard, please, Capo. Take me hard."

"Have you ever been fucked in the ass, little princess?"

"No."

"I'm taking your ass, right here." He grabbed my conditioner and squeezed the cold, viscous liquid down my crack. "Are you ready?"

"I don't know." I was nervous and admittedly aroused.

He fucked my pussy hard and wedged his fingers in my ass. "Your little ass is so tight. It's so sweet."

His fingers sliding in and out of me, stretching me, opened up new pleasure. "Oh, that feels so good."

He took his dick out of me and lodged it at my pucker. "You ready for me to fuck your ass?"

"Yes."

"Relax."

I tried to relax as he pushed forward. I had to brace against the tile, and he couldn't get in.

He reached around and put four fingers on my clit and his lips on the back of my neck. "Relax, sweet girl. Let me take you. Let me own you."

I groaned with the rising warmth under his fingers and relaxed. The head of his cock slid into me, and the invasion made me tense. I gasped.

"You are so fucking beautiful." He put his other arm tight around me and grabbed my breast. I felt bound and secure, unable to do anything but let go. "This ass was made for me."

He jammed forward, and I screamed, getting hot shower water in my mouth.

"What do you want, Contessa?"

He was asking if I was all right, and he waited for me to answer before he moved again. I needed a moment to breathe and took it. I shifted my hips until I felt better.

"I want you," I said. "I want you to fuck my virgin ass so hard."

He gripped me harder and pulled his dick out. The pleasure was overwhelming, reaching right to my clit, where his hand still gripped me.

"Take it," he growled in my ear as he slammed into me again.

"Oh, God. Fuck me in the ass."

"I love it. I love fucking your ass."

He pumped hard, rubbing my clit and stretching my ass farther than I thought possible. I kept whispering *take me take me* as the feeling of an impending explosion built. I went far away in my mind, past words, past thoughts, pain, pleasure. I was only his fingers and his cock, knowing me in a way I'd never been known before.

"You're going to come," he said. "I can feel it."

I grunted. The fuse sparked close to the keg, crackling and bright.

"Come on. Give it to me."

My ass clenched and pulsed around him, and my legs dropped under me. He held me up as I had the most powerful orgasm of my life, a slow motion detonation, every piece of flak airborne in its own sweet time, trailing smoke behind. I didn't realize I was screaming until the last bits of fiery shrapnel floated to the ground, as if I'd been unconscious. I woke to Antonio thrusting hard, slow, with a different rhythm.

"...in your ass, Contessa, *si, si, si...*" he whispered in Italian, sweet words I didn't understand.

"Come, Capo. Come inside me."

His groan was loud and final. A few more thrusts, and he molded his chest to my back, our rising and falling bodies matched in time.

"Bene."

He kissed my shoulder. He pulled his dick from me, and I sucked in a breath.

"*Bene* is right," I said.

He stood up straight, and I turned around.

"Now we should shower, no?"

I laughed, and his smile lit up the room. We washed and toweled each other dry.

"Can you stay for a few hours?" I asked. "You can still slip out in the night."

"I have to take care of Uvoli, still. There are consequences to what happened with you and Bruno, and me. I have to talk with people." He reached for his clothes.

"I thought I saw him at Zia's."

"He's not my crew. He's a free agent. We keep him close. I'm saying nothing else."

I snapped his jacket away. It had his burned pine smell all over it. "Let me keep this then. To remember you when you're pretending you don't own me."

"While I'm telling lies about you?" He dropped his clothes and pulled the jacket from me.

"Tell me the lies. For practice."

He kissed my cheek. "I will tell them I fucked her once, and she got attached. But she knows the DA and will cause us trouble if she's hurt. I'll say I don't trust her. She means nothing to me."

"Like you said about Marina?"

"It was the truth about her." He pushed me onto the bed. "About you,

I'll lie. Say you're not the most beautiful woman I've met. You're not sexy. You're cold, unpleasant. Nothing a man would want to keep."

I touched his face, his lips, his stubble, his insane lashes. "What would it be like to be your girlfriend?"

He kissed my cheek and jaw. "We'd be friends first. And no touching."

"No touching?"

"No kissing, no touching."

"That wouldn't work."

He kissed my chest and breasts gently, little flicks of his tongue on my nipples. "You'd live with your parents, and I would come to visit you. We would sit and talk in the garden. Your mother would cook for me, and I would sit at the table with your family." He moved down to my belly, exploring every inch of it. "I would see you at church. Other men would talk to you, and I'd chase them away. Your father would hate me for a while. Then he would approve. I might touch your hand when no one is looking."

He got up on his knees and opened my legs. "I would fuck other women and you'd understand, because we hadn't even kissed." He brushed his lips inside my knee. "Then I'd ask your father for your hand, and when he said yes, I stop fucking other women." He ran his tongue inside my thigh. "You'd plan the wedding, and I'd work. I'd build myself. Being young and blind, I wouldn't see that you're now a target for my enemies."

He kissed my pussy gently. "You'd cry on our wedding night and call me a brute." His tongue flicked my clit. "You'd tell your mother I'm an animal. I'd promise to never fuck you like that again. I'd promise to be tender always." His tongue ran the length of my lips, circling the clit twice, then back to my opening. "It wouldn't matter. You'd be part of my life. My world. You'd get hard and cunning to survive, or you'd stay gentle and die."

"Antonio," I whispered, "can you do it like that? Can you do it gentle?"

He crawled up until we were face to face. "*Come vuoi tu.*"

I pushed against him, feeling his hard cock on my pussy. My ass was sore, but I wanted him again already. He guided himself in, and I took him slowly, his shaft angled to rub against my clit.

"Oh, that's nice." I groaned.

He rocked against me, pushing all the way in. "You're so sexy. I love watching you walk, how your body moves under your clothes. How beautiful. How straight you are for the world, and how you bend and cry for me. I want to go so deep in you we have the same thoughts."

His eyes were unguarded, open, warm for me. The swelling in my pussy blossomed as I looked into his face. The sight and feeling mixed, becoming a swirl of emotion and sensation. We moved so slowly together that I felt everything, every inch of skin touching, every firing sliver of pleasure.

"I'm close, Contessa."

"Can you come with me?"

His face contorted with effort. "Soon. I'm trying to stay slow."

"You're amazing, Antonio. Amazing."

The last word barely made it out of my mouth as I was overcome with electricity. He jerked, slammed into me, and I cried out. He'd put me over the edge. I clawed his back as he jerked and thrust, growling my name. I spread my legs farther, feeling him against and inside me. We came as a crawling, rolling, single creature, as if we were having one orgasm. Even afterward, our breathing was the same and our hearts beat in time.

"I need to see you again soon," he said into my cheek.

"You'll come secretly in the night."

"Yes. I will. Be ready."

Downstairs, the door opened and banged shut.

"Maybe not so secretly," I said.

"Ah, this is the director?"

"Yeah."

"Is there another way out?"

"No," I said. "But I trust her."

He got up. "Good for you."

WE WENT DOWNSTAIRS TOGETHER, dressed and clean, to find Katrina standing in front of the television with a quart of salty vanilla ice cream and a spoon.

"You're up early," she called over her shoulder. "Did I wake… Oh, hello," she said when she turned. "Nice to see you again, Mister Spin."

"Katrina, you're up late. Or early, perhaps?"

She put her ice cream down and jammed the spoon into it. "Because I'm amazing!" She threw her arms up like a cheerleader.

"Oh dear, what now?" I crossed my arms.

"I got post-production financing!"

"Oh my god! How? Who? What?"

She said the next part so cheerfully, as if painting on a cartoon face. "Scott Mabat." She did a little jazz hands shake.

"What?" I yelled.

"*Gesu Christo*!" Antonio exclaimed.

Her knees bent, and her hands went from jazz to *stop*. "I have a plan."

"This better be good, Directrix."

"I take the money, start post, and get fresh financing from this German investor who's been sniffing around. I can keep the energy up, then just pay him off when the German money comes in."

"That guy"—Antonio pointed—"is a lowlife. Okay? He is worthless shit, and he's sick in the head. How much did you get from him?"

"Hundred thou," she said.

Antonio and I groaned.

"That's what it costs to finish a movie, guys. And that's cheap. I'm sorry but these are realities."

"Screw the Germans," I said. "I'm giving you the money."

"No, you're not."

"Yes, I am. I'll pay the note, and you'll be done with it." I turned to walk Antonio out. "Come on, I'll finish with her."

"Hey, Spin," called Katrina as I opened the door. "You should come to the wrap party Saturday night. Strong chance of epic."

"I'll think about it," he said.

I pushed him outside and closed the door behind us. The stars were drowned out by the light of Los Angeles.

"You're coming up with that kind of money?" he asked.

"Yes. My family is well-off. I have a trust, and I can use it for whatever I want."

He put his fingers on my chin. "I know all about your family. If Scott wants cash, you do not transport it by yourself. And you are not to see him without me. No negotiating."

"We're supposed to be a secret."

"Call him, don't see him. I'm serious. You don't know what you're exposing yourself to."

I put my hands on his chest. He'd left his jacket upstairs for me, and I felt his muscles through the shirt. "I'll stay away from all the loan sharks in Los Angeles."

"Please. I ask only this, please."

"How are you getting home? You came in my car."

"Don't worry about me."

I pulled away a little, so I could see the entirety of his face. "Don't feel pressured to answer this question."

"I won't."

"Did she stay gentle? Or did she become cunning and hard?"

"She stayed gentle."

I didn't feel right pressing him further. We kissed again, and I let him go.

Chapter Twenty-Nine

A movie opening with Daniel seemed like the easiest, most convenient way to make sure Antonio and I didn't look attached. If he needed us to be a secret as long as possible, a few public sightings with Daniel Brower would do the trick.

—I'm going to a movie with Daniel—

He didn't return the text. I thought nothing of it. We were in stealth mode after all.

BIG GIRLS WAS A HUGE, star-studded drama about a hot-button issue. The script was built for award-winning performances, and the director had a long career of pushing talent to the limit. So even without any car chases, explosions, aliens, terrorists, or trips to outer space, the film had been declared one for the historical lexicon.

I'd noticed the bald man outside the morning after Antonio left, and again when I'd gotten home from set. I saw him through the window, sometimes smoking or poking at his phone. I'd gotten close to him once, just long enough to confirm I didn't know him and the walking-through-dirt scent of Turkish cigarettes emanated from him. I didn't mention him to Gerry when I confirmed I'd go to the movie with Daniel or when I met my ex outside the limo door.

I'd ended up agreeing to everything just for the sake of convenience. Even uptight, rich bitches had to deal with parking woes in Hollywood that were ameliorated with a limo.

"You look stunning."

"No flattery tonight, Dan. I'm just here to keep you from biting your nails."

He smiled and stopped me before I got in. "There are four guys in there. One is a bodyguard. The other three are going to talk my ear off about the press conference tomorrow."

"That's fine."

"I brought you this." He out held his hand. In his palm sat my engagement ring. I'd thrown it at him, huge stone and all.

Daniel had scrupulously saved to get me a ring that wouldn't embarrass him in front of my wealthy family. It hadn't mattered to me, but it mattered to him. He took me up to the Griffith Observatory on a night when Saturn was close and bright. He helped me onto the apple box as the astronomer showed me how to look into the telescope. There, with Saturn's rings as close and tangible as they'd ever be, he slipped the ring on my finger and said, "This ring around our world, Tink."

I picked up the ring. Did he say that? Or did he say, *my world?* Did it matter?

"You don't have to give it back," I said.

"The wronged party keeps the ring."

"No, the one who initiates the break up surrenders it. You would have stayed if I'd let you."

"Just take it." He opened the door. "One day, maybe you'll put it on again."

I got into the car, holding the ring. There were indeed four men in the back, and they did indeed talk strategy the whole way to the theater. Though I understood what they were talking about and I would have had plenty to contribute before the break up, I felt disconnected. It just wasn't fun anymore. I was watching animals in the zoo discuss their escape, but I was already outside. I'd moved on.

Cameras flashed, and Daniel answered questions as we entered. I smiled. I'd done it a hundred times, yet I couldn't believe I'd almost agreed to a life of it.

Right around the middle of the movie, the heroine and her husband had brutal, bruising sex, and I thought of Antonio. I wanted it again. Hard and fast with a side of hair pulling intensity, him grabbing me from behind as if he would tear me apart. When the movie ended and I stood, a drop of warm fluid escaped my underwear and ran down my thigh. I pressed my legs together to stop it.

"Are you okay?" Daniel asked as we got into the limo alone. The others seemed to have been dispensed with. "You seem flushed."

"I'm okay."

"I meant what I said." He touched my jaw by my ear, a move that had always made me shudder. "You are beautiful."

"What are you doing?"

"I'm seeing if I lost you," he whispered, coming close to me.

I pushed him away. "No, Daniel. Just, no."

"I still love you. You know that."

I took a deep breath, and said something I never thought would be true. "I'm sorry Daniel. I don't love you anymore."

The mood in the back of the limo changed with an almost audible snap.

"It's him—"

"It's not."

"I can bring him up on murder charges tomorrow."

"I don't care."

"Fuck someone else," he pleaded. "Fall in love with anyone. Not him. All right? Just not him."

"It's over, I told you."

"He's a murderer." He looked as though he immediately regretted saying that. "I have no control around you. You leave, and I fall back into the guy I was because I can't be that guy around you. God, Tink, you were my valve."

"Daniel, I—"

"No, stop. Let me explain. I'm going to stick to the issue. This guy, I can't even say his name right now. That nice peacetime we've been enjoying? It's over as of last week. It started with a fistfight with one of his soldiers, and snowballed into what you've been seeing on the news."

Impassive. I couldn't let on, not even a little. What we intended to keep a secret in Antonio's world had to remain a secret in mine as well. Daniel wasn't above using his position to administrate his personal grudges.

"Daniel," I said firmly, "do not get distracted. You're trying to win an office in the second biggest city in the country."

"Not without you!" His voice got tight and sharp, his litigation voice. The voice of a man with a list of righteous grievances. "He killed Frankie Giraldi and Domenico Uvoli."

Uvoli. Bells rung, but I kept my face impassive.

"He came here for the men who raped his sister. Two, he tracked down and killed. The third, he's still looking for."

Nella. The sister he'd left behind.

"Do you want to know what he did to them?" Daniel asked.

"No." It felt ugly to be told like this. "Stop it."

"He castrated them, then he choked them with their own genitalia. In front of the men he needed to take over their businesses. What he did to find them, I can lay it out for you. You'll never say his name again."

"Stop it." I felt filthy hearing things I shouldn't from a man whose hurt was so apparent. "If you have proof, you need to prosecute. If you don't, you shouldn't gossip."

"It's not gossip when I'm talking to you—that's what I'm trying to say."

The car stopped at the building where Daniel and I used to live together. He looked at the front door, leaning over so he could see up to the eighth floor. Was he homesick? I didn't have the courage to ask.

He sat back. "When I failed you, you threw me out. I never blamed you, but I'm fighting for you. I'm going to win you back. Hell or high water, Tinkerbell. You'll be mine again."

Daniel opened the car for me and led me to the door, *his* door, without another word. I wondered if he could smell the Turkish cigarettes as he walked back to the limo looking more determined than ever.

THE TEXT CAME when I was almost asleep, from a number I didn't recognize.

—Sweet dreams, Contessa. I will see you soon—

I jumped at the phone.

—Come now—

My message bounced. The screen announced that number had been disconnected or was unavailable. I was relieved he'd sent me a text but disconcerted that the number was unavailable. What if I needed him?

I couldn't sleep. I put my hand under the sheets and slipped it beneath my underwear. I was soaked by just the thought of Antonio. My clit felt as sensitive as an open wound. I felt powerful, furious with desire, and I was going to come. My fingers wanted it as much as my engorged pussy. I counted to twenty, then I came forever, crying out for no one. When I was done, I cupped my pussy and looked at the ceiling, thanking God for the release.

My phone rang. Again, I didn't recognize the number. "Hello?"

Just breathing. A swallow.

"Antonio?"

No. It was a woman. On the off chance she was on a borrowed phone, I hedged my bets.

"Deirdre? Katrina?"

A sniff.

"Marina."

Still no answer. Just a weeping woman. What if she was me? What if Antonio was cheating on her? What if I was the mistress this time?

"Are you okay?" I asked. "There's no point calling if you're not going to tell me off or something."

"He's one of us," she croaked. "Not you. He's not one of you."

"I understand," I said, even though I didn't really.

"He thinks..." She choked a little before continuing. "I know him. He thinks you can make him something he's not."

"I don't know what he thinks, Marina. You should ask him."

She shot out a little laugh that must have soaked her phone in snot. "Maybe *you* should ask him."

I was about to answer, but she hung up.

Chapter Thirty

Imagine being cooped up in small spaces with a hundred people in your age group, eight to eighteen hours a day, strictly focused on a project's completion. Imagine long waiting periods where you talk at length about the project and the most important thing in the world—the state of cinema. Imagine you connect intellectually and spiritually with those people. Imagine you can't connect physically because you're so busy.

Now imagine the party at the end of it.

"Honestly, I want to wait to hear from the Germans," Katrina yelled over the music.

It was the first time she'd been willing to entertain a serious discussion of my offer, and only then because she had a few drinks in her. Katrina and I had gotten a downtown loft that was between owners for the party. The rental and cleanup were paid for by the last pennies in the budget, and some sneaky dealing on my part paid for a DJ and open bar. People had melded into a simmering mass of hot, wet flesh pulsing with the music. The loft, someone's future overpriced home, had turned into a nightclub without the safety permits.

"If they fall though, I want a piece," I said. Meaning, a piece of the pie. I tried to couch it not as a charitable offering but an investment in something I believed in.

"You heard from crying lady again?" Katrina asked to change the subject.

"Nope." I hadn't heard from Antonio after his good night text, either. I didn't know what that meant. Did he plan to just come and go as he pleased? Were sweet little texts I couldn't respond to some kind of leash?

"Well, epic party ahead," Katrina said. "Maintain speed through intersections."

She grabbed my hand and dragged me into the middle of the loft where the thump of the music was the loudest and the press of bodies hottest. With the floor shaking, the kisses from the camera man, the bumping and grinding, and the gleeful exclamations over the music, I got diverted. Michael came up behind me, put his arm around my waist, and moved his hips with mine.

I let go. No Katrina and her money woes. No Antonio or his secrecy and lies. No Daniel, period. Just a fine-looking, nice man dancing behind me, a few more in front of me, smiles all around, and a feeling that I'd been part of something bigger than myself.

When Michael moved his arm, I kept dancing for a second. Then I felt a *whoosh* as an area behind me opened up. I turned with the music just in time to see Antonio throw Michael against a table. Michael bounced off the top and fell cleanly, like any actor worth his salt had been trained to do.

"Antonio!"

If he heard me over the music, he made no indication. He stepped forward, stiff and enraged. Michael, being the class clown, spread his legs, waggled his brows, and dodged. Antonio caught his wrist, the motion so fast and effortless that Michael was slammed against the wall with his arm twisted behind his back before I took three steps. A circle of stunned people surrounded the two men. Antonio was such a ball of power and rage that no one dared come near him.

"Maybe you shouldn't let her out by herself then," Michael grumbled when I got close enough to hear.

Antonio twisted his arm harder. I put my hands on Antonio's shoulders, tightening my fingers to make sure he felt them and knew it was me.

"Capo," I said in his ear, "he's my friend. Please."

Antonio's face was contorted in rage, and Michael was trying to smile rakishly through the pain. I pulled Antonio back, and he stepped against me. Michael turned and shook his arm out, giving his attacker a hot look.

"I'm sorry," I said, taking Antonio's hand.

"Put him on a leash," Michael said.

I feared Antonio'd take the bait and attack the actor again, but personal insults didn't seem cause for violence. He squeezed my hand and looked down at me, working his jaw.

"You have no right," I growled as the crowd dissipated.

"I have the only right. I'll hurt anyone who touches what's mine."

I knew we were being watched, so I smiled and touched his face. His jaw was tight and tense.

"Put a smile on your face or someone's going to call the cops," I said.

He stared at me with white hot intensity.

"I said smile."

He shut me up with a kiss. I must have tasted of sweat and hormones. The one beer I'd had was probably stale on my breath, but we kissed as if I was clean and fresh from the shower. Our tongues curled around each other, eating each other alive. His hands crept up my wet shirt, slipping under my bra.

"No," I said, turning away. "You can't just kiss me and make everything okay."

His mouth was on mine before I even finished. I pushed away with my arms, but my mouth had a mind of its own and stayed locked on his. My resolve melted like butter in a frying pan, leaving a streak of bubbling grease behind.

He put his hands on my face and moved an inch away. "You're mine. That means no pretty boys on the dance floor. No fake dates with the district attorney."

He must have seen me with Daniel on the news. Maybe in the paper. Maybe the man with the smelly Turkish cigarettes had told him.

"I'm not telling him anything about you," I said.

"I know you're not. In my heart, I know you have too much grace for treachery. But he wants to fuck you. I don't like it."

I wanted to draw the rules out for him in a cold, businesslike manner. But I couldn't, and it wasn't just his beauty but the intensity of his gaze. Something spun inside him, some toxic lava. It terrified me, and it was the thing I wanted most. How could I draw lines around that? Was there a law I could lay down that it would obey?

"I can't see you with anyone else," he whispered into my ear. "It makes me crazy."

"We're supposed to be discreet. This isn't helping." He pushed his erection against me, and I gasped. "And where have you been? Your phone's disconnected."

"I've been busy."

"What the hell does that mean?"

"You're asking questions."

"I don't have the right to ask questions? Still?"

He held his finger up to my face. "I fuck you. I take care of you. That's what I offer."

"It's not enough."

"You American women make me crazy."

I closed my eyes for a second, getting a hold of myself. I couldn't fight him like this. He'd only come back at me like a bull.

"Tell me," I said. "Tell me what's happening. Where have you been? Are you all right?" I took him in, his eyes blacker, deeper from the moonlight coming through the window. "Don't tell me facts. Your truths all sound like lies anyway. I don't care about names and dates. I don't care about the situation. Just tell me about you. I want to know you, Capo." I touched his chest with the flat of my hand. "I want to know your heart."

"No, you don't."

"Let me know you."

"Contessa," he said so tenderly I barely heard it.

"Let me know you," I repeated. "Let me in."

He brushed a strand of hair off my cheek. "You dance with your friends. I don't. You see movies. I don't. You have a good life. I have something else."

"Come with me. You can dance too. We can go out to movies with friends, do all the things people do."

He put his arms around me and kissed me fully. When I slipped my hands under his jacket and felt the lump of a gun holster under his arm, he stiffened. I kissed him harder, because the feel of it had dumped a bucket of desire between my legs. I clutched him, the gun on the inside of my forearm.

He shook his head. "You turn me around every time. You're going to make me soft."

"A soft man wouldn't say that."

Something changed in his face. His jaw got tight again. "No, a soft man would." He grabbed my hand. "I'm taking you now, Contessa. And not gently."

We were in a room full of people. I had no idea what was on his mind, but he pulled me to the back of the loft and through the kitchen, which had been stripped to the lathe. He pushed through a metal door and yanked me into a fluorescent-drowned hallway with cracked walls and mottled concrete floor.

He rushed me into a dark closet and slammed the door behind him. Brooms and mops fell around us when he grabbed me, pulling my hair back and hitching up my skirt. The painted-over window let a little of the streetlights in, and when my eyes adjusted, I saw the fire in his eyes. Was this his reaction to a moment of softness?

"You're going to get me killed." He ran his fingers over my pussy roughly. "That make you wet?" He jerked my hair.

"Mercurial, much?"

"I will not die because you made me weak." He put me on the edge of the slop sink. I leaned on my hands, and he jerked my legs open.

"Fuck me then, you son of a bitch."

He ripped a gaping hole in my panties and shoved two fingers in me. With his other hand, he released his erection as if it was a weapon. He took his fingers out of me and put them on my throat, thumb and middle finger on each side of my jaw, pressing me to the windowsill.

"I fuck you, and you take it, do you understand?" Without waiting for an answer, he shoved his cock all the way in me in one thrust. The wind went out of me, and his hand on the throat kept me from speaking. He said, "You're mine. I am who I am, and I own you. That's all it is."

He fucked me hard and dirty. One hand pinned me by the throat, not choking me, but letting me know he was there, and the other hand spread my knee wide. My ass was balanced on the edge of a sink, and somehow, as rough as he was, his hands kept me from falling.

"You take it. Take it."

"Yes, yes," I croaked, pressure building every time his cock went in me.

He hooked his pussy-soaked fingers in my mouth. "Come, Contessa. Do what I tell you. Fucking come."

In three painful thrusts, I had to obey. I shuddered and cried out into his fingers, coming for him, only for him. He ground his teeth and plowed into me so hard, the pain was muffled by another rising orgasm. Still he came at me, punishing me with his dick, and still my body rose to him. He slowed, and I thought he was done, but he pounded twice more, lengthening my climax.

"Please stop." I gasped. "Please, Capo. I can't take it."

He sighed, shifted his hips, and gathered me in his arms. I wrapped my legs around him and rested my head on his shoulder.

"You're going to be my death," he said. "I don't know what to do. I feel weak around you. I'm going to slip up."

"I want to be there for you, but I can't. I can try to stay out of trouble," I said.

"I'm not worried about you getting into trouble. I'm worried about trouble coming to you. I'm worried about spreading myself too thin. Il have enemies all around me. Every man wants his own thing, and not every man can have it."

I felt a light vibration at his hip. He ignored it and pulled his lips along my cheek, then to my ear.

"A bunch of my crew broke off. Is that enough for you to know?" he said.

"Yes."

"It's my fault, and it's going to take time to make right. I'll have someone on you."

"Will you come see me?"

"If I can."

His phone vibrated again. We kissed briefly before he dropped me, stepping back to button up his pants then his jacket. He checked me out and, finding me presentable, kissed my cheek and took my hand.

Back in the loft, in the middle of the crowd, he kissed my hand then stepped back. He bumped a girl in a tiny skirt then Michael. Michael held up his hands, and Antonio did the same before he spun on his heel and walked out, one hand on his phone.

Katrina crept up behind me. "Got a live wire on your hands, girl."

Michael passed by, a pretty girl on his arm, and said, "No dancing,"

I slapped his arm, but he walked to the dance floor with his new girl as if that sort of thing happened all the time.

Chapter Thirty-One

Someone knocked at my door early the next morning. Katrina still wasn't home. I'd left the party twenty minutes after Antonio.

Looking out the window, I saw a bald man in jeans and a long black jacket. He was smoking. Would answering the door be stupid? Would that be getting myself into trouble? I decided not to risk it and let the curtain close. I waited one minute, then two, then looked out. He was gone, and a little package had been left behind.

I opened the door and peeked at the package without picking it up.

CONTESSA

SAME HANDWRITING as the cards on Antonio's flowers. I brought it inside and opened it. A phone dropped into my hand.

THIS DEVICE IS SECURE. My number is on it. Please only use it for emergencies. And be very safe.

I CHECKED and saw one number in the contacts with an area code in Nevada.

The front door opened, and I jumped. It was Katrina, and her lip was split.

"What happened?" I asked.

"He picked me up." Her breath hitched in a loud sob. "I got in the car, I didn't think anything of it. He said I lied about who I was. That I couldn't pay him back because no one was going to buy my movie."

"What did they do to you?" I said with an edge I didn't recognize from my own throat.

"The lip. It'll go away. I'll just make my vig until I prove him wrong"

I did something I'd only done once before, on the side of the road with a Club in my hand.

I lost my temper.

"What do you mean make your vig? Do you live in one of your goddamn movies? Who the hell even knew that fucking existed anymore?" I paced.

Katrina cried. She'd never seen me like that. *I'd* never seen me like that. I didn't even know who I was.

"I'm calling the cops!" My hand was shaking so hard, I couldn't dial before Katrina snapped the phone away.

"Central?" She spat the name of the LAPD's Downtown division like a curse. "Are you fucking with me? They're a bunch of blabbermouths. The editor of the *Calendar* has every one of them on the take. If this gets out, I'm finished."

"When what gets out? That he pulled you into a car and slapped you around? No. No. A thousand times *no*. I'll call Antonio."

"No! I don't want to be rescued by your boyfriend. That's weird. Forget it. Just forget it. I've handled douchebags like this before."

"How much do you need?"

She leaned on the back of the couch and pressed her fingers to her eyes. "A thousand for last week and a thousand for next."

"Interest compounded minutely if you don't pay." My arms were crossed. I was so mad, all my compassion had run away in fear.

"I can pay it all back when I get distribution. He just..." She drifted off, and tears welled again. "He didn't know about the lawsuit I lost. He found out. I think it just... I don't know."

"For someone so smart," I said, unable to stop myself, "you leave yourself open to the stupidest mistakes."

I stormed into my bedroom. My closet held a few thousand in small bills for emergencies. I counted out three grand and stuffed it in an envelope. I called Antonio from my new phone then hung up. Was this an emergency? Did he just tell me to stay away from Mabat because he was being protective? I really didn't want to bother him when he had so much going on. I'd apologize later for disobeying him if I had to.

I went downstairs. "Come on. I'm delivering it personally."

KATRINA DROVE. The place was in East Hollywood, a trashy nightclub as big as my childhood living room. *Vtang*. I had no idea what it meant, but it was in big, flat red letters on the front, bathing the people in line in blood.

The bouncer, his hairline a receding M, moved the rope before we'd even slowed down. He ushered us past the register for the cover and into a room so dim I wouldn't have been able to tell the girls from boys if there had been no high hair involved.

I was still mad. I didn't know how I'd held onto it that long, because anger wasn't my forte. It was unattractive and uncontrollable. It pushed people away and for the most part, achieved nothing. This anger was mine, though, and it was a caged mink about to get skinned.

The bouncer nodded to the bartender and opened a door to the back room for us. We passed through then down steps, past a smaller door, into an underground office. I should have been scared, but I was too pissed off. Even when I saw four men lounging around the room, two playing backgammon, one on the phone, and one tending blood on his knuckles, I wasn't afraid.

Before anyone had a chance to explain our presence or introduce us, I spoke. "Which one of you is Scott Mabat?"

One middle-aged dirty-blond man in a black leather jacket, bent over the backgammon board, raised his hand slightly, the pointer extended to say, *one second*.

"Scotty, come on," the skinny guy across from him demanded. He pushed aside a tiny cup with a lemon peel in the saucer.

"Shut the fuck up, Vinny," Scott said.

"This is a fast-paced game."

Scott moved his piece. "Not when I play it." He stood. "Kat, nice to see you so soon. Who's the friend?"

"She's—"

"I'm the money." I wanted to throw the envelope down and storm out, but common sense cut through my anger. "I'm putting up her interest, and I'll be paying off her loan next week."

He stepped around the desk and slowly opened his top drawer. "Cash."

"Cash."

"I recognize your face." He flipped through a folder. "You marrying the district attorney?"

"No. Let's get this over with. I have last week, this week, and next week on me. I'll get you the—"

"Whoa, whoa, lady. Don't rush. Kat, did you explain that our terms changed?" He spoke to her as if she was a child.

I wanted to kill him slowly.

"No," she said.

I'd never seen her so cowed. She was the fucking Directrix, for Chrissakes.

"This is the contract," he said. "It's easy as shit. A moron could understand it. The studios give you a ream they nail together. You go to the Giraldis, they don't even write shit down. You're lucky." He flipped me two stapled pieces of paper. The contract was in bullet points and looked as if it had been the result of a hundred generations of photocopying.

"Point four," he said with his arms crossed. "Kat, would you like to read aloud to the class?"

She held out her hand for the pages. Was she insane? That docile girl couldn't direct a movie.

I read point four myself. "'Recipient has made no misrepresentation of their ability to repay the loan.'" I shrugged. "Okay, so?"

"So?" he said. "*So!*"

Throats cleared and chairs squeaked. A heightened intensity vibrated in the room.

Scott pointed his rigid finger at me as though he wanted to stab me. "This bitch didn't tell me she was *poison*. I put up half a mill on an Oscar nominee, not a whining cunt no one wants to touch. Her fucking shit's gonna be at the CineVention selling to Latvia for five G."

"A little underwriting would have gone a long way, Mister Mabat."

The guy whose knuckles were now fully bandaged snorted a laugh.

"That's fucking funny?" Scott said.

Knuckles shrugged. Scott, a man who could not be rushed through a game of backgammon, picked up a dirty coffee mug and bashed Knuckles in the back of the head so hard his neck seemed to shake back and forth like a seizure. It happened so fast, Knuckles's head had dropped to the table before either of the other guys could stand to aid him.

"This was easy money." Scott pointed the cup at me. There was blood and a single black hair on it. "A no-fucking-brainer. Terms changed. There are no prepayments. There's a thirty-year schedule she's keeping." He slapped the cup down. "We'll be happy to take it out of her ass when she can't shell out."

I was scared finally, but I didn't flinch. Knuckles was conscious and being tended by his two compatriots. Katrina sniffled behind me.

"Shush," I said to her. I held my chin up to the loan shark. "You will take the prepayment, plus five thousand, and you will be happy with that."

"Oh, really?"

"Really."

"Or what? You getting the mayor after me? I'm all grown now. He can't do shit."

I pressed my lips together in a smile. "He can't. But if you knew my name, you'd know I have a family. And if you knew anything about how they settle debts, you'd back away slowly." I pulled the envelope out of my jacket and plopped it on the desk. "I suggest you do your research before dismissing my offer out of hand."

I dragged Katrina out by the forearm and didn't look back. I pulled her up the stairs, through the club, and into the street. I walked with my shoulders straight, confident that I owned everything in my sight. My friend blooped the car and got in. I followed and got into the passenger seat as if I was being chauffeured. It wasn't until Katrina stopped at a light on Temple that, in order to release the tension, I started crying.

Katrina rubbed my back. "Look, I'll pay what I can, and he'll get bored of me at some point. I mean, he can't make it so bad that I go to the cops." She laughed bitterly.

"Your memoir is going to be a blockbuster."

"*How To Ruin a Perfectly Good Career in Two Years*."

"*The Girl With the Busted Kneecaps*."

"Maybe I'll make him fall in love with me. I'll be Katrina Mabat."

"Oh God. no. You'd drive him to his ultimate death," I said.

"I think you should back off. Self-preservation is honorable."

"I'm paying him off and walking away. You'll release your movie, and everything will be back to normal."

She sighed and left the dead weight of it in the air. There was a shadow and a *clack clack clack* at the window that I recognized from my car breaking down in Mount Washington. Bald guy. Cigarette.

"Who's that?" Katrina asked.

"My shadow." I rolled down the window. "Hi. Can I help you?"

The smell of turned earth overwhelmed the air coming into the car. He handed me his phone. I hesitated.

"Spin," Turkish Cigarette Man said. "He wants to talk to you."

"Wow, Tee Dray. Wow, okay? Weird and possessive much?"

I took the phone. I had to stop myself from calling him *Capo* in front of Katrina.

He took the moment's pause to demand my attention in a tight voice. "Contessa?"

"Hi."

"You were in an Armenian nightclub? This somewhere you usually go?"

That was him asking me what I was doing without making assumptions. His tone was a coiled spring. He needed a flat truth, or he would wind himself tighter.

"I was seeing Scott Mabat."

He was silent, but in the background, I heard the mumblings of men, as if he was in a crowded room.

"Antonio?" I said.

"Otto will take you to me."

"No, I have—"

"He will pick you up and carry you." He would have been shouting if his voice had been raised, but he kept all the power and tension while practically whispering.

I knew then why he was capo. I hung up on him. I wouldn't disobey him, but I didn't have to tolerate the tone either.

"Kat," I said, "this guy's driving me to see Antonio. We're going to follow you home first and make sure you get in the door, okay?"

"Okay, Tee Dray." Her voice was suspicious even as her words were compliant.

I turned to Otto. "Okay?"

He held up his hands in surrender and smiled. Both of his pinkies were missing. "It's no problem." He had a thick accent.

He opened my car door. I started to get out, but Katrina put her hand on my forearm.

"Thank you," she said.

"It's no problem," I said in Otto's accent.

She smiled. "You're pretty badass. I didn't know that about you."

"Me neither."

Otto had parked his incredibly nondescript silver Corolla two spaces down, and he opened the back door for me.

When he got in, I said, "The car smells nice."

"*Grazie*. There's no smoking in the car. Still smells new, no?"

"It does."

"Okay, I take your friend home, then we go, okay?"

"Yes, sir."

"WHERE ARE WE GOING?" I asked after we'd walked Katrina to the door.

Otto tapped on his phone from the front seat. "The office. But I confirm now."

"How long have you been watching me, Otto?"

He shrugged and pulled out. "A week. I sleep in the car. But no smoking in it. My wife, she's mad I'm not home, but I have a job to do until the boss tells me to stop doing it."

"I hope you get to see her again soon."

He waved the notion off with a flip of his four-fingered hand. "Spin, he save my life. She just make me crazy all the time. Watching you? Like a vacation."

"How did he save your life?"

"That is a long story, I promise."

"I have time."

He made a motion of locking his lips and throwing away the key. "Let him tell you. But he won't. He is too *modesto*."

"Antonio Spinelli? Modest?"

"Like a priest."

I bit back a laugh.

Chapter Thirty-Two

We approached East Side Motors. The yellow and black sign faded orange in the dimming light. The parking lot was clearer, so we pulled in without much trouble. Antonio stood in the middle of the lot in a black suit, waiting. The security lights cast a sunburst of shadows around him.

Otto pulled up. "*Buonasera*, boss."

"Thank you, Otto," Antonio said as he opened my door. "Go on inside and get coffee, then go home and rest."

"*Grazie*," Otto said and disappeared through the garage door.

Antonio took my hand, and I got out of the car.

"Contessa," Antonio said softly, his face deeply shadowed in the artificial light.

"Yes, Capo?"

He pushed me against the car. "I told you not to see him."

"He slapped Katrina around. I'm sorry, but I couldn't wait for you to take care of it."

"And did you take care of it?" His hands moved up my rib cage, thumbs tucking under my breasts.

I looked down. "Not really. He won't take prepayment. He made threats."

He held my face in one hand, a little too tight, to make me look him in the eye. "He threatened you?"

"He threatened Katrina." I pushed him off me. "I want to go home. My God, how did I let myself get stuck here?"

I pushed him hard, and he stepped back. Having gotten out from under him, I walked to the open gate. I didn't know where I was going. I guessed I'd have to call a cab. I could wait for it in the *pupuseria* down the street, but I knew he wouldn't let me go. I still wanted the freedom of that open gate and that dark street and those empty sidewalks. I heard him one step behind me, then he grabbed my forearm.

I twisted and yanked away. "Stop!"

His gaze was dark and unreadable for the second I saw him. He shifted, a blur in my vision, then he became a force of movement against me. He picked me up at the waist and carried me over his shoulder. I would have screamed, but he'd knocked the breath out of me. All I could do was watch the light shift on the blacktop as he carried me across it.

I pounded his back, but I was helpless. "Antonio!"

"Be quiet."

"Stop!"

"*Basta*, woman." He avoided the garage where Otto had gone and opened the door to the dark office without breaking his stride, passing the water cooler and the reception desk. He smacked open his office door then slammed it closed with his foot.

With a lung-emptying thud, I was dumped into a chair. He leaned over me, so threatening and powerful that if he demanded it, I'd have told him the sky was beneath my feet.

"Listen to me," he growled, putting his hands on the chair arms. "I will kill any bastard who touches you. So you walk into a room like that again without me, you'd better want the man dead."

He meant it. From the tightness in his lips and the lines in his brow, I knew he wasn't speaking metaphorically. He'd kill for me, and it would be my responsibility.

"I'll admit I was scared, and you were the first person I thought of," I said. "And the last person. But in between that, I was afraid of getting you involved."

"You're involved. I'm involved. We can't go backward now. You said you saw that stupid punk face to face, and I went crazy. I saw you with that other ass, the one who cheated on you, and I went crazy. I don't have a brain when it comes to you. You know how much trouble it could be for me if I get arrested for something stupid? Like beating that guy with the ugly Porsche? But I thought he kicked you, and I lost my mind."

"You didn't even know me."

He continued as if I hadn't spoken. "When I was a young, they called me Tonio-botz because I'd go off over nothing. But I'm a man now, and I don't do that. Tonio-botz was a garbage kid who had no control over himself. But he's back every time I see you."

I was scared of him, for him, about him. I was also turned on. I touched his face. "I bet he wasn't so bad."

"Please understand."

"I do. Would you kiss me?"

With breakneck speed and intensity, he kissed me, using his tongue without prelude as if it was a dick shoved in me. I leaned up and he knelt back until we were both on the floor.

"Here." I pulled his wrist and slid his hand between my legs. "Feel how wet I am." I pressed his hand under my skirt to my damp panties, moving until his pinkie touched my soaking skin. "It's never been this easy, and it's you. This is how I react to you. It terrifies me."

He sucked air through his teeth. "We're even then, Contessa."

"Take me now, please. Fuck me scared."

He slipped two fingers in me all the way, pressing as if he wanted to get his whole hand in, and I spread my legs as if I wanted exactly the same thing. He put his face to mine until he took up the curves of my vision. His breath fell on my open mouth as he watched me react to his touch.

"I want to fuck you so hard we have the same skin."

"Yes," I gasped, reaching for his belt.

A knock came at the door. "Spin? You in there?"

"Fuck," he grumbled, then shouted to the door. "What, Zo?"

"Uh, sorry, but uh, we got word from Donna Maria. And you said—"

"All right." He removed his fingers from me.

Zo didn't get the message. "You said if we heard from her that—"

"Zo! *Basta*! I'll see you inside." He straightened my panties and skirt. "I'm sorry, Contessa. Business calls. You and I will share a skin later."

"Can Otto drive me home?"

"I'm sorry, but you're not going home tonight. I'll have one of the guys go to your house and pack you a bag. But until I take care of Scott Mabat, you're staying at my side." He stood, erection apparent under his pants.

I was still splayed on the floor. "Antonio, really?"

"Really. It's like the kids' shows. When the song comes, the bouncing ball tells you when to sing the words." He put his hand out to help me up. "Just follow along."

WE CROSSED the parking lot holding hands, and when we went into the pitch dark garage, he squeezed my hand. I heard men talking and a *thup thup* sound.

"Follow along," he said and opened a door in the back.

In a low room decorated in wood paneling and cigarette smoke, a handful of men faced the same direction. Zo crooked his arm and straightened it quickly. A *thup* followed, and the others reacted by exchanging handslaps and cash.

Darts.

An Italian flag draped one wall. The chairs were wooden and well worn, like the desk and linoleum floor. I recognized a man in a fedora from outside Zia's restaurant. Silence fell on the room like a lead curtain.

Antonio kissed me on both cheeks, left first, then right. He stared me in the face for a second before facing his crew. "*Signori*, this is Theresa. Theresa, you've met Lorenzo."

Zo came up to me as if for the first time and took my hand. "*Piacere*." He kissed me on each cheek, right then left, and stepped back.

"Otto, you're still here?" Antonio said.

He stepped forward and took my hand. "*Piacere di conoscerla*." He kissed me the same way, left then right.

"Good to meet you," I said.

"Now go home," Antonio said. He indicated a man in a checked jacket and receding hairline. "Enzo, meet Theresa."

"Very nice to meet you," he said in a clean California accent I wouldn't have noticed in any other group.

"You, as well." I counted three more. Fedora was next.

"Niccolo, this is Theresa."

"*Piacere*." He kissed me quickly, in the middle of counting a stack of bills, as if the whole process was inconvenient.

"Nice to meet you, too."

"Last, Simone, I'd like you to meet Theresa."

"Good to meet you!" The only blond in the crew, he shook my hand like a car salesman and smiled big, only kissing each cheek when Antonio shot him a look. He did it right then left, and the mix-up meant we almost kissed on the lips. He laughed.

"Enzo, Niccolo," Antonio said, "go get the half-Armenian *strozzino*. Call me when you have him. Zo, bring the lady to the little house then pick her up a bag."

Otto, Enzo, and Niccolo left, chattering in deep voices.

"Antonio," I said with warning in my voice.

"The ball with the music," he said. "Please. Call your roommate and tell her Zo's coming."

"I have work tomorrow."

"I hope so." He whispered in my ear, "I'll come to you. Just wait."

Paulie burst in. "Hey! I heard there was a formal introduction."

"Hi, Paulie," I said.

"This is Theresa," Antonio said.

Paulie joyfully kissed my left cheek, then my right, and took me by the shoulders. "Welcome. Good to have you."

"Thanks," I said.

Paulie turned to Antonio. "We taking care of the Donna Maria thing?"

"Yes. Let me get Theresa set up, then we'll talk about it."

Chapter Thirty-Three

The little house stood up into the foothills behind a hundred feet of allergens. It could have been in the Tennessee mountains for all its foliage and acreage. A skinny kid of about nineteen with an acne problem sat on the porch. He stood when Zo and I drove up.

"Don," Zo said, "this is Theresa. The boss formally introduced her tonight."

"Huh," the kid huffed, as if surprised. "All right, then. *Piacere*." His accent was terrible, but he kissed me on both cheeks, left then right.

"Donatello's gonna be on the porch. He's keeping his eyes on you so, don't worry about him." Zo punched the kid in the arm, and he almost fell over.

"Thanks," the kid said.

"This is a safe house, isn't it?" I said.

"Used to be. Now it's just safe."

He took me through the two-bedroom house, which looked more lived in than any safe house I'd seen in movies. I saw old world touches all over in the unfinished wood and hand-painted ceramics. The quilt on my bed was deep burgundy, the oil paintings showed seashores and mountains, and the kitchen, the only ultra-modern part of the house, had a basket of fresh fruit on the counter.

"This is Antonio's house?" I asked.

"Yeah."

"It's smaller than my loft."

Zo shrugged. "He likes it that way."

"Can you bring Katrina? It's her I'm worried about."

"Boss has it covered. He takes care of his people. And after tonight, you're with us." Zo kissed me on both cheeks again and left.

"KATRINA? ARE YOU ALL RIGHT?"

"I got a shard of swan in my foot, I want you to know."

I was curled up on a strange couch, in a strange house, with a strange guy on the porch to protect me. I had the news on and muted. The ticker moved, and the heads talked. "There's a guy coming to get a bag for me. Can you put some stuff in it?"

"Cups? Plates? Saucers? What do you want?"

"Are you okay?" I asked.

"When I'm not crying, I'm fine. God, I botched this."

"We'll make it right. I don't know how, but we will. It's a good movie."

"I'm going to my parents in the OC tomorrow. I'll stay a few days and get my shit together. If he chases me there, my dad will just shoot him."

"Great plan."

She sniffed. "Do you want the electric toothbrush? Or a regular one?"

"Regular. I don't intend to be gone long enough to charge the electric one."

"Okay. I gotta go. Michael's coming over."

"Really?"

Daniel's face appeared on the screen. The ticker told me he was doing the unprecedented: opening a major case against an organized crime family at the tail end of a mayoral campaign.

"Reckless asshole," I mumbled.

"Excuse me?"

"Nothing. Have fun with Michael. And, Kat?"

"Yes?"

"There are going to be men around watching you. Stay calm, okay?"

"Jesus, Tee Dray, what are you into?"

"I don't know, but I think I'm up to my eyeballs."

I SLEPT on the couch until the navy sky faded into morning cyan. He came to me in a haze of pine and musk. His lips were my awakening, the hard firearm at his back a reflection of the hardness between his legs.

"Capo," I whispered through my sleep.

"Ah, Contessa. I could barely talk tonight. All I wanted to do was make peace so I could fuck you every day and night." He pulled up my shirt and kissed my belly.

"Is this about the trouble with your men?"

"Done for now. Tie up loose ends tomorrow." He pushed up my bra.

I wove my fingers in his hair when he sucked my nipples. "I can go to work?"

"Shh. No talking." He pulled away and got on his knees, looking at me. He yanked at my skirt and panties, slipping them off. "Spread your legs." He shrugged out of his jacket and pulled off his shirt. "Touch yourself." There was a sense of urgency about his manner as he wiggled out of the last of his clothes.

I watched him with my fingers between my legs, stroking my hardened, wet clit. "I want you so bad." I moaned. "I want you inside me."

"Shh." He put his cock at my opening. He thrust forward.

I put my hands on his shoulders, letting the thrust of his hips take me. He took my hands and pinned them to my sides, wrapping his arms around me tight. He pressed the whole of his body to mine as if he was trying to crawl into my skin. If he did, I couldn't have stopped him. He had me powerless under his weight, restrained by his desire. My legs were free but pinioned by the fulcrum of his cock.

"Every day," he whispered, "I'll take you like this. In the morning, before coffee, I fuck you. At night, I fuck you harder. In our bedroom, our living room, our kitchen, I'll love you in every room. *Mi amore,* I'll break you with my love and put you back together. And when I retire, you still call me Capo because you're mine. Always mine."

His lips spoke into my cheek. I felt wrapped in him, past, present and future. I had no whim or hunger outside the building pleasure in my legs and safe pressure of his skin and muscle.

I gasped. I was going to come. I wondered if my explosion would be held down, tamped by the weight of his arms and the swirling affection in his words. But my orgasm came in a flood. My back arched, and my thighs got stiff. I saw nothing, heard nothing, felt nothing but Antonio. His weight, his breath, his scent, and his pleasure, concurrent with mine, swirled together inside my skin, and I, inside his.

WE STAYED WRAPPED around each other for a long time, just breathing together. I was so tired, I fell asleep under him. He whispered *mi amore*, kissing my neck and shoulders, then relaxed his arms.

"My Capo," I said. "Always."

"You should sleep." He brushed wet strands of hair from my face as if it was of great concern. "I brought your bag."

"I hope she packed work clothes."

"You stay here today. I haven't taken care of the *strozzino* yet."

"Antonio, please. I have to live."

He pressed his fingers to my lips. "What do you think happened last night?"

"I followed the bouncing ball."

"You are under my protection. My crew recognizes you. They can't touch you, and they will protect you. But you also have a responsibility to us to stay out of trouble. For a few days, things will be disrupted. Bruno and Vito, they're doing their own thing. I didn't want that. Vito, with the young girls…" He rubbed his eyes. "I don't like it, but…" He looked up and crooked his neck as if shaking off the thought. "We have to pay tribute to another family, so everyone recognizes them as their own thing, not just us. This has to be completed before I can let you walk around without an escort."

"What?" I sat up, and he moved off me.

"I couldn't isolate you and keep you safe. This was the only way. You're untouchable now, as long as you obey the rules."

"What are the rules?"

"Do not talk to the press or police. Not talk about our business with anyone. Not ask questions." He held up his hand to my pending objections. "You can ask *me*. But no one else. I have all the information. My men only know some things, and if they talk, you get half the story. And I know what can hurt you."

"You might have mentioned this before all the double kissing happened."

"What am I asking? That you be loyal? That you come to me first? Only the saying of it makes you sit up and cross your arms."

I huffed. Of course he was right. Of course I had no intention of ratting him out or investigating him further. It was indeed the list of rules that bristled me.

"This needs to be on a probationary basis," I said.

"One minute probation," he said then kissed me, his hand tight on my jaw, his tongue prying my mouth open. He stopped. "My minute's up, Contessa. Are you still mine?"

"You are my Capo," I whispered. "But I'm mad at you."

"Get in the shower then before I fuck you again."

KATRINA HAD PACKED everything I needed. One set of work clothes, one set of regular clothes. Shoes, toiletries, and a note.

TEE – Thank you for everything. You are a shining star. I promise not to let you down. You'll be proud of me one day.

BE SAFE, okay?

THE DIRECTRIX

WHEN I GOT out of the bathroom, Antonio held up my phone. "What are we going to do about this guy?"

There was a text from Daniel.

—need to speak with you in person
by tomorrow—

"What are we going to do about you looking at my texts?"

"As long as you're talking to him and the thing is face up on the table, I'll look."

"You don't trust me?" I asked.

"I do."

"I think you're missing an opportunity to get some inside information, Capo."

He crossed his arms and narrowed his gaze. "Contessa."

"If I don't see him, he's going to get suspicious. He's just opened a case against, I'm assuming, you? Knowing I might be with you? Let me see him and find out what he wants."

"You're going to spy for me? I don't want that from you, ever."

"To be honest, I just want to go home and have kind of a normal day. You know, one where I don't see a gun or take part in some ritual I don't understand."

"And you need to see Daniel Brower to do that?"

"He's not a loan shark or a baby capo looking for territory. He's not going to hate you any more than he already does, and he'll never touch me. What's the harm in me putting on my work clothes and taking a lunch?" I put my hands on his forearms, and he dropped them. "We'll be in public. I promise." I slipped my hands around his waist and held him close.

He put his arms around me and kissed my head. "*Come vuoi tu*."

Chapter Thirty-Four

Enzo drove me home in a charcoal grey Ferrari and left me in the parking lot. I went right to my car and made it to work just in time.

Pam was business as usual, dozen red roses on her desk notwithstanding.

"Good morning," I said.

"Morning."

"What do I have today?"

Pam rattled off a list of meeting and conferences. I texted Daniel.

—What time today?—

—Stuff exploded. Tomorrow ok? Before lunch, 30 min?—

—No prob—

"Can you reserve the big conference room at eleven thirty tomorrow?" I asked Pam.

She tapped around. "It's free. Who are you meeting?"

I looked over her shoulder. The blinking cursor required an answer to who would be in the room with me. "Daniel Brower."

She tapped it in, her expression sour under her rhinestone-tipped horn rims. "You know, polling this morning shows he's in the lead for mayor."

I plucked the card from the roses. "I knew he didn't need me to win."

Tonight.

I smiled to myself. Tonight, indeed.

I TRIED to keep my mind on my meetings and rows of numbers. I smoothed things over between two accountants on my team while thinking about Antonio's body. I didn't know how much longer I could stay at WDE. I hadn't been fully engaged in my job in months. After spending time with Antonio, the job felt like a blunter, dimmer version of life.

I kept Antonio's phone in my pocket. When it rang during a meeting, I excused myself and answered in the hall. "Capo?"

"Paulie."

I might have blushed, as if he'd walked in on my dirty thoughts. "Hi, Paulie."

"I'm coming to pick you up from work. Is six okay?"

"Sure. I can leave my car in the lot."

"See you then."

OUR VALET WAS in the alley behind the building, and Paulie's Ferrari fit right in. When I came out, he was leaning against it in the shade of a bougainvillea hedge, smoking a cigarette.

"Hey," I said. "What happened to you?" I pointed to my lower lip, indicating the split on the bottom of his.

"Fell on a guy's fist."

"You should watch where you're walking."

"He's taken care of. You can tell your friend the loan's forgiven."

"I'll give him his money. I don't want to steal it," I said.

"Don't worry about it."

He opened the passenger door, and I got in. He obviously didn't want to discuss the money. I'd wait, but I had every intention of making sure Katrina's production was clean.

"Where are we going?" I asked.

"San Pedro."

"We going to the beach?" I asked facetiously. San Pedro did indeed have a beach. It was also home to the loading docks and a notorious organized crime stronghold.

"We have an office down there."

"Of course you do."

With that, he drove into the traffic of Wilshire Boulevard.

"Where are you from, Paulie? You sound American."

"Here. Born and raised. Pure-blooded Angelino dego."

"Have you always been, um, in the life?"

He flung his hand back, as if indicating everything behind him. "Few generations. I'm as in it as Spin."

"And you guys partnered? I mean, were you here first? Did he just muscle in or what?"

"He told me you were full of questions."

"Did he tell you how frustrating it is to not ask any?"

He swung south onto LaCienega. "Doesn't occur to me. I stay inside the lines. Safer that way. No questions because everyone already knows the answers."

I didn't say anything all the way down to the 10 freeway. He went east, and the wind drowned us out.

Paulie started talking as if he'd been working on his answer the whole time. "Spin came here with a bloodline, which is important. Gives him credibility, you know? He came right to me and asked for my permission to do some business. Did it exactly right, too."

"I can't imagine him asking permission to do anything."

"Wasn't like I couldn't tell right away he could run a crew. And I'll tell you, it would have been stupid for me not to partner up."

"Why?"

"Because I like money, that's why," he said.

"He knows how to get it, I presume?"

When he didn't answer, I thought I'd said too much, pushed him past his comfort level. He rubbed his lip as he changed lanes.

"How did your family get their money?" he asked.

"Generations of stealing followed by a few generations of legalized thievery. Now it's all compounded interest."

He laughed. "You're honest."

"Sometimes."

"I'm going to be honest with you then."

"Oh, this is already so much better than that meeting I cancelled."

"My partner, he likes you."

I was going to joke about being relieved but decided against it. This seemed very serious to him, so I shut up.

"He introduced you. That doesn't happen every day. He's got girls who are in the life. Like family." He turned to me briefly then looked back at the road. "Do you know what I mean by that?"

"I think so."

"Okay, so none of them are anything. But you? He's lost his shit. He's pissing himself. After today, shit's gonna change, and I don't know if you can handle it."

"Are you sure he'd want you telling me this?"

"I'm not telling you anything you can use. Reason is, and I'm being honest here, I don't trust you."

I watched the train stops in the center of the 110. The road was relatively clear. Paulie kept left, and everyone got out of the way.

"I guess I don't blame you," I said.

The paper bag-brown sky of San Pedro crept over the horizon. Giant chair-shaped cranes loomed over the portal to the sea.

"Thanks for helping with my sister that night," I said.

"No problem."

"You were very level-headed."

"Thanks. You too."

Chapter Thirty-Five

Paulie pulled into the docking area with a wave. Yellow and black striped barriers went up everywhere, allowing a right, then a left, to an alcove inside a parking lot that housed two trailers and a couple of cars.

"You really know how to schmooze a girl, Paulie."

He winked at me, and we got out. I followed him to two red shipping containers fifty feet from a sheer concrete drop to the fouled water of the harbor.

"Okay, kid, here's the deal," Paulie said. "You're not going to care for this, but you're going in there with me. I am not going to hurt you. I'm not going to hurt anyone you care about. I'm telling the truth when I say you need to see something."

I hadn't been nervous. I knew Antonio was at the end of this journey, so I'd felt safe. As Paulie spoke, I became unsure and my heart pounded. The container had no windows or doors. Once I went in, I could be easily trapped.

"Let's go then," I said.

He grabbed the silver pole and yanked it down with a clack. He swung the door open, and it creaked so loudly I was reminded of a horror movie. When the triangle of light cut the dark tunnel, I had second thoughts.

"I'll leave the door open a crack," Paulie said.

"You coming in with me?"

"Right behind you."

I didn't feel safe. I didn't feel threatened, but I didn't delude myself into thinking Paulie would jump a pack of wolves for me, double kiss or not. I stepped up to the entrance anyway. Maybe curiosity drove me. Maybe a quest for self-destruction. Maybe I wanted to grab a little badass cred and put it in my Prada bag or walk in riskier shoes.

Two steps in, I heard wet, arrhythmic breathing. Then the door closed, and the box went dark.

"You said you were leaving the door open," I said.

"Oops."

The light flicked on, drowning the tunnel in flat, industrial illumination. A man was curled against the wall, his ankle chained to a hook on the side of the container. I'd thought I was nervous and scared before. But when the door opened again, I understood what it felt like to jump out of my own skin.

Paulie laughed. He leaned on the wall casually tapping his phone.

Zo stuck his head in. "There you are."

"Come on in," Paulie said.

"Hi, Miss Drazen," Zo said. "How you doing?"

"I'm fine."

Zo glanced at Paulie then the guy.

"She's cool," Paulie said. "Let's see him."

Snapping the door shut, Zo crossed the length of the shipping container in about four steps. He kicked the guy to semi-consciousness. "Hey, asshole."

He picked up the man by the back of his collar. His face was beaten bloody, but I still recognized Scott Mabat. Zo plucked a bottle of soda from his jacket pocket and shook it before tossing it to Paulie. Paulie nodded as he passed me, tapping the bottle cap to his forehead as if tipping his cap to me. It left a dot of condensation. The soda must be ice cold.

"Time to get up, Scotty." Paulie opened the bottle into Mabat's face.

"Fuck!" Scott yelped.

"Welcome back."

"Fuck you!" He spat blood.

"I know it's been a rough night. So I brought you something pretty to look at." Paulie yanked Scott's face around until I was in his line of sight.

Shit. I had to decide what to do quickly, and I decided to do what I always did. Show nothing. Give nothing. Own it.

"Where's Antonio?" I asked.

"Taking care of business. He's on his way."

"Fucking frigid bitch," Scott said.

"Same wonderful sense of humor, I see." I said.

Zo laughed long and loud then petered.

Paulie capped the soda bottle and turned to me. "So I have a problem, and I think you can help me solve it. Scotty here is the victim of my partner's protective streak. I didn't know he had one. But it's there."

Scott coughed and sputtered. "I'm gonna fucking kill you." He stared at me then coughed again.

"You're being paid, Mister Mabat. I have the money ready to be wired." I clipped every word, keeping it business despite the piss I smelled on him. I refused to be sick. I refused to even have a feeling about what was happening. Now wasn't the time for feelings, only thoughts. Cold ones. I couldn't get muddied.

"Fuck the money," Scott said. "I'm getting your friend's tits."

"See," Paulie continued, before I could snap back at Scott. "I have this trust thing with you, like we talked about. So I looked into you, your whole family. You're clean, but a couple of you got your fingers in shady pies. Your father could teach me something about the business."

"And you could teach Scott something about the importance of research."

Paulie's mouth tightened, and I knew he was holding back a smile. "You hear that, Scotty? You taking notes?"

"I'm gonna put my fist up her little Viet-cong ass," Scott growled at me.

"Yeah," Paulie said. "Scotty over here is touching on something I'm getting to."

"Make her suck my fingers after."

"Shut up, douche." Zo slapped Scott, sending a splash of blood to the wall.

I noticed then that there was no blood on the walls or floor. A gruesome observation, but it told me that he'd been beaten and moved there.

"Personally," Paulie continued, "I like you. I think I mighta fucked you if Spin wasn't already whipped. But here you are, hanging around the neighborhood, DA's girlfriend, looking for shit. So I'm nervous. Then there you are, being introduced, and I can't say shit. Even if it's common sense, I gotta button it because those are the rules. Everyone's got rules but the women."

"I got pulled in. You forget."

"No. I didn't forget, and I don't care what you do on purpose," Paulie said. "This whole thing with Vito? Spin was already pissed he had a valet thing on the side. A straight job, no less. But then he beat his ass over some bullshit about a girl he didn't even know. And why? Because he's pussy whipped. Then Bruno partners up with Vito, and I got two guys Spin's after, guns blazing. He's beating on their friends trying to find them. Four days, my partner didn't make no sense. Four days he forgot the rules, and everyone runs to Donna Maria looking for help. It gets so bad he's gotta ask permission from another family to do what's his right to do. Now I'm dragged in, thinking you must have a magic cunt."

Scott scooted around on his knees. His hands were tied behind his back, and one shoulder looked dislocated. He needed a hospital stay.

"Here's what I told our boy here," Paulie continued. "I told him I'm not gonna kill him. I told him you were an accessory to all this. And I told him he couldn't touch you. You are protected, by us, indefinitely. This will keep my partner happy, and you alive, because this guy's pissed." He pushed Scott down with his foot. "Right, you Armenian fuck? You're pissed, right?"

Scott tried to spit on him, but gravity put the spit back on his face. Paulie leaned closer, in spit range, but Scott didn't appear to have a drop of saliva left.

"You're gonna take it out on someone, aren't you?" Paulie asked.

Scott smiled through a bloody mouth.

"You sold him Katrina," I whispered.

"Maybe. That's up to you."

He stepped back and let Scott and me look at each other. Worry and fear crept through my skin. Resist them though I might, I wasn't calloused to this. I was a nice girl with a beach house and perfect grades.

"Well then, Mister Patalano, it looks like I'm going to have to figure something out." I turned to leave, but Paulie held me back with a hand to my shoulder.

"I'm not done."

"I disagree."

"You can run to the DA. You can run to daddy. But I know your father better than you do, even if I never met him. Our families aren't strangers, if you know what I mean. And the DA? Don't get me started. Your girlfriend has a couple of family here in Orange County. A few friends. She disappears, it's in the news this week, and next week London Westin's worn-out pussy's in the papers."

He reached in his jacket. He was going for his gun. I think my panic must have been visible then, because he held out his hand to calm me. He slowly pulled the firearm.

"I have a solution for you," Paulie said. "You want to earn my trust? If you earn that, you and your girlfriend will be under my protection. This guy won't touch either of you." He handed me the gun.

Zo spoke up, "Paulie, whoa! The fuck?"

"Shut up, Zo." It sat in the flat of his hand like an offering. "Take him out. Problem solved."

Scott laughed, lightly at first. Maybe a smarter person than I am would have deduced another solution. Maybe a more naturally manipulative person would have stalled long enough to change the course of events. But I was empty. I took the gun. It was lighter than I expected. Easier to pick up. Maybe I thought it should weigh some more supernatural amount, equal to the death inside it.

"Take him out, and you're going to solve all kinds of problems," Paulie said.

"You're nuts, you know that?"

"I'm hedging a bet. It's a million to one you have the spine for it. And I gotta be honest, I want you out of the picture."

"Paulie, come on," Zo said.

"Shut the fuck up, Zo." The man with the bow lips stood close to me, engaging in a staring contest I had no intention of losing.

"She can't get made, no ways," Zo pleaded.

I said softly, "This is a very risky proposition."

"No, it's not."

"Shit." Zo was freaking out. "Pauls, what if she misses and hits me?"

"Pick him up," Paulie said without releasing me from his gaze. "Let her get a good shot."

"I'm not killing anyone," I said.

"My money's on you not even pulling the trigger."

"Does Antonio know about this little bet with yourself?"

As if in answer, Paulie's phone buzzed. He ignored it. "He's not here right now, is he? He's busy taking out two perfectly good guys he alienated because of you. I'm here cleaning up this mess he made because of who? Yeah. You."

Scott had stopped laughing, the blood on his lips crusting over. Paulie squeezed my hand with the gun in it. He looked at it, and I followed his gaze. The gun was hard and black with flat surfaces and squared edges. A cop gun, not a cowboy gun.

I slipped my finger in the metal loop around the trigger, cupping the handle in my palm. "You misread me, Mister Patalano. You think I'm some sheltered little girl who never had to fight for myself. But I've spent my whole life fighting for myself. Just not the way you think."

"Prove it." His phone buzzed again.

Was it Antonio? Could I stall long enough to get a bye in this little game?

"She can't earn no bones anyway, Paulie, come on!" Zo was near hysteria.

"Aw, the little girl has a gun?" Scotty said.

I didn't know what was wrong with him, why he didn't just roll over or shut up. I didn't know what had to happen to make him continue taunting his attackers until they killed him, but whatever it was, Scott Mabat was in self-destruct mode.

So I pointed the gun at him. "I could shoot you right now."

"You don't have the balls. My dogs will rip that girl in the middle."

He didn't threaten me. He'd never threatened me, only Kat. As if he thought that in self-preservation, I'd just let her get pulled into a basement by him and his cronies. And he'd leave me unharmed at the door. Paulie's word must really mean something.

"I'm going to shoot you, Mister Mabat, unless you allow a prepayment and keep your hands off Katrina," I said.

"You're not shooting anyone."

"Keep making me angry."

"I bet she tastes like soy sauce when she cries."

My hand tightened to the point of no return. I pulled the trigger. Tight. Tighter, until the tension in the thing released, and the trigger bounced back.

Nothing happened.

Scott broke into hysteria.

Zo's eyes went wide. He chanted "Holy shit holy mother of Jesus," over and over.

I let the gun swing from the trigger loop, finger extended. Paulie looked both impressed and pensive as he held out his hand for it. We didn't have a chance to exchange a word because the door opened with a creak.

Antonio stood in the rectangle of light. "Paulie." The word was a statement with a serious undercurrent of darkness, violence, and unspoken threats. "What is she doing here?"

"Nice to see you, too. What took you so long?"

Antonio stepped inside, taking in everything, his hands, knuckles already bloodied and bruised, coiled for something. Zo shut up as if someone had stapled his mouth shut, and Scott, for once, was reduced to silence.

"You said you were in the trailer," he said.

"I moved him."

Antonio reached me and took the gun then put his other hand in mine. I realized that with everything we'd done together, we'd never held hands. Not until I was afraid to hurt him or get blood on my cuffs did I feel his fingers laced in mine.

"What the fuck are you doing, Paulie?" Antonio asked.

"Good luck with this one," he said.

Antonio pulled me through the door, and I followed because I had no choice. Though the container had been lit, the afternoon sunlight made me squint. I held my hand up to block the sun as Antonio pulled me toward his Mas.

He opened the door for me. "Get in, and do not make me put you in."

I got in. He came around the front of the car. We watched the open door of the red shipping container. No one came out. Antonio backed out of the parking lot in a spray of gravel.

"What the fuck—"

"He picked me up from work," I said.

"What did he tell you?"

"Nothing. Then we went in there, and Scott looked like that. Did you do that to him?"

"I didn't want you to see that. It was supposed to be that I finished getting his guys to understand my position, then we worked on Scott. Then you gave him his money back, and you were done."

"Well, I did see it. You hurt him. One of his eyes was sealed shut."

"I woulda done worse if Zo hadn't pulled me off him." Antonio drove in a rage, pulling onto the freeway as if he wanted the car to eat it. "He just wouldn't stop fucking talking. This is what I was telling you. This is who I am. This is what you do to me. And Paulie? He doesn't trust you. He showed you so you'd run away from me, right?"

"He wanted me to shoot Mabat in exchange for Katrina's immunity."

"And what happened when you wouldn't?" he asked.

"I did."

"You what?"

"I pulled the trigger."

I saw that he was confused. He was probably thinking: Had Scott been quiet when he got there? Did he look dead? Who was the woman sitting next to him? Was there a whole new set of problems to solve?

"You think you're the only one, Antonio. You think you're the only one with a little murder in him," I said. "A little temper? Well, I knew there were no bullets in the gun, because it was so light. I knew it would just click, but I was sorry it was empty. I wanted to spray his brains all over the wall. He's a waste of a man."

Antonio pulled the wheel hard right at eighty miles an hour and screeched to a stop at the shoulder. If that was what it was to be mercurial and impulsive, I understood the appeal. Every moment felt like living at the height of awareness, every sense sharpened to a fine edge.

"God help me," he said. "I've ruined you."

I touched his arm, but he pulled away.

Chapter Thirty-Six

"Antonio," I said.

He didn't answer, just kept his wrist on the top of the steering wheel.

"Capo."

"Don't call me that."

My face got hot, and my loins tingled as if I'd been dropped off the first hill of a roller coaster. I wanted to look at him, but I couldn't. I wanted to check his hands for bruises and accuse him of worse violence than I'd wanted to commit. I wanted to make excuses and demands. I looked at my own hands, free of blood or bruise, but they were shaking.

"Antonio, what's wrong?"

He got off the freeway downtown. "It doesn't matter."

"I think it does."

"We'll still protect you."

"What? Wait. I don't understand. What happened to everything?"

"It's just done, Theresa. Over." He shook his head, eyes on the road and avoiding my gaze.

I blinked, and a tear fell. What had I done? How could I have done differently? How could he shut me out? "This was Paulie's plan? That you'd hate me?"

He didn't answer. He'd turned to stone right in front of me.

"Brilliant," I muttered. "He's a fucking genius."

"Nice mouth."

"Fuck, fuck, fuck!" I hit him on the arm.

He yanked the car over, screeching to the curb a few blocks from the loft. He drew his finger like a rod, rigid and forceful, as if he could kill me with it. "Do not hit me again."

"What happened?"

"This is not what I want. I'm in the life. I'm damned, I know this. I cannot come home to a woman I'll share hell with." He slapped the car in park and turned away from me again, as if seeking answers in the half distance.

"You would have done the same to protect someone you cared about," I said.

"I would have beaten him to death with the empty gun. That's the point, isn't it?"

"I'm not understanding the point."

"Please just go. I don't want to see you again."

His words tightened in my gut, twisting my insides to jelly. "Antonio, please. Let's talk—"

He sped the car forward and around a turn, barely stopping to drop me in front of my house. "Get out."

I waited for him to change his mind. Maybe if I reached out to touch him, he would relent, but he seemed so radioactive that I couldn't. I took the phone he'd given me from my bag and handed it to him.

"I don't want it," he said, still not looking at me. "Give it to the poor. Just go."

I was a coward. I couldn't fight for him. I didn't know how. I got out, and though I didn't look back, I didn't hear him pull away until I was safely inside.

MY HOUSE WAS EMPTY. Every surface gleamed. The dishes were put away. The broken swans were gone.

I stepped out of my shoes and looked around for any sign of Katrina. She'd left a few old-style bobby pins, but everything else was gone. She'd always kept most of her stuff at her parents', I reminded myself. I had a family. I could call any of them. And what would I say? They'd walked me through Daniel. Would they walk me through another man? One I couldn't talk about?

I put the phone he'd given me by the charger, and it blooped with an auto update to the music library. Tapping and scrolling, I found he'd left me music ages ago, before I'd squeezed a trigger. Puccini, Verdi, Rossini. Antonio liked opera, and it didn't matter that I liked it too.

I put on *Ave Maria* and shuffled the rest. Went to the refrigerator, didn't open it. The sink, empty. Back around the kitchen.

I made a third and fourth circuit around the island, as if spooling my pain around it. Antonio, my beautiful, brutal capo. He wanted me to be clean, and I'd sullied myself, debased myself, not with sex but violence. I was supposed to be his escape, and I'd walked into a trap where I was empowered to commit murder. For all intents and purposes, I had.

And there were witnesses. People who didn't like or trust me. They'd pat him on the back and tell him to move on to a woman who knew her place. To get cunning and hard and live, or stay gentle and die. A woman who knew the rules. A woman from his world. He'd whisper *mi amore* in her cheek while he held her. He'd make her eggs and protect her innocence with his life.

All of his sweetness would go to her. All of his brutality would stay at the job.

Chapter Thirty-Seven

My face hurt. I remembered the feeling from when I found Daniel's texts. I iced my face, broke out a new toothbrush, and went the fuck to work. Shit, I'd done this before. I was an old hand. I wasn't going to shake off Antonio that day, and maybe not that week. But I had to, didn't I?

Despite my game face and strong words of self-reliance, Pam saw right through me.

"What happened?" she asked.

"Nothing."

"Uh-huh."

"Can you get me a meeting with Arnie?" I asked. "Fifteen minutes. Tell him it's urgent."

"Don't forget your eleven thirty with Daniel Brower."

I noticed she didn't call him a dickhead, and I raised an eyebrow. Pam stared at me, and I looked over her shoulder. I recognized the faces on her computer screen.

Two mug shots. Bruno Uvoli and Vito from the valet service. I leaned in. Vito's mug shot was for an arrest for the sexual assault of an eleven-year-old girl. Bruno's DNA had been found at the scene of his cousin's death, ten years earlier. No charges.

They'd been shot down assassination style in an abandoned suburban house in Palmdale. They'd just been found, but it was assumed they'd been killed the previous afternoon.

Antonio. All I could think about was Antonio assassinating two men and finding out I'd almost done the same.

"Miss Drazen?" Pam sounded concerned.

"Did you get me Arnie?"

"Ten fifteen. Are you all right? You turned white as a sheet."

"I'm going to go catch up on my email. Hold my calls."

I didn't check my emails at all. I wrote Arnie a short, concise letter of resignation. I was done wasting my life with anything I didn't love.

ARNIE KEPT me far longer than fifteen minutes, trying to work out consultancies and flexible hours, more pay, a promotion, a new title. He asked me where I was going. When I said, "Nowhere," he believed me and wished me luck in the most sincere voice I'd ever heard him use.

I saw Daniel's team before I saw him: a handful of men in suits huddled by the window and a woman I recognized. Short, slim, with a professional dark bob, and sensible shoes. Clarice. From her outfit, no one would ever guess she liked being called a filthy whore while sucking a taken man's cock.

I felt absolutely nothing about her presence, and that was a relief in itself.

"Hi, everyone," I said as I approached. "I'm ready. Who's joining me?"

"Just me," Daniel said. "It's my only chance to get rid of these guys."

Clarice grimaced in a valiant attempt at a smile. I led Daniel into the glass conference room where Antonio had threatened to kiss me in front of everyone. We sat at a corner of the desk, me at the head and him at the side.

"You rang?" I said.

"How are you?" he asked. "Besides in no mood for small talk."

"I'm fine. I see you hired Clarice back."

"She was the best speechwriter I ever had. I figured if you weren't coming back to me…"

"Makes sense." It did. It made all the sense in the world. "I'd prefer it if you didn't tell her about anything about what happened between us or about my relationships."

"You said it was over with you and Spinelli."

"So? She has a big mouth, and every thought she's ever had is on her face."

He sighed. "Yeah, I know. Honestly, there's no pillow talk because there's no pillow. I have no time right now for any of it. Did you see the latest polling?"

"Heard about it."

"It's partly Clarice," he said. "She knows her job. But it's also taking action against crime. Caution doesn't play. That's a fact."

"I would have talked you out of it."

"Yeah, well, there you have it."

I didn't realize I was still attached to my work on his campaign until that underhanded non-insult. "Ouch, Dan."

"I'm sorry. I didn't come here to give you a hard time."

"Oh, good."

He leaned forward, getting into his business posture. I saw that his fingernails were cleanly cut, and his hair didn't flop, and his hands didn't seek purchase on old habits or tics.

"You left some notes behind with Bill and Phyllis," he said. "You had a lot of questions about a cluster of buildings in Mount Washington. They brought it to my attention a couple of days ago."

I remembered how to tamp down my emotions and how to control my expression. "I didn't find anything. That's why I didn't bring it up."

"I know. But some of that property was managed by a law firm with one client who was killed by the current owner," he said.

"You lost me on the killing part."

"I'm going to let a judge decide that. In the meantime, I'm getting together a warrant. I wanted to let you know ahead of time. If you left a tube of lipstick there, or a tampon or whatever, you'd better go get it."

I laughed a little to let him know what I thought of his warning.

"What?" he asked.

"You're protecting me?"

"Yes, I am."

"They're not going to forget Catholic Charities. The press might have brushed it off as an interesting photo op of nothing, but if my stuff is on that property, dots get connected. How would it look if it comes out that you sat on your hands for almost a month while a war started? It's going to look like you swept it under the rug because I was involved."

He set his face in a look he'd never given me before. It lacked any compassion or grace. It was the look that scared witnesses. "I want to be clear, so I'm only saying this once. This is the last time I will speak to you as an insider. This is your last concession. If I need to subpoena you, I will. If you have a shred of DNA over there, remove it, because once I walk out of here, I won't hesitate to drag you down with him."

I stood and held out my hand. "Thank you for your consideration, Mister Brower."

Instead of shaking it, he held my face and kissed my right cheek then my left. Though Daniel was as American as apple pie, it felt like a final good-bye.

Chapter Thirty-Eight

Did I have hours? Days? Was the time between now and Daniel's warrant measured in minutes? And what did I want to do about it?

I put the top down on my dented car as I drove home, as if the extra smog intake would clear my head. But the 10 freeway at rush hour was no place to get my head together.

Antonio had dumped me in no uncertain terms. I owed him nothing. If he got dragged into a black and white tomorrow, it would have nothing at all to do with me. But that image of him in cuffs, for anything, made me pull off onto Crenshaw.

I still had his phone. I swallowed my pride and dialed, heart pounding from the first ring, then the second, then the voicemail announcement. I hung up. I didn't know if I was being ignored or if some smaller insult was being hurled, and I didn't want to think about it.

I plugged the phone into my stereo and listened to Puccini. Could I call East Side Motors? Should I just go? It was about five fifteen. The drive would take me a good forty minutes.

I headed east. When I passed downtown, I'd decide.

I SAW smoke on the horizon as I went east on the 10. Wildfires were a fact of Southern California life, especially at points north and east of Los Angeles, so I thought nothing of it. Then the traffic on Figueroa was diverted to

Marmion, and I heard sirens and saw flashing lights on the flats, not the wooded hills. I parked and walked a block south and two east, smoke choking me. A crowd had gathered at the curb, and the police were hard-pressed to keep them safe from their own curiosity.

"There are underground gas tanks," one cop said to a guy who wanted to cross the street. "They blow, and you're gonna be grease. So get back."

The man got back, and I stepped in his place for half a second to confirm what I knew to be true. East Side Motors was up in flames.

I walked to my car. I knew where Antonio's house was, more or less, but it was very close to the shop, and the fire trucks had blocked off that street. He wasn't getting out without being seen, and neither was I.

I scrolled through my phone, the one without Puccini and Verdi. Did I have Paulie's number? Zo's? Would any of them listen to me or would they just be relieved I was gone? I needed someone I could trust. Someone who had an emotional enough connection to Antonio that I could count on their loyalty.

I felt fit to burst. I needed to tell Antonio what Daniel had told me. I didn't need to make sure I didn't have any tissues at his house. I didn't need to clear myself of malfeasance. I needed to make sure I'd done everything to get him out of the way.

It occurred to me late, almost too late. Too late for me to claim innocence.

I was bait. I was doing exactly what I was supposed to do: going to Antonio and leading the authorities right to him.

"Daniel, you fucking bastard."

I'd never felt so used, so whored in my life. I drove away as fast as I could with the top down, west on Marmion. Was my phone tracked? Who knew what Daniel had done while we were together. If he felt no compunction in tracking my credit card purchases, why wouldn't he track my phone?

At a red light, I wrote down a number from my call history then tossed the thing in a bus stop garbage can. It smacked against the back of the wire mesh and dropped onto a pile of ketchup-covered fast food bags.

I unplugged Antonio's phone and called the number at the next light. If his phone wasn't secure, I didn't know what would be.

"Hello?"

"Marina? This is Theresa Drazen. I'd like to meet with you."

She barked a laugh. "About what? I told you he'd never be with you."

My heart jumped into my throat, as if deciding it needed to be eaten rather than tolerate this. I swallowed hard. "It's business."

"I'm not in the business."

"That's why I want to talk to you."

She didn't answer right away. "What then?"

"It's not what you think. Where is good for you?"

"Dunno. Things are a little crazy with the men right now."

"I know. I'm on Marmion, if that helps."

"Yeah," she said sharply, as if coming to a decision. "Sure, yeah. Come by Yes Café, off La Carna. Ten minutes."

"Thank you."

She didn't hear me apparently, because she'd hung up.

Chapter Thirty-Nine

Yes Café had plastic-wrapped sandwiches and lousy coffee. The half and half came in little plastic cups with peel tops. I sat in the wooden chair and looked out the window and playing with Antonio's phone. It felt like reminiscing about Antonio, even though the thing was clean of anything but music and a short call history. He'd given it to me, he'd left me, and now it was all I had.

I read the local paper, which reported the same things as the bigger papers: The spate of violence in the city. Bruno Uvoli's nasty history which may or may not have included having a hand in the death of his cousin, Domenico Uvoli. Vito Oliveri's penchant for young girls. Nothing new but the insinuation that they had it coming.

Marina was twenty minutes late. She came in from the parking lot in the back, all heels and tight jeans, makeup and shiny hair. I hadn't realized how young she was, maybe her early twenties. Dew hung on her like the morning, and I felt a twist of jealousy for the fact that she was so fresh and pretty.

"Hi," she said, clutching her purse strap over her shoulder.

"I'm sorry to bother you."

She shrugged and sat. "It's fine."

"Did you tell Antonio you were coming to meet me?"

She looked at me sheepishly.

"It's fine either way," I said.

"I gotta go soon, so if you want to say something?"

I took a deep breath. "I trust you to bring this to Antonio because you care about him."

"He won't like me getting involved."

"I know. He can take it out on me if he wants." I leaned forward, hands folded. "I happen to know that the district attorney is getting a warrant to search *l'uovo*."

She looked down, shifting her mouth to one side.

I continued. "I don't know when he's serving it. Tonight, tomorrow, next week. So if you could tell Antonio personally as soon as you can."

"Well, the shop is kinda burning down. And uh, I hear things got hot with some of the other guys. The other, um, group."

She was so unpracticed, so raw in her immaturity, I didn't know whether to feel threatened or sorry for her naiveté.

"You seem different than you were on the phone the other night," I said.

She turned pink. "You're intimidating in person."

"Well, in the interest of not making you any more uncomfortable, I have nothing else." I picked up my bag.

"Wait," she said. "You need to tell him what you told me. I don't even know what you're talking about. Do you have a little time?"

Did I? Was I looking to get involved even more deeply? By a woman who perceived me as a threat? Did I want to go home to my empty loft? Or start the round of calls to friends and family to ensure I had things to do and places to go for the next few days? Or did I want to exist in Antonio's sphere for another hour?

"Sure," I said.

SHE DROVE up the hill in her Range Rover. I followed her lights on the unlit roads. We were a few miles west of the car shop. She stopped on the top of a hill. The concrete ditch of the L.A. River was beneath us.

"This it?" I said.

Below were makeshift shacks occupied by the homeless, some more complex than others. Across the river was Frogtown, but no one would walk across the muck of a dry river bed for that.

"Marina?" I turned to ask her where we were going but stopped short.

She was holding a little silver gun.

"Jesus Christ." I held up my hands.

"What did you do?" she asked. "Tell me. What did you do to make him love you?"

"He doesn't—"

"You're *lying*. He does. You made him crazy. He's still crazy."

"I didn't do anything Marina, I—"

"He's destroyed everything because of you. First, he dumped me, then he threw Vito Oliveri under the bus. And Bruno? Bruno was a good guy. But he saw what was happening, and he tried to get you so he could put some sense into Antonio. It was just going to be an example."

"He let Bruno live, Marina. I was there. He could have killed him. He had his wits about him."

"Bruno was *made*, you dumb Irish bitch. He can't kill him without warning every other family in Los Angeles he's gonna do it. They're coming from the old country to kill Antonio, and now I'm going to save him by killing you. The cause of it all."

I didn't know if it actually worked like that. I wasn't in her world. Maybe if she brought my head to Donna Maria Carloni and whoever was coming from the old country, that would be helpful to Antonio. Maybe the spell I'd woven around him would be broken and he'd start making coherent decisions again.

I stepped back, hands still raised. "You understand if you murder me, you'll go to jail. Is that what you want?"

"For him, I'd go." She straightened her arms and aimed for my heart.

Smart girl, unfortunately. It was a safer shot than the head. Her hands tightened. I would be dead in a second. I wasn't sure my arm would reach when I extended it for the gun. She moved, bending her elbows, and it went off with a flash and a pop.

I didn't feel any pain, just a pressure and a blank space in my thoughts. The world went sideways, then I heard another crack, and—

nothing.

Chapter Forty

The pain came first, as if someone had put a sharp clamp on the side of my head. The sounds came afterward. People shuffling, metallic clacking noises, short laughs, all men. The acoustics indicated I was in a small space. And the smell was wet, sticky earth.

My mouth was dry, and I moved my tongue.

"What's the date?" said a voice. *That* voice.

I didn't know the answer, but I opened my eyes. Lights and colors were blurred as if thrown into a blender.

"What's your name?"

"Contessa," I croaked.

"Good."

I blinked, squeezed my eyes shut, and opened them again. The room was tight and low, with dirt walls and ceiling. Enzo and Niccolo passed by, yammering in Italian, and over me was…

"Capo."

"Shh. Please. You got a good knock on the head."

"Where am I?"

"Under *l'uovo*. But I'll say no more."

"Where's Marina?"

He shook his head. "She's fine, but stupid. Otto found her and you just in time. She's being sent home to Naples tomorrow. How is your ear?"

That must be the searing pain on the side of my head. "Hurts."

"It caught a bullet."

I got up on my elbows and looked around. I saw a door on each side of the room and a wall lined with racks of rifles.

"I wanted to tell you something," I said.

"Marina told me."

I noticed then that he wasn't touching me. He wasn't holding my hand or stroking my cheek. His fingers were laced together between his legs.

"Thank you. The warning about the DA is very helpful. We were clearing out anyway. Paulie's gone."

"Why?"

"Why? He put you in a terrible position. We, ah…" He looked at his hands. My vision had cleared enough to see the red scratches on his fists. "We fought. He set the shop on fire. I don't know who he will align with, if anyone. But not me." He stood. The ceiling wasn't much higher than his head.

"Antonio," I said, "where are you going?"

"I have a war to prepare for. Otto will make sure you get home safely." He walked toward the door like a doctor satisfied the patient would live.

"No," I said, suddenly lucid. "Don't. Please."

"Nothing's changed, Theresa."

"That's right." I swung my feet around, and they found the floor. I was sitting on a wooden bench. "Nothing has changed. You feel the same. Deny it. Deny you love me."

"I don't love you."

"You're lying."

"Contessa—"

"Don't call me that until you admit how you feel."

He closed the door, shutting out the sounds of the men. "What difference would it make? I won't destroy you. If I take you in, you'll be miserable. You'll spend your life never knowing who I am or what I do. You'll have to accept that I may go to jail for years, and you can't leave me, even then. It won't be tolerated. That's the better scenario."

"And the worse one?"

"You learn to tolerate me." He put his hand on the doorknob.

I knew that if he went into the other room, only Otto would come back. It would be the last I'd see of him. So I jumped up and stood in front of the door. The world swam. I tried to lean on the wall, but my stomach turned over, and I was sure I would fall.

Antonio's arms went around me, holding me up. My senses came back, and I pushed him away.

"Admit you love me." I touched his face, feeling the stubble on his cheek and the exhaustion emanating from him. I wanted to make it all go away, to give him peace.

"It wouldn't make any difference," he said.

"Admit it."

"I loved you the second I put my eyes on you. It doesn't matter."

"Let me love you back."

"You have a life to live."

"I have nothing." I stroked his lip, and his hands remained at his sides. "I've danced enough. I've seen movies. I've been in every pool in Malibu. I've travelled. I've dated. Worked on a political campaign. Met stars. Had a job. I've done all that. What I've never done is love a man like you."

He turned, ever so slightly, and kissed my palm, letting his eyes close. "What if you die from loving me?"

"What if I die from not loving you?"

He kissed my cheek, and I melted into him. I thought I'd never feel those lips again, and when I did, I groaned.

"Please," I whispered. "I'll follow you anywhere."

"You're going to get hurt."

"Hurt me, then. I'd rather get hurt than live a lie."

He put his forehead to mine and wove his hands behind my neck. It increased the pain in my head, but I fell into it, wanting his pain as much as I wanted his pleasure.

"Contessa, you make me crazy."

"I know."

"I don't know where you'll fit in with me. I don't know your place."

"My place is beside you."

He leaned back, and I felt the loss of his touch deeply. I needed more. But he put his hand behind his collar and took off his medal of St. Christopher.

He pressed it into my palm, one hand over mine, one under. He looked into my face as if watching a storm gather. The metal was hard on my skin and warm from being close to him.

"Are you sure you want to never feel safe?" he asked. "Are you sure you want to always look behind you? Are you sure you want a life without people you trust?"

"If you're with me, yes."

"Are you sure you can love a man who's damned?"

"Only you. Damned or saved, I want only you."

"I have a problem, my Contessa. It's been eating me alive since I kissed you. I want you, and I don't know how to have you. I want you beside me.

I want my world and your world to be one. To see you laugh in the morning. To see you weep my name at night. I am not ever afraid, but with you, I am. I'm afraid I won't have you, and I'm afraid I will."

He turned my hand over until my palm was facing downward, clutching the medal. He leaned down and kissed it, fingers, knuckles, wrist, and looked up at me. His eyes were felony black, lips built for declarations of love, jaw set to break barriers.

"I can't let you go," he said. "I want to be that man who can make you breakfast and raise children without always looking behind his back. I am going to make myself worthy. I am going to get out so I can't hurt you. But I can't just walk away from what I do, and I can't turn away from you. God help me, every time I walk away from you, I only see hell in front of me."

I put my hands on his face, letting the chain slip over my thumb and dangle. "Don't walk away from me. It kills me when you do."

"This life, it's impossible to pay every debt and go straight."

"Pay what you can."

He took the chain and opened it. I leaned into him so he could put it around my neck and fasten it.

I laid my head on his shoulder and pulled back. "Ow. My ear."

He turned my head to get a good look. "It's barely a scratch." He kissed my neck, moving the chain to put his tongue on the skin where my neck and shoulder met.

"I have a headache," I said, pushing his ass forward until I felt his erection at my hip.

"I'll fuck you gently. You'll come long and slow. Your head will forget its ache when you shed tears." He reached under my skirt from behind.

I groaned.

"Shh," he said. "My men are on the other side of this door." He pushed me back onto the bench and spread my legs. *"Mi amore."*

He kissed inside my thighs, moving my panties aside to lick so slowly I almost came with anticipation. I grabbed his hair, but he wouldn't suck. He only used the tip of his tongue on my clit.

"Antonio," I whispered. The hard bench bit my back and the room was rough hewn from the earth, yet I'd never felt so comfortable, at home, safe. "Always be my Capo."

He slid my underpants off and planted himself between my legs, his dick out and ready for me.

"What do you want?" he asked.

"Fuck me," I said with conviction. "Fuck me now."

He put one of my legs over his shoulder, opening me for him. He moved my body like a precious thing, then he slid his dick into me. I was so wet, he got the whole length of him in with one try.

"*Come vuoi tu,* Contessa." He moved out then in again, every inch a breath of intention to keep me safe, to keep me pure. But most importantly, I felt his intention to keep me. His voice dropped, and his words sounded more like prayer than surrender. "*Come vuoi tu.*"

Epilogue

There was plenty to be worried about. Paulie had turned on Antonio, Daniel was after him with renewed vigor, and I rarely had in idea of where exactly I was running to whenever Antonio took me to a new location. He'd left the Maserati in a nondescript garage built into the side of a hill because it was too conspicuous. He spoke in Italian with some of his crew, and a pidgin of English terms I didn't understand. I spent a lot of time alone, sequestered, protected, bored to tears.

Daniel was an unfaithful creep, but I had been completely integrated into his life. A partner, at least outside the bedroom. Was I always going to have to choose between sex and respect?

The second night after he gave me what I wanted under *l'uovo*, he started to take me up to the little Spanish house.

"I've set it up," he said. "It should be safe for you." His smile was meant to transmit confidence, but I saw the effort.

He pulled the Mercedes SUV up the hill, slipping his hand between my thighs. My legs reacted immediately, spreading for him. I thought maybe partnering in only the bedroom might be the better that being a complete part of his world. His body could break a woman's heart, who knew what his business could break?

I put my hand on top of his before it reached my crotch.

"Antonio, what's happening? Can you tell me?"

He paused, taking a hairpin turn by pressing the heel of his hand against the wheel. I had no cause to feel safe with him, but I did.

"I cannot," he said, his arm out the open window. "Not completely. There's talk, and it's cheap. I can't react to it as if it's truth until I know."

"Know what?"

"If two families are trying to unite with a marriage. If they are, it's trouble. One organization will be too big." He shrugged. "If it's Paulie trying to work with the Sicilians, he'll be too powerful for me to fight."

"You still do that? Marry for business?"

"Of course."

He took a softer turn, glancing at me, then back at the road.

Of course.

That was why they kept mistresses.

It was on this thought that Antonio swerved left at a fork when I knew the Spanish house was to the right.

"Get down!" he shouted, grabbing a fistful of my hair because that was what he reached first and yanking my head onto his lap.

"What?" I shouted into the cavern between the bottom of the dashboard and the pedals.

The gunshots answered. The passenger window shattered, and the gravity in the car changed as my cheek slid across his lap and the sounds of cracking, popping, screeching flooded my ears. A wood plank from a fence shot through the window, missing me by an inch. I still couldn't see past Antonio's feet on the pedals, but when the car stopped the feet were gone. I knew the car was sideways from the pull of gravity, and rocking back and forth ever so slightly.

"Theresa!" Antonio called me from a thousand miles away.

I said his name.

I didn't.

It was no more than a groan.

Wake up. Wakeupwakeupwakeup.

I heard a click and my hips slid away from the seat. He'd taken the belt off.

Another smash, like a pop and a crackle, and I woke up enough to realize the sun roof had been broken. I turned. Blinked. Mentally rooted around for the boundaries of my body.

"I'm fine," I said, twisting a little more. The jagged-edged rectangle framed and flattened Antonio so perfectly he looked like a renaissance portrait. My battered mind was surprised when he reached in. The car rocked and creaked.

"Slowly, Contessa. Don't move suddenly unless I tell you to."

I wrapped my hands around his forearms, and he did the same.

"Do I have you?" he asked.

"Yes."

"Slowly. Let me pull you.'

I let him guide me out the sunroof. We were on the edge of a cliff down into the San Gabriel Valley, having broken through a fence in the back of a little Victorian bungalow. The Mercedes rocked at the edge held up by a patch of bushes and a busted clothesline.

"Look at me," Antonio said.

I turned. He held me in his gaze, brown eyes serious and supremely confident at the same time. If I just did what I was told, I'd be all right. I was sure of it. His hand was scratched. Had he been thrown clear? How do you survive that?

Until my hips got stuck in the window.

"What do I do?" I squeaked. What kind of partner was I? I was totally unqualified to be his equal in this or anything. I was going to get pulled off a cliff by an SUV any minute. My heart raced to the point of pain. I wanted to run away, scream, and cry all at once.

"Go back in a little and twist," he said. "Slowly and be calm. Put the widest part of you at the diagonal part of the window."

He glanced at the road. Were they coming back? Would they just shoot us here, like this?

When he put his gaze back on me I got calm again, shifted back in, twisted, pushed, causing the SUV to rock and creak.

"Exhale," he said and when I did, he pulled me with all he had. The SUV creaked one last time before I separated from it, sprawling on the ground with him. It pitched down the hill another ten feet, the front hitting something with a crack and smash.

I got to my feet. My knees were barely holding me, and a shoe was missing.

Antonio looked down the hill then toward the road.

"They were trying to kill you." I said. "Who were they?"

"Spin!" I heard the voice before I heard or saw the car up above, on the side of the road.

"Were they after me?" he growled, "Or you?"

"What's the—"

"Spin! You down there? Hurry up!"

"This is over." He said it as if he didn't hear Otto calling his name. I didn't know what he meant, so I took his arm. He yanked it away. "I cannot do this."

He walked away from me, up the hill to Otto.

Would he get in the car and drive away? I ran to him and caught up at the road.

"What do you mean?"

He cut the air with his flattened hands. "Done."

Otto barked with urgency when we crested the hill, his Italian full of spit and percussion. Antonio nodded and barked back.

"Get in. Quickly. *Andiamo*." He opened the rear door. "They're coming."

I had a million things to say. Denial. Refusal. Venom. Sweet phrases to get him to see the light, but his jaw was set and he breathed such certainty the pit of my stomach dropped out.

I got in the car. I thought he was going to get in after me. I'd talk to him. Plead, beg, curse, demand he see it differently. But he closed the door and walked to the rear of the car. I twisted to see out the dust-covered back window. Another car, driven by Lorenzo, had pulled up behind.

Otto got into the front seat of the car I was in just as Antonio opened the driver's side door of the one behind us and shooed Zo across to the passenger side.

"Otto, wait," I said.

"Sorry, miss," he said. "I got a lotta orders and no time." He pulled away. The road was straight enough for me to see Antonio get into the driver's side, but we went around a corner before I could see which direction he went.

RUIN

Preface

Though the Downtown Gate Club is a figment of my imagination, there are tunnels under Downtown Los Angeles. Because they are closed to the public, I went to the tunnels in Pendleton, Oregon for my research. My LA underground is based on those. Any actual differences with the actual LA tunnels are just too damn bad. I do my best with what I've got.

Chapter One

THERESA

Everything bled. The sun bled gold over the skyline. The deep blue horizon bled over the map of the streets. The trapezoid of light bled across the carpet as the day passed. The smog bled into the cloud. From the tower, I presided over silence.

I didn't know how many hours a day I sat in front of that window, looking out over the breadth of the Los Angeles basin with its endless ocean of greys and browns, wondering where he was and where I was and how many hours were between us. Wondering if I'd eaten or if my motionless night at the window had been cut by sleep or if my open-eyed diligence was to end in another day of bleeding the hours of life into the endlessness of death.

He was gone. He didn't talk about what he did, but I was sure the sun draining onto the blanket of the basin was blood shed by him or his men or on his behalf. I feared it was his. Everyone's blood looked the same once spilled, but his, running the same color as a polluted sun, would have brought me to tears.

The most tender symptom of aging is the reduction of choices. I'd wanted to be everything when I was a girl: a scientist, a politician, a financier, a lawyer. But I'd made a choice to be nothing, bleeding options from a wound where my heart had been pulled out, inflated to ten times its normal size, and put back.

Time had passed in that bland grey apartment. People had come and gone, like Zia Giovanna, Antonio's aunt who ran a restaurant in San

Pedro, and Zo, one of his associates, a sweet man who had no problem beating the life out of someone. Others with names and accents came, bringing food, clothing, comfort, and I still had no idea how I'd gotten there.

Not physically. I remembered the multiple cars, the handoffs in desolate places. But I couldn't recall the single decision I'd made that had yanked me from my world and into that place, high above the city, where I knew no one, had no connection to the things I'd spent years building, and had no influence on decisions made about my life.

I was able to leave.

People watched me, but I could have eluded them if I'd gotten my mind to wiggle around options and choices. With a well-built strategy for escape, I could have left in a blaze of light or the thick of night. I had a phone. One call to my father, and my confinement would have been over. Or to Daniel. I could manage anything I set my mind to, even if I was watched. And I wasn't being kept against my will. Not really. Not in a way that was decidedly illegal, but only in a way that left me staring at the breadth of the city and out to the horizon, bleeding time.

Until he came.

He barely knocked when he entered. Maybe the *whickCLAP* of the lock should have been as good as a knock. Or the mumbles of him and the guy outside, with his voice an interlocking puzzle piece to something in my brain. Something with needs. Something desperate. But every time he came to the apartment, I was surprised and relieved and hungry, like a woman who was so starved she hadn't even entertained the thought of food until someone slipped a bowl of stew through a flap in the door.

I paused when he closed the door behind him. I never knew which Antonio I was getting when he walked in. It didn't matter if he was in jeans and a polo shirt or, as was the case that day, a jacket and sky-blue turtleneck. He could be any one of ten incarnations.

"Contessa." He tossed his keys on the end table.

I said nothing. Not yet. I was afraid speaking would break the spell, and like that, he'd disappear in a flare.

He shrugged out of his jacket, revealing the brown-leather shoulder holster that creased his sweater. He wore it in my presence. He trusted me. He wasn't afraid, and as he walked toward me, the straps cutting his frame didn't scare me either. The gun made me bold. The scruff on his face and the circles under his eyes made me compassionate, and the line shadows bleeding from his feet to the side of the room in the late sun made me angry.

"Capo," I said when he was a step away.

He gently reached for my cheek, and before he could embrace me and sweep me away, I tilted my body back and slapped his face.

I hit him so hard his neck snapped ninety degrees until he was facing the window. The sound of skin hitting skin rang against the walls.

And I felt not an ounce of regret.

I raised my hand again, and he grabbed the wrist. He was not gentle when he drew it down, nor when he stepped toward me, pushing me back against the table. His breath was hot on me, his body a field of energy. His hips pressed against me so forcefully his erection hurt through my clothes.

"Did you want to tell me something?" Antonio let my wrist go so he could put his hand up my shirt. He shoved my bra out of the way and grabbed a nipple, pinching to pain.

"Where were you?" I gasped the question. All the accusation and anger heated to a sticky, molten mass between my legs.

"It's business."

"God," I groaned. "Go to hell."

I tried to wiggle away, but he grabbed under my arms and threw me on the table. I swung; he dodged and held me down with his weight while peeling my pants off.

"Did you hear me?" I growled.

"I heard you."

I kicked at him, twisting. I fell off the table with a crash, pants halfway down, and I flipped so he wouldn't have me helpless on my stomach. He grabbed my ankle and dragged me across the room. My shirt rolled up, exposing my skin to the burn of the carpet, which matched the burn between my legs.

"You're not understanding your place, Contessa."

He whipped my pants off. In the split second before he grabbed me again, I scuttled to my feet and backed up.

"My place? It's next to you."

"It's under me." He came for me. I slapped him again, hard, the force of my body behind it, but it didn't stop him that time. He took me by the arms and threw me on the couch like a rag doll. I lay there with my legs splayed, my elbows under me, looking up at him with a clenched jaw as he undid his pants.

"Don't you even think about it."

"I'm not thinking about it." He wedged himself between my legs and pushed my knees apart. "I'm doing it."

I slapped him again, twice in the face, three times in the chest, and he ignored all of it as if he were under attack by mosquitoes.

"Fuck you," I said when he slid his cock along my soaked cleft, not entering me but teasing, even as I lashed out at him. I got a good shot to the neck, and he latched my wrists together in two of his fingers, binding me with his flesh.

"Say 'fuck me,'" he said, putting his other hand on my throat.

"Fuck you," I whispered.

He moved his hips, sliding the length of his cock on my clit. He leaned down, and I smelled the burned nicotine on his breath.

"Wrong. Say what you want."

My pussy pulsed for him, and while my hands and shoulders thrust against him, my lower half pushed into him.

"You're hurting me."

He pressed his dick on me harder and hooked his fingers onto the side of my jaw.

"Say it."

"You're garbage." I was clothed in him, a corset laced tight with desire and pain. I wanted his fingers to dig into me and find my filth, my foulness. Only he could find it and grind it out. There was only one way to do that. There had only ever been one way. "Fuck me. Fuck me hard, you worthless piece of shit."

With a twist of his hips, he was right there. I felt him. I moved against him, the slickness of my pussy an open invitation.

"Do it!" I said as loudly as I could manage with his hand on my throat.

"Beg."

"No."

He slid along me again, a strafing of pleasure between my thighs. I moved with him involuntarily, shifting so that worthless and beautiful man would rub me.

"No?" He said it as if he were speaking to a child.

"Fuck you."

"No."

"Please."

"Now we're getting somewhere." He let go of my wrists, and I balled up my fists and pushed against his chest, even as I pushed my hips against him.

"Please, Antonio."

"Please, what?" He unstrapped his gun, letting it drop to the floor in a tangle of leather and iron, and pulled his sweater off.

"Please, fuck me good." I punched his chest. "Fuck me hard. Use me like the punk you are."

He slammed into me, taking my breath away, before I'd even finished the sentence, and time stopped. He had me pinned, and I accepted him, pushing myself against him. It was the only direction I could move in.

"This good, Contessa?" he said in my ear. "This how you want it?"

My mouth was open, but no words came out. Only vowels. With every thrust, a wave of hot-pink pleasure came in, and then another.

"Capo," I groaned. "Fuck."

"Those words," he whispered.

"Destroy me."

"You're ruined, *amore. Rovinata*."

And at the thought of being left a ruined piece of flesh and bone, I burst into flames of sensation, crying his name, be it Capo, or Antonio, or my own personal dance with death. I claimed him to the heavens.

Chapter Two

ANTONIO

I was taught that a woman needed to be protected. She needed stability. Tenderness. A woman needed to feel safe and build a home for a family. A woman needed a future, a hope of comfort. She needed a man who'd stand between her and danger.

The securest place for Theresa was with her ex, Daniel. I admitted I was already failing to put her in the safest situation, because I'd die before letting him have her.

My father, who ran the entire olive trade in Napoli, never told my mother a thing about how he got his money. He made two children with her. He made her an honest woman. He gave her all the things a woman needs until she threw it back at him because he couldn't leave the business. She threw his name away; she took his children; she made herself the target of contempt. I'd always thought my mother was the one with the broken heart, because my father was a cold, cruel man.

One night when I was maybe eighteen, he came to the mechanic shop, drunk. He didn't drink much, but it was his birthday, and my father did not like birthdays.

I had a Fiat on the lift. Grease up to the elbows at midnight. The customer was demanding, and wanted his car right away. I'd had to leave my father's birthday party to finish the job.

"*Figlio,*" he said.

"Papa." I didn't look away from the transmission. It was a tricky thing.

"You have a woman now. You're going to marry her." He'd told me before that he liked Valentina, so I didn't expect he was about to give me trouble about it.

"If her father agrees."

"He will. I'll make sure of it."

"I'd rather win my own way." I always did things my way because it made my mother happy when I was away from my father's influence. But I liked my father; he taught me a lot, and I felt like a man around him.

He sat in silence for a while.

"What's on your mind, Papa?"

"When are you leaving for Milano?"

He was obsessed with my going to law school. He asked a thousand questions about it, how much it cost, how the year was broken up, who my compatriots were. But he never got to the point until that night.

"August," I answered.

"I've talked to every capo. None will take you for their *consigliere*."

"Have you talked to yourself?" I looked away from the car long enough to make eye contact.

And it all became clear right then. He was worried I'd become like him. Even though he watched over me and gave me jobs, he was of two minds. He'd send me on an errand with one hand, because he didn't trust anyone else, and with the other, he'd tell me to go to law school in the north to be away from the *camorra.*

"You will never be my *consigliere.*" He tilted his chin up and rocked his hand at the wrist, two fingers up, which he did when he meant to be taken seriously.

"I'll be a prosecutor." I smiled up at the transmission. I had no intention of being a prosecutor or a defender. I wanted to do family law, and he knew it.

"I want you to keep that woman," he said.

"Yes, Pop. *Bene.*" My father could have had any woman, but he pined for my mother, who despised him. He'd never change for her or her children. He'd never try and be a man he wasn't. He was a crook and as damned to hell as they came, and he knew it. He'd risk me being a non-*camorra* lawyer for the love of keeping me from being like him.

At the time, it seemed easy. The path was straight and clear. My father taught me how to hold two opposing ideas in my mind at once, but he never taught me how to live those opposites.

How distorted the path must have become, to have gotten me to America. To Los Angeles, of all places. I was neither *consigliere* nor lawful. Neither husband nor free. And now, I was twisted with that red-haired beauty I could never resist or deny. I'd been on a death-march from the minute I saw her, with her porcelain skin and blue eyes. She was a swan, gliding across the floor, so straight that I had to see her bend.

Then I saw that mistake on her shoe, that imperfection inside that perfect package. It was a sign that I could have the unattainable, and when I touched her arm and spoke softly, she bent to hear me. She smelled like sweet olive trees, and she blushed like a virgin when she saw the paper on her sole.

I wanted to make her come from that moment. Not just come. I wanted her lost in such pleasure that mascara would streak across her china-white cheek.

"*Amore mio,*" I whispered after I exploded inside her.

"Capo," she groaned. "Fuck."

"Those words." She had been so pure when I'd met her. Innocent, yet mature. Her purity was a choice. Sinful words never left her lips until I demanded them, and every time I touched her, she lost a little more spotlessness and came closer to me. Closer to the animal I was. The only moral choice would have been to leave her, but I couldn't. Not because of guilt, even though I had a little of that. But her pull on me, and mine on her made it impossible for me to leave her, even for her own sake. I never felt so helpless in the destruction of graciousness as I did with my Contessa.

"Destroy me," she said, as if I had to be told.

"You're ruined, *amore*."

She put her hand on my cheek and put her blue eyes to mine. Was it wrong to want her again? Was it immoral to have a desire that grew with the destruction of the object of it?

"Where were you?" she asked. "I don't even know how long you were gone."

"What's the difference?"

"It was too long."

"I agree."

"You should make peace with Paulie," she said.

How was I supposed to tell her that my old partner would not abide her in my life? He'd been very clear about that. As much as I loved Paulie like a brother, I couldn't choose him. The last time I'd thrown Theresa from my life, my future had blinked out like an old bulb.

"I can't," I said. "That's over."

"But, Antonio—"

I put my finger on her lips. "What did you do today?"

"Nothing. I can't leave here."

"Yes, you can, but Otto has to go with you."

"Shouldn't he be working with you? Whatever it is you're doing. Which you won't tell me."

"My most trusted man is with you. As he should be. And if he's not around, you call me, and I'll find someone for you."

She sighed and looked past me to the ceiling. I'd been with many women in my life. I'd cared for some of them and loved only one before Theresa. She was the first who seemed so contented and discontented at the same time.

"You can go shopping," I said. I almost offered her money, but the last time I'd done that, she'd laughed at me. Her reaction to my suggestion wasn't much better.

"Shopping?" She turned her eyes back to me. "Are you joking?" The foul-mouthed girl who begged me to fuck her was gone. She was back to her haughty self. I wanted to fuck the arrogance right out of her, rip away the coating of innocence and take her to the dirty, sexy core again, because it was mine. Only mine.

"Get something nice for me," I said.

"Antonio." She put her thumb on my lip. "I need something to *do*. I need a *life*."

"I can stay the night."

She sighed again. There was something I wasn't getting. Some key to a door I couldn't find. She wasn't fitting into my world. She had nothing to do, and she didn't need me for anything, not support, not money. Nothing I was taught to give a woman was right for Theresa.

She got up, clothed only in her poise. "Someone's going to notice when I'm not around, and when they do, they're going to tell someone else. And before you know it, you're going to see my face on the news, and you're going to wonder what the hell happened. So for your own good, Antonio, I'm telling you: tomorrow I'm leaving, and you're not going to stop me."

She spun on her heel and didn't look back on her way to the bathroom.

We weren't going to last, not as a couple. Not as lovers or sinners. She loved me. I owned her. Her heart was branded with my name. But she'd loved before, and she'd survived. She'd leave me as a matter of practicality.

I avoided death and imprisonment. I protected my territory and my partnerships as a matter of honor and business. But I didn't fear losing those things. I'd had nothing in life, and having nothing again brought no fear.

When she walked to the bathroom without looking back at me, though, I felt fear.

She was my second chance to be whole and clean, and to have a life I'd failed at.

I wasn't losing her.

But I was.

If I kept her under lock and key, I'd lose her. If I tried to keep her too safe, she'd evade me. If I worked to hard to keep her away from my business, she'd want to know more. She was right; she needed a life. I was going to have to provide her with one.

Chapter Three

THERESA

I think he bruised me. Or, more likely, I bruised myself on him. I was going to ache the next day, but if he wanted my body any time between now and then, I'd give it to him.

I leaned into the mirror. The sensitive skin of my neck was reddened and raw where his scruff had abraded me. It didn't matter. It wasn't as though anyone was going to see me anyway.

He came in quietly, no slammed-open door or yelling or grabbing. He just stepped in as if he had every right to.

He took my shoulders. The hands that had hurt were so gentle now, exerting just enough pressure to pull me back and kiss my shoulder. His lips curved themselves to the slopes of my body as if they'd been constructed for my pleasure alone.

"Contessa," he whispered, "I want to ask you something."

"Yes?"

"What do you want?" he asked.

"I don't know. You. I want you. But I don't know how to have you."

"What if you don't have me? What if you're had? You leave it to me, and I'll take care of you."

"Antonio, we talked about this. I have money. I couldn't give it all away in this lifetime."

"I don't mean money."

In the mirror, he considered my shoulder, and brushed the curve of my arm with his thumb like a lit fuse slowly burning.

"What do you mean, then?"

"I mean your safety," he said. "Give me your safety. Abandon any idea you can take care of yourself."

I turned to face him, and he pressed me against the vanity. "But I can take care of myself."

"No." He held a finger up. "You can pay for things. You can manage a political campaign. You can walk into any room and talk to anyone. In your world, you are the Contessa. In my world, you are helpless."

"So, what are you going to do? Send me out in a suit of armor?"

"Don't tempt me." He gave a smirk, and I loved and feared it at the same time.

"Antonio, really, what are the odds Paulie is going to do something stupid to me to win this battle with you? I come from a very large, notorious family. I was engaged to the District Attorney. I'm not trying to throw that in your face; what I'm trying to say is—"

"You're not untouchable."

"I'm not saying I'm untouchable. I'm saying messing with me would be crazy. Suicidal. I'm not only protected by you; I'm protected by the world. It's just who I am. Honestly, my disappearing into this apartment for too long is going to cause more of a problem."

"How?" His eyebrows arched like landmarks, and he looked as if I'd just told him Santa Claus was at the door.

"There are places I go and people I see. Even if I have no life that you can see, someone is going to notice I'm not picking up the phone or taking lunches at Montana's. I'm not saying it's easy to prove an absence, but someone's going to connect that with you and me at Catholic Charities. Someone ambitious and smarter than me."

"Not too many of those around," he said.

"Well, thank you. But the facts remain: I need to be let go without a fuss from you. And soon." I poked his chest. He pulled my arm up by the wrist and put it around his waist. "You said you were going to leave the world. Under *l'uovo.* You said you were getting out. Give Paulie your business and come with me."

"You need to watch more movies," he said.

"Believe me, I've seen plenty."

"Then you know I can't just divide my business and walk away. Even with everything the movies get wrong, they get that part right. And with everything the FBI thinks they understand, they get that one thing right: I can't just walk away. I can't surrender in the middle of a fight."

"Why not, if you have no more skin in the game?" I said. "Why wouldn't they just let you go?"

"Imagine this. I act like a reasonable man. I divide everything and walk away. I promise you, I'd be a dead man as soon as I turned my back. And you ask why. Why? It's because I have information. I've done things."

I started to ask what, but his expression shushed me.

"Without my family to protect me, I'll be picked up by your ex and questioned. Accused. I can either talk or not talk. If I don't talk, I go to jail, where I'll be murdered to keep me from talking. Or I'll talk, and I can choose between a witness protection program, where you can't join me because of who you are and how well-known your family is. Or I can be murdered in jail for talking."

"What if I made a deal with Daniel to leave you alone?"

He held a finger up in my face, jaw clenched. "Do not—"

I took his wrist and kissed the inside, on the rough, blue tattoo of Mount Vesuvius. I'd asked him if it had hurt to have it burned into such a sensitive area, and he'd laughed and said he practically slept through it.

"If you made peace with Paulie, you wouldn't have to worry about him killing me."

He pressed my hands together between us. "It's been quiet these few days. Zo is working on rebuilding the shop. The Sicilians, Donna Maria and all of them, have stopped complaining that the Neapolitans are fighting. I'm just starting to breathe."

"Can I speak my mind?" I said.

"How can you not?"

"I don't trust her patience. When a political opponent doesn't respond to an attack or an offer, he's not just sitting there waiting for something to happen; he's gathering ammunition. The worst thing you can do is give him time to arm himself."

He pressed our hands together pensively then kissed my fingertips. "You have a devil of a mind, Contessa."

"What are you going to do about it, Capo?"

He stared down at our pressed hands as if considering something. "There is something distracting the Sicilians. A wedding."

"They can't plan a wedding and run a business at the same time?" I said.

"Not their wedding. It's a wedding between a Neapolitan family, the Bortolusis, and a rival Sicilian family, the Leis. This doesn't happen often. Sicilian mafias have a tower of payoffs. Don, boss, underboss, capo, on and on. I'm Neapolitan camorra. We're smaller. We don't step on each other.

We don't have all these people to answer to, just the capo then Napoli if something goes bad."

"Like with you and Paulie?"

"Like that," he said. "But we don't marry across organizations. Sicilians and Neapolitans don't have a matching structure. It's more trouble then it's worth. So it's just not done. Because marriage is for love when possible, but for business, when necessary."

"And this one is business?"

"Yes. And it's a problem, a big problem, because it makes them too powerful, now. And Donna Maria Carloni needs to answer it or get crushed. She has a granddaughter, raised in Sicily, a good match for a nice Neapolitan boy."

"Do not even tell me you're short-listed."

He smiled. "They have someone. Nice boy. Little *stupido*, but he'll do for her."

"And what's your job in all this?"

"My job is to fuck you until the neighbors think I'm murdering you."

I kissed his cheek, his chin, his lips. He was erect in less than a minute, and when he carried me to the bedroom, I fell into a suit of armor.

Chapter Four

ANTONIO

I'd gotten used to helicopters. I'd seen them in Napoli as they blasted along the coast, taking tourists along the beach or finding lost boats. But helicopters—Los Angeles style, with their low circles over a block or house—were a different experience.

The first time I'd been exposed to the loud *thup-thup-thup,* I'd been near LAX, having just gotten off the plane in order to do the dirty business of avenging my sister's rape with certain death.

"It's called a double-double," Paulie said. I didn't know him yet. He was just the guy who'd met me at the airport and driven me to a restaurant for a hamburger.

"It's huge." I held the humungous thing in one hand and a soda, which was also too big, in the other. In Napoli, we didn't eat like that until the sun set.

We stood in the parking lot because there were no seats, and Paulie said it would be more private anyway. He leaned against the red Ferrari and bit into his burger. Sauce dripped down his chin, and he caught it with a napkin. "It's good. Try it."

As soon as I lifted the sandwich, the helicopter came into range. I looked up then back to Paulie.

"Don't worry about it," he said. "Not us."

I looked up again. The helicopter turned in circles over the skies.

"It's three hundred meters away," I said.

"Is that far or near? What the fuck is that?"

"Close. And low. No one cares?"

"Would you eat the thing? Jesus. I'll eat it if you don't want it."

I was hungry. I put my soda in the tray that sat on the hood of the car, and bit down.

"It's good," I said, trying to ignore the low-flying helicopter with the letters LAPD painted across it.

"*Molto bene*? Right?"

"Don't."

"Don't what?" he said.

"Speak Italian. Ever again, please. It's like gears grinding."

"Fuck you, dago motherfucker."

"*Porci Americano.*"

"Oink oink, asshole," he said with a mouth full of food.

I replied, but I've forgotten what I said, and the sound of the helicopter drowned me out anyway. But in the past weeks, the sound of helicopters has reminded me of Paulie and of what had happened to our friendship because of a woman.

"What do you want to eat?" I asked, when the sound of traffic helicopters woke Theresa. "I'll have Zia bring it."

She rolled onto her stomach, tucking her hands under her thighs. "She hates me."

"She doesn't hate you."

"She won't look me in the eye."

"She doesn't trust Irish Catholics. It's not personal." I drew my hand over her ass, which was snowy and pure. She didn't fidget in her nudity, didn't try to cover herself or play at modesty. Not with me.

"I want to see Katrina," she said. "She's been calling."

The movie director, Katrina Ip, had started the trouble in the first place. Theresa was financing her movie. I supported her talking to Katrina, just not as long as Paulie was acting crazy. "Not yet," I said. "Soon."

She rolled over and got out of the bed. I grabbed her by the wrist. I think I had her more firmly than I'd intended, because she tried to yank away and couldn't.

"This is not a joke," I said. "This is not a competition for who has control over you."

She growled. The guttural sound of it stiffened my dick. I pulled her harder. "The first time I lost a woman I loved, it was easy to get my vengeance, but it didn't bring her back. Nothing brought her back. The second time, when my sister was hurt, they were ready for me. I did what I had to do, but now the consequence is that I can't go home. If anything happens to you, the consequence will be my death. I'm ready to die if anyone takes you. But they won't kill or hurt you because I was lazy or because you were proving some point about your independence."

"You can't sustain this, Capo."

"I can. As long as Paulie sets himself against me, you're a target."

She softened, moving into me, so I didn't have to grip her so hard. "And the next enemy? Who is it going to be? If you win with Paulie, that only sets you up for the next challenge. I can't live like this."

She balled her fists in frustration. I pitied her. She hadn't been born into this. She didn't understand it.

"Let me ask you a question," I said. "You have a, shall we say, infamous family. You aren't unknown."

"I've worked my whole life to be normal."

"Good job. You've been shopping recently?"

"Before you holed me up?" she asked.

"Yes."

"I went to Rodeo on—"

"To the grocery store. To buy towels. Sheets. Soap. Have you ever washed a dish?"

"Yes, I have," she said. "But I see your point. Even if it's irrelevant."

I pulled her onto the bed and wrapped my arms around her. "Tell me about that scar on your lip, and tell me you haven't always been protected."

She rested her head on my chest and didn't say anything. I thought she'd fallen asleep. I was considering how to get out from under her, so I could do what I had to do for the day, when she spoke.

"We rented a cabin every year, up by Santa Barbara. It was a campground, but really, more of a pretend-rustic resort. And there was this kid who lived in the area. He was older then me. I think I was seven when we first met, and he was eleven or twelve. He lived in an RV with his mother, and they just had it arranged so he could go to the schools up there. But, every year I found him by this narrow little river at the edge of the campsite. I was the youngest girl of seven, and I was so sick of my family. My mom just talked to the other moms and drank wine. And my dad talked business with his friends. So boring. And this guy? He was wild. We climbed trees and went past every fence we were supposed to stay behind. I think I was the kid sister he always wanted. Or maybe not. Because…"

She stopped herself to sigh, wiggling around until she was looking up at me. "I was thirteen, and he was older. We met in the same place, the Thursday of Labor Day weekend. After dinner, same as always. It was different. I was different. We sat on our rock and talked for a while. He showed me his high-school ring, and then he kissed me. You know, I didn't think about how young I was. I just thought I liked him. And maybe I loved him. Or, maybe I just wanted to. But, God, I never told anyone this before."

"You can stop."

"He put his fingers in me. I came right there. I just about died. And he… he came, too, all over my shirt. I never even touched him, which I didn't know could happen. And it was such a mess, and I was so surprised that I laughed. I didn't mean anything by it. It was nerves, and it was funny. But I must have hurt his feelings because he hit me, and his ring caught my lip. There was blood everywhere. And that's the scar right here. I told my dad I fell, and he didn't say a word the whole way to the doctor. Got two stitches. When I got back to the cabin, I realized I had cum all over my shirt, in front of my dad and everything."

She laughed to herself, a soft chuckle that sounded like nerves. I touched the scar. You could barely see it unless you were the type of man who looked for damage.

"What happened to the boy?"

She rolled over until she faced the ceiling. "They found his body at the bottom of the gulch the next morning. The rocks can be really slippery. I slept in until lunch because of the pills the doctor gave me. If I'd gotten up, who knows what would have happened?"

"What do you think would have happened?"

She stared out the window then back to me. "I would have found him. But I was spared that. Same as I've been spared everything."

Chapter Five

THERESA

I'd told Daniel that story, up to the kid at the bottom of the gulch, but I'd never mentioned the silent car ride, or the sticky adolescent semen all over my shirt. I had never felt safe telling him. Daniel had a suspicious mind, same as Antonio, but he was the DA, and ambitious, and there was no statute of limitations on murder.

From my window perch, I watched Antonio walk out of the building and toward the bench where Otto sat. Antonio had entered the camorra to avenge his wife. Then he came to Los Angeles to avenge his sister, and as much as he wanted me safe, and as much as I wanted to live, I didn't want to be the reason for his vengeance. I could ruin his life while I lived, but in dying, I could destroy his soul, so I stayed. For the time being.

Daniel was on television again, talking, talking, talking. I could count his bullet points off on my fingers, and they'd gotten tighter and meaner, undoubtedly due to Clarice's influence. There was a distinct lean away from previous talk of generic crime fighting and more emphasis on organized crime. Antonio and I had gotten out of the yellow house, *l'uovo,* with whatever the DA had needed before they got there with his warrant. That fact burned Daniel. He'd planned everything to a T, except the traffic caused by the arson of Antonio's shop and me shutting off my phone.

There would come a day when near misses weren't going to sit well with Daniel anymore. He wasn't biting his nails or flipping his hair back, but his ambition was challenged, and there was something a little feral about him. No one liked looking foolish. No one liked failing. But Daniel played a high-stakes game, and the more he tried to win, the more I felt like a cornered chess piece.

Chapter Six

ANTONIO

Zo waited in the driver's seat of my car, under the building's sign, which read *The Afidnes Tower* in big gold Grecian letters.

"Hey," Zo said as he ripped into a sandwich. "You want some?"

"No. Where's Otto?"

"He went to feel up his wife eighty percent worth." He laughed at his joke.

"You need a break?" I said.

"Me? Nah. We got a bunch of permits cleared for the shop. Had to do a little song and dance, but fuck, I feel like, you know, useful when I'm building shit. Or you know, when I'm telling a bunch of other guys what to build. And I want the shop up and running so that *stronzo* sees it and sees it good."

"All right, all right. Easy." I slapped his back. "Go take care of it."

"You got it." Zo gave me a thumbs-up and got out of my car. I took his place and headed for a little empty storefront on the east side.

My cold feelings toward Paulie surprised me. There wasn't a woman alive who had meant as much to me as Paulie had. Maybe not even a human being. I had no brothers, and my father had been a shade of a man until I walked into his coffee shop at eleven years old to settle a dispute.

But Paulie, though a *camorrista* deeply connected to the Carloni family through a couple of generations of business ties, had earned my trust in the first few minutes at the airport.

I'd been photographed on the Italy side like a criminal, but once I'd arrived in Los Angeles, I was a dot in a newspaper photo. I stood a second too long under the arch of the international terminal, overwhelmed by the size, the multicolored crowd, and the expanse of space and light. The public address system went on and on about loading and unloading, lines, flight times, gates. I smiled through security, had my bag inspected at customs, and got taken aside briefly for questioning. It was easy on the Los Angeles side.

I went outside to noise and smog that wasn't much worse than Napoli, which was urban to the teeth at the center and more and more pastoral the closer you got to Vesuvio.

Paulie stood by a chrome pillar that was stained with an old spray of blackened soda. He wore skinny jeans, white shoes, and Ray Bans, which he flipped up when he saw me.

"You Racossi?" he asked in shitty Italian.

"Spinelli," I replied, nervous about my just-passable English. I felt vulnerable without a weapon, and he must have felt like that, too. As far as I knew, it was impossible to get a gun into the airport, even for people with connections.

"Donna Carloni wants to talk to you," he said.

"I'm not here to get involved. I'm here to finish some business and go home."

I dragged my bag and walked away. He caught up, crossing the street to the cabs with me.

"I don't think you can refuse." A bus stopped near us, beeping when it kneeled, the driver shouting over an intercom for passengers to exit through the back. The noise was enormous, and the heat was oppressive.

"I don't take orders from Sicilians." I didn't know if that came off right in English. In the end, it was Paulie who helped me understand the nuances of the language. But on that day, I could only use the words I knew.

"You need her say-so to finish this business you got, or she's going to get in your way. And let's face it, you don't know up from down. If she offers you help, you oughta take it." He stepped in front of me. "She sent me because I'm *camorrista*. Like you."

"There's enough off-the-boot in your blood. I can see it."

"Jesus, man." He showed me the inside of his left wrist, where a tattoo of a volcano was drawn. The high peak was on the left. I took his wrist and pulled the skin. It wasn't pen. It was real. I didn't want to trust it. Anybody can get a tattoo.

"This is Vesuvio from the Pompeii side," I said, dropping his hand. I pulled up my left sleeve and held out my wrist, where the active side was drawn on the right.

"I know, man. Dude got it from a book. What do you want me to tell you? Nobody's actually been to fucking Naples."

"No," I poked his chest. "Nobody has been to Pompeii." I walked off, heading for what looked like a taxi stand.

"What are you going to do?" he said, chasing me. "Walk up and down Sunset, showing a mug shot? You're gonna get pegged for a narc by the gangs and for a dago criminal by the cops before your tourist visa's even up."

"I have leads."

"Not as good as mine. Come on. I know what they did to your sister. And I know why." He stepped in front of me and dropped his voice. "I'm going to be honest. They got a big chunk of the east side, and I want it. Give me a chance to do business and avenge a lady at the same time."

Something about the guy's straightforwardness appealed to me, and the fact that he'd known I'd be there intrigued me.

"I see," I said. "My father told Donna Maria I was coming."

"I can't say whether or not there was a phone conversation last night. I got nothing. 'Cause, you know, on the surface, he don't even agree with you being here. On the surface, he wants it taken care of on the Naples side, by Neapolitans. By him. Not you. You're a *consigliere*, dude. You don't get to do vendettas."

"But you do."

He shrugged, confirming it with the gesture.

"And a contract gets you made," I said.

He gave another gesture with a bobbing head that seemed affirmative.

"If I go with you," I said, "that doesn't mean I'm agreeing to anything."

He smiled. "You ever had an In-'n-Out burger?"

"*Scusa?*" I didn't known if he was propositioning me, or what.

"A burger. You hungry?"

"Yes. I am."

"Let's go then," he said. "You're gonna love it here."

I never did. But I paid my debts, and the price of allowing the vendetta to take place was two years of my life in the service of a Sicilian. It was worth it.

Chapter Seven

THERESA

Eventually, I did need to leave the apartment. I picked up some things from the loft—cash, valuables, toiletries, even Daniel's engagement ring—then went shopping on Rodeo, which was a complete waste of time, even after I'd dropped a few grand. I ignored a call from Katrina and my eleventh text from Margie. I wasn't interested in explaining myself to anyone, since I couldn't even explain myself to myself.

Otto took me back to the *Afidnes Tower.* I stood there, waiting for an approved activity. Or a signal that I could move back home safely. Would Antonio allow tonight to pass without crawling between the sheets with me?

As Otto and I waited for the elevator, I texted Antonio.

—I'm back from lunch. I'm thinking of jumping out the window—

—Let me jump you first—

—Tonight?—

—I have something to show you first—

I was formulating a snappy retort, something along the lines of a grownup show-and-tell, with nudity, when Otto opened the door to the apartment. I was shoved back so hard the wind went out of me.

I never realized how big Otto was until I tried to see past him and couldn't. His shoulders turned in, as if his arms were in front of him. The fact that I knew he was pointing a gun said a lot about what I'd been through.

"It's all right," said a man's voice on the other side of Otto's bulk. "We're friends."

"Like hell," said Otto.

"Ask her," came a woman's voice. "Sometime before you crush her against the wall."

"Margie!" I pushed past Otto to get to my sister.

"You know these people?" Otto asked as I hugged Margie. I didn't know who the man was. He was mid to late thirties, maybe, or late twenties with a ton of extra experience that aged him ten years. He had dark hair and light-brown eyes, but he wasn't Italian. And even though he wore a pinkie ring, he didn't look mob. Not that it meant anything because mob or not, he and Otto had guns leveled at each other as if they meant to shoot first and deal with the handcuffs later.

Margie had her red hair up in a chignon, and she wore a snappy business suit as if she'd cancelled a meeting to break into my fake apartment.

I left Margie's arms and stood between the two guns. "Guys, really?"

"Who are you?" Otto asked.

"Will Santon."

"He's with me," Margie said. "That's all you need to know."

"And you?" he asked Margie.

"She's my sister." I put my hand on Otto's wrist. "They're okay." I looked him in the eye, transmitting sincerity and seriousness, until he lowered the weapon.

"*Mi dispiace*" he said to Margie. He shot Will a dirty look before stepping out the door. I clicked it behind him, and before I could let Margie know that Antonio would likely interrupt us in a few minutes, she reached behind me and slid the chain on the door.

"What is wrong with you?" I asked.

"You should try answering your phone."

"I was busy."

"Doing what?"

Will interjected as he removed files from a briefcase, "Hanging around Alberto Mongelluzo, apparently."

"His name's Otto."

"No it's not. Otto's the Italian word for eight." He holds up his pinkies. "You should ask him how he lost these. It wasn't a golfing accident."

"Who are you, again?" I asked.

Margie sat in my chair. "Mr. Santon freelances for my firm, and today, he's doing me a favor."

"That's a fucking answer?" I said.

"Correct use of the word fuck. Well done."

"Don't be a bitch. And no clever quips. Just answer."

She sighed. "I think I liked you better when you acted like a lady. But all right; before you tear my face off, Will works for me. He finds things out, does research, and kidnaps my sisters when necessary. He's a good guy. You should be nice to him."

"Antonio's going to show up about five minutes after he finds out you're here."

"That's the problem, isn't it?"

"I'm making tea. Do you want any? Or is it just bust in and run?"

"Coffee," Margie said.

"Dark and bitter, I presume?" I stormed into the kitchen before she had a chance to answer.

Why did she make me feel like a prepubescent? Was it because she was more of a mother to me than my actual mother, who popped designer pills between emotional outbursts? Margie had earned the mother role by giving me affection and gaining my trust where no one else had, but her methods were drastic and overbearing, and apparently included breaking and entering.

"You broke into this apartment because you don't like who I'm sleeping with?"

"'Don't like' is mild. Very Old Theresa. New Theresa would say something more colorful. So I'll tell you this. The guy you're fucking terrifies me, and I'm just going to spoon-feed you some sense before Daddy gets wind of it."

A phone rang in the other room. I peeked in, wondering if it was Antonio. Santon placed piles of files on the coffee table and answered his phone. Margie dialed hers. I heard everything while I slapped the pieces of the coffee maker together.

"Good evening to you too, little brother." She turned to look into the kitchen. I ducked away. "You have Will Santon's team flying to Vancouver to watch Kevin Wainwright?"

Margie, single at forty-seven, had never been in love as far as I knew. She'd been a model of sharp, dirty, cut-and-dried sense; even her tone over the phone to our brother was tidy and utilitarian. As if love made sense. Love didn't stay on budget or check to see if the ledger balanced. Love didn't care if all things were equal. Love bathed the books in red, shredded documents, spent more than it brought in one month and paid too much income tax the next.

When I came in with cream and sugar, I heard Jonathan's voice, made tinny though the phone as he shouted, "Physically and irrevocably hurt."

"You know, Jonny," Margie said, "I don't mind you getting paranoid and crazy, but you're doing it on my dime."

Jonathan growled something, and I went back into the kitchen.

"Now you're getting nasty," said Margie pointedly, yet without an ounce of upset in her voice. "I gotta pull him, Jonny. I'm sorry."

She hung up just as I came back with the coffee. "I just lied for you."

"You want a medal?"

"I'd like some appreciation."

"For coming into my apartment uninvited? Because I didn't answer your texts in the right amount of time? Because you don't approve of the man I love?"

"Oh, it's love now. Great." She tossed her phone on the coffee table and grabbed a cup. "I've never seen anyone make a good decision for love."

"Love is its own decision," Will cut in. "It chooses you."

"Thanks, Delta," Margie said. "You can engrave that on your headstone." She turned back to me. "You already made it clear you wanted nothing to do with what I had to say. I stopped caring what you wanted when Dad asked if you were really with that guy from the Catholic Charities thing."

"What did you tell him?" I said.

"I laughed. But he knew I was evading." She snapped open a briefcase and swung it over to Will. It was his, and she was hurrying him.

"He can't control who we're with," I said.

"He does like to try."

"And you?" I glanced at Will, then back to Margie. "What is it you're trying to do?"

Will cut in. "We're educating you." He removed a file and opened it on the coffee table.

Antonio. Even his mug shot made me tingle: the curl of his smirk, the jaw set in anger, the tousled black hair. He was younger in the photo and had a reckless edge. His mouth was shaped for a different language, and the lines around his eyes were somehow unset, reversible. He watched me from a wallet-sized rectangle stapled to a document that told me what had been implied but never stated.

"Antonio Spinelli is the bastard son of Benito Racossi." Will put his elbows on his knees, the angle of the sun cutting his face into dark and light sides. "By the time he found out who his father was, he'd already made a name for himself as a petty criminal and pickpocket. He went to his father to settle a dispute between himself and another thief who'd stolen a shipment of his bootleg cigarettes. He was eleven. A prodigy, even by Neapolitan standards."

"Look at you." Margie, arms crossed, leaned back in the chair. "You got a face like a brick wall. You don't want to hear it, because you already decided you don't care. This mug shot, it's Interpol's. He was accused of killing the men who killed his wife."

This story wasn't new or shocking, though I guess it should have been. I guess if anyone else heard their lover had murdered someone, they'd be upset. But I wasn't just anyone. I was a savage.

"She took a car bomb that was meant for him," Will said. "He was visiting a client in a neighboring town. His business partner drove, which saved Spinelli's life and ended his wife's. He killed the two guys allegedly responsible."

"And?" I flipped through the file, moving quickly past the photos of the bodies of the men who'd killed his wife. Allegedly killed. "It's just a theory. Do you want me to say, 'Oh, darling, welcome home, let me take your coat, what exactly happened with your wife?'"

"You could start by asking about the real-estate-assessment racket," Will said. "Go on to the money laundering, the car insurance fraud out of his shop, the sideline in tax-free cigarettes, and the occasional truck hijack on the 60 freeway."

"If that's not enough to make you ill," Margie said, "I don't know why you even need a car-bombed spouse."

It didn't make me ill. Not a bit. It made me curious and hungry. And a little turned on. I was fascinated not by the wife but by the web of underground criminal activity and the way he'd mastered it. He'd turned East Los Angeles into his own marionette theater.

I hid my excitement behind a cold stare and a raised chin. As if she saw right through me, Margie got out of her chair and looked down at me. "I'm trying to say things so you hear them. I love you. I want to protect you. How has he protected you?"

"Maybe it's time everyone stopped trying to protect me." I stood up. I'd heard enough facts I already knew and the rest was conjecture. "Will needs to go back to doing whatever he was doing for Jonathan, because there's nothing here to fix."

I started to leave. Margie took my shoulder. "Please, Theresa. It's going to get worse, and you're going to be a target."

"How could it be worse?"

"There's a wedding," Will said, gathering his papers and files.

"I know all about it."

"It's a serious imbalance. No one knows how it's going to be rectified, but it won't be bloodless. All I have to say is Spinelli will have to get involved. His life isn't his own. Never was."

"Speak clearly, Mr. Santon. Tell me what you mean. You didn't come all this way to make insinuations."

His mouth curled into a knowing grin. He was a nice-looking man with brown eyes and scruffy black hair he'd tamed into something conservative and nondescript. "You really are all cut from the same cloth," he said warmly.

"Enough, Delta," Margie cut in. "Get to the point."

He cleared his throat and sat back. "To correct the imbalance, Donna Maria Carloni is going to have to have a granddaughter marry into a nice Neapolitan family with ties to the old country. The most likely candidate is a young lady named Irene. She's just been flown in from Sicily, where she was educated in the old way. She is unsullied, if you will."

It was funny, what came to mind. Will was describing a young woman educated in a particular way to achieve a certain goal and groomed in behavior and speech, much the way I'd been.

"Well," I said. "I hope she likes it here. If she can stay a virgin for fifteen minutes, I salute her."

"Oh, she'll stay a virgin," Margie said. "Because the Neapolitan who was supposed to marry her has disappeared."

"The *stupido*?"

"And his girlfriend." Will handed me a picture of a nice-looking couple on the beach. He was dark-haired and bulky, smiling. She was cute as soda pop, mousy blond and cap toothed.

"Theresa," Margie said softly. "Get out while you can. It's chaos."

"You were there when the thing happened with Daniel. You saw me. You saw what I went through. You want that again?"

"I'll take it over a funeral."

"I can't; it's too late. I love him, and whatever he faces, I face with him."

"You might face it without him. He's part of a world you don't understand; he'll cut you out, and you won't even know what hit you."

"You don't know anything," I growled. "You're so closed off. You're so scared. You run every piece of information through your worry filter, and nothing gets through unscathed. You calculate everything that can go wrong, and when you're done doing it for yourself, you do it for the rest of us. I think you were happiest when I was alone and not taking any risks. You need to stop. You need to let me try and be happy."

"I can offer this," Will interrupted. "I know you won't take protection from the authorities because of Daniel. But I can offer it to you separate from that. I have contacts in the military who can keep you safe from Paulie Patalano, Antonio Spinelli, Donna Maria. All of them."

"I don't even know you."

"It's through me," Margie said. "Limited-time offer."

"Thanks for the offer, Margie," I said, "but I have mistakes to make."

As if summoned by the word "mistake," the latch turned, and Antonio walked in as if he owned the place. A second passed, or a fraction of one, during which all parties assessed the imminent threat of danger. Antonio was armed, as was Will; I knew that much. If either of them was worth his salt, he would smell it on the other.

"*Buongiorno,*" Antonio said with a smile. The three of us stood. I went to him, kissing each cheek. He put his hand on the small of my back.

"Antonio, have you met my sister, Margie?"

"I haven't," he said, smiling to her and offering his hand. They shook.

"Nice to meet you," she said. "This is my friend Will Santon." They shook hands, as well. The distrust in the room was palpable, multiplying exponentially, like compound interest on a bad loan.

"Tea? Coffee?" I offered, half joking.

"A butter knife for the tension, please," Margie said.

"Something serrated might help?" Antonio offered.

"You'd know, apparently."

"Margie!"

"I don't like niceties," Margie said. "They bore me."

"Of course, then." Antonio spoke the words with one hand extended, as if offering peace, and the other firmly planted at the base of my neck. "Let's skip all that. How can I help you?"

"You can let my sister answer her calls."

"Your sister does what I ask her to because she knows what's best for her."

The conversation was going nowhere in a big hurry. If I knew anything about Margie, her intention had been to leave the apartment with me, and she wasn't walking out any other way. If I knew anything about Antonio, she was going to have to walk over a dead body to do it. So, either the unstoppable force and the immovable object were going to have a meet up, or I was going to step in between them.

"I can pick up my phone any time, Margaret. But I don't want to. I'm sorry; I wasn't trying to worry you or stress you out. But you really have to step back and trust that if I'm not answering the phone, I'm busy. I want you to consider that no news is good news." She started to say something, and I held my hand up. "I'm not in a bit of danger. Boredom is my biggest problem right now. Antonio," I said, turning to him, "you tell my sister you're bossing me around, and she's going to get a SWAT team in here. Personally, I don't need the aggravation."

"I'm sorry, then," he said, facing Margie. "Of course, she's a grown woman, in America."

I held my hand out to Will. "Mr. Santon, thanks for coming. I appreciate your candor. I hope we never meet again."

"Feeling's mutual," he said as we shook on it.

I separated from Antonio and went to the door with a cold spot at the back of my neck where his hand had been. I opened it. Otto was waiting in the hallway.

"I promise I will pick up my phone from now on, as long as you don't unleash a stream of neuroses on me."

Margie brushed her skirt down and composed herself, which meant, in Drazen parlance, that she was about to unleash a torrent of The Truth According To Margaret, and nothing could stop her, not a word, gesture, or forward tackle.

"I'm fine with being dismissed like a child, and I'm fine with you not taking my advice. I can walk out of here without a problem. But when the last asshole did things I don't even want to talk about, I was the first one you called. And I was the one who stood by you for the whole thing." She slashed the air with the flat of her hand, the gesture filling in for words like bawling, suicidal depression, the inability to move, long bouts of self-doubt, reproach, and loathing. She'd been with me for every minute of it, and with that karate chop, I relived it.

"And I want you to know," she continued without pausing, though my brain had hitched, "that the next time you call me because you're in over your head, and you can't handle what's happening, I will pick up the phone, and I'll be there for you again. And I won't even say 'I told you so.'"

"Thank you," I said, because there was nothing else in my vocabulary for that speech. She tilted her head down and left, with Will close at her heels. He and Antonio nodded to each other. I shut the door softly then pressed my back to it.

Antonio's face betrayed nothing but perfection. I felt cornered by his beauty, soothed to inaction. I slid away so I could think.

"We have to talk," I said. "And you're keeping your pants on for the entire thing."

"You're going to talk," he said, holding up a finger and stepping so close our bodies shared the same heat. "And I'm going to keep my pants on."

He leaned forward until I took a step backward, and in the second of slight imbalance, he grabbed my shoulders, directing me into the chair behind me. I didn't know what to ask first. He looked down at me with a fully visible erection, and the whole pants-on rule seemed really badly thought out. "You're going to take these pants off. Then you're going to spread your legs so I can see everything, and you're going to tell me what they said to you."

"Why do you need me vulnerable to hear this? Don't you trust me?"

"I don't need you vulnerable," he said, leaning down and hooking his fingers in my waistband. "I need you accessible."

"I'm going to tell you everything. You know that already."

"Then it's only right you should enjoy it."

He yanked my pants down. They were loose, silk things and came off easily, taking my underpants with them. I tried to get up just to prove a point, but he pushed me against the chair. "Spread your legs, Contessa."

I didn't. He pushed me down with his right hand and took my knee in the other, wrapping his fingers around it easily and yanking it to the side. I gasped as the rush of fluids drenched me. He slid his hand down my chest and kneeled in front of me.

"Your sister is an honest woman," he said, kissing my mound and working his way down. "So it's not important what she said, only what she thinks."

His tongue, honed to a point, slid down, parting my skin. The invasion was delicate and sweet, warm on warm, wet to wet, and I melted into the chair.

"I don't care about any of it, Antonio."

"Really?" He kissed my clit, folding his lips around it, closing them, tightening, sucking just enough, and releasing. "Tell me what you don't care about."

"You want a list?"

He licked me harder in response, and I pushed myself into his mouth, running my fingers through his black hair. He awakened a galaxy of burning stars that turned in the universe between my legs.

"She thinks you're a killer, a criminal. Money laundering, insurance fraud, oh, God, just like that. Keep doing that thing." He slid a finger into me and rotated it, not saying a word, but with his eyes, he told me to continue.

"You're going to hurt me," I gasped as his tongue swirled. "She's afraid for me." The burning points of heat and light coalesced into a bright center, and when he moaned, his mouth vibrated against me. I wanted to tell him more, but I couldn't when the galaxy spun into itself and exploded, my orgasm a black hole of wordless ecstasy.

When I could speak, I said, "Now. Take me now."

But he was already there, pants down, glorious cock stretching me open, his weight on me the comfort and security I needed. The protection Margie thought I wasn't getting was him and me together: his thumb in my mouth, his dick owning me, his control and dominance frightening, deadly, and indispensable.

He came with a grunt, and I was right behind him, screaming his name again, tightening my legs around him, bucking as he held me still.

Through the post-orgasmic haze, I could barely hear his soft words in a musical language or feel the light kisses he laid on my cheek and neck.

"Capo," I whispered.

"Contessa."

"I wasn't finished."

He picked up his head and looked me in the eyes. "You feel finished."

I laid my hand on his cheek, stroking the short hairs, their resistance pleasing my skin. "I need to finish what I was saying. About Margie."

"You don't have to finish." He sighed and straightened his arms, putting twelve or so inches between us. "She's more or less got a point. I'm bad for you. And you have a point also."

"I do?"

"I think I've been wrong. I think if I keep you here, trouble will find you. So, get out. Go do… I don't know. Find your life."

"Oh, Antonio…" I didn't know whether to assure him that my life was with him or thank him for coming around to giving me space.

"But please, be safe. Can you do that for me? Until Paulie is calm."

"What happened to the *stupido* and his girlfriend?" I asked.

He put his fingers on my lips. "Not now. Just tell me you'll let Otto take you around."

I promised. I'd keep as safe as I could.

Chapter Eight

THERESA

Katrina's post-production rental was on the west side in some in-between neighborhood. The low-slung buildings in a three-block radius had been painted yellowish beige and sprinkled with Spanish roof tiles, black soot, and garish signs in three languages.

Otto walked me to the double glass doors that faced into the parking lot.

"Where will you be?" I asked as we passed into the small reception area.

"I have to check it out. Then I'll be right here." With a pinky-less hand, he indicated a leather chair by a plastic plant.

"You can grab a cup of coffee if you want."

He smiled and nodded, but prior experience told me that he wouldn't get himself a cup of anything.

The receptionist, a young Hispanic girl with straight hair down her back, said "Which project?"

"*The Lion In the Sand*?" I said. "I think they're in edit."

She checked her computer. "They have a bay on four."

Otto took me upstairs, and when we left the elevator, I turned to him, saying nothing but giving him a look. He understood and nodded.

"I'll be here." He indicated a bank of couches.

"Thank you."

I went past the double doors alone.

Katrina leaned into the monitor. The overhead lights were dimmed down to nothing, leaving only the four glowing editing-bay monitors to illuminate the trays of half-eaten burgers. The room smelled of men and salty food. Her editor, Robbie, tapped keys. Michael Greenwich's face, all lion and rage, filled the screen.

"This is the best take," Robbie said. He motioned to his assistant. "Rob, call up number four."

Katrina leaned back. "I'll look, but I think you're right. TeeDray, what do you think? You marked four as the best." She tapped my set notes.

"Look at four again. But this is it. I mean, who can tell anything on set?" I shrugged, and Katrina eyed me as if I were lying. She grabbed our Styrofoam boxes and went to the door.

"Let's eat. You look like you could use it."

The light in the hall was blinding on the white walls. Burgundy doors lined the corridor. Each had a little square, meshed window at eye level, and behind them came the sounds of screaming, music, crashes, whispers, and groans. Editors didn't understand moderation of volume, and headphones would have given them a headache after twelve hours of chopping up scenes.

Katrina led me to the lounge at the end of the hall, which consisted of plywood boxes covered in grey industrial carpet that matched the floors. No windows. No tables. Dated movie posters. There was a vending machine that reminded me of Antonio and, in front of it, a brown-splat stain that would never come out, no matter how hard they shampooed.

"What the hell is wrong with you?" Katrina flipped open the Styrofoam box and shoved my well-done burger toward me, pushing it against my thigh. I moved so she would have room to open hers. Her burger would be rare. She liked it squealing as it went down.

It had been a week since I'd seen her. I hadn't answered any texts but had left a voice message when Antonio told me it was safe for her to come home. I believed him, because he knew his business.

"Well?" she said with a mouthful of fries.

"I don't know where to start." My fries looked like a bundle of Jack Straws. I tried to pick one up without disturbing any of the others and failed.

"Throw the first scene out," Katrina said. "Always."

"I'm in love with Antonio."

"That was fast."

"Yeah," I said.

"But?"

I looked up at the walls to think for a second and was hit with a poster for Good Fellas. I laughed to myself. Even in that bland, windowless room, he hung over me. "I understand him. It's weird. There's this connection. I get what he's saying, and I know what keeps him up at night. It sounds crazy, but I know what's in his heart."

"That sounds pretty good."

"It's different. With Daniel, I knew what was in his mind. I knew what he was thinking; I just didn't know what he was feeling. Obviously, or that whole Clarice thing wouldn't have gotten past me." I brought my burger to my lips and bit it. It tasted like every other well-done burger. The texture was grey and leathery. Flat. Boiled dry. Katrina's burger dripped when she bit into it. "With Antonio, I'm alive when he's there. It's chemical. My blood goes crazy."

"Wow."

I shrugged. "Yeah."

"Oh, for Christ's sake, Tee. What's the problem? Speak. You're boring me."

"It's complicated."

She chewed slowly then took a pull of her soda. "I'm waiting."

"How is the edit coming?"

"Fine. I think I got most everything. Michael's in Montana doing a spelunking movie, so if I need pickups, I'm screwed. Why don't you tell me why it's so complicated?"

"It just is."

"Oh, for the love of God. He's in the mob. Just say it."

"Katrina!" I said.

"Please, sister. I wasn't born yesterday. One, he was having you followed by that guy with no pinkies. Two, it's all over the news that shit's going down. Your ex is taking out the flamethrowers and threatening the biggest prosecution since Robert Kennedy in like, the sixties. Which I'd blow off, except I met Antonio and yes, he's hot, but also… he's got a whole connected thing happening. Three, you disappeared in a poof after the wrap party."

"I did not."

"You talk on the phone and don't tell me where you are. Have you even been to the apartment?"

I put my burger down. "Antonio is a businessman. His office was burned down. His partner split and took half his team. He's rebuilding, and I'm there for him."

"Uh-huh. Fine. And what else?"

"What do you mean?"

"You have no job. You're not talking to me." She leaned forward. "A lot of fucking, huh?"

I pulled out a fry and it rubbed against another. Five more shifted in the container. "There is sex." I bent the fry against my tongue and folded it into my mouth. "And it is life altering."

She smiled and raised her eyebrows, delighted for me. I couldn't tell her about my ennui, or the level of protection Antonio felt he needed to build around me. I couldn't tell her that, from the outside, he deserved every indecent name I called him during sex and that it turned me on. How far he would go, his life on the fringes, the unknowns about him, and even his insistence that I bend to the will of an outlaw turned me on. And I feared that, without those hours of languor in between our meetings, the desire for him to dig out the aching filth inside me would disappear. And I needed it. I needed him to treat me like a rag doll while I called him an animal. I needed to see that animal turn pure, to feel him slowly get gentle, to hear his growls subdued into whispers. Thinking about it in that little room, under a Good Fellas poster, melted my legs into a pool of lust.

"Have you considered this might be a rebound thing? From Daniel?"

"Sure," I said. "I've considered it then dismissed it. If rebound things always felt like this, they'd last longer."

My phone dinged.

—downstairs in 10 minutes—

—I'm busy—

I didn't know why I bothered. I was done with Katrina. She was busy; she had a life, dreams, and work. I had appointments.

"Is it him?" she asked, poking at her own phone.

"Yeah."

—Eleven minutes. No more—

—Say please—

—Per favore, Contessa bella—

—Flattery is unnecessary—

—So are your clothes—

"What are you smiling about?" Katrina asked, flopping down the lid of her Styrofoam box.

"Not this burger." I closed mine. "You don't need me for anything, do you?"

"Just stay in touch. Your notes get a little scribbly toward the end."

Chapter Nine

THERESA

The Maserati came down Cahuenga and parked in front. Otto's Lincoln must have been dismissed because it was nowhere in sight.

The top was down, and Antonio was in aviators and snug jeans, his boots making a *clup-clup* on the pavement as he came around to open the door for me. "Contessa," he said.

"Capo."

"How was your afternoon out?"

"Thrilling." I sat down, and he closed the door behind me. When he got behind the wheel I asked, "Short notice to give a girl."

"Ten minutes is enough time to get down the stairs."

"Maybe I was busy."

"Were you?" He put the car into drive and twisted to see behind him before pulling out. His leather jacket stretched between his shoulder blades.

"Hardly the point," I huffed.

"Exactly the point." He pulled into the street and headed south with the wind in his hair, the sun on his glasses, and his skin a rich olive color. When he smiled at me, I forgot the point entirely.

"Where are we going?" I asked.

"Back to the east side."

"You won't give up over there, will you?"

"It's mine. I never give up what's mine." He turned to me for a second. "Ever."

"So, if you kept that territory, where did Paulie go?"

He smirked, eyes on the road. I wasn't supposed to ask questions, but if he expected me to stick to that, he was sorely mistaken.

"Is he a businessman without a business?" I used air quotes.

"There is nothing more dangerous than a man who has lost everything fighting something he fears."

"What does he fear?"

Antonio pulled onto the 10 freeway. My hair went nuts, spiraling like cotton candy in the wind. He put his fingers on my thigh, pushing my skirt up. I put my hand on it as he moved it deeper, grasping the flesh.

"Tell me," I said.

"Your legs are closed."

"I'm in a convertible on the 10."

"Open them. *Adesso*. I want to feel if you're wet."

"Antonio, really." A big rig came up on the right. If the trucker had been looking out his side window, he would have had a clear view.

"Pull your skirt down over my hand and spread your legs. One knee touching the door. All the way. Don't argue, or I'm going to pull over and spank you for every trucker on the freeway to see."

I was wet. I had to be. I pulled my skirt over his hand and put my bag on my lap. He grabbed his jacket from the back and put it over the bag.

"Good enough," he said. "Open up."

I spread my legs. The city streaked by in swashes of grey, blots of billboard colors, and flecks of palm-tree green. The only constant was the flawless umbrella of blue sky.

"You didn't answer the question," I said. He changed lanes, blinker and all, and slipped his hand under the crotch of my panties.

"*Dio mio*, you are soaked. What were you thinking about?"

He rubbed my clit gently, one stroke along the length.

"Paulie's business." I opened my legs wider.

"Really?" He leaned back and draped his left wrist over the wheel while drawing sticky circles around my opening with his right middle finger.

"No."

"Tell me."

"I was thinking about your mouth."

"*Bene*. What about it?" A BMW came up close on the right, and I ignored it. If I looked at them, they'd look back. The car was red, and I was throbbing.

"Your lips," I gasped. "Between my legs." He moved so slowly I thought I'd explode from the rush of blood.

"More."

"Kissing me. Sucking. God, Jesus Antonio. How can you drive and do this?" I could barely see past the nest of hair whipping around my face, but I saw his smirk clearly.

"The left hand doesn't know what the right is doing." He grasped my clit between his thumb and forefinger, changing lanes again so he could blow the speed limit that much better.

"God!"

"More," he said.

"And you put your tongue inside me, and rub your teeth on my clit."

"You are dirty, Contessa. And detailed. Do you want to come?" He let the pinch go and rubbed with the pads of his fingers.

"Please."

"Sit still."

I caught sight of him, between the spaghetti of red hair, glancing my way and smiling.

"Yes," I said. "Yes."

"Keep your legs open." He dragged all four fingers over my hard clit once, twice, the bumps and ridges of his fingertips a pulsing rhythm at seventy-five miles an hour.

"Yes."

"Keep still. And no shouting." He ran his fingers over me. Even though it was autumn, I was sweating, muscles clenching, nerves firing. My jaw went slack then tightened when he flicked his nails over me.

Without an outlet in movement or sound, I felt everything. My body connected with wires of pleasure, tightening with the orgasm, twisting, my ass clenching, my pussy pulsating for a cock to fill it, grasping for him in waves. The white noise of the freeway was consumed by my own vortex, and any cares about people seeing me disappeared.

His touch got lighter and lighter, prolonging my orgasm. It went on and on. I closed my eyes and got lost in his fingers, my silence, and stillness.

When I finally stopped coming, Antonio removed his hand from under the jacket and got off the freeway.

He put his fingers in his mouth, and when he stopped at the red light, he brushed his pinkie over my lower lip, painting me with our mingled juices.

"You know what made Paulie crazy enough to break everything he worked for?" Antonio asked.

"It was me, wasn't it?"

"Yes. Partly, it was you."

Chapter Ten

THERESA

We made a few more turns, but I more or less knew the neighborhood after the night Marina had tried to shoot me. We were probably five blocks from his burned-out auto shop. He was committed to the neighborhood, for sure. If I owned a business on the east side and someone set fire to it, I'd never want to cross the LA River again.

He didn't say much after revealing that I was not only a target for Paulie because of the feud, but the reason for the hostility in the first place. As if he knew I'd need a minute to absorb the new information, he just drove and waited.

"Where are we going?" I asked.

"I'm driving around until you ask what you want to ask."

"I thought I wasn't supposed to."

He stopped at a light and twisted to face me. "Go ahead."

"Can't you just say what you want without me trying to ask the right question? I'm not the lawyer in the car, here."

"Apparently. And your hair is a mess. Your lips smell like pussy. Did someone just finger the hell out of you?"

"Antonio! You're deflecting."

"I am, Contessa. *Mi dispiace*. This has been obsessing me, and the only time I don't feel obsessed with it is when I'm around you. When I'm around you, I want to pretend it's all gone away." He drove, but with purpose, not as if he was killing time waiting for my question.

"This is going to be a constant battle, isn't it?"

He smiled a devil of a smile. His parents had skimmed from the very top of the gene pool to make that mouth. "If you make things into battles, yes, they are battles." He pulled into a narrow alley and parked in front of a garage.

"Why was he scared of me?"

He opened his door. "Come." He went around the car, keys jingling, and opened the door for me.

"I'm being really patient," I said.

"Yes, you are." He planted a kiss on my lips, and I tasted my sex on his mouth, from the fingers he'd licked. "Women scare him. Especially the wild, unpredictable ones."

"Me? Wild and unpredictable?"

We put our arms around each other, and he led me out of the alley and to the street. The row of buildings was connected, and flush with the street in the old tenement style, with storefronts on the first floor and one story of apartments above.

"To Paulie, you are," he said.

He stopped in the middle of the block. The storefront was empty. A large window had crusty bars in front and cracked glass behind. The door was original to the building, which looked as if it has been built just before the depression and not updated since. On the right of it stood another empty storefront that had been updated in a grotesquely ugly way, with chipped brown stucco and a poorly installed vinyl window. On the left was a store with a purpose I couldn't divine, with hours posted and the sign in the door flipped to "Closed."

"What do you think?" Antonio asked as he unlocked the front gate.

"I think it needs a coat of paint."

The gates creaked, and he slapped them home with a metallic smack. "What color would you like?" He fingered a bouquet of keys.

"Capo, what's happening? You can't turn this into an auto shop. It's in the middle of the block."

He opened the door, turned, and flipped on the lights. He repeated a version of his previous question. "What would you turn it into?"

I didn't answer but stepped past the door, onto a linoleum floor covered in grease and dust. Metal racks lined the right; stacked round tables stood on my left. I glimpsed a dark back room that looked like a place where unpleasant scientific mysteries waited to be solved. "A clean room, first," I said.

"And then?" He jingled his keys. He seemed relaxed and happy, leaning on his right hip slightly, shoulders sloped, face waiting for something joyful, and I knew what our visit was about.

"Capo." I took two steps toward him, with my arms out. "Has anyone ever told you that you're sweet?"

His hands took me by the waist and drew me close. "No."

"You are."

His head tilted slightly, and his cheeks got narrow, as if he sucked them in. His eyes were hard and defensive. I remembered who I was dealing with and how little I knew him, but I refused to be scared.

"I don't want a store."

"The shop is close. I can watch you. And you'll have something that's yours."

I wanted to protest that I had plenty that was mine, and I did. I had a condo. I had money. I had three-thousand-dollar shoes. And if I wanted a store in one of the worst neighborhoods in Los Angeles, I could have one very nicely arranged without his help.

I tamped back all of my resistance because the store was a gift, and a thoughtful one. Most men gave women flowers or jewelry; Antonio gave buildings. I didn't need a dozen roses, and I could buy myself a diamond necklace, but I could see the value of Antonio's gift.

But I didn't want a store. I didn't want to be handed a life.

"Can I think about what to do with it?"

"*Si!* It's zoned for food, not liquor, but any licenses you want…" He held his hands out and said no more. I was sure I could get it zoned as an amusement park if I wanted.

That store was his dozen roses and box of candy. It was completely useless. Pointless, even. In a moment of peace, he'd tried to give me what he thought would make me happy.

"Thank you, Capo. Can I take time to decide what to do with it?"

"Of course."

I reached up to kiss him, twisting my fingers together behind his neck. His tongue hit mine, filling my mouth with aggression and lust. His hands went up my shirt, shoving my bra out of the way with his fingers, thumb teasing my nipple as he pressed his hardness against my hip. Would he take me in that filthy store? Knock me against the metal shelves and drag me into the dark back room? Yes. Yes, he would.

He kicked the door shut. And that slam threw me off for a fraction of a second, so that when the other sounds hit, I thought they were echoes of the door. When Antonio threw me to the floor, I thought it was part of his seduction. I was primed for hard, lustful, thoughtless sex.

But the door kept slamming, and his weight on me was not amorous. His breath came in gasps on my neck, hot and sharp, and he held my wrists down hard enough to bruise.

Glass broke, plaster popped, and what I thought was the crack of a slamming door was no less than the constant *pop pop pop* of gunfire. And my body under his, with the threat of death a sudden stink in the room, was on fire.

Chapter Eleven

ANTONIO

It stopped. I didn't know if the guy with the gun was reloading or getting out of the car to finish us off. So when I had a second, I let go of Theresa's wrist and pulled her up. It was not graceful or chivalrous. I had no time to apologize, and she didn't have a second to ask what the hell had happened. I pulled her into the back so fast she almost tripped. It would have been fine if she had fallen. I would have preferred to have dragged her.

No windows. It was dark and infested with a cloud of flies louder than mere machine guns.

I heard her say my name, a question in her voice. Next, she'd ask who, how, and why. Only the last question had answers.

Because there was no peace. No truce. Because my name was Antonio Spinelli, and this was my life.

"Antonio." She pulled against me when I got to the back door. I yanked her close.

"No questions now." I growled it harder than I should have, knowing I'd regret it in retrospect.

"Your car."

I turned to her. The light from the front room reflected blue on her eyes. I held my hand still on the door.

The car. A blue Maserati, parked in the back like a cursed beacon.

We stared at each other. She was right; we were trapped.

The windows were boarded. I peeked out, holding her hand. She wasn't shaking. She wasn't even sweating, but her lips were parted, and she looked ready to fuck. I considered taking her, but gunshots wouldn't go unnoticed, and a yellow Ferrari pulled up next to the Mas. It was the man himself.

"Stay behind me." I unlocked the door.

"No, Antonio. Wait." She was flushed, but still sharp. Her eyes flashed, scanning my face. Oh, she wanted to fuck all right, and yet, she seemed more alert, as if her arousal was mental as well as physical.

Paulie, who had been a friend to me, sent a chill up my spine when he got out of the car and stood on the hood.

"Spin!" Paulie shouted. "Come out."

"I should go in front," Theresa whispered.

Paulie held up his hands. "I got nothing. I'm unarmed. I promise; I ain't gonna do nothing."

"He'll never shoot me," she said.

Paulie called out before I could answer. "If I wanted you dead, I woulda come in and done it already."

That son of a whore. He knew it would bother me that he had control. And if I asked for concession for Theresa, if I made sure she walked away, it would be perceived as weakness.

"You stay here," I said.

"He knows I'm here. He could have come in the front. Listen."

"I got a news flash out here, Spin." It was Paulie again. Like the buzz of a fluorescent light that you couldn't fix.

"We have to go out side by side," Theresa urged.

"Listen to me," I said. "Do not speak. Do not make a move. Do not insinuate yourself. Do you understand?"

"Antonio, but—"

"You will stay behind me, not because he'll shoot either one of us. If he kills me, he's a dead man, and he knows it. If he touches you, his life isn't worth anything. But if you come out at my side, I will look weak. Do you understand?"

That last statement was a lie. I wanted to protect her in case Paulie had lost his mind or brokered a deal for my life that I didn't know about. A man has to live with himself and God, and I'd already alienated God.

"Behind this wall right here." I touched the wall by the doorframe. "Stay in arm's reach."

I tried to remind myself that that was Paulie out there. That was a guy who had helped me avenge my sister, who laughed at my pronunciation then helped me get it right. That was a guy who'd thought of us as partners from the minute he met me at the airport. He jumped down from the hood of the car then pulled his gun out of the holster and dropped it in the front seat.

The *thup-thup-thup* of a helicopter came over the distance.

"They're coming, Spin. Come on. We got about five minutes."

I opened the door. It was brighter outside than I'd expected, and I fought to keep my hand from shading the sun. It would look like a sudden movement.

"Come in, then," I said.

"Where is she?" He kept his hands out, an unusually wise move from him. I would have shot him dead if he'd reached for a pocket.

"You try and kill us, and you want to know where she is?"

Theresa stood right at my side but behind the wall, unmoving. I could smell her perfume and shampoo. I could hear her long breaths and the ticking of her watch.

I did not sense fear on her.

If she'd been scared, I might have moved too quickly or made a rash decision. If she'd been whimpering or crying after being shot at, I might have put a bullet in Paulie without a second thought. But she wasn't afraid. Thank God for her.

"I aimed over your head," Paulie said. "I was trying to get your attention."

"You were always impulsive. Always reckless." He grinned and looked at his shoes for a millisecond.

I'd enjoyed and feared his impulsiveness at the same time. He'd been valuable, but I'd so often had to smooth over an overzealous shakedown or unnecessary insult that, in the end, I stopped letting him manage politicians by himself.

He still needed me. But I didn't need him, and that scared him. He wasn't breaking with me because of his ambition; I had to remember that. This break wasn't about money, and it wasn't about power. It was about fear.

"I wanted to tell you something. It's gonna hurt, Spin. Gotta admit."

"About?"

"This thing we have—"

"You," I said. "This is your grudge."

He admitted nothing. He'd already said everything he was going to say the night he burned the shop. He wouldn't tolerate me with a woman so deep in the establishment's pockets. He would never trust her. He would never trust me. I had to choose between him and Theresa. I tried to understand why he'd make such an ultimatum but came up empty-handed.

"You heard about the Sicilian virgin's fiancé?"

"*Stupido*?" I said.

"Nice Neapolitan kid. But yeah, a little dumb. He and his girlfriend just washed up in Malibu. You know why? He refused to marry a nice Sicilian virgin because he already had a girlfriend. *Stupido* is right. Made enemies on two continents.

"And?" I didn't want to talk about it in front of Theresa.

"Numbers Niccolò. Our accountant. He's mine. I'm the future of this side of town. You know why?"

"Is that what you shot at me for? The accountant?"

"Niccolò's playing the odds. I got the bloodline for the virgin. She's mine now that *stupido* is dead." Paulie glanced up. The helicopters had gotten closer. "I know you're there, Princess," he called out. He jumped from the hood of the car to the uneven ground of the alley. "Don't get too comfortable. This asshole's shit's gonna be mine in a few months." He got too close. Not to me, but to her.

Something took over me. It was the old Tonio-botz, the man who wasn't much more than muscle, bone, and rage. Even if Antonio was a thoughtful man, Tonio moved quickly because he didn't think.

Paulie had never seen that side of me. He didn't know how swiftly I'd react to him addressing Theresa, even if there was a wall between them. He didn't know I didn't give a shit about his restraint, and he didn't have his guard up when I grabbed the front of his shirt. The defense came up, but it wasn't fast enough.

I heard the *thunk* of his head on the brick wall. When he tried to push away, I leaned all my weight on him.

"Don't talk to her, Paulie. Not a word to her."

It was too late. She came out from behind the wall and leaned in the doorframe with her arms crossed.

Chapter Twelve

THERESA

Had I gone through my adult life without once thinking I was going to die? Had I never been threatened? Never almost been in a car wreck? Had I never been in the wrong place at the wrong time?

When Antonio threw himself on top of me, while his chest rose and fell as the gunshots broke the windows, I knew I'd never tasted life as closely as I had with that man. The blood rushing between my legs, the juice collecting there, every point of light in my life dropping to that point was painful in its speed and intensity. I thought I'd explode from the desire for his cock before a bullet could even touch me.

Then it stopped, and all I could think about was his mouth and his neck and his sweat, scented with worry and adrenaline. I knew we were in grave danger, and I'd follow him through it. I'd follow him anywhere.

I'd followed him through the store, my ears dulled from the shots, while outside, Paulie waited with his threats and talk of the virgin, the wedding, and a poor, stupid boy sold into a marriage he didn't want and who was killed along with the woman he loved.

Even after that, when Antonio pushed himself against Paulie, close as a lover and angry as a pit bull with the stink of savage rage coming off him, I didn't panic because I didn't need to. All my passion, rage, panic, and arousal stayed tightly confined behind a hard black shell.

Antonio and Paulie were evenly matched, physically, but my Antonio was stronger in his fearsomeness and clarity of purpose. He would never back down, not until he stood over his enemy in victory. His determination was clenched in his jaw and held fast in his fists.

Leaning in the doorframe with my arms crossed, I saw the meaner man take advantage of the weaker one and the force of their bodies against each other, the intensity of Antonio's face, the force of his arms, and I wanted those tight lips and that rigid cock between my legs.

"Antonio," I said.

"Get inside," he growled, his fingers resting on Paulie's cheek and tensing, tensing, until a shadow of a divot appeared in the skin. Their bodies were so close they could have been one person.

"This what you like, Princess?" Paulie grunted. "You like a thug? You think you can make him into a gentleman?"

Antonio pulled his gun out and leaned it against Paulie's head. "I should kill you for what you did already."

As if knowing where his bread was buttered, Paulie relaxed his body and kept his eyes on me. "Theresa, you see what he is? Go back to your lawyer. It's safer."

"Contessa. In*side*."

I didn't move. I couldn't. He was going to shoot him. It was clear as day.

Antonio leaned his elbows on Paulie and chambered a bullet. "This is for the good of everyone," he said.

"After what we been through, it comes to this? You're going to shoot me for a woman? I killed for you, man. I stuck a dead dick down a dead throat for you."

"Antonio. Don't." I was whispering, but I knew he heard me. At least, his ears heard me. There was nothing less than murder in his eyes. "Please."

"I wish I coulda tasted that magic pussy, Princess," Paulie said. "Must be something."

"Inside, Contessa. Don't make me say it again."

I stepped back into the doorway, into the shadows, shaking my head and mouthing the words *don't do it don't do it...*

"Pray, Paulo," Antonio said. "Say it with me. *Ave Maria, piena di grazia.*"

I could still see them in the slit of light between the jambs. Paulie cringed. "The Lord is with thee."

Antonio stepped back and aimed the gun.

"Tu sei benedetta fra le donne."

"And blessed is—" Paulie's voice hitched, and he continued. "The fruit of thy womb, Jesus." He leaned into the wall, but sagged, eyes shut tight.

"Santa Maria, Madre di Dio, prega per noi peccatori."

"Now and… now and…"

I stepped into the sunlight, softly. Antonio had moved backward, to the Ferrari. He leaned in the window and quietly removed the gun, his own weapon still trained on his partner.

"Finish, Paulie."

"At the hour of our death."

Paulie opened his eyes.

"*Amen*." Antonio pulled the trigger. A spray of brick dust flew out of the wall above Paulie's head, dredging his hair, and he barked a sound that was neither consonant nor vowel but a mingling of both.

Or maybe I made that sound.

"See?" Antonio said. "I shot over your head."

Antonio grabbed me by the arm and pulled me out of building. The last I saw was Paulie stumbling back as if he couldn't believe he was alive.

Antonio practically threw me into the Mas, taking off before the helicopter got over us. I had my hands over my mouth to stifle all the emotion that wanted to spill out.

"Contessa," He rolled the top up and drove slowly and legally. "What?"

"He's right," I choked out. "If something happens to you, it's my fault."

He pulled over, slammed the car into park and took my wrists in his fingers. "Listen to me."

I couldn't see him. I couldn't see anything. It was all too big. Too overwhelming. He was ready to shoot his best friend, right there, for me.

He pushed into me until all I could see was his face, his hands cupping my cheeks in my peripheral vision. I inhaled his smell of burned forests and charred cities, his voice of salted caramel. He was my world, right then, and my heart rate slowed.

"Listen. To. Me." He took a deep breath, and I felt it and mimicked what he did, calming myself by tuning my body to his. "I am responsible for the years of my life," he said. "Nothing you do will change them. This position I'm in is my own. And now, you're in it. We can talk about that later. But now, do you hear the sirens?"

I listened. Nodded.

"The shop is a half a mile away. We have only a minute to leave or we're going to be found here."

"We didn't do anything. We were just standing—"

"If I'm here, there are questions. If I'm not, there are layers of paperwork between those shots and the owner of the building."

The *thup-thup-thup* of helicopters was a few blocks away, over the store. Paulie would have left the scene, and we were just two people in a parked car, but we couldn't ignore the impending descent of the law.

I took a long blink. The crisis was over, and there were only three things left: Antonio. Me. And God.

Could I keep two realities in my head at the same time? Could I believe he was good and sound, even though I knew he committed murder while he was with me? I feared it would become too much, some day. The struggle would eat my soul until all that was left of me would be my body, the physical manifestation of ache, need, and desire.

Chapter Thirteen

THERESA

I knew there would be ramifications to Paulie's near-death experience. I'd have to deal with all of it, and yes, I was going to have to deal with my responsibility in his current state of affairs. I breathed once, twice, and I put my fear, arousal, and self-loathing behind a thick shell of ice and control. I knew it swirled underneath, an ever-growing, self-propagating ball of hysteria.

The size and power of that ball terrified me. Once we were in the car, I hardened the shell around it. Blinked. Breathed. Swallowed. Became myself.

Antonio drove like a model citizen. The police sirens died out; the *thup* of the helicopter faded away. I could tell he was trying to be calm and to breathe evenly. Eventually, his grip on the wheel loosened, and he leaned his head back on the seat.

"Will they find us?" I said. "Or Paulie? Or anything?"

"The building is owned by an offshore trust." He took a pack of cigarettes from his jacket pocket and poked one between his lips. "The police will find nothing. The insurance company will get a bill." He offered me the pack, and I declined. He pocketed it and pulled out his silver lighter. "Case closed." He lit his cigarette and snapped the lighter shut with a *clack*.

Antonio drove. Smoked. I wondered if this would be our new small talk. Instead of the weather or the financial markets, would we share a quick description of police activity and the traceability of ownership?

Since the Mas had been parked in the back, no one would know it had anything to do with the shooting. If they did know, they expected it there. The possibility that everyone in the neighborhood kept silent for their own protection occurred to me.

Antonio coiled like a spring, pushing on the steering wheel, even as he drove like the sanest, soberest man alive.

"I am going to fucking kill him." He slammed the heel of his hand on the steering wheel. "What did he think he was doing? Son of a whore. He could have killed you."

"I'm fine."

He put his hand on my cheek. His touch lit my skin in a crackle of firing nerve endings. "I'll rip him apart if anything happens to you. If he scratches you, I'll drive a knife into his heart. Do you hear me? He'll be dead before he hits the ground."

I groaned. I didn't want him to kill anyone, but I didn't want him to stop talking. "You don't need to kill for me."

"Killing him would be kindness if he hurt you." He curled his fingers into a fist. "If anyone hurts you, I will kill them."

Our lust was all mixed in with viciousness. I wanted to take it and swallow it without reservation, even if I blew apart from the intensity of it.

I took his hand and put it on my breast. "What if you hurt me?"

"*Basta.*"

"Take me, Antonio. Hurt me bad." I slid my hand between his legs. He was hard.

He turned a corner, and I saw the yellow-and-black East Side Motors sign. It had a dusting of soot on the bottom. A trailer with a logo for LoZo's Construction had been pulled onto the lot, a man sat in the back of the truck, feet dangling, eating a sandwich. Charred wood and plastic were piled to the left; burned-out cars had been moved to the right. The office side of the building was burned to the beams. The garage fared better, though there had been some damage. Antonio pulled into the garage. It stank of grease and flame. Thickness and sharpness stung the back of my throat. If black had a smell, it would be the inside of that building.

Antonio got out of the car and lowered the gate, shutting the space in darkness except for the wall connecting the office, which had burned off at the top.

I got out of the car, feeling my way along the side of it.

"Antonio? I—"

I felt him beside me a second before his hand grabbed a handful of hair and bent me over the hood of the Maserati, holding me there.

"You want it to hurt?" He pulled my skirt up and dug three fingers into my pussy as if he owned it.

"Yes, yes. Do it." I was pinned. He yanked my panties down halfway then put his wet fingers back inside me without warning.

"If you scream, there's no one in here to hear you. And you're going to scream loud enough to bring the rest of this building down."

I pushed my hips against his fingers, feeling violated and needy at the same time. I needed him to go deeper, to touch me where it hurt most. I was going to break from the inside out of he didn't bend me into nameless shapes.

He took his hand off the back of my neck and pulled my thighs apart. A gust of air cooled the wetness between my legs. He spanked my ass.

"Open your legs."

I didn't have a chance to obey before he kicked my knees apart. His tongue descended on me, the flat of it taking me from clit to asshole. His fingers worked inside, gathering moisture as his tongue worked my clit, not gently, but sucking like he meant to eat it, teeth grazing painfully, leaving waves of pleasure behind.

"Fuck me, Antonio."

"Not yet." He sucked on my clit then licked it, drawing his tongue over my ass. I'd never felt anything like it, and I cried out.

He used his fingers to wet my ass while he gave his tongue to my clit, sucking hard, then licking.

"I'm going to come, you fucking—"

"Come."

"Make it hurt!"

He shoved two fingers into my asshole and I came, pulsing around him, arching back and pushing my pelvis against the car.

"Stay still," he said when I shuddered and twitched. His cock slid into my ass, which was smooth from saliva and pussy.

"Yes!" I shouted. "Fuck!"

"Does it hurt?" he said in my ear then bit my shoulder.

"No." I wanted to hurt, to break, to get lost in pain. I was crusted and black, hardened to steel on the outside, while inside, a molten swirl grew every day I was with Antonio. The pressure of it bloated me, and the gunshots in the store had only tightened my hard-bitten skin into a translucent, paper-thin shell. He had to break it. He had to crack me and let it spill.

He jammed himself in harder, but I was too ready and too needy to think of the stretching as anything but pleasure.

"Do it until I break," I hissed. "Make me cry." I swung back at him, but he took my wrist and twisted it, pinning it against my ass.

"You're going to cry, Contessa. But not in pain." He put my knee over the hood of the car, and he got in even deeper, groaning. He went slowly, rotating his hips gently.

"You won't weep from being hurt. Not from me. You're going to shed tears from coming so hard you forget who you are. And when you return, you'll remember you're mine, and you'll cry then too." He pumped me hard, once, and I screamed in surprise. "And you'll cry again."

"Harder."

He didn't go harder; he slid carefully out and back into my ass, letting me feel every inch of him. I cursed him. He intended to make good on his promise but took his time with it, shifting my hips downward until my pussy was pressed against the hood of the car. It rubbed against the hard metal.

"You think you want me to hurt you. You don't even know what that means." I felt rocking, rocking, his hips and mine, the hood of the car, his hand holding my arm back, the escalation of pleasure on my clit, my empty pussy throbbing for something to fill it. "You have never tasted death," he said into my ear softly, as if it were a secret.

"Make me taste it." I heard the desperation in my own voice, the pain of need.

"I can't bring you back."

"Put it on my tongue. Take me all the way. Please."

"No," he said.

In the dim light, his face close to mine, I saw his jaw clench, his eyes get hard. He pulled me back by the throat and put his other hand between my legs. I don't know how many fingers he wedged into my cunt while his dick was in my ass, but I was full and covered too, with and his warm wrist on my wet clit and his body above mine. I felt protected under his thrusts, even if I'd never be safe again. I let myself crack. The fissure opened and the molten lava poured, pressing against the blackened case of control, smashing it until I screamed as if I were being rent open.

I was made of heat. The cold shell shattered into sharp-edged chips and floated away in the fiery river. I was consumed so completely I screamed in the pain of loss and pleasure of emptiness.

Antonio, the catalyst for my dissolution, the destroyer of my façade, put his lips to the back of my neck. I didn't know who I was anymore, but I was his.

And I wept.

Chapter Fourteen

THERESA

Two bathrooms had survived the fire. Antonio let me take the nicer one. I washed up and came out sore and emotionally drained. I didn't have a thought in my head, only a need to see him.

I heard him before I saw him, rattling off in Italian. I'd never had a talent for languages, but right then, I wanted to learn to speak to him in his. I wanted to sing with him to that same song, to tell secret jokes in the same melody.

I followed his voice to his burned-out office. He was freshly scrubbed and brushed, poking a charred two-by-four with the toe of his dress shoe. I kissed him. His mouth was minty and soft. His face was clean, and when he touched my cheek, his tenderness was a balm on the damage he'd inflicted with those same hands.

He said a few short words over the phone and clicked off.

"What would you say if I sent you away?" he said.

"Sent me away?"

"Back home. My home. I think if I can't protect you, my father can. Until things blow over here. Or until I can go back there."

"There is no way, Capo. No way in hell. I have a family here. I have friends. I can't just get sent away. It doesn't work like that. And I won't be away from you."

"If Paulie ends up running an empire, whatever happens will be my fault," he said.

"The last thirty-four years are my own. And the last couple of months are mine, as well. If something happens to me, it's not your fault. It's mine. I own this."

"No. You don't. I dragged you into hell. Now I have to get you out in one piece."

He put his arm around me, and we looked through the space where the window had been, onto the broken glass and carbon chips that made up his shop, like an old couple on a porch, reminiscing about how the neighborhood used to be.

"What are you going to do?" I asked.

"About?"

"Your accountant?"

"Dime a dozen."

"He went to Paulie?" I asked.

"Everyone loves a winner."

I leaned against a circular-saw table and crossed my arms. Antonio put his hands in his pockets.

"You just nearly blew Paulie's head off," I said.

"Give me credit. If I wanted him dead—"

"And he shot at us."

"He was aiming over our heads." By his tone, I could tell Antonio wasn't defending Paulie but mocking his excuse as one would mock a child who blamed his baseball bat for yet another broken window. "Asshole. I don't want to kill him; I want to rip his heart out."

"I mean it. We have a deal."

"I know, Contessa. We have a deal. I hope to God that you live to be the most beautiful old woman in history."

"I need you to end this, Antonio. Before I lose you. This has to stop."

I put my arms around his waist, and he held me so close I felt the blood in his veins.

Chapter Fifteen

THERESA

I woke up the next morning in a panic. My rib cage felt like a twisted coil around my lungs. I needed to get out of bed, or my spinning brain was going to lift me six inches off the mattress.

I couldn't think about Antonio, where he was or who he was meeting. He'd conducted his business his whole life without getting killed. I had to assume he knew what he was doing.

Daniel was a talking head again. Polls were looking better, but the outcome was touch and go. The local elections were scheduled for March. Four months. I knew Daniel. He wasn't done with Antonio and me. He was gathering clouds for a February storm.

My phone buzzed. I snapped it up without even looking at the caller.

"Tee Dray," said a familiar voice.

"Directrix. How is it going? Do you need me?"

"Uh, yeah. Have you ever been in for questioning?"

"By whom?" I asked.

"LAPD. I lost half a day of edit."

"What did they want?"

"Why don't you come by? I have some questions about your notes. It would really speed things up if I had you around this afternoon."

KATRINA HADN'T BEEN SHELTERED as a child. Her parents hadn't had a lick of money until middle age, and by then, their daughter had been exposed to enough of the realities of Los Angeles. She knew how to answer questions from the police, something I'd given exactly zero thought to my whole life.

"What happened?" I whispered as she walked me down the hall.

"Remember the day your hot boyfriend came with food for the crew?"

"Yeah?"

"They wanted to know about that." She stopped at the editing-bay door. "They wanted to know what he was wearing, where you went for dinner."

"What did you tell them?"

"Everything." She opened the door.

She went in like it was nothing, and I got in behind her and slammed the door closed. We were alone in the darkened room with only the blue light of the monitors highlighting the curves of her face.

"Like what?" I asked, my tone an accusation.

"What?" She shrugged. "He came. He brought dinner. To seduce you, I figured. And nice job, by the way…"

"Were they asking specifically about *me*?"

"They're lawyers. They don't need to ask. But yeah, that's what they were getting at."

I tapped my fingers on the back of the chair. There was an equation at work, with Daniel sitting to the right of the equal sign.

"He said he was done protecting me," I said. "Looks like he meant it."

"Have you done anything? What happened with Scotty?"

The loan shark Scott Mabat, had shaken down Katrina for her post-production money, threatened her life, refused payment, and eventually run afoul of Antonio. He'd landed in the hospital and was back on the street in a week.

"I pointed a gun at his head and pulled the trigger." I said it as if delivering the news at nine. Who knew what looking death in the face had done to him? If he'd felt threatened enough, he might have gone to the cops, which would have eventually led him to Daniel.

"You what?" Katrina said.

"It wasn't loaded."

"Okay, Tee." She held her hands out as if pushing me away. "This is way, way out of my league right now."

"I didn't shoot him."

"What do you want, a cookie? Holy fuck. Holy fucking fuck. You're pulling triggers on people?"

"He was going to hurt you," I said.

"Oh, no. No no no no. Just, no. I would have gone to the cops."

"And lost the movie?"

"Which I'm going to lose anyway, right now, if my script supervisor and the woman financing postproduction shoots people. Holy fuck, no! They can freeze your assets. Then they can stop post. Everything here can go to hell! God dammit, Theresa!"

"Next time someone threatens to gang-rape you, I'll just give them your address."

She growled, closing her eyes and clenching her fists, as if the anger inside her had to be released before she could say another word. "God, Tee Dray!"

Quick as a snake, but with better intentions, she wrapped her arms around me, squeezing my elbows to my sides.

"Can you lighten up? I can't breathe." I pushed her away. "Did the lawyers ask how you were financing post?"

She pulled back and dropped into a chair. It swiveled and squeaked before stabilizing. "No."

"Then why do you look so guilty?"

"They asked if Antonio was involved with the movie. I said no. He just brought dinner that one time, and it looked as if he was trying to get into your pants. They asked if he did, and I said I wasn't sure. And before you get upset, that's the best answer to give them, because it's all about the doubt, and since I never saw you actually doing it..."

"I get it," I said.

"So, they asked every detail of that night, and if I'd seen him again, and I told them I saw him at your loft the night you banged up your car."

I sat down. I had entered a non-emotional state, and I just took in everything she said. Much could be missed if I got upset or let her push my sympathies.

"From beginning to end, Directrix."

"They said Scott went to the hospital. He wasn't coherent for days, but when he started talking, he implicated *me* in getting the shit beaten out of him but wouldn't say anything else. Now, I was at my parents' place in Orange County, and there's a credit-card trail and a dozen people who saw me getting drunk at my old hangout. So, first they threatened me, but I knew they had nothing. Then they started asking questions about you and Antonio. I denied everything because I never thought you'd be involved. And I still can't believe it. Still."

She looked at me as if I'd just lied when I'd told her what had happened in the shipping container.

"Wait, wait," I asked. "Did they come because they wanted to know about Antonio's involvement? Or because they wanted to know if you had something to do with that scumbag getting beaten up."

"You said scumbag."

"Why did they come?"

She swiveled in her chair and hit the spacebar on one of the keyboards. The monitor flashed brighter. She faced it.

"They were fishing." *Tap tap tap*. I was being shut out.

"Katrina."

"I don't know you anymore. I mean, I thought at first it was all crap. I thought they had it all wrong about everything. You know, like it was just Danny being a dick. But you? *You*? You scare me."

When she looked up at me, her eyes were big and scared and determined all at once. She'd grown up with good parents in a bad neighborhood and had a healthy fear of anything illegal. "This is all I've ever wanted my whole life. I had it and lost it. I'm getting it back. My job. My work. This movie is happening. I can't let anything get in the way."

"Is my financing it getting in the way?" It hurt to even say it. Giving her money felt like the only productive thing I'd done in my life.

"I don't know," she said.

"Fine. We'll talk about this later."

"Don't be mad."

"I'm not. I understand. I can't…" I swallowed. I could barely continue. "It's not right if I sully your work."

"It's not that." She turned toward me then away.

"It is, and you know it," I said.

"I keep thinking it would be easier if I could just get a studio to back me again. Even without LAPD hanging over the thing and the paper trail back to a loan shark. Michael's amazing. I might cut together a trailer and see if I can get Overland behind this picture. The odds are impossible, but what the hell, right? I mean, after I got Scott involved like some film-school amateur, I deserve the problems I've gotten. It's my responsibility to get out of them."

"Just let me know." My voice must have been thick, because she stood up and put her hands on my shoulders.

"I don't want to hurt you."

I backed up. I didn't want her hands on my shoulders, and I didn't want to talk anymore. I felt filthy, and I had a compulsion to leave before she saw the depth of my wickedness.

She was worried about hurting me, but she had it backwards. I was the one who wound up hurting her every time I tried to help her. God damn Daniel for not just leaving her alone, and God damn me for not finding a way to shut him down. I went downstairs with my head held high and my shoulders lowered from the weight on them. Otto opened the car door for me. I was a princess with unearned graces, a sparkly package with a bomb inside. I couldn't live like that. I couldn't go about my business and watch people get hurt without taking action.

When Otto stopped at a light, I leaned forward. "Are you going to eat lunch?" I asked.

"Now that you mention it..." He patted his stomach.

"How about In-n-Out? You can get me an Animal Style."

His eyes lit up. "Great idea."

I know I smiled, but I was so angry I could barely think. I transmitted none of that in my face or body language. I knew anyone who saw me wouldn't know what was going on in my mind, or sense my heart palpitations. Except Antonio. From day one, he knew what my body was doing when no one else did. Good thing he wasn't there to see me thinking through what I wanted to do to Daniel.

Otto pulled into the lot, and while he was waiting on line, I slipped away. I didn't like doing it, and I knew he'd get into trouble, but I needed to breathe and to make my own decision about how to handle Katrina.

Chapter Sixteen

ANTONIO

I tried to make peace with Paulie because Theresa had asked me to and because she was right. Doing things for Theresa's sake was getting to be a habit.

Donna Maria Carloni agreed to broker the peace, and surprisingly, Paulie agreed to show up. I'd been Donna Maria's *consigliere* for two years, and I was convinced Paulie wouldn't let her broker anything. I was wrong.

I never should have been in the life. My father saw that it would eat me alive, but from the minute I walked in to him and demanded vengeance for Valentina, and he took the demand from me and gave it to one of his men, I was in. I didn't even want to be, but I had changed, and the power and freedom that came with being *camorristi* became a need. He had no other way to protect me from myself and from the people coming after me.

Since then, not one second of my life had been my own. I was the property of Benito Racossi, his *consigliere.* His right hand, protected and enslaved. Then I moved on to be Donna Maria's *consigliere* as payment for a debt. I was never my own man.

I must have been confusing for Theresa. I had to appreciate that. I was reluctant to expose her to the life but, at the same time, drew her in. I worshipped her virtue while destroying it. I murdered men even as I feared God's justice. My mother had told me that a man who held the idea that he was good in his right hand and the knowledge that he was damned in his left was destined to live half a life.

The hills were a sunbaked brown and dark grey-green, thick with brush and spotted with chunky rocks, like Naples, without the ever-present shadow of *Vesuvio,* still and silent but boiling inside.

I turned in to a nondescript dirt driveway that any casual observer would have missed, which led to the ass end of Whittier Narrows. No one was supposed to live there. It was a preserve, not meant for residences, but Donna Maria Carloni's dead husband had worked it out forty years ago and created an inviolate right-of-way. To attack Donna Maria, a person would have to trespass on government land, and then pass a gantlet of cameras. She ended four underbosses with her own hands to regain her husband's perch at the top of East Los Angeles's mafia pyramid.

I made a hand sign to tree-perched camera: one thumb pressed against the center of my pointer finger, where the scar was. The white gate appeared a hundred feet later with another camera mounted on top of it. It opened.

A quarter mile along the brushy dirt drive, I tipped my head right, then left. The still unripe fruits of the olive trees hung heavy. The last time I'd been there, two weeks before, they'd been harvesting on rickety wooden ladders. I'd been politely summoned and told that Vito had to be dealt with. I found him trading in pictures of girls—babies—and threw him hard enough to dislocate his shoulder. We didn't do that. *Camorristi* did not keep prostitutes or traffic women. We did not make money on the backs of children, and we did not ever sexualize them.

But although that was offense enough to get Vito killed, what broke my crew was the valet parking. Men opened little businesses like that to make extra cash. It was a simple thing, but ended with him betraying Paulie and me.

He started the valet business to do something honest. The little shit pedophile was trying to go legitimate, and for that, for doing what I wanted to start but didn't think I could finish, I destroyed him. I let my temper get the best of me. I chased him. I shot at him. I pulled him out of his house in Griffith Park and threw him down a hill. And from that point on, my reputation as a man who kept control of himself and his crew spiraled downward. It happened faster than I thought it could.

In the weakness came an opening, and in the opening, men's ambitions flowed. One man's ambitions made him chase Theresa down the freeway to kidnap her. Another trapped her into attempting murder.

A *camorrista* accepted that death could come at any time, for any reason. The sins of a boss were visited on his crew. It was a trade we accepted. We could be killed, but our families and our women wouldn't be touched. And when I became the boss of our corner of Los Angeles, I grew eyes in the back of my head to watch for the knives.

The *camorristi* didn't answer to Donna Maria, but we didn't ignore her either. We did our business because if we actually had the desire to band together, it would be more trouble for her to fight us than to take the loss.

The house lay low to the ground with a corrugated tin panel jutting over the doorway. Potted succulents and cactuses covered the cracked concrete and walls. From the outside, with its rows of citrus trees on the right and left and the sweet smell of the olive trees, it felt like being back in Naples.

I got out of the car. The alarm went on with a chirp. Useless automation. There was no safer car in California.

"*Consigliere*," came a voice from behind me. I didn't turn around but put my hands out, palms in front.

"Ruggero," I said. "That's not my job anymore."

I felt his hands on me, checking my shoulders, waist, back, and heels. He was a big guy and a pussycat. Even though I faced the other direction, I know Skinny Carlo was next to him. Skinny Carlo was sixty-five kilos, drenched in seawater, but he was responsible for much of Donna Carloni's dirty work.

"You run around unarmed like one." Skinny Carlo had a voice like a serrated knife.

"I left it in the glove compartment." I turned and flipped him the keys. They twirled in the sun a second before he snatched them out of the air. "It's loaded and cleaned. Treat her nice."

"We wasn't expecting you for an hour. She's not seeing no one," Ruggero said.

"Right."

I walked into the house.

Donna Maria was not interested in how things looked. She preferred misdirection. So, her home looked like a Sicilian ghetto house, decorated with faded floral curtains and browned crocheted table coverings underneath chipped porcelain figurines of children. She'd had eleven babies and had shipped them all back to the mother country to be educated.

I walked through the dark house to the backyard. I was convinced she slept in the dirt somewhere on her eight acres.

The sun seemed brighter back there. Not just vivid, but merciless. Stacks of hutches on both sides stretched back into a distant orchard, and in the wood and wire boxes were animals. There were rabbits to the right and, to the left, small creatures with fur so sleek they could only be minks.

In front of me stood a table three feet high with wood sides and wire mesh stretched over the top. The mesh was crusted with black.

The boss of the biggest Sicilian family east of the Los Angeles river was a handful of sticks wrapped around the middle with twine, no taller than five-two and starvation thin with hair that had more salt than pepper. She made her way to us with the surefootedness of a woman whose feet hadn't bothered with pavement in a while. In her right hand she carried a twitching white rabbit by its hind legs and, in her left, a two-foot shaft of hard wood. As soon as I saw it, I took my jacket off and draped it over the back of a chair.

"*Consigliere*," she called out. Even though we both spoke Italian, I could barely understand her; the Sicilian accent was as thick as tomato paste. "I expected you."

"I'm here, but you have no *consigliere*."

"There are no Italian lawyers to be had. Not for love or money." She wiggled the rabbit back and forth. It squirmed a little, dropping its ears.

"American ones know the system well enough." I rolled up my sleeves. This was not particularly messy work, but I still needed be cautious, and I couldn't avoid the work altogether. If I demurred, I'd lose the advantage of my lineage and culture.

"I won't lower my standards." She handed me the club. It was blacker on the business end and slicked brown and smooth on the grip side. "Americans are weak and mouthy. They don't show respect, and they die with secrets on the way out of their mouths."

She held the rabbit out over the wire-mesh table.

"They love life too much, Donna." I tapped the back of the rabbit's head, getting my aim right, favoring accuracy over strength. It was the only humane method, and if I hesitated for one breath, she'd notice. This, like everything, was a test.

"And you," she said. "Do you like running your crew more than sitting by my side?"

"I do." I brought the club to the back of the rabbit's head, where the ears met the neck. The death was soundless, with only a hollow thud to alert the universe that it had happened.

"You were doing fine at it, too." She held out the rabbit and let it bleed out of its nose and mouth onto the black gravel. "Until a couple of weeks ago." She shook it a little, letting the last of the blood fall away.

"I had it under control." I took the dead rabbit from her and held it over the grass by its heels as she twisted a valve on the side of the house and picked up a hose. "I admit I failed with Paulie. I didn't expect him to turn on me."

"That's very grown-up of you. And that's why you made a good *consigliere*. You know when you fuck up." She hosed down the rabbit until its fur was matted and flat, and there was no blood on the surface. I turned it so she could get the back, letting the fouled water drip onto the gravel until it flowed clean. She shut off the hose, and I put the rabbit on the grate.

Back home, small animals peeked out of the ruined mountains to peck at the garbage and city families were so poor that a piece of meat didn't get away just because it ran fast. Despite my father's position, my mother had run the house as a single parent, and rabbit and raccoon were frequently on the menu.

"So," she said, opening a small knife. "You came early for the rabbit cacciatore, yeah?"

"I came here for an indulgence."

"Ask." She passed me the knife by the handle side. She wanted to me to do the honors. That was her way of saying I was favored because of my background, and to refuse would be to throw her favor back in her face.

"I have a woman." I cut the skin inside the rabbit's thigh and up to the gut.

"I've heard." She smiled and took out a beedie, a short, black cigar with a smell that reminded me of the garbage piled on the side of a Neapolitan highway.

"She's a good woman."

"She was in bed with that *sbirro*."

I slashed inside the rabbit's other thigh, right through the animal's penis. "That's over. She's loyal to me." I held the rabbit's hind legs and yanked the skin off it then looked at my boss with the inside-out animal in my hands. "Once this thing with Paulie is done, I don't want her looked at or questioned. She's with me."

"You say this is a small thing."

"It is," I protested.

"In America, yes. You can have your personal life. You marry for love. But that's not where you're from. Not with the job you have. You don't own your life."

I cleanly slashed the rabbit's center muscles from gut to neck. Green-grey organs spilled out onto the mesh. I realized I was wound tight from fingers to core. I switched the knife hand and flexed my fingers.

She was a skinny thing, the donna, but she was formidable, ruthless, and protected. Too many men had made the mistake of underestimating her. Even though I knew my fingers could break her neck, those fingers would be attached to a dead man before they even touched her.

"You, *consigliere,* are part of something bigger than yourself." She picked up the hose. "You are a man of traditions. And you are not just any man in this tradition. You are a prince. Do you think a prince can just marry anyone he wants? He has his king to consider. His country. The blood of his children. His own future." She sprayed the rabbit carcass down, and the grey entrails fell onto the mesh. "You want some sweet pussy, you keep it. But you don't marry it. Everyone knows this. You don't contaminate your family or your business."

"Let me worry about my business. You worry about yours."

"I am." She took the carcass from me. "You've heard about my granddaughter and Patalano?"

"Suspected."

"Well, I wanted to be the one to tell you anyway. Paulie Patalano is taking Irene. He's going to be a powerful man. You ready for that?"

"I can handle it." My phone buzzed in my pocket. It was Otto.

"Good. Come inside," she said.

"Un momento."

She went and left me. I picked up. "Otto."

"I'm sorry, boss. I lost her."

I closed my eyes. Jesus Christ. Where could she be going? Why would she sneak away? I cursed everything: my vulnerability, my love, my powerlessness. The only thing that kept me from leaving to sniff her out was the knowledge that Paulie wouldn't do anything while we were supposed to be negotiating a truce.

"Find her. Just find her."

Chapter Seventeen

THERESA

The Downtown Gate Club was in the middle of the city, down a turn to the left on Venice Boulevard and a right on Ludwig Street, where the streets took on a little curve, and the trees shading the rare brick row houses stood farther from the curb. A couple of blocks of oddball houses in the last sweet corner of downtown made the perfect enclave for those daring enough to make that neighborhood their home.

A person from the north might pass it by without noticing it. But old-money Angelinos who found Bel-Air tacky, those born into a level of privilege it might take decades to wean from, knew better. They knew to turn down the driveway of a brick building with stonecarved window treatments that sat ten feet from its neighbor. The building had been one of a row of businesses as early as the eighteen-fifties, complete with basements and stone foundations.

"Miss Drazen," the guard said as he pulled out his clipboard. "You here for the LA Democratic Summit?"

I was, and I wasn't, but I needed to get past the gate, and if he looked at the clipboard and found I wasn't there, he'd let me in but not check me into the Heritage Room. "I'm here for Daniel Brower."

"I just saw him." He opened the gate.

The DGC was visible on satellite, but from the street, it was surrounded by enough houses and foliage that passersby wouldn't notice an eighteen-hole golf course. Transplants didn't know it existed. LA natives knew it was there, but few had been inside. The club didn't try to go stealth; it simply wasn't glamorous or flashy. It wasn't a desirable place to be, outside of certain circles, and the board did everything in its power to stay under the radar.

I left my little blue BMW with the valet. He eyed the dent on the passenger side and said something polite before coasting away. A tall man in a uniform opened the glass and brass door for me.

The Heritage Room was as old as the club, somewhere on the order of one hundred and fifty years old. The walls and floor were stone, and the ceiling crisscrossed with beams the thickness of a ship's mast. The "Heritage" in question was the heritage of success, which tended to follow all its members. Glass cases held trophies, medals, photos, certificates, and plaques from elite tournaments. When my father had brought me there at the tender age of eight, I'd been impressed by the shiny artifacts, the high ceiling, and the marble. I'd stared at the pictures of my father and grandfather, trying to discern the real men through the oil paint and how their own moods and words came through the canvas. But not much came through. The men were painted to erase their Irish heritage. They looked like mouse-haired WASPs. I hadn't thought about the dulling of the fire in their hair since I was an adolescent, and seeing it again irritated me anew.

"Theresa!" Gerry came out in a light-grey suit and dress shoes, smiling at the dozen straitlaced politicians dotting the room. Gerry was Daniel's political strategist. I'd spilled my guts to him one night, when he picked me up from set, and I'd been wondering about the state of my sanity.

"Hi, Ger."

He kissed my cheek and gently led me to the doors that opened out to the golf course, where we couldn't be heard. "To what do we owe this surprise visit?"

"Wanted to talk to Dan."

"He's in the conference room." I stepped toward it, and Gerry put his hand on my shoulder to stop me. "Wait."

"Yes?"

"Let me get him."

"It's fine. I know about Clarice. It's not going to be a scene."

He twisted his face into a half smile that meant he was going to say something difficult. "I know you'd never make a scene. Neither would he. And Clarice isn't here yet. But it's not that."

I crossed my arms. "Describe it, then." A fake laugh echoed through the room. I recognized the ex-mayor Rubin right away.

Gerry took a deep breath, calculated to let me know the conversation was hard for him. "Who you're seeing is going to get out. Eventually."

"Oh, you're kidding—"

"You can't pretend it won't have a negative effect on his candidacy. And I'd hate to say this thing is in the bag so soon, but if—no, *when*—he wins, it's going to be a pressure point, even if you don't keep showing up."

"Theresa?" Daniel had found me. He put his hand on my shoulder.

"Hi, Dan."

He kissed me on the cheek, and Gerry cleared his throat, looking around to check if anyone had seen.

"Take it easy, Gerry," Daniel said, his hand still on my bicep.

Gerry smiled and folded his hands in front of him. "This is lovely. So happy we're all getting along. Now"—he opened a wooden door with a window set into it and dropped his voice—"get the fuck out of sight."

He pushed Daniel past the door but did it gently, by the hip, so it didn't look like he was being pushed. Then he closed the door.

The office belonged to the Heritage president, and some of the oldest medals in the club's possession were shelved there.

I wanted to break all of them. As soon as the door clicked, I turned on Daniel, keeping my voice at a low growl. "Do not ever, ever send your team of pit bulls after my friends. If you want to know something, you come to *me*."

"This is about the director?"

"Don't play games," I said.

He sat down on the leather couch as if I'd said nothing at all. He'd learned something from me, apparently. I was the one who got calm during a fight, and he was the one who flew off the handle. Well, that was about to change, because I suddenly understood what it meant to deal with a passive aggressive.

"You went to Katrina about Antonio. That is not acceptable."

"You should sit down." He sat back with his arms in front of him. But I knew all about his strategies and body language: the position of his arms and what it transmitted, how he could speak without speaking, and how he could say two things at once. Adopting a pose was a big part of what Daniel and I did together, and hands in front was meant to project a simple honesty, even when it was a lie. "My office is following leads on a money-laundering scam through a restaurant in San Pedro. It's public knowledge."

I remained standing. "I don't want you harassing my friends."

"I don't want you fucking a known criminal while I'm running for office, but we don't always get what we want."

I didn't know what I'd expected. The visit was impulsive. I hadn't prepared Daniel, and I hadn't prepared myself.

"You're turning your professional bailiwick into a personal vendetta."

"Give me a break. You want a personal vendetta? I've got your sister Margie on wiretapping. Your brother has a few shady real-estate deals in his portfolio. Another sister's got two potentially illegal adoptions. And the other one, fuck. What the fuck happened at Westonwood sixteen years ago? And as for your father, don't even get me started on his disgusting personal tastes, which everyone knows and no one talks about. I've had a personal vendetta to protect you and your family, and let me tell you, it's wearing thin. I could take your entire family down faster than I could take Antonio Spinelli down. But I don't because of what we had. Because I respect it. So don't come in here and tell me how to do my job."

I threw my bag down next to him and stepped forward until my knees were in front of his. "Daniel, let's talk about respect. What it means."

I leaned over, putting one hand on the arm of the couch and one on the back, bending until my lips were at his ear.

"Tink, please." He tried to push me away, but the effort was half-hearted.

"Respect isn't treating me like I'm made of sugar. Because I'm not. I'm made of cum and saliva. I'm made of salty sweat, and I taste like fucking. I sound like an orgasm that's so hard you can't even scream, and I fuck like a closed fist."

He turned to me until his breath was on my cheek. I heard him swallow.

"Do you want me?" I knew the answer. "I can feel your fingers twitching. You want to stick them in me. You want to see if I'm wet. You're confused because I don't usually make you this hard Because you *respect* me. Women you respect don't make your balls ache."

"Jesus, Tink." He was barely breathing.

"You're hard."

He reached for my breast, and I caught him at the wrist and pinned it to the back of the couch.

"If you knew me, you'd respect me. If you respected me, you wouldn't threaten my family. And you wouldn't even breathe my lover's name."

He deflated, though his dick was still rigid under his trousers. I stood straight.

"Since we're doing threats, let's talk about the illegal campaign contributions, the filthy texts. There's enough borderline stuff I know about you to sink your career. But if you fuck with me, it's going to be my civic duty to tell the *LA Times* about how I helped you with your struggles with overseas taxation."

"You wouldn't."

"Fuck with me," I said. "Please. I want you to. I want to shed a tear, telling the *Times* about how we opened accounts for the express purpose of your tax efficiency two weeks before you lobbied to pass laws against them."

I crossed my arms and set my mouth. We stared at each other.

"This sounds like an impasse," he said.

"Then we understand each other."

I backed up and reached for the knob. Quicker than I would have thought possible with that rod of an erection, he got up and put his hand over mine. "How is he going to react to you being here? Is he going to be able to hold himself together long enough for you to win his war for him?"

"You're implying I'm being used?" I asked.

"Implying?"

"Dan, you don't know the half of it. And it's not my responsibility to tell you anything." I pushed my bag farther up my shoulder and faced the door, putting my fingers on the seam at the jamb. "But I will tell you this: he is genuine. Maybe not in the ways you care about, but I've never been loved the way he loves me. He loves me recklessly, to the misuse of everything else in his life. What kind of woman would I be if I let him get careless for me?"

"He's playing you."

"He's not. I've been used before, and it didn't feel anything like this." I stole a glance up at him. I'd hit him just where I wanted to.

A soft knock came through the wood of the door. I looked through the frosted glass to the light-grey shadow of Gerry.

"We're on," Gerry said.

Daniel opened the door.

I said a few hellos to the people I'd known in my past life as they filed into the conference room, and I walked out unscathed.

Chapter Eighteen

ANTONIO

I could smell the rabbit cacciatore from the yard, where I swirled a jelly glass of sweet wine and walked along the rows of hutches. A slinky mink nibbled on the wire of her cage, and I leaned down to stroke her nose. Paulie was due in fifteen minutes. We'd make a cautious peace. He'd marry Donna Maria's granddaughter and run an empire. And then?

Then, I'd make the impossible happen. I'd get out. It had to be done. Even if I got out of Los Angeles to avoid Paulie, I'd be expected to continue in the life, and Theresa would never fit. The only option was to secretly unwind everything in my life and live the rest of it out with her. I didn't know when or exactly how. I didn't know if it would be done during peace or war. But I knew it would be done. Then my Contessa could be released from the cage I had to put her in.

Far in the front of the property, I heard a car engine get louder then stop. It was Paulie, undoubtedly. I didn't react to knowing he was there, close enough to shoot at me again.

Fabric rustled behind me, and I turned. "Hello," I said to the girl before me. Her mane of dark curls contrasted with her white shirt. She had Donna Maria's brown eyes, without the hardness.

"Hi. Grandma said I should come and see if you wanted anything."

"Anything?"

She shrugged and smiled. "Sure."

I handed her the empty jelly glass and spoke to her in Italian. "You're from Sicily?"

"*Si.*" She took the glass. "I mean, no. I was born here, but I've lived there since I was six."

"And you're how old now?"

"Twenty."

She looked about that, with her lips parted in a smile and skin so smooth she looked like a painting. She looked as if she'd never cried a day in her life. She reminded me of Valentina, my wife, and I was blindsided by the memory. She had been one of the truly beautiful things in my life, before I became everything my mother tried to stop me from being.

"What's your name?" I asked.

"Irene."

"I'm Antonio."

"I know. Grandma said."

"What else did she say?"

She smiled and looked away then looked up and swung her hand out, speaking English in a thick Italian accent. "'Go find the man outside and get him something. Stand up straight. He is Antonio Spinelli, a prince. Treat him like one.' Then she threw me out."

"I'm no prince."

"*Camorrista* from a long line? Kind of prince-like."

"A bastard son."

"Or just a bastard?" She kicked a hip out and shot me half a smile.

"For such an innocent-looking girl," I said, "You flirt shamelessly."

"At home, I don't get to. My mother won't let me look a man in the eye. Here, it's expected. I kind of like it." She looked me in the eye and waggled her brows. She was cute. We walked back to the house slowly, hands in pockets.

"What you're doing is very dangerous," I said. "If you pick up bad habits here, the boys back home will start talking. Then they'll start doing. It's not flirting anymore after that."

"You sound like my father." She flashed a pout worthy of a 1940s Hollywood drama.

"He's a wise man."

"All business." She waved me away. "Cigarettes and gasoline. But he won't let me smoke or drive."

I laughed. Poor kid. Then I realized she'd told me her father's businesses, and thus, her lineage.

"You're Calogero Carloni's daughter?"

"Yep. The Princess of Sciacca! I want to die. Jesus."

"Hey, watch your mouth."

She puckered it in response.

"Why did you come here?" I asked. "To Los Angeles. College?"

She laughed. "You don't know?" I stopped and she stopped with me. We faced each other. "There's a wedding in a few weeks. I'm expected. So are you, I'd think."

"I never miss a wedding if I can help it."

"I got a light-blue dress," she said. "What color are you wearing?"

"Haven't given it much thought."

She shrugged and turned on her heel. I noticed her feet were bare. "Someone else was here for you. Should I bring the wine to the dining room?"

"Please."

She went ahead of me, her hips flirting with me while her face was turned away.

I walked back to the house. As if a box had opened and giggles came out, it was suddenly populated with children. Three ran past, screaming and bumping, none taller than waist high. They joked in pidgin Italian from deep in the south of the boot and colored with Anglicisms. I swore I heard one say, "Dude," before rattling off a series of baseball stats.

"Don't shoot."

I heard Paulie's voice but didn't need to look around. "You'd be dead if I wanted you dead."

"Yeah, yeah. I don't expect an apology."

"I don't owe you one."

Donna Maria shuffled in from the dining room. "You two quit it."

She slid open a big wooden pocket door, revealing a small study with heavy chairs and dark fabrics. A deeply masculine room, it looked inherited directly from her late husband.

Paulie went in first. Two men were at either side of the window. They had risen to their feet when the door had opened. One was Skinny Carlo; the other was a clean-cut gentleman in a full suit, about forty years old. I didn't recognize him.

"Carlo," I said as Paulie sat.

"Spin," said Carlo.

I turned to the man I didn't know. "Antonio."

He didn't say anything. The cuckoo clock over his head ticked loudly. I could hear the gears grinding.

Donna Maria shuffled in. "Don't mind him."

"I'll forget to mind him when I know who he is."

"He's from the old country."

"Mine or yours?"

She laughed to herself. A clear, crystal Virgin lighter, about the size of an eggplant, wobbled when she sat behind her desk. It had a brass metal head that flipped up to reveal the flint. These things made better paperweights than lighters, but that didn't stop old Italian ladies from buying them. I'd seen about a hundred of the monstrosities in my life.

"There's only one, but if you have to know…" She waved her hand at the stranger.

"Aldo," said the man. "From Portici. I'm sent to make sure this runs smooth. So we don't have any trouble with our friends from the south." He spoke in an Italian I knew well, the spiraling tones of my hometown clicking together like gears.

"I don't need to be watched."

"He ain't watching you." Donna Maria sat back in her chair, her body filling in the worn spots in the leather. "He's watching me. Ain't you, Aldo?"

Aldo didn't answer.

"All right. Let's get down to it," she said. "This thing with you two, it's bad for business. Not just your business, but mine, because if I gotta get into it with you to keep the peace—"

"It wouldn't be a peace," Paulie interjected.

"You can put it back in your pants. As an interested third party, I'm just here to make sure all's fair and send you two on your way. I don't need to tell you that what's done in here is done. What's agreed is law. What is said is true under God and the Holy Virgin. Yes?"

I made the sign of the cross. Paulie and the two men sitting behind Donna Maria did the same, even though it wasn't their job to agree; it was their job to listen.

"*Bene,*" Donna Maria said, fingering a piece of paper. "We got a nice chunk of territory east of the river and north of Arroyo Seco. Biggest hunk of camorra territory in the country. You guys got tobacco, real estate, protection, and something happening with a garment factory on Marmion. Good job, that. No tributes to pay, either. Nice to be Neapolitan."

Paulie snickered. I lit a cigarette with my own lighter. She didn't know all of what we had, but she didn't have to. She only had to know that within our territory, she could push all the drugs she needed without interference, and though she didn't officially run prostitution, she managed to squeeze cash out of a few pimps working in the soot of the

110. We split the local councils and brokered the bigger politicians individually. When shit broke out with the gangs, we negotiated the area as a solid block. It was a good system, and I was invested in keeping it intact. We loved peace. Peace was profitable.

"I have a proposal," I said. "Geographic. Split at the railroad tracks. I take east."

"You take west," said Paulie.

"The shop is mine. What's left of it."

"Split along the foothills through Avenue 37," offered Donna Maria.

"That cuts the commercial district by half a mile," Paulie said. "Do this. He gets three blocks at the edge of the foothills, and I get the outer ring up to the river and the arroyo"

"Fine," I said. That gave me the garment factory and the shop. That was all I needed in the end. He could have the commercial sector if he thought he could make any money off it.

"When he bails on us, I get his stake," Paulie said.

"What?" I said.

"*Eh*?" Donna Maria said.

Oh, that son of a whore going to try and corner me. I should have shot him when I had the chance.

"See how easy this was?" Paulie continued, holding his hands out to indicate the room, the people, the agreement. "I would say, normally, he's just going to grease me first chance he gets, but he woulda done that yesterday if he coulda." He turned to me. "I ain't afraid of you. I'm a made man. If you take me out, you're gonna lose your dick. So I been trying to figure what you're doing. Sat up all night, thinking. Tick tock, all night, listening to that clock, and it wasn't till the sun came up that I realized. You're getting your shit in order. You want out of the life."

There was a dead silence that was filled with the ticking of the cuckoo clock and the laughter of the children outside.

Donna Maria laid her gaze on me. I didn't have to answer the charge, serious as it was. I didn't have to entertain the challenge or defend myself. I could leave it hanging with a laugh and a wave of my hand. But with Donna Maria looking at me, and the clock ticking over Aldo's head, I knew I had to counter the charge.

"Let me tell you something. My great-great-grandfather carried a *carabina* for Liborio Romano when the *Atto Sovrano* was nailed to a tree. And not a generation has passed without an olive tree being planted for us. Not one grows that my grandfather didn't oversee the pricing, and my father, even now, fixes the price of every kilo. My family is in the orchards, from the roots to the leaves, and you think I can run away from that? The blood beating in me is Napoli. It's this life. I'm *camorrista,* blood and bone. And do not ever, ever bring anything like that up again. It's an offense to my father and my father's father."

A heavy silence followed. Even the children were quiet. Only the clock went on and on.

Paulie leaned on the arm of his chair and stroked his chin with his finger. I know I betrayed nothing, but he was a little too confident. "I know who you are. And there's another piece of this deal. You drop the *inamorata*."

Donna Maria broke in. "We don't discuss the women, Paulo."

"That's the deal, or I'm out. Theresa Drazen goes."

"You can't lead like this," Donna Maria said. "You'll end up dead."

"Well." Paulie fingered his phone. "So you know, it's not just 'cause I don't like her face. It's because she met the district attorney at the Downtown Gate Club today for a private chat."

I burned from the inside, as if my spine were a fuse, and my heart was a bomb; the spark coursed from my lower back upward.

"You're lying," I said.

"I ain't. Got this text right here from a good source. Gerry Friedman from the mayor's campaign." He held up the phone for Donna Maria. She put reading glasses on and read while Paulie continued. "He wants her to fuck off, too. She's poison. But that's besides the point."

I didn't want to see his fucking phone. I didn't think I could read a word of it through the haze of rage I was holding back. I didn't know what she was doing with Daniel, but I wouldn't have her tried and found guilty by that *stronzo*.

"My split's east of Cypress Avenue," I said. "And south of Merced."

"What?" Paulie twisted in his seat to face me. "You can't redraw this now."

I looked at Donna Maria when I said, "Yes, I can." She did not flinch. This was going her way, I realized.

"No, fuck you." He shot up, pointing at me, looking at Donna Maria. "What's this asshole playing at?

Normally, the person who stands first has seized the power in a negotiation. My father taught me that, but I taught myself how to change that without getting up.

"Ask him," Donna Maria said.

"What the f—?"

He didn't have a chance to drop the curse before I swept his legs from under him. He lost his balance and caught himself on the edge of the desk. I swiped the crystal Virgin from the desk and hit him on the temple. Blood sprayed on Carlos's shirt, but he didn't move, even when Paulie went flying into the sideboard. Dishes fell, Paulie grunted, yet I didn't hear a peep from behind me. Just our breathing and the ticking of the cuckoo clock.

"It's all mine, you *stronzetto*. All of it."

I pulled him up by the collar. His eyes rolled to the back of his head, but he reached and slapped me. I barely felt it. Theresa had slapped me harder.

"Come on, Paulie. This is too easy."

I dropped him, and he caught himself on the sideboard, wobbly. I almost felt bad. He'd been a brother to me until he broke with jealousy over a woman.

"You're a dead man," he grunted, his hand reaching for the bloodied lighter that I'd put down. I moved it an inch farther away. He reached again.

I looked back at Donna Maria. She had her arms crossed and was leaning back in her chair as if the TV was playing a rerun. Carlos was smiling, and Aldo frowned but hadn't moved an inch. The clock ticked as always. I turned back to Paulie, who seemed to be getting his bearings.

Paulie's fingers touched the blood-streaked crystal Virgin. Her head had fallen off, and she was just a lower half with a butane lighter sticking out of her.

I moved it another inch farther. "How many times will I have to make you pray before you understand?"

He didn't answer but hitched himself up. I put my weight on him, pinning him under me. Stuff rattled on the shelves. I picked up the statue and put it in his hand.

"You mention Theresa again, I'm not going to kill you," I said, wrapping my arms around his neck and pressing his artery shut. "You're going to beg to die."

He became dead weight in my arms, and the crystal Virgin fell out of his hand. I picked it up.

"I've cleaned blood off that thing twice already," Donna Maria said.

"Third time's the charm." I poked a cigarette out of the pack and lit it with the Virgin Mary's brass butane head. "He'll come around in a few minutes."

"I'll deal with him," Aldo said.

"You got other problems," Carlo said to me. "This woman. The one he's talking about?"

"Yes?" I suddenly didn't want him or anyone to utter her name.

"You going to do something about it?"

"Yes, but I'm going to have to miss the cacciatore. My apologies to your daughter."

Chapter Nineteen

THERESA

I wasn't in the habit of going to church anymore. It was a requirement before I turned eighteen, but once I got to college, I could beg off with studies and activities a little too easily. Once I was in my twenties, no one pretended the requirement would stick.

I still knew what to do. Stand up. Sit down. Kneel. Stand. Kneel. The standing and kneeling seemed strategically placed at the end of the mass, when legs got wobbly and the evening's fast made attention hard to keep.

Margie stood next to me in a *contrapposto* pose, as if she were simply too impatient to be in that big stone box with its waxy smell and bleeding Jesus.

"You called me here to tell me you're worried?" I whispered. "Why didn't you just call me?"

"I needed to see you. And now I'm worried more."

Margie always had a sense of when things were wrong with us. Back before I knew how to get in trouble, it amused me. She could take one look at Fiona and know when she was using, or talk to Jonathan for ten minutes to know he was having trouble with his wife. The only one she couldn't read was Daddy. But no one could read him.

"I'm fine."

"I heard you went to see Daniel today."

"Jesus—"

"*Shh.*" Her hush wasn't drawn or loud, and sounded more like *chh* than a soothing naptime sound. "Will is watching you."

"Watching me?" The church broke into song, and we stood, the organ drowning out our words, and the voices of the crowd keeping me from hearing the pounding of my heart.

"He's good," she said.

"I don't want to be watched. I'm a grown woman."

"Too bad. We need to talk, you and I. Right after communion."

"No."

The woman in front of me turned around to glare, and I glared right back.

"You are in deep, playing the DA against the mob, you're—"

"Shut up, Margie. Just shut it. I'm not talking about it with you, ever."

"I will not sit back and watch you destroy yourself," Margie said.

Every muscle coiled, every breath came short. I wanted to yell, to push, to fight her on everything. I wanted to say words that would cut her, about her spinsterhood, about her lost opportunities, about her authority to mother any of us.

Luckily for Margie, the woman in front made it her business to shoot us a librarian stare, and I got to funnel my anger into her.

"Turn around and mind your business," I said.

Margie looked at me as if I'd lost my mind, and maybe I had.

I didn't smell burned pine when he stepped next to me, probably because of the weight of the incense. Nor did I feel his closeness, probably because the nave was packed, but when he put his hand on my arm, and I felt the lightning of his touch, I knew it was him.

"Contessa," he whispered.

I looked up at him. Gorgeous thing in his jacket and shirt, hands gripping the pew in front, all squared-off knuckles and throbbing veins. Those hands needed to be on my thighs, clawing my back. Even in church, I had ungodly thoughts.

The hymn ended, and everyone sat in a rustle and clatter.

"She's worshiping, for Chrissakes," Margie said.

"Good," Antonio said, snapping up a bulletin. "So am I."

He knew the words, as did I, and we recited the responsives until Margie seemed distracted.

"I have to talk to you," he said.

"OK." I pushed against him, feeling him next to me, his solidness against my tipping form, rocking with the music as if the rising phrases of the hymn made him denser and made me more viscous.

"Were you at the DA's office today?"

I went cold. My skin curled in on itself, and the backs of my thighs tingled with an adrenaline rush. The music sounded as if it were being sung through a funnel.

"Not the office. I saw him at a club."

We faced each other, standing in church with our hymnals open. "Was this an accident?"

"It wasn't what you think."

"What do I think?" he asked.

"You think I want him, I—"

He took my hand and pulled me out of the pew. Margie looked more irritated than frightened, and I shot her a smile to keep up the ruse but then yanked back for half a second long enough to say to my sister, "Never. And stop asking."

But I admitted to myself, as he pulled me out to the vestibule and down the marble stairs, I was afraid. I didn't think he'd hurt my body, at least not in a way I wasn't begging for. He could, however, hurt me with his anger, his disappointment. And though I hadn't given the trip to see Daniel a second of thought, I probably should have.

"Listen!" I yanked back at his hand at the bottom of the stairs, but he yanked me and swung me through a doorway.

The choir dressing room was ancient with wooden lockers built in the Depression. So, when he slammed me against them, there wasn't a clatter of sheet metal, but a *thunk* as my body rattled.

Antonio grabbed me by the wrists, locking them together in two fingers and holding them over my head.

"You think I'm worried about him?" He put his finger to my face. "I spend not one minute of my life thinking about that man with you. He's not even a man. He's not worthy of you. He's one of a thousand rats on the bottom of a sinking ship."

"Then what's the problem?" My question came out in a gasp because my body gravitated toward him, arching to press against him, just as he arched in the opposite curve to keep his face close to mine.

"Why did you see him?" I could have kissed him, but I moved my head against the locker door, turning my face toward the arched lead-glass window. I wanted him, not in spite of his anger but because of it.

"He went to Katrina. His team grilled her, and I don't like it."

"What did they grill her about?"

He knew damn well, but he wasn't going to assume. I noticed that about him. He never assumed anything or jumped to a conclusion.

"You," I whispered.

"Me."

"You."

"And you told him what?" he said.

"To stop. To leave you alone. That if he didn't, I had enough on him to make his life a living hell."

"Do you think you maybe should talk to me first, before you do crazy shit?"

"No." I twisted and pulled my hands down. He let them go but increased his weight on me, pushing me against the lockers. "You barely let me out of an apartment that's not even mine. I highly doubt you'd let me see Daniel."

"Because it's stupid and dangerous."

"It's what I have to give. And it's useful to you. And go to hell if you don't like it. I will never, ever sit still while he's after you."

"I'm already going to hell. *Grazie*."

I pushed him away, and he grabbed my jaw, holding me still while he put his nose next to mine and spoke into my mouth. "You're a loaded gun. Do you see that? You're from a different world, but you smell like home to me. I haven't been to Napoli in ten years, but whenever you're near me, I smell olive flowers. My heart gets sick with thirst, but the water is poison."

"Antonio—"

"I'm drowning, Contessa."

"What are you talking about?"

His face got tight, holding back a flood of emotion. His fingers pressed harder on my face until I took hold of his wrist, pulling it down. He let go.

"Talk to me," I said. "Just tell me."

He looked confused for a second. Overwhelmed. Then, as if the dam had burst, he wrapped his arms around me and put his mouth to mine. It happened so quickly that I didn't kiss him back at first. I couldn't breathe; he held me so tight, but I got my arms around him and my mouth open, pulling him close, pushing as much of myself as I could into whatever part of him was within my reach. Thighs, hips, hands, shoulders, lips bashing lips, tongues forceful on tongues. It wasn't even a kiss, or at least, not like one I'd ever had before. It was a slap, a punch, the use of force, a coercion of two worlds into uncomfortable cohesion.

The kiss never got soft and only ended when he jerked himself away.

"Talk to me," I said in a breath.

"The thing I want most is the only thing between me and getting it. You are everything that will destroy me. I should go back to who I was. But you made me dream I could be free, when I'd forgotten I was in prison."

"Is this about you being honest? Is it about me seeing Daniel? Antonio. If I hurt you, just tell me how. Let me make it right. Let me help you get out."

He caressed my face with both palms with a tenderness that shouldn't have been able to contain such intensity.

"Sweet olive blossoms," he said. "That was God's message to me." He stepped away, and the space between us became a sigh. He held his hand. "The only way out is through."

Chapter Twenty

ANTONIO

I wanted to kill her. I wanted to worship her. I wanted to fuck her. I wanted to fill her so deeply she broke from the pain, screaming my name.

There would be no end to the trouble. She would cause it then escalate it then make it impossible for me to change my life enough to make it stop. She was dangerous, undefendable, and powerful in her own right.

She was going to be the death of me, and I was suicidal. I would kill for her, or I'd be killed by her, but no matter what, someone was getting anointed in oil and put in a pine box. God willing, it would be me and not her.

I kept the top up and the windows closed after the church. I was still at a rolling boil, and she sat back and said nothing, about that or anything, as I drove her up the hill to my little Spanish house. It was in slightly better shape than when she'd seen it last. The walls were plastered, but there was dust everywhere. The kitchen had been ripped out and the bathrooms were down to the bare necessities, but the bedroom was beautiful in spite of all the mess.

I'd tried to integrate her into my life before, but with half measures. I'd introduced her, thinking it would shield her, and it did, as long as my crew was my crew. Once that broke, she wasn't above getting hurt for betraying us, nor was she considered one of us. I was back to square one, and only when she admitted to seeing the future mayor did I realize how vulnerable she was.

I'd protected my wife. I'd protected her life, her virtue, and her ignorance. In the end, only her virtue survived, and I knew in that church basement that it was the most useless of her qualities. Only her life had been worth saving, and I'd failed at that.

Had Valentina known about my history, my father, and the world I'd turned my back on, she might have been more careful. She might have known what to look for. But I'd treated her as if she were an amusement park: a separate world, free from reality, where I could pretend I was something I wasn't.

I didn't want that for Theresa. I couldn't leave her. I was not a good man. I wasn't even decent. But with her, I could find an honest place in the world. Because she was worldly and sophisticated but still virtuous, I knew she could teach me to be the same.

In the seconds when I held my Theresa's jaw and she kept a firm grasp on my wrist and looked at me without fear, I recommitted to my plan to become a better man. I would have her and leave the life my father had denied me and that I'd rushed into despite him.

She was the only one who could take me there but only if her eyes were open and only if she wanted us as much as I did.

I didn't even want to think about it, but I had to. Tomorrow. Now, I was drunk on her scent, smelling the orchards of my youth, when I was just a fatherless child and not the end of a long line of bastards.

Chapter Twenty-One

THERESA

We snaked up a familiar hill. He'd been quiet the whole drive, only acknowledging me by taking my hand and squeezing it. At a red light, he looked at our hands together. I wanted to ask him what had changed, but the light went green, and the car took off.

The only way out is through.

I didn't know what he'd meant, but in saying that, he'd changed. He got tender. He kissed my lips and said, "Come home with me?"

I didn't know where that was, but it could have been old Napoli for all I cared. I would have gone anywhere.

"I'm sorry, Antonio. I wasn't trying to cause you trouble. I was trying to help you and Katrina both."

He didn't answer explicitly. He could have said it was all right. He could have shrugged or kissed me again. In the end, I let him take me to his car.

"Why here?" I asked when we stopped at the end of the drive at the Spanish house on the hill.

"This is my house." He opened my door and led me out of the car and up to the house.

"I thought the place on the east side was where you lived."

"Before this house, I had the small place for me." He unlocked the door and swung it open. "I got this because I realized I wasn't in this country temporarily. I was never going back, so I thought I'd settle in. Act like I really lived here."

"I like it."

"Good." He put his hand between my legs, wedging it. He bunched my skirt in his fist and curled a finger over my crotch. "Because I'm about to fuck you in it. You ready to scream?"

"I think we should talk," I said, not really meaning it. I wanted him to take me before he could tell me something I didn't want to hear. My legs opened to take his hand, and my skin tingled.

"After. We have plenty to discuss after."

"Capo," I whispered.

"*Sei mia.*" He got his finger around my clothes until he found where I was wet. "*Questa è mia.*"

"What does that mean?" I asked. My hair was still a nest of wind, and it stuck to my lips when I spoke.

"This"—he slipped his fingers over my pussy—"is mine." He put his other thumb in my mouth before I could answer, pressing my tongue down. "*La tua bocca è mia.*"

I nodded and pressed my lips around it. He tasted like church when he slid his finger from between my lips. When it was out, I said,
"My mouth?"

"Mine."

I couldn't take it anymore. I unfastened his pants and we kissed. I was at his command, no matter what he wanted, no matter what his plan.

He pushed me to my knees, and I collapsed to a kneeling position, looking up at him when he put his thumb back in my mouth. I stroked his cock, so thick and ready, the thumb a small piece of flesh in comparison. "*La bocca,*" I said.

"*La* mia *bocca,*" he replied. "My mouth. *È tua.* Is yours."

"*La mia bocca è tua.*"

"Excellent. Now I'm going to use what's mine."

I opened my lips, and he took them.

He was cruel. He put his cock in my mouth and held my head still while he pushed forward, down my throat. He shoved past my gagging, past my breath, and I let him. When he let me go and drew back, I sucked in air, paused, and then looked up at him.

"*La mia bocca è tua.*"

I opened my lips to let him take me, let him fuck my throat raw. He took a handful of hair and pulled me forward, sliding his cock in my mouth, stroking the bottom of it on my tongue.

"*Sei mia,*" he growled between his teeth then pumped down my throat again. The bottom half of my face dripped with spit and throat gunk, but still, he kept his cock in my face. It was uncomfortable, painful, degrading, and yet my nipples hardened and my panties were soaked with wanting more.

When he was as big as I'd ever felt him, and his firmness matched the weight of my ache, he took his cock out of my mouth and held it there, the tip almost touching my lips.

"*Apri*," he said, eyes at half-mast. "Open."

I opened my mouth, and he started to come into it, leaving a bitter trail on my tongue. He pulled out and moved against my face, coming on my nose, my forehead, groaning into it, until he looked down at me and smiled.

"Oh, *Dio*, Contessa."

"You like it?"

He chuckled and kneeled with me. I smiled, and semen dripped in my mouth. I laughed. I couldn't help it.

"You look like a wedding cake." He wiped his thumbs across my cheeks.

"It doesn't really come off." I licked my lips and wrinkled my nose. "And it doesn't taste like cake."

He laughed, rubbing the moisture down my forehead and across. "I anoint you in the name of the father, the son, and the holy moley."

I laughed so hard I nearly choked, and he laughed too, even as he tried to wipe my face with his undershirt. I put my face up against this chest and wiped it all over him and laughed so hard tears rolled down my cheeks.

"Woman!" He pretended to be angry but wasn't. Who could be angry while laughing and wearing a shirt covered in spunk?

He picked me up and threw me over his shoulder, singing some Italian song on the way to the bathroom, while I pretended I didn't love it.

He put me on a pink-tile vanity built in the 1950s and ran hot water over a washcloth.

"What happened before church?" I asked. He opened my legs and settled between them. "You didn't just barge in because you had a bad dream."

He wiped my face tenderly with the hot cloth. "I had a meeting with Paulie and the head of the Sicilian family that runs the east side."

"What was it about?"

"Splitting territory. That's how it started." He kissed my damp cheeks, one and then the other, then gathered my shirt at the hem and pulled it up. "Arms up."

I put my arms up, and he peeled the shirt off.

"Did it go okay?" I asked.

"It went fine. I'm not worried about territory. I only have to make it look like I'm worried." He unhooked my bra, and I wiggled out of it. "I have to be at full attention. I have to rebuild the shop, take care of my men, and make good decisions."

"I sense there's a 'but.'"

"But I'm preparing to leave. I'm thinking about it every day. Then Paulie announces you're sitting with your ex, in a room."

"It wasn't—"

He put his finger to my lips. "*Basta,* woman. I know you're not going back to him. I own you, remember?"

I nodded.

"No one trusts you. They think you're going to sell me out, and then they'll be next. So, we hear you're with him—"

"Gerry," I said. "He made the call. He's got contacts with the city council in your neighborhood. I have a feeling you know the politicians pretty well, too."

He smiled. There was a world of knowledge in the way his face fell into it. "Yes, of course."

"Well, Gerry doesn't trust me for the same reasons Paulie doesn't. He made sure you heard all about it." I put my hands on his chest. "I know I didn't grow up with what you did. But you have to know I can keep my mouth shut. I will never betray you."

"You betrayed me already by being there. By not telling me." He put his hands under my knees and squeezed them against the sides of his waist. "I know it was done with a pure heart. But don't do anything like that again."

I bristled at being told what to not to do, and he must have sensed my discomfort because he drew his face close and kissed me with those satin lips, flicking his tongue across mine.

"You realize that you just told me stuff," I said. "Real stuff about your business."

"I can't do this without you. I can't even protect you unless I put you by my side. It's the only way."

I didn't know how to answer that because I didn't know what it meant in a practical way, but from his face and his voice, I knew what it meant to him, as a man, as a leader, and as my lover.

"*Come vuoi tu,*" I whispered.

Chapter Twenty-Two

THERESA

We spent the night in the heavenly expanse of his bed and woke up with the songbirds. The first thing I felt was pain between my legs. How many times had he taken me? Just thinking of it, I felt a familiar ache, and I reached for him, but he wasn't in the bed.

"*Buon giorno*," he said from the side of the room. He was already dressed in slacks and jacket and was pulling his cuffs from under his sleeves.

"How can you be up?"

"I have a lot to do."

"Such as?" I said.

He sat on the side of the bed. "My shop is a wreck. Zo needs to rebuild it. I need to make sure my territory is secure. And I need to prepare a way for us to leave." He slid the sheet off me, exposing my nudity to the morning sun.

"Where will we go?"

"Where do you want to go?" He smirked, running his hands along the length of my thigh.

"With you," I groaned.

"Men die trying to leave because they make it public. So this is our secret, even from your sisters and your friends. Do you understand? It's a matter of life or death."

"Yes," I said.

"You're with me. You're in the life. You are mine for everyone to see. One day, we'll be gone."

"I have a family, Antonio. I can't disappear."

"I know. For now, you're beside me. No one will hurt you."

"You keep saying that."

"I mean it," he said.

"Good. I want to go to Zia Giovanna's. I want to look at the books."

"No." He cut the air with the flat of his hand. "*Assolutamente, no.*"

I sat up straight, naked from the waist up and not caring a damn. "You say you want me to be integrated. You say you know you can't keep me locked up. You say you want to share with me."

"Not in the business. If you do something you can be accused of, your consequence is on me."

"I know Daniel's been looking at Zia Giovanna's. He told me it's part of a fraud investigation. And I know you lost your accountant to that motherfucker in the Ferrari." His eyes widened in shock. I was a little surprised at my language, as well.

"The books are clean," he said.

I got down on my knees, letting the sheet fall from me. "You have no idea what Daniel's people look for. You have no idea what they miss, and you don't know what they catch. I know it inside and out. It's wasteful to not use me." I got up and stomped to the bathroom, turning before I got to the door. "I can fuck a felon, but I cannot fuck a fool."

Lightning fast, with criminal agility, he picked me up and threw me on the bed. I landed on my back with my legs spread. I opened them farther.

"So, felon or fool, Capo?"

He kneeled over me, hands between my legs like he owned everything there. Two fingers in. Out. In. His lips covered gritted teeth.

"You're going with Otto," he said, taking his slick fingers up to my clit.

"Yes, Capo," I groaned as he drew his fingers across it. "But I miss my car. Can he follow me?"

"Agreed. But about the books, you look; you don't touch."

"Fuck me."

"You'll wait." He pinched it and I cried out. "That's punishment for calling me *tonto*."

"Oh, you bastard." My smile belied my words.

He laughed to himself. "At least that. At least."

Chapter Twenty-Three

THERESA

I felt energized for the first time with him. Embraced. Accepted. Maybe it would even work. Maybe the solution really was to go deeper in. Dante and Virgil needed to go to the deepest circles of hell in order to find the way out.

I bounced out of bed and got ready. Otto waited outside, smoking with his four-fingered hand.

"Miss Theresa," he said.

"Hi, Otto. Can you take me to my car?"

"I'm taking you," he said. "And no running for food. We go; the car moves, and it stops when we get there."

"I'm sorry. I hope I didn't get you into too much trouble."

He opened the back of the Lincoln. "Enough trouble for one man in one day."

I got in. He didn't talk much on the way to the west side but just asked where we were going. I breathed as the city went by. I breathed deep into my chest, inhaling relief and a sense of belonging, if not with Antonio's world, then with *him*.

I opened the door to the loft I shared with Katrina. The air smelled stale and the surfaces had a fine layer of dust. It hadn't been that long since we'd been there, but the lack of activity had a psychological effect on the space. It felt forlorn and empty. I went right upstairs and showered and changed. Forty minutes later, I was back in Otto's car; then I got into the car I'd renamed the Little Blue Beemer and headed east to Zia Giovanna's. The Lincoln followed. I had at least the impression of freedom.

I touched my St. Christopher medal, pinching it between my thumb and second finger. Antonio could guarantee my safety from many things, but he couldn't protect me from derision and dislike. I'd have to turn that around myself.

The restaurant was packed with a lunch crowd, hipsters and businessmen who must have been from the media center down the street and a few moms with strollers parked alongside their tables. I went right to the kitchen. Zia Giovanna scuttled between the row of hanging tickets and the stove while waitresses filed in and out with heavy dishes.

She looked up, saw me, and went back to scanning her orders. "*La Cannella*. He said you'd be back."

"You know why I'm here, then?"

She plucked a ticket off the rail and put it under a plate. "In the office."

I paused, waiting for more, but she continued managing four burners, two other chefs, and a line of waitresses. I went to the office.

There wasn't much in the room, just an ancient beige computer and a few dozen sticky notes with bits of Italian scrawled on them, some with curled, greasy edges and rectangles of bright color where another note had been on top for too long. On the desk, which was actually a shelf with two filing cabinets under it, were two bank boxes of documents.

I got to work.

I DON'T KNOW how long I stood over the rows of numbers and figures. I don't know how many rivers and eddies of money I followed, keeping my eyes on the big picture and letting the errant details expose themselves, but at some point, it got dark, and Zia Giovanna entered with a sandwich, coffee, and wine.

"You need to eat," she said.

"Thanks," I said, concentrating on a little notebook of expenses. I'd honed in on a few things and gotten down to the nitty-gritty.

Zia Giovanna just stood there with her hands on her hips.

"What?" I said.

"You've been in here seven hours."

"I'm not done."

She snapped the book away. "Eat."

She put the tray on top of the ledgers. I sighed. I was hungry, and the hot tomato sauce made my stomach rumble.

"It's chicken *parmesan*," she said. "Not even on the menu, but Antonio likes it. So I made a batch. You might as well eat it."

"One minute." If I ate first, I'd forget something. I slid a slim packet of notations from the pile and disconnected a page from a printout. I snapped up a couple of the dead sticky notes that had numbers I understood, and I sorted through the ledger for all the other red flags I'd identified. Once I knew I had it all, I handed Zia Giovanna back her tray with half a sandwich on it.

"Thank you," I said. "*Grazie*, I mean." She made me nervous; I didn't know why.

"You didn't finish."

"The numbers don't talk to me if my stomach is full."

She made a face that made me feel as if I were a sick, crazy, exotic bird. Then she left, and I got back to work. I dammed a river of money, put signage on a river of cash, rerouted a flow of expenses, and took a pile of papers to the kitchen. Zia Giovanna had gone to manage something on the floor, and I worked quicker without her.

Dinner was at a lull, and the kitchen was empty. One waitress flirted with a sous chef who was cutting blocks of chocolate with a band saw. I went around a corner and opened the back of the pizza oven, stepping back when the blast of heat hit my face. The wood was good and hot, smoking and red. The paper would disappear in the flames, along with my spotless character.

As I stood by the flames with the documents over it, I paused. Was I really doing this? Was I really going to cross over? My impending action was not just illegal. It constituted aiding and abetting criminal activity. This was jail time. It was my soul in flames.

I hoisted the papers and books to oven level and was about to throw them in when I felt pressure on my arm. It was Antonio.

"What are you doing?" he said.

"Cleaning up the books."

He took the pile of papers from me and closed the oven. He looked stern and almost confused.

"You are with me, but you're not to endanger yourself. We're going to put these back. You're going to watch it. If anyone asks, as far as you know, the boxes have everything. *Si*?"

"*Si*, Capo."

Zia Giovanna pushed him out of the way and pulled the stack of papers from me, muttering something in Italian. When Antonio spoke softly and patted her on the back, I knew he'd accepted an apology.

"Listen to me." He pinched my chin. "That you would do this with your own hands, it says a lot. But those books are clean."

"No, they're not." I held up my finger. "You might know your business, but I know mine. You have income streams at the beginning of every quarter that make no sense at all. Your expenses would break the bank of a corporation. All we have to do is get rid of—"

"*Basta.*" He put his hands up.

"No, I'm not going to *basta*. You're going to *basta*. Either this accountant you had sucks at this, or he was setting you up. I'm going to hope for the former, and you can worry about the latter, but—"

He silenced me with a kiss, a mouth-filling, brain-wiping kiss. By the time he pulled away, I'd lost my train of thought.

"I'm crazy," I whispered to him.

"Sit with me," he said.

"Don't try and shut me up. I want to say what needs saying."

"*Come vuoi tu*."

A corner table had been set with red wine and bread. Antonio pulled the chair out for me and sat across. "I got us *osso buco*. Zia Giovanna wanted to give you the same sandwich you left on the desk."

"She's tough."

"In her old age, she's softened. When I was small, she held my nose to open my mouth more than one time. And she was a devil with a wooden spoon. I have scars."

"I haven't noticed any."

"You have to look harder next time." He poured wine. "We can talk here. About the books. I'm not an accountant; I can't see what you saw."

"It was bad."

"I want you to tell me, but this is the last I'll hear of it. I don't want you involved."

"You sent me here," I said.

"Not for this."

I took a deep breath. He was stubborn and for good reason. He was right; I had no business in his world. He needed me to stay out, not only to protect my own purity but because my ignorance of the rules meant I could blunder with my words or deeds. And the stakes were very high: prison, or death.

I extended my hand over the table, and he took it, sliding his over mine.

"I don't want to be in your business," I said. "I think it's stupid and dangerous, to be honest. Maybe because I've never worried about money. I've never wanted for anything, so I've never had to consider stealing it or killing for it. But the things I've wanted, really wanted, haven't come to me, either. I'm thirty-four years old, and I've never been married. I don't know how many kids I can squeeze in before it's too late. And everything has a habit of falling down around me. But I don't want this to fall apart. You and I. It's the most impossible thing I've ever been a part of, and if we're not both on board, if we're not both making every effort to be together, it's going to get taken away from us. I promise you, Daniel isn't done. He can take you away from me, and the only thing that's going to keep him off you until the election is knowing that I'm willing to lower the hammer on him. And I will, Antonio. I will. I can end his career. As God is my witness, if he comes after you, I can destroy him, and I will."

"If he fell off the earth tomorrow, ten more would take his place," Antonio said.

"He says the same about you, I'm sure."

The waitress brought two plates of saucy, sloppy stew, and though I didn't want to pause the conversation, I was starving.

Antonio put his napkin on his lap and waited for the waitress to leave before speaking. "This isn't the tradition. Even if you grew up next door, you'd be limited. You have to accept that."

"You said you wanted to be with me the right way. To get out of this whole thing."

"That's between us."

"Exactly. And if we're trying to do the same thing, then I need to help you. If that means keeping you out of jail, so be it. I'd be serving a greater good by getting involved."

He didn't answer but pushed his food around. I couldn't believe what I was arguing for, and there was a good chance he couldn't, either. I was asking him to let me into a criminal life. I was begging to get in so I could get him out. I'd lost my mind, but it was what I wanted.

"Don't think this is easy for me," I said. "I'm of two minds about it. I can't believe I'm asking to commit crimes so you can stop."

He smiled at his plate, pensive. "You keep two opposite ideas in your mind at the same time. It's the only way to survive."

"Let me survive with you."

He put his fork up against the edge of my plate and pushed the plate toward me a eighth of an inch. "Eat."

I put a piece of meat in my mouth. "It's good."

He ripped a piece of bread from the roll and dunked it in the sauce. "Have you ever been to an Italian wedding?" He blew on the hot sauce.

"Are they like in the movies?" I asked.

He leaned over. Holding the dunked bread with one hand and cupping his other hand under it to catch any errant sauce, he held the bread up to my mouth. "Did you know, when Italians came here and opened restaurants, they started serving butter to go with the bread. Butter is a luxury where I'm from, see? So, they were giving what they saw as a luxury."

I bit down on the bread, and he pulled it away while I chewed.

"The expensive places here," he continued, "they give you good olive oil. Which is wasteful. Where I'm from, the bread is for the sauce."

"This has what to do with an Italian wedding?"

"There's the way back home, and there's the immigrant way, which has fake luxury. Tons of it. It's embarrassing."

"Yes, Antonio."

"Yes, what?" he said.

"The Bortolusi wedding." I took another forkful of meat and sent it home with a mouthful of rich burgundy. "I'll go with you."

"I can't take you."

My fork clinked loudly when I put it down. "Are you serious? You think Paulie's going to try something at a wedding? I thought you guys worked it out."

"Doesn't matter. I'm just letting you know where I'll be that day," he said.

I wanted to throw my fork at him.

Having given me the information and laid down the law, he settled into a few bites of *osso buco*. Then he looked at me over the rim of his wine glass and caught my expression. "What?"

"How is this 'getting out by going through'?"

He raised an eyebrow as if I'd just asked him to bend me over the buffet. "Forget it."

"You decide to bring me closer, then you keep me in a box all over again."

"I'm figuring out how to do this, same as you."

"You have to take some risks."

"Not with your safety," he said.

"If you bring me, it will show that whatever I said to Daniel that day didn't hurt you."

"Or that I'm a fool."

"It's business. Your family is undoubtedly in the middle of a negotiation with the Sicilians, but am I right in thinking nothing's locked down yet? As far as the details go, I mean."

"You're right," he said.

"If you bring me, it empowers you. It's going to disarm them. They're going to wonder what the hell you're thinking." I took a bite of meat and chewed slowly. "Also, it'll scare the hell out of Paulie. There's no use in having a bazooka unless the enemy knows you have it. If you want to keep the peace, that is."

He sipped his wine, avoiding my gaze. It wasn't like him. I could have asked what was bothering him, but I had the feeling I knew the answer.

I was right again.

Chapter Twenty-Four

THERESA

We passed the night in the cocoon of the bed. When I was with him, my isolation was acceptable, simply a way to be close, to hear his stories uninterrupted. He talked about the color of Naples, the veiled identities of the camorra, the family he called his own and the one he inherited when his father came back into his life.

"Your father really loves you," I said, propped up on my elbows. He leaned on the headboard, stroking my shoulder with a fingertip. "He gave mixed messages, I admit. But he only wanted what was best for you."

"He was trying to keep me safe as *consigliere,*" he whispered, brushing his thumb over my cheek. "*Consiglieri* are lawyers who advise bosses, so they aren't meant for vendettas. But I had to send a message to the men who killed my wife."

"Did you send the message?"

His lower lip covered his upper for a second. He slid down into the sheets and wove his legs into mine. "You're going to ruin me, Contessa."

"*Rovinato,*" I replied.

He laughed. His eyes lit up, and his cares fell off him. I wondered if I'd ever get to see him smile once a day, or even once a week. As beautiful as he was on any given day, he was a treat for the eyes and heart when he laughed.

Chapter Twenty-Five

ANTONIO

"There's talk," Zia Giovanna said, twisting a fistful of dough into a long beige tube. She insisted on making her own bread at five a.m., even when it would have been more economical to leave the bread making to bakers. "My sister tells me they're whispering over there."

Zia Giovanna's sister was my mother. Both held advanced degrees in gossip and hearsay, so in their garden of chatter, a seed of truth often sprouted leaves and flowers of beautiful lies.

"How can they hear each other over the traffic?" I didn't want to hear her little rumors. I had a ledger spread on the stainless counter. The office had become claustrophobic in seconds. I had rows and columns of numbers to organize since Numbers Niccolò had taken off and left me with them. I wasn't a numbers guy. I could do the basics, but past that, I'd always had people to organize the larger concepts into smaller processes. Niccolò seemed to have done his job of hiding and cleaning money through the restaurant by means of misdirection and sleight of coin. Theresa had been dead right, though. Once she showed me where the trail led, it was very obvious he'd done a terrible job.

"When you came here, I told you to stay away from Donna Maria. Sicilians. You can't trust them. They're animals. You didn't listen. You never listen."

I could do numbers and listen to her scold me at the same time. One took up the attention of my brain, the other, my heart.

"But you run." She pounded her dough, pulling and twisting. "And you sit by her as *consigliere,* and that puts you in her sight. She knew Paulie was going to fuck up. He's American. He can't do anything the right way, the patient way. Even though he wanted Theresa out, he couldn't do it right. A smart man would have waited to marry into the family then taken you out but—"

"*Aspetta*. What are you talking about?"

She looked like she was going to cry. She slapped a ball of dough down. "Paulie's wedding is off. He's weak. They're all talking about you beating him, and they're looking at you to unify the families."

"What?" I said.

"Your father stepped in. He thinks he has you. He says it will be done. His Neapolitan interests and the American Sicilian. You and Irene."

I held my hand up. "Slow down."

"Make this go away." She pounded her dough, flattening the tube in one place. "Tell them you want the red-haired one. She's all right. She won't hurt you. She won't force you."

I couldn't make it go away. I had no way to undo what was done, and if all Napoli was already whispering, it was unlikely my father could undo it without brutal consequences, not just to me, with my disposable life, but to Theresa, who was under my care.

I needed to get out more than ever, and as difficult as that would have been anyway, it had just become nearly impossible.

Was I committed to this? Or was I going to make half efforts? Leaving the life, breaking so many ties, and slipping away was always a nice fantasy when I couldn't find my way through a problem or when the light at the end of the tunnel turned out to be an oncoming train.

After I'd lost Valentina, I'd made choices. I'd gone in with my eyes open, and having made those choices, I never questioned the fact that I'd earned all my own troubles.

Chapter Twenty-Six

THERESA

Katrina's text woke me from a dead sleep. I swung my arm for Antonio, but he was gone. He'd left me alone in his little Spanish house. He must have trusted me with the silver.

—Can you come to the editing bay?—

—Why?—

It wasn't like me to question Katrina, but I was half asleep, and I missed Antonio already. I should have been thankful that I was out of *The Afidnes*, but I wasn't. I felt like I'd stepped out the door to find the stoop had disappeared and the sidewalk was open beneath me.

—Because you were a part-time script supervisor, and you're half the team that put the half shots in order and I'm confused right now—

—Fine. Give me 20—

Otto waited outside.

"Do you ever see your wife?" I handed him a thermos of coffee.

"It's the arrangement," he replied. "She knows what I have to do, and she accepts."

"She's very generous."

"She is."

"I want to take my car. Can you follow to the post-production place?" I helped up two fingers. "No burgers, I promise."

He agreed to follow close, and I let him, not making a move to lose him. I knew his proximity relaxed Antonio, and that was important to me.

"What's up?" I asked Katrina when she opened the glass door.

"Nothing." She wouldn't look at me.

"Nothing? Describe 'nothing.'"

She walked a pace ahead, looking at the floor. "The type of nothing that's just unpleasant." She reached the door to her editing bay and put her hand on the knob.

"Katrina?"

"I didn't have much in the way of choices," she said. "I had wonky location permits and my financing was, you know, questionable."

"You don't need to review a shot list. That's what I'm getting."

"I hate my fucking life. Really." She opened the door.

Daniel sat in the biggest chair, one leg crossed over the other at the ankle.

This was how a poor kid from Van Nuys got to be a mayoral candidate. First, he showed up where he wasn't wanted, and he was ready. He was armed with information, and he had a plan. He surrounded himself with people who could help him, and he cut the rest of them loose. He was ruthless in his pursuit, hungry, careful, and above all, shrewd.

"Sorry, Tee," Katrina said.

"It's fine. I have this."

This was how a poor kid from Carthay Circle became an award-winning director. First, she did what other people wanted, as long as they stayed out of her way. She understood the hierarchies of power as they related to her singular goal. She understood personalities and could make judgment calls about how to play them for and against each other. She apologized for it, and she never pushed far enough to make enemies, but she knew how precarious her situation was, and she protected the twelve inches of upper-floor ledge she stood on, because one wrong move, and she would have been in midair, calculating the hardness of her skull against the acceleration of gravity. And since she'd already fallen, and had to climb the building again, she was especially careful of her footing.

What kind of person can love two people like that?

The kind of person who could love a killer, I decided, as I sat in front of Daniel, and Katrina closed the door behind me. I was the kind of person who was rotten inside, whose very core was drawn to the ambitions of others, no matter its form.

"The last time you came to me, at WDE, you said it was my last chance," I said.

"I did. And nice to see you, too."

"I said I'd ruin you, Daniel, and I meant it."

He smiled. I found myself disarmed by it. It wasn't a political smile but something more genuine that I remembered from the very beginning of our relationship, when he was starting as a prosecutor. That was before he'd been beaten down and had to be built back up.

"No, actually, you didn't mean it," he said. "You and I, see, we're in this tension. You got me in the palm of your hand, but I have you in my pocket."

"Really? Interesting. Tell me." I settled into the chair, swinging it so the back was to the computer screens. I betrayed nothing.

He said nothing immediately but looked at me up and down as if considering something he hadn't seen before. "You look good."

"Thank you."

"Different." He put his hand out, cupping me in space. "I noticed it last time, but I was so thrown by you showing up I couldn't pin it down."

"I'm the same. Maybe the eyes that see me are different."

"No, not that, but maybe something else. You were always… I don't know the word."

"Do try," I said. "We spent so much time talking about how you looked and how you came across, so now it's my turn. I'm curious."

"By outward appearance, you're the same. Aloof. Ladylike. Perfect."

"And inside?"

"Feral," he said.

"If you'd known that earlier, things would have been a lot different."

He shrugged. "No way to tell. But, things have changed. And I'm not looking forward to this conversation the way you looked forward to the one you brought to me at the club."

"Oh, just get to it Daniel. Katrina needs her editing bay."

He nodded decisively as if changing gears. "I was thrown by our last conversation; I admit it. But I know you, and even if you've changed, well, I don't think you've changed that much. You're very protective. I know exactly what you have on me and how much it will hurt me. But if you send me down the river, I have enough on your little sleazebag to put him away. And you don't want that. I know he's got you around his finger. How he did it, I don't know. I thought you were with him to spite me, but I think I was wrong. He really has you."

"You have nothing on him, or you would have charged him already."

"I may. His accountant is running with Patalano now. If I catch Patalano, I have the accountant. Then I can get Spinelli. And guess what? He'll tell me whatever I want about whatever I want, in order to save you."

"Me?" I said.

"You."

"What—?"

"The attempted murder of Scott Mabat. Did you forget that? Scott hasn't. Because I traced the financing of this little picture right here." He indicated the room, the computer, all Katrina's work. "Big chunk led to him. So after we saw Katrina, we went to him. He didn't look too good. And I have to say, once I heard him tell his story, I didn't want to believe it. I didn't even want to think about it."

I swallowed. I'd known the gun wasn't loaded, but who would believe it? My face tingled, and I tightened my grip on the arms of the chair. I wasn't going to react. I knew how to do that. I knew how to present whatever emotion I needed to, and in this case, I needed to project confidence. I knew Daniel. If I showed him a crack, he'd wedge himself into it. "You have the testimony of a known loan shark against mine?"

"By the time this is done, I'll have Patalano and Niccolò Ucci telling the same story."

"I dare you." I leveled my gaze at him, consciously relaxing my jaw muscles as if whatever strength I had took no effort whatsoever.

"What happened to you?" he asked. "Inside. Where is Tink? Where's the woman who wanted to do the right thing, the good thing?"

This was how an heiress became a criminal. First, she didn't want for money. She wanted only to be normal and good. She flew under the radar her whole life, making sure there was always someone next to her who shone brighter, talked faster, and laughed louder. Then the sun she circled shifted, and she became disoriented and dizzy from being thrown out of orbit. She bumped into a dark planet and broke, from the force of the impact, into millions of white-hot pieces, blasting apart into a firestorm of euphoria, a soundless roar of exultation in the vacuum of space.

Daniel, as if reading my thoughts, continued. "I don't even know you."

"You never did. But in all fairness, I didn't either."

"This exciting for you? Running with this crowd?"

"Was it exciting for you calling your mistress a dirty little slut? I'm going to assume it's a yes, for the sake of my point. It all comes from the same place. We can only pretend we're clean inside for so long before we crack, and the darkness starts spilling out. You fucked her because you had to, to stay sane. I'm with Antonio because it's the only sane choice. I'd go crazy if I had to go back to who I was."

He leaned back, fixed his tie, and crossed his legs again. "I don't want to send you to jail. I know you think I don't care, but it would break my heart to hurt you. I have to try one last time."

"Try what?"

"To save you."

The screensavers on the computers went out, bathing us in a false daytime darkness. Feathers of light fell beneath the room-blackening shades.

"In a few weeks, there's a wedding," he said. "It's at the Downtown Gate Club. Is he taking you?"

"No."

"Don't lie, Tink."

"He's not."

"Make sure he does. I want you to be there on time. Wear your best gun-moll dress. During the cocktail hour, I want you to pass something to the bathroom attendant." He put a small manila envelope on the desk.

"You're a damn member, Daniel. Can't you give it to her yourself?" I said.

"They're going to sweep it before the place settings are laid out. IDs checked. Everyone's frisked for wires. And there's a mole on my team. I can't let it leak."

"What makes you think I won't tell Antonio?"

"I expect you to, and I expect him to stay quiet to protect you. Everyone's walking out in one piece. You're going to put an object in the tip tray, and you and your lover will ride into the sunset, for whatever that's worth. If you don't pass it, I'm having both of you prosecuted. And there will be no witness protection for you. You don't know enough to be worth it to the Fed."

I rocked in the chair, my eyes getting accustomed to the lack of light. I was in a terrible position, and I knew that. I had internalized my situation quite nicely in less than thirty seconds, because I knew Daniel. I knew when he was serious and when he was bluffing. It had been my job to know for too long, and it was a job I had a hard time quitting.

"I think I always knew you were like this," I said. "When we were together, I had a feeling that once I stopped being useful to you, I'd lose you. I think that's why I always tried to be a part of what was most important to you. I told myself I did it because I enjoyed it, and to a large extent, that was true."

"You never lost me. This is business."

"I never had you. I made myself a part of your career because I knew that if I didn't, you'd find a woman who would. So I'm going to tell you something about Antonio. I'm not useful to him. He wants me as far away from his business as possible. Maybe I enrich his life. Maybe I drag him down. I don't know, because I don't know what love is anymore. I only know that no man has ever loved me like he does. If love is part of our better natures, he's a saint. And if it's part of our basest instincts, he's an animal."

He sat still in his chair, hands on the arms, as the hard drives behind me wound down with a *whirr*. Then he smirked.

"You his Madonna ? Or his whore?"

I smirked back. The question didn't offend me, which was why I could answer honestly.

"Yes."

Chapter Twenty-Seven

ANTONIO

Barnsdall Park was a perfect private place. It was an outdoor setting yet private in its expansiveness, with crannies of bushes and low walls and a sheer drop onto Hollywood Boulevard. It would have been difficult, if not impossible, for anyone to casually listen to my call. I sat on the ledge overlooking the city as the sunrise bled red over the hills.

"Antonio," said my father, "*Come stai?*" In the background was the sound of Neapolitan traffic. He must have been in the city.

"Good, Pop. How are you?" I spoke in Italian, but my mind had always been elastic with language, and I knew I'd stumbled on my native tongue.

"You have an American accent," he said. To him, I sounded American. To Americans, I sounded pure dago. I was a citizen of that in-between place where no one would accept me as one of their own anymore.

"It's been a long time," I said.

"You sounded American in the first five minutes." He went behind a door, or closed the window, because the white noise stopped as if cut off at the knees.

"It's an efficient language. Easy to learn. You should try it."

"Sounds too German. All this *chop chop chop*."

"Well, it's good for fast decisions," I said.

"And bad for small talk, son. You didn't call to chat about phonetics. Not at this hour of the morning. What time is it over there?"

"Almost seven."

"Did you leave her in the bed alone?"

That made me smile. "It's almost like we're related. You and I."

We sat inside a pause. I watched the light traffic on Hollywood Boulevard, and he let me.

"I heard Donna Maria won't have Paulie Patalano in her family," I said. "She doesn't think he'd be strong enough."

"News travels fast when there are women involved."

"And she's looking for another match for Irene, because she knows the Bortolusis will crush her."

"There's only one match, son," he said.

"With Valentina, you took care of all of it. You brought me in. I said I'd give my life to the cammora. I let you make my decisions for me in exchange for vengeance."

"You said there would never be another woman. I believed you. I figured, he's my son. I know how he is." Regret coiled around his voice. "If I don't make this match, we're going to be crushed."

"I want out," I said.

"If anyone else questioned me, they'd be in the hospital asking forgiveness."

"I won't do it."

"They all say that. Your sister said it, then she fell in love with him."

"Then she was raped to prevent the marriage. Do you think any of this makes sense? Do you think we should maybe stop this?" I couldn't sit still. I jumped off the concrete wall and paced the jogging track, keeping my eyes off the horizon and focused on my feet.

"There's more American in you than the accent," he admonished. "This is not your choice. Not after the first one."

"These decisions were mine. And this one is mine, too. I'll do it with you or without you. With you is simpler."

"It's too late, Tonio. You gave up your life." He was angry, growling at me in a way he'd had no chance to do when I was a kid. "I told you this when you were my *consigliere*. I warned you it was the worst decision you'd make. And when you left my side to go over there, chasing them, I told you then, too."

"I'll sell the businesses. Peel off territory. Stop taking tributes. Just tell me what I have to do to get out."

"Nothing. You don't get to go back; that's the end of it. If you don't care about your own life, at least think about the woman. The one you're fucking. They'll kill her same as the last one who got in the way of business."

Stupido. God, that poor kid. Donna Maria killed his girlfriend, without a word of remorse for it.

"I know you think you can protect her," Benito said. "But know this. They'll kill you first then her. There's no message if she lives. And don't make a mistake. There are a lot of them. If they want you dead, you will die."

"How, then? How do I do it?"

"Don't let them smell weakness, son. If you want to out, you have to find your way. Don't whisper a word, even to me. I will try and stop you."

I watched the blood of the sun pour onto the city and knew that, years before, I'd sold my hopes in the name of vengeance.

"*Capito*," I said.

"*Bene*," he replied. "After the Bortolusi wedding, you and I will discuss your courtship. It will be very traditional. You're lucky. She's a nice-looking girl. It could have gone much worse for you."

I rubbed my face. I'd never been less attracted to a woman in my life. I hung up without telling him that.

I drove up the mountain and through the flatness of the valley, up into the freeway split of the Angeles National Forest, where a man could be alone with his thoughts.

I didn't blame my father for what he was doing. I'd taken a *camorrista* vow to be at the service of the family. The camorra worked the way it worked because marriage was a business deal. My father was the result of such a marriage, so why should it have been different for me? The fact that he'd never been forced to marry was the result of luck. There had been neither necessity nor opportunity.

I drove faster. I had no business doing it. I was endangering everyone else on the road, but the faster I drove, the faster I thought. The other cars, and the mountains on either side, faded into a blur.

Benito Racossi, my father, counted me lucky with Valentina. I'd married the woman I wanted to marry. She had been outside the life, and I was finishing law school. My father was proud and grateful. My mother had even spoken to him for fifteen minutes without a fight.

I pulled onto an exit that wasn't an exit. It was no more than a bastard turnoff onto a dirt road. No gas stations, no fast food, just the potential for a city. It was a space set aside for something, someday. The freeway turned pencil thin in my rear view, and up ahead, the mountains went from shapes against the sky to solid masses of green and brown. I'd hoped to drive into a wall, but it didn't work that way. I knew that from home. The roads to Vesuvio twisted and rose gently until ears popped and the car slowed, but in increments. Halfway up the mountain, I'd realize I'd made a choice to go there.

And Nella, sweet Nella, my sister. Raised outside the camorra, she was promised to a man against her will then fell in love with him anyway. Like animals, a rival family gang-raped her to prevent the marriage.

I thought about what might happen to Theresa if I refused to marry Irene. That stupid man and his girlfriend had washed up on the sand because they'd refused.

But he'd been weak. What if I wasn't? What if I started with Donna Maria and killed every single son of a whore beneath her until I had what I wanted?

No. Even if I was successful, I'd be more deeply trapped in the life than ever, and Theresa might not survive it. I had to do better.

I pulled the car over and looked east. Indeed, I'd gone halfway up the Angeles mountains without feeling it. I looked out over the washed-out colors of civilization, the gas stations and fast food joints, and the stucco houses and dots of cars. They looked like plastic debris caught on a slowly heaving sea of dirt and dry grass.

I felt as if the world reorganized around the *camorristi,* spinning up and away. We nailed our feet to the ground with spikes of tradition while the whipping winds of modernity threatened to rip our bodies off at the ankles. And if it succeeded? If we let ourselves be yanked into the air? We'd fly and fly and be unable to walk when we came down, crippled by our fear of change.

I couldn't murder my way out of it.

I couldn't walk away. I was hobbled.

But maybe, just maybe, I could run.

Chapter Twenty-Eight

THERESA

Daniel's envelope had a set of seven flaccid wire lengths with plastic nodules on top, and it took me a second to identify them as earpieces. I was about to call Antonio. I wasn't going to keep a word Daniel said secret. I owed him nothing, and I owed my Capo everything.

I went to the Spanish house on the hill. The door was locked, and the Mas was parked out front. I went around to the side, where I could hear Puccini through the leaded glass windows. I called his name over and over but got no reply. Finally, the obvious occurred to me, and I texted.

—Capo? I'm outside—

The music went off. I waited, but he didn't come out. I went to the front of the house and found him by my car, driver's side open. A plume of smoke curled from his perfect lips.

He was smoking. That never boded well. He never lit a cigarette when everything was all right.

"You need to go," he said when I was within earshot.

"I have things to tell you." Did he hear I'd been in the same room with Daniel again? That wasn't my fault, and if that was the source of his anger, he was going to get an earful about waiting to talk to me before making assumptions.

"I'm sorry," he said. "Just go."

"Whatever it is—"

His face was stone cold. His mouth was set so hard the last wisps of smoke came from his nose.

I crossed my arms. "What?"

"It's not you—"

"It's you. I know. I've heard it. And I agree. It is you. It's all you. I'd be at work now, pushing numbers and fighting through protocol meetings, if it wasn't about you. So, what's this about now?"

He dropped his cigarette to the ground and stomped it out. "I'm leaving."

"I'm coming."

"You can't."

"Like hell," I said.

"I have two choices. I leave quietly, and I'll be hunted the rest of my life until they find me and kill me. Or I kill everyone who demands the marriage, and I protect you at the same time. Those are the two. There is no third."

"Another consolidation, to match the marriage in December."

I must have surprised him with my immediate understanding and my lack of emotion about it.

"Yes," he said.

"What century is this? Don't do it. Just say no."

"The last man who said no washed up on a beach with his girlfriend."

"The girl's going to get a complex."

"I'm sorry, Contessa. I'm willing to die. I'm willing to say no and leave the life, even though one day they'll kill me. But I keep thinking no matter what I do, I hurt you. And *that* I'm not willing to do. If I go away, and I'm not around anymore… sure, they find me. I don't care. Eternity is a long time. Another fifty years on this earth isn't much, by comparison. But, without you, it's wasted."

"And that's your plan? Run away and get killed to protect me?"

"I'm not dragging you down anymore."

"I thought the only way out was through."

"Don't ever doubt I cared for you," he said.

He walked back to the house. As soon as he walked back through that door, he'd be gone. He'd close the door and lock it. Then I could text all I wanted; I could call and I could come with a battering ram and a police warrant, but he'd be gone.

I ran ahead of him, wedging myself in the doorframe.

"One more time," I said. "Then I'll let you go. I'll never see you again. But one more time."

He was on me so fast I didn't have a chance to put my bag down. His lips crashed into mine, his arms cocooned me, and my knees came out from under me.

He shut the door behind me and pushed me with his lips and his intentions. I pulled his jacket off, and he undid my hair. His face an inch from mine, his palms on my cheeks, he kissed me, and in that kiss there was more love than I thought a human heart could contain.

"I want you right now. Right here. One more time for the rest of our lives." He kissed me with a mix of gentleness and depth. "Just a moment with you." His words were breaths made of desperation and heat. "Please. Indulgence. Saintly indulgence before the devil finds me."

It couldn't have been that cut and dried: marry another woman and live; stay with me and die. It couldn't have been that simple. But his mood wasn't nuanced; he needed me. There was no use denying it. Practical matters would have to wait.

"Take me." I raised myself. "How do you say it?"

"Fammi tua." Even as he said the words, his hands were already up my shirt, feeling under the side of my bra and where the underwire creased the soft flesh. I turned and put my arms around him.

"Adesso." He pushed his hardness against me, and I swung a leg over his waist to get him closer to home.

"Fammi tua."

His hands crept up my skirt into my panties, finding the split in me, following the wetness.

"Fammi tua!" I cried. "God, is it my pronunciation? *"Fammi tua!"*

"You are my heaven." He hoisted me up, leaning me against the rock of his dick. "I can't say no to salvation."

He carried me upstairs, kissing me, and laid me on the bed. A full suitcase fell onto the floor, spilling everything.

He pulled his pants off. God, that piece of meat between his legs was a beautiful sight, and when he pulled his shirt off, the shape of his body looked built to fit into mine, every curve and line angled as if calculated match to my desire.

Where was I going? What life was I living, without him? I'd be an empty shell of a woman.

He fell on top of me, yanking my clothes off until we were naked together.

"Wait." I pushed him away.

"I will not be told what to do."

He looked at me with such intensity that I knew he wasn't talking about me telling him to wait.

I laid my hands on his neck. "Daniel found me today."

"That son of a whore… if he touches you…"

"He wants me to go to the wedding and pass the bathroom attendant a bunch of bugging devices. He'll hurt you if I don't do what he says."

"I'll be gone. Dead, probably."

This man was willing to die rather than live without me. I wanted to save him, but maybe I'd be damning myself if I told him the extent of Daniel's manipulation. Even the fact that I was willing to use my safety as a bargaining chip made me wonder about my motives. "He'll file charges against me."

"You're not compelled to pass listening devices around, Theresa."

"The attempted murder of Scott Mabat. The loan shark."

His breath was deep and sharp. "When I murder Paulie, it will be for that."

"You said you wouldn't," I said.

But he would; I knew that. If he wasn't protecting a relationship with me, and the opportunity arose, he wouldn't hesitate to kill Paulie.

"I don't know what to do," he said as if admitting to a crippling weakness he'd hidden his whole life.

"Yes, you do." I brushed my hand against his cheek.

"I don't. There's no solution."

"There's always a solution."

He just shook his head. He believed it. He'd done the math and come up with the best, most selfless solution he could. Walk away.

"Fight, Antonio. Fight for me."

"I am fighting for you," he said.

"Fight harder."

He whispered it back to me. "Fight harder." Then he smirked, shaking his head a little. "Of course. I'll die fighting for a life with you. If they kill me for it, my fate is set. I'm marked for hell. I'm damned, and once this life is over, we're separated for eternity. So while I'm on this earth, every second I have is yours."

"And my seconds and my minutes and hours are yours. Will you take them?"

"I am yours, Contessa." He kissed my breasts and belly. "*Solo tua.*"

The particular strain of his voice, hinted with both intensity and hopelessness, gave me pause. But it was a short pause because his tongue was between my legs, finding ridges and edges, working around my core and then upward, tickling my clit.

He came up to me, face to face, leaving me still wanting his tongue. He hitched my hips up and slid his dick into me. "Forever. Everything I do with you is forever."

"Wait. A second. Wait. Just. Ahh." He fucked me so hard every thought went out of my head. He fucked the brains out of me, the common sense, the grounded quality he loved so much. I was gone. Every thread of maturity, wisdom, and care was gone.

I'd been his long before that moment. He owned me the first time he put his body on mine, since the first thrash of violence on my behalf. He'd owned me the minute he wanted me, even before I wanted him.

But it wasn't until he spoke to me in vulnerability, until I heard panic, until he came to me with nothing, that I owned him.

It was only at that moment that his salvation came under my care, and I became responsible for my own destruction.

Chapter Twenty-Nine

THERESA

We planned our annihilation like two chess players in the park, both hitting the clock after each move, thinking and rethinking assumptions, motivations, and methods. He was brilliant, and with each passing day, in my bed or his, we spoke of things no one should speak of and avoided any talk of failure.

Failure was death. And our deaths would mark our success.

It was one thing to agree to live with someone, to settle on committing to sickness and health, good times and bad, and to promise to live until living was no longer possible. It was a completely different thing to promise to die with them. And that was what we agreed to.

Antonio Spinelli and Theresa Drazen, two people from opposite sides of the world, with barely a language in common, whose bodies fit together like modular forms, were going to die.

The decision to die came at the end of a series of decisions. The first was to be together. The second was to fight together. The third was to leave together. The rest followed from there, because even before Hemingway, all good stories that were carried to their inevitable conclusion ended in death.

Our story would end in the death of Daniel's pursuit, of Paulie's threats, and of Antonio's status as a slave to his life. It would end in the death to my relationship with my family, my friendships, and my access to a few million in trust. All of it.

And most days, I was elated about erasing my past. How many people can start fresh with nothing on their backs? It was bliss to sit in serious talks with Antonio, even sprawled on the bed with a sheen of sweat, stained in his love, mind clear enough to think of some dirty nuance that needed to be managed.

"Daniel is still a beneficiary on my life insurance."

"Does it matter?" His mouth was taking my nipple in small bites.

It didn't matter because I had enough wealth already, and because it was too late to change the paperwork. It only bothered me because I didn't want Daniel to have my money.

"No, I guess not." I was stretched out, naked, on my bed.

"I'm supposed to meet my future wife the day after the wedding."

"A date?"

"Chaperoned, of course," he said.

"God, I hate this. I hate how I feel. I'm actually jealous of this poor girl."

"I'm going to stand her up by dying. That would make me the second promised Neapolitan in a row. Maybe she'll marry Paulie after all."

He handed me a little blue booklet: my passport. We'd agreed to die around the time of the Bortolusi wedding. We'd made plans for after our deaths, but still hadn't decided on how we would die, how our bodies would appear to be obliterated, or how we would slip away.

I flipped the passport open. The pages felt real, with crisp paper in multicolored shades. There were even some stamps in it already. In my picture, I looked optimistic and clean, like a middle-school teacher travelling on Christmas break.

"I have mixed feelings about the name," I said, tossing my fake passport on the bedspread.

"Persephone? The goddess of the death?" He kissed me from above, hands on either side of my waist, his upper lip pressing against my lower.

"She was abducted into hell."

"She kept running into the wrong types of men." He kissed between my breasts, moving the St. Christopher medal aside with his teeth. I put my arms around him, letting him move above me like the shifting sky. "And poor you, with only me at your feet."

He moved his lips over my belly and hips, and I over his, until our mouths could worship each other properly.

Chapter Thirty

ANTONIO

She understood. I thought she wouldn't. I thought she'd dismiss how serious our power and our traditions were. But she was from an old-fashioned family. I don't think I realized that until Thanksgiving.

"I want you to come," she said over the phone as I stood in the driveway, watching Zo go over building plans with his workers. Someday the house would be done, even if I never lived in it. "Thanksgiving is important here."

"I can't."

"I want you to come. That should be enough."

"No. It's that simple."

I couldn't believe we found the time to argue about something so mundane. It felt like practice for real life.

"I'm not some kid looking to show you off. I want you to meet these people. They're important to me. Do you understand what I'm saying?"

I did. And maybe I didn't want to go for just that reason. "I want to talk about this when you're in front of me and I can occupy your mouth with something besides your demands."

"Don't avoid this," she said.

"*Ti amo,* Contessa."

"I'll text you the address. I expect you there."

I'd found myself in the position of trying to talk her out of our escape plan. She would be better off without me. And I tried to convince her, but only wound up fucking her. I tried to slip away, but she caught be by my dick and had me.

I'd promised to protect her. It was a promise I realized I couldn't keep. I felt resigned to the difficulty of the path and also to the potential of it. The trick to dying without dying was to make arrangements without making arrangements. The strategy was to not break up, to not stay together, to not *change*. And the question I'd pose to her when she was in front of me would be, "Would I go to Thanksgiving dinner with your family under different circumstances?" I didn't think I would. Not yet.

"This has to be done," my father said over the phone as I opened the door to the basement. Lorenzo and I clattered down the wood stairs.

"I understand." Zo handed me a box on handguns. I had an armory under the house that had been moved from *l'uovo*. I had the phone tucked between my shoulder and ear as I pointed to one of the guns and mouthed the word *ammo*.

"She's a nice girl," my father said. "You've met her?"

"Yeah."

I chose the one thing I'd need: a small handgun, built for a woman's hand but large enough to stop a man. Zo took a box off a shelf and shook it. Full.

"When this is done, I want you back here. This is going to put a lot of vendettas to rest. You and Irene will be safe."

What was the answer? What would it be if I were going to live past the next few weeks?

"No," I said taking the box from Zo and heading upstairs. "I'm not going back."

You didn't say no to Benito Racossi. You said yes, boss. But I wouldn't have said yes. I would have said no and gone to Napoli anyway.

"Is this about *la rossa*?" he asked.

"Yes."

"Bring her."

"She's American, Pop. It doesn't work like that here." I pocketed the weapon and put the rest away, and we clattered back up the stairs. Zo shut the light and closed the basement door behind me.

"It's all right. I'll figure it out," I said. The conversation with my father was such a play. I felt like an actor reading lines.

"You always do, son. You always do."

I didn't think he knew what was going on, but he was suspicious. I could hear it. We hung up soon after. Zo put the box of bullets on the kitchen counter.

"Who's this for?" Zo asked.

"Wedding gift."

"Nice. She's hot, you know? You gonna, you know, get to know her better?"

"After the Bortolusi wedding."

"What are you going to do with the rich one?" He opened the little gun, popping the clip.

I shrugged. "She can stay around if she wants. I can handle two. What are you doing?"

"Loading it."

I took the gun away and put it back on the counter. I knew all too well what Theresa was capable of, even with an empty gun.

"I need a favor from you," I said. "If something happens to me, I want you to watch after Theresa.

"Why would something happen to you?" Zo was never the most fruitful tree in the orchard.

"I'm the last one. And if I don't take this Irene girl, Bortolusi doesn't have any real competition. Donna Maria's going to have to handle it herself, along with Paulie and the other camorra bosses who spend more time fighting than making money."

"Well, nothing's gonna happen to you."

"Well, if something does, you take care of Theresa, or I will come back from the dead and make you a very sorry man."

"In that case…"

"I trust you, Lorenzo. I want you to know that. Next to Paulie, you were the guy I trusted most."

"Paulie didn't work out so good."

"So, don't fail me. Don't fail me."

I didn't mean to be fatalistic, but it was hard not to be. There would come a time when the father I'd just hung up with, who I hadn't known the first decade of my life and who'd always had my best interests at heart, despite everything, would write me off as dead. And the friend here, in front of me, who was building and rebuilding my life, would be unreachable.

I was making the project seem easy to Theresa, and it wasn't. That decision was going to break her heart before it healed her.

"Something going on, Spin? Something you can tell me?"

"Yeah, and I think I need your help. I can't do it by myself. But I need to trust you. You need to take this to the grave."

"Okay." He seemed unsure.

I snapped a drawer open and took out a knife.

"No, no, no. Come on man…"

I cut the web between my left thumb and forefinger, drawling blood.

"Give it here," I said, holding my right hand out. Zo gave me his hand, and I cut it. We shook with our left hands, a mirror image of gentle society.

"On *San Gianni,* do you swear silence?" I asked.

"I swear it on the five stars of the river."

I let his hand go and yanked off a paper towel.

"You cut deep," he said. "What the fuck?"

"*Forza,* my friend. You're going to need it." I unrolled a towel for myself. I felt relieved to have his help. I couldn't prepare the way without him, because there were two paths. Theresa and I needed out path secured, even though it would never be tread. And I needed another path. It needed to be a separate one, yet connected at the beginning, with props and plans and a clear way for me, and me alone.

Because she wouldn't be coming with me.

Chapter Thirty-One

THERESA

We ended up at Sheila's most holidays. She had the children, and apparently their schedules held places in the pantheon. The Goddess Tina of the Late Naps needed a sacrifice, as did Evan, God of the Special Diet, and Kalle, Goddess of I Will Only Go Wee In My Own Pink Princess Bathroom.

It was easiest to just go to into Palos Verdes. Anyone who couldn't make it just didn't make it. It was impossible to herd eight siblings anyway, even if Daddy had tacitly agreed to be someplace else for a business function.

RPV, as it was called, was set deeply west and south on the map, and was practically inaccessible by more than one freeway, making it unmanageable for even the richest commuter with an actual job. A famous movie director's wife had started her own RPV-based Montessori school in her basement just to avoid having to bring her equally famous children to the Montessori school over the hills. Sheila described it as strictly a matter of geographical convenience. The children within a two-mile radius joined in, walking to school in packs and creating a true neighborhood enclave of a type that had once been the American norm, but with more money involved than most people would see in seven lifetimes.

Sheila answered the door, her more-blonde-than-red hair disheveled, cut into a bob, and her flip-flops showing off a weeks-old pedicure. She didn't even say "hello" when I was beset by children whose red-topped heads bobbed and swayed like the flames of birthday candles.

"Did you bring wine?" Sheila asked when I got through the door. Tina had latched onto my leg and insisted on being carried on my foot.

I handed my sister the bottle, and she snapped it from me with one hand while picking an oatmeal-crusted plastic spoon off the floor with the other.

"The turkey didn't make it." Her Pilates-toned ass worked the yoga pants as we walked toward the kitchen. "I'm having one brought in." Sheila's voice rose and fell in a childlike singsong, often ending sentences in a question. But underneath that sweet exterior rolled incredible rage. Pushed the wrong way, she reacted with blinding, illogical anger. So she didn't let much get to her anymore, or she'd lose control.

"What happened?" I asked.

"Dog got it." She swung her hand has if it didn't matter. "The mess was anthemic."

"Anthemic?"

"Like an anthem. It's the new 'epic.' Only Jon's here so far. Alma?" She turned to her helper, barking instructions in Spanish. The kitchen was indeed a mess, but without the usual holiday smell of good cooking. Just the food. All product, no process.

I heard men outside and saw Jonathan with David. My brother was instructing his nephew on the proper windup for some pitch, using an orange as a prop. The kid pitched it into the yard. I slid the door open.

Jon picked another orange off the tree and lobbed it to David. "You're opening your hips too soon, so you're getting zero power from the lower half of your body."

"Hey," I said. "Whatcha doing?"

"Basics. Again," David said, winding up.

"Wait, wait. This whole thing is in the hips. That's why you kick your leg. So don't forget to turn them."

David wound up and pitched into a tree about fifty feet away. The orange smacked against the trunk, bouncing off and landing in a pile of half-green oranges collecting on the grass.

"That's in the stands. You just took out Jack Nicholson. He's going to sue your ass."

"See, it's because you're making me turn my hips like that," David protested. He was ten and a funny kid, sixty-five pounds soaked in saltwater.

"It is not," Jon said.

"David." I sat at the table. "Your uncle knows."

He rolled his eyes so hard his brain should have been in his line of sight.

"Here." Jonathan poked him in the arm. "Watch."

He pulled another orange off the tree and pitched it into the tree trunk. It landed three feet below David's, even though its velocity had been much less.

"You just gave up a double pitching like a pussy." David grumbled.

Jonathan laughed. He had infinite patience with David's crappy attitude and stunted attention span. "Get out of here, kid," he said. "Go play Minecraft."

David rolled his eyes again, bobbing his head as he skipped off. Jonathan threw himself into the chair beside me.

"Uncoachable, that kid. Just raw energy all wrapped in IQ points."

"I wonder if you'd be so patient with your own kids."

He shrugged, fondling a short glass of whiskey with nearly melted ice.

"Sorry," I said. "I shouldn't have brought it up."

"Nah, Jessica's miscarriage was a long time ago."

"I feel like you guys never recovered from that."

"We took each other for granted. That's what we never recovered from. And me, I'm over it entirely. She stopped taking me for granted fifteen minutes after she saw me with someone else. It's sad."

"Where is this someone else?" I asked.

"I should be asking you. Where's the guy you were trying to not ask about at lunch? The one who says… what was it? *Come vuoi tu?*"

I think I blushed. It was easy to talk about his ex-wife and their failed attempts at children. Talking about my beautiful Capo made my skin prickle.

"Working," I lied.

"On Thanksgiving? Talk about taking someone for granted."

"Oh, Jonathan. Do we need to get laid?"

He nearly choked on his whiskey, and I realized I'd never spoken like that around my brother. As innocent as the words were, the sentiment was not from the Theresa he knew.

"Okay, okay!" He held his hand up in surrender. "I'll lay off the guy."

"Which guy?" Sheila asked from the other side of the screen door. Before I could answer, she continued, stepping back. "This guy?"

Beautiful even from behind a screen, Antonio stood, smiling and holding a bottle of wine. Sheila slapped the door open. I think I must have been smiling right back at him.

"Napa, again?"

"It's from Campania." He handed it to Sheila, who stared at him a second, smiled, and then went back into the house. I was stunned. I hadn't seen Sheila blown back by a man in a long, long time.

"Antonio, this is my brother, Jonathan."

They shook and exchanged how-do-you-dos. Daniel had been the last strange man I'd brought to a holiday function, and he'd melted into the scenery as if he belonged there. But I wasn't worried about Antonio. There were so many men and women, friends and others, who came to Sheila's dinners, that Antonio's presence would be noted but not focused on.

"So, Theresa's told me all about you," Jonathan said.

"Really?" Antonio said.

"No, actually, not a damn thing."

"Don't mind him," I said to Antonio. "He's got all my worst qualities."

Antonio folded his napkin in front of him. "Then you must be a shrewd yet reckless man."

"You aren't describing my sister. You can't be."

"You're implying I'm not shrewd?" I said in mock consternation.

"I'm implying that, for you, a four-inch heel is reckless," Jonathan said.

The doorbell rang, and the chaos began.

Chapter Thirty-Two

ANTONIO

I couldn't count all the adults at the house, much less the children, who were more restrained and more present than the kids in Napoli. I didn't trip over them. They were both more self-possessed than kids from home and wilder. They were shrewd with adults and seemed unable to negotiate their own squabbles or feed themselves. But I was so busy trying to remember names and faces of the adults that I didn't have time to give the children any of my reserves of memory.

I remembered Deirdre but pretended I didn't. I shook hands with Fiona and Margie and made a point of remembering them because they were siblings. Men came and went; there were boyfriends and husbands, and some were half a relationship I didn't understand.

"Thank you," Theresa whispered to me between conversations and questions I didn't want to answer.

"For you? The world."

"How are you holding up?" she asked as we walked the edge of the property where it fell to the beach. Beneath us, the waves crashed against the rocks.

"Which one is your mother?"

"My mother isn't here yet."

"Margie still looks at me like she doesn't approve."

"She doesn't approve of much," she said.

"I bet her husband is an unhappy man. Which one is he?"

"Doesn't have one."

"Too bad," I said. Our hands swung together as we walked along the property, leisurely heading back toward the house. We were still too far from anyone for eavesdropping, and the water made a good mask for our conversation.

"I'm thinking you need to come to the Bortolusi wedding," I said.

"How's that going to work while your father negotiates the value of your cock with the Sicilians?"

"You took on this dirty language with both fists, didn't you?"

"There's no other word to use. Does it bother you?" she asked.

"It makes me have to keep myself from taking you by the hair and putting you on your knees."

"Quick. Change the subject."

"If you come, it looks like a strategic move. It looks like I can walk any time, or that I want to."

"Keeping your frenemies on their toes," she said.

"Exactly." We'd gotten close to the house.

"Shall I ask for olive oil with the bread?"

Just as we came in from the patio, there was a crash from the kitchen, the volume and length indicating a mishap of some scope. It barely paused the conversations around us.

"None of the women are going to the kitchen to help?" I asked.

"She has a staff, but I was just thinking…"

Jonathan came up behind Theresa with his whiskey drained to the ice. "She kicked me out," he said.

"Does she need help?" Theresa asked.

"Would she admit it?"

She looked up at me. "Sheila might kick Jonathan out, but from me, she'll take help."

"Andiamo."

"Jonathan, can you take care of Antonio? Make sure he doesn't step on a toe."

"Mom's not even here yet," Jonathan said.

She play punched him in the arm and went to the kitchen to see what had happened.

I tried not to look at her bottom when she walked away. She never swayed it or asked for attention with it, but her posture was so straight and proud, the result of such effort to remove sex from her gestures, that I got hard just looking at her.

But her brother was right next to me, and looking at his sister as if she was naked wouldn't make me a friend. I didn't know what future I had with Theresa, but I was sure getting kicked out of her sister's house at Thanksgiving wasn't going to help.

"You're the only boy," I said to Jonathan. "Of how many?"

"Eight."

"Protecting all these women. Sounds like a full-time job."

"You have a sister, then?" His Italian was accented, but fluid and nuanced. I had to remember not to underestimate him.

"Back home," I said. "Just one, two years older than me."

"She know everything about everything?"

"But, of course. How I breathe without her help, I always wonder."

He glanced around. I knew the look. He was seeing if anyone was listening. At least one of them must have spoken Italian. "Even after you came here looking for those *bastardi*?"

"Yes."

Though the shift in the conversation hadn't caused half a second of pause, and our faces betrayed nothing, it was as audible to me as a magazine clicking into place.

"Heard you missed one," he said.

"I haven't forgotten." I was being watched, indeed, by the redhead with the vapor cigarette and one of the men.

"Good."

"I think that's the only big failure in my dossier," I said.

Jonathan nodded. "We've decided to overlook it."

"No Italian!" Theresa had returned. She put her hand on my back. "Not fair. I don't know what you're saying."

"Did Sheila need anything?" Jonathan asked.

"Besides a mop? No. And she's letting the kids toast the s'mores before dinner."

They exchanged a look that seemed more intense than it needed to be.

"Oh, Jon don't tell this story," she said.

"Why not?"

"It's… I don't know. Inappropriate."

At the word, he took on a glint of mischief and leaned toward me. "Our dad took us to the club whenever Mom was unavailable, meaning *incapacitated*, and the nannies had the night off or were overwhelmed.

"Which was most of the time." Theresa was cutting in on the conversation despite her misgivings about appropriateness. "The 'overwhelmed' part, I mean."

"Yeah. Of course, he'd go off with his cronies to the Gate Bar to drink, and we'd be left in the TV room. Which had this big screen. At the time, this was a big deal."

"Oh, and movies on prerelease."

"Right. R rated, too. But mostly, we'd wander around, and at one point we got to the carriage house. It was me, Theresa, and Leanne, who was old enough to know better. But we saw these lights on and who knew, right? Maybe there were baskets of candy or some coke or something."

"We were too young for that."

"I think Leanne was dabbling. So. Hell, if there wasn't something going on. Out on the patio, it was so damn dark, but we smelled a barbecue and found it happening at the carriage house. A bag of marshmallows was right there. It was closed. The boxes of graham crackers and chocolate were, too. Leanne wouldn't let me have any unless there was no one inside. So we checked."

"How old were you?" I asked.

"Eight," he said. "By the way, it was the last time she got candy out of my hand. Anyway, so, you know, the carriage house was like a guesthouse for dignitaries, right on the Downtown Gate Club grounds. It had everything in it. A kitchen they never used, a little pool, and a sitting room, which we snuck into."

"It seemed like a good idea at the time," Theresa said.

"So, we're in there. And we hear this noise, like this slapping. And we're all curious. Oldest of us is what, eleven? And, get that look off your face," he said to me, "It's not what you think."

"It's ten times worse," Theresa said.

"We peek around to the living room, and then, I mean the slapping gets louder, and there's this…" He lowered his voice. "Woman, bent over the couch, with her bare bottom out, and a guy. Big hairy motherfucker of a beast, hitting her ass with a slab of meat."

I didn't say anything, because I hadn't heard that exact idiom before. But Theresa burst out laughing.

"I think it was a raw flank steak," she blurted out.

"Wait, what?"

"She covered my eyes. So sure, if she knows the cut of meat, I believe her."

"*Mio Dio*." I didn't even believe what I was hearing. I had to hold in an attack of laughter, because Theresa was taking over the story.

"The guy… he hears something, and he stops. We run. Leanne pulls us in some crazy direction—"

"She has no sense of direction. She gets lost putting her contacts in," said Jonathan.

"And we end up in the bedroom diving for a closet. We make it, but we hear the guy stomping down the hall, yelling in Russian."

"Czech," corrected Jonathan. "And I tell them, I whisper, 'You're my sisters, and I won't let him spank you with meat.'"

Though he'd kept his face straight until then, none of us could hold it in any longer. I laughed so hard I thought my guts would drop out of me. Theresa had tears streaming down her face, and Jonathan tried to finish the story between bouts of laughter. "Leanne, I mean she was horrified. She said, 'No one's spanking anyone with meat, Jon.' And then this one"—he pointed to Theresa—"says, 'he was just tenderizing it for the grill.'"

"I was protecting your eight-year-old mind!" Theresa said.

"Wait," I said. "You were talking? In the closet? Did he hear you?"

"We were in the tunnel by that time." Theresa wiped a tear away, then seeing what must have been a quizzical expression, she said, "There are moveable panels in the closet. All the kids knew about them. The carriage house used to be a speakeasy. There are tunnels under it that go across the street. From prohibition."

"Ah." I said. "So you got away?"

"Yeah," Theresa said. "There's one spot where it bent to a grate under the parking space outside, and if you stood one kid on top of the other, you could open it. I have no idea if those panels are still there. I'm sure they've been sealed during a renovation or something."

"They closed the connection between the carriage house and the grate," Jonathan said. "I was trying to lose my virginity a few years later and ran into a wall."

"It has to still be there," I said.

"It's all still there. Trust me. But the grate's not connected to the house any more. And that was the best escape route, too. Landed across Gate Avenue. Remember?"

"All right!" Sheila called out from the kitchen. "We're not waiting for Mom. So if you all want to eat, the caterer is here, and we're ready to go!"

Chapter Thirty-Three

THERESA

We ate like kings and queens, princes and princesses. I didn't taste any of it. I was memorizing Leanne's slovenly ponytail, Sheila's lilting singsong, Margie's clipped wit, Deirdre's errant curl and sober scowl. Jonathan said nothing of importance, deftly avoiding any meaningful, personal subject matter as if he were in some sort of pain he didn't want discussed over dinner. I wanted to corner him and ask what was happening. But then he told some joke and got a witty rejoinder from Margie. He laughed. I smiled at my brother and wondered how I would make it through the rest of my life without hearing his laugh.

Antonio put his hand on my knee and squeezed it. I put mine on top of his, and we looked at each other. I felt a third hand on my knee. It was smaller, softer, and slick with grease.

"I wanna hold, too!" I peeked under the tablecloth. It was Kalle. She had a turkey leg in her hand and poultry bits all over the front of her sequined dress. She had a lump of Play-Doh in the other hand. It smelled of dry bread dough.

"Can you wash your hands first?"

"No! I don't like to wash my hands!" She left a big stinker of a three-year-old's handprint on Antonio's pant leg.

For some reason, when she giggled at the shape of the grease stain, a lump rose in my throat. I smiled through it and excused myself. I got myself together in the bathroom. I had to choose between my family and Antonio, and I loved this family, at least my siblings, but I didn't want to be without my Capo. Not for a month or a year. Too much of my life had ticked away while I'd been doing things that made me unhappy. I'd settled for the wrong choices, followed the wrong people, and betrayed myself for too long. I was doing what I wanted, no matter how much it hurt.

Sheila was waiting for me on the way out.

"Theresa? Are you all right?" Her lilt, as if she spoke to a hurt child, would have driven anyone else crazy. It might have had that effect on me, but at that moment, I needed it.

"This guy? He's not hurting your feelings is he? Because I'll be happy to rip his spine out." Even when making death threats, her voice was gentle as a lullaby.

"Him? No. He makes me very happy. I think I'm just tired, and I had too much wine."

I hugged her tightly. I couldn't let it go too long. I couldn't cry on her shoulder. If I did, she'd know something was wrong. But in my mind, I said goodbye to her and to all of them.

Antonio didn't ask me anything until the car ride back.

"Do you need to back out?" he asked. "I won't mind. I'll understand."

I ignored him. I knew I could back out. "Are you supposed to propose to this girl or something?"

He pressed his lips together as if he didn't want to answer. I waited.

"After the Bortolusi-Lei wedding."

"How soon after?"

"Very soon. There's all kinds of formalities. I have to ask Donna Maria first, then have chaperoned visits… and on and on. But they won't suffer the power imbalance too long."

"I think we should die at the wedding," I said. "I think everyone should see it. I mean there are easier ways, for sure, but they'll be questioned."

"What did you have in mind?" he asked.

"We don't need to just die," I said. "We need to be obliterated. Let me finish working it out, but I think the wedding is the place to do it."

He nodded, as if understanding the gravity of what I was saying. As if he saw me shaking, he said nothing more on the drive to the little Spanish house.

I had given no thought to death, unless I wanted to be paralyzed with fear. I was afraid of neither pain nor hell, but death? Death crippled me.

It was the thought of nonexistence that took my breath away. The idea —and it was only an idea—that we ceased completely was no comfort. I felt only terror, because I wondered what my life had been in the first place if my consciousness could be so utterly snuffed. And in those moments that I allowed myself to feel, and thus fear, my nonexistence, the shattering vulnerability of my corporeal self overtook me until my skin crawled at the thought.

Was my consciousness made of carbon and electrical impulses? And was I more than that consciousness, or less? Contemplating death made me question life. Consciousness was all that I valued, and if I ceased to think when I fell into that infinite sleep, what exactly was the living me?

I would go with him into death, into that deepest of vacuums. But our death would be special, a birth into a new life together. Everyone else had to go into blackness alone, to hold up the earth or to fuel a fire.

We just hadn't worked out how exactly we would die. And then, in the middle of the night, it came to me.

"Antonio," I whispered, turning and finding his eyes already open.

"Yes?"

I caressed his cheek with the backs of my fingers, and he kissed them.

"Fire and tunnels."

The answer was fire; that had never been in question. But there was always the matter of an escape route, and it came to me on the drive home on Thanksgiving.

The tunnels under the carriage house were part of a ten-acre system under downtown, built inside basements for deliveries, initially, then for drunken escapes from the underground speakeasies in the 1920s. Each block had its own network of basements and tunnels, and, in the case of the Gate Club, there were only two ways to get off the city block. The first was down the grate and across Gate Avenue to an unused trapdoor in a driveway; the second was the speakeasy way, through the carriage house, across Ludwig Street and into a residential basement.

The grate was in a small parking lot. We couldn't use it without being seen going down it, so that option was out. The carriage house had no cameras to protect the privacy of important people, and the walls were thick for the same reason. It was perfect.

"You drew this?" Antonio said when I handed him the map. He was freshly showered. His lashes looked darker and thicker, like black-widow legs.

"I wanted to get it right."

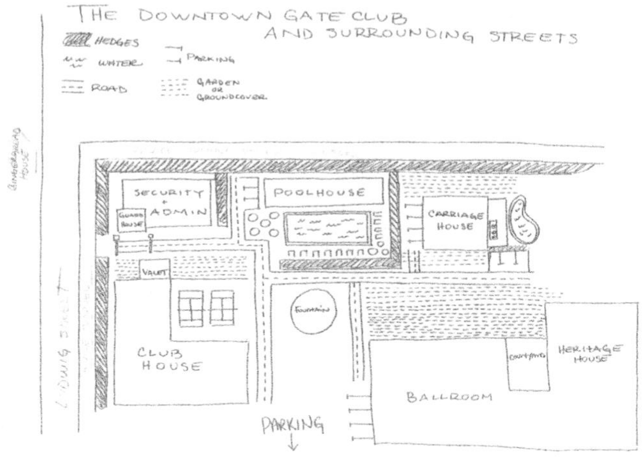
THE DOWNTOWN GATE CLUB
AND SURROUNDING STREETS
HEDGES
WATER
ROAD
PARKING
GARDEN OR GROUNDCOVER
SECURITY + ADMIN
GUARD HOUSE
POOLHOUSE
CARRIAGE HOUSE
VALET
FOUNTAIN
CLUB HOUSE
COURTYARD
HERITAGE HOUSE
BALLROOM
PARKING

"YOU REALLY DO NEED A LIFE."

I swatted him. "*Basta*."

He cocked an eyebrow at me, and I pointed to the map. "Okay, this is the layout. As I remember it, the tunnels went from the carriage house, across Ludwig, into the gingerbread house. It's really long, but if we run..."

"And you want to blow up the house?" He said it as if it were a possibility, but it sounded absurd to my ears.

"Yes," I said, embracing the absurdity. I picked up a red marker and drew on the map.

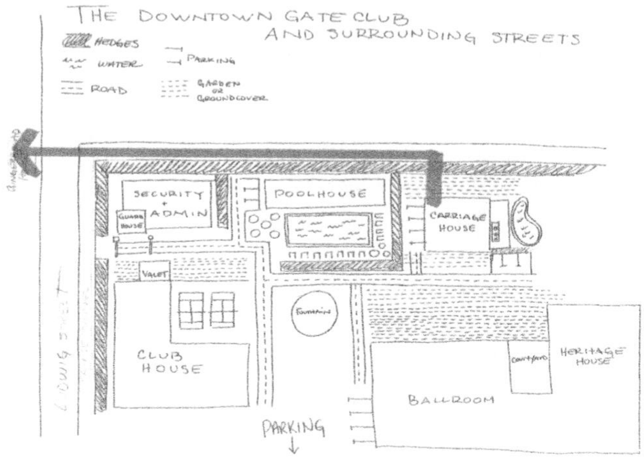
THE DOWNTOWN GATE CLUB
AND SURROUNDING STREETS
HEDGES
WATER
ROAD
PARKING
GARDEN OR GROUNDCOVER
SECURITY + ADMIN
GUARD HOUSE
POOLHOUSE
CARRIAGE HOUSE
VALET
FOUNTAIN
CLUB HOUSE
COURTYARD
HERITAGE HOUSE
BALLROOM
PARKING

"HERE TO HERE. Done. The service tunnel is straight because they used it for deliveries."

"But there's another way?" he asked.

"Yes, but it's not connected to the house. There's a grate here. I don't know how we'd get to it without being seen."

He took the map from me, and the red pen, and drew his own lines, at one point plucking his own black pen from his pocket for an accompaniment. I loved watching him work, the concentration. I wanted to work with him, to see that part of him all the time.

"This is how it's going to go," he said. "According to you and your brother, there's a tunnel across Gate, not connected, and a grate we can't get to. But we can."

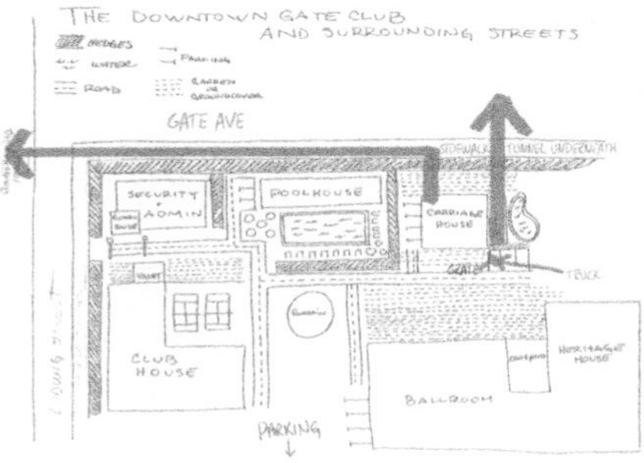

"HOW?" I asked. "The grate's right there. You can even see if from the ballroom if you just look through the trees."

He winked at me. "You check out the way across Ludwig, and I'll see what I can do about the short way."

Chapter Thirty-Four

THERESA

I could go look at the carriage house, under the pretense of planning a stay there at some point after the Bortolusi wedding. I could even put a deposit on the place, as if I were expecting to be alive to throw an actual party on the grounds. But that would be a paper trail. It would be known that I went to look at the carriage house weeks before the wedding that was the scene of my death. And Daniel was blindly ambitious and emotionally void, but he was not stupid.

So, I had to look at the other side, and that was where I got lucky. The gingerbread house across Ludwig Street was for sale. It sat in a tiny residential enclave in the middle of downtown, protected by a Historic Overlay Zone.

A two-foot-high plastic A-frame sign sat by the streetlight, with the address written in chalk under the words "Open House!" Three white balloons had been tied to the corner with blue grosgrain ribbon. The breeze had twisted the ribbons into a stiff braid by the time I got there. I parked on the corner and walked as if I wanted to check out the block.

The houses sat close together. None were the same; none held to a stylistic similarity. The gingerbread house was the only one of its kind for miles around, with swooping peaks and dormers, shingles that curved over the edge of the roof, and a red door. Grey stone covered everything from the porch floor to the path leading to it. The windows were small, plentiful, and painted blue at the crosspieces.

The house had been staged in period-appropriate furnishings, except the kitchen, which has been redone in glass tile and stainless, probably to raise the sale price. Couples milled about, looking in closets and trying to find reasons to buy or not. They made notes and whispered, talking to each other about the real-estate market and its pattern of booms and busts. I smiled noncommittally at everyone and drifted between rooms. I opened the cabinet under the sink. It was filled with cardboard boxes. Whoever lived there hadn't moved out all the way yet.

"Hi there!" I turned, taking my hands off the knob as if I'd been caught peeking in a friend's medicine cabinet. In the doorway stood a woman with cornrows and a white smile, clutching a clipboard to her chest. "I'm Wendy! Did you sign in?"

"No." I smiled back. I intended to neither sign in nor explain why.

"Were you interested in the neighborhood, or gingerbread in general? Because we have another one in West Adams."

"Is it in the overlay?"

"It is."

"And the renovations here," I indicated the kitchen. "Approved by the historic district?"

"All the modernization by the previous owners was approved." Her smile hid something.

"And before that?"

"If you were planning to do any remodeling to the basement, there are some adjustments you'd need to make. We have a very rare basement in this house. It was modernized without approval ten years ago."

"Can you show me?"

"Us too," said a man who had been taking down the model number of the microwave.

Wendy perked up. She led us down a narrow stairway that twisted in the middle, down to media room with industrial carpeting, leather couches, and a screen that took up the entire space. One window set high in the wall looked out onto Ludwig Street. I touched the wall under it.

"This is a fully functioning media center, but as you know…" She nattered on about Historic Preservation Overlay Zones and districts, the rules that had to be abided, how her agency would help buyers navigate the process, and why the media room was still a great addition.

But I was thinking about tumbling into that same basement through the trapdoor, stinking of old dirt and Fiona's cigarettes, falling face to face with an oil-heater tank. The basement back then had been dark as hell, with the only light coming from the moon through the street-level windows. I'd navigated piles of fabrics teeming from boxes, an old gas grill, and a plastic Christmas tree with light strings still on it.

I lost myself in the memory of that near-illegal thing, running my hand over the wall where the oil tank had been set. It could have been defined as breaking and entering, maybe. I hadn't been elated or paralyzed, but had entered a zone where my senses tingled, and I focused on one thing only: getting out. I calculated the time, the distance back across the street, the likelihood everyone upstairs was asleep. I checked out the window to see if the car was in the drive and wondered if I could climb through it without looking like a burglar.

That had been the only time I'd crossed the length of the tunnel to the house on the other side, and the gritty trip back to the club had been uneventful. But I poked the memory to see what had changed, and just about everything had.

I looked at the one remaining window then down. The wall beneath it was solid, and cool to the touch, as if stone through and through. The panel to the carriage house tunnel had been bricked over. The tunnel out was a dead end, literally and figuratively.

We'd have to figure something else out. The tunnel was blocked, and we couldn't use the grate exit.

—Where are you?—

I didn't know if I'd ever get used to Antonio just demanding my location, but knowing we were in a special circumstance, I tamped down the offense and went outside to call him.

"I'm looking at a house," I said. He'd know what I meant.

In the background, I heard sirens and men shouting.

"Are you all right?" I asked.

"I'm fine."

"What are the sirens?" It wasn't unusual to hear sirens in the background when someone called from outside, but they'd never caused my chest to tighten and my breath to shorten before.

"Don't get in your car. Otto will come for you."

I didn't ask. He wouldn't tell me over the phone.

As if he'd been nearby the whole time, Otto showed up ten minutes later with a half-eaten sandwich in his lap.

"Hey, Miss Drazen. You have the beemer?" He opened the door for me.

"It's down the block. What happened?"

"The blue Mas is gone. Pieces of it are still falling outta the sky."

"What?"

"Car bomb."

"Is he all right?" I asked, even though I knew he must have been, or he wouldn't have called.

"Everyone's fine. Spin caught a bit of shrapnel in the leg. The thing went off when he unlocked it. I'm telling you, that shop has taken a beating. They gotta start over."

"Who did it?"

"We got our ideas." He said no more.

Chapter Thirty-Five

ANTONIO

I never saw the bomb that went off in Napoli, the one that had my wife declared dead. It had been a column of smoke over the mountains. Then, when Zo met me halfway down the mountain to tell me what had happened, I didn't breathe until I saw the circle of black and the carcass of the car.

The bomb in Los Angeles was so different I didn't make the connection right away.

The shop had just come back to life and was populated with men hauling wood, wielding nail guns, and shouting to each other. They'd gone to the Korean pizzeria for lunch, leaving tools behind and work undone, but the garage had been reframed already.

When I unlocked the Mas as I was heading toward it, my mind was on Theresa and how she'd fare without her family. I doubted she'd make it, yet I had to believe she would. I was thinking I needed to choose whether to believe she could stay by her word or to doubt her when the car hopped as if animated. The motion was barely visible, and the tires never left the earth, but only became more circular at the bottom, losing the weight that flattened them to the ground.

I only had time to kiss the ground, as if I'd kicked my own legs from under me. The sound deafened me, blasting the top of my head, velocity of the air pushing me back an inch or more, and a rain of glass followed for the next sixty seconds.

I spent that entire minute convincing myself to breathe, because I'd never been that close to a car bomb.

My life was getting simpler and simpler. I was being pushed through my options one by one until I had none left. Seemingly all at once, I'd gone from having a few enemies and a couple of soured relationships to being a target.

The forensics unit was in the process of clearing every scrap of glass and metal; every speck of carbon and dust went into a bag. I was treated like a criminal, not like a victim, even when I sat outside the back of an ambulance. I was questioned for an hour about my whereabouts that morning (Zia Giovanna's, which was verified) as if I'd blown up my car for the insurance money. Once they realized who I was, the tone of the questioning changed. My shop was cordoned off with yellow tape, and the contractors were questioned. I knew they'd walk away untroubled and come back the next day. They were my men. If they weren't trustworthy, they wouldn't work for me.

I went through the questioning before an EMT saw the blood on my trouser leg and pulled me into the ambulance, sitting me down as if I couldn't do it myself. She was insightful and gentle, with a straight brown ponytail I might have taken a try at pulling in the past.

"What kind of car was it?" she asked while she cut my pant leg, her plastic gloves wrinkling at the knuckles.

"A Maserati Quattroporte."

"This year's?" She spread the pant leg open. A piece of metal was lodged in the muscle of my calf.

"Last year's. I liked it too much to get a new one."

"Nostalgia. I get it. This is going to hurt, Mr. Spinelli." She squirted the wound with a blue liquid that stung nicely. But I knew that wasn't what she was talking about.

"This your shop?" She didn't look me in the eye. She was pretty, even as she held onto the metal with a pair of sterile pliers. Carefully, she pulled the metal out of the muscle. It did indeed hurt.

"Yeah. Past five years or so."

"Looks like it's taken a beating."

"Rough month," I said. She pulled out the last of it, holding it up for me to see.

"The car was blue, huh?"

"Custom paint."

She plunked the metal into a tray. "Nice." She squirted the green liquid to clean the wound. It wasn't that bad. The expectation of pain was always worse than the actual thing.

"Looks pretty good," she said, peeling the skin away, looking for debris, and squeezing her liquid in the crevices. "I can take you to the hospital if you're worried about scarring."

"Scars are the proof we've lived."

She looked up at me. "You're going to have a really nice bit of proof here."

I took my cigarettes out. I needed one. Not for the gash in my leg. I didn't care about that. But the bomb made a good impression as a message. The bomb was a flexed muscle, a chambered bullet, teeth that were bared and ready to rip a throat. But only if necessary. Next time I wouldn't be so lucky, in theory. That was what I told the police.

I leaned my head against the side of the truck and let the pretty EMT clean my leg. I wondered what the hell I was doing, and why. Money? Power? My vengeance was complete. I had nothing. My family was an ocean away. I had no partner. My business was burned down. I wasn't the lawyer I'd wanted to be. I had no future outside of a beautiful woman who would tire of my secrecy soon enough. I wished I'd been inches from that car, because I was exhausted from running, from hunting, and from keeping secrets.

Otto pulled up across the street, and my Contessa got out before the Lincoln had even come to a full stop. She was my hope, that woman, standing so straight as she crossed the street. She could rule the world. She already ruled me.

Chapter Thirty-Six

THERESA

We didn't say anything to each other when I saw him in that ambulance. We didn't need to. I sat next to him and held his hand. He waved Otto away. The EMT put bandages on him without a word, other than instructions on dressing his wound the next day. Then she left to take care of someone else.

"Those were nice pants," I said.

"I have more."

"Who did this? Paulie?"

He shook his head, leaning it on the side of the truck. "No. The Sicilians are watching him. This was the Bortolusis. I'm the last *camorrista* prince. If I'm gone, there's no merger."

"And you're going to the wedding? I think I should forbid it."

"It'll be the safest place in the world on that day. Paulie's been too quiet, and it's you he wants."

"That's our last day on earth."

He squeezed my hand. "*Si*."

"When you leave, there's going to be a power vacuum. Paulie's going to try and fill it. I'm thinking I have a couple of days to plant a seed in Daniel's head about him. Just put him on a trail. That'll get my ex off of thinking about where our bodies went, and Paulie will be preoccupied with sworn statements and such."

He huffed a short laugh. "My God. You have the heart of a capo, do you know that? You could have brought Sicily to its knees. No don would stand against you."

"I'll call Dan tomorrow."

"No." He squeezed my hand when he said it. "Make an appointment for the day after the wedding. Say you have something on Paulie. Say you're checking it out."

He seemed so melancholy, so much a swirling black pool of sadness, that I was drawn in with him.

"Can I take you home to the loft and feed you soup?"

"Ah, Contessa, I have to—"

I stood. "You have to nothing. Get the hell up, Capo." I held my hand out, and he clasped my wrist.

"No don could stand against you." He smiled as I hoisted him then grimaced when he leaned on the leg.

"You need to lean on me?"

"No. I'm all right."

"Antonio."

"Yes?" he said.

"Next time you do something like this, you need to tell me first. I was worried. I don't want to panic like that again."

He stopped and faced me, a smile playing on his lips. "Are you saying I blew up a Maserati? My favorite car? To what, set a pattern? To get the next one to look just as real? Come on, that car cost a hundred thousand dollars."

I crossed my arms. "All of Zo's guys are gone. He always leaves one to sit with the tools. He eats lunch out the back of the truck, but not today."

"Contessa, even if I had done such a crazy thing, I wouldn't have told you. You'd try and stop me and get yourself hurt."

"One day, you'll see me as a partner, not a responsibility."

He put his arm around my shoulder, and we walked back to my car, his bloody pant leg flapping against his calf as he tried to hide the fact that he was limping.

Chapter Thirty-Seven

THERESA

I laid him out on my couch and fed him minestrone I'd poured from a can and heated in the microwave. He complained about the saltiness, demanding I try Zia Giovanna's the next time I was there. "When she makes it, you can taste everything. This, I don't even know what's in it." He took the bowl from me and put it on the side table then pulled me on top of him.

"What are you going to do about Zia Giovanna?"

"How do you mean?" he asked.

"Daniel's taking those books, and I don't know if I caught everything. He's going to have your accountant. He won't prosecute an old woman. That would be political suicide. But the restaurant?"

He pressed his lips together into a fine line. "Without me, she'll go back to Napoli with her sister."

"Come on, Antonio—"

"Not everything needs to be controlled. There are no formal charges against her. She can go any time. It's like you. No charges in the thing with the Armenian. If I were gone, he'd drop it."

He was dead wrong, about Zia Giovanna at least, and I didn't know if he was lying to himself or just to me.

"I had a thought," I said.

"Another one?" He stroked my hair.

"Greece," I said.

"I don't speak Greek." He pulled my shirt up and slid his fingers under my bra, the tips bending my nipples.

"Weather's nice. Government's totally corrupt." I groaned at the trilling sensation between my legs. I pushed myself down on his erection. "After we bounce around. When we've erased everything. We can settle there. Fuck on the beach every day."

He got my shirt and bra off in one movement. "That would be nice."

"Nice?" I unzipped him.

"*Simpatico.*"

"That's better, Capo."

I stood up and wiggled out of my pants, naked before him in seconds. He held his hand out, and I took it, putting a knee beside him.

"*Tu sei preziosa per me.*"

"I have no idea what that means."

"*Io ti farò del male per proteggerti.*"

I straddled him, putting his dick against my wetness. "Nothing. You get nothing until you translate."

"You think this stupid wound will keep me from taking you?"

"*Fammi tua,*" I said into his ear.

"Your accent is terrible."

I slid myself against him. "*Fammi tua.*"

"To save the world from your Italian, I'll tell you what I said. It was, 'I'm going to fuck you easy and slow, until your bones turn into jelly, and you forget how to beg me.'"

"When? I want you to fuck me. Please."

He moved my hips and shifted until a sharp upward stroke was all that he needed to impale me. I gasped. He grabbed my ass cheeks and pushed deep into me until I felt the pressure inside.

"Is this what you want?"

"Yes."

He rocked against me, his body rubbing my clit, and I threw my head back.

"Like this?" he asked.

"Faster."

"Faster what?"

"Please."

"*Per favore,*" he said.

"Oh, no. I can't."

He stopped moving and smiled an evil grin, brown eyes glittering. "Say it so I can hear it."

"Per favore. I want it."

"Lo voglio."

"Lo voglio, Capo."

I leaned forward, and he gathered me in his arms, holding me close and controlling my movement. *"Sei così preziosa per me."* He whispered it over and over as the heat between us built to a red throb, slowly, in a rhythm that went from pleasant to tortuous without changing.

"Wait for me," he sighed.

"Per favore," I cried. "Faster, please."

"Wait for me."

I nodded but had no words until he said, *"Si."*

He held me to the rhythm, and I felt every step of my orgasm: the foothills, the climb to the mountain, and then the volcano dripping lava as I cried for him. My face pressed to his, my mouth opened wordlessly, and he put his lips to my tears and came into me, clutching me as if he'd never let me go.

Chapter Thirty-Eight

THERESA

I lived in an unreality where my life was marked in days. And having made that absurd, stupid choice to end my life, I lost my mind.

Antonio was shrewder than I was. He wanted to leave everything alone and let it sort itself out. I wanted to leave a neat little world behind me, where everyone could be happy. Anything less seemed cruel. I kept twisting contingencies around in my mind, trying to find the best and worst outcomes and to fix all I could without raising flags. What damage could be prevented? Was there a single favor I could call in and never repay?

There was.

I didn't tell Antonio. We'd be long gone and he could be pissed at me as we fucked on a beach on a Greek island. The thought of a rabid hate-fuck on a beach made me smile, in public, on an elevator to the Century City penthouse, where ODRSN Enterprises had its offices.

"Daddy," I said when he turned the corner and entered the bright, sparkling reception area. My father was in his sixties. He still stood straight at six foot four, wearing a four-thousand-dollar suit and a face still handsome enough to turn heads.

"Theresa." He handed a folder to a tall, blonde receptionist. She slipped behind the glass desk and answered the phone, smiling like a robot. My father had impoverished the family trust. Then Jonathan had rebuilt it and sold it back to J. Declan Drazen. Since then, my father had been a businessman worthy of the original Irish-born Jonathan O'Drassen and just as bad a parent as the Irishman.

"What brings you out here?" he asked.

"Looking for a job."

"Really?"

"No."

He laughed and led me into the corner office. The windows were on a slant, as if it were a greenhouse where all the plants had been removed and replaced by an expansive desk and maps of Los Angeles everywhere.

"I'm glad you came by." He indicated a leather chair and sat in the seat next to it. "I've been meaning to talk to you since Thanksgiving."

"It's my turn to say, 'really?'"

"Tell me first, how are you doing since you left WDE?"

"Fine. I've been working a little on my friend's film."

He leaned back. The leather of the sofa squeaked. "It's not like my daughter Theresa to not have any plans. Fiona, yes. Leanne, sometimes, but you? You always were very sensible."

"It's not like I need money to live."

"You never wanted to live on your trust."

"I'm just in between things."

He shook his head slowly.

"You don't approve?" I said.

"You're all past my approval. Which is too bad. But no, since you asked, I don't. I heard about this man you took to Sheila's?"

"And?"

"Is he the reason you quit your job with nowhere to land?"

The visit had been a mistake. He did what he always did: he took control of the conversation and made me uncomfortable before I'd even gotten to the reason for my visit. And he'd do it until I either blurted out what I wanted or left without mentioning it. He had that way of interacting. He just wanted to make us squirm. He wanted to take the rug out from under us. It was his *way,* and even when he'd been called out on it, he'd laughed. Only Margie could manage him, God bless her and God fuck her.

"I quit my job because I was miserable. I have nowhere to land because I hadn't set anything up. I hadn't even thought about it. I've spent my whole life inside a sensible little box. I got tired of it."

"So you went 'outside the box'? That's very cliché, Theresa. I'd say you're better than that, but you're not a creative soul. I thought you were at peace with that."

His tone was so gentle and sincere that his words didn't sound insulting. I knew they were, but he wasn't trying to offend me, so I took no offense. He had a way of cutting deep without letting a person put up a defense.

"I am, but I've been thinking about what to do, anyway. There's a trust I need released to my discretion. There's only one left that you still have control over."

"I know the one. What were your plans?"

His interest was piqued. He knew I didn't want to pack it up my nose or blow it on the ponies.

"Antonio's aunt has a restaurant in San Pedro. It's being investigated for fraud, and I've looked at the books. It's clean, but broke. He can't help or he'll be accused of laundering money through it. He's pulled out completely. She's a nice old woman. The restaurant is all she has. I want to help her."

"How nice of you." He didn't believe a word of it, or at the very least, he didn't care.

"And because I know nothing is free with you," I said, letting the first part of the sentence sink in. He nodded. He didn't care what any of us thought of him. "I can donate half to the Wilshire Golfer's Club. I can finance a renovation. I think the carriage house could use a touch-up?"

He waved my suggestion away. "They haven't done anything in eighteen years. They won't fix that thing until an earthquake flattens it, and it's already survived two."

"You name it, then."

"For this man? This mobster?"

"For me," I said.

He looked out the wall of windows. "Have you ever wondered how I have so many children and so few grandchildren?"

"There's Sheila."

"She can't make up for the lot of you. Margie's a spinster. Carrie is off somewhere. Fiona, thank God…" He rubbed his eyes with a thumb and forefinger, as if truly troubled. "It's the men you girls choose. I don't know where you find them."

I could have made a crack about the example he set, but to what end? He was too old to change, and I was too old to take what he said personally.

"I'll tell you what," he said, taking his fingers from his eyes. "Make a good choice, one good choice, and I'll release the funds."

"Define a good choice."

"Whatever this phase is, finish it. Go back to who you are. Start making sense again. Then go back to Daniel. I'm sure he's apologized. Am I right?"

"Dad, really? What will this solve?"

I shook my head. This was a waste of time. Dad had done his share of philandering, enough to put him and Mom on opposite sides of the house. I should have expected that kind of old-world nonsense.

"Is this business?" I asked. "Are you looking to have the mayor in the family?"

"I know what makes sense when I see it. That's all."

He did, and Daniel and I had always made sense, always been perfect on paper, and that was how Dad saw everything. He never understood actual human emotion, which was how we ended up having a conversation with him thinking the ridiculous was possible.

"Just think about it," he said. "My insistence might be a favor in the end."

"I will."

When I stood, I saw a picture on a shelf, a big one of the ten of us at the Santa Barbara campground, each in our own world. Margie looked more a sister to Mom than a daughter. Jonathan, at twelve, was already bursting with puberty. Fiona's hair was tangled. And there I was in a button down shirt and lace collar, chin up, skin without pimple or blemish from sheer force of will.

"This was the year after," I said, stopping in my tracks.

"After what?"

"The boy."

"Which one?"

"The one at the bottom of a ditch," I said.

"Yes?"

"I went through middle and high school convinced you did it."

He held up his palms, one finger still wrapped in a ring that didn't mean what it had decades before. "These hands are clean," he said and denied it no further.

Chapter Thirty-Nine

THERESA

"I need your phone," Antonio said, standing over me in a jacket and trousers. I'd grabbed his pillow and pressed it to my face, breathing in his burned-pine smell.

"Why?" I grumbled into the pillow. Why was I so relaxed in that happy limbo between living and dying?

"Because I need to put a detonator in it."

It was a normal weekday-morning conversation. It wasn't even exciting or titillating, but right and real in a way nothing in my life had been before. I shuffled around in my bag and handed him the phone. He took it and pulled me to him, pressing my nakedness against his clothes.

"You have a call from your sister," he said, holding the glass to face me.

"Of course I do. She must be scolding me about something."

The text came up first.

—Jon is at Sequoia. Heart
attack. Looking at a bypass
where the fuck are you?—

My hand covered my mouth. I'd ignored my phone because nothing seemed as important as what we were doing, but Jon at the hospital? I hadn't expect that.

Antonio held his hand out for the phone. "What is it?"

"He's thirty-two."

"Who?" He looked at the text.

"I have to go see my brother." I stepped away and headed for my pile of clothes. I had no intention of bathing or delaying another second. Antonio just stood in the middle of the room, my phone in his palm.

"We should call this off," he said.

"Let me see what it is first."

"You love your family."

"Antonio!" I shouted. I hadn't meant to shout. "Just let me go see him, okay? Then we can decide."

SEQUOIA TOOK up a few city blocks on the west side, the hub of a medical community with research centers for spokes and uniform and equipment suppliers at the outer rings.

I found Jonathan sitting on the edge of his bed with tubes all over him. He looked drained of everything but frustration. Sheila sat in the chair by the window, tapping on her phone like she wanted to poke through it. Under stress, the rage came out.

"Hi," I said, kissing his cheek. "You look good."

"He wants to get out of here," Sheila said.

"They're holding me until I'm stable," he growled. "And I'm feeling more unstable every hour."

"What happened?" I asked. "You're hardly old enough for this."

"Can I not review this again?" he said.

"Honestly," Sheila said, all the singsong gone. "It's just his youthful indiscretions catching up with him. But if you make him tell the story again, he's going to chew your face off, and it's not worth it. He needs a bypass. He's going to get it. End."

"They do them during their lunch hour. It's just which lunch hour that's the question." He laid back. I sat in the chair next to the bed. A tray sat next to him with a plastic container that was empty but for a piece of cut pineapple.

"They're letting you eat pineapple?" I asked.

He looked at me as if I were crazy then followed my gaze to the container. "That's Monica's."

"Where is she?" I asked. "Is this is the new girl?"

"She comes at night," Jonathan said.

"Mom thinks she's a gold digger taking advantage of Jonathan's infirmity," Sheila piped in. "So she comes at night, and we avoid the drama."

"That's ridiculous," I said, pointing at Jonathan. "How can you do that to her? Do you love her or not?"

"She doesn't need the aggravation. Believe me."

I shouldn't have cared about some girl I'd never met. I shouldn't have cared about one of my brother's dalliances. But he was so young and so sick, and I was disappearing in a short time; I felt as if the smallest problems were dire, and that if I had one tiny bit of wisdom to offer him, I owed it to him because it would be the last.

"Commit, Jonathan. Just commit."

I walked out a couple of hours later, after laughing and crying with them, knowing I'd take my own advice to heart.

Chapter Forty

THERESA

I felt as if I were studying for a test. We drilled day in and day out. We drilled in the shower and in the bed. He fucked me and wouldn't let me come until I got all the answers right. He still had my phone, so I called Jonathan from his phone. My brother invariably growled at me because he wanted to be out making money or bedding the new girl. Then Antonio would begin again as soon as I hung up. He was a rough taskmaster, demanding perfection.

How is it going to go, Contessa? Say it again.

First thing, I deliver the earpieces to the bathroom attendant. I come back. During the cocktail hour, before they introduce the bride and groom, I go outside.

Why?

I'm meeting you for a fuck. There's a florist's truck in the parking space over the grate. The florists are setting up the ballroom. I go in. The florist is owned by a business associate. You made the truck and sold it to them. I go in the false bottom. You have left a brick of C4 and a handheld crowbar under the chassis.

What else?

Guns.

What am I doing then?

Asking Donna Maria permission to marry her granddaughter.

Then what?

I wait for you.

Wait for me, Contessa, no matter what you think you hear. No matter how long you think it's taking. I'll be there. We'll run across the street and blow up the truck.

And there will be two explosions, because C4 explodes twice.

In the chaos, we come from the grate in the street and get in the car.

What kind of car is it?

A Porsche.

Perfect. No one would believe it was you.

Do you have it?

I have it.

Chapter Forty-One

THERESA

It wasn't my wedding. I wasn't wearing white. I didn't have bridesmaids or an excited family. I hadn't chosen the venue or the catering, but in a way, I was coming out of the event a woman entangled with a man to the death. We were committed, tied in ropes of lies and deceit, each able to destroy the other if we escaped the net.

I wore a short grey dress with matte silver-bugle beads. The looseness of the skirt made it easy to move in, with heels that were more comfortable than they looked. In my bag I had lipstick, credit cards, jewelry, and an obscene wad of cash. I'd memorized my account numbers and passwords for my overseas banks.

I heard Antonio come into the loft, downstairs.

We'd never discussed getting married. It was too soon, but with the intensity of our commitment, I wondered if we'd both been too busy with practicalities to bring it up or if we were simply scared of making it official.

He came behind me in a black tux that fit him without an errant crease or curve, brushing his fingertips on my arms. His touch was still perfect, still arousing, designed to bring my skin to life. He dropped my phone on the vanity.

"It's done," he said.

"I press the home key?"

"Yes. Three seconds. But wait for me. We can both detonate. If we're not together, one has a good chance of blowing the other up."

He kissed my bare shoulder and looked at me in the mirror. "You look like a queen."

"How do I taste?"

"Like a woman."

I shuddered, arching my neck until the back of my head was on his shoulder. "You didn't have this power over me three months ago."

"And you? You were just a figurine on television," he said.

I turned, put my arms around his neck, and pulled him to me. "A miserable one."

He cast his eyes down. "So many things could go wrong today."

"Nothing will go wrong."

"Wait for me. You have to wait for me."

"I'll wait in the tunnel under the car, I promise," I said.

"You don't come out until I'm there. Then we exit the tunnel together. I checked. It's open on the other side."

"Yes, boss," I whispered.

"*Ti amo,* Theresa. Please don't ever doubt that."

I kissed him because the doubt he forbade me was all over his voice. I knew he loved me, at that moment. I knew I had his heart and owned his soul. Today.

But maybe he was wondering about tomorrow. Something was off.

I didn't want to doubt our plans. I wanted to be on a plane to Greece as Persephone, goddess of the underworld, with my Adonis next to me.

"You have to know," he said, "I'll always take care of you. I'll always think of you first. You're precious to me."

"Can you get that suit off and show me?" I hiked my dress up to show him the terribly impractical garters I wore.

He looked at them with a ruefulness I didn't understand, drawing his finger around one of the legs and yanking it.

"Do you want to be late?"

"I don't see that it matters. Come on, Capo. I'm wet. You're hard. Give me that cock one last time before we die."

With a quick stroke, he ripped them, reducing them to tatters in seconds. He threw me onto the bed. "Open your legs," he said, undoing his belt. "Show me your pussy."

I bent my knees and spread them apart. My pussy cooled when the air hit it. I kept my eyes on Antonio and then on his cock as he pulled it out. "I love you, Capo."

He kneeled on the bed then licked his hand and pressed it between my legs, entering me with three fingers. "Wet to the death, my love."

He didn't make me beg but fucked me without preamble. I thought, as he drove into me, growling my name, wrinkling our good clothes, that this was the man I was fucking forever. I dug my fingers in his hair and said his name over and over until I could no longer form words.

Chapter Forty-Two

ANTONIO

I was a bad man. I knew that when I met her and when I stood at her door the night she called me *Capo* the first time. And I knew that when I came inside her on the day she planned to disappear with me.

She didn't know she wasn't going anywhere with me.

She was going to live. She was going to get over me and find herself a lawful man to take care of her and fuck her gently. She was going to have children who lived as citizens of decency, and I'd twist in hell, knowing that she'd mourn for a little while and then find happiness.

Chapter Forty-Three

THERESA

The club was not its usual self. A line of long black cars backed down the block as each driver and passenger was identified, cross-checked and let through. Or not.

Why was I nervous about going through? I felt as though I was about to star in a musical production where there would be no encore, no repeat performance, no ovation. And under those nerves was a lightness I could only describe as elation. I was leaving everything behind and starting fresh. The possibilities were endless and had been barely scraped by my imagination.

Antonio, driving a three-year-old Alfa Romeo, reached over and took my hand, knotting the fingers together in my lap. "You all right?"

"Yep."

"Wait for me." He inched forward in the line. "Remember."

"How do you say it in Italian?"

"*Aspettami.*"

"Will you take me to Italy some time? My sister lives there."

He took his gaze off me, and turned in to the gate, stopping at the guard station.

"Well?" I asked.

"Yes. Sure." He squeezed my hand and let go.

"Hello, Sir," the guard said. He wore a boutonniere in his uniform, a little white carnation wrapped in green and fastened with a pearl-head straight pin. "Can I have your name?"

Another security guy took down Antonio's license plate number.

"Antonio Spinelli," he said.

"And you, ma'am?"

"Theresa Drazen."

"Can I see some ID?"

We showed him. He checked our photos and took the license numbers down.

"Romance in America," Antonio said, quietly joking.

"Movie stars and mobsters get the same treatment."

"In Italy, they'd just shoot anyone who made trouble. To avoid the war, you play nice."

"We're about to ruin the whole party," I said.

"We are mad, aren't we?"

"We are." I squeezed his hand. "Let's do this. Before I go to the truck, let's enjoy this. Let's forget everything and dance for one hour. Let's be who we could have been. Just Antonio and Theresa, with a real future and boring pasts. I'll act like my biggest problem is whether or not you like my dress. And you'll act like yours is how to get under it. We'll be the most thrilling things in each other's lives."

He touched my lip, turning it down, then stroked my chin. "You already are the best thing I have."

"Pretend I'm also the worst thing."

"I haven't earned the life you just invented for me."

"Mr. Spinelli?" The guard leaned down, our licenses on a clipboard.

Antonio turned from me. "Yes?"

"Sorry about the wait." He handed the licenses back to Antonio. "Can you get out of the car?"

"No problem."

We were frisked. My bag was rooted through. They fingered the space behind my ears and looked inside them with the same little handheld lights doctors used, apologizing the whole time. Across the way, on the line of cars coming the other direction, another couple was getting the same treatment. Then the guards smiled and nodded, letting us through as if patting down guests was normal.

Chapter Forty-Four

ANTONIO

Was it wrong to give her good memories of me when I knew I was leaving her? Yes, it was. I should have been making her hate me. But if I was going to keep two conflicting ideas in my mind at the same time, one was going to sweeten the bitterness of the other.

I was being selfish, but her suggestion that we enjoy the wedding appealed to me, and I couldn't let it go. So after we gave the valet our keys and walked into the Heritage House, I guided her with my hand at the small of her back, which she relaxed into as if she belonged there. When the champagne went around, I took two glasses and gave her one, looking deeply into her eyes when we toasted.

"Am I getting dirty looks?" she whispered to me.

"Not today."

If any part of our plan failed, by the next week, she'd be the *camorrista* whore. But I'd be long gone, and no shame would be brought to anyone. That day, to everyone but a few, she was just a woman I'd brought to a wedding.

"And Paulie's not coming? You're sure?"

"I'm sure," I said.

Donna Maria sat at a small cocktail table with Irene and Carlo, shaking hands with subjects who passed. Irene wore a blue shift dress that went to the floor. There was no sign of the hypersexed little flirt I'd seen in the yard. She avoided looking at me.

By the dais, Bernardo Lei and Giacomo Bortolusi, the fathers of the

Neapolitan bride and Sicilian groom, respectively, held court as if this coronation were the end of years of competition, when in fact it was only the beginning.

"We have to go pay our respects," I whispered to Theresa.

"Can I get drunk first?"

I removed the empty champagne glass from her hand and led her to the line.

"I once met the Queen of England." Theresa said quietly.

"Really?"

"Elizabeth. My whole class went. It was a trip to London, and you know, private school. Los Angeles. Rich people, blah blah. I wasn't even nervous. And when it was my turn in line, and I said 'How do you do?' exactly like I was taught, I could tell she was just bored out of her mind." She tilted her head to the right slightly to see the front of the line, the curve of her neck begging to be touched and bitten and licked to a bruising. But I couldn't touch her. She turned back to me. "These guys don't look bored."

"This is the height of their lives. A business arrangement disguised as a marriage."

She squeezed my hand. "Have you ever thought of just doing it? Maybe it won't be so bad?"

"How could I go back to earth, having kissed heaven?"

I didn't know if I was leading her on. I wondered if speaking the truth to her in those last hours would just make the separation worse. Would it make the sting of her hurt be lengthier or go deeper? Would the venom course through her veins longer, or would she just have some honest piece of me to hold onto after I left?

"Master Racossi!" Bortolusi bellowed. He knew my father and was his main competition in the cigarette trade. He was ambitious, cruel, and ruthless.

"I go by my mother's name," I said as I shook his hand, looking him in the eye. I was famously unashamed of my bastard lineage, and I wouldn't take any shit about it.

And he knew it. That disconcerted me.

"This is Theresa Drazen," I said.

He took her hand and kissed it. She was perfectly gracious, neither too proud, nor coy, nor embarrassed.

"Pleasure to meet you," she said.

"I recognize that name."

"I have a big family. You might have met one of my sisters. I have six."

He laughed and nodded then turned back to me. There was a line of people behind me, waiting to meet the father of the bride, but he took the time to put his hand on my shoulder. "A little bird told me I'll be seeing you back home in a few weeks."

"You shouldn't listen to birds," I said. "They chirp what they hear, not what they know."

He laughed, but there was no humor in it. We shook hands with the gentle Bernardo Lei, who made no insinuations. Then we met the groom, who was boisterous, half drunk, half bald, and a bride who beamed with pride. Despite the reasons for the union, it looked like a good match.

"Shall we dance?" I asked. "I think we have time for one."

"He said you were going back to Italy? I thought you couldn't?"

"If this goes through, everything's forgiven. Come on, let's go dance. I'm not looking for absolution from anyone but you."

Chapter Forty-Five

THERESA

I was glad I didn't speak Italian. It meant I could smile through the half conversations and small talk Antonio endured on the way to the cocktail room. I didn't have to attach meaning to any of the looks I got. I only had to pay attention when he was addressed in English.

"Consigliere," an old woman said from a seat we passed. She wore a black dress and shoes, no makeup besides years of sun, and brown eyes sharp and clear.

"Donna, it's been years since I was your consul," he replied in English with a rote, joking tone, as if they'd been through this a hundred times.

"It still has a nice ring to it. I haven't met the lady."

I put my hand out. "Theresa Drazen. Lovely to meet you."

"Maria Carloni. I'm sure you've heard of me."

I swallowed. Smiled. Ran through my mental rolodex, cross referenced her with Daniel, in the subcategory 'nice things felons do.'

"Yes. Of course. The Catholic Woman's League."

She laughed in the way an old woman does when she can, because she's old and she doesn't give a shit what anyone thinks anymore.

A young woman in a modest blue dress handed Maria Carloni a drink. She was lovely, with olive skin and brown eyes the size of teacups.

"You've met my granddaughter, Irene, Mr. Spinelli?"

"I have." He took her hand and bowed a little. "Nice to see you again."

She didn't meet his gaze but curtseyed. Something in the gesture was formal, yet intimate, and I felt a surge of jealous rage I worked to cover with a noncommittal smile.

I wasn't introduced.

Antonio took my hand and pulled me away. But as fast as he got me away, I heard Irene mumble, '*puttana*,' under her breath. I was no scholar, but I knew what that meant.

Things had to be normal, right? I had to act like we were just walking out of here and going home and fucking. I had to act as if nothing had changed, and nothing ever would. I had to do things any typical woman would do on any particular day.

So I turned and smiled at her, then put my fingers to my lips and blew her a kiss.

"What are you doing?" Antonio asked.

"Being nice gets tiresome."

"Contessa."

"Yes, Capo?"

"You make a beautiful cat." He pulled me two steps toward the piano player. "But you're already dangerous when your claws don't show."

He turned me until I faced him. It was too early to dance, but he put his arms around my waist and pressed me against his body. I laid my fingers on the back of his neck.

"She's cute."

"I'm sure she fucks like a log in the woods."

I smiled. He had a way of saying the exact right thing.

"The flowers are beautiful," I said. "Did you see the truck? I saw it pull around to the Heritage House side."

"They're setting up the ballroom now. I made sure they were late."

"Bad, bad capo."

"It's what I do." The music stopped and people stood. "Ready?" he said. "We're moving over."

The party shifted to the Heritage Room, which I knew intimately. A big room that was part of a big building, with few doors and high ceilings gilded to the teeth. It was our last stop before we escaped this life. I reached for my phone.

"Who are you calling?"

"I didn't talk to Jonathan. And I'm…"

Dying.

I clutched the phone, trying to find the words for what I'd forgotten to do.

Antonio laid his hand over mine. "No, Contessa. Just leave it. I'm sorry. Come on. You were the one who wanted one dance. Let's have it."

He pulled me into the center of the room, which had been fashioned into an ad hoc dance floor. The band struck some tune from the eighties, a happy kickoff. We were the first ones on the floor.

He pushed my hips away with one hand and pulled me back to him with the other. We turned, stopped, and kicked together. I must have been smiling because I squeaked with delight when he turned me and smiled back. The world blurred outside our movements. It was only us, stealing a dance, a moment, the space around our bodies an indefinite haze that had no bearing on our coupling.

I forgot for a minute of that. I forgot everything except the places where his body pressed to mine, and his skin touched my skin.

When it was over, the band didn't stop but went right into the next song. Antonio pulled me to him. "There are two more songs before they introduce the bride and groom. We're sitting them out."

"You're a good dancer," I said. "Wherever we go, let's make sure we dance."

He nodded. "We're here."

We sat at a round table with two other couples I didn't know. He greeted them in Italian, introduced me, and put his hand on my back when we sat. He glanced at his phone and cursed under his breath.

"It's early. The truck. They finished setting up the ballroom already."

"Let's go, then." I grabbed my bag.

"The doors are open. No one will see us go. It's pointless."

"I'll go then. I'll keep them there."

He put his hands between my knees, like a teenager who couldn't keep his hormones in check. "Go do what you have to do in the bathroom. Now."

"Why? I mean, who even cares if I do Daniel's bidding?"

"Trust me."

I squeezed his hand and stilled my heart long enough to look into his eyes. I was doing this for him and for us. I was doing it to be a different person and finally shed my skin of pretense.

I kissed his lips and stood.

"Okay, Capo. I'm going."

I carried myself, more than walked, to the bathroom, slipping in with my head held high. I gave my hair a quick swipe in the sitting room then went to the area with the sinks and the attendant.

Her chair was empty.

Of course it was. I was a good fifteen minutes early. I put on lipstick, smiling at two women who came in and snapped the stall doors shut behind them. A third woman in a pale-blue dress came in, coyly swaying her hips. She puckered at me, as if she expected me to be there.

"Hello, *puttana*," she said.

"Everyone in America knows that word, Irene. You're not getting it past me."

The attendant came in. She looked vaguely Romanian. Her name pin said *Codruta*, and she did not make eye contact with me.

Irene blushed a little, shrugging. She played with her curls. I put on more lipstick, patting it with a cloth towel. When the two women in the stalls came out, I made room for them, but stayed by the sink. My hand was in my bag, around the tiny envelope, but I had no idea when I'd get to pass it over.

"He'll never marry you," Irene said when the two women were gone. "He'll always run away."

"I'll chase him."

"He's not keeping a whore when he's married to me."

"Then I hope you like anal sex."

Her look of abject horror was priceless. Codruta suppressed a laugh. I let mine out, chuckling and sliding my bag off the vanity. The bag got behind a stack of towels, and they fell to the floor like dying white butterflies.

"Oh, I'm so sorry!" I said.

"It's fine," Codruta said. I kneeled down to pick up the towels and slipped the envelope between two, handing the short stack to her. "I've got it, thank you." She looked at me pointedly, nodding ever so slightly and pressing the envelope's bulk between her fingers.

"You're welcome." Then, looking at Irene in the mirror, I said, "It's really very hot. You should try it."

That was cruel, but I couldn't have helped myself. Not one bit. I was only human, after all.

I walked out the door and through the cocktail hour as if onstage. Invisibility was not the objective. Antonio wasn't at his seat. I kept a noncommittal smile on my lips as if I were going for a pleasant screw in the back of a flower truck, and no more.

I don't know if, even at the height of my scandal with Daniel, I'd ever felt so exposed, so watched, so in need of the poise and control I'd been famous for. The goal, in both instances, was to be seen, noted, and found unthreatening.

A few stragglers wandered outside, mostly smokers and some younger girls in short dresses, discussing their makeup into their compacts, as if announcing the brand of their blush into a microphone. I paused until one of the saw me then glanced around as if looking for something.

Breathe, breathe, breathe.

The truck came into view. It turned out to be a van. Deep blue, with flowers bouncing around white clouds. A man got out of the driver's seat.

"Hi," I said. "Are you the florist for the Bortolusi wedding?"

"Yeah."

"The mother of the bride says the orchids on the dais smell."

"Smell?"

"I don't speak Italian, but it was something like toilet. She's pretty pissed."

He sighed and slammed the door. "Well, hell. Let me check."

I knew he wasn't going to be able to get near the mother of the bride until after the introductions. So all I had to do was get into the truck.

I thought I might hesitate, but I didn't have to. The truck windows were black with tint. The blue seemed more saturated than normal; the smooth coolness of the handle seemed sharper than the weather should allow. The click of the driver's-side door, as it opened, seemed loud enough to wake the dead.

It swung open easily. I got in and closed the door behind me with a *phup*.

New-car smell. Fragrant flowers. An Egg McMuffin. I slid into the back and lifted the carpet. Potting soil dropped like a waterfall, gathering in the crease. I peeked underneath. It was just like he'd said, a ring and a loop.

I could still hear the music of the second song. He'd come in less than five minutes. I'd be waiting, just like I was told. I yanked up the door.

There was engine stuff down there, just as I'd been promised. But somehow, enough space had been made for a slimmish man to get through. Past that was the drainage grate. It was smaller than I remembered. Or I was bigger, because everything about the iron circle looked the same.

Reaching down until my legs splayed above me, I found the box bolted under the floor and opened it. I found the micro crowbar and a gun. When I picked up the gun, I felt the weight of the bullets, and I swallowed. The situation was real. Very, very real.

The space for the C4 was occupied with a brick that looked like clay and smelled like Play-doh. Weird.

"They smell fine!" I heard from outside. Sounded like he was talking on the phone. "I don't know what she's on about."

"Fuck!" I whispered.

Should I get out and sit in the back as if I were waiting for my boyfriend to show up? Or get the job done and slip into the hole?

The voice got closer. I put the crowbar to the side of the grate and dug it between the dirt and the metal.

No. It was heavy. This had been Antonio's job. I was going to have to pull up, back into the truck and act like a horny woman at a wedding.

"Hey!" I froze. It was Antonio's voice from outside, followed by a mumble from someone. Then Antonio. "I don't know. She said it was the purple? And there are white? Go ask. Who the fuck knows?"

I wasn't big enough to do Antonio's job. The grate was too heavy, and my arm wasn't long enough. I got out from the trapdoor and put the micro crowbar and the gun into my purse. I heard footsteps on the asphalt. *That must be him. God bless him.*

I put my feet into the hole under the truck, and lowered them until they hit the grate. I wiggled, bent my knees a little, wiggled farther, prayed I didn't get stuck, and shifted until my knees were on the grass and my torso stuck out the bottom of the truck.

"God help me," I whispered as I picked up my arms and slid down. My dress stayed up and I was naked below the truck. "Ever the *puttana,*" I grumbled, sliding down. My breasts caught on a tube or tank or something, and I shifted again.

I hoped Antonio would get there soon, if for no other reason than to laugh his head off.

I heard voices. One was Antonio, sharp and loud. The next I also recognized, but I didn't have time to have a feeling about it before the truck shook.

The truck shook again, and I heard something hit the ground outside.

Paulie: "Who's saying *Ave Maria* now?"

Antonio, with a grunt: "You are." *Bang. Shake.*

And then there was nothing.

The music started again from the Heritage House. People would start milling as the salads went around; then they'd sit. And I was here, half in and half out of a truck. I let my breath out and twisted, sliding, falling into the bottom of the truck as if it had given birth to me.

I looked back up and wondered if I should I close the trap. We were supposed to be coming together, but Antonio was apparently dealing with Paulie, and I had no idea if he needed me or if staying put was the thing to do. The carriage house was twenty feet away. I could make it across to there from under the car without being seen. I couldn't hear anything from the car, and that concerned me more than anything.

Aspettami.

I was supposed to wait, but I was sure Paulie hadn't been anticipated, and I had no excuse to be on my belly, under a florist's truck. I'd figure something out. I'd told him I'd wait, and that meant he'd take whatever action he needed to with the assumption that I was going to be under the truck. I scooted back and got my fingers into the dirt at the edge of the grate. The leverage was better, and I could get it up and slide it over if I could get the micro bar under there.

The party picked up across the field. I could hear the music and shouts of laughter. But over that, I heard a *pop* from the carriage house, and that was it. Some reactionary hormone flooded my bloodstream. I wasn't lying there another second, waiting for the plan to get even more screwed up. Without thinking clearly, because all I could think was that everything was off, and Antonio was hurt, I scuttled from under the truck and ran to the carriage house in my heels, flattening my skirt at the same time. I was sure I was full of grass and mud. I was sure that I couldn't return to the party looking like that, but I was also sure Antonio and I weren't going back for a dance and aperitif.

The house was bathed in the flat light of sunset. I took three steps and cast a three-foot-long shadow over the grass. I flattened myself against the wall, listening. Stuff was getting thrown. Things were breaking. I trotted to a window, but it was obscured so I couldn't see in. Only out. Damn the privacy of the privileged.

The door sat inside a cut in the wall, and I slipped inside it. The knob didn't turn. It never did. Even when I was a kid, the front door had been a joke, a double-reinforced barrier against an unknown enemy.

Fuck it.

I ran around to the back of the house. The patio looked the same as on the night Leanne and Jonathan and I had come across the uneaten steak-and-s'mores dinner. And like that night, the sliding door was open enough to get through.

Nothing had changed, but the dining room table was off kilter and a bunch of porcelain knickknacks were in pieces on the floor.

Not a sound came from another room. Not a crash or a scuff, or a word, and that concerned me. I was tempted to call out Antonio's name. I needed to know he was all right, that he was there, and to let him know I wasn't waiting under the grate.

But I didn't, and I think that saved my life, because as I approached the bedroom I heard a thud, and a breath, and the words in an exhausted gasp… "Too easy, motherfucker. That was too easy."

I should have run, but that hadn't been Antonio's voice. Tiptoeing, I peeked in then flattened my back against the wall. In that flash of a view, I saw Paulie, hunched, breathless, face bloody on one side, and a set of legs that only could have been Antonio's.

I had a gun.

He'd given it to me for a reason, and if that wasn't his intention, what was? I reached into my purse for it. Things clicked. My clothing rustled. It must have sounded like a klaxon in a morgue, because Paulie, who was not an idiot, and was as much of a killing machine as my lover, heard me and sprung into action.

I was an accountant. I paid attention to the machinations of money. My talents were on paper. I was not a specialist in the art of physical confrontation.

So, when Paulie snatched the bag away, I just stood there, stunned. And when he grabbed my arm and threw me against the bedroom wall I flew like a rag doll, smacking my head on the corner of a marble tabletop. My vision collapsed into shattered webs of light with blackness at the edges.

"Well, well," Paulie said. "What a sweet little present this asshole gave you."

My vision cleared to a pinpoint of clarity, with him at the center, my gun in one hand and my bag in the other. He dropped the bag on the floor.

The circle of clarity widened. I blinked. Tried to move. Paulie held the gun, checking it for bullets, popping the clip, slowly, as if he wasn't worried about a damn thing. The room swam a little when I moved my eyes away from him.

Antonio faced away from me, his head in a pool of blood. He wasn't moving.

Oh, fuckjesusmotherfuckerhell.

"I know you're pissed he was promised to Irene," Paulie said. "But to get him in here for a screw then shoot him? Man, you women are just nuts, you know that?"

I tried to say Antonio's name and failed. I got my feet under me and braced myself against the wall, which swam and rolled.

Paulie crouched on his haunches. "You want to do it yourself?" he asked. "He shelved you, you know. He'd keep you for a fuck, but he was marrying that girl, no matter what he told you." He dangled the gun in front of me. "You want to take this cheating asshole out?"

Past the gun, with my focus improving but confused, I saw Antonio's finger move. Just a twitch. Was it a death spasm? Some relic of life left in him? Or was it the result of an intention?

"I won't." I croaked.

"Man, you Drazens." He shook his head in mock pensiveness. "You got this badass rep. But, buncha rich pussies if you ask me."

My wits had returned. I glanced at the pile of crap on the floor, located my phone, and put my gaze back on him.

"Why are you alone, Paulie?" I asked. "No one love you anymore? Couldn't find an ally to take out an enemy with?"

He smirked. "In the end, it's on me." He grabbed my hand and put the gun in it. "And you, Princess." I yanked my hand away. He pulled his arm back and swiped the gun across the side of my face.

I think I flew. I think things fell and crashed, because a bolt of light followed the one that came from the impact of the gun. I went out of my body a little. I was blind and dizzy again. My stomach upended. I felt my hand levitate and something hard go into it. This was Paulie, putting the gun on my hand. I felt him over me, talking in my ear.

"Say something dramatic. Like you're in a movie. Something like, 'If I can't have you, no one will.'"

The phone. If I could get to the phone, I could blow up the truck. If I could blow up the truck, there would be enough of a distraction to get away. Or he'd run away. Or Antonio would wake up if he had a breath of life in him. Anything was better than this.

"Irene wants you," I rasped, blinking blood from my eye. "She told me in the bathroom."

The grip of his hand over mine loosened. I didn't have much control over my limbs, with half my brain checked out, but I pulled and yanked against all resistance, from his hand, the floor, the wall. The advantage was enough, and I got away.

The phone. Face down. There. I dove for it, but Paulie put his foot on it.

"She said what?"

"She said I could have Antonio. She was fighting for you." My fingertips touched the phone.

He moved it an inch farther. "Why should I believe you?"

And why should he? I drew lines and connections in my mind and, through the haze, found an answer that could buy me time.

"She texted me to meet her there. In the bathroom. To tell me." I lurched for the phone, and he shifted it another inch. "I'll show you."

He paused, standing above me, considering.

"I have no idea what she sees in you," I said. "So don't ask."

He smiled down at me. "If I see one tap on that glass I don't like..." He moved his foot. I grabbed the phone and pressed the home button for one, two...

Three seconds.

Four.

Five.

Paulie tilted his head, watching.

Six seconds on the home button.

Nothing exploded.

On seven, he knew there were no texts, and I knew there was no bomb. He kicked the phone from my hand.

"Worthless." He dropped on me, knee first, knocking the wind out of me, and wrestled the gun into my hand. He pointed it at Antonio. I tried to wiggle away, but he had me under his weight.

Antonio gasped and heaved, getting up on his elbows. I croaked his name and he turned.

"Say goodbye." Paulie squeezed my hand around the trigger.

Antonio rolled, and as if consciousness was equivalent to utter situational awareness and agility, he was on his back with his gun at Paulie's head as the pressure on my hand became enough for the trigger. A bullet lodged itself into the floor where Antonio's head had been. Every surface on my body got red hot as I realized I'd almost shot him.

"You're aiming over my head," Paulie said, taking my moment of surprise and using it to shift the gun back to Antonio. His hands were hot on mine, and once Antonio rolled, the sweat poured off them despite his cocky words. "You got blood in your fucking eye."

"Let her go, Paulie."

"When you're dead, brother. When you're out of my way. You been a drag on me from day one, and I've had it." He squeezed my hand. My palms were dead dry. How did I do that? How was my body an icebox in the face of so much menace?

But Paulie's hands were greased, strong and slick with sweat. I fought against him, and he tried to force me to shoot Antonio, moving the barrel across the room when his target moved. The pressure was too much. The trigger snapped, Antonio rolled, and a bullet landed in the wall in a *pop* of plaster dust.

Antonio's gun went flying and a line of blood opened up on his arm. The bullet had grazed him before hitting the wall.

I screamed, and an ice-cold, thoughtless panic took hold, because that man was my only chance at life, my one last gift of happiness and intimacy, and I'd shot him. I couldn't feel myself breathing.

Paulie moved me with Antonio, so the gun stayed pointed at him. But he had to move his elbow off my shoulder to do it, and I yanked myself away. His hands slid over mine, and I twisted, the pressure on the trigger still hard enough to discharge the gun. I took out a lamp.

Paulie and Antonio dove for Antonio's fallen weapon, and Antonio lost, rolling away as Paulie stood and pointed his gun at him.

"How do you like this, you fucking dago wop motherfucker?"

Antonio had his hands up, sitting akimbo, one shoulder to the wall. "You do this, you're going to have to answer for it."

"Fuck you!" he moved the gun when he spoke with his hands, pointing at his ex-partner with his unladen hand. "You leave us, you leave me, for her, and who answers for it. Huh? You don't. You dropped everything we had for a little pussy."

"We had business."

"Business? I loved you!" He blurted it out, and before he even got to the third word, I saw the shock and horror on his face.

He wouldn't let Antonio live after admitting that. It was all over his face. And after half a heartbeat, his body responded, leveling the gun at Antonio and pulling the trigger.

"No!" I heard my voice but didn't feel the shout in my breath. I swung to Paulie and squeezed my weapon. And after the very raw memory of almost shooting the man I loved, I did something in the ice-cold emotionless place I dwelled in.

I knew what I was doing.

It was not an accident.

And as if he saw my intention on my face, Antonio yelled my name.

But it was too late. Of my volition, I squeezed my fist more tightly, by an infinitesimal amount, and shot Paulie in the head. A bloom of red broke out under his wide-open eyes, and his head thunked down.

Sweat broke out in my palms, and the gun clanked to the floor, splashing in the growing, comma-shaped pool of blood.

My corruption was complete.

Chapter Forty-Six

ANTONIO

I moved, and he missed. And when he went down, it took me a second to realize why.

I played at standing straight, but my eyes had fog in front of them, and my balance was uneven. Even with my senses at fifty percent, I knew what was happening, and I gathered what dexterity I had to stand. To yell her name. Then, I had to hope she'd missed, even at a meter from his face.

Theresa, my Contessa, who stood straight and aimed her words like arrows, didn't miss. I didn't know it from the drop of Paulie's body because I wasn't looking at that. I was looking at her, only her. My grace. My sweet olive blossoms rotting on the branch.

She dropped the gun, and the sound cleared my mind.

I scooped it up.

"Capo," she whispered. Whatever cold, collected woman had shot Paulie was gone, and she shook from elbows to fingertips, eyes wide, lips parted. She had a sentence to finish, but apparently not the breath to do it.

"Get back to the truck," I said, putting my hands all over the gun. "Be seen. Wait. Just wait. For once…"

I sounded angry. Maybe I was. I grabbed the gun by the trigger and pointed it at Paulie, who looked like a mannequin. A bleeding one. The blood still poured out of him. He wasn't dead.

Gesù Cristo; that man was always thick. I used to think it was funny. I used to think it was good to be the brains of the operation.

He was impulsive. Stupid.

And I was muddled.

He'd helped me. He had a big heart that hurt. He'd helped me do wrong and right, and of course, he'd made everything balanced in an unbalanced world for a little while.

What was happening to me? I straightened my arm to finish him off. Behind me, Theresa sniffed. I turned. Her face was wet with tears, and the careful makeup she'd done for the wedding was smeared down her cheeks. She pressed her lips together.

Would shooting him save her? Would it make her happy and bind her to me, or would it break her?

That was my only concern: how it would affect Theresa, her heart and her life. I didn't even care if it would make her love me less, because it didn't matter anymore.

"Don't leave me," she whispered, her mouth wet with tears. "Please."

I wanted to say I'd never leave her, to hold her shoulders and say the thought had never crossed my mind. I wanted to say I'd never lied or snuck around or given up on her. But I had. In the guise of making her life easier, I had.

"I have to." I dropped the gun on the floor. It was stained with my prints. The whole mess would land in my lap, but I'd be dead, gone, and she couldn't step in the way of it. "Tell them you were hit in the head. Unconscious for the whole thing."

"Don't." Her voice was no more than a breath.

"You probably have a concussion." My voice was hard and distant. I didn't know how else to speak to her. She'd shot a man. She'd swung her arm to aim at him and squeezed the trigger. Her face had been as cold and hard as my voice, and she made no mistakes about the gun being loaded. She knew, and she'd shot to kill. Would I see anything else from now on?

"Were you seen coming in here?" I asked.

"Maybe? Probably? I don't know."

"Go back to the truck. They'll be here soon." I didn't want her to see me go to the closet. She knew where the tunnel was better than I did. "Go."

"There was no C4 under the chassis."

"Just go!"

"You think you're leaving without me."

"I was, I am…" I looked over Paulie's slow bleed then back at her.

We had to move.

No. *I* had to move.

I was leaving to protect her. She didn't have so much thrown at her that she couldn't manage. Daniel would never prosecute her if I were out of the picture. I was the one with the problems. I was the man with the baggage, and she was…

She wasn't innocent. Not anymore. Not with her running mascara and red eyes. Not with the bruise bubbling above her ear, or her grass-stained dress, or the powder burns on her hand.

I prayed God would forgive me for loving her, and feared only the devil would answer.

I picked up the gun and put it in my waistband.

"Antonio, no. I—"

"*Basta,*" I said, opening the closet door. "I love you, Contessa. Your madness is silent and your sanity makes a racket. Now is time for madness." I pushed the hangers out of the way.

I found the false wall where she and her brother had described it. I ran my fingers over the edges but couldn't find a way to open it. She came up behind me, reaching between my legs and wedging her fingers into the corner between the floor and the wall.

"You have to go where children can reach." She pulled, and the false wall shifted. I took the edges from her. We were hit by a blast of air that should have been stale and dusty but wasn't. I knew she noticed from the deep breath she took.

She opened her mouth, and I sensed an objection coming out of it.

"Listen to me. I bought it the way I bought everything. It's not traceable. And yes, I was going down this tunnel. Alone. And I was never coming back. That was the plan, but it changed. I have to get something, and I will come back in a few seconds."

I put my finger to her lips. We had no time for explanations. "Be mad," I said. "Your sanity is there."

I ducked into the tunnel and down the stairs.

Chapter Forty-Seven

THERESA

I must have been crazy. I'd intuited that he was leaving me when I was under the truck and couldn't lift the grate. No one could. It had been locked or bolted since I was a kid. And the C4 smelled like Play-Doh, which was made of wheat. C4 couldn't smell the same. Wheat didn't explode.

Stupida.

Standing in front of the tunnel with the fresh air coming from the other side, probably the result of Antonio reopening the basement, his plan became clear. He was going to leave me there and escape through the tunnel across Ludwig without me. But Paulie intervened. Damn Paulie, and bless him, because without him, I'd be under the truck, waiting like a good girl.

Paulie bled in the other room. I steeled myself against the horror of what I'd done. If I stood in that dark closet another minute, the steel was going to melt, and my madness wasn't going to be so silent.

I stepped into the abyss. It led to a wooden stairwell with steps higher than they were wide. I remembered that.

I put my other foot on the step.

He'd said to wait under the truck, and I hadn't done it.

I should wait now.

God, please let him come back to me.

Let.

Him.

Come.
Back.
Please.

I WAITED, and because I waited, I heard them coming. Maybe someone had heard shots, or maybe they'd seen the break-in of the florist's truck without a loving couple rocking the back. Maybe Daniel's minions went looking for me to thank and, discovering I wasn't there, came looking. I didn't know. But I knew there was a traitor's body in that room, and I knew I didn't want to explain what had happened.

I closed the closet door and shut the panel behind me.

It was pitch black, and if I remembered the stairs correctly, they were treacherous and rotted.

"Antonio," I whispered into the darkness. Was he gone?

Above me, I heard the clopping and shouting of people entering the carriage house and doing what needed doing. I wondered if they knew about the tunnels and whether there was someone from my world who would check.

My fingers grazed the stone walls. I'd seen them in the light. They were made of big rocks, cut into cross sections of multifaceted dark-grey ovals and mortared together with beige cement. To the hand they were rough and sharp, not cut but cracked.

Prepared to be in the tunnel under the grate, I snapped my keys from my bag and juggled to find the little LED light. I clicked it.

The service tunnel was five feet wide with a concrete floor cracked to dust and rock. The ceiling joists were thick, bare wood under slats and below them, Antonio stood, pointing a gun at me. His head had stopped bleeding, and in his other hand, he held a silver suitcase.

"Theresa," he said, lowering the gun.

"Antonio? Where are you going?"

"On my way back." He must have seen me look at the suitcase, because he held it up for me to see. "This is the C4."

"They're coming."

He looked up as if that would help him hear through the dirt and wood above. The thumping of booted feet and shouts of serious men came through the layers of ceiling and floor.

"I was going to die in the house and escape through the tunnel, the long way, to Ludwig, while you were safe under the truck."

I stepped toward him, my LED moving the shadows across his face. "We have to do your plan, but with two."

He pressed his lips together and looked down. He took my hand. "*Si,*" he said. "We will."

A shout echoed over the walls, and he and I jerked our heads up. It was close, but not so close. In the closet maybe. Maybe they'd opened the door.

I felt his breath on me, short and shallow, and his eyes were a little wider under his bloody forehead. I put my hand over my mouth.

"*Adesso!*" he snipped, "And put the light out."

I did. He tugged me with him into the darkness. I tripped and he yanked me up. "A little ways, and I'll put the suitcase at the halfway point between the end and the closet stairs. Then we run." We came to a point where glass insets in the sidewalk let a little illumination through. It was night, and the spots of blue lamplight made more shadow than brightness.

"If people are coming, by the time we get there… we have to give up."

He jerked me forward, until the only barrier to me falling was his body. "I. Don't. Give. Up. Any. More." He said it through his teeth.

"I don't want to kill anyone else today."

In the dimmest of light, his brow shading his expression, he whispered, "I can plant it here, before they come down. There will be a bomb between us and them, but we need to be protected."

"There's a well," I said. "Fiona used to throw her empty vials down there."

I didn't give him a chance to answer. It was my turn to yank him to where we had to go, clicking my little light on when it got too dark to see. I pulled him through a room with a ditch that smelled of dried meat and over to a rotted-wood platform with a water pump. It keened to the side.

I found the rusted iron ring in the center and pulled up a wooden circular lid. Antonio shone his light down it. It was dry as a bone, and smaller than I remembered, with no vials, as if someone, some kid or some adult hiding something, had filled it in.

"Plant the bomb behind the wall and—"

"Get in," Antonio growled, dropping the suitcase.

"But you won't fit."

He knocked my feet from under me and caught me, carrying me in both arms, and as effortlessly as he did everything, he put me into the hole.

It was a tight fit. I couldn't fit a kitten in there with me, much less Antonio.

"Two explosions," he said. "Wait for them both. Then come through the house across Ludwig Street.

"Where will you be?"

"There."

Shouting, close by. Voices on stone. They'd found the partition and moved it. I thought we'd have more time. There was no chance he would get close enough to the closet to block the way and then back to safety in time.

"You have to detonate now," I said. "Before they come down. You'll never make it."

"Two explosions. Wait. Then get out and run to the house. The car is in the back. Don't stop until you're in the car."

"Wait!"

"I have to put this thing by the stairs, back there, to keep them from coming down. No more delays."

Before I could answer, he slammed the lid back on.

Darkness. Silence.

I knew the distances all too well. The halfway point between the well and the house, under the street, was too far for him to get to, and that suitcase would blow in some cop or security guard's face. If he left it close to where we were, the time it would take for him to get to safety would cause the same result.

He would die. And in the middle of the realization, the explosion hit. The earth seemed to move against me on the left and expand away on the right.

He couldn't have gotten away. No one could run that fast.

I wanted to get out. I needed to see where he was, but I had to wait, and the second explosion came on the heels of the first. I cringed because it came so fast.

I didn't wait a second longer than I had to. I shook the ringing out of my ears and put my hands against the trapdoor. It was red hot, and I snapped my palms back with a curse.

Closing my eyes and steeling myself, breathing, counting *three, two, one…*

I punched the wood. The burning sensation was nothing compared to the hardness of the surface against my inexperienced hands. But it moved, just a little, shifting to the ledge and over. I saw the room above in the crescent of space between the well edge and the lid, bathed in flickering red light and letting in a blast of heat.

I shifted and wedged my foot above me, pushing at the lid with the soles of my feet, and kicked upward. The lid creaked and shifted, the circle breaking at the diameter. Beyond it, the ceiling smoked. I scrambled out of the hole, careful not to touch anything that could have been hot.

The air was scorching and the smoke thick enough to burn my eyes and throat. I crouched and got out of the room and into the service hall.

There, I saw the origin of the fire, where the hundred-year-old roof beams burned and the smoke was thicker than sour cream. It was closer to the carriage house, as if Antonio had actually walked back the way we'd come to set the bomb off, which would have made his way back to the house even longer.

Could he have made it to the house, between closing me up and the explosion? I tried to remember how long the interval had been. Ten seconds?

I couldn't think about it, but as I scuttled to the house across Ludwig Street, digging into the recesses of my memory to recall the way, the seconds ticked, and I knew there was no way in hell he'd made it. No. He'd planted the bomb near the carriage house to block whomever was on the way down.

Pockets of fire raged in the corners, and smoke billowed in angry curls. My chest burned, my feet found every fracture and crack in the ground, and the heat felt like it was blasting at my back until I eventually found the end of the tunnel to the house across the street.

The door was ancient and heavy. My eyes burned so badly I couldn't do more than feel for the hundred-year-old knob and deadbolt. They were hot to the touch, and I cursed. I picked up my skirt and shielded my right hand with the fabric then licked my left hand and quickly turned the deadbolt. I opened the door and closed it behind me. The air in the stairwell seemed seven hundred degrees cooler. I took it in as if I'd never breathed before, and my lungs punished me by feeling as though they were being stabbed with every gasp.

After a couple of blinks, I looked up. The stairs were the same as they'd always been, and at the top was a rough-hewn oval where Antonio had broken through the wall.

Antonio.

Fuck.

I ran up the stairs. Tripped. Fell. Got the hell up. I ran again and reached the dark basement, falling palms-first onto sharp plaster chips. I screamed. It hurt badly. I looked down, and even though I couldn't see well past my singed eyes and the room's darkness, it was obvious my hands were burned.

I swallowed. That hurt, too. It had been worse than I'd remembered down there. I'd been intent on getting out, getting to Antonio. I hadn't even known I was in hell. And where was he? Was he still down there? What if he was burning to death on the far side of the tunnel, and I was up here with my feet on cold plaster, waiting?

I thought about going back down. I saw myself wandering through ten miles of tunnel, calling his name. I knew I shouldn't have let him put me in that well. I shouldn't have let him close the lid or walk away or any of it. I should have protected him the way he protected me.

And that was what he'd done. He'd protected me every step of the way. He'd put me under the umbrella of his love, and I'd done nothing but stand in his way. I'd made it my business to assert myself, and in doing so, I'd put him between me and death.

"Antonio." I whispered, but no one answered. I didn't even know who I was calling to in that dark basement. He wasn't there. He couldn't have made it and closed the door behind him. It was just me, with a murder on my conscience and my docket, on the run, alone.

Don't stop until you're in the car.

"Get it together," I said to myself. I could cry about Antonio another day. Today, I had to make his death worthwhile. I breathed, even though it hurt, and looked over the basement. One stairwell went up to the house; I knew that. A blast of cold air came from another shorter, rough-hewn exit that led right outside. I heard the sirens through that opening and went to it.

The fresh air hit my face like a Freon blast. The yard went back a hundred feet and was surrounded by cinderblock and cast iron. A white car waited by the exit, which led to a back alley. I couldn't tell the make, but it was nondescript, looking like a million other cars in the city. I walked to it, wondering how I was going to open the door without bloodying the handle or drive without touching the wheel. And then, ten steps in, I berated myself for worrying about my stupid problems after what had just happened, and I had to fight an emptiness and uncertainty I'd never felt before. The plan had been to go to Tijuana then drive south to Guatemala, and fly to Greece under different names. I couldn't remember if I'd promised to stick to the plan. Was it the right thing to do? Did it even matter without him? I put my head on the cool roof of the car, listening to the sirens a block away. I prayed that no one was hurt, that I could gather the strength to drive away alone, and that Antonio was in heaven.

The smell of burning wood that saturated my clothes reminded me of him, and I decided I'd never wash that fucking dress. We'd tried everything together. We'd done crazy things, wild, irresponsible shit. My God, I'd shot someone. I was a murderer for the rest of my life. I'd killed two men: Paulie, on purpose, and Antonio through sheer recklessness.

My breath hitched, and though I tried to hold back the tears, they came nonetheless. A minute to cry. I had to just take a minute to breathe, mourn, and cry.

Like angelic comfort from the firmament, a hand came on my shoulder.

It was a cop, maybe, or some other authority figure come to arrest me, or Daniel gently comforting me before handing me over for a hundred infractions. Then I felt a hand on the other shoulder, and through the smell of burning wood that saturated my clothes, hiding all other scents, came a voice.

Chapter Forty-Eight

THERESA

"Passenger side, Contessa."

I spun so quickly I got dizzy and fell into Antonio's arms. I was saved, pulled from the jaws of despair. I didn't care why or how, just that it was true that he was with me.

"What? Theresa? What's wrong?" He pushed me away, and when he saw I cringed, he looked down. My hands were up, in front of me. He took them from underneath.

"*Gesù*, what happened?"

"I thought you were dead," I said.

His ripped shirtsleeve dangled off his elbow like bunting. "Not yet. I run faster than you think." He held his finger to my face, first pointing then stroking the length of my nose. "But next time we go to a wedding, the worst that will happen is you get too drunk to dance."

"I don't drink at weddings."

He put the hand without the ripped shirtsleeve on my cheek and kissed me in the dark yard, with the crickets squeaking their mating call and the *thup-thup-thup* of the helicopters getting closer.

"You ready to go?" his mouth whispered into mine before he kissed me. God, I couldn't believe I thought I'd lost that hungry mouth, those lips, soft with intention, framing a brutal tongue. I couldn't touch him because my hands were still raw and burned, but he pulled me closer in that kiss. I wanted him to tear me apart against the side of that nondescript white car.

But I pushed the kiss off before I could ask and he could be tempted to comply. "You driving, Capo?" I barely had enough breath to finish the sentence.

"Si, amore mio."

He walked me to the passenger side and held the door open for me. His arm was bloody under the torn shirt, but he didn't say a word about it. He knocked on the hood of the car as he came around, as if sending me a message that everything was all right and that he had it under control, and when he got in and the gate opened, I knew he did.

The car pulled into the street, and we drove south, to our life.

Epilogue

THERESA

Tijuana was filthy. A year ago, I would have been happy to leave because of that alone. The heat, even in December, the layer of crud on everything, the narrow alleys that smelled of piss, and the stink of old tequila and beer in the air would have been enough to get me on a plane early.

We had no phones, no way to be contacted. We were gone. Poof. Disappeared. I never felt so free in my life.

"Terrified," I said to Antonio. He looked as if a layer of worry had been scraped from him. He looked younger, even.

"Fear is a good thing," he replied, leaning over the bar, tilting his glass bottle on the bar surface, leaving an arc of condensation behind. We'd stopped in a small hotel that looked as if it was going to give up any minute and collapse into a pile of wood and dust. "Keeps you honest."

I hadn't been afraid when we'd crossed over the border into Mexico. He'd packed clothes and cash and hid his wounded arm under a sleeve. It hadn't been so bad, nothing a little unguent and a kiss couldn't fix. My hands had second-degree burns, and though they looked awful, I only had to fold them to hide them. I had nothing. He thought I wasn't coming, so I had only the clothes on my back, the crap in my bag, and some valuables I wouldn't part with.

We'd crossed the border when the traffic was so dense we would have only gotten stopped if blood were dripping from the trunk. Then we made it a point to laugh and joke as we went through Border Patrol, as if we were no more than a loving couple looking for a fun weekend. I think we were so high on adrenaline that nothing was easier than manic laughter.

The explosion had made the news immediately. It had been contained in the tunnel. The report stated no deaths and one injury.

"They're not saying we're dead," I'd said.

"It's been an hour," he'd replied, but he furrowed his brow.

"I saw that tunnel. Nothing would have survived it."

"Things happened we didn't expect. Our exit wasn't clean."

"I'll go back and die again," I said.

He laughed and drove the Toyota safely and sanely southward. I talked when I didn't want to think about my family. I knew my memories of them would cloud and get distant until I could only remember little things. I played with the radio, and before we even hit San Diego, the news of Daniel Brower's collapse as mayoral candidate hit the airwaves.

The TV was on in the bar, hanging above us, blaring Spanish, the light shining through the miasma of cheap Honduran cigarettes. Antonio could only decipher some of the news, but the pictures told the story. They showed an Italian wedding, joyful yet staid, and a room full of people, each with a story, each living a different version of the events until suddenly, arrows were superimposed on the screen, pointing at three men in suits.

As one, they whipped off earpieces as if in pain.

"What happened?" I asked.

He leaned his back on the bar, looking very pleased with himself. "When you pressed your home key…"

"No bomb. Thanks for that."

"They got their wires from the bathroom attendant. Then you put this radio signal out. A very loud, high-pitched squeak. Very loud. His little team was exposed. He looks like the ass he is."

I must have gotten sullen. My face, which hid everything from everyone else, was pure bright-yellow signage to him. It always had been. From the minute he beat some guy on the hood of a car, he'd known what I was feeling.

He put his fingertips on my chin. "It was for your own good."

"You didn't want to fight for us. You were just going to leave."

"I didn't want you to spend your life fighting. I want life to be easy for you. I want you to be happy. If I humiliated him, and he lost the election, he'd back off troubling you. I'd be gone. You'd be happy. That's all I ever wanted. More than wanting you for myself, I want you to have a good life."

"If it hadn't worked out the way it had—"

"Don't."

"Are you upset that we're here, together?" I asked.

"I'm upset that you scarred your soul for me. That's the biggest sin I live with."

"That's not what I asked." I looked at my orange juice then at the specks of pulp on the side of the glass, as if they could help me divine what he was thinking.

"Theresa," he whispered then drifted off.

"Never mind," I said, waving it off. "It is what it is. I think I'm just tired." I shut down. I didn't want to talk anymore. I wanted to pretend everything was perfect. If we'd been alone together I would have taken my clothes off and tried to drown my sorrow in pain and pleasure.

But being let off the hook wasn't going to fly with him, not for one second. He put his beer down and took my head in his hands, thumbs on my cheeks and fingers at the back of my head. "Listen to me, and listen very, very carefully. We have a difficult list of things to do, and I need you to be the woman you are, the woman who can run the world. So, I'm going to say this once. Are you listening?"

He was so intense, so close. He couldn't lie or obfuscate from that distance. "Yes, Capo."

"I didn't dream of this moment. I did try to leave you, but it was for your own good. I wanted to free you. I admit I was ready to walk away. And I admit that when you shot Paulie, I decided you had to come with me to protect yourself from being accused of his murder. I had to tell myself I was protecting you. But, my Contessa, I was so happy to be forced. I felt it was a gift. I had an excuse to take you and have everything I wanted. I can't lie to myself. Yes, I want to protect you from being hurt, but I just want you. Plain and simple."

"Antonio, You've been trying to get away from me since the minute we met. If you do it again, it will be the last time. My heart can't take it."

He nodded, looking at the bar surface. "I didn't dream God could make it possible for me to have you. But He made it impossible for it to happen in any other way. Do you see what that means? It means I was destined to defile you. I live with that every day. My destiny is to destroy."

"Maybe I was destined to be destroyed."

"*Shh*. Listen. I want you to have a normal, sweet life, but I can't give you that. I will never be that man for you. Never. But here you are, with me. I am happy, and I carry the weight of my guilt for that happiness. So, don't fool yourself; I don't just want you, I hunger for you. My skin needs your skin against it. My mouth needs to taste your mouth. I. Am. Happy. But my soul has never been so stained."

I swallowed a tablespoon of gunk. "I'm sorry," I said through my tears. "I've made such a mess."

"I forgive you. Can you forgive me?"

"I love you. You are my only, my one and only. And if I have to turn my life upside down, or go to hell to be with you, so be it."

"That's not to be undertaken lightly."

"It never was. Never," I said.

His eyes scanned mine as if deciphering the full meaning of the message: that I'd always understood what being with him meant and had grabbed it with both hands from the beginning. I never shared his doubts, and I think, for once, that comforted rather than troubled him.

"If I ask you this, I want you to answer it after you think about it. Don't rush."

"Ask what?"

He breathed lightly, almost a sigh, then brushed his fingers over my cheek. "Will you be my wife?"

"Yes."

"I told you not to rush."

"I'll tell you again tomorrow. Same thing. Yes, yes, yes."

We crashed together, mouths open, lips entangled, arms tightening around each other for the first moments of commitment, nothing between us but love.

The bartender wiped around our glasses, whistling. Antonio held my face fast to him then kissed my cheek and whispered in my ear, "I just heard your name on the news. They aren't sure we're dead."

"We failed, then?"

"We were only buying time. We need to go."

"No time for a good-bye-to-Tijuana screw?"

"Plenty of time for that later," he said.

I smiled, imagining "later." His body was mine, and I watched it move as he put a few bills on the bar and pulled me toward the door, every finger a lightning rod for my desire. I took a glance at the TV and jerked him to a stop. He followed my gaze up there.

Jonathan's name was in the little tape below a reporter who stood outside Sequoia hospital.

"What is she saying?" I thought I was speaking in a normal voice, but I barely breathed it. I scoured my mind. Had Jonathan been at the wedding and I didn't know it? Had he been hurt by something I'd done?

"Something went wrong. The heart, like you said," Antonio said, knotting his brow as he deciphered a language he only partly understood. He pressed his lips together the way he did when he was reluctant to say something. "It's bad." Antonio shook his head. "I don't know all the medical words, but they say he will die."

The TV flipped to a *futbol* game, and the bar patrons cheered. The room suddenly smelled sweatier, wetter, and more florid than it had.

"I like your brother," Antonio said.

I didn't answer. I didn't have words. I had only a dead weight in my chest where a light heart should have been. I couldn't swallow. I couldn't feel my fingertips. Where had my elation gone, and my need for Antonio and only Antonio? Was it that easily swept away?

"We'll keep the news on in the car," I said. "Maybe they'll say something else."

I walked out into the heavy heat of the street. It was December, and I was sweating. The concrete flower boxes and indecipherable color-soaked graffiti that had charmed me on the way in seemed to mock me now, and the bent street with its dented cars no longer spoke of a charming over use but instead invoked an angry entropy, a sick god of destruction. The plaster cracks over every inch of the city twisted themselves into a net that wanted to catch me and drag me away from Antonio.

"I want to go somewhere with winters," I said when he caught up to me. "Can we do that? Can we live somewhere with snow?"

"You need to go back."

"No!" I shouted it to block out the knowledge that I needed to go, more than anything. I'd underestimated the pull of my family. I'd left them as if they'd always be the same, for the something different that Antonio embodied, and they changed as soon as I turned my back.

A man in a straw hat, one of many passing us, turned to watch as he walked.

"I can't do anything about it," I said, slashing with my arms. "I can't donate my heart. I'm using it."

He took me by the wrists stilling them. "Contessa, my love. He's your brother."

"I can't. I made a choice. I chose *you*."

"And I chose you. I am yours. You are mine. I'm going to make you my wife and steal your name from under you. But if you turn your back on your family, you won't forgive yourself if he dies—"

"Don't say that!"

"It's a reality," he said.

"I'll forgive myself fine. I can turn my back on my brother because I can't help him. He doesn't need me. My presence is meaningless."

He paused, looking across the street at the *putt-putt*ing, half-functioning cars and the stacked stucco buildings. Then he looked back at me. "I won't let you take the rap for Paulie."

"Are you serious?" I said. "You think I'm letting you take the blame for that?"

"My prints are on the gun. You will not go to jail for Paulie, as God is my witness."

"You brought me here to keep me from taking that rap, and now you—"

"No," he said. "I brought you because I love you. Because I need you. Because heaven gave me a reason to have you."

"And what about Irene? And Donna Maria?"

"I didn't promise you this would be easy. It's ten times worse now."

He shook his head as if he wanted to say things and didn't, as if words wanted to tumble out, and he held back the tide. I balled my fists and steeled myself for a fight. Jonathan had six more sisters and two living parents to care for him. A prodigal sister wasn't necessary. If I went to see him, it would be for me, not him, and despite what Antonio might think, I wasn't feeling selfish.

"If this happened in twenty years," I said, "when it was supposed to, we could slip back without a problem, and I could see him. If we go back today, we destroy everything."

He held his hands out. "Isn't that what we do?"

I wanted to cry with frustration. I shook my head, looking into the traffic, the noise, the bedlam we had more than embraced. We'd gotten on the cliff of normalcy and jumped into the chaos face first. Of course, that was what we did. I couldn't deny it anymore.

"I don't want to," I said.

"He's your brother."

"And damn him for it."

Antonio kissed me slowly in the fetid heat, and I tasted the sweat of his cheek, the beer on his tongue. His lips were a promise, a blood bond, a kiss of greeting and good-bye, and the years in between.

"I won't let anything happen to you, Capo," I said.

"I know."

"Are you sure about this?"

"Yes." He sighed and looked up, as if seeing the narrow street for the first time. "I smell the beach."

"Let's walk on it," I said. "We can decide what to do together."

He slipped his arm around my neck, and we walked to the end of the block. The beach was a right turn and a few blocks away. We traversed it three times before our plan was set, and then, as if it was our job to dive headfirst into chaos and ruin, we began.

RULE

Chapter One

DANIEL

There was soot all over everything. Black ash and dust. Big stones made newly small. The size and shape of the Carriage House of the Gate Club had changed from the foundation upward with an explosion, much like my career. The building remained but had withstood the equivalent of a San Andres earthquake.

"She's not here," Kylie said, out of breath. She'd barely broken her run from the ballroom, in heels and a tight skirt, to deliver the news. "But she's on the tape and—" She stopped short and turned green.

The spot where a barely breathing gunshot victim had been found—male, early thirties, possibly Paulie Patalano, possibly not—was splattered with blood, bone, and flesh. A dozen crime scene technicians took pictures and laid markers.

"Don't look," I said, using my fingers to direct her eyes from the corporeal mess to my face. "Did you check the exit tapes?"

She swallowed hard and looked at me. "So many people are crowding out at once, it could take days to sort through."

My stomach had started churning as if poked with a sharp stick. And I had to stand up straight, because she'd taught me to do that. She'd made me a man, and in the wreckage of what I'd done, and with every bit of information that came to me, it became more clear she was gone. The tunnel had been sealed shut on the outside. She'd been lured down there, or that piece of shit had, and she'd followed him. Then…

I couldn't dismiss Kylie to do her actual job of assisting Gerry in spin management, because if I sent her away, it meant I had no more leads and Theresa had been in that tunnel when the explosion hit. A ruckus broke behind me. Four men in smoking, wet rubber jackets came out of the closet. Aaron, the chief of police, approached them with questions, and I heard *collapsed. Nothing left.*

"Not much but junk down there," one of the firemen said as he handed a digital camera to a forensics specialist, and I saw a picture of the scene. "We're yellow taping it. It's not safe."

The forensics guy flipped through the pictures. A button. A diamond ring half-buried in the detritus underground.

I knew that ring. I'd chosen it. I'd gotten a bigger stone than I could afford. A stone that matched not my budget but my aspirations.

All the noise in the room fell away. Because that ring meant Theresa had been there, but it meant more than that. It meant nothing was cut and dried.

Why had she been wearing that ring? If Spinelli had wanted her to marry him, he would have gotten his own damn ring. I put the puzzle together. Was it that easy? It had been only hours since the Bortolusi wedding ended in fire, and the solution was already in my hands.

The question was, did I share my guess or keep it to myself? I wouldn't tolerate anyone shooting it down, because if I was wrong, she was dead, and that wasn't bearable.

"Kylie," I said, bringing the young intern away from the noise and clutter of the investigation. "For the past and next twelve hours, get me flight manifests into and out of Rome and Milan."

She cocked her head. "What are we look—?"

"Just get them. And Palermo and Naples."

I'D CHEATED ON HER, ruined her ability to trust in men. I hadn't spent one minute being faithful to her or doing what I'd promised, then I'd manipulated her, used her, done everything to push her into the arms of a man who destroyed her.

I didn't even know how to be pissed at Spinelli. I kept redirecting the energy back at myself.

It was my fault she was in the position she was in, whatever that was, living or dead. I'd pushed her, with my distaste, toward a criminal. I'd used her to plant bad earpieces and tried to manipulate her back into my bed. But even before that, I'd set her up. I'd left her crying and broken and wondering what was wrong with her. I'd betrayed her for years behind her back. Whatever happened was my responsibility, and if she was dead or a mob wife, I had to save her to save myself.

If that meant the mayor's office and the governor's mansion would go to someone else, then fine. Suddenly, gaining political office and losing my soul seemed like a fool's choice.

The seed of an idea grew in my head, watered and nourished by the reams of minutiae that came into my view over the following hours. Small things were my job. Details that fit together like a puzzle, telling a story of guilt or innocence, were how I put men in prison. And later, retelling that story to thousands of people became another part of a job I wanted and would do anything to gain.

The idea that grew, though, wasn't the story of how the Bortolusi wedding was handled, or who shot Patalano. It wasn't a story around how we would nail Spinelli. The story that grew was the tale of my own life being lived differently. It was a story of opportunities I had missed in choosing my life's ambition. It was a story of freedom and, wrapped up in it, was the story of a life lived parallel to Theresa.

The story was a deal with God. If I made up for the pain I'd caused her, I would lose the election and be free of my ambition. Then what?

Who knew? Maybe a life with her. Maybe without. But a life where she was somewhere safe in the world and my responsibility for her hurt would be gone.

If she was alive. And that looked less and less likely. Her phone was dead. Her apartment hadn't changed. Her family was dealing with their own crisis and hadn't been able to get her on the phone.

I let everyone prove she and Spinelli were dead, and I wove the story of her life in the midst of it.

The details came in. I let my staff run in circles, because the story I built wasn't for them. It was for me. I was a full-on fuckup no more. That was my new story.

Theresa hadn't taken a bag with her.

The stash of cash was missing from her closet.

Years ago, the tunnel had led to a house across the street, but it was blocked by rubble and brick.

That ring. That ring that ring.

They'd split. It was so obvious to me, yet my staff was easily misguided. I told stories. It was what I did.

Did I have to save Spinelli to save Theresa? That was my only concern. I didn't want to. I hated him. I hated him for breaking her down.

But if I was going to stop bullshitting myself and do the job, I had to consider it.

I was exhausted when the manifests came across my desk.

"You have a press conference on the wedding in three minutes?" Kylie almost asked.

"Why do you look like I'm going to snap at you?"

"I was supposed to get you into makeup seven minutes ago, but these came and I forgot."

I stood and got my jacket on in the same move. "Don't worry about it. Looking tired's going to help more than hurt." I picked up the manifests and walked into the hall before I'd even gotten my arms through both sleeves.

"What the fuck, Kylie?" Gerry said, walking with a purpose, flanked by the usual team. I was sick of seeing them already.

"Leave her alone. It's better." I flipped through the manifests. The third set I'd seen with nothing nothing nothing… "These are incoming to LAX." I handed them back.

But they caught my eye when I handed them over, and I saw two names right next to each other.

SPINELLI ANTONIN M 35A

SPINELLI TINA F 35B

I SNAPPED THE PAPERS BACK. The flight was arriving in two hours. Impossible for them to get to Italy then back. Physically impossible. Was this some sort of trick he'd set up to misguide me? Or was every assumption I had made incorrect?

I was about to have Kylie set up a car to go to LAX after the press conference, but I decided against it. I was telling this story hour by hour, and I didn't need anyone sending it off the rails. I'd get there myself.

Chapter Two

ANTONIO - FIRST NIGHT IN TIJUANA

She slept on her side with her hand resting on my arm and her toes pivoting against my calf. The bed flattened the side of her against it, so the curves above were accentuated in the moonlight. Her left hand was turned palm up, the burn ointment doing its work.

I didn't want to wake her, so I ran my hand along her neck, shoulder-to-ear-to-lips parted in innocent peace.

Paulie was dead because of me. He had been a confused, violent man I used and loved like a brother. And where was my grief? I rooted around my deep corners for it, but I was empty. I only had love for the woman who had killed him. That hand on my arm was murderous and capable. I should have been repelled by its touch, but I wasn't. I was connected to the soul who wielded it.

When she'd pulled the trigger, I saw the intent in her eyes. It terrified me in a way that was coiled tightly with exhilaration. This woman was no more than a stranger and no less than a kindred animal.

Everything happened too quickly after that. The practical matter that I couldn't leave her took a backseat to something bigger. I couldn't put a name on it. Not yet. I couldn't call it something I didn't understand. But she belonged to me. Her eyes, fluttering in sleep, were mine because they saw what I saw.

And still, that didn't begin to define it. It wasn't something I felt. It wasn't lodged in my heart. This possession wasn't the stuff of operas and art. It was made of bone marrow and earth. Roots and reality. I could almost touch it, but still, I couldn't find the words in any language to describe it.

I touched her bottom lip, as if words would be released. She sighed and rolled onto her stomach, her elbows making a V on either side to keep her burned hands to the cracked ceiling.

The whole way to Tijuana, I'd wanted to fuck her, to see what was different, to touch this definition at the center and unearth its meaning. To dig through our separateness and feel what it meant to own someone. Until then, I would be at this same loss for understanding. I'd had half a hard-on the whole way south, and it wasn't the curve of her breast under her shirt, though that was as arousing as always. She was beautiful, and I knew she always would be to me. The source of my arousal was deeper. I wanted to fuck her to find this shared core.

But there had been matters. Things. First thing, get past the line in the sand. Then get a place to hole up for the night. As we'd waited in the bar for the hotel to clean the room, we found out about her brother.

Jonathan, who I'd met once, was as sick as a man could be. I couldn't take her from her family just yet. I couldn't do that to her. As if he were my own family, I had to go back, for her, for our shared fate, for that connection in the marrow. I didn't even want to return to LA for myself, but knew I was going as surely as my balls ached.

So on the beach, I'd spoken to her about plans. None of it meant anything, because plans changed in the doing, but we agreed on a goal and a first step, which had to be undertaken immediately.

I called my father, who cursed me for breaking his heart with my death on the one hand and being alive with the other. He'd arranged the marriage I'd run from.

"Do you understand what this means? Do you understand the level of betrayal?"

He was almost too enraged to speak, but he gave me the number for a man who knew a guy who could forge two passports.

I thanked him, but he'd hung up before I finished. My father's reaction hurt me, but it hadn't surprised me. I didn't know if I could ever repair things with him. Which was too bad. I loved him.

I ran my hand over the slope of her back. She didn't wake up.

We'd found a little hostel with the entire desert in the backyard. I spoke a little broken Spanish to the man behind the desk. When I signed us in as Mr. and Mrs. Spinelli, she blushed and got the smile people get when they can't help themselves.

The passports wouldn't be delivered until the next afternoon, and I had business to attend to. Important business.

I'd closed the hotel room door behind us. The room was done in cheap Mexican artifacts imported from China. The air conditioner hummed, and the windows were shut tight. The white curtains hung dead in the heavy afternoon air, and the flies were too lazy to buzz.

Theresa had slipped her bag off her shoulder onto the straight wooden chair as if she had all the time in the world, then peeked at herself in the peeling dresser mirror at the foot of the bed. She'd touched the bump on her head.

Against the sound of crickets and her breathing, I ran my finger along the angle of her shoulder blade, remembering the afternoon.

"I know what you're thinking." She'd passed the bed. The mattress was as high as a slice of bread over a metal frame.

"The bed will creak? I think it will, and I don't care."

"There's too much, Antonio. Too much to think about. I'm anxious."

If she hadn't said it, I wouldn't have known. Not a line of worry crossed her brow.

"Get on that bed, Contessa, before I give you something to be anxious about." I bolted the door.

"I don't feel like it."

I pushed her onto the bed, and she fell in a sitting position with her hands behind her. Her denim-covered knees parted slightly, and when she tried to cross her legs, I yanked them open.

"I mean it," she'd gasped.

I got hard remembering that little bit of resistance I'd had to get through.

"Give yourself to me," I'd said.

"Not now."

I wedged myself between her legs, and she fell supine. "Give yourself to me." I pushed my cock against her.

She put her hands on my chest and pushed me away. I took her wrists and held her hands over her head. She cringed. I let her hands go, and she held them up to me.

They were red. Streaks of white crossed the palms where they'd blistered. When I looked in her eyes, the bump on her head laughed at me. I'd gone to the tavern and walked on the beach with her and not tended to her injuries. I was already a failure as a husband, and we weren't even married yet.

"Stay here," I said, getting up. I was out the door and on the street in seconds.

I had crossed the border a different man. Had it been the border? It was only a line in the sand. Or had it been before, on the drive south? Or the moments when I let her think I was dead, and I couldn't do it, couldn't leave her with the corpse of my best friend and a warm gun. The thought of leaving her there seemed wrong. Against the laws of physics and logic. I had been trying to be *forte* and turn my back, find some other life to ruin. I couldn't. I was a selfish brute. I was worse than my first wife's accusations. An animal. A destructive force wherever I went.

I'd gotten got a tube of antibiotic cream, burn ointment, and white tape and gauze from the drug store, then I ran back. I was paranoid, convinced I saw enemies ducking around corners and behind doors. Would I always look for them? See them? When we got out of Los Angeles the second time, would I be able to live like a normal man? Ever?

When I'd gotten got back upstairs, she hadn't moved. It might be the first time she'd actually obeyed me.

The bed creaked and bent when I sat on the edge. "Let me see your hands."

She held them out, and I bit the end off the burn ointment.

"I'm sorry about this. This is not how we start." I gently coated her palms with the clear gel.

"We're not exactly normal. Ow." Her wrist twitched, but she didn't pull away.

"Are you sure you want to marry me? You're committing yourself to a man who gives you burned hands."

"Oh," was all she said.

I looked from her hand to her face. Her eyes were cast down, only slivers of blue visible from my angle, but her answer was in the shape and twitch of her mouth. Her lips were held tightly together, narrowed, straight across, and her cheeks dimpled. She was trying not to smile.

"I mean it," I said, capping the tube. There wasn't much I could do about the bump on her head besides clean it off. I pulled her hair away so I could see it. "You'll have to learn to speak Italian so you can curse me like a good Neapolitan wife."

The smile broke into a full crescent of teeth. "I'll invent new words to curse you with. Promise." She put her fingers on my shirt buttons and slipped them through the holes. "Now get this off. Your arm and your head need attention."

I got out of my shirt. I thought she wanted to get us naked so I could take her, but the sleeve stuck to my bicep and hurt when I ripped it away. I looked at the raw wound, bordered in gunpowder and angry pink between the split skin.

"This is going to scar," she said.

"More proof I lived."

She spun on her bottom, hopped off the other side of the bed, and padded to the sink. She snapped a worn white towel from the rack and wet it, twisted it into a rope to get the last of the excess water out, then sat next to me.

"No crying now," she said. "Be a big boy."

She pressed the towel to the wound. It hurt enough to make me bite back a grunt, but I didn't make a sound as she cleaned it off. She patted my head with the same cloth. The blood there had been wiped away on the drive down. We'd covered it with my hair so we could pass through customs.

"This already looks better," she said about my head. "You have amazing healing powers. The arm though…" She dabbed my arm again.

"I guess you'll clean the children's knees with a wet cloth too? I can see it."

"If the children have gunshot wounds, you're the one who's going to need first aid, Mister Spinelli." She squirted my arm with antibiotic gel and ripped open the packet of gauze with her teeth. She didn't remove the gauze from the envelope. Didn't move.

"What?"

"I was so busy thinking about myself. I didn't even think about children."

I took her chin and pointed her face at me. Close up, I could see tiny pieces of grit inside her scrape. "We're out."

"I don't feel out."

With the other end of the white towel, I patted the bump on her head, cleaning it. "You're out. I'm out. We go back to being civilians. We just have to get into LA without being seen and back out again. Should be easy."

She plucked the gauze from the paper package and looked around for the tape. "I don't want to be a burden to you." She taped the square of gauze to my wound, swallowing her nerves. "I'm scared, Capo."

I took the tape and put it to the side. "You're not to be scared."

I'd said it as if it were an instruction. I should have soothed her, but I didn't know how. So I kissed her. I kissed her long and hard. To suck her fear out of her. To eat it alive and spit out the bones. I pushed her back onto the mattress and kissed her harder. Her hands stayed burn-side up, but the rest of her body arched up to meet mine.

I moved my hips against her, the clothing between us getting hot with friction. "Give yourself to me, and I'll fuck the fear from you."

Her eyes fluttered closed as I pushed myself against her, increasing the pressure until I thought I'd burst.

"Your answer, Contessa," I whispered in her ear. "Your answer. Answer. Answer." I was ready to get off her if she said no, but I knew she wouldn't.

"Take me," she breathed. "You crazy, beautiful bastard. Take me."

I got up and peeled off her pants, yanking her legs open so I could see her pussy. She tried to close them, and I pulled her legs open again, bending the knees.

"Don't move." Standing over her, I got my pants off. I was going to fuck her so hard that we were one person, to touch that sameness between us so I could understand it.

Two fingers in her, and she was soaked. She bucked against the thin mattress, and when I ran my wet fingers over her clit, she cried out. I wanted to taste her, to tease her, to spend hours swimming in our heat. I wanted to fuck her hard and fast. Plant myself inside her and drive to the finish. I wanted to fuck her mouth, her ass, her cunt, her very being. I didn't know how to do all the things I wanted to do to her.

I got on my knees quickly, pulled her seam apart until everything was exposed, and I ran my tongue over her. She dug her fingers into my hair as I fucked her with my tongue and hands. Two fingers in her ass. A thumb in her pussy. My mouth sucking her clit. Other hand squeezing her nipple tight to hold her still. When she came, all of Mexico heard.

I didn't wait until she breathed. I had to have her. My spit had to be on her cunt when I fucked it, the last of my fingers in her ass still. She was so wet, so soft when I fucked her, and her mouth was open, unfucked. Unacceptable. I rolled her over so she was on top. I pressed her tongue down with three fingers and took her face too. I was everywhere inside her. Ass and mouth and pussy. All mine. All of it.

And still, a few hours later, in the dark of night, with her breathing next to me, touching every part of her as if committing to a sacrament, I didn't know what we were. But I knew I'd have to leave her alone on the earth. One way or the other, they would get me. Going in or going out. I was a dead man and something else. I was the man who would prepare her for his death.

Chapter Three

THERESA - NEXT MORNING

Jonathan had tried to kill himself when he was sixteen. It had been over a girl, my friend Rachel. At the time, I'd thought it was because they split up, but it had been much, much more complicated. He'd suffered, and I hadn't been there for him, not in the way I should have been. I was beating myself to a pulp over it in the hostel, brushing my thumb over Antonio's arm. I would be there this time, and as stressful as it was to go back to Los Angeles, reestablishing that balance released a different source of tension.

"This has a texture," I said, running my fingers over the volcano tattoo inside his left wrist.

He'd just brought me to orgasm twice, and I was on my stomach, getting my brain reorganized. Once I'd stopped screaming in ecstasy, he'd opened the windows. Children played in the street two stories down, and we spoke softly as if they could hear us.

"It's not a tattoo. Not really." He got up on his elbows and held out his wrists. "The shape is cut with a knife, and they rub ink from a pen on it."

I looked closely. Every line was a bump. "Blue pen?"

"I asked for the blue. I liked it."

"Did it hurt?" I stroked the lines of Vesuvius.

"Yes."

"It's dangerous to cut the inside of the wrist. Did it bleed a lot?"

"Are you going to ask me if I cried?"

"I know you did."

He took me in his arms and kissed my face. "Like a baby."

I looked at the ceiling for a second as his hand trailed up and down my body like a boat on still water, leaving widening wakes of sensation.

I rolled over. The window faced north, so the morning sun was cool and soft. "We have a few hours before the passports come."

"I have plans for you."

"More of the same?"

"No, I'm sorry to say," he said, sitting straight up. "I've left you vulnerable. We are going back as civilians, but that doesn't mean we go back stupid."

He took the gun off the table and checked the ammunition. He pivoted on his ass then stood above me with it, naked, shoulders at an angle that balanced the pedestal of his neck. His waist, his hips, his tight stomach with a line of hair leading to the perfection of his half-erect cock, all were meant for me.

He snapped the gun closed, reminding me of everything hard and hot and dangerous. All the reasons we were going to hell. I felt two jolts. One between my legs. The other in my heart.

"I did it," I said. "With Paulie. I shot him. I held the gun, and I pulled the trigger. That's on me."

"Because he was coming at me."

I sat up. Paulie had been coming at Antonio, and if I was ever unsure whether or not I'd kill for him, I wasn't anymore. But in the haze of thinking Antonio was dead, to needing to stay completely and utterly calm for the trip to TJ, to finding out about my brother and planning for our return, I hadn't had a moment's peace to think about what killing for him meant.

I looked away from Antonio at the foot of the bed. Past the wrought-iron footboard, the mirror stared back at me. I was naked, hair hanging over my shoulders in a post-coital nest. I looked as I always had, and him above me, dark hair contrasting with the whiteish walls, body lithe and tight and perfect, dark eyes with lashes longer than should be legal. The mirror couldn't see Antonio's taste in my mouth, his cum dripping from me, my aching pussy. It couldn't see the change in my brain caused by the sex and the safety, the dam of avoidance dropping and the torrent of truth.

I held up my right hand to block my face in the mirror, and I saw something I shouldn't. The little black stain was probably caused by the dirty mirror, because when I turned my palm around to look at it directly, it was red from a burn, not black with sin. Downstairs, a child's scream turned to laughter. I pressed my lips between my teeth.

Antonio looked down at me. "Theresa?"

"I didn't…" I pressed my finger to his lips. "I can't accept that you forgive me."

He sat down, twisting to face me. "You didn't mean it."

Mean it? What did that even mean? No one *means* to shoot anyone, except psychopaths and nihilists.

"I did mean it."

He pulled my fingers away from his lips, but I shook my head violently and put both hands over my face. I couldn't look at him, or anyone. Especially not myself. That mirror, it bothered me. It flattened everything into truth.

Antonio straightened like a shot, straddling me. He took my hands from my face and filled my vision. The eye of the storm: a place of peace and calm, and the most dangerous space to be in. The eye made you complacent and comfortable, and the next minute, while you were enjoying the cloudless sky, you'd be swept into a violent wind.

"Theresa," he said, his accent like music, the concern on his face as real as his taste on my tongue. "Contessa. *Amore mio. Ascolta.* We are animals. You. Me. The kids playing outside. We wash ourselves. We cook our food. We speak in big words and have ideas. But we are animals. We fuck and we shit, and when we have to survive, we kill."

We kill. Did that mean everyone, or just me? Just us? Just the family I'd forced my way into for reasons that even I couldn't articulate?

"No. I don't believe that," I said, knowing he was right no matter how I let the light hit it.

He cupped my chin and held my head fast, as if keeping me still would ensure I heard him. "Your life will be easier if you accept it."

What about me deserved an easy time of it? I'd never earned the ease I'd been given, and now that I'd done what I'd done, my worthiness was even more questionable. His eyes met mine, and I saw nothing but the depth of his troubles. Decades' worth of weight. Would I add mine to his? Would I harp on my sin until he took responsibility for my corruption? I could break him. I knew that. If he thought I was destroyed beyond recognition, he'd take it all on himself.

"I'm fine," I said. "Just adjusting."

"Don't adjust too much. If something has to be done again, it's for me to do."

"I know." I turned away, and he let my chin go. "Trust me."

"First thing, we don't separate. I am with you always. If you need defending, I'm going to do it."

I admired the way he assessed and took control of a situation. I admired his passion and heat, his old world attitudes and how he was willing to bend them to accommodate his respect for me, and how unwilling he was to let go of his responsibility to protect me from all the evil I'd brought on myself. I couldn't have asked for better, and that made me want to shield him from the worst of me.

"I love you, Capo."

"Say you understand."

"I understand. We stay together. All the way back to Los Angeles."

"And you do not pick up a weapon to defend me. As long as I'm alive, I am your weapon," he said.

"You're not dying."

"Say it. Say I am your weapon."

"You are my weapon."

"I see you, beautiful Contessa. Don't think I'm blind."

"What do you mean?" My voice was sharper than I wanted it to be. I was afraid he saw my emotional discomfort and mistook it for guilt. But it wasn't guilt he saw. I'd turned my back on heaven when I pulled that trigger, and I felt no regret. I didn't want him to see the empty hole where guilt and sorrow should have been.

"You don't have as much practice at this, and today, before the passports come, I'm going to teach you to defend yourself for the day I may be gone."

"Please don't say that."

"Call it a sleep then. I need you to know what to do if I sleep."

I nodded, because I knew what I'd do if anything happened to him. I'd find the bastards who did it, and I'd put them to sleep with Paulie. I was a talented psychopath. I had a real God-given gift.

I kissed Antonio so he wouldn't be able to look in my eyes and see what was broken and what was whole. He owned me with his lips, protected me and told me I was worth saving when I felt less than worthy. I loved him for trying, for telling me how precious I was without saying a word. I wanted another hour with him, so he could fuck me so hard I became the human he thought I was.

Chapter Four

THERESA

It felt hard and warm, the surface supple to the touch, with curves designed to comfort the force of a closed fist.

"You know how to use it?" Antonio asked, even though he knew the answer.

The long brushy desert behind the hostel was perfect for target practice, and the owner didn't seem to mind bullets flying as long as we didn't disturb or shoot the guests. It was as good a pastime as any while we waited for passports to be fashioned out of lies.

I took aim at the empty Coke bottle, putting the pin of the front sight into the notch of the rear sight. Squeezed. Missed.

He smiled on one side of his mouth, lips full in the blasting Mexican sun, face cast in hard shadows that accentuated the flawless angles of his face. "I can see that it bothers you."

"What? That I missed? Everyone misses. It's a small object, and you put it far away." Was I whining? Maybe.

"But it bothers you."

He put his fingertip on the back of my neck and started to say something, as if he would teach me how to shoot. That was why he'd brought me out here. Before he could start, I leveled the gun on the bottle and squeezed, expecting to waste a bullet.

The bottle shattered.

He pressed his hand to the back of my neck.

"I'm getting anxious." I pulled the trigger again. A *ping* echoed over the rocks when I hit the bottle just at the edge. It spun then fell. "Every hour that passes... I might miss him."

"I think we can make it," he said.

"Then what?"

He ran his hand down my neck. "The Carlonis can't find out we're alive. I shamed Donna Maria by running from her granddaughter. She'll want me dead and pay good money for someone to do the job. But these are the American mafia. They watch too many movies. The Italians I think I can make peace with. Once that's done, I'm going to marry you."

"Can't be a big church wedding." I bent my elbow until the gun pointed at nothing but the sky. "Not without family."

"No. Maybe." He ran his hand up my arm and over my body until he found my chin. I felt safe and loved when he looked at me like that, eyes shadowed by the sun but still intense enough to compete with its blaze. "I want something so badly, and I'm afraid to even say it."

"Why?"

"I don't want to tempt God."

"Say it." I felt more than heard the breath he took. "God can't hear you out here."

His glance toward the heavens was almost imperceptible. "I want to go home. I want to take you into my family. To make you a part of... we've always looked for a new life. Maybe that was the mistake. Maybe we need to make the best of the old life."

"How? I don't even know how."

He leaned forward, and I leaned into him until I felt his stubble on my lips. "Me neither," he said. "But come home with me and try. Come home with me."

I wondered, not for the first time, when it had happened. When I'd fallen in love. When I'd committed myself so irrevocably. When the thought of a world without him hadn't seemed grey and flat.

It wasn't the sex. It wasn't the way he fucked me as if he wanted to peel my skin off and enter my soul. It wasn't the way his unreasonable demands made me wet rather than angry. It wasn't the violence, or the knowledge that he would do anything he had to in order to get what he wanted. He'd murder, steal, hurt himself. Hurt me.

Nor was it the way he took on responsibility for my brother as if Jonathan was his own. Daniel would have asked me what I wanted to do then explained why he was too busy to be with me for it. Or we'd talk about what to tell the media. But my problems would be inconveniences, puzzles to be solved. He wouldn't own them. Antonio owned me, meaning my body, my soul, and my family. I didn't know how to own him with the same surety. I didn't know how to want things for *us*.

But he was teaching me how to be his. When we'd arrived in Tijuana, I'd been under the influence of such momentum, I couldn't imagine going in reverse, not even for my family, not even to see Jonathan one last time. Antonio had slowed me down, pushing against the inertia of movement from here, to there, to the goal that blinded me. Thank God for him, in that moment and every moment since. Thank God for his level head and his perspective.

Except now, behind a filthy hostel as we waited for our fake passports.

Now he seemed desperate as he whispered, "Come home with me. Be a part of me."

I could have just said yes, but there was no lying between us, not even to make the other happy for a second's breath. "They'll never accept me."

He nodded and stepped back, his hand dropping off me. His white shirt and linen pants clung to one side of his body when the desert breeze picked up, and they fell in a graceful drape when it died.

"You have one more bottle, and two bullets," he said. "You're a little to the left, so when you aim, you have to compensate."

I aimed carefully, holding the gun at the sharpest point of the triangle of my arms. Squeezed. I had no idea how far off I was, but the bottle was unimpressed.

"Little right," he said, putting his fingers together.

I tried again. Another fail. I shrugged.

"Missing bothers you," Antonio said, taking the gun. "I see it in your face."

"It's not a big deal. I have you."

"You do. And if you never destroy another bottle, you're still perfect." His eyes grazed my body, running over it in a zigzag, as if imprinting the details into his mind. I felt brazen and desired, the center of a vital universe.

"Do we have time to go back to the hotel room?" I asked, imagining his body twisted around mine, his rough hands on my ass, his mouth on my...

"No," he said, popping the empty mag and sliding in a new one. "Because… don't look. Don't change anything, but… take this." He handed the gun to me, sliding his fingers over my wrist. "There's a man behind the water heater at the back of the hostel, and one behind the big rock to my right, back there. If they kill me in front of the right witnesses, they get my title. My territory. My crew. So I can't reclaim it when I return."

"What?" I didn't move, but the conversation had turned so casually, I felt like a purse someone had turned upside down and shaken.

"They're going to try to take me alive."

I had to take a second to absorb what he said. "How did they find us?"

"The forger, maybe. There might not be any passports." Nothing about him indicated panic. He looked as if he were about to stroll in the park.

"Don't leave me." I choked on the words.

"Are you ready?"

I barely took a breath when I nodded. I was ready.

The whole of my vision went as far as the light that surrounded him, and the hard metal of the pistol between us became a world. I didn't see either of the men he spoke of, only a light patch of dust behind the shed.

"One behind the water heater," he said, tipping his head to the hostel behind him. "One behind the big rock to your right."

"What do you want to do?" I asked as if considering where to go for dinner.

"As soon as I raise my arm, drop to the ground."

"Then why the gun? If you're putting me in a defensive position?"

"Only shoot to survive."

"I'll shoot anyone who tries to hurt you."

"Don't. Trust me."

I trusted him. I did. The salt of the entire visible world was at my command with him. I feared nothing. Not death, not pain, not my own sin. God was my ally, and evil was my slave inside the quiet torrent of his eyes.

I trusted him to protect me, but not to protect himself for my sake.

He squeezed my hand, then he walked away, his own gun sticking out of the back of his waistband.

What happened then happened so quickly, I didn't have a chance to think about the feeling that he was shrinking in my vision, or the way the landscape seemed to squeeze him into a smaller space. He was ten steps to shelter. I still didn't see anyone. My gun weighted seventy pounds or more, and the Sicilians, who wanted him alive more than they wanted me dead, were waiting until he was close enough to get a clear shot.

That, I knew.

And I knew he walked slowly to draw them out.

And I knew the pain in my chest that grew with every step. The twisting feeling, as if my lungs were being played like an accordion.

I was afraid. Desperately afraid.

And my patience ran out like a broken hourglass.

I raised my arm and pointed the gun at Antonio's back as if I could ever shoot him. "Capo!"

He didn't spin toward me but pulled the gun from his waist, and shots, everywhere, pinged, popped, cracked against the mountains. I dropped, but not like a child in an earthquake drill. I dropped with intention and pointed the gun in the direction of the shots behind the boulder, while Antonio dropped and rolled to aim behind the water heater.

A rough scrape to my right left a divot in the dirt, missing me by inches. I'd never felt so vulnerable. So distant from my sun, like Mercury cast into Pluto's orbit. Like a child in an earthquake drill that turned out to not be a drill at all.

I exhausted my bullets and froze. Antonio rolled. Alive? With no more forward movement to take and the center of my orbit down, I was out of ideas, out of thoughts, only knee-deep in a fog of fear that I hadn't kept pressure on the guy behind the boulder long enough to keep Antonio from getting shot in the back. Oh god, he was out there, alone, and I was light years away.

He rolled onto his stomach and took another shot at the water heater.

One thousand years passed in a split second.

Then the explosion.

I screamed as water poured from the water heater, bathing the sand in a miniature ocean that grew and flattened while the noise and light of the pilot light hitting the broken gas line sent flames everywhere. Cracked masonry. Smoke. Steam. If I had been confused and afraid before, I was wrecked when I tried to stand.

Until he came to me. Through the dense air, he came and yanked me up. As if slapped back into reality, I felt safe again. My guts stopped twisting, and the world slipped back onto its axis.

"What the hell were you doing?" he growled.

"If they thought I was going to kill you, they'd shoot at me, not you!"

He squeezed my arms so hard, I thought he was going to cut off my circulation. His jaw was tight against his skull and his lips were parted. I wanted to kiss the snarl right out of him, but he pulled me into the smoke and steam. I ran with him, step for step, in complete synch like the winners of a three-legged race. If gunshots still rang out, their sound was muffled by the roar of the flames we headed right into.

Heat. My skin didn't have time for sweat, just hair-curling heat. I didn't ask what he was doing by pulling me into it. I just did what he asked, and I feared nothing.

"Get to the street!" he shouted, pointing left while keening his body right.

"No!"

"Theresa!" He said my name like a command.

We had no time for words. Under the thunder of the flames came another gunshot. I felt nothing, but Antonio looked at my arm. Following his gaze, I saw where a bullet had torn my sleeve. The edges smoked from the heat of the projectile, or the fire from the water heater. It didn't matter. The calm in his face was gone.

He dropped to a crouch, pulling me with him. "The street."

He had soot across one cheek, and his face glistened with sweat. I couldn't change his mind about sending me away from danger, I knew that. I also knew I couldn't stand being away from him for a second.

He curled his fist and held it up as if keeping his patience inside him. His voice held a tension between uncontrollable rage and forced peace. "I'll be right out. I swear it."

I nodded. Took one step backward. The hostel was five steps away. The water heater was set away from it by ten feet, so the building hadn't caught fire, but it was only a matter of time before that escape route was closed off.

"Go!" He pointed at the hostel then took off at a run in the other direction.

The flames and the space around him squeezed him tight as he got smaller, and I couldn't stand it. I followed him.

Antonio stood by the boulder, looking down. A man crawled from the other side in a dark zip-up jacket and jeans, leaving a trail of blood in the sand. I knew him but couldn't place him. Young. Goatee. With the way the desert sun lit his face, I almost lost the memory, but the goatee jogged it. I remembered a night on Mulholland when I brandished an outdated car security device. I'd been ready to kill this man, and Antonio dragged me away, promising to do it himself. Antonio had obviously let him live so I wouldn't have his death on my conscience. And there he was, armed and ready to return the favor with murder.

"Bruno Uvoli," I whispered.

Antonio made a *tsk* sound and shook his head. "His brother. Domenico."

Domenico pointed his gun at Antonio, and my spine turned to ice, but I didn't hear any shots. Out of bullets? Maybe. Antonio took three steps toward him and pulled the gun away, standing over Domenico with his own gun pointed.

"Antonio," I said.

He looked at me then at my ripped sleeve where the bullet had almost hit me. "Go back."

Domenico had his hand up to fend off death. His leg was bleeding where he'd been shot. Had I done that? I hadn't seen Antonio shoot at the man behind the boulder. It could have only been me.

"You fucking bitch," he said.

Antonio cocked the hammer.

"Don't," I said. I had followed him intending to do no more than close the space between us. I hadn't intended to stop him from killing the second man. "It doesn't do us any good. And we're on foreign soil."

He was going to shoot, or so I thought. Instead he lowered his gun and licked his lower lip. He took a single step back as he put the weapon away. "You're right."

My eyes met his with an emotional click. He'd heard me and acted accordingly, as if I'd had the thought for him. Everything in that moment was right.

He took my hand and guided me toward the hostel, which had already cleared out, and through to the street. We ran across. Traffic had stopped, and dozens of people watched the flames.

I slowed. I didn't see anyone hurt but wanted to check, just to be sure. Antonio yanked me down the block toward our white Toyota. A Cadillac with the size and paint wear of a cruise ship pulled out from behind our car. Antonio ran to it and leaned into the driver's side window, where a straw-hatted man in his fifties turned the wheel.

"I'll trade you this car for mine," Antonio said as sirens got louder in the distance. He pointed the Toyota's key fob at the nondescript car we'd come in. He pressed a button, and the car squeaked. "Title's in the glove compartment."

Smoke rose from the desert behind the hostel, lighting the evening sky orange. A woman cried out behind me, bolting across the street. Two teenagers brought out a man with a bloodied shoulder, and she kneeled in front of him.

Guilt. There it was. I felt it for the innocent people I'd hurt. No more explosions. That guy was in pain because of me, and I didn't like it one bit.

Caddy Man shifted his hat, looked at Antonio, then past him at me. I smiled coyly, as if this was no more than the act of a crazy-ass boyfriend.

"Transmission's no good," the man said in a thick accent. "Bad." He laid his hands flat and wiped the air with them.

"It's okay."

The exchange of titles and keys was made in fifteen seconds, and our bags were removed from the Toyota in another five. Antonio drove away in a beat-up boat of a Cadillac with me in the passenger seat. An ancient fire engine pulled up behind us, and four police cars passed us coming from the other direction, sirens blaring and lights flashing red and blue.

Antonio put real weight on the gas pedal when the police cars passed. He pulled onto a scraggly highway, going in a direction I couldn't figure out. The car went into fourth gear and stayed there no matter what speed we went, lurching and jerking.

He looked ahead with an intensity that couldn't be attributed to the dark of night, one hand tight on the top of the steering wheel and the other draped out the window. The highway was mostly empty.

"Antonio?" I said.

No answer. Nothing moved but the small adjustments of the steering wheel.

"Antonio. Are you all right?"

Nothing.

"Antonio!"

He jerked the wheel, swerving to the side of the road in a crunch of sand and rock. The car pitched, flopping gears as the sheer length of the thing kept inertia from throwing us overboard. He slammed it in park and, in the same motion, reached for me. I didn't like the look in his eye. It looked like murder.

When his hand went around my throat, I liked it less.

"You did *what*?" He was stuck on some old conversation, as if rewinding a tape and playing it randomly.

"What are you talking about?" I asked, grabbing his wrist with my hands. He was holding me still, not choking me, but it was uncomfortable.

He thrust himself across the seat. Nothing stopped him. No armrest. No brake. Just a leather surface he put his knee on to get leverage. He was livid. Spitting mad. Hair in front of his face, beautiful mouth curved into a snarl.

"You drew fire to yourself?"

"It was—"

"*Basta!*" He put his face an inch from mine until I smelled bullets on his breath. "You do this again, and I'll…" He gritted his teeth so hard he couldn't speak.

"What?" I croaked. "What will you do?"

He pulled me toward him, fingertips digging into the space behind my jaw. I leaned into him, taking my hands off his wrist so I could push closer. I wasn't afraid.

"You do not—"

"What are you going to do, Capo?"

He didn't soften. Not a millimeter. He did not waver. He pushed me back against the door, and with his other hand, he twisted me around until I lay sprawled across the front seat.

"This is a fact, and it's a threat. You get killed, and I am as good as dead. Kill me first. If you die, you should just kill me."

I put my hands on the sides of his face. "It was the right thing."

His thumb stroked under my chin, and he lowered his head to put his lips to my cheek. "No. Don't… ever… do that again."

"I'll do what I have to."

He let me go and got as far up on his knees as possible under the car ceiling. I gasped as he reached for his waistband.

"There is one thing you have to do." He popped his button and held up a finger. "Stay still while I fuck you. That's your job. Spread your legs. That's all."

"You're so fucking backward." I tried to get up, but it was cramped in the car, and Antonio pushed me down. "Get off me."

He didn't get off me. He yanked my pants down with one hand and pressed on my breast with the other. He ripped off my jeans, stripping me of my shoes. "I'm going to fuck sense into you."

I had arguments on top of wisdom. I had logic and strategy on my side, but he pinned me like an animal and pulled my leg up until my knee was at my ear.

He slapped my ass and paused.

I groaned. "I'll do it again if I want."

"And I'll spank you for it if I want."

He slapped my bottom three more times. God, I should have been humiliated, but it woke my skin, sending a fire of pleasure through me. I couldn't move. Bone to skin, I was made viscous from the intimacy of indignity.

He pulled my legs farther apart, and I let him. He was hard with me. Merciless. His roughness silenced me into short breaths.

"Who's backward?" he growled. "Who has her legs open? It took me nothing to get you naked with your pussy out." He jerked up my shirt. "Now your tits. I can do anything to you. You're going to take my cock, and when you do, I want you to know I'm never letting you alone again. I own you, and you'll do what I tell you."

Before I had a chance to erase the thought, he rammed into me. My head was bent into the door handle, and one leg leaned on the dashboard as he took me without regard to my pleasure or pain. Outside, cars blew by so fast, I felt the air pressure change. I reached for him.

He swatted my hands away and pressed them to the window. "Look at me."

And I did, because he was still the most beautiful man I'd ever met.

"Never again. Say it." He pressed into me, deeper than deep, rubbing my clit with his body. "Look at me."

"Always, always."

"Never look away again."

He thrust into me again and again, and the fullness between my legs grew like a balloon ready to burst. I could have looked at the intensity in his eyes forever. There, I could believe he'd always be by my side, that I'd never be afraid again, that the safety he promised was real not just for me, but for us.

I believed it. In my heart I did, for just a moment, and the orgasm that came in that moment became tangible, with its own weight and mass. He let my wrists go and leaned on me. For those few moments, his roughness was gone, and he made love to me while I came, clawing his back as if that would get me inside him.

He buried his face in my neck and stiffened, releasing into me. He groaned again and again, then he was done.

He whispered my name. "Drawing fire can get you killed. There is no world without you in it. Nothing. I'm not talking about despair. I've lost people. This isn't me being a child. There is one universe. Just one. And it's between us. If you destroy that universe, you destroy me. Do you understand what I'm saying? You cannot do that again. Ever. For me."

"I was scared," I whispered. I could barely hear myself over the cicadas.

"I know." He dragged his lips over my cheek and to my throat.

"I was scared you were gone. That you'd be hit while I couldn't reach you."

"I know." He picked his head up and looked me in the eye. "I don't want you to be scared ever again. I'm going to teach you how to survive without me."

I pushed his chest so I could look him in the eye. "Enough of that."

I took his hair in my fists, I was so angry at him. How could he even consider that nonsense? Some idea that he was mentoring me for a life of misery?

Cars had been blowing past us sporadically, so the presence of another car on the highway didn't surprise me until it slowed down, and a car door slammed.

"Oh, crap," I said, pulling myself away.

Antonio picked his head up while holding me down. "Stay."

"I'm naked."

"That's why I'm staying here."

I heard the crunch of footsteps outside, and my door opened. Upside down, the man in the dark brown shirt looked ten feet tall, with a cowboy hat and a silver star like a sheriff in the old west.

Just above me, the underside of Antonio's chin cut a triangle into my view of the night sky.

"Spinelli," the Tijuana cop said with a tinge of annoyance.

"Oscar."

"Hotel rooms too expensive for you?"

"We couldn't find parking."

"Get dressed, fucking gringos."

He slammed the door, and Antonio and I wiggled back into our clothes.

"You know him?" I looked behind us. Looked like that cop and another, shorter guy.

"His daughter."

I stopped what I was doing and looked at him.

"She got into trouble with a guy." He buttoned his pants. "Some drugs. The guy ran to LA, and I brought him back to TJ."

I jerked my legs through my jeans. "So he owes you?"

He buttoned the last button of his shirt. "Why?" A smile stretched across his face as if he knew what I thought but let me meet him there.

"How fast does this thing go?"

"In fourth gear all the way? Even this shit American car can hit a hundred fifty."

I made the rest of the journey in my imagination. He'd start the car and take off. We'd be followed for a time so the cop could say he did his best, but they'd give up, report us, and move on. We'd have nowhere to go. No passports. No way back. Then for sure we'd never get back to Jonathan.

Antonio caught my train of thought. "I don't think he'll chase us far."

I put my hand on his knee. "I have a better idea. There're no passports coming, right? If the forger sold us out? There's only one way out of here."

WHEN WE GOT out of the car, Oscar held out his hand to shake Antonio's. Oscar looked older, early fifties, when I was right side up, and his deputy looked to be a couple of decades younger. We made introductions in the middle of the desert, the afternoon wind forcing us to shout.

"You're in the shit, my friend," Oscar said.

"Keeps life interesting."

"Okay, I get it, but letting you walk's gonna cost you. You get outta LA with any cash?"

"I did," I interjected. I had a few hundreds in my pocket and no more. "But not to let us walk. We need to get back over."

Oscar, looked at his deputy, then at Antonio. Tipping his head to me, he said, "Live one you got here. She know she's jumping into the lion's mouth?"

"You can do it." Antonio waved as if it was nothing. "You got a badge. You can do anything."

Oscar laughed. "How? Tell them not to look at you?"

"Yes."

Oscar looped his thumbs in his belt as if they were too heavy for his shoulders to carry without support.

"People see what they want to," I said. "If they trust you, we can get across."

He laughed so hard his elbows shook. "You want me to be your coyote?"

I didn't want to look at Antonio. I didn't want to see his disapproval or disdain. Didn't want to see the thousand reasons this wouldn't work. But I did look at him, and he was fixed on Oscar, steady and strong.

"Yes," I said. "We want you to be our coyote."

"You know what stinking coyotes get paid?"

"Money isn't an object, generally speaking," I said, now totally out on a limb, "but transferring it can get sticky. So I think you may owe Antonio more than an escort out."

Oscar huffed. "One ride still pays for two." He held up two fat red fingers.

"I will find a way to pay you if we get across alive," Antonio said.

"And not into the hands of the Sicilians," I blurted.

"If they have you," Oscar said, "you'll be paying me from the grave."

Chapter Five

ANTONIO - SEVEN WEEKS EARLIER

I didn't know how I felt about her.

I wasn't used to thinking much about how I felt or what I wanted. If I wanted a woman, I made sure she was someone who knew *omertà*, the law of silence, and practiced it. I was a lawyer and former consigliere, and I had too much information in my head to leave unprotected. So I found women already in the circle. I never had to even tell them to keep quiet. I didn't worry. If I was attracted to a woman outside the circle, I didn't fuck her. That was all.

But this one? Theresa? I wasn't even in control of myself with her. It was easy to see her on the television and admire her. The way she stood brought out her curves, and her eyes let you into a mind that turned and churned with something spoken in a language only she knew. She was inaccessible through that screen. I didn't have to think about what I wanted to do with her body because I couldn't touch it.

Then when I did, my mind was poisoned and I thought of nothing else.

I fucked her to get it out of my system, then thought, maybe one more time. If I could crack her and hear that language spill, I'd be done.

In the shop office, with Paulie giving me a hard time about the Catholic Charities donation from the day before, I thought about how I could bend her until she broke just one more time.

And that was when Daniel Brower drove into the lot.

I'd never seen a man so bold in my life. He walked onto my property as if he had a right to be there. As if he had an Aston Martin making a high rumble when low was required. I saw him across the lot, through my office windows.

Paulie took his foot off the table. "What the—?"

I turned my back to Brower, who still had half the property to cross, in his beige jacket and flapping black tie. Paulie stood and put his hand on his weapon, which he had no license for whatsoever.

I waved my finger in the direction of his gun. "He's alone, and I know what it's about. Put that away."

Paulie had never looked at me with distrust in all the years I'd known him, but then, I saw it. It was so obvious, it jarred me.

I caught myself. I was acting as if I had done something wrong. I wasn't doing something wrong. I was doing something stupid. There was a difference.

"This is personal," I said.

He must have read my face, because his body went slack at the same time he rolled his eyes to the ceiling. He was so American. "You banged his wife."

"They never married."

"Jesus fucking Christ, Spin. We agreed not to do this. We agreed no women get in the way of business."

I shrugged. She'd been more than worth it, but I couldn't tell him that any more than I could tell him that I intended to do it again.

A knock at the door before it cracked open, and Lorenzo poked his head in.

"Let him in," I said before Zo could announce him.

Paulie stood and buttoned his jacket, which did nothing to hide the bulge under his arm. "Do not fuck with me on this."

Before I could decide if I should feel threatened or not, Brower came in. He looked naked without his security detail and trail of press.

"Danny DA," Paulie said with a thick coat of disrespect.

"Mister Brower, come with me." I indicated the door.

Before Paulie could protest, Brower and I were on our way into the lot. I didn't want to argue with Paulie in front of the DA, and I didn't want to shame him by asking him to leave.

"I know what you're here about," I said as we walked behind the building. We barely had room to walk two abreast. Oil cans stacked against the chain-link fence blocked the view of the graffiti'd cinderblock wall on the other side.

"You have no idea," he replied.

"One man's trash," I said, smiling. "You threw her away."

"Don't tell me she's your treasure. Let's skip all that. Let's not pretend you have a bone in your body that can feel anything. No one has time for discovery."

I didn't care what he thought about me, or his opinion of my intentions with Theresa. I didn't even know how I felt about her. But oddly, I couldn't read him.

"You have something," I said. "So why not just tell me what it is?" I tried to act casual, as if he had nothing on me.

"I know about your sister. I know there were four men who gang-raped her."

He did it on purpose. He used words that opened my glands and filled my bloodstream with violence. I wanted to choke him, and he smiled as if he knew it. He was trying to weaken me with my own bile, and I was letting it work.

"That was in Napoli," I said. "It's not your business."

"Four Neapolitans from a rival family. Three are dead, and you took their territory."

"I already thanked God for striking them down."

"You lit a candle to yourself," he said.

"You going to arrest me? In the back of my property? No. You didn't come here unarmed, by yourself, to take me in."

"I came to make a trade."

"This should be good."

"Do you want to hear it?"

I wanted to check him for a wire was what I wanted to do. I wanted to walk away, because there was no good end to this. He wasn't offering me anything that would benefit me. It wasn't in his nature. But I wanted to hear it, because it would tell me more about him than about me, and he was not to be underestimated.

I reached inside my jacket, and Daniel didn't stiffen or flinch, as if he knew I wouldn't pull my gun on him. He was confident of it even in his bones. That in itself was cause for concern.

I took out my cigarettes and lighter.

I poked out a cigarette for him, and to my surprise, he took it. I lit his, then mine, watching him for signs that he didn't smoke. But he blew a ring.

"I know what I did," he said. "I know, in the end, it'll fuck me. People don't vote for men who can't be monogamous. They think it means I'm not focused. Well, fine. Just fine. I'll fix what I can and fuck the rest. But Theresa takes it on herself. She thinks there's something wrong with her. And this is a problem for me, because there's nothing wrong with her."

"I agree."

I'd gotten to him, because his lips tightened. I knew he was imagining us together, and that made me happy. I'd fuck her again just to see that look on his face one more time.

"I know men," he said. "I know how we are. She's not some whore. She's not a tool in your drawer. She's sensitive, and she's been hurt enough."

"By you."

"By me."

"What do you want me to do about it?" I asked.

"Here's what you're going to do about it. You're going to take whatever happened yesterday and file it under stuff in the past. You're going to politely refuse to see her again. You'll leave her the hell alone, and she'll find someone else."

"How noble of you."

"Fuck you."

"No," I said, stamping my cigarette under my shoe and speaking softly. "Fuck you."

I walked off, back to my office, to my life, to figure out what I wanted to do about this woman. I wouldn't be told who I could and couldn't fuck, but I wouldn't be pushed toward her in the name of spite either.

"Spinelli," Daniel called behind me.

He didn't seem flustered. He didn't shout, he just said my name, and that made me listen. I stopped at the corner and looked at him as he flicked his cigarette through the chain link.

"I know where the fourth man is. If you want him, you know what you have to do."

Chapter Six

THERESA - THE RETURN TO LOS ANGELES

Oscar had gotten us into the back of a truck without being seen. He kept making jokes about being a newly minted coyote, since it seemed Antonio had rescued his daughter from one. I sensed an edge to the jokes.

"You didn't sleep with her, did you?" I'd whispered in a free moment at the depot.

"No. Can't speak for Paulie though."

"Jesus. He's not going to try to get back at you for that?"

The truck had come before he had a chance to answer, and we were all smiles and handshakes.

Hours into the journey, I'd forgotten all about Paulie's indiscretion. I was getting antsy in the back of the truck. It was dark outside, so it was black inside. The hours blew by in the *hup-shh hup* of the tires hitting regular seams in the road. The heartbeat sound made me anxious about Jonathan. We'd made the deal to take us all the way to Los Angeles, and the drive seemed to take forever.

"Do you smell that?" Antonio said in the dark.

I felt him next to me, a stalwart presence that kept my pounding heart from exploding. "Smells like trees."

"Olive trees. There are olive orchards in southern California. We must be passing a stretch along the 5."

I nodded and took his hand, memorizing that scent. It was important to Antonio. It reminded him of his childhood, and it seemed as if knowing an olive orchard when we passed it brought him closer to me.

"What's your mother like?" I asked.

"Sick, always sick. Since Nella… since the thing with those men, she doesn't get out of bed much. But she talks on the phone and leans out the window. When you meet her, she'll make you listen to opera. She'll tell you Italian culture has nothing to do with crime. And she's right. We're aberrations, my father and I. She'll show you art and read you poetry. She'll play you opera until you can sing it in the shower."

"I love opera." I was charmed by the idea of meeting his mother. It seemed like a fantasy that could happen. "And your dad?"

"Never. You'll never meet him. By running away from this marriage, I put him in a terrible position. If I see him again, fifty-fifty chance he'll kill me. Let's stick with my mother for now." The dim light glinted off his teeth when he smiled, but what he said couldn't be more serious.

"Opera and art then." My mind wandered to my own mother, her cultured aloofness, and my brother's love of art.

"Jonathan's probably fine," I said into the dark after a long silence.

"Yes. Probably."

"Fine. I'm sure of it." I recited it more than said it. "Fine."

Because I couldn't see Antonio, when he squeezed my hand, I felt every bit of his skin, his warmth, the pressure of his touch. We'd be home soon. The border patrol hadn't checked the back of the police van. We just withstood the heat, the stink of gunpowder and old sweat heavy in the bare box.

Oscar had been so confident, he'd sat us in the back without a contingency plan, and he'd been right. He'd taken our guns though. Antonio had been reluctant, but Oscar wasn't moving armed passengers. End of story.

Antonio and I sat next to each other on the wood bench, barely moving, ready for everything to go wrong. We weren't resigned to failure, only sitting in a state of preparedness.

"I don't know how I can face my family after what I've done," I said. "I hurt them. I try not to think about it… but I'll have to deal with it."

"Don't explain to them. You're back, and that's all there is to it."

"I'm not worried about explaining. It's… of everything I've done… I wronged them. All of them. They love me, and I made them grieve for nothing."

"You should sleep," he said.

"I can't. I can't think about anything but losing you and facing them."

"Do you still have the medal I gave you? The St. Christopher?"

"Yes." It lay flat against my chest. I forgot it was there most of the time.

"Touch it."

I did. I couldn't discern anything but an overall bumpiness on the nickel-sized charm. He put his arm around me and pulled me toward him. I didn't feel as though I was resisting, but apparently I was.

"Down. Put your head on my lap."

I rested on him, letting his thumb stroke my cheek. "That medal came from my great-great-grandfather, one of the first *camorrista*. It protects you from harm. All harm. Even when you beat yourself, you're protected."

"What about you?"

I felt a shrug in the movements of his body. "I don't need as much protecting."

I sighed. Arguing was pointless. "You should sleep too."

"I'll sleep when I'm dead."

"Stop that."

He pulled my hair off my face, stroking it gently back. "It's inevitable. One day, Theresa Drazen will close her eyes." He drew his fingers gently across my eyelids and down my cheek. I felt the need for sleep cover me like a blanket, as if my limbs and senses were in the first stage of shutting down. "She'll close them while thinking a happy thought. About when she was younger, and she and her husband drove across the border in a police truck, before he got old and ugly."

"You will never be ugly." It took an enormous amount of energy to get those five words out, but they needed to be said.

He continued as if I hadn't said a thing. "This is the day she'll remember. The day her brother's heart was healed, and she and her husband made peace with the Sicilians. The day they went to live in the olive orchards. When you close your eyes for the last time, it will be this day you remember as the first day of the long happiness of your life. You will smile your whole journey to heaven."

I didn't know if he said anything else. My thoughts started to go pre-dream, and I was far away from the heat and smell of the truck, held down only by Antonio's touch on my cheek and the thrumming of the wheels on the road.

I woke with a mouth full of white school glue when the truck jerked to a stop and went backward, beeping. The light through the tiny windows in the door was daylight bright, then grey, as if we'd glided indoors.

Antonio's head rested on the side of the truck, but his eyes were open. "*Buongiorno*."

"Hi. You look good for a guy who slept sitting up." I rubbed my eyes. He couldn't possibly look that good on no sleep, but he did. Unshaven. A little rough around the edges, but still perfect.

He cupped my chin. "I want you to be ready for anything." He gently pulled me up so he could stand. "I don't know what we're going to see when those doors open."

"As long as you stay with me, I'm ready."

The windows in the rear bay doors were set so high, Antonio had to stretch himself to see through them.

I heard a conversation outside the truck. It sounded like English, but I couldn't string two words together. Contentious, sharp, businesslike. Antonio rubbed his eyes and sighed and motioned me to him.

"What is it?" I tried to get tall enough to see through the wire-meshed windows, but I couldn't.

He didn't answer, just looked at me for a few seconds, then took my hands. "Listen to me, this is not negotiable. This is the rule. Whatever I do, you stick to the story we agreed on."

His tone was so sure, so confident, as if I were an employee and he were the head of operations for Theresa and Antonio Inc., I got a little ruffled.

"I'm not agreeing to anything until you tell me what you've got on your mind."

He put his finger up. Tightening his voice like a rubber band wrapped twice around something just a little too big, he got his tone down to a low, tight-jawed growl. "We don't have time for this. Just do what I say."

I put my hands on my hips, more to give my body a message from my mind, because my physical self wanted to do whatever he said, almost as a reaction. But my mind was infuriated. "Tell me first."

The clack of the lock echoed in the empty space, and he let go of me.

"Do not defy me," he said.

I didn't have a second to tell him I didn't want to defy him, only know what he had planned.

The back door lifted, clattering open as it slid up.

There wasn't much like the squawk of a police bandwidth, both urgent and incomprehensible. Like the scrawl on a prescription pad, it was only clear to the initiated. I tingled from between my shoulders to my fingertips, as if my central nervous system demanded I do something violent.

We were supposed to be dropped by Sequoia in a building Antonio's company owned. Had the cops infiltrated it? This was bad. So bad. My skin got tight around me, cutting my ability to breathe, to think, to see a foot in front of me.

The muscles of my hand tightened and the skin…

No. That was Antonio. He was holding my hand. I took a short breath, all my lungs would hold, and looked at him. He oozed a type of awareness and alertness that made me feel safe next to him.

I exhaled, and my chest opened. It would be all right. Whatever it was, I could handle it.

Half a second later, with my every nerve ending on fire, the front cab doors slammed shut, and the man pulling up the truck door was revealed.

It was Daniel. The squawk was from two cops passing behind him.

"What the—?" I gasped, realizing we were in a loading dock in the First Street police precinct.

"I knew it!" Daniel cried, pumping his fist. "God! You!" He pointed at me. "You're just… sight for sore eyes doesn't even begin."

He took two steps into the truck and put his arms around me, invoking God and Jesus in a litany of gratitude I didn't feel I deserved. He rocked back and forth, squeezing me until I thought I'd suffocate. I turned my head just enough to see Antonio. His face was impassive, but the clenched fists at his side told me how he was reacting to the hug.

"Dan, I can't breathe."

Daniel pulled away but held my shoulders. "Are you hurt?"

"She's fine," Antonio said, putting his hand on my shoulder.

Daniel didn't seem the least bit threatened. He was so close to me, I could see the white rings around his blue eyes. "What happened?"

"It's a long story," I said.

"We thought you were dead."

"I know. I… we escaped. They were after him. They had Paulie lure him into the Carriage House and—"

"Slow down, Theresa," Antonio said. We'd gone over the story and who would tell it.

"No! I won't!" Was I being too petulant? Did the lady protest too much? To hell with that. I had to sell it and sell it fast. "It was the Bortolusis. They were afraid Antonio was going to make a marriage that would compete with them, so they planted a car bomb at the shop then tried to do the same at their own wedding. Those people are nuts, Dan. They won't leave him alone. He needs protection."

"And you ran," Daniel said, crossing his arms.

"Damn right we did," I said.

Daniel looked over my shoulder at Antonio, who held up his hands. He'd slept sitting up and had a day and a half of growth on his face, but the sparkle in his eyes made him look as if he'd just stepped out of the shower.

"I make no accusations," he said, "and for my own protection, I don't argue with her. But we're back."

"And the shooting of Mister Patalano?" Daniel asked.

I swallowed a bucket of ice.

"Shooting?" Antonio said casually, as if talking about the weather. "So he's not dead?"

"Not entirely."

"I was there when he shot himself," Antonio said, shaking his head in mock disappointment. "He always had this problem. He couldn't hit the side of a garage."

"We'll see what forensics comes back with on that. In the meantime, come with me. I have something to show you."

Chapter Seven

ANTONIO - SIX WEEKS EARLIER

The day I killed the last man who'd raped Nella, I forgot my own name.

I did it four days after Daniel came to me with his name in exchange for turning my back on Theresa. Four days after I kicked her out of the shop because I suspected she was partnering with him, even while I didn't believe it. Four days of making sure Daniel's man was really the culprit. Knowing I might be getting set up, I killed him anyway.

At the time, I'd been confused. Confused about my purpose in life, which was vengeance for my sister. Confused about how to proceed now that I'd killed the last of them, and confused about this woman who wasn't supposed to mean anything to me.

I felt a curious emptiness when I stood over his body. Brower had given me his name, and despite the fact that the DA thought I was an animal who would kill anyone, I had to check his facts.

It all lined up.

Four days of forcing myself across the town, asking questions that would only be answered when accompanied by gunshots or a beating so deep inside Griffith Park, the threat of starvation on broken legs was real.

Four days of petitioning old Italians to let me finish my business.

Half a day of chasing him, because he knew I was coming. When I finally stood over the rapist fuck after the light had gone out of his eyes, a piece of myself went with him.

That was it. I was done. I had no more vengeance to wreak. I had no more debts to pay.

I dialed my mother's number to tell her Nella was safe, that the men who'd raped her were gone forever. Down to the last one, they were wiped from the earth. But I couldn't tell her. I couldn't make it real. I had to figure out what it meant for me first. I drove to the mountains and took a dead dirt road up, up always up, and walked past a yellow-and-black gate until I could see California in front of me.

What would I do now?

That empty space filled itself with an ache I couldn't control. I even felt it happening and pushed it away. Denied it. But the anger-shaped space inside me changed into a vacuity designed for her sweet smell and her cinnamon hair, the sound of her laugh, her tone when she was haughty, and the silk of her skin in my hand. She took up residence, kicked off her shoes, and sprawled out inside my soul.

I couldn't have her. It was crazy. But the place where the want for vengeance had resided was filled with the want for her, as if I had a proscribed amount of space for desire in my heart and it had to be occupied.

I felt the warmth from my chest to my fingertips as she infected my blood. Every part of me vibrated. I had agreed to stay away from her. I'd made a trade. Vengeance in exchange for erasing her from my life.

But in exacting the vengeance, she became impossible to erase, and when I got a call that Bruno was going to grab her because he was ambitious and stupid, I had to nip it in the bud. Not to protect myself, but because I needed to send a message. Theresa Drazen was not to be touched.

I couldn't be with her. My world would break her, and hers would never accept me. I was fine with that. Just fine. Up to the point where she was hurt. Then the space in me where vengeance was, that was now filled with thoughts of her, widened a little, and the old rage seeped in.

At exactly the right time, I found out she was being chased up Mulholland Drive. We found her wielding a stick against a man who had made his bones at twelve.

"Make no mistake," I said after closing her car door. Her eyes were cast in shadow from the car roof, until she moved, and I saw her broken. "I will hurt you to protect you."

Her lips parted another millimeter. I had to bite my tongue to keep from kissing her. I was trying to scare her, but I hadn't. I'd excited her. It was in the curve of her lips and the growing tension between my legs.

"Now go." I turned my back to her. I heard her back up, and the glare from her headlights swung against the trees and disappeared.

Lorenzo got off Bruno when I approached. Bruno's hand was shot up, and he had one foot in nothing but a black sock like old men wore. Paulie kept a foot on Bruno's shot up hand and a shoe in his mouth to muffle his screams. I stood over Bruno, considered the flame at the tip of my cigarette, then looked at him again, stretched before me.

"Bruno," I said, flicking the ash on him. "How are you?"

Paulie removed the shoe. Bruno spit defiantly, but gravity sent it back in his face. Paulie put his foot on the man's throat. I'd had that done to me once. It was very uncomfortable, and the next day I'd looked as if I'd danced with a noose.

"What did you think you were doing?" I asked.

He grunted. I didn't know if he could even pay attention to me with the fear of death clouding his vision. I retrieved the shoe that had been pulled from his mouth and tapped it on his forehead.

"Don't you know nothing, *stupido*?" Paulie mangled even the simplest Italian words. "You can't get to us through a woman."

I crouched until I took up all of the frame of Bruno's vision. "He's got a point. Now, you have my attention. Did you have something you wanted to tell me?"

He snorted, choking on his own snot, eyes blood red and narrowed.

"I can't hear you." I put my hand behind my ear. "Was it my number you wanted? Maybe call me and ask me on a date?"

He shook his head. Snorted.

"Liar." I pinched his cheeks until his mouth opened, then I jammed the shoe back in, sole-side down. "Did you want to say hello? Join my crew? I need someone to clean the floors. They're filthy. People walk in with dirty shoes. It's disgusting. No? You're shaking your head, so all right, if you didn't want to ask me on a date and you don't want to work for me, then I'm going to assume you didn't want to send me a message. I'm going to assume you wanted to fuck Theresa Drazen. Is that correct?"

He shook his head as much as he could.

"Now you're lying. Everyone wants to fuck her. I want you to lie to my face, you piece of shit." I pulled the shoe out of his mouth. A trail of saliva followed. "You were going to do what, once you caught her?"

How he had the energy to spit in my face, I'll never know, but I respected his nerve.

Paulie did not. He took his foot off Bruno long enough to kick him in the cheek.

I yanked Bruno up by the collar and pinned him to the side of the car, then got in his face, daring him to spit again. "You have no manners, Bruno. This a Sicilian thing?"

"Kill me. I dare you."

"Tell me what you thought you were doing."

"I was going to teach you a lesson," he choked out. "Give her a little of what those Neapolitans gave Nella. In honor of the last one you killed."

He said it through his teeth, biting back tears. He wanted to beg for his life. I could smell it on him, yet he was pushing me.

I was ready to be pushed. I'd killed a man the day before, and there was an inertia to violence. Once set in motion, it tended to stay in motion.

But vengeance didn't have the same inertia. I was filled. I should have been enraged by what he said. Insulted. Offended to the core. But I felt none of that. As I squeezed my fingers tighter around his neck, what I felt was fear that by staying away from Theresa, I was creating a vacuum where other men would go, and they would use her to take action on their own vendettas. She wasn't one of us, so they wouldn't suffer any consequences. I was leaving her wide open, and the thought of something happening to her drove me insane.

Nothing seemed more natural and right than standing over Bruno Uvoli and taking his life. Because he was an animal, an affront, and mostly because he'd tried to hurt her.

In that moment, I decided to have her. To protect her. To satisfy the longing in my heart. For my own salvation. Once that was decided, I couldn't kill the man. I had to earn her.

I pushed him against the car. "Get in."

Paulie flicked his cigarette to the ground. "Where we going?"

"Sequoia," I said. "I know a doctor who can take care of this little shit's hand."

"What the fuck?" Paulie exclaimed.

Bruno looked at me suspiciously.

"He's going to send a message back to his people." I dropped my cigarette and stamped it. "This vendetta is done. And unless you want to see more blood shed, stay away from Theresa Drazen."

Chapter Eight

THERESA - FIRST STREET PRECINCT

Daniel put his key into the service elevator. I hadn't been in it before, as it was used to transport suspects and convicts from the precinct offices to the prisons and courts.

Antonio looked at our escape route, at me, at the elevator, then back at me.

Daniel held the door open.

"If I didn't know you better," Antonio said, "I'd think you were setting us up."

"You, I'd set up," he replied. "If I could figure out how to bring you down without taking her with you." He tilted his head toward me.

There seemed to be a sort of brutal honesty I hadn't been aware of between the two men. As if they had a shared history.

"She stays here," Antonio said. "I'll come up with you. I'll answer any question you have. But she goes to see her brother."

Daniel appeared to consider something. He made all the right signs, gave all the right clues. A pause. A breath. Eyes slightly elsewhere but still present. A tap of the finger. As if he was checking things off a list I'd provided him, years ago.

I had no idea if he was faking or not. He'd gotten that good.

"Fine," he said.

"No, absolutely not." I walked up to Daniel until I was practically in the elevator. "You have nothing on him, or you'd have a rear flank of police and he'd be Mirandized already."

"I never said I was arresting anyone. I said I wanted to ask questions. And his confession's inadmissible considering the evidence hasn't even been gathered yet and, thanks to him, my reputation in this town is shot to hell. So you can come, or I can force you. And I'm at the point where I've got fuckall to lose, so if I were you, I'd just come along for the ride."

"She goes," Antonio said, stepping past Daniel into the elevator.

Daniel held the doors open. "He's right. You should go."

Antonio leaned against the back wall and folded his hands in front of him. He knew the law. He'd let Daniel spin while I saw Jonathan. It was the smartest thing to do. But with Daniel between us and my lover boxed in, a little empty spot opened up. A spot that told me I was alone, adrift, not enough.

"No," I whispered.

"You need to see Jonathan. You don't have time for this," Daniel said.

My sinuses suddenly pinched and tingled. "Is he all right?"

"No..." He drifted off as if trying to formulate the right way to say what needed saying, and unless he'd taken serious acting lessons, he wasn't faking the distress in his voice. "He's really fucked up. Bad. You have to see him by tonight, or it might be too late."

"Too late? What kind of too late?"

He shook his head, and my chest tightened. "The worst kind. I'm sorry."

"It was routine stuff when I saw him," I protested.

"It happened fast. Look, I'm going to question you, I promise you that, but I like Jonathan, and you need to see him."

"Go, Contessa," Antonio said from behind Daniel. "I have this."

I couldn't save Antonio, but maybe I could. I wasn't powerless. But if I told the truth, that I'd shot Paulie, I wouldn't see my brother. I could admit to the murder at any time. Tomorrow. The next day. No amount of time would change the facts, but in that time, Jonathan could be dead.

Daniel moved out of the way, and the door started to shut. Antonio was cut into a straight line by the edge, then bisected, then almost gone behind the scratched metal door. He'd be gone in another fraction of a second, cut off from me by rebar and concrete, floors and ceilings, men and women who would become obstacles to my wholeness and safety.

I stuck my hand in the elevator door before it closed, and it bounced back with a rattle. "I'm coming up."

"Theresa..."

"Contessa..."

I stepped in.

"I was trying to save you from grief," Daniel said as the door slid shut again.

"Too late," I said, standing next to Antonio. I watched the red numbers flip as we went upstairs into the belly of the LAPD.

Chapter Nine

THERESA

"Who is this?" Margie asked.

I was hunched in the corner of the precinct bathroom with Daniel's phone. The first thing they'd done was take Antonio away and put him behind a door, and my sense of orientation went with him, as if I'd been airlifted and dropped into a foreign nation. My ex gave me his phone and told me to call my sister, whose first reaction to my voice had been silence. Her second had been disbelief.

"It's Theresa, I swear. I—"

"We're all going through five stages of a loss, here. Mom is still on denial and Sheila's on anger, and you're calling me like it's hey-how-do-you-do time."

"You're in the same stage as Sheila."

"What was Fiona put away for?" she asked.

"What?"

"Prove you're you. And tell me who she was in with."

"Oh, please, Margie, we don't have time."

The lights buzzed above me, casting the bathroom in a light that seemed to suck away brightness rather than add it. I'd put my family through hell. Avoidance was futile.

"She was put away twice," I said, resigned to doing this.

"Which time?"

"The first time."

I couldn't hear her tapping her foot, but I knew she was.

"Fiona went to Westonwood for stabbing her boyfriend. Jonathan was there for suicide. Both were caused by a girl named Rachel, who was my friend. Who Daddy seduced. Enough?"

She paused then spoke quietly. "Thank God. Thank thank thank God a million times you're not dead. Where are you?"

"I'm at the First Street Station, on the bathroom floor."

"You know what? I have no idea what's happening with you, and I'll care about it tomorrow. You need to be here."

"I know. I'll be there, I promise."

"I'm not trying to be graphic. Just blunt," she said. "Jon has irreparable damage to his heart. It's not going to go well without a transplant. And maybe you don't care. Maybe this new life you have is more important than the old one. That's fine. But—and this is not for me, it's for Jonathan—see him. Okay? Just see him. Then go back to whatever it was you were doing."

"Okay."

"Don't make me come after you."

"I'll be there. I swear."

"All right. Then you can tell me why you're not dead."

My bitter laugh bounced off the green tiles as I hung up. I had to be a big girl and leave the building without Antonio.

After washing my hands, I looked down and did what I always did since the night Antonio and I met. I checked my shoes. A little square of toilet paper was stuck to my right heel, still white and flat, hanging on for dear life, hoping for rescue from the trash.

Come on, Theresa.

I picked it off. I should have thrown it away. But it reminded me of meeting Antonio, of those months and years before, when I felt incomplete, and how that had changed with him. I knew a piece of paper couldn't bring that back. Only I could. But I couldn't toss it without tossing the feeling away, so I put it in my pocket.

I took a deep breath and went into the hall. It was full of cops and lawyers, little metal carts with file boxes stacked high. Linoleum floors scuffed in the middle and shiny where they met the walls. I knew this place. I'd met Daniel here a hundred times, back when the doors didn't mean a thing to me. Nothing behind them had been of interest.

"Daniel!" I said when I saw him opening one of the nondescript doors.

"Can you go to the waiting room?" he asked.

"No. I need to see Antonio, then I have to go to Jonathan. Then after that, you and I are going to talk about what happened at the Gate Club."

"You don't call the shots, Theresa." He said it without reproach or vindictiveness. A man with toes everyone seemed to step on regularly, he said it so gently, I wondered if he was trying to ease me into a new reality.

"Phrase everything I just said as a question."

"Mister Spinelli is occupied," he said.

His insistence irked me, but I didn't feel in a position to argue further. But I couldn't just walk without talking to my Capo. If Antonio was occupied, it was probably Daniel who was occupying him, and there was a good chance he was behind the door Daniel was about to enter.

I stepped back. "Fine."

"Don't go far, Tinkerbell."

I turned and walked away slowly. As soon as I heard the door squeak open, I spun on my heel and pushed past Daniel, through the door, and into an empty room with two folding chairs.

It was dark. The only light was from a window looking onto the adjacent interview room. Antonio sat alone at a metal table, in a beat-up wooden chair. If he knew the wall to his left was a two-way mirror, he didn't show it by moving a muscle.

Daniel closed the door behind him. "You should go."

"I'm going to bang on the window and shout."

"No, you're not. The room is soundproofed and it doesn't look like a mirror on the other side, first of all, and second of all, you're leaving."

He reached for my wrist, but I pulled myself away before he could get a good grip. A door opened, and at first, I thought it was the door to the room I was in, but it wasn't. It was the door to Antonio's room.

Daniel muttered, "I didn't want it to go like this."

I glanced at him, his shoulders slouched, his eyes closed. I turned back to the interview room. Antonio was standing. In the doorway was a woman about my age and a boy of about ten. She had a cascade of black hair and olive skin. Her lips were full and sexual, and her limbs were lanky and long.

The boy.

Well.

The boy was a young version of the man I loved.

I lost the ability to swallow. Once I saw them, I couldn't keep my eyes off Antonio. He could be stoic with the world, but he'd always shown his emotions to me. When he saw who entered the room, his face betrayed his heart. His joy was unmistakable as he said something in Italian.

"She heard he was dead and came here."

Nella. It must be his sister. She was just stunning. A heartbreaking beauty with brown eyes that had seen too much and a quiet confidence that I tried to embody over the feeling of being incomplete.

"She's been in Sorrento," Daniel said compassionately. "In hiding. She wanted to get her son away from the mob."

The woman ran into Antonio's arms, and I stared as he embraced her, pressing his nose to her hair. They spoke in Italian, rushing through words I couldn't understand. He touched her face and kissed her cheek.

"I went looking for you and found two Spinellis on a manifest from Naples. I thought it was a ruse you'd set up. But it wasn't. Obviously. It makes me kind of almost believe your story."

Antonio got on one knee to speak to the boy, his nephew. I'd never seen a man so happy. Even in that gritty box of a room, he shone with contentment, as if he was where he belonged and with the people he was meant for. His family. I knew then that I had to go back to Italy with him. If I was in jail twenty years, thirty for shooting Paulie, I'd meet him under the olive trees at sixty. He needed to be home with his family, and I'd be with him, no questions asked.

"The only thing was the names were so close," Daniel said, leaning on the mirror, watching me. "Are you all right?"

"I'm fine." Why wouldn't I be? I was witnessing Antonio speaking softly to his nephew as if the child was his own son. "Close to what? The names?"

"To you. Antonin and Tina Spinelli. It seemed like a ridiculous subterfuge."

Wait.

Something was wrong.

"Tina?" I asked.

"Short for Valentina."

I rummaged around the dark corners of my mind, looking under memories and details. I was snapped out of it when the little boy slapped Antonio's face and screamed at him in Italian. Valentina pulled the boy back and held him, her eyes welling up with an apology.

"Valentina shortens to Nella?"

Daniel didn't answer right away. He waited until I'd turned from the scene to look at him leaning against the mirror, eyes cast down. He fidgeted with his fingernail, gave it a quick bite. Stopped himself.

"Daniel. What is it?"

"Tink, I don't know how to say this."

"Don't call me that." Before the sentence was even out of my mouth, I uncovered the name from a mental file box of things that were precious to Antonio in the past.

Daniel let me know that what was written in that file was right. "Valentina is his wife."

I thought, in that moment, Daniel would be a vindictive dick. But he wasn't. Not with my hand covering my mouth and my eyes filling up.

Over.

Everything was over.

"Theresa. I'm sorry."

His apology was a backdrop to the scene in the interview room. Antonio spoke softly to her, Valentina… his wife… as she held her…. no… *their* son. He put his arm around her. What was her scent? Did he remember it? Even with his eyes closed, he looked as though everything was coming back to him.

He was home, and I was on the other side of a wall.

Chapter Ten

ANTONIO

I'd had a life once. I was a family lawyer. I practiced keeping families together because I'd never had one. Valentina had married that man. She married an optimist with a future who had escaped a life in the shadows. She married endless potential, strength, contentment.

The man she was married to the day before she died was a monster. She'd watched me become everything she loathed, everything my mother had tried to save me from. Valentina watched me fail and drew away away away. I didn't even realize she was a stranger until her car exploded over the hills of Naples and I didn't know where she was driving to.

The despair. There was nothing like it. No experience in my imaginings. No anguish so great I could kill man after man to eradicate it. But I dampened it. I buried that optimistic man and all his possibilities and I steeped myself in what I was to become.

An animal. A hell-bound murderer.

And…

And before Valentina was brought in, Daniel Brower had asked me questions that didn't make sense, about Italy, about my whereabouts ten years ago. My relationship with Paulie took up no more than three minutes. I couldn't turn the questions on him because there were two cops in the room, and my personal history with the district attorney was dangerous territory.

I knew he was hiding something. I knew he was beating around a bush. I knew he was playing a game of his own making when he dismissed the cops and said the interview was over. They shut off the camera and started out.

"And Theresa?" I'd asked as Brower was the last one out the door.

"Don't worry about her."

"Don't dismiss me."

"I'm not dismissing you." Brower held the door ajar. "Believe me. You fucked me royally. I'd never dismiss you again. But you're about to hurt her, and I thought I could stand that. I was wrong."

Before I could tell him he was wrong about that too, he closed the door, and my denials died on my lips. I'd never hurt Theresa. I'd take death for her. Eat it with a spoon. Embrace my damnation to save her. She was my hope, the call to that earlier self I thought had died.

In the minutes between the door closing and opening again, I unraveled the components of our predicament and tried to find a way through. She'd confess to shooting Paulie even if I swore I'd done it. The evidence might back her up. I had no idea what forensics would find. Hopefully the Carriage House had been such a mess nothing could be proven. Hopefully there had been so many criminals in such a small space that doubts would arise. But mostly, I hoped that the district attorney loved Theresa enough to protect her from what she'd done.

What simple worries. What facile hopes.

I forgot all of them. They imploded. A windshield—smooth, simple—cracked into an unpredictable web of joy, horror, confusion, completion.

And disbelief.

In the first second of seeing Valentina, I thought I was looking at a ghost. Or a different woman. Or a trick of the light. She was older but the same. She was… my God. My heart went up and down at the same time. It went to the heavens with joy and dropped out of me like a stone, because my grief was for naught, and my anger had been misdirected.

And still, even with her hand on the shoulder of a boy who looked exactly like my father, I didn't believe it until I held her and smelled the grass in her hair. It was her. I felt nothing but confirmation, a clicking into place of a memory with a fact.

I had questions. Too many. Where? How? Why? And they were drowned out by the sound of a windshield cracking slowly into a million complex shapes that would never fit together again.

She'd done to me what Theresa and I had attempted to do to everyone else. She'd faked her death. Her resurfacing was the perfect vengeance for the wrong we'd done.

"Antonio," she said, the Italian lilt a hymn from her lips.

Her voice brought me back ten years, to the rustling olive trees, the trickle of the fountain in the *piazza*, the thick smell of soil. She ran into my arms, and I had to catch her or she would fall.

"Valentina? Is it you?" Her cheek felt the same when my lips touched it; the smell and taste were the same. Though I felt all the tenderness in my heart for her and all the joy in the world that she was alive, another crack appeared where my love should have been. I pulled away, more confused than I thought possible.

"It's me, *amore*," she said.

"I know, it's just… how?"

"We have forever to talk."

Did we? Forever? Another crack. Another discomfort lodged in my gut where I thought I couldn't be less comfortable. I held her face and called for the old feelings and found only happiness. An overwhelming yet generic pleasure that she still existed.

She cast her eyes down. "This is your son, Antonin."

Her voice was cool and distrustful, and it hitched, as if she spoke through her own pane of broken glass.

I had to look at him. *Dolore*. That was the only word for it. Pain. In him, and in me, and between us. I didn't know children. All I saw was a little man and missed opportunities. Misused lives. Broken promises. And maybe the hope that they could be fixed. Maybe some wrongs could be undone. Maybe even a man like me could get a second chance to do something right.

That must have been what my father felt when he saw me for the first time in eleven years. That was why he'd brought me into his world and tried to keep me from it at the same time. In that crack of realization, that I would do the same with my son as my father had done with me, Antonin let me know it wouldn't be easy. He hit me. I deserved it.

"Antonin!" Valentina cried, taking the boy and looking at me. "I'm so sorry. He's confused."

The blow hurt my face but cracked that moment of hope that he needed me to fix him. Little Antonin was perfectly fine without me. I'd only undo the good work his mother had done.

"We're all confused," I replied. *Andati in pallone*. I could only feel this confusion in Italian. As soon as I put eyes on her, I knew what she was feeling.

"No," she said defiantly, her Italian as cutting as it was musical. "No, we are not all confused."

Chapter Eleven

THERESA

I had to do something. I had to walk. Think. Speak. I had to see my brother. I had to plan the next few days.

I had to do a lot of things. But what I wouldn't do was have the same complete mental breakdown I did when I found out Daniel was cheating on me. So I dedicated myself to shutting out the image of Antonio looking at his wife as if he'd finally come home. Blot out the way he touched her cheek. Erase the sound of them speaking to each other in a common language. I had to focus.

I sat in Daniel's empty office with my hands in my lap and recited a litany of prime numbers, focusing my energy completely on three numbers ahead, imagining the shape of the digits, occupying the lowest parts of my mind on garbage so the higher parts of my mind could attend to the important things. I had returned alive. I was all right. He was all right. And maybe this crazy screwed-up situation was the best thing for him.

Daniel entered with a glass of water. "How are you doing?"

I took it and put it on the desk. "Thank you. I'm fine."

19. 23. 29. 31.

He sat across from me in an old green chair. The leather squeaked from his weight when he shifted forward. "I'm kind of relieved. I thought he'd killed her. I thought your judgment had gone fully out the window."

"And now you think I was being reasonable?"

"No. But at least I don't think he's in the habit of murdering his wives. Just his business partners."

"He didn't. I did." I tried to swallow the admission back. It wasn't necessary to confess just yet, but in my weakened state, the truth was a powerful balm.

"Yeah," he said. "Sure. You did it."

He didn't believe me. Or he didn't want to. I tried to care, but I was broken, split apart, an incomplete measure of a person.

I couldn't come up with a reply, because all of my energy went into remembering Antonio's reunion with his wife.

Focus.

Wife.

An unbreakable bond under God. I'd been bedded, repeatedly, by a married man. I was the other woman. The whore. The one left behind. Big words, explosive ideas, hurtful phrases pushed into my consciousness like a TV left on to a bad show I couldn't stop watching.

37. 41. 43. 47.

"Theresa?"

"I'm fine. I think I should go to the hospital."

"I can take you."

"Sure." What had he smelled when he put his nose in her hair? Hope? Togetherness? Completion? "I'm just a little…" I spun my hand at the wrist. There was a word, but I couldn't think of it because I was trying to get to the primes over a hundred, where it got complex enough to sustain me. I had to shut off the TV in my head. *She stayed gentle. She stayed gentle and died.* "He told me she was dead."

"He thought she was."

He thought she was. Why was it taking me so long to process things? Why couldn't I turn the TV down? *He thought she was dead.* Right. Okay. So I wasn't half the whore, and he wasn't a liar. He'd asked me to marry him.

Don't cry.

Meaning Daniel was telling it right. Antonio wouldn't have asked for my hand if he thought he had a living wife.

Don't.

Cry.

Focus.

53. 59. 61.

"She's been in hiding. She wasn't in the car when it exploded. It was a setup. She and her mother-in-law set it up. She'd disappear until he finished and came home."

I shook my head. The prime numbers clattered around. "Why?"

"They hate the mob, his mother and his sister. Valentina's no different. From what she says, they were fighting a lot about his new line of work. So his mother convinced her Antonio would get clean and return. Told her he knew she was alive. So she waited until she found out he'd died in an explosion in downtown LA."

"And she was pregnant when he left."

"Yes."

"It's an Italian opera, isn't it?"

"Except you're not fat, and you can't sing."

I felt my face stretch into a smile, but my mind was still working on the TV. The tuning had changed, but the volume was the same. Antonio hadn't known. He must be as confused as I was. I worried about what he felt. What he would do. About him as a person who had resigned himself to losing someone he loved and then found her in a police station.

"I don't understand what you have to do with this," I said. "Why I'm not being questioned by the police. Why you know. Any of it."

"Everyone knows Spinelli shot Patalano. That's first. You'll be questioned, trust me, but you're not a suspect. Not as long as I'm the district attorney. And the way the mayor's race is going since the wedding, I'm going to be DA long enough to put him in jail and keep you from throwing yourself to the wolves for him."

I nodded. I'd do what I had to, but I couldn't put it together right then.

"Theresa?"

"Yes?"

"Did you look like this when I hurt you?"

I shrugged. "I'm going to do better this time."

When I said "this time" as if it was a done deal and I had no hope of feeling whole again, I took a sharp, involuntary breath. I cleared my throat. *101. 103. 107. 113.* No. One was missing.

Daniel put something in my hand. "This is yours. It's the only thing I gave you of any value."

I looked down at a soot-covered engagement ring.

"You're too good for me," he said, closing my hand around it. "I had no business asking you to marry me. And he had no business being with you, whether he knew about Valentina or not. I don't want you to settle."

107. 109. 113. 127.

"You're a real fuckup," I said.

"Yeah. But I'm a good DA."

That was the truth. He was even a great DA.

I put the ring at the top of my thumb and let it rest there. Stupid thing. I'd been so excited to get it. I'd felt completed. I'd thought Daniel and I looking up at the solar system together was what it meant to be fulfilled. But it had been precarious, and I was a different woman now. Bone to flesh, I was different. I'd run away, shot a man, been shot at, died, come back to life. I'd gone nose to nose with danger and walked away stronger. I didn't have to make common choices anymore. Antonio had freed me of my own expectations of myself, and I could be whomever I wanted.

"You know Donna Maria's after him," I said. "He has a price on his head."

"There's not much I can do until they try to kill you."

"Is his wife safe?"

"Probably not. Why?"

My tears had dried up, and the rote repetition of numbers that kept me from thinking of Antonio and Valentina in that room dissolved into sense.

"I'm glad you have him," I said. "He's safer with you."

He pressed his lips together. "I can't much longer. I have nothing yet."

"You can't throw him to the wolves."

"I can't keep him in custody. Believe me, I'd love to lock him up, away from you."

I imagined Antonio getting gunned down on First Street, two steps out of the building, cars screeching away, return shots fired, a movie in three dimensions. A man dying, bleeding out, his wife and son finally reunited with him. The drama was epic, and I didn't see how it could happen differently. "You need to protect him. They're after him. He was supposed to marry Irene, and they killed the last guy who tried to get out of it."

"I know."

"We almost got killed in Mexico."

"He's a big boy."

He wasn't budging.

"What about her? The wife? And the boy? Are you going to be responsible if something happens to them?"

"They're staying with me."

"That's a little off book, isn't it?" I said.

"There's no rulebook for any of this. And like I said, my reputation barely matters anymore. The election is a formality."

"So keeping a beautiful, vulnerable woman at your place..."

"A married woman and her child," he said.

"You really hate him."

"Hate's a very strong word."

"Protect him, Daniel. If only to keep my heart from breaking again."

He gave every appearance of considering it. His gaze drifted to the half distance with a little tilt of his head, a lowering of his eyelids, half a swallow. *Tick, tick, tick*. I had no idea what was going on in his mind, except I did. There was a veracity about him. An honesty that you could see on people who'd had an epiphany. Those who had taken a hard look at themselves and made choices based on what they saw.

He'd never be a politician, but he'd become a man.

Chapter Twelve

ANTONIO

I loved Valentina. She never gave up on anything. She fought endlessly for things that were destined to die. Her grandmother's rotting crochet tablecloth. A bird with a broken foot left at the door by our cat. Her Fiat.

We'd met on a rainy day in Napoli because she wouldn't let that hunk of metal go.

Some cars needed to be put out of their misery. The little ones that didn't go far enough on a liter of gas. The big ones that didn't go fast. The cars so dented and bruised they hurt the eyes. I could keep a car running a long time. Slow, inefficient, or ugly, I'd fix it even if I wanted to kill it. We had that in common. We let things live too long.

"Take this one, Tonio!" Imbruzio had shouted from his office.

He was fighting with his mistress over money. I could hear them through the door every first and third Monday of the month. She cooed. He excused. She scolded. He got defensive. She whined. He comforted. She cried. He cried. She shouted. He put his foot down. Then either she stormed out or the desk legs started creaking. The putting down of his foot was the critical juncture, and when Imbruzio told me to take the little Fiat cutting a turn from the narrow cobblestone street into our tiny lot, he and his mistress were in the comfort/cry stage.

I put down my lunch and stepped out of the office into the rain. It had been drizzling all morning and had just increased to a light rain. A thunderstorm was imminent, and she looked like a bird with a broken wing.

The Fiat was smoking like a Turkish cigarette, rattling and clanking up to the garage. The car itself had a rust problem, a dent problem, needed a paint job, and shook so hard I thought the carburetor's idling pin might not just be screwed too loose but was probably missing entirely. When she got out of the car, the little sheets of water turned into a deluge, and the sky lit up as if it were on fire.

I'd gotten the car running again. Cars and vengeance, I didn't let either go. *La vendetta di cent'anni ha I denti da latte.*

Yes, we had that in common. We held onto things.

VALENTINA WAS PISSED. Before she even opened her mouth, I knew she was about to start crying. Antonin had been pulled out by Zia, my aunt. Who knew the whole time. And my mother. And my wife.

I was holding a chest full of anger, but held it back. Too many things were moving. Theresa. Paulie. Daniel, that fuck. Losing control would do nothing.

She felt out of place. Awkward. Angry. Sitting primly on the bench at First Street Precinct, she was a tightly wound coil of unhappy confusion.

"You don't look happy to see me," I said once she and I had sat down. Being able to speak about things in my language was a relief, but of course, I couldn't talk to her about anything real.

A Los Angeles police woman came in with bottles of water. I opened Valentina's and put it in front of her, then I gave myself a moment to think as I drank from mine. Valentina didn't even look at hers, and I needed much more than a moment.

"And you?" she asked.

"I'm happy to see you. You have no idea. I mourned you for a long time."

"I mourned you for a day."

I twisted on the bench so she and I faced each other. I needed to see her to read her.

"Somewhat smaller investment."

"Oh, shut up." She rubbed her eyes. "This lawyer met me at the airport and told us he was taking me to see you, and I didn't believe him. I said I didn't trust lawyers."

"I'm a lawyer."

"I waited too long. I got comfortable where I was, doing what I was doing. I work in a fabric factory. I do the books and operations. And it's good. I manage a little team. I never would have left the house if things hadn't happened the way they did."

"Happened?" As if she had no hand in it. As if she hadn't disappeared of her own free will. As if her love hadn't been a rose with thorns.

"Years just went and went," she said.

"And then I was dead."

"I was going to stay home. But Antonin wanted to see your face, even if it was at a funeral. I couldn't tell him there was no body, so what was I supposed to do? Refuse him? And your mother, she's broken a hundred times. She couldn't leave. So between the two of us, we decided Antonin and I would come."

"My mother *knew*?"

"For Antonin, she thought it—"

I slammed my hand on the table. "Damn you!"

"This!" She pointed at me. "This is what I'm talking about. This craziness. Yes. She hid me. She hates what you became."

"You could have just left me."

Her eyes, huge and almond-shaped, pouted at me. "You would have found me and dragged me back. Me and the baby. I didn't want that for him."

She was right. I would have hunted her, and when I found out she was carrying a child, that would have been it. I would have had her watched, and another opportunity to leave never would have presented itself. She would have been stuck with a man she loved and hated, but mostly hated.

"You're right," I said.

She raised an eyebrow. "I'm right?"

"You hate me. But I wouldn't have let you leave."

"I don't hate you, Antonio. I never hated you." She touched my hand gingerly, then laid hers flat over mine. "Seeing you—" She shook her head.

And there I was, thinking I'd had fake death sorted out. Theresa and I had caved to the temptation to come back to life in less than twenty-four hours. Yet for ten years, Valentina had resisted the temptation to find me.

She was good.

Where did I find these iron-spined women?

As if summoned by my thoughts of Theresa, the door opened, and Brower came in. "Valentina."

Calling her by her first name like that, he irked me, twisting the edges of my discomfort. It was too familiar.

"You're required down the hall," Brower said.

"*Scusi,*" she whispered before she spun on the bench and slipped out. I imagined it was her son, *our son*, she needed to attend to.

Brower was left. I stood. I wouldn't straddle a bench with this fucker in the room. I would break his head open with it. He closed the door and stepped toward me until we were nose to nose. I was in his territory. His building. I couldn't touch him, and he knew it.

He sat down and indicated the bench across from him.

"What did you think you were doing?" I asked.

"Can you sit?"

I didn't move. I could sit, but I didn't want to be across from him. Didn't want to be on an equal footing.

"There was no easy way to tell you," he said. "It was going to suck no matter what."

"So you tried to spare my feelings?"

"Your *feelings*? I couldn't give a shit. Are you going to sit? Or do you think standing puts you in some kind of position of power?"

He sat with both elbows on the table, palms up. I assumed he was going to tell me about Valentina. How he found her, what he intended to do with her.

I sat.

He tapped his fingertips together. "I know you guys. I know how you operate, and you know why."

"Because you pick the olives and uproot the tree at the same time?"

He smirked. "Spoken like an Italian."

"Spoken like a man who can keep two conflicting ideas in his mind."

"The skill of criminals and priests."

"Which are you?" I asked, because in a way, he was both.

He stopped tapping his fingertips and folded his hands together. He took a long time to answer—too long, as if he was searching in a file for what he wanted to say and couldn't find the paperwork for it.

"You know what I think of you," he said.

I nodded. I didn't need a list.

"But that aside, I'm conceding defeat. You win," he said.

"I don't believe you."

"I thought Theresa was dead, and I died with her. Everything died. Even my desire to hurt you for it. When I realized she was alive, I swore I wouldn't make her life difficult any more. Which means I'm not taking revenge on you for hurting her, or stealing her, and I'm not coming after you for fucking me up. I don't care if you think I'm a coward for that."

"Not for that."

"Touché. But I'm not done. We have conflicting intel regarding the price on your head for bailing on Irene Carloni. As low as half a million for your corpse. Alive, we've heard up to two million."

"Alive is nice. They get to torture me." I smiled at him. I wasn't afraid of torture or death. I'd been hurt before, and I'd be hurt again.

"I assumed it was because if the murder is witnessed and documented, she gets your territory."

"Money is a great motivator."

"They also want Theresa. Quarter million."

My hair stood on end. My fists balled tightly enough to stretch the skin over the knuckles to white. I put my hands under the table.

"Who told you this?" I asked.

"Fuck you."

"No. Fuck you."

We regarded each other over the table. It didn't matter who the mole was. What mattered was that the life I'd promised Theresa wouldn't happen.

"And your wife and child?" Daniel said as if reading my mind. "Once they find out they're here, she'll be a target. Never mind the fact that if you'd married Irene, you'd be a bigamist. Let's focus on this. You're going to be followed everywhere. You're going to be in constant danger. Even if I wanted to cut you down, I wouldn't. All I'd have to do is step back and watch. Except for Theresa, who's so upset you're married, I don't think she's absorbed that she's going to get killed."

"You told her? That's for me—"

"Do you even know her? Do you even know what you made her? She doesn't hear the word 'no.' I told her to stay in the hall, but she was in the room before I could close the door."

He jerked his finger at a wood panel on the wall. I hadn't given it a second look until that moment, but when I trained my eye directly on it, I saw the translucence. Theresa had seen the whole thing. I tried to piece together my reaction to Valentina. Had I kissed her? Held her? Spoken a tender word in English?

"The safest thing to do would be to keep you here," he said. "But I can't. I don't have enough on you." He stood. "And you need to protect Theresa, because I can't do that either. I've tried, and I have no resources. Not like I did before the wedding."

The facts were damning. If I hadn't made that last unnecessary volley against him, he'd have the power to protect the woman we both loved. The result of my vengeance was vulnerability.

Daniel opened the door. "I'm sorry to say, you're free to go."

"And Valentina?"

"She'll be in touch."

Chapter Thirteen

THERESA

I finally left Daniel's office drained, wrung out, a shell of hard skin around an empty core. I'd have to get to the hospital in a cab. That was all I had to do. That was what I'd come back for. After seeing Jonathan, I could let my world crumble. I could make decisions, run, stay, thrive, die. But this thing with my brother had to be done first.

I felt pressure on my elbow, then at the base of my spine, and lost control of my direction and will just as I caught the scent of burned pine. I couldn't spin around to face him until the door was shut and he was pushing me against the wall of an empty room.

"Antonio," I said firmly, "stop it."

"Stop what?" A lock of his hair dropped in front of his eye, and his lips parted with the tick of the last T. "You can't leave without me."

I pressed my hands to his chest and pushed him away, but I couldn't move him. "I know." I paused to see if he could tell what I meant. "About Valentina." I watched the flick in his eyes as they moved across my face, looking for my feelings on the subject. Feelings I was desperate to hide. "I'm happy for you."

"Are you?" He took my wrists and snapped them over my head before I could resist. He pressed his body into me and spoke so close to me that his lips brushed my cheek. "Why?"

"Don't be stupid." I tried to wrench away, but he held my hands fast and immobilized my hips with his. My body didn't care about wedding vows or another woman. My body wasn't worried about moral complexities. My body surged with lust at the feel of his dick against me.

"Men are dead because of her," he said through his teeth.

"She's alive, Antonio. And you have a child. This is your chance at life. It's staring you in the face. Don't you see? You go back to her. Tell Donna Maria that was why you couldn't marry Irene, that you knew. She'll forgive you, and you can go home."

He bent his knees until our eyes were level. "And you?"

I looked him in the eye. If I obfuscated even a little, he'd think I didn't mean it. "I cop to shooting Paulie. I tell the police, not the DA. I convince them. I can do it. You walk back into the life you lost. It's perfect."

He let my hands go but left his hips against me. "Perfect?"

"It's like a puzzle clicking into place. This is your only chance. It's a gift that she's back. Just make your life what you want."

I was a weakling. When he cupped my chin and brushed his finger along my cheek, I turned enough to trick myself into thinking I was resisting, and I put my gaze on the floor, because I couldn't look at him.

"I saw her, and it was shocking. I'm only a man. I thought all the things you think I did. That I could go back. That I could have another chance. I admit it. But the truth? It's more frightening. I kissed her cheek and felt nothing. Like kissing my sister. Or a stranger. I'm not that boy anymore. I'm a man. I'm made of everything I've done and everything I want, and I don't want a life in Napoli with her. That's the idea of who I am. I want a life with you, because you accept me. All of me. I am whole with you. Only you."

I could have fallen into him so easily. I could have broken myself apart and fit the pieces into a shape resembling sanity and morality. When he leaned in to kiss me and I felt his breath on my lips, my body bent to fit him, whoever he was and whatever he wanted.

The door snapped open, and he turned quickly to address what might be a threat. But it was Margie, looking unusually nonjudgmental. I guessed she got sick of waiting for me to get a cab to the hospital.

"Are you coming?" She looked at Antonio as she passed us. "Or do you want to stay here until they find enough to Mirandize?"

He laughed and took my hand, following Margie's brisk pace down the stairs. They spoke another language as they walked. Not Italian, or even English. They spoke lawyer.

We got into Margie's silver Mercedes without her or Antonio breaking the constant stream of jargon regarding Daniel's ability to hold him.

"I wish he'd kept you," I said, sliding into the front seat.

"Why?" Margie asked as she closed her door.

"They want to kill him. As soon as he gets out of this car, they can shoot him. Then when he leaves the hospital. And it's not like he can go home."

Antonio sat in the back, his shoulder against the door. Light slid over his face when Margie reversed, then it fell back into shade, then light again. Gorgeous in the light. Magnificent in the dark. Light. Dark. Light. Magnificent. Gorgeous. His lips relaxed to speak. Those full, soft, married lips.

"Don't worry," he said.

"I want to trust you on this, Antonio, I really do. But you can't stop bullets with bossiness or good looks."

"They would have killed you too."

"I wish you guys would talk about something normal." Margie snapped the ticket out of the parking machine and made a right. "Like cancer."

"It's hard to be normal with this guy."

"I know how you feel," she replied. "Listen, I know the director of neurology at Sequoia. I defended him on a thing. We can get his parking spot. It's secure. I'll coordinate with Antonio to get you both out of the hospital. Do you have a place to stay?"

"Not yet," Antonio said.

"I got that. You have a phone?"

"No."

"Let me take care of you tonight. I'll get you a burner, and you can call him. But please, don't leave fucking town until we know what's happening with Jonathan. Please. I know it's risky for you." She looked at him in the rearview.

It didn't matter if he liked her. He wouldn't refuse her. No one could.

"It's fine," he said. "We came back for him."

"You're all right for a reprobate thug, you know that?"

"You can be a character witness at my sentencing."

They went on like brother and sister the whole way to the hospital, while I looked out the window and reminded myself that my relationship with him was coming to a close.

We parked deep in the underground lot, past a separate gate, in a spot right next to the elevator. Antonio held the car door open for me, but I couldn't look at him, even when we stood in front of the elevator doors.

"Mom's medicated," Margie said as the doors slid open with a ding. "Sheila's managing her anger. Deirdre's sleeping on a chair. Dad turns up in the halls sometimes. Jon's girlfriend is the emaciated specter on the verge of tears."

"Three short?" I asked.

"At the moment."

Chapter Fourteen

THERESA

Returning to Los Angeles had been dangerous and stupid. Our journey back had the potential to ruin our lives. If we'd continued with our plans in Mexico, Antonio would never have reconnected with Valentina. I wouldn't be considering admitting to shooting Paulie. We would have gotten married, bought a house, had children.

But we came back for Jonathan, a fool's errand that wouldn't do anyone any good. When I saw my rake of a brother in that bed—tubes sticking out of him, hair a mess, skin battered in flour—I was glad I had come.

I sat in the chair beside him. "If you're up, I'm over here."

"I'm up," he said, slowly turning toward me. Machines beeped incessantly, and a hiss of a medical apparatus underscored every other sound in the room. "You look like hell."

"You look great. I saw your girlfriend on the way in."

"She's beautiful, isn't she?"

"Yes."

I thought he slipped out of consciousness, or maybe he was gathering strength to speak. But his eyes closed, then opened halfway.

"She won't marry me. I asked, and she ran off."

"Why?"

He held up his hand, or he attempted to. He had too many tubes sticking out of him to do it properly. I held it down and squeezed it.

"Pledge open," I said.

"Dad's making trades with her. He bought her house to keep it from foreclosure."

A seemingly kind gesture in my father's hands always required a payment. You might not see it. You might not understand the depth of it, but no favor went unsettled.

"And I'm stuck in this damned bed," he said. "She doesn't know what she's getting into. I don't know how else to protect her."

"I don't blame her for saying no," I said. "No one wants to be asked out of desperation."

"I'm not desperate," he protested. "I'm pressed for time. And Dad..." He took a few deep breaths. "I'll kill him."

"You need to get better first," I said, as if that might give him some hope and strength. Looking at him, the very idea of recovery was as ridiculous as the idea of him dying.

"What if I don't get better?"

"She'd be a widow."

He swallowed, leaving a long gap between the word "widow" and our next words. I smiled to myself. If Antonio died, he'd have a widow, and it wouldn't be me.

"I realized something today," I said. "I realized what I thought of marriage. I think I took it all for granted, with Daniel. I just said yes because I did. Because I could, and it seemed like the next stage of life. But it's sacred. It's holy. Let no man tear asunder. We have to mean it when we say it. No one should rip up a contract God wrote. I'll go to hell for plenty I did without thinking, but I won't go for a crime I chose while knowing better."

He didn't answer. His eyes were closed, then he tightened them and looked at the ceiling. "What's today?"

I counted days from the Bortolusi wedding. "The nineteenth."

"Merry Christmas."

That was Jonathan, naturally deflecting from his seconds-span of unconsciousness with glib sarcasm. I'd miss him if he were gone. Even if I lived far away under a different name. The world would feel less sardonic and far too serious without him in it. "What do you want under the tree? Besides a 'yes'?"

"I want her," he whispered. "I asked for the wrong reasons, but I want her."

"It's forever, Jonathan." I put my elbows on the bed and my hand on his shoulder. "Do it for the right reasons. Don't do it because it's convenient. Don't do it because you're scared. Marry her because you love her and your life wouldn't add up without her. Can you do that? Can you promise me you're not forcing it? It would break my heart to see you propose because you wanted to give yourself a reason to live."

"What's wrong, Tee?"

"I don't think love should be taken for granted, and I don't think you should keep on a path of least resistance."

"This is hardly… the Italian guy. What's happening? You're acting strange."

"Can you honestly say that if you were healthy, you'd marry her?"

"Yes. But we'd have a proper engagement."

He was sure. Through hid glassy eyes, I saw a rock-solid surety. Antonio must have been that sure when he'd asked Valentina, but me? I wasn't beating myself up, but the circumstances had brought his proposal on too quickly, and after seeing his wife alive and well, I couldn't assume his feelings for me would withstand her return. Even if he'd meant it when he asked me to marry him, everything had changed...

Jonathan meant it. He did. Daniel had meant it. But Antonio couldn't.

I fished in my pocket and came up with my soot-stained ring. I pressed it into his palm. "Try again, and use this. Give it back when you can buy her her own."

His hand didn't close around it at first. God, he was so messed up. Was he even conscious?

"The last time I saw you," I said, "you were killing oranges for sport and making jokes in Italian. This is… I don't know. A wake-up call."

I had to spend the rest of my life doing right. If I had to answer for my actions, I wanted to be able to stand up and say that I had definitively and consciously decided to be better, do better, be a person I could be proud of.

"I never joke in Italian."

"Sorry to make it about me," I whispered.

He smiled a little then held up the ring so he could see it. "I'm boring right now. And all anyone talks about is me. Where did you get this? They said you went on the run? Did you start robbing jewelry stores?" He lowered his hand as if he were too weak to hold it up.

I didn't know how much of this conversation he'd remember, if any of it. "Someone really wanted me for a while. You've met him."

"Daniel won't be happy. He still wants you."

"How do you know?"

"I know regret when I see it," he said.

"He'll tell himself he cares, but we cancel each other out. We add up to nothing. Trust me when I say I'd rather break up for the right reasons than get married for the wrong ones. With him, or anyone else. I'm either first in line, or I walk."

"You're not the uptight priss I thought you were. You're a priss with a purpose. I'm proud of you."

"You thought I was an uptight priss?" I said with a smile. I'd never thought of myself that way, but maybe I was.

"I think I underestimated you. I'm sorry."

"Don't be. I can't explain why I feel okay about it, but I do."

"Thank you." He held the ring in his fist as if he were afraid to lose it. "Pledge closed."

"Pledge closed." I kissed his forehead. It was cold, and my heart ached for him. "I'll try to come back, but you might not see me for a while."

Chapter Fifteen

THERESA

I left in tears. My family was in the waiting room two doors down, and I craved them. Margie and Sheila, even Mom, whose hugs felt like being loosely wrapped in chicken wire. I wanted them. A week ago, I'd wanted to get away from them, but on that day, all I wanted was to be a pack animal. Surround myself in them. Drown out thoughts of Valentina and soak in family love.

I touched my St. Christopher medal before I got in their sights. I'd avoided facing my family on the way in because I needed strength for Jonathan.

Mom sat by the window, face slack with medication. She's been on the worst of them, then gotten off them, then on again. Her expression was as deadened as it had been during her Thorazine years. Margie and Sheila talked with their arms crossed, and the singer stood to the side as if she didn't belong. We'd have to fix that. I'd hold her first, then hug Mom, then Sheila, and I would apologize for running away. I wouldn't explain the unexplainable, but I would go deep into my gut for the regret and gratitude they deserved.

Except I never got to the waiting area. One minute I was walking down an empty hall wide enough for two lanes of traffic, the linoleum shining in vertical stripes where the lights were reflected, and the next, my feet didn't feel the pressure of my body. I was pulled out of the hall so fast I didn't have time to scream, even if a sweaty hand hadn't been covering my mouth. My shoes slipped on the floor, and my knees dragged. I no longer had control of my body.

A door slammed, then there were steps. I clawed at my attacker. Male. Huge. Not Antonio. As I got thrown down a flight of concrete steps, I knew, even as my vision swam and my stomach flip-flopped, that I was alone. As alone as I'd ever been. No one was coming.

The man looked like the guy Antonio didn't shoot in Tijuana. The one behind the rock. Domenico. Bruno Uvoli's brother. I remembered it when my lungs emptied as he grabbed me and, as if he just couldn't be bothered to carry me down the stairs, tried to thrust me down the next flight.

At the last second, I grabbed his ankle. My weight, which already had significant torque, pulled him down with me.

Bodies in motion tend to stay in motion, and we did exactly that. Elbows, knees, hips, the corners of the stairs, and gravity all battled for space. In those two turns, the civilized parts of me peeled off as if by centrifugal force, whipping away, leaving the basest, coarsest version of myself. The raw rage and adrenaline. All action and forward thrust. I considered nothing but action.

When we got to the next landing, I twisted until my hand was free, and I reached between his legs, grabbing for the soft flesh there. I squeezed, twisted, and pulled all at the same time.

Domenico's howl woke me from my fog. He reached for me, and I couldn't get away without letting his balls go, so he got my hair and jerked me around.

"You fucking mick bitch." He went for my throat with one hand and pulled his other fist back.

I kept squeezing the flesh between his legs. His hand tightened on my throat. The edges of my vision dotted black as he cut off my circulation. I kicked at him but hit nothing, and fight turned to flight as I waited for him to smash my face.

But the blow never came.

Domenico was pulled away from me, mouth half open, eyes popping as if I was still twisting his balls.

In the whoosh of air as he was drawn away from me was the scent of campfires in a pine forest. Choking on my bruised esophagus and hurting everywhere, in a stairwell that should have been guarded but obviously wasn't, I felt safe again. I got my legs under me.

"Theresa." His voice, unflustered by anything but simple rage, cut through my pain and disorientation.

"I'm fine."

I wasn't. I was beat to hell, more shattered than I ever had been in my life. Yet I was fine the second I heard his voice.

Antonio held Domenico against the railing with his left hand while he pounded his face with his right. His knee was wedged between the man's legs, immobilizing him into a back-arched position. His face was red.

"Chi ti ha mandato?"

I scanned the stairwell. Why was no one coming? How had this even gone on so long? The camera hung in the corner like a wasps' nest, but it was turned all the way around.

"Chi ti ha mandato?" Antonio insisted, glancing at me quickly. "I'm going to fucking kill him if he doesn't answer."

Domenico made gacking noises in his throat.

"I don't think he speaks Italian," I said through a throat full of sand.

Antonio tightened his grip. "Too bad he can't pray in God's language." He got up in Domenico's face, jabbing his knee between his legs, and whispered, "Who sent you?"

Domenico puckered his lips as if to speak through layers of spit, and Antonio turned his head a quarter to hear.

"What? *Che*? I can't hear you?"

Since Antonio hadn't loosened his chokehold one iota, there was nothing to hear. My lover was being unnecessarily brutal. Cruelty wasn't necessary. I should have been horrified, but I wasn't any more dismayed by this than when Antonio had made Paulie recite the Hail Mary with a gun to his head.

"Antonio," I said, "we don't have time. I don't know why no one's here, but it won't last."

He looked me over, lingering on my throat, which must have been a shade of red that was about to go black and blue.

I turned to Domenico and said calmly, "Who sent you?"

Antonio loosened his grip a little.

I continued. "I've seen him kill people. And I'm no angel either."

How could I revel in it? How could I align myself with the most savage part of the man I loved? And how could I feel so right about it? So empowered by murder?

"P-P-P..." the man sputtered.

Antonio and I exchanged a look and understood each other very clearly. Antonio removed his hand.

"Patalano," he croaked. Domenico looked at Antonio expectantly, then me, breathing hard.

A beat passed before Antonio spoke low and with forceful intent. "Liar."

In one fell motion, Antonio bent and scooped Domenico's knees and pulled them up. The railing became a fulcrum and the man's body a plane, and he tumbled down the space between the stairs. I heard banging and grunting, but I didn't look. I only had eyes for Antonio.

Then it stopped.

Antonio wasn't breathing heavily, as if he'd expended zero energy, physical or otherwise. His gaze burned my skin, peeling it off and looking through me. I felt vulnerable and soaked in desire, bare before him and still safe.

"You're made for this life," he said.

"I'm made for you."

Below, someone screamed, and the camera behind me whirred to life. He took my hand and pulled me upstairs. He took the steps two at a time, not as if he was rushing but as if the steps were simply too small for him, and I kept up. I didn't know how, and I didn't know why, because he hadn't told me where we were going. But hand in hand, step for step, in a pine-scented breeze, I made it to the top landing.

"We don't have time," he said without breaking his pace. "There are no cameras here, so we could get out. Paulie's here. The place is crawling with his family, but it looks like Donna Maria found me."

Antonio turned back to me as he shouldered the door, checking on me. Admiring. Connecting. Yanking that spiritual tether between us.

Before the door clacked open, I noticed the floor and walls shaking in a consistent rhythm. Not an earthquake.

He yanked me forward, pushing the door all the way open and drawing me onto the roof where a helicopter waited. The pressure of the air almost slammed the door on me, but he held it. The rotors spun against the orange haze of the setting sun, and a man crawled out of the cabin to hand Antonio his headset.

"You got clearance to Montecito," he shouted over the whip of the rotors. "Maintain at two thousand. Call in at squawk oh-three-five-one."

"Got it."

Antonio motioned to me and headed for the cockpit. I ran after him.

"Are you joking?" I tried to gather my whipping hair together and failed.

"Get in."

"We can't run away!" Even as I said it, I knew how ridiculous I sounded. Of course we were running away. "And you can't fly this thing!"

"Yes, we can, and yes, I can."

"You didn't tell me you had a pilot's license!" I yelled over the wind.

"I don't. Now get in before I pick you up and belt you in like a child."

I hesitated, and Antonio didn't have time for that. He picked me up by the waist and tossed me into the helicopter. I dropped into the bucket seat just as he reached for the belt.

"I have it." I tugged the belt. "Just promise me you've done this before."

"It's the only way to get around Capri."

He went around to the left side and slid in, buckled in, and put his headphones on as if he knew what he was doing. I put on mine. He reached over to my headset and snapped the broadcast function off.

"If you kill us, that's fine," I said. "Do not kill anyone else."

He turned to me and raised an eyebrow before pulling the helicopter off the roof. The bottom dropped out of my gut, and I gripped the edge of my seat.

"I think the word in English is 'ironic,'" he said once we were airborne. "You don't want to kill anyone by accident?"

"You want to discuss this now?"

"Yes."

I lost my train of thought when he swerved east and my stomach twisted.

"I can drive anything," he said. "They all work the same. This just has forward and backward plus up and down." He dipped again, high over Hollywood. "Like this."

We swerved across Wilshire, north toward the hills and the Observatory.

He leveled it and took out a pack of cigarettes. He offered me one and I refused. He bit the end of one and slid it out.

"I hope Domenico's dead," he said, clicking open his lighter as if he wasn't flying a helicopter at the same time. "I told you once, I'll kill anyone who touches you."

He was dead serious, almost bored. As if stating the date a war ended or began. As if vengeance was no more than a mathematical equation that needed to be solved. And it was the sexiest thing I'd ever seen. Almost as sexy as the knowledge that I'd kill for him with the same seriousness.

"Capo," I said to get his attention.

He shifted his attention while keeping the helicopter at a steady level.

"I don't know who I am with you, but I like me better now than I ever have. I'm scared. And elated. But the wife. Your wife—"

"Stop. We are not discussing her."

"We have to," I said.

We crossed the twisting thread of the LA River, which actually had water in it from the recent rains.

"You are my life. It doesn't matter what I am, or what I've done, as long as you're mine. Nothing in the past matters. There is you, and nothing else." He didn't look at me but kept his eyes on his work. A cluster of taller buildings appeared ahead, and he headed for them. "My one job," he said, holding up a finger, "is to make sure you know how to protect yourself when they finally kill me."

"Stop it."

"It's very clear to me. Do you know why I didn't confess to doing Paulie? Because if they send me to jail, I can't protect you. And yes, I have to protect Valentina too, because I made a promise to her. But it's not the same. Do not make the mistake of thinking it's the same."

He looked at me, a world of confidence and confusion churning in his eyes. Both and neither. I read him like a book and understood that he knew what he had to do, even if he didn't like or understand it.

I wasn't as sure. I didn't know what I had to do. I wasn't as confident that I could keep him alive or as comfortable with the moral ambiguity of the past week.

I gripped the seat on our descent, but he landed the helicopter smoothly.

He winked at me. "Easier than the beach."

"You'll have to tell me how you managed this," I said.

"I'm surprised you don't know already." He snapped off his headset. I unbuckled as he got out and crossed the front of the craft to my side.

"I'd just like a straight answer," I said.

He held out his hand, and I took it. "You come from a very powerful family, Contessa. They are no less organized than mine."

I should have been insulted. Shocked. Confused and curious. But I wasn't. I was frozen in place as I remembered everything I knew and had been told. My father's way of moving mountains to get what he wanted. Margie's way of making things happen with a phone call. The way people who hurt us wound up ruined or dead.

Was I made for Antonio by dint of my genetics?

Was I an animal from birth? Had the real me been dormant all this time?

I took Antonio's hand and slid down into the whipping wind of the landing pad. I felt a twinge of guilt for even touching a married man, but I stifled it. We had too much to do.

He paused for a moment as the rotors wound down. His head keened a little, peering inside me. "Some things are in the stars. I was meant to protect you. And you were meant to rule."

Chapter Sixteen

THERESA

Antonio hustled me down the stairs, waving to the pilot who was waiting for the craft. Montecito Hospital was less luxurious than Sequoia, but it spanned four city blocks.

Antonio seemed to have planned everything in the half an hour I'd spent giving Jonathan my ring. We careened down two flights of stairs before cutting through a bridge across Pacific Boulevard and catching an elevator. Everyone faced the door, and he pulled me into him until my shoulder blades touched his chest. He put his finger on the back of my neck, drawing on it from my hairline to the place where my spine disappeared under my shirt. I shuddered, and his dick got hard before we made it to the lobby.

I had no idea what to do about that beautiful erection, or what it did for me.

Or what it made me. The interloper. The other woman. The siren call to a taken man's filthiest desires. Not a speechwriter in sensible shoes, but an accountant and a killer with the grime of Tijuana still in her hair.

I was all those things, and more. And less.

I followed Antonio to the parking lot, listing them in no particular order.

Tramp.

Trash.

Fool.

"My god, Spin," Zo said when we got to the deepest level of the parking lot.

I hadn't said a word, because I didn't know what role to speak from.

"You look like shit," he said, hugging Antonio and kissing each cheek, left then right. He pointed at me and apparently chose courtesy over truth. "You look nice, of course."

Whore.

Slut.

Mistress.

"It's about a mile away," Antonio said with no preamble. He opened the back door for me and sat in the front with Zo.

I didn't mind being his whore, his one and only plaything. The shoe fit, and I wore it with pleasure. But being his mistress, his second, ate at me. He had a wife, and I wouldn't be the one to break that, nor would I become what destroyed my own life, no matter the circumstances. I wasn't exonerated because we hadn't known she was alive.

"Where are we going?" I asked in the car, feeling like I didn't belong there or anywhere.

"Up a hill." Antonio twisted in his seat to face me. "You're taken care of. Don't worry."

I'd made a concerted decision not to think about Valentina while we were getting out of the precinct, but in the backseat of the car, with him unintentionally using a phrase for the whores of married men, I lost the battle for my own composure.

"Stop looking at me," I said. I couldn't do this in front of Zo. I couldn't break down. I had resources. I'd kept myself from falling apart in worse situations. Goddamnit. My chin wiggled, and my sinuses filled up. I couldn't recall a prime number over two.

Antonio put his hand on my knee. I let my fingers slip around his, and I closed my eyes, just feeling his hand around mine. A deep breath. His presence in the car. The glue that held my mind together.

"Don't," he said.

I nodded, squeezing my eyes shut against tears.

"You are first," he said, reading my mind.

I didn't want him there. His left hand was on mine, with its bare ring finger. I pulled my hand away. "You're married. I can't touch you. It's not right."

He snapped his seat belt off and thrust himself over the front seat, extending his body back to me and leveraging himself against my knees.

His body bridged the front and back. His face was an inch from mine, and his smell of the forest after a fire consumed me.

"Sit down," Zo said a hundred miles away. "You're gonna get us pulled over!"

"*Sei mia,*" he whispered.

"Don't kiss me," I said. "Just don't, I'm—"

But he did, and so gently that the kiss itself was a request for a kiss. I squeaked involuntarily, because I didn't want to kiss him. I didn't want to do what I'd said I wouldn't do. I wanted to stay strong in my conviction that until we worked out what was happening with his wife, there would be no touching, no kissing, no nothing.

And he ripped all of that away. In the first microsecond of the kiss, when his parted lips brushed the length of mine as if introducing themselves for the first time, I lost every ounce of will I had against him. I needed him. I wouldn't make it through this without some part of his body against some part of mine. I was going mad, surely. Mad with violence or mad with need, but mad mad mad.

I opened my mouth, and his tongue greeted mine. It wasn't a lusty kiss but a joining. A reassurance. A nod to our connected destinies.

I put my hands on his cheeks, and he pulled back ever so slightly.

"I'm scared," I said. "And I love you."

"She admits it," he said, smiling. "*Amore mio,* you may have to carry our love alone, but it won't be heavy."

"It will be, and I don't have the strength."

He pulled back to kneel on the front seat. Before turning toward the windshield, with his left hand on the back of his seat and his right on Zo's headrest, he said, "Then it's agreed. We live. We live, and we share the load. *Dimmi di sii*?"

His confidence was infectious, and I let myself believe him for a second before spiraling back into doubt. "*Si, Capo. Si.*"

"Great," Zo said. "I don't know what you're talking about, but there's a cop two car lengths behind."

Antonio slapped Zo in the back of the head and twisted back into his seat.

Zo stopped at the end of a twisted path, at a modern little house with no windows in front, and we all got out of the car.

"What's the plan?" Zo asked, rubbing his forehead.

"Tonight we sleep." Antonio clapped Zo on the shoulder. "Tomorrow we plan. Give me your piece."

Zo unbuckled his shoulder holster and gave it to Antonio.

"Grazie," Antonio said, then motioned at the car. "You have one in there for Theresa?"

The crickets creaked, the wind crackled through the palm trees, and Zo looked at Antonio as if he'd lost his mind.

But Antonio just stood straight with his hand out. "They took everything on the way up."

Zo reached into the glove compartment and took out a small gun. He checked for bullets and slapped it into his boss's palm. "She know how to use it?"

"Blow your left nut off from ten meters."

"All right." He shrugged, resigned. They shook hands, and Zo drove away.

Antonio punched a code in the door, and we entered. He dropped the weapons on the counter with a clatter. The back of the house overlooked the San Gabriel Valley. I saw the barest of furnishings. A couch. A table and three chairs. Blinds, not curtains. Not a single painting, picture, or scuff mark broke the white expanse of the walls.

"This your house?" I asked.

"It's your sister's. I've never met a fixer like her."

"Margie? God, I—"

He crushed me in a bruising kiss, and I responded by accepting it, yielding to what was right, what fit, what made sense. His hands yanked up my shirt, his tongue owning mine.

I pushed him away. "Stop."

Whatever agility he used to hurt people, he used on me, twisting me around, pushing me against the window overlooking the valley and tying my shirt until the tension held my hands behind me. *"Cosa c'é?"*

"I just..." His scent distracted me. His breath in my ear. The hard-on pushing into me. My body made excuses, but damn it, I had a long explanation planned, one that was well-suited to a sane and civil dinner or a car ride. "I can't. I... we need to talk about—"

He clamped his hand over my mouth and pulled my head to his shoulder. "I don't want to talk," he hissed into my ear. "I want to fuck."

I couldn't make more than an *mmm* into his palm. He pulled off my shirt, freeing my hands, while keeping my head stable against him.

"Pull your pants down, Contessa."

I grunted a *no* and tried to shake my head. I was sweating and spit covered his hand, but he held me.

"You're going to pull your pants down right in front of this window. And you're going to be quiet when I fuck your pussy. Not a word. No talking. No yelling. Then I'm taking your mouth, and you're going to swallow all those words."

I begged with my eyes, but we'd done it rough so many times.

He was so serious, squeezing until he dented my cheeks. "Pull your pants down. Let me see it."

He pulled me back until I could see us in the window. He was hidden behind me except for the hand covering my mouth and the face growling into my ear. I swallowed. I saw my hard nipples in the window's reflection, and if I took my pants down, he'd feel how wet I was.

"Don't make me take my belt to your ass before I fuck it."

I heard and felt him undo his belt with his free hand. I made a sound in my throat. He looked at me in the darkened window. I wasn't allowed to protest.

"Look at us, Contessa. Watch when you give yourself to me." He locked my head forward, and I watched him put his hands down my pants. "*Adesso*"—his wrist disappeared below my waistband—"put your hands on the glass. Let's see how much you want to fuck."

I shook my head, but he pushed me forward, and I had to hold my hands against the glass to keep from falling. Cruel. He was so cruel. And my body was lit from within by his brutality.

He slid his hand to where I was soaked for him and put two fingers inside me as if he had every right to. My knees nearly buckled.

"No!" I said it behind his hand and knotted my brows, rattling my vocal cords.

If this wasn't serious enough for him, if he didn't hear this cry of mind over body, we were over. I swore it. My better self needed to be heard.

Chapter Seventeen

ANTONIO

She always resisted when she was tense, and I always forced my way through. This was us. This was how we were. I felt better afterward, no matter how I felt before, and our ferocity always lapsed into tenderness.

But she was crying, and she meant it. She wasn't playing. I was about to hurt her, or I'd done it already.

Had I lost her?

My pain was almost physical. I took my hand off her mouth.

"Let me go," she gasped.

"Why?"

I didn't know why I asked. To fill the space, maybe. I stepped back with a heavy heart. I'd done something wrong. Maybe too rough? I didn't have a minute to ask what exactly had gone over the line in the sand for her. I didn't have a second to make it up to her. She buttoned her pants and walked out of the room.

I didn't know the layout of the house, so I followed because I didn't want to lose her. I didn't fear much, but I did fear having her too far from me, and if she went outside, I thought I'd never see her again. That was a reality to me. Her disappearing into a puff of smoke, or getting shot or taken when my back was turned. I'd let her see her brother for thirty minutes while I met with her sister, and she wound up getting dragged down a stairwell by Domenico Uvoli.

I turned a corner in time to hear a door slam. She'd gone into a bathroom and closed the door without even turning on the light.

I knocked. "Contessa? Open this now."

"Pounding on the door is not helpful."

Had I been pounding? I realized my fist hurt. "Let me in."

"No, please. Just leave me alone."

"I will break this door down."

"Go to hell. I'll climb out the window."

A window? Was she *botz*? Was she trying to drive me to the edge of a cliff? Because jumping out the window and rolling down the scrub-brushed hill half naked was not all right. My blood got hot with the thought. My skin tingled and curled on itself. If she knew that I was sure she'd be picked up by some *stronzo* as soon as she was out of my reach, she would have come out of that fucking bathroom right then.

"This is your last chance to come fucking *out*!"

No answer, just the sound of her weeping on the other side.

Fine. At least I knew she was in there.

I checked the objects in the room. Nothing. Carpet. Blinds. Electrical outlets. Enough. That was enough.

I tore down the blinds with my bare hands. She must have thought I was having a temper tantrum, and maybe I was. She'd separated herself from me by not telling me what I'd done, then again with that door that I could have torn off the hinges.

The crossbar that held the blinds separated from the wall, tearing plaster. I yanked off a vertical blind, cracking it. I used the edge of a piece to start unscrewing the plate from an outlet.

"Are you in there, Contessa?"

I needed to keep her in the bathroom. If she crawled out the window, I would rip the mountains off the earth and fling them at heaven.

"Are you there?" I shouted.

She sniffed.

"I don't like too much talking," I said. "Too much can get misunderstood. So if you say straight what I did, I can apologize and we can finish fucking. But you sit there behind that door, then we're fighting, not fucking. That, I do not like." I finally got the plate off.

She mumbled something.

"I can't hear through the door."

I got the plate off the outlet. It left a nice hole in the wall that would work for leverage.

I pulled up the blinds by the crossbar, extending them to their full length. I jammed one end in the hole in the wall the plate had covered, bending the outlet until I had room, then put the other end against the doorknob.

"It's too much. It's just too much. I can't… we can't… this is wrong."

I bent the crossbar so it wouldn't slide closed. Adjusted. "What's wrong?"

I felt a little less angry knowing she was inside and staying there.

"You're married. I can't get past that."

I didn't even address that concern. It was ridiculous. I went outside. The vegetation at the side of the house was overgrown, and I walked through the brush like a bulldozer, breaking any branch in my way, angry as the floodlights at the back of the house. The rear wall was five feet from a near-sheer drop into the oblivion of the canyon, and at the back wall, the bottom of the bathroom window was six inches over my head.

I tucked my thumbs under the window. It was locked.

"Open this window," I shouted.

"Are you nuts?"

I could see the top of the bathroom door. Saw the geometry of it change then snap back into place. She was trying to open it.

So eager to get away from me. Oh, this would not continue. Not for another second. I was going to make her understand that she was not to hide from me. Not to run. Not because of Valentina or anything. She was mine, and what was mine stayed in my sight until I decided it was safe to leave it.

I knew how to break a window. I'd broken a few dozen. I didn't want to scare her or cut her, but that window was getting broken or opened, and I was getting in there to explain to her what all this meant.

Of course, no rocks in Los Angeles. You had to buy fucking rocks. Sick place, this, where you couldn't find a rock to break a window. I lifted a flat flagstone from the path, exposing fat white grubs and a sprinkling of ants.

I tapped the stone. I loved that woman. She was as much mine as a part of my body, and she was upset about Valentina. I understood that. Sure, who wouldn't be upset? But my wife had nothing to do with her. With us. With the fact that I couldn't think about what to do about Valentina, or the son I hadn't known I had, or anything, with Theresa on the other side of a wall

"Theresa," I called as I put the stone on the windowsill and climbed up. I heard the shower running, and Theresa was nowhere to be seen. Good. I wouldn't have to ask her to move to the back wall. Clinging to the siding and the wood window frame, I touched the rock to the top edge of the bottom window. *Tap. Tap*. Then something stronger, until the window cracked. I pressed the stone to the glass, and the crack widened into a poorly-defined web. A chunk popped onto the bathroom floor.

She poked her head past the curtain. Her eyes were red and swollen, and her hair stuck to her face. "Antonio, just leave me alone."

I reached up and in, twisting the lock. "No. I'm not leaving you alone. Never."

I slid the window up and crawled into the bathroom. My shoes hit the floor when she turned off the water, and I snapped the curtain open. She faced me, skin textured in drops of water, and she covered herself, ashamed of her nakedness.

"Put your hands down."

"I need space."

"You do not. You need to come back to me naked. That body you cover? It's mine. Every centimeter of it."

She shook her head and looked down into the middle distance. "I saw her. When she came into the room. I was behind the mirror."

I took mental inventory again. The moment when I saw Valentina… what had I done? Had I kissed my wife? I didn't think so. Had I held her? What had my expression been in that moment when all my grief and vengeance came to nothing?

"I know. Did Brower do this? Did he make you watch? Because I'll kill him."

"No," she said. "I forced my way in. He tried to get me away. But I'm glad I saw. I wouldn't have believed it otherwise."

"Believed what?"

"Can I get dressed?"

"No."

"She's your fate. I'm just a distraction." Her face dropped, fell apart, and she started crying. Her hands left her breasts and the space between her legs and covered her face.

I wanted to punch whoever had made her cry. I wanted to avenge her every pain, but how could I take vengeance on myself?

"Contessa…" I put my arms out for her.

"Don't touch me!" she shouted as if I were a scorpion in her bed. "You don't get it. You don't belong to me. You never did. We didn't know. All right, that's fine. But I won't be the one to break a marriage. That's forever, Antonio. Forever. Until death. You really need to think about that."

"There's nothing to think about."

She stepped out of the tub, and I stopped her.

"*Aspetta,*" I said, looking around the floor. I pulled up the blue glass-coated rug and flipped it. The underside was safe. I put it in front of the tub and moved out of her way when everything in my body told me to get in her way. "Step on that."

"Don't tell me what to do."

"Your feet are bare. There's glass all over."

Her jaw jutted out, but she stepped on the upside-down bath mat. "You old world guys... you think it's fine to have a wife and fuck a mistress. Don't think I haven't been on the other side." She held up her hand. "And before you even speak, I know this situation is different." She dried herself off, apparently unaware of what her naked body did to me. "It's crazy. Your dead wife shows up because she thinks you're dead. There's no precedent for this, I know. And its irony isn't lost on me. But you're not seeing this situation for what it is because you figure you can keep on sleeping with me while you figure out what the whole 'Valentina and a son' thing means. Well, I don't figure it that way."

She poked her feet through her pants, and I watched her beautiful legs disappear into the fabric. My balls ached. My thoughts were disorganized. All I could think about was getting inside her, like an adolescent.

"The way I figure it," she continued, wrestling on her shirt, "you just had a priority shift, and you have to shift back to your wife." Her head stretched through the neck of the shirt, and her red hair left wet splotches on it. "You belong with her. You speak the same language. Same country. Same community. Your dream to go back to Naples and live in peace? You can't have it with me. You'll never have it with me."

She tried to open the door to end the conversation but couldn't. She pushed, but I'd wedged it closed very effectively. She yanked the door back and forth. "Damn it, Antonio!" She smacked the door so hard she had to cradle her aching hand.

I took her injured hand and turned her back to the door. She had defiance in her face, and I wanted to wipe it away with a fuck so hard we'd both break.

"You listen to me," I said, getting close to her and putting up my finger so she knew I meant what I said. "I want what I love, and I love what I want. What I want is you. You came to me as a lady and now you are a queen. I've never met a woman like you. I don't even deserve you, but I have you. And having you, I'm not giving you up. Not for an old promise I made when I was a boy. Not for a place that rejects me. Not for a family that won't have you. Your world is my world. Our world."

"You have a child."

Her eyes blazed, and her words were the end to a story. She was right. I had a son who was a stranger. I would never shirk my responsibility to him, but I needed a minute's peace to get my head around what that meant.

"I'll take care of him. Don't worry. That's outside all this."

She shook her head slowly. "It's not enough."

"I don't have anything else."

"I love you. But I won't share you."

"I'm not asking you to share."

"In the eyes of God?"

I pushed myself away from her. "You choose your sins like a woman."

"I'll kill for you again, because I love you still. I'll kill for you a hundred times. But I'm not touching you. Not like a lover."

I saw white hot. Did she think she was going to walk away from me? She was wrong.

"No other man will lay his hands on you as long as you live."

She looked as if I'd slapped her, and I had a moment of regret. I'd only spoken the truth, but maybe I spoke it too soon. Or too hard.

"Capo," she said softly, "there will never be another. I'm ruined."

She blinked, and a tear fell. Then another. I wanted to kill the man who'd hurt her.

Chapter Eighteen

THERESA

I'd made every effort to keep Valentina in a little compartment in my head. To stick her in a box, mark it "LATER," and keep it on the shelf. But when Antonio tried to fuck me in the safe house, the box rattled off the shelf and fell to the floor, breaking apart in a spray of unwanted news.

He is taken.

He has a son.

He will never be happy with you.

He made a promise.

There was more, some more hurtful than others. Some had a comma and the phrase "and you love him," following, as if to drive home the point that not only was all this true, all this mattered. In the bathroom, I stabbed myself with those phrases and tried to wash them from me in the shower.

I knew he loved me. There was simply no question. I'd never been loved the way he loved me. With him, I felt important and whole. Without him, I was a piece of a person.

How pathetic. How old world.

"I'm ruined," I repeated with my back to the door, not to sound pitiable but to shine another light on it. He'd ruined me with his love, branded me with an outmoded way of loving that I wanted more than anything in the world.

"No." He laid a hand on each side of my head and stretched his arms, looking at the floor between his feet. "I'm the one who's ruined. I was left a widower of a wife I loved, and I fell in love again. I can't leave the wife; we have a child together. And I can't leave the woman I love. I can't be with either."

"You can go back to her. It's best for your family."

"No. I cannot."

"Why not? Because you feel sorry for me? That's just—"

"No!" He spoke so sharply I jumped. "No one should feel sorry for you. I pity the man who feels sorry for you. Do you feel sorry for a starving tiger today? Or the animal she rips apart tomorrow?" He stood straight and sliced the air with his hands. "No. You can't get rid of me so easily. I'm not turning my back on you. You're mine. You'll always be mine. We live together, or we die together. There is nothing in between."

I shook my head, pressing my lips together as if tightening them against the words that wanted to come.

"There isn't a good end to this," I said.

"It's decided."

He was out of his mind, but I didn't know how to talk him back to reality. We didn't both have to be miserable. A measure of happiness could be meted out if he'd just accept that he couldn't, and shouldn't, have me.

But he seemed determined to let me drag him down. Then fine, he'd have his damned way. I'd be present at his side, and I'd protect him from harm, but no more.

"There is no sex," I said. "No kissing. No touching. I do not have affairs with married men, and I don't play second fiddle. We're partners. Business partners. Which means if you're up shit's creek with the Sicilians, I am too. It means however we decide to remedy that, I'm right there with you. You can't put me in a box and lock it until it's safe for me to come out. That's not what this is."

"Nothing will happen to you," he said, softening.

"Well then"—I put my hands on my hips, feeling taller and more powerful than I had even ten minutes before—"nothing will happen to you either."

His lips were on me so fast, I didn't have a second to turn away. He smelled so right, and the arches of his body on mine were such a tight fit, I forgot they were a wrong answer brought on by a flawed assumption.

I pushed him away. "I mean it. Do not test me. The next time, I bite. Your tongue will go back in your mouth a bloody piece of meat."

He smirked, the asshole, and slinked closer without touching me. "I'll die before I kiss you again."

In contrast to my voice, his was silken, as if he was saying the exact opposite, that he would kiss me. Maybe not today. Maybe not tomorrow, but he would kiss me.

My heart sank right into that thought. I wanted that kiss. Wanted it ready to be given when I was ready to take it. I turned my face a quarter of an inch, just enough to feel the heat of his cheek on my own.

Did it matter? Since we were doomed anyway, did it matter if I kissed him or not? Logic cut both ways. If I couldn't see further than the length of my arms, what was the difference? I had no future with him and no future without him. No future. What had I sold myself for? For this? A guy with a wife? Of all the ridiculous, irritating, miserable, shitty choices in men.

"You know what?" I said. "Go to hell. You're a piece of shit. And that's not foreplay. I hate this. I hate everything about it. I hate feeling committed to you, because everything about it is wrong. I hate loving you. I hate myself for standing here right now, wanting you to fuck me." I felt the muscles of his face change. He was smiling. I pushed him back. "That was not an invitation. I hate you for turning me into your side piece, and I don't care if you meant it or not. I don't care if you knew. You know what I care about? The damned facts. You made me a mistress, and I made myself a whore for loving you. And shut the hell up. Don't defend yourself or what's happening here. I'm mad, and I'm staying that way."

I took the doorknob in both hands and shook the door. It was wedged shut by something on the other side. I punched it, which was the very definition of ineffective, and it hurt my hand. I pressed my face against the painted wood.

"Theresa," Antonio whispered, putting his hand on my shoulder.

I leaned into it, because I was soothed wherever we connected. "Don't touch me."

"Get away from the door then."

He dropped his hands, and I stepped back onto the upside-down bath mat.

Antonio kicked the doorknob once then again. It bent. One more kick, and it hung by half a screw. On the other side, something *thupped* to the carpet. He opened the door.

I walked through the bedroom and swept up his phone, wielding it like a sword. "I'm using this."

"To do what?"

"To call my sister."

His shirttail hung in fangs at his thighs. Hair stuck up in a sexy disaster. Pant cuffs an ombre of dirt. I'd never seen him look so helpless. I wanted to hug him and tell him everything would be all right.

"Get out," I said.

He stood stock still. I didn't know what to expect. He'd drag me to my knees and put his cock in my mouth, or he'd leave me alone. I half wished he'd take control of my body, force me to bend to him, so I didn't have to be responsible for choosing him.

He spun and strode out of the bedroom, snapping the door closed behind him.

Chapter Nineteen

THERESA

The closet was dark as sin and hot as hell. I'd been there an hour and had just gotten through to Margie five minutes before.

"He needs a heart," Margie said. "That's all there is to it. He's got a shredded valve, and there's not enough blood in the world to make up for the leaking."

"We're really going to lose him." I huddled in the corner. My eyes had gotten used to the light from under the door. Two wire hangers hung above me, and under me were dust bunnies and nylon carpet.

"Change the subject," Margie said. "I can't talk about this anymore. It's making me want to punch someone." She entered a crowded space. I heard voices and a whoosh of white noise. "You're alive. That's the good news. Everyone's happy, but you ducked out without saying a word, and they're scared you're going to do something stupid. Or disappear again. Or die like you mean it."

"I want to." That was the wrong thing to say. I was heartbroken, but Margie was on the front lines of real tragedy. "Not really," I said quickly. "I'm sorry, I'm being—"

"Please. Be dramatic. Talk about small things that seem big. Is he getting a divorce or what?"

"I don't think so," I said, hugging my bare knees. "He can get an annulment."

"And make his kid a bastard? Sure. Good thinking."

"Maybe she'll divorce him?"

"She waited for him a long time," Margie said.

"I'll talk to her. I'll explain that he's different. Maybe I can convince her to leave him, because he won't do it. Out of guilt or shame or some kind of feeling of responsibility." I was grasping for control, looking for something I could do, some action I could take to bring his body and soul back to me. "Maybe she'll tell him to fuck off if she knows he loves me. If I tell her."

"Mom wants to talk to you."

"Can I not?"

But she never answered.

"Theresa?" That voice. So flat and patrician. Jonathan called it *haute vox*.

"Mom."

She didn't say anything, but she sounded wet. I heard a half a breath and a ladylike sniff. Mom didn't cry, so she tried to hide her hitched breaths and clear the mucous out of her throat with a rattle instead of a snuffle. I'd never heard much emotion from her, but what I was barely hearing was a soft sob from most people. For my mother, it was blubbering.

I could have been mistaken, confusing tears with allergies, until she spoke through lungs that wouldn't stay still and a nose full of snot.

"I thought I was losing two in one day."

"I'm sorry, I… we had to disappear," I said.

"You didn't see us on the way out today, and I was scared you were leaving again. Theresa, my baby. Don't… please don't do this."

"Do what, Mom? I'm back. I'm here."

"I wanted you. Did you know? You and your brother surprised me, but you were my special gifts." She broke down into sniffles and hics.

I was frozen. I didn't know how to react. I'd never heard this sappy story of her feelings about her last two children. "Mom…"

"And I'm losing the two of you."

I touched my St. Christopher medal to protect against hating myself for what I'd done. "I'm here. I'm not going anywhere."

Why did I say that? Would I have to stick to it? Was I cursing any chance I had of working things out with Antonio? I wasn't ready to make that bargain. Not yet. Other deals with the universe were still pending, but this was no time to take it back.

"Where are you?" said a voice that wasn't Mom's. The new voice was bent with rage at the same time it was lilting like a singsong meant for a child's ears. Only my sister Sheila could do that.

I opened my mouth to tell her then realized I didn't really know.

"Where are you?" Sheila growled and sang.

On a closet floor, feeling like an ass for getting upset over a man when my whole family is falling apart. "I'm fine," was the only lie I could articulate.

"Oh, bully for you. Really? Did you do this on purpose?"

"Do what?"

"Fall off the face of the earth? Let us all think you were dead?" Her phrases made hairpin turns around razorblades.

I wanted to tell the truth, spill everything. I was sure I'd get lacerated on a lie. "Sheila, I can't answer that."

"Oh, for the love of fuck, how could you? How could you do that to people who love you?"

She said everything I'd feared hearing when I came back, but I thought it would come from Margie or Mom. Instead it was Sheila, who had always had too many children to focus on me.

"I'm sorry to inconvenience you," I said. "I've been a piece of furniture in this family my whole life. I haven't asked any of you for a thing, and I promise you, I never will."

It was the perfect time to hang up, but I couldn't. I'd done enough walking away.

"Don't pull that," she growled. No one got away with anything as far as Sheila was concerned. "Any one of us would have jumped in front of a bullet for you."

I was a pathetic woman crouched in a dark closet, but when she said that, and I heard the love behind her anger, I felt worthy in a way I hadn't ever before.

"Maybe I didn't want you to," I said. "And I promise you the whole situation is more complicated than I can explain over the phone."

"I'm so pissed off, I can't even swallow." But she wasn't. She'd said her piece, and she was on her way down from her rage high.

"Well, get used to it. I'm not a piece of furniture anymore."

"You were always the one we could count on to not change."

"I'm sorry."

"Don't be. Not for that. The other stuff, yeah. I'm still mad. When are you coming?"

"Soon," I said, lying again. It was possible I could be with my family some time before my brother's funeral, but my own funeral was the likeliest event.

"I'm going to corner you, and you're going to talk to me."

"Okay."

"Okay. Good." She seemed fully calmed. "I have to go."

She hung up. I dropped the phone as if it had turned into lead.

I stayed in the dark, hunched over and paralyzed with conflicting emotions. The shower turned on. I waited for Antonio to finish. Then waited a few minutes more before I couldn't wait another second. I opened the door and padded into the living room. The kitchen island separated the two rooms, and Antonio stood under the island lamps, hair still wet, cigarette dangling from his lips, with the guts of his gun all over the counter. He clicked pieces together, *snap clap snap*.

His hands stopped moving when he saw me. I'd seen him magnificently tired, exhaustion making him look more feral and beautiful, but in that cone of light, he looked as if he'd been unzipped and emptied.

"Hi," I said.

"*Buona sera.*" He slapped the last piece into the pistol. "I've been trying to find the right words to tell you. I keep choosing then unchoosing."

I'm a wreck, everything is fucked up, I love you, I can't have you. You could get shot any minute, my brother is dying, and I can't see him. I feel like a half-played game of Jenga. Pieces of me keep getting pulled away and added to the load.

"I don't want to talk," I said.

He didn't say anything. Didn't even look at me in that way that made me feel eaten alive. He just put his gun down carefully and held out his hand. I took it, and he led me to the couch. He lay flat, and I crawled on top of him, lying thigh to thigh, cheek to chest. When he put his arm around my back, the weight of it secured me in place, pressed the anxiety from my ribs, and I slept with his heartbeat in my ear.

Chapter Twenty

THERESA

I dreamed I was chasing something through the halls of WDE, but I didn't know what. I only knew I wanted it very badly. My father stood behind Arnie Sanderson's wooden desk, knocking on it while saying *it's in here it's in here*. His voice wasn't his voice but a hive of bees in his throat.

I woke with a stiff neck to Antonio's cheap burner phone buzzing.

"Be still," whispered Antonio when I tried to raise my head. He wiggled until he got his phone out of his pocket. "*Pronto*?"

I opened my eyes and rested on him, letting my vision clear. How long had we slept? Longer than I thought I could. The light outside was dull grey, and the birds made a racket. Zo was on the other end. I heard his choppy Italian. I wondered if Antonio's voice would still sound like music if I could understand what he was saying. Maybe if we got out of this and made a life, I'd learn Italian and find out the answer, or maybe I'd just go on loving the way he sounded, listening to what he was feeling instead of what he was saying.

He tapped his thumb to two of his fingers, making a list for Zo. He swallowed and added a third thing. Zo laughed. Antonio did not.

"*Bene. A dopo*. He tapped off.

I got up, and he sat on the edge of the couch.

"You look beautiful," he said.

"What did Zo want?"

"Marching orders. I don't know what they did without me for two days."

"I want to see Jonathan," I said.

His silence was too heavy. Too obvious.

"You can pick the time if we have other things to do first. Or…"

I realized he had a set of concerns he wasn't sharing, and the look on his face told me he wasn't just going to tell me what he was thinking. He was calculating his next move.

"Say it, Antonio. What are you going to do when Zo gets here?"

"I need you to wait for my call before you leave for the hospital," he said. "I'll send Otto or come myself."

Ah. That was it.

"We need to stay together," I said.

I knew he wouldn't agree. I knew my demand was the first salvo in a series of shots meant to keep us together, and I knew there would be a fight. When he just smiled at me as if I'd not alarmed him but charmed him, I knew something was wrong.

A car pulled up outside.

"That's Zo," Antonio said without even looking out the window.

Antonio leaned into me. I wasn't supposed to touch him. I was supposed to shun his body, but I already failed when I slept on top of him and let the pace of his breathing soothe me to sleep. So there was no harm in letting him put his arms around me. I could pretend nothing had changed. Valentina was dead, and she'd stayed gentle forever. A memory of some past time, some past love of a man who didn't exist anymore. I let him kiss my neck because she was gone and he was mine alone.

The hug lasted two seconds before Zo knocked.

Antonio peeked out the window and opened the door immediately.

Zo stood there with a white plastic bag. "Good morning."

"*Boun giorno,*" Antonio replied, taking the bag and giving it to me. "Your wish for a toothbrush has been granted."

"Lorenzo, I think I love you." I hugged him hard.

He patted my back noncommittally, and when I looked at Antonio, I knew why.

"I'm going to give these roses a rest," I said and dashed to the bathroom to run the brush over my teeth.

There was still glass all over the floor. I stepped carefully onto the overturned rug.

"I'll have to pay your sister for the window," Antonio said as he closed the door behind him.

I ripped open the packaging on two toothbrushes. "Better do it before she sends a collections agency for you. Oh, he got the cinnamon flavor. I like that." I handed him the blue brush and loaded it.

"I want you to consider something," he said before putting the toothbrush in his mouth.

I'd never seen him do a simple cosmetic chore. He'd always been this effortlessly perfect man. Invulnerable. Capable. He could solve anything. Even during the ridiculous ritual of tooth-brushing, he looked as though nothing could touch him. I think I stared at him too long, brushing the enamel off my teeth.

He spit. I spit. Like normal, whole people, neither of whom was committed to anyone else. I got that nagging feeling of incompleteness, and I chased it away when I wiped my mouth. I had no time to feel sorry for myself.

"What am I considering?" I took the brushes and wrapped them back in the plastic bag.

"Staying here for a few hours. Maybe until tonight."

"I'm sorry?"

"I'll have a TV sent. Books. Anything you want. And someone will come to watch you."

My initial reaction was rage, then insult, then a stew of annoyance, sadness, dismissal, and disgust. I ran my fingers through my hair, making sure the mirror showed nothing of my messy emotions and all the neat and proper thoughtfulness I wanted to project. He caught my stare in the mirror, and I smiled at him.

"Well?" he said. "I won't be too long. I can take care of this today. In and out. Easy. Then I'm going to get Valentina and send her home."

"What about your son?"

"I won't turn my back on him, but he's not safe here."

"He might need a father." I kept my face completely straight when Antonio broke our gaze. I wasn't even half done. "And I mean, you know, one who's alive. One who can teach him to stay out of trouble in Naples."

"Like my father did? I'd do more harm to that child than you know."

"You're wrong, but you'll never know if you're dead. And her? Well, it's going to have zero net impact on her life if you die. She goes home and picks up where she left off. But me? Selfish me? I get to sit here and wait to hear you got killed." I turned from the mirror and looked at him. "I know you're inaccessible, maybe forever. I know I'm all wrong in the head to think I need you, but I'll never feel right without you. So I'm going with you. If you die, I die. If there's a miracle and you live, then fine. You take your wife and your family, and you move on. But me? Sit here and have my life preserved in a jar while you do this? So I can what? Be destroyed when the news comes that they killed you?"

"I have nothing if you're hurt."

"You have a wife and a family. Do you not get it? You have something to lose."

He balled his hands into fists and held them up. "You make me fucking crazy."

I pressed my lips together. I had to consider if I was simply irked that Valentina was probably going to enjoy his company today while I was not. Or was I annoyed at having to put off a trip to Jonathan? We were on our way out of the bathroom before I realized he'd said something I'd missed. He was at the bedroom door when I stopped.

"Antonio."

He turned, hand on the doorframe, pointer finger bent just so in a way that made me want to put it in my mouth. "Yes?"

"You said you were going to do something quick before you see Valentina."

"Yes."

"What was it?"

"Do you need the day's itinerary every day? Do we need to hire a secretary?"

Oh, no. That wouldn't do. Not at all. We'd come too far together for defensive nonsense.

"Today. I need your itinerary today," I said.

"I am not going back to my wife, if that's what you're worried about. I may see her for practical matters but—"

"Do not treat me like a toy."

"Theresa," he said softly, "let me take care of business."

"No. Not when I don't know how far you can go without getting shot at. Not when Otto might come back and tell me you're dead. I won't get in the way, but I won't be left behind."

He held up his hands in surrender. "I tell you what. Wait for Otto. He'll take you to your brother. We meet up after."

"After what?"

He shook his head just a little and strode out to the living area where Zo waited.

"I'm not some bored housewife you have to keep occupied."

He said something to Zo in Italian. A command, because I'd never seen one of his men do anything other than exactly what they were told.

Zo reached into his back pocket. I must have been moved by some form of trust, because my attention wavered enough for me to wonder what Zo had, what time it was, if we were going to get picked up by the Sicilians before we even got out the door, then I was airborne.

"What—?"

Antonio had slung me over his shoulder and carried me into the open kitchen. I fought him tooth and nail, though I didn't know why. I only knew he was forcing me onto the counter, trying to get control of my left wrist.

"Calm down!"

I clawed his face.

"Spin, really…" Zo's voice drifted off when the handcuff was slapped on my wrist.

"Little help here, Lorenzo!" Antonio cried.

I kicked Antonio, and he moved about three inches before wrapping his arm around me. I wiggled and wrenched myself away, but he was strong and vicious, slapping the other cuff around the drawer handle. I was trapped.

Zo held up his hands, muttering, as if he wanted nothing to do with anything about anything.

Antonio stepped back, breathing heavily. "You are a piece of work, woman."

"Where are you going?" I pointed at the stove. "I'm going to burn this house down if you don't tell me right now."

He gathered his gun. "I am the boss, Theresa. I go where I need to, when I need to. If I tell you, it's not for your approval. It's for your information."

He glanced at Lorenzo then turned back to me as he stuck his gun in his waistband. Of course, if he didn't tell me, it would look as if he had to hide things from his woman. I'd put him in a position.

"I'm going to meet Donna Maria Carloni. Right now," Antonio said. "I need to clear it up. I need to tell her I was already married and show her the trouble I saved her. Present it like a favor. It's easily done, and this all gets done."

"And what if it's your territory she really wants?" I yanked against the drawer. It opened but didn't come out. "You're delivering yourself into her hands. She kills you, and she gets it? Is that right? It's as good as a marriage, but she doesn't have to share."

"If she wanted my territory so badly, she would have done it already."

"Bullshit. She wasn't threatened before. There was no Bortolusi union. You know how people act when they're cornered."

"I am not taking you to a den of snakes!" he shouted. "End. No more. You brought this on yourself by insisting you can do things you shouldn't. Otto's gonna knock first. If anyone else comes in here, shoot them in the fucking head. If I'm not back in two hours"—he dropped a phone and gun on the counter—"call somebody."

"I'm calling someone as soon as you turn your back," I spit out.

"That's enough of a head start." He strode out.

Zo gave me an apologetic look before following. I yanked the drawer hard. It didn't budge. By the time I figured out how to get it out of the counter, Antonio would be long gone into the den of snakes.

Chapter Twenty-One

ANTONIO

When she'd lain on top of me and fallen asleep, I stayed awake for hours. Her chest rising and falling, her legs on mine, her breath on my neck, the blossom smell of her—I was trapped inside her. In the lack of movement, the absence of logistical puzzles, the only thing I heard in my head was:

A quarter million.

The amount was serious, and it floated over her head and under her feet, weightless because of her ignorance of it. She knew she was in danger but didn't seem to understand what the price tag meant. The Carlonis were not messing around. Word would get out in less than a week, less than another day even, and she would be hunted worse than me, because she was a woman, and vulnerable, and if I was out of the picture, they'd get her. As ferocious as she was, they'd get her. I'd be too dead to stand in front of it.

My first thought was to attack. Go into the Carloni compound guns blazing. But the odds of winning that battle were small, and Theresa would be left alone. She had a vengeful heart and would get herself killed trying to get to the Carlonis.

She was the priority. Her long life. Her health. The price on my head was manageable. As soon as I'd started making money in Los Angeles, I became more valuable dead than alive, as my business would transfer to my murderer.

I had to extricate her.

Meet Donna Maria in a neutral place. Tell her about Valentina and trade my territory for Theresa's safety. I would be free, Theresa would be safe, and maybe I'd be out of the business. Maybe if they let me live, I'd walk. More likely, she'd make up a debt. A term to serve as her consigliere again. Which I'd do, if I could just have Theresa.

It seemed so easy. But with the list of things that could go wrong as long as a man's arm, I had to leave Theresa behind. By promise or force, she couldn't join me.

When it became force, I decided I was at peace with it. I'd make it up to her. I walked out of Margie Drazen's safe house relieved.

"I need to get Donna on the phone," I said to Zo. "I need a neutral place."

"Got it, boss." He plucked his phone out of his pocket.

"We're ending this without blood."

I heard the gunshots as I was about to get into the car. If I'd just gotten in and driven away, she would have been safer, but she was fast. She came out of the door with a wrecked kitchen drawer in her left hand and a smoking gun in her right. She put the gun in her waistband and yanked the handle off the drawer front. It clanked to the ground, and she looked at me expectantly.

"We should take the 210 to the 5. Should be clear at this hour. You can unlock the bracelets on the way." She got into the backseat.

Zo stood by the driver's door with his phone in his hand. "What should I do?"

I was supposed to know. I was supposed to control my woman. I was supposed to be the boss and bark orders that were obeyed. "Don't call yet. Take us to Zia's and have the crew meet us there."

I'd have the whole car ride to think about how to do this as painlessly as possible.

Chapter Twenty-Two

THERESA

I had a sense that something would happen, some idea that the culmination of my life was upon me. Anticipation overtook me on the way to San Pedro. My heart fluttered, and my skin felt the touch of my clothing. My fingertips felt kindled, as if I could touch inanimate objects and set them afire.

I looked at them to make sure they weren't reddened from heat or crackling with the future, but I found that though they looked the same, my way of seeing them had changed. They were no longer just fingers but kinetic devices designed for a fate they leapt to fulfill. They wanted to quicken finally. They wanted to lock into the network of life and vitality they'd only gingerly caressed. *Use me*, they said. *Take me. Make me an instrument for your heart's purpose.*

I was distant from the city around me. The lights of South Central, Compton, Torrance were a projected screen showing a fairy-tale reality of hell-on-earth that I was distanced from, yet intrinsically a part of. There was no middle ground, only the peaceful coexistence of extremes.

I was here. And not here. I was the breakneck pace between who I was and who I was to become. I couldn't breathe from the force of my own velocity.

Even when we stopped in front of Zia's, I was a vibrating buzz of connection and purpose, still in my seat, moving toward a new version of myself. Antonio opened the door for me, and I stepped out of the car as a new thing. An as-yet-unseen and undefined creature.

I felt, as I stepped into the parking lot, that the ground was fitted to me and carried me. When he held my hand, I gathered the power of all the stars in heaven and let him pull me to the earth.

Nothing could touch me. Not death, not hurt, not a fear that I was incomplete. Only he could get near me.

I was a wave form of potential, vibrating upward to suffocation and dissolution. I held his hand as tightly as I dared, because I didn't want him to catch fire.

Chapter Twenty-Three

ANTONIO

I rode in the front because I didn't want to be next to her. I didn't want to touch her or hear her. Not even her breathing. I didn't want to catch her olive blossom scent. I wanted to be as far away from her as possible. Mostly because I wanted to fuck her and protect her, and she wanted neither.

Well, no. The fucking she wanted but refused. The protection, she needed.

I got angrier and angrier in that front seat. Up. Down. Sideways. I couldn't move in any direction because of her. I couldn't run, and I couldn't attack. She was being impossible and unrealistic. A fool of a woman. Chaos. She was fucking chaos. From the minute she walked into my life with toilet paper on her shoe, she had been a wrecking ball.

I got out of the car intending to tell her to stop this. I needed to say it in a way she could hear. I needed to be more clear. I opened her door, thinking I'd get in and explain it in the backseat, maybe get my fingers inside her to make the point.

Yes. That was the way.

But when I opened the door, I knew I had to rethink my strategy. Beautiful and strong. The weight of life on her. Every muscle meant for survival. An instrument of death and life. She was a bird who'd molted into a deadly carrion, sleek and lethal. How then? Had it happened when she chose to shoot a kitchen apart rather than be left behind? Was it her commitment to me even though she thought I was unavailable? Was that it? What had changed except for the way she fit into the world?

The puzzle of the air and space around her had always clicked to meet the way she walked and spoke. But when she got out of that car, the world changed to meet her on her terms.

I got in front of her, stopping her. She would be impossible to control. She scared the hell out of me. Since the day I met her, she had been frightening, and it had only gotten worse. My life was spinning out of control, and it was her, all her.

She stood on the curb, chin up, with a face that asked what could possibly be the problem? What on earth was unusual about her demanding a part in a negotiation with a Sicilian family to get the quarter million death-price off her head?

"What's here?" she asked. "This isn't some mob boss's compound."

"It's a restaurant. I'm meeting with my crew."

"And then?"

"I'm handcuffing you to something you can't shoot, and I'm taking care of business."

"Handcuff me to you."

"I don't know what to do with you," I said.

"Feeling's mutual."

I felt the shake of rage. I had to hold it back. What did I want to say? I wanted to explain the rules and expectations, because if she was going to be by my side, we had to be of one mind. Yet that was crazy. It wasn't allowed, and it could get her hurt.

"You insist on this course. Repeatedly," I said. "We should be in bed right now. My only problem should be how many times I can get my dick in you in a day."

"Grieve for that dream," she said. "Because it died."

Chapter Twenty-Four

THERESA

Once I said the words, the juices started twirling in my own heart. Our dream of a quiet little life was dead. Deal with it.

Behind me, Zo took off to get the crew, and it was just Antonio and me on the sidewalk.

The little chained sign in the glass door of Zia's was flipped to the CLOSED side even though, behind the print curtains, the lights were on. I tried to walk toward it, but Antonio blocked the way.

"Listen. They won't want to accept you. Do I need to tell you the reasons?" he asked.

"I'm a woman, and I'm from the right side of the tracks. That cover it?"

"Yes. But I ask only that you hide what you're made of for now. Until you need to show it."

"What am I made of?" I asked.

Antonio put his thumb and forefinger on either side of my chin. It would be hard to remember he was married. "I haven't figured it out yet."

"*Bene,*" I said.

Antonio backed up and let me in, then followed. The door slapped closed behind us.

The restaurant smelled of bleach and tomato sauce, and it sounded like the buzz of fluorescent lights and tension. The lunch crowd hadn't shown up yet; neither had the waitstaff. Only the smell of food drifting from the kitchen gave any indication that the captain was at the helm.

Antonio reached back and drew the bolt on the door. As if summoned by the *clack*, Zia came to the kitchen doorway, wiping her hands with a white towel. The space between her and Antonio was tight with strain.

"Tonio," she said.

"Aunt."

Zia's chin wrinkled then straightened. *"Mea culpa. Per Tina. Per Antonin."* Her voice cracked, and fat tears dropped down her cheek. *"Per tutti."*

Antonio didn't move. No one moved. Forgiveness hung in the air, refusing to touch down. People couldn't die from tension in a room, but if they could, we would have at least passed out from the toxins.

"I'm sorry too," Antonio said finally, in a tone that had no room for apology, only an accusation.

Zia snapped her towel and draped it over her arm. *"Tina è per strada. Stu venedo qui."* She sniffed once then spun on her heel and walked back into the kitchen.

Antonio looked stricken.

"What did she say?"

"I'll take you home," he replied, taking my arm.

"Wait, where's home?" I shook him off. "And in what car? What did she say?"

He was still trying to guide me out. "Let's just go."

"Stop it!" I folded my arms. "What did she say?"

He looked at the ceiling as if asking God for help, just for once, a little help.

Outside, a car door slammed. Zia's was on a short block, adjacent to a real estate agent and an optometrist, so there wasn't much street traffic. The car door got Antonio's attention.

"Let's go out the back," he said.

"What's happening? You're scaring me." I followed his gaze outside. Through the curtains, I saw a man in a suit open the passenger door of a new Honda and a woman got out.

Not just a woman. Valentina Spinelli.

And the man in the suit turned around. Daniel.

Antonio took my hand and pulled me toward the kitchen. I yanked him back.

"Do you see?" he said, indicating the two people coming toward the door as if the situation were obvious. To him, they were a speeding tornado and we had to seek shelter.

"You're as white as a sheet," I said, tugging him back. "You're not afraid of death or torture… but your wife and me in the same room terrifies you. What do you think is going to happen? We're all adults." I brushed by him and took three big steps toward the front door.

"You can't be here," he said.

"You have to deal with this. It won't go away by denial."

He went rigid and lowered his head so he looked me in the eye. "We. Are. Leaving."

My eyes locked on his. I reached behind me, stretching, and turned the bolt on the front door. *Clack.*

A whoosh of cool air blew in as Daniel opened the door, and there was Valentina, in the same room as me. Breathing the same air. Haughty and righteous, wearing her skin as if it were a suit of armor, straight where I curved, long where I was short, she clutched a little bag in front of her and tilted her chin up.

"Antonio," she said.

"Valentina," he said.

"You won't call me Tina, all of a sudden?"

"Come stai, Tina?"

"I learned a little English."

"Fantastico. Mi dai il cappotto?"

"Don't make your girlfriend feel left out," she crooned.

"Can I take your coat?"

"I have it," Daniel interjected.

Was I wrong to find the whole thing delicious? All of the emotional upheaval of the last few days had inured me to the threat of his wife. I'd already surrendered to her. I'd already accepted what her existence meant. I was already crushed under the weight of it. Her presence in the same room as us couldn't hurt me.

Daniel slipped off her coat, and I felt not an ounce of jealousy for that either. I doubted Valentina Spinelli would let Daniel get one over on her.

"Aren't you going to introduce us?" Valentina asked, one eyebrow raised. She didn't move but comported herself perfectly. She reminded me of me.

So that was it.

That had been the initial attraction. She and I couldn't have been more physically opposite, but Antonio had seen both deeper than that and less deep. Because her comportment wasn't courteous. She attacked by staying still and asking a question designed to make her husband feel ill-mannered and to draw attention to discomfort.

I didn't like it, but I understood it.

"My name is Theresa," I said, holding out my hand.

She waited a half a beat then shook gently. "I am Valentina. Valentina Spinelli."

"Nice to meet you."

She was far away, taking her own counsel. She had no intention of giving an inch. I'd seen that look in press agents and lobbyists who knew they had the upper hand and had no intention of budging.

"Zia!" Antonio called. "Let's get something to eat out here!"

Zia came out and, seeing Valentina, said a greeting in Italian and kissed her on both cheeks, twice. They chattered in Italian for a minute while Daniel fidgeted. Poor guy.

"*Si, del vin rosso per favore,*" Valentina said.

"No," Antonio cut in as if putting his foot down for the benefit of a defiant child. "No wine."

I thought he would get his way, as strange as it was.

"You are still bossy," Valentina said in choppy but quick English before addressing Zia. "A chianti."

"No! And that is the final word."

Zia looked from Valentina to Antonio, not knowing what to do. I didn't know what his objection was about. Did he find it unbecoming? Was it too early in the day? I'd had a drink or two in front of him, and it had never warranted this level of protest.

"I could use a glass myself," I said.

I went to the sideboard. It was lined in clean white cloth napkins. The grey tray was loaded with silverware, and the empty water pitchers were stacked neatly. Above, wine glasses hung. I snapped up five, wedging the stems between my fingers.

I put the glasses on the counter then flipped up the end of the bar and walked behind it. The floor was coated in a black rubber honeycomb mesh half an inch high. My feet bounced when I walked. I'd never been behind a bar before, and everything seemed neat and compartmentalized. I located the fridge immediately.

I stared at it. I was nuts. I couldn't diffuse the tension in the room with a little wine. I was an outsider.

To hell with it. I opened the fridge door and resolved to choose a damned bottle and do what I was supposed to do. Serve wine and celebrate the continued and uninterrupted life of Antonio Spinelli.

As if I'd called him forth with my mind, his scent filled me. The knowledge that he was close melted the skin right off me.

"You'll never make a good Italian wife unless you learn to obey," he said in my ear.

He said it in good humor, trying to relieve his own part of the tension, but it was a stupid, hurtful, wicked thing to say, especially with a fuckable growl that acted as a whisk for my arousal and anger. I didn't know whether to spread my legs or spit in his eye.

I put a random bottle on the bar with a smack, trying to look casual. As if I didn't want to kill him for saying that stupid thing. Though I wanted to eviscerate Antonio with a steak knife right then, I didn't want to undermine him. I didn't want any of them to think he'd shown poor judgment in being with me. I didn't want them to think I was a liability or that his wife was more refined and mature. I wanted to leave, walk out the front door as if it just happened to be what I was doing at the moment. No more, no less.

I didn't know where I was going. I just had to get out of that cramped restaurant. The December air hit me full in the face, and I wished for a jacket. But more than that, when I got outside, I immediately calculated the width of the street, the movement of the cars, the foot traffic, the rooftops. I was completely exposed. I'd never felt that while walking across the street before. But every window was a gun perch, and every car was a moving crime scene.

I wasn't concerned for myself but the fact that I was drawing Antonio out into the open.

Antonio came out of the restaurant, dinging the bell, and our eyes met across the seven-foot expanse of the street. Miles between us, and close enough to kiss. He could take one leap and be on me in the most pleasing agony.

"Get out of the street," he said, pointing into the restaurant. "Anyone can take a shot at you here."

I tore my eyes from his and went to the covered driveway that led to the parking lot behind the restaurant. Jesus. I was backing myself into a corner. I wondered if I could hop a fence, then I felt him behind me, and before I even got to the back lot, his hand was on my neck.

Time stopped. I didn't know how much longer I could do this.

Chapter Twenty-Five

ANTONIO

The back of her neck, bare except for the stray hair that got out of the rubber band, was warm under my fingers. When I touched her there, getting my finger under the gold chain that held the St. Christopher medal, she stopped, like an animal with an instinctive reaction not to obey but to listen.

"I want you," I whispered in her ear. "Only you."

"I know," she said. "But am I what you need?"

The scent of the food in the restaurant and the idea that any man knows what he needs triggered the memory that had haunted me for years.

My mother never made risotto, but Valentina had been raised in the north, so she'd brought the dish with her. It had to be stirred constantly. If the spatula stopped moving, the grains could get hard in places. For a consistent texture, not one grain could be still for one second. Nor could the temperature fluctuate. Hot broth went in to increase the moisture without cooling the pan. If she put in cold broth, the rice grains would crack into mush. It was a balancing act she did without even thinking.

She had no family to speak of, so she made mine into hers. My mother and aunt loved her, and she loved them. We'd lived in a small house in the outskirts of Napoli. Two bedrooms, a barely finished kitchen, and a back-yard big enough to farm in. The winters were mild, and in summer, we buried our trash twice a day in a hole by the back fence because of the humidity. An apple tree took root where we put the garbage, so we moved our digging spot.

She had been making dinner when I saw her last. I was leaving for the night in an hour, and I hoped for a fuck before I went. But she was making risotto for dinner, and I couldn't stop the process, nor could I skip eating entirely for the sake of the pressure on my dick. She was cooking, and that was all there was to it.

I couldn't tell her where I was going. That was a given. When I was a mechanic, then a law student, then a lawyer, she didn't have to ask where I was going, because I wasn't going anywhere. Work-school-work-study-work.

I'd told her I would take care of the men who had hurt my sister, then I was done. *Stupidi*. She and I both. I hadn't cleared my desk of all of them while she lived, and there was no "done." Ever.

"I have to go," I said. "I'm sorry. I have to miss supper."

"Antonio!" She indicated the risotto as if it were its own reason. And it was. It couldn't be stored or refrigerated.

"I'm sorry, it's business."

She slapped the spoon on the edge of the pot and put it down. Watched it bubble for a second before starting to stir again. She'd never ruin a risotto just because she was angry at me.

"Business. You do mental Olympics to make excuses for yourself," she said, twirling the arm that wasn't stirring the rice. Her nails were trimmed but unpolished. Her hair was thrown up in a quick pile on her head that I wanted to take down and pull from behind.

But no. There was no hair pulling, and there was no "from behind." That had been agreed, but I could still imagine her on her hands and knees. My mind was my own.

"Oh, you think?" I snapped up a spoon. "Maybe I'll leave tomorrow and show you Olympian stamina tonight."

"Stop with your filth." I wedged a little risotto onto the edge of the spoon, and she swatted me away. "I'm serious. Do not dismiss me."

She was always serious. Her mother said it was because she had a heart condition. Even a misunderstanding could start the pains. I'd never seen any such thing until the night of our wedding, when I'd pulled her hair and she had palpitations.

I popped the bite of risotto into my mouth. It was delicious. Perfect. I remembered that bite of risotto for years after that day. The layers of flavor coated my mouth no matter how much bile I walked around Los Angeles with.

I'd dropped the spoon into the ceramic sink and clasped her at the rib cage. My hands went nearly all the way around her. I could ask her to keep stirring while I fucked her. That would be fun. But not only was that position off-limits, the kitchen was as well.

"Tell me about my excuses then."

"I won't tell a man what to do," she lied, and I smiled. She was so bossy. "But, Antonio, I cannot do this anymore. I cannot watch you go away overnight and not know if you're coming home."

"There's no safer job in Napoli." I brushed loose strands of hair from her neck. "Consigliere is a protected position. If anything happened to me, every capo would make sure I was avenged."

She slapped the spoon on the edge of the pot. "And you'd be in hell." She turned her back to the stove, letting the risotto sit. "I can't live like this anymore. What you do is wrong. It's against God. I won't be a part of it anymore. I won't raise children like this."

I took the wooden spoon and reached around her waist to stir the rice. "You don't like the nice things I buy you?"

"I don't care about them."

She must have forgotten how unhappy she had been when we had nothing. She nagged me to change jobs, work harder, go back to fixing cars.

"And the children? When they come, you're going to want things for them? We can buy a bigger house with what we've saved. Public lawyers don't make shit."

"I mean it, Antonio. Stop now. Today. Stay home tonight."

"And?"

"And what?"

"What do I get if I stay home tonight?"

She stared at me with her almond eyes, lips pressed together, and all the filthiest things she might let me do went through my mind.

"You get to go to confession and have your sins removed."

"And then?" I was such a hopeful bastard.

She put her hands on my chest. "You go to heaven."

"In the bed? Or maybe against this counter?"

She nudged me away and turned back around. "The kitchen isn't for that." She snapped the spoon away, grumbling, "Dirty boy."

I was suddenly very, very angry. She didn't have to promise me anything. She didn't have to give me any part of her body she didn't want to. But she pushed and pushed, and I was expected to do as she asked for the love of the same shit.

I put my hand on the back of her head and curled my fingers, grabbing a handful of bunched up hair. I yanked her head back. I was playing with fire, but I didn't know how to stop myself.

"Ow! Stop!"

I spoke right into her ear. I wanted my words to be so tight between us, the air didn't even know what I said. "I'll tell you when I'll quit this job. When I come home and you've got your palms on the counter and your skirt around your waist. When I spread your sweet cheeks apart, and you say, 'Yes, Antonio baby, fuck my ass.' And I stick a finger in your cunt and you're wet."

"Stop it," she said, crying.

I pulled her head back harder. I was so fucking mad, I didn't care if her arrhythmia went crazy and I spent the night apologizing in a hospital. I was on some kind of track and I couldn't get off. "When I take your juice to wet your asshole, and when it's wet, my cock goes one, two, three, right inside. And you sit the fuck still and take it." I let her hair go with a jerk. "That's when I'll stop doing what puts food on the table."

I left before I did something stupid. I had a panino from the street cart for dinner, and I never saw her in Italy again.

Chapter Twenty-Six

THERESA

His hand rested on the back of my neck with just enough pressure to let me know he was there. I didn't need the reminder. I knew he was present. Knew he loved me. I'd just needed a moment to breathe.

"You have to stop touching me," I said.

He swung in front of me. The sunlight hit the edge of his face. The rest was veiled in shadow. I could still read him clearly, as if the light was his lust and the shade was his rage. All he had to do was turn his head slightly to be either bathed in brilliance or drowned in shadow.

"I don't know how many times I have to say this—"

He stopped talking when I pulled away from him, backing into the brick wall. "I know. You can touch me any time you want. I've heard it."

"Don't take this lightly."

"Lightly? I'm the only one taking your life seriously." I touched his lapel. It was bent a sixteenth of an inch and needed straightening.

His shoulders dropped an amount equal to the bend of his lapel. Enough for me to notice. It was a half measure of resignation, another half measure of vulnerability. My fingers trailed the edge of the jacket seam, as if they were caught in a groove. He looked down at their journey, his eyelashes the length of black widow legs, lips parted just enough to emphasize their fullness.

"I'm only a man," he said. "I'm not a saint."

"Not a devil either."

He flicked a speck of something off my shoulder, smoothing the fabric.

"I don't know what to do. And that alone is uncomfortable. I always know what to do."

I pressed my hands to his chest but didn't push him away. "I can't reassure you. I can't say we'll figure it out. I can't see the way through it."

"We don't divorce. It's not done."

"I know."

"I could kill my mother for doing this."

"She was protecting a life she knew you'd want back," I said. "And before you protest, you want it back. I know you do. It's exactly the life you described to me in TJ. It's a good life. I get it. I want it with you, but I don't know how to get there."

I expected him to resist and tell me I was his life. That was the script. He was supposed to reassure me in no uncertain terms. But he wouldn't look at me.

"This is what it means to get older," he said. "Your choices get less and less."

"You can get there. You can do it. You can have it all. If you manage to get forgiveness from Donna Maria, you need to step back and think about it."

"I should leave you behind?"

"Yes. I think if we can unravel this, then that's how it has to go." A hairline crack appeared in my heart. I knew I was right. This was solvable if I gave him up. If I didn't, it was a mess.

"It's decided then?" he said gently, and the hairline crack deepened.

"Yes."

"You'll be safer that way." He put his lips to my cheek, and my body trembled.

"I will," I lied. I could never go back to who I had been. Never. "I'll live a long, safe life."

"Without me." He kissed my neck, and the shimmering arousal that ran though my body seemed not hindered by the flood of melancholy but abetted by it.

"Without you." My hips found their way to him as if by magnetism. His every kiss to my neck, his every breath in my ear, was a contradiction to the words he spoke.

"And I'll go back home with my wife and fuck her sweetly for the rest of my days?"

I couldn't give him more than *mmm* from deep in my chest because his hand brushed over my hardened nipple, coming back for a second pass with the backs of his fingers. I thought I should push him away, but my body wasn't taking instructions.

"I'll be happy," he whispered in my ear then kissed it. "We'll buy a little stone house, and I'll spend the rest of my life with a sweet, useless little pet."

"Don't bad-mouth her."

He pulled back until we were nose to nose. "She fucks like a plucked chicken."

I had to bite back a laugh, and Antonio smiled so wide, I fell in love with his face all over again.

"Don't—" I said.

"Don't what? Don't change? Don't look back at my past and see clearly?"

"Don't smile like that. You melt me. I can barely stand straight."

"Let me catch you."

He put his lips on mine. I bent under him, yielding completely to his mouth, the rhythm of his lips, the force of his tongue. I allowed myself to hope that there was a way out, and at the same time, the hope lived with resignation.

I didn't want that kiss to end. It shouted down my confusion. I wanted to drown in it. Take my last breath with him. Die connected in a painless flood of arousal and sorrow. But through the window came the pop of a wine cork, and he straightened.

"Let me take you back to the house," he said, his voice covered with a thin sheet of urgency. "I swear I'll meet you there."

"Do you not want me to talk to your wife?"

"I don't want her to talk, period."

"This intrigues me." I slipped away from him and strode quickly back to the street. I opened the restaurant door to Daniel filling the glasses. "Don't you have a campaign to run?" I felt my face getting red in the warm dining room. "You've been socializing without talking politics."

"Gerry wants me out of the way until the trick you played at the wedding dies down."

He handed Valentina a glass. She swirled it, avoiding eye contact with me.

"Sorry about that."

He handed me a glass. "No, you're not."

"No. I'm not."

Behind me, Antonio spoke sharply to Valentina. "*Non bere quell vino.*"

"Salute." She raised her glass and, in a single open-throated gulp, poured the entire contents down her throat.

Antonio groaned as Valentina clacked her glass on the bar and made a swirling motion above it with her finger. Daniel refilled it.

"Sit down for *primi,*" Zia said as she burst through the swinging doors with a tray of manicotti. She set it in the center of a round table, which had already been set for four.

"Grazie, Zia! Bene!" Valentina said with an enthusiasm I hadn't noticed before. She grabbed her glass and the bottle and sat.

I sat across from her, and when Antonio placed himself next to me, I whispered, "Isn't Zia eating?"

He made a *tsk* noise with a shake of the head and placed his napkin in his lap.

"What about Antonin? Where is he?" I realized the question was just on the other side of inappropriate when it was all the way out of my mouth.

Valentina took the half-empty glass from her lips and answered. "I sent him home. It's hell here. I don't know how you stand the smells. Car exhaust. It's everywhere. When I was first married, I had to scrub it out of my husband's clothes every day. I will not have my son smell like street grease."

"He took a plane home alone? To Europe?" Daniel asked, sliding a cheesy tube onto her plate.

"Non-stop flight. We do it all the time. Only Americans circle their children like helicopters. Give me another one please." She indicated the manicotti and brought the wine to her lips again.

"Tina, enough," Antonio said, reaching for the glass.

She slapped him away. Had I thought she was haughty and controlled? Because she didn't seem that way anymore.

"Tell me, Tonio, what have you been doing here? Besides pretending you're dead and letting your girlfriend drink all she wants?"

"Avoiding this guy." He smirked, pointing his fork at Daniel.

I took a slice of manicotti and watched as Valentina shoveled down half of one neatly and efficiently.

"You fail at this," she said after she washed it down. "He's right here."

Daniel smiled and pushed his cheese around the plate, obviously finding this whole thing very amusing. He filled her wine glass, and she graced him with a beatific smile. God, she was stunning. A thoroughbred.

I got Daniel's attention and mouthed, "More wine."

He grinned and got up for another bottle.

"What else?" She swirled her wine around as if she was baiting Antonio.

"Just running my business."

"You mean your criminal empire?" She bobbed her head when she spoke, a graceless gesture and a sign that she'd had a glass too many.

Antonio dropped his fork. "*Basta*, Tina."

She turned her palms down and shook her hands, telling us to be quiet because something important was coming. "I work in a fabric factory, at the desk, and there's a little *salumeria* on the corner. And the little men sit outside it talking like they're so important. Little *mafiosi*. They come into the factory and take their money. Their tribute." She flung her hands around like butterflies. "They try to take me to bed. You know what I say to them? Your little *pistola* matches your stupid bald head. Both in your pants. Both can't shoot."

"More wine?" I asked.

She pushed her glass to me. "*Grazie*. And all of the *mafiosi*…" She held up her pinkie. "Like this. You can't be in the organization unless you have an okra between your legs." She put her thumb and pointer finger two inches apart, then held up her hands to Antonio as if he'd objected, which he hadn't, except to rub his face in embarrassment. "Not Mister Spinelli, of course. With that *cetriolo*."

I almost spit my wine. Daniel pressed his lips together so he wouldn't bust.

She was on a roll, addressing Antonio with a hand cupped as if handing him a golden piece of advice. "My God, you are going to kill someone with that thing one day. This is what I thought." She put her elbow on the table and wagged her finger at him. "I thought you couldn't be *mafiosi* because…" She put her hands up, a foot apart. "But no. Time passed, and you were just like the rest of them."

She poured wine down her throat and turned to me. "You can have that thing."

I think I went red. She was imagining me with that beautiful dick, and I felt my barest lust exposed.

"No one woman can keep up with him. He can manage two," she said.

"Not in America," Antonio said. "Here, it's one woman, one man."

"Sometimes," Daniel mumbled then leaned back.

She stretched her neck and tilted her head as if bringing her ear closer to Antonio. "*Che*?"

"Don't pretend you haven't heard of it," Antonio growled.

We'd been through hell together, but this? This was a million times worse.

"*Monogamia*?" Valentina said with disbelief. "Not for the men in the organization."

"For this man, it is. I'm sorry, but this *cetriolo* is for her only." He took my hand, and though I was proud of that, I also had to shake the feeling that she shouldn't see any affection between us. "I love her. You waited, I know you waited, until I was the man you wanted me to be. But she took me as I am."

"A thief and a killer?"

"Alleged," I said, keenly aware of Daniel's presence.

She bent her head slightly left then right, left then right, pursing her lips. "We don't divorce. We aren't American. I will fight you."

"I don't want to fight."

She huffed as if that was the first time she'd heard him say such a thing. "You won't make our son a bastard either. I will curse you to hell."

"I'm going to hell anyway."

"Can you just fuck her and leave me alone?"

"That's not up to me. It's up to Theresa."

She faced me, full-on, as if expecting me to answer the big questions of her life with a half-eaten manicotti in front of me, my ex on my left, and the love of my life on my right.

"Way to drop it in a girl's lap," I said, taking my hand from Antonio's.

Valentina swooped up the second bottle in one hand and her glass in the other. She came around the table and bent over to whisper, "Let's go, *troia*."

She strode out to the back, ass wagging like a flag, the swinging doors kissing behind her.

"Did she just call me a whore?"

"Worse. Don't follow her," Antonio said. "She's not right in the head when she drinks."

He started to get up, but I put my hand on his shoulder and pushed him down so I could stand. "Stay here and help with the dishes." I snapped up my glass and went out the back.

Chapter Twenty-Seven

THERESA

Zia had something going on in the kitchen that smelled like meat. I was still hungry but didn't pause long enough to ask what was bubbling. Valentina stood in the tiny parking lot, by the dumpster, filling her glass. She had the bottle out to fill me up before I had two feet out the door.

"What do you want?" she asked.

"You're the one who waited around ten years. What do *you* want?"

"I want my life back." She put the bottle on top of a car.

"You gave it up because you didn't like it."

"The life before he was consigliere for his father. This one I'm talking about. He was very nice. He was a sweet man."

Nice. Sweet. Was she talking about someone else? Her eyes were cloudy, and she held on to the edge of the gate to steady herself. Wine was indeed a bad idea.

"Antonio's a lot of things," I said. "Sweet isn't one of them."

"He used to bring me strawberries, in summer, from the fruit vendor on Via Scotto. So expensive. And beautiful. He took the leaves off and fed them to me."

I imagined that was true. Of course he'd bring gifts and tributes. It was the sweet part that tripped me up. He must have had the act down pat. He'd wanted this gentle girl and lied to himself to have her.

"He brushed my hair." She touched it, remembering in a drunken stupor. "Every night. When I had headaches or felt faint, he rubbed my forehead until I fell asleep. If I was tired, he carried me up the steps, and he sang to me. He can't sing a note, did you know? He's terrible."

She smiled to herself and sniffed. She didn't seem stupid or easily fooled. Valentina was heartbroken and drunk, but I didn't think Antonio could lie to her about who he was. It was possible that somewhere in that bossy, demanding, vicious man, there was a gentle, sweet husband who brushed his wife's hair and brought her strawberries.

"I'm sorry, Valentina," I said. "I think that's all in the past now."

She continued as if I hadn't spoken. "And he changed. I drove him away. I threw him away. I thought… I don't know what I thought. I dreamed he'd change and I'd go back to him, but I knew it was crazy, and now it's not so crazy."

She wiped her eyes with the back of her hand. "He's in there." She poked her chest. "And now I take responsibility. You are young. You seem all right. Maybe you don't have to be a *troia*? Maybe you can find your own man? Because I'm going to have my husband again. I waited ten years. I can take as many more as I need." She raised her finger as if making her point, but when she took her hand off the hood of the car, she wobbled and put her hand back.

"He's mine." I spoke as gently as I could. We weren't going to have a catfight. I had no time for it. "I'm sorry. I'm not going to scratch your eyes out or anything like that, but when you sober up, you need to go home. To Naples."

"Napoli," she corrected. "*Naaah*-poh-lee."

She let go of the car again, and when I caught her, she pushed me away and put all her weight on me at the same time.

Daniel rushed out from the restaurant. "Jesus, Tink, what's going on?"

"What do you think? And stop calling me that."

He got himself under Valentina, and she put her arms around his neck.

"I got a call from Gerry," he said once he had Valentina properly balanced. "He put together a fundraiser tonight. I have to go prepare."

"Good luck."

He squinted in the winter sun, hair dropping in front of his forehead in the way I used to love. Valentina rested her head on his chest.

"Spin says she's not a puker," he said.

"So you guys talked."

He nodded. "I had to tell him I wasn't fucking his wife. Guy thing."

"Ah. Well. Good luck tonight. With the fundraiser."

"Yeah." He shook his head. "I think I ran out of juice. Even before that fiasco at the wedding, I lost energy for it. So I don't know."

"You can't drop out. Ten more weeks."

He laughed to himself, as if I'd misjudged ten weeks as too long or too short, but I'd somehow misjudged everything.

"I parked in front like a dope," he said. "I'm walking out of a storefront for an Italian crime family—"

"Tell them you were looking at the books—"

"Practically carrying a camorra capo's wife."

"Wife!" Valentina interjected loosely, flopping her arm up before pointing at herself and collapsing.

"You're finished in this town," I said to her.

I started away, but Daniel called to me.

"Tink, when we have enough evidence on who shot Paulie, we're taking him in." He indicated Antonio with a jerk of his head.

I faced him fully and took all the defensiveness out of my voice. I wasn't protesting, I was stating a fact. "He didn't do it."

Without waiting for an answer, I went back into the restaurant.

Chapter Twenty-Eight

ANTONIO

Otto and Lorenzo pulled up out front just as Daniel went out the back for the women. He'd told me he wasn't fucking Valentina, which I could have told him. I wasn't giving him permission either. He was still on the other side of the line, and I wanted him to stay there. I reserved the right to break his legs over that or anything.

Otto closed the driver's side door, scanning the street as always. Lorenzo got out of the passenger side. And no one else. They walked away from an empty car.

Could they not find the others? Or were they coming separately? Normally that wouldn't even give me a second's pause, but a bit of doubt crept into my head. Something wasn't right.

Zo came in first. He didn't make eye contact. Otto came in in the middle of lighting a cigarette. I sat at the bar as Zia came out with a tray of something that steamed.

"How many are coming?" she asked, putting the tray in the center of the table.

"Two more," I said. No one disagreed.

"The staff will be here in half an hour. So sit!"

Otto and Zo mumbled thanks and sat for lunch. When Zia passed me again, I put my arm around her. I didn't say a word, just kissed her forehead. She'd been good to me, and I might always be angry at her for hiding Valentina, but I had to forgive her or more than my love for my wife might die. She patted my arm and pushed past the swinging doors.

Otto leaned back in his chair, cigarette between his third and last fingers. Zo sat with his hands folded over his crotch and cleared his throat.

There was a heavy silence I didn't understand.

"Simone and Enzo?" I asked, sitting.

Zo put his hands out then back down. More silence. A pot banged in the kitchen.

"Come on, Zo!" Otto shouted.

"I can't say it."

Otto stamped out his cigarette as if nailing it to the ashtray. Then he clapped twice. "Welcome back!" Otto came at me with both hands out. He planted them on my neck and kissed my cheeks twice. "You look good for a dead guy! *Gagliardo*!" He patted my shoulder and kissed my cheeks again.

"You kiss me again, you're going to have to marry me," I said.

"I have a wife," Otto replied. "This guy"—he indicated Zo—"he's single. Give him a kiss, would you?"

"I think Zo fucked me already," I said. "Where are the others?"

Zo made a noise that was a cross between a groan and an *ah*. "They ain't coming."

"Excuse me?"

"We… uh. The day you was gone, we made a pact with Donna and now… they got families. They don't want another war."

"They're cowards!" Otto shouted, but I didn't hear him.

There were a million reasons to make peace. Strategies within strategies. It depended on who my people thought had killed me. If they thought it was the Bortolusis, which was what we'd intended, then the allegiance would be to partner against them.

"You made a pact? For what purpose?" I asked.

Zo looked stricken. "Business."

"I'm glad you didn't marry that bitch," Otto said, as if trying to pull solidarity from the jaws of anarchy. "I don't want to work with the Sicilians. I never liked it. You ever been to Palermo? It's backward, like they got their own pope. I don't want to answer to a man I never met. Never shook his hand. Nothing."

Otto was talking for the sake of talking, because no one was hearing him. It was Lorenzo and me in the room.

"I'm sorry to speak ill," Otto continued. "But Paulie, he was dangerous. I'm sorry you had to do what you done with him, but I'm glad I don't gotta worry no more."

"Lorenzo," I said, "you didn't tell me this was your plan."

He faced me full-on. He wasn't afraid of me, and that concerned me.

"So?" he said. "This way we didn't have to avenge you. Because I didn't want to avenge a guy who wasn't dead."

He was right. He could have used my death to start a fight that might have brought him millions if he won. But he'd opted for the path of right and found a way to navigate it. Not bad for a baby don. Not bad at all. Except he hadn't maintained the loyalty of the crew. Because they were gone, with a bigger love for peace than their own lives.

"They already tried to kill us," I said. "And the crew, they don't realize it's me today, and it's them tomorrow." I had a finger up, talking to Zo but seeing Enzo and Simone. "If we were in Napoli, that would be a given. You cannot trust Americans. Cannot. They turn on you the minute there's a risk. Nothing gets done alone." I pushed my wine three inches left. Two right. "Americans. All lone guns. Let me tell you something. That fails."

"I'm with you," Zo said. "You was dead, but now you're not and they put a price on your head. It's changed. But some guys don't change so fast."

The wine became offensive to me. Liquid celebration turned bitter by betrayal. I threw it across the room. It hung in the air in a streak of red then splatted everywhere.

Theresa walked in from the kitchen just as the glass landed, and I felt a deep shame at my tantrum. She deserved better. She deserved a man who could solve problems. But my thoughts were like pigeons in the piazza, a sea of cohesive grey scattered to the wind by a running child.

"You got this," Otto said, seemingly unaffected by my tantrum. "I don't know how. But as long as we can get close, we can attack. And that gets the price off your head because if you kill her, you run her business."

That was the last thing I needed. But he'd given me an idea if I could just get my head around the execution.

"No," I said. "There are too many ways to die."

Theresa came up behind me and put her hand on my shoulder. I slid mine over hers and stayed that way for a second. I was surrounded by treachery, but she was behind me, like a balm.

"You guys eat," I said. "I have business to attend to."

Chapter Twenty-Nine

THERESA

When he took my hand and stood, making eye contact, I melted a little. He cut through the business, the violence, the calculation, and took me to the kitchen. My cognizance of the space his body occupied sharpened like a razor. I was nowhere near his dick, but I was aware of it. My body was aware of it. My nipples hardened as if that could get me that much closer to it.

"What happened?" I asked.

"I am being betrayed."

"By who?"

"Possibly all of them."

"What do we do?"

He took my hand, and I let him because I felt no will outside my desire. He led me past Zia scrubbing a pot and greeting the lunch staff, to the office where I'd looked at the restaurant's books a million years before. The same squares of yellow sticky paper covered the wall, and the same beige computer hissed and hummed. He snapped the door closed and pushed me against the shelf that served as a desk.

"Let me have you," he growled. "Today. Now. *Adesso*. I don't care about anything but your body. I can't think without it. I'll get a divorce. An annulment. I'll murder anyone who comes between us. I'll promise not to. Anything. But I want you. Please. Call it a fuck of agreement. Call it a fuck for good-bye. Call it a *che sera, serà*. I don't care. But don't tell me I'm married to someone else. There is no one else."

I didn't want to believe him, because everything about what he was saying was wrong. But I did believe him. From the soaking arousal between my legs to the tips of my toes, from basest parts of my lizard brain to the intellect in my frontal cortex, I believed him.

I didn't believe the world would cooperate, but I didn't want the world inside me. I wanted him. His… what had Valentina called it?

"What does *cetriolo* mean?" I asked quietly.

His mouth twitched on one side as if he was trying not to smile. "You call it…" He cleared his throat and rubbed his eye as if he were so embarrassed he couldn't even see straight. "A cucumber."

"No, that's not what I call it at all." I spoke only in breath, my eyes on his luscious mouth. Those lips. On me. On my neck. On my body. My resistance slid away, lubricated by Valentina's dismissal and the shape of Antonio's mouth.

With a tilt of his head and a *tsk* of his tongue hitting the roof of his mouth, he had me.

"She doesn't seem to care if you fuck me," I said.

"She said that?"

"More or less. She seems to want every part of you but your eggplant."

His eyes lit up, and his mouth tightened in a smile. I'd given him as good as a "yes."

"It comes with the set," he said into my neck.

"Give it to me. The whole package."

I kissed him, pushing my body up against his. We wrapped our arms around each other, and pressed together, the outline of his erection was tight against me. He pulled back, and I drank in the lines of his face, the texture of stubble on his cheeks, the espresso of his eyes. Our lips came together again in an explosion of shared desire.

He pulled my shirt and bra over my breasts in one move, releasing them. "I missed these," he said, squeezing a nipple. "You are *magnifico*."

I groaned his name when he took my breast in his mouth. "I won't let you go," I said in a gasp. "I know I said I would, but I can't. I'm so confused." He sucked the nipple hard, and my last word came out as a squeak.

"I'm not." He opened my pants. "Fucking is very simple."

I was going to do this. I was going to break my promise to myself into a thousand pieces.

"Your body is mine." He kneeled in front of me, kissing my belly and the triangle where my legs met, slipping my pants down as he went. "I'm going to do what I want with it. Trust that I want what's right for it."

"I trust you, I just…" My words fell into breaths when his hands caressed my ass.

"Trust me. Trust that I won't leave you. Not from being careless or reckless. Not if I can help it. Not for a woman in my past." His eyes became brown disks warm with a pure decency I'd never seen before. "I will never leave you. I need you. Tell me you understand."

I didn't. Not at all. But I believed his intentions. "I trust you."

He lifted my feet from my jeans and kissed inside my legs, my knees, his tongue waking my skin as if from a long sleep. He spread them apart, pushing me back onto the desk. "You're going to let me fuck you so hard, you remember me forever. There is no such word as 'no.'"

My head rested on the wall, and he kissed where I was most vulnerable. The hair on his face scratched my sensitive thighs, but when his tongue reached my center, the discomfort was forgotten.

My feet tingled. My heart went code red. I couldn't see an inch in front of me. His tongue coursed up and down, exploring every inch of me. He put the tip of his tongue to the tip of my clit.

"I'm so close, I'm so close," I breathed.

He sucked on my clit in response, and I went rigid, using my arms to lift myself from the desk, mouth open, eyes shut, thinking nothing more than *oh god oh god oh god*. He slipped two, maybe three fingers in me, and new sensations opened, as if it hadn't been full enough before, and tears streamed down my face.

My hips dropped back to the desk. He stood over me, beautiful and cruel, and took out his cock.

"Wider," he said. "Spread them wider."

I did it, holding my legs open with my hands. I wanted to split myself in two for him. When his dick touched me, I thrust toward him, hungry for it.

"Capo," I prayed.

"Take it. All of it," he growled and thrust into me completely in one stroke.

I was so wet he got in all the way, burying himself inside me. He paused there, eyes half lidded with pleasure, and pulled out slowly.

"All of me," he whispered then slammed back in. "Because you trust me."

I touched his face, and mouthed, "I trust you." as he thrust into me.

My fingers memorized his face, the textures and lines, to the tempo of his rising urgency. *I love you I trust you I love you I trust you.* Warm pleasure spread over my body like spilled milk, until I was covered in it, toes curling, back arching, legs stiffening. I held back a cry and came for him, only him.

When I came down, he gathered me in his arms and kissed my neck while he fucked me until his breathing sounded out in short bursts.

"I'm going to come so hard in you."

"Yes," was all I had. No other word would do.

I felt the pulse at his base as he came with a groan. Antonio the invulnerable became vulnerable, and he opened himself to me in his parted lips and slowing thrusts, emptying his violence inside me where it could do no harm.

He pressed his lips to my cheek for a long time, only moving them away when there was a knock at the door. And though I felt the flood of all my previous concerns, including his estranged wife and the shadow of impending death, they didn't soak through. I trusted him.

He pulled away as if he sensed what was about to happen, the way cats and dogs know when an earthquake is coming. In the restaurant, glass shattered, and Antonio stared into my face, listening. A car screeched away.

"It begins," he said. "Are you ready?"

"No."

"*Bene*. Because I am."

Chapter Thirty

ANTONIO

"*Bene*," I said into Theresa's neck. Olive trees and fresh air. How she did that in Los Angeles, I didn't know.

She didn't have to go to Napoli to make me happy. She brought it with her wherever she went. I didn't want to leave that room, because I had an idea what the broken window was about, and I knew it meant I might never bury my face in her neck again.

A knock at the door.

"Spin." It was Zo.

"*Due secondi*." I stroked Theresa's breasts, and her nipples got hard all over again.

She bit her lip and her skin turned into a field of goose bumps. Outside, Zo shuffled away.

"Lean back," I said, and she did without question. I pulled her shirt and bra down, adjusting them so everything went in its place.

"Thank you."

"You're welcome," I replied, kneeling in front of her. "I want to give you an option, because you're a grown woman, and I know you won't take it because you love me." I'd intended to pull up her pants, but I stroked her legs because they were supple and perfect and meant for my hands. "But if you need to go, ever, then I will let you go." I slipped up her pants. "Even right now, if you need to walk out, I won't stop you. When we're in the middle of the storm, if you need to leave, I won't think less of you. Because there is going to be a storm, my love. I think you can handle it. I do. But if you can't, don't even say good-bye. Just turn your back and go."

I meant all of it, and I didn't. If she left, I'd be half a man. No plan I made would ever work without her. But I had to give her the option as much as I needed to hear her say she'd leave if she had to. I needed her full consent.

She didn't say anything at first. She let me fasten her pants and straighten her clothes. She let me put myself back together and button up. Then she answered.

"If I can't hack it, I'll walk," she said. "As an act of loyalty, I'll turn my back on you."

"Is this your wise mouth? It doesn't sound like it, but I need to be clear. I am going to make a deal with the Carlonis. Zo has proven it can be done. But I'm not him. I pose a bigger threat, and I have more to lose. It may go south."

"No sarcasm. I mean it. It's a promise between us."

I believed her, and in doing that, I was free to make any decision I needed to in order to save us. I opened the door feeling like a whole man.

Chapter Thirty-One

THERESA

As we strode out to the dining room, I decided I meant it. If things got too hot to handle, I'd walk because he wanted me to. I'd walk because it was the best way to prove I was loyal. I'd leave him behind if that gave him comfort. I'd do it because he didn't try to force me. Didn't pigeonhole me. Gave me the choice to do it or not based on what I thought, felt, knew, and expected. He didn't try to think for me.

When we got out to the front room, the trouble was obvious. A brick lay inside a spray of broken glass. Zia was screaming at Zo, who was trying to soothe her. A man with a broom waited at the edge of the spray to sweep it up, and the waitstaff set up the room as if the broken window was no more than an obstacle to a final goal.

Otto had gone outside to look down the block with his hand on his waistband. He came back in looking sheepish. "Missed them."

The brick hadn't been touched. They were more worried about the person who threw it, which made sense. But there was a rubber band around it, and that couldn't have been a mistake.

Zia turned her attention to her nephew and rattled off what must have been a litany of southern Italian cusses. I thought he apologized, but after only a few words, she threw up her hands and stormed to the kitchen, giving the guy with the broom the go-ahead.

Antonio hoisted the brick, tossing it up a few inches and catching it. The blue rubber band that looked like it had been taken from a head of broccoli held a piece of paper to the weight. He tossed the brick up and down until he had the attention of everyone in the room.

Otto lit a cigarette. Zo leaned on the booth and crossed his arms.

"Come on," Zo said, flapping his hand. *"Presto."*

Antonio took the paper from the rubber band. I took the brick so he could unfold the note. He let me look over his shoulder, and though that meant a lot to me, and seemed symbolic of a real trust between us, it was useless. The short handwritten note was in Italian. He pressed his lips together, and his face tightened. He was angry. He wanted to vault into action. I knew him at least that well. But he kept it together long enough to read it out loud.

"Shit," Zo said.

Antonio glanced at me. "The Carlonis. They say they're going after Valentina."

"No deal then," Zo mumbled.

"No deal." The note disappeared into Antonio's white-knuckled fist.

"Daniel," I said. "She left with Daniel."

Chapter Thirty-Two

THERESA

His look went from red hot to ice cold in the time it took for him to pull me to the kitchen. No words were transmitted between us. We weren't telepathic. No. We were something deeper.

"What?"

His tongue flicked over his bottom lip. Almost a nervous tic. The first one I'd ever seen on him.

"I can't," he said as if he'd made a full statement.

"Can't what?"

He ran his fingers through his hair. "They could hurt her. Or kill her."

"What do you want to do?"

He didn't say anything.

"Antonio?"

"I want you to know I love you. I am yours. Only yours."

He was trying to reassure me as if he was about to do something that would hurt my feelings.

How sweet.

How stupid.

"You want to go get her. Just say it."

He said nothing, frozen between his wants and his obligations, or his past and his future, or between his wife and his mistress. I put my hands on his biceps, and regretted it instantly. His body was a warm, automatic friction against mine, and I had to take a deep breath before I spoke.

"We can't let her die," I said. "I won't make you choose."

He breathed. I hadn't realized he'd been holding his breath, but relief poured off him. Somewhere in the kitchen, the door to the fridge clacked open, waitstaff yelled, stoves flamed, and a shovelful of broken glass tinkled into a garbage bin.

"*Grazie*."

"I am beside you."

He raised an eyebrow. "I can't bring you with me."

So that was his conflict. He knew he had to get Valentina but worried about dragging me back into danger. In that moment, I loved him for his loyalty more than anything else. I was relieved he'd never considered abandoning her, and annoyed that he still considered me an asset to protect rather than use.

"If you leave me behind, I'll follow."

"No."

"We live together or die together, Capo. You said it."

"I lied." He pulled out his gun, clicking it open, then closed it.

I crossed my arms and leaned on one foot. "She was with Daniel last. Do you know how the Sicilians are getting into his place? They can't just stroll in and start shooting."

"Yes, they can. Danny-boy's worked with them for years."

My face got red hot. I was ashamed of my ignorance and my naiveté.

He saw the prickly heat of shame on my skin and flipped the gun around. He handed it to me grip-first, blocking everyone's view of it with his body. "Keep this, and pray for anyone who sneaks up on you."

"I'm going," I said, taking the gun.

"You are not. If you die, if you're hurt, if you so much as cry again—"

"You need me. He's the fucking district attorney. A mayoral candidate. How are you getting in? Because I'll tell you how I'm getting in. He fucked me for seven years. I'm walking in."

When would I stop being surprised at how fast he was? He had an arm carried by electricity, landing at the back of my neck in a fierce grip. "Are you trying to piss me off?" he hissed, his mouth kiss-close, bending my head until my face met his.

He didn't scare me. Not one bit.

"Yes."

"It's not working," he lied, the lead weight of rage heavy on his voice.

"His security detail knows me. From. All. The. Fucking."

The dishwashers chattered in Spanish, and I realized our intensity was a lousy shield.

Antonio let me go. "*Dio mio,* woman. When this is over, I'm going to take you to a place no one knows, and I'm splitting you in two."

"Take me," I whispered, pausing before I finished… "with you. You'll never get past security without me. And they'll just walk in and take Valentina into a field and shoot her, if they haven't already."

He pressed his lips between his teeth as he always did when I was getting to him. "You are to stay with me at all times."

"All right."

"You do not let your attention wander."

"Yes." My god, every command turned me on.

"You do not use your weapon unless we get separated."

"Yes."

"I am your weapon."

"Yes." I was barely breathing.

"Say it. Say I'm your weapon."

"You are my weapon."

He put up his finger. "I don't like this."

"Yes, you do."

Chapter Thirty-Three

THERESA

When Daniel and I had moved in together, he rented out his tiny condo a block from City Hall. Once the tenant's lease was up, he returned to it. The proximity to the civic center made campaigning easier. He needed security, and he needed a place that was easy to care for. Antonio held the building's brass-and-glass front door open for me. Zo came in after me.

"You sure you don't want to wait in the car?" Zo asked.

"We're going in together," I replied "You don't need to watch me."

The lobby was a stark study in white and wood. Everything was in its place, but nothing was exactly right. I didn't know what I had been prepared for. Nothing and everything. I was prepared to see his wife, alive and beautiful, a cinderblock wall shaped like a supple woman between Antonio and me. I didn't want to meet her and I didn't want to save her, but she was important to him, even if he wouldn't admit it, and I didn't know how he'd bear losing her again because of his actions. He carried things around. He held grudges and pain. I walked into Daniel's building for Antonio, for his health, for his peace of mind. Because I loved him, and it wasn't about me.

That aside, it was too quiet. The security detail I'd promised to get Antonio through was absent.

Zo lumbered behind me like a loyal puppy while Antonio moved like a cat, as if he was only checking territory he already owned. The front desk wasn't manned, so all my talk of getting Antonio past it was for nothing. I stopped him with a *tsst* sound. He turned, eyes everywhere, and I indicated the closed circuit monitors behind the security desk.

They were off.

He nodded slightly, paused.

"I know what you're thinking, and forget it." I moved my lips but no more sound came out. *Live together. Die together.*

His eyes lingered on my mouth. I didn't know if he understood me, but my thoughts went dirty, and a weight of wetness dropped from my spine to the space between my legs.

"Let's go," I said and went toward the elevator. "We have a nice Italian woman to rescue."

I didn't have the key to Daniel's place, but as we walked down the soft white hall upstairs, I saw a keypad outside his door. Zo checked his watch. Antonio touched his jacket under the arm, where his gun sat in its leather holster.

It was up to me. I didn't know how many digits, and Daniel didn't have a commonly used password for the daily business of getting into the easy stuff.

I put in his birthday.

Red light.

His childhood address in City Terrace.

Red light.

His social security number.

Red light.

His phone number.

Red light.

His mother's phone number.

Red light.

His phone number backward.

Red light.

"Contessa," Antonio said, "let me shoot it."

I held up my hand. If we wanted to get in and out, we had to make as little mess as possible, and I wanted to prove my worth. Had to prove he'd brought me here as more than a burden, and I factored into the situation as more than a dead weight with a murderous streak.

I put in my birthday, just to keep my fingers moving.

Green light.

"Excellent," Antonio said, pushing the door open. "What was it?"

I didn't answer. I didn't want to lie, but I didn't want Antonio to get distracted by the fact that my birthday was the code to Daniel's loft.

Zo pulled out his gun and held it up. Antonio reached into his jacket. I still had the hunk of metal in my waistband, and it was staying there. If this went down the tubes, I didn't want to kill anyone else.

Antonio put his other hand on the knob. "You ready?" His voice was couched in a tenderness I sometimes forgot he was capable of.

"I'm fine, Capo. Let's just get her and go."

He swung the door open.

I smelled gunpowder. Antonio tried to hold me back, but I beat him into the big room. My footsteps echoed. Zo closed the door. Antonio checked the corners then leaned against the doorjamb to the bedroom. I swallowed, wondering if she'd be sleeping or naked. But he shook his head. There was no one.

The kitchen was open to the larger room, with a bar creating a psychological barrier. I touched the shiny marble surface. I heard a creaking sound. I looked around. Didn't know where it came from.

I pressed my fingertips together. There was a white powder on the pads from touching the marble.

The creaking came again.

Antonio came toward me.

Zo checked the bathroom. Nothing.

I rubbed the powder on my fingers and listened to the interminable creak.

Slap. A shoe clonked down onto the counter, and I jumped. I looked up to where it came from, and Antonio followed my gaze.

I screamed.

Daniel was hanging upside down from a beam in the ceiling, ropes around his calves, feet free but squeezed enough that his remaining shoe dangled from his toes, the other foot covered in just a sock. He moved back and forth slightly, the rope creaking against the beam. A silver rectangle of duct tape covered the bottom half of his beet-red face, and his hands were tied behind his back.

"Get him down!" I shouted.

Zo jumped onto the counter, but anyone could see it wasn't high enough. The rope was still six feet above him.

"Antonio!" I shouted his name in supplication. I didn't know what to do, but if I prayed hard enough to the right god, some answer would come. "Get him down!"

Antonio put a barstool on the counter and hopped on it.

No. That was too unstable and wouldn't reach the rope.

I stepped back and yanked the gun out of my waistband.

"*Basta,*" Antonio cried. "Wait!" He grabbed Daniel by the chest and steadied himself.

I stepped back and aimed.

"Let me do it," Antonio said, because I could as easily shoot Daniel as get him down.

But I was upset, and it was too late for sense.

I squeezed the trigger before worrying about it too deeply, and the rope that held my ex-fiancé by the ankles cracked. Daniel fell, and Antonio broke his fall. Both tumbled to the floor.

Antonio twisted out from under him, and Daniel rolled onto his back and I saw his face. It was swollen with blood, veins popping.

I didn't think about what I was doing. Daniel had broken my heart. He'd soiled my soul. I thought I'd never trust another man because of him. But he drove me to Antonio. I'd loved Daniel for seven years. I'd given him everything I had, and he'd given as much as he could.

I burst into tears. I cursed through them, unaware of Antonio or Zo. I hated this. Hated what had happened to Daniel. Hated that I'd caused it in some twisted way. I couldn't remember a bad thing about him, though I knew there was plenty to complain about. I only remembered being included, being validated, feeling as if I was part of a team with a larger purpose. I remembered all the good works he'd done, his compassion for the marginalized and underrepresented. I remembered him before he'd thought he had a chance to make anything of himself, and his wide-eyed joy at the thought that he could be polished into a man who could make a difference. All of that unknotted itself from the cheating, the manipulating, the double-dealing, and the strands of my vision of him separated. I saw him for the complex person he was, and appreciated what he was, what he could have been, and how very wrong he was for me despite all that.

"Contessa," Antonio said gently.

"Get that shit off his face!" I clawed at the duct tape.

Antonio took the other side and ripped it off, leaving spots of blood on Daniel's mouth. Daniel coughed as Antonio got his hands untied.

"Oh my god!" I said through tears. "Jesus, Dan! Dan."

He rolled facedown on the floor, holding his head at the base of his neck. I looked at Antonio, who crouched with his elbows to his knees. I must have had a question written all over my face, because he answered it without me speaking.

"Blood's flowing out of his brain. He's got a headache you can't imagine."

"I'm going to kill them," I said. "He could have died."

"He still might, if there's a blood clot. I never told you about my uncle."

"Should he stand up?"

"I don't think so. Give him a minute." Antonio crouched on one knee, without jealousy or rage in his eyes, and slipped his fingers along my jaw. His touch was an embodiment of tenderness and strength, and though the facts remained, it helped me see through the tangle of my emotions.

I couldn't just sit there. Zo was wiping down surfaces we'd touched. Antonio was hovering over Daniel to see if he would survive. I went into the kitchen and snapped open the door over the sink. He'd organized the cabinet the way I had when we lived together. His medicine was boxed by pain killers, cold and flu, skin care, etc., with a little plastic cup for water. I tapped out a headache pill for him. Four came out, I was shaking so hard.

When I'd said I wanted to kill whoever did this, I was serious. My feeling of bright white rage would only be relieved with the death of someone, or their howls of pain. Was that why Antonio felt he needed to right wrongs with murder? I got it. I really did. And if his life was cut short, I knew I would get myself killed avenging that death.

"Don't fucking touch me," Daniel said. He was on his back, hands over his eyes.

Antonio took his hand off Daniel's arm just before I crouched down.

"Here," I said, putting the pills in Daniel's palm.

"This is so past anything I had in the cabinet."

"I know."

"Valentina," he said. "Did you find her?"

Antonio and I exchanged a look.

"No, what happened?" I asked.

He groaned and tried to sit up, wobbled. I snatched a pillow from the couch and put it under his head. It was a bed pillow, I noticed, and the blanket was spread as if someone had slept on the couch the night before.

"They came in, Domenico Uvoli and another guy. I thought they were going to give me a hard time about the Bortolusi wedding, so I hid Valentina. But they were fixing this rig up, and she started screaming. They were really here for her. They kept asking… fuck. We have to get her." Daniel wasn't talking to me. He was talking to Antonio. "She went pale and fainted. She didn't look right."

"Not good. That's not good," Antonio said. He didn't look alarmed as much as he looked as if he was controlling his unease. "You're the DA. You should call the police." His voice didn't mock Daniel, but it had the weight of a rhetorical suggestion.

"I will. And in the time it takes me to explain it all, they'll kill her."

"What do you want me to do about it?" Antonio asked.

I didn't know if he was seething because Daniel had stepped on his territory with me or with his wife, and I didn't care.

"Antonio," I growled. "It's not the time for a pissing match."

Behind me, Zo's phone buzzed. Meekly, he reached into his pocket.

"They have you on speed dial, Lorenzo?" Antonio said.

"Your burner don't hold a number or do shit, so… it's on me." He shrugged and answered then immediately gave the phone to Antonio.

He stood up, straightened himself, and spoke. *"Pronto."*

Daniel stood, wavered, got his bearings.

"Signora. Buon giorno."

That was all I caught. The rest was a tangle of syllables I didn't understand. Zo understood though, and by watching him, I could gauge the level of worry I should feel. Daniel spoke enough Spanish to communicate with his constituency, and Italian wasn't that far off, so his sharp breath worried me as well.

Antonio, however, was very calm up to a point. Then he changed completely. *"Valentina?"*

I couldn't pretend to understand any of what he said after that. The words were just a sharp music, slicing me apart with their song. He was gentle with her, and he was upset, looking at the ceiling while he listened to her voice. I couldn't hear a thing. He turned away from all of us slightly, the angle of his body courteous and inclusive but sending a message that the conversation was not for my ears.

His voice was reassuring, confident. I couldn't help it—I leaned in and caught just enough of her voice to hear hysteria and tears.

He lowered the phone, tapped the glass a few times, and put it back against his ear. *"Shh, Tina,tesoro. Shhh. Cinque secondi. Non dire nulla. Respira."*

He spoke to her as if she were a child. There was love in it, but not as a husband to his wife. If I'd ever doubted him, I stopped completely when he was gentle but not tender with her. She was silent but for a few sniffs, and he closed his eyes. What was he doing?

A female voice came over the phone and barked in Italian. Antonio put the phone down, and I saw on the screen that the line was dead. He tossed the phone back to Zo, who caught it.

"What did they want?" Zo asked.

"To prove they had her and she is upset. To pull my heart around so I do what they want."

Daniel leaned on the arm of the couch to stand. "We have to get her."

"I'll get her, Brower. Just stay out of it."

"She didn't look good when they pulled her out. I know she was scared, and they had me by the balls."

"Shocking."

"She was white as a sheet. Sweating."

"Do you know where she is?" Antonio asked. "Did they say anything?"

"No. Not that I understood." He looked chastened, and I wanted to slap Antonio.

Antonio gestured to Zo, who gave up his phone as if reading his boss's mind. Antonio laid down the phone.

"You set the recorder?" Zo asked.

"Yes." Antonio tapped the screen. "First, we need to figure out where they have her. Then we discuss the rest."

Antonio fiddled with the phone and came up with his call to Valentina. She was hysterical; I hadn't heard that. I felt sorry for her. She was totally out of her element. I didn't need to understand the language to understand that much.

"Shh, Tina, tesoro. Shhh. Cinque secondi. Non dire nulla. Respira."

She did quiet down, and the background noise became audible. Indoors, yet the sound of a siren came through. And someone talking. Two people. Professionals. But I couldn't hear the words. Then another siren with a different cadence.

And a beep.

An odd beep.

Then more hysterical Italian chatter from her, and my deep, heartbreaking pity for her.

Antonio played the five seconds of silence again. Siren. Talk. Siren. Beep.

"The hospital," I said, leaping forward. "She's in the hospital. The first siren is an ambulance. The second is police. The only time you're getting those two so close is in the hospital. And the beep. It's an ECG monitor. I remember it from my brother."

Antonio pressed the phone to his forehead and closed his eyes, as if thinking hard. "She has an arrhythmia. This is why she looked pale to you. And why she has no business with wine." He spoke to us but seemed deep in his own world. "Zo, get Otto and find out if his daughter still works for the medical supply company. See if she can make some calls. Find out which hospital."

Chapter Thirty-Four

ANTONIO

I didn't tell Theresa what Donna Maria had said. The details were irrelevant.

SHE IS SAFE. For now.

You, we will gut.

"SHE" was Valentina. The gutting was assumed to be literal. Donna Maria had used the word *sbudellarlo,* which had a particular Sicilian connotation. It was used for the most disloyal offenders. The ones who broke *omertà* and gave information to the police, who stole, or who married outside the business.

AND IF YOU don't come to us by tomorrow night, we will open her up. Don't think I won't for this shame you visited twice on my family now. My granddaughter still has no husband. It will not go unanswered. You have twenty-four hours to present yourself, or she's dead.

I WASN'T afraid of that or anything, but Theresa would go after anyone who hurt me, and she would get herself killed by less talented and more experienced hands.

I held out my hand for Theresa. "We're taking care of this, Mister Brower."

"What are you going to do?"

"We're going to find her first," I said. "Then we're going to send her home."

"What do you need me to do?"

"Keep the police off us," Theresa interjected. "I don't care how."

Daniel nodded. "Today. No problem. I can't guarantee tomorrow."

I held out my hand, and he took it. "Take care of that head," I said.

"Sure, sure." He still looked a little red in the face. "Don't let this asshole get you killed."

She hugged him. "Go to the fundraiser if you can."

When she hugged her ex, and he rubbed her back, I had a sudden sense of wholeness with her. I'd changed. What a fool I'd been. Not a fool but a man in a box. A box I'd been raised in but had had every opportunity to break out of. A man nailed to the ground by tradition and conformity.

When I'd first seen her on the news, next to him, I admired her purity because that was what I thought one admired in a woman. It never occurred to me that she could be more. Though I'd come to respect her ability to do what needed to be done when the air was on fire with bullets, my mind didn't truly expand until I saw her inside her old life and knew she didn't fit. My world unfolded and laid itself before me. I'd loved the wrong reasons inside the right woman and made excuses for the love. But I'd known it the whole time, hadn't I? The way she aligned herself with Daniel. The way you could tell she meant more to him than a docile little wife. She was the power behind him. The fearless, intelligent, fierce lioness.

I didn't know what to do with her or myself. Now, today, she fit with me and I with her. But tomorrow? I'd been a man without a nation for a long time, and now I was a man without friends. She was mine, and she fit me where it counted, but not where it counted with everyone around me. They'd turn on us. As soon as there was a moment's peace, we would be targets, and she wouldn't let me stand in front of her. I'd tried handcuffing her, leaving her, diverting her, yet she bent herself toward death.

I had no answer. I only knew if she died, I was going with her. It was the only way.

Chapter Thirty-Five

THERESA

I could never predict his moods. He was businesslike and managerial while figuring out the whens and wherefores of the coming twenty-four hours. He called Otto and got us a car. Half an hour later, we were in a nondescript lot in Silver Lake, walking up to a white Porsche. Otto leaned on it, holding up the keys.

"Did you talk to your daughter?" Antonio asked, snapping the keys away.

"She needs time."

"We'll be in Paseo. If she can't, you need to call me." He opened the passenger side of the Porsche, staring at me as if he wanted to eat me alive.

"Does Otto know how you feel about Porsches?"

"His idea of a joke. And the sooner you get in this shit car, the sooner you're out." He pulled out of the lot and threaded through the back alley and out onto Sunset.

"Where are we going?"

"We own a building on Paseo Del Mar. Not a luxury, but I'll be fucking you so hard, you won't even notice." He glanced over with a gaze like a starving cat.

"Before that, I need to know we have a plan," I said as he made a left, using his signal, keeping it under the speed limit. No sharp moves.

"A plan? We're going to find out what hospital she's at and grab her."

"And then?"

"I can't predict the future. No. I can. I'm going to fuck you tonight. I'm going to fuck you until Otto calls or until you're in a thousand pieces on the bed. Whichever comes first."

A thousand pieces on the bed. I knew what that looked like. It looked like me, naked, sated, catching my breath. Sore everywhere. Drenched in sweat and the smell of pine. Barely conscious with not a thought or worry in my head. It sounded so good, I didn't want to derail it. I wanted it to happen as promised.

But as we drove west, I had a nagging question, and I was sick of dancing around it. I needed a plan. *We* needed a plan. I played a game of Whac-a-Mole in my head. Every time the issue popped up, I smacked it down, but it popped up again.

"Antonio, I…" I didn't finish the sentence because he smiled at me and looked at me as if I were the last woman on earth.

"Yes?" He pulled into a narrow alley behind a little house that was packed against its neighbors.

I could press him about his wife, or I could take what was mine and discuss it later, after I was in a thousand pieces on the bed. I was sure there was no right choice. "I hope this place has a washing machine."

He snapped a key off the car's ring and dangled it in front of me. "Go in while I put this in the garage. And get your clothes off. If you're not naked when I get in there, I'm taking my belt to your ass."

I turned red from my cheeks to my chest, where my nipples hardened under my shirt.

"Go," he whispered.

I got out and walked up the wooden steps to the back. The little porch was clean of dust, dirt, and personality. No one lived there, of course. When I unlocked the back and went in, I knew I was right. There was a pot on the stove, but it was spotless. The lights went on, and the kitchen could have been a hotel.

I realized how few times Antonio and I had made love in anything that resembled a permanent home. His unfinished house in the hills. His temporary space in Mount Washington. The loft I shared with Katrina. That was as good as it ever got. And now we were in another generic space, probably owned as a business loss. The likelihood that he and I would ever have a marriage bed was unlikely, and I got sad for a second before I remembered his demand that I be naked.

I felt like hell. Filthy to the core. I took off everything and found a washer/dryer in the closet. I threw everything in, dumped in some soap, and snapped the lid closed.

"What about mine?" Antonio asked from behind me.

"You're fast," I said, opening the lid.

He responded by peeling off his shirt, a fast reveal of the perfection underneath. The hard abs, the straight shoulders, the line of black hair from his navel to the heaven below.

He threw his shirt into the wash then got out of his pants. He was fully erect, and I found my need for a shower turned up a notch.

The rest of his clothes went into the wash with a swoosh. I turned my back to him and snapped the lid closed. I pushed buttons. I didn't even know which ones. The colors were mixed, and I didn't know if I'd put the right amount of detergent. Hot water? Cold? Rinse? His body was against mine while I turned dials and pushed buttons. He grabbed the hair at the back of my head.

"Where do you want it?" he whispered in my ear, his cock at my ass.

I trembled then turned. "I need a shower, Capo."

"All right." He leaned into me and reached behind me to pull the dial. *Click*. The water whooshed as the machine filled.

"Oh, you do laundry?" I cooed.

"Tonight, I do laundry and you."

I kissed him through a smile, and he carried me to the bathroom.

Chapter Thirty-Six

ANTONIO

I knew what was on her mind. I wasn't stupid. But I didn't know how to soothe her without fucking her. I didn't know what to say that would be practical. She was hiding her worry from me, and that bothered me. I didn't like it. She needed to be completely open.

The bathroom had no towels and only little chips of soap, but we managed to clean each other with what we had.

"You make a lot of bubbles with a little soap, Capo. I admire that in a man."

She was coated in white drifts. I ran my hand down her body, cutting through the glaze to her bare skin. She put her head back and let the water run through her hair, the impossible shade of strawberry blond turning dark brown. We had no shampoo. She just wet it then looked at me with her lashes stuck together and beads of water on her lips. I brushed them away.

"You were going to tell me something in the car," I said.

She looked away. "Yeah." She shut off the water. "I guess we have to air dry."

We found sheets in a drawer under the bed. White flowers on blue with worn spots. But clean. Better than I'd expected.

"Are you worried she's in the hospital?" She was naked still, arms out as she flapped the top sheet over the bed. "I mean, she could be sick."

"It was the arrhythmia. They're lucky they brought her in, or I'd kill them for not taking care of her."

She didn't say anything. Her silence was enough.

"Theresa, she's my responsibility."

"I know. I'm not blaming you. You're honorable. If you felt differently, I'd think less of you. You can't just throw someone away because they're not convenient right now."

She crouched to tuck in the sheet. I'd never seen her do a domestic chore. I knew she couldn't cook, and she hired out the cleaning. I never would have married her in my youth. Wouldn't have even considered it.

"I have no cause to trust any man in the world, but I trust you. I don't know if that says more about you or me," she said.

"It says something about us."

"And I know you're not going to get confused and start fucking her. Or leave me to start over with her. I don't know how I know that. It's just… part of me still thinks you should." She tucked the sheet around the bed, across the foot, and back up to the side I stood on.

She stood and put her hands on her naked hips, and I couldn't take not touching her for another second. I put my arms around her waist and kissed her face.

"We were always complicated," she continued, "but this? I don't even know what this means. I don't want to tell you what to do. It's your culture. Your family. Your values."

"This bed is a disaster. I've never seen a sheet so crooked in my life."

"Don't change the subject."

"I'm not changing the subject."

She pulled her face away to look at me, mouth pursed, head tilted just a little to express disbelief.

"You know who can make a bed? My wife. And fast. She practically had the sheets trained to make themselves." I was a brute, of course, to bring her down before bringing her up. "You want the values of my culture? In those sheets were everything. If a woman could cook and care for the house, she was everything a man needed. And I was the luckiest man on earth. But who am I now? Am I the man who values straight sheets? Is that what I want anymore? And if I don't care about the sheets, or the cooking, what do I care about?"

"If you're telling me you love me, I know that. But a plan. I need a plan." She seemed exasperated, as if she wasn't getting through to me.

I pushed her onto the bed. I wanted to rumple those sheets. Shred them. I straddled her and put her hands over her head as if that would shut her up. I was getting to something, and I had to speak it or lose it. "You. There's only you, Theresa. I can't figure it out, and I don't have time to tonight. Who am I anymore? I don't know. I'm a different man now. So you want a plan, but I can't make one because I don't know what I want besides you."

"You have me," she said.

I let her hands go. She was still concerned. It was in her voice, as if she wanted to add something but didn't because I was on top of her naked and only half dried-off.

I rolled onto my back. The ceiling was a popcorn pattern with chips missing in the shapes of islands lost in the sea. "When I was a boy, I knew my side of the piazza. I was the little mayor. Sophia sold cigarettes, Vincenzo sold fruit, and they'd give me some for running errands, though I tell you, Sophia was a hardass. Made me work for it."

Theresa got up on her elbow. "Her product was more expensive. Vincenzo could give you a bruised reject. She couldn't."

"True, true."

"Did Vincenzo have strawberries in summer?"

"When I was a kid? Never. I had him get them for me special later, though. I was a mechanic. I couldn't afford them but…"

But Valentina loved them.

"I like them better than cigarettes," Theresa said.

"Sophia's smokes stank to high heaven anyway." She touched my face, stroking my cheek as if appreciating something seen for the first time. She looked breakable, but I knew otherwise. "I want one now that I mentioned it."

"Is that how you made money? Running errands?" she asked.

"I was fast. You shoulda seen me run. Via Duchessa to Via Concezio in seventeen seconds. I took care of business. Made sure my uncle got to the docks, made a little money where I could. Went to school sometimes. Everything had a place. When I went to work for my father, the places were different, but there was less chaos. Men did what men did, and women did what women did, and it all fit. Who I was as a child still fit in that world. It wasn't what my mother wanted, but it was something I understood. I didn't have to think about it."

I looked at the islands on the ceiling. The longer I looked, the more there were. It was a regular archipelago up there.

"And now it's all different." Her voice came over the popcorn waters as undulating music. "The rug's getting ripped from under you, but not all at once. Piece by piece."

I turned to her and put my hand on her face. "I told you once that you were making me soft."

"At the wrap party."

"That day, Daniel Brower had a press conference. I went to see him because he'd been to that movie with you the night before. I didn't know what I wanted from him, except to keep away from you. He said he wouldn't. I felt powerless. I thought I was going to go insane." Remembering that moment, I felt helpless all over again. The feeling had been new at the time. I would never get used to it. "You've been making me soft since we met. And now I'm lying here telling you this bullshit. I should be fucking you."

"No." She straddled me. I put my hands up, and she held them. "I should be fucking you."

"Oh, really?"

"Yes, Capo."

"Well. Let's see how you do then."

She hitched up a little and guided herself onto me. She felt perfect. Built for my body. I was consumed by her. I took her hands again, and she leveraged herself against them. She leaned down, and I held her, let her be the boat on my sea as the islands above formed and reformed. I closed my eyes and felt her softness in my hands, all warmth and curves. When I felt her stiffen and shake, I released inside her.

We slept in each other's arms, and the last thing I saw was the chipped ceiling, no more than part of a room in need of a paint job.

Chapter Thirty-Seven

THERESA

Los Angeles nights were cold, and if the heat wasn't on in the safe house you happened to be staying at and the stash under the bed wasn't equipped with a blanket, you huddled for warmth. At some point in the night, Antonio and I had unwrapped and rewrapped ourselves around each other, and his heat kept me warm under the flimsy sheet. When I woke, I thought he was asleep, but when I turned and looked at him, hoping to see him in restful peace, his eyes were open.

"Shh," he said. "Someone's outside."

I thought he should be moving, standing, something. It took me a second to feel his arm and an uncomfortable hardness under my pillow. He was holding his gun. He was more alert than he appeared, trying to lure whoever it was into a false sense of security. I reduced the pressure of my head on the pillow, wedging my shoulder under me so he could clear the shot easily if he had to. I stiffened at the knock on the back door.

"He's a polite intruder," I whispered, and Antonio smiled. Who wouldn't be safe with this man in her bed?

"It's one of my guys," he said, throwing off the sheet. "Get dressed."

I'd tossed our stuff in the dryer in the middle of the night, so we unloaded the clean clothes and wiggled into them. Being grunge-free felt good.

"I should have put that toothbrush in my pocket," I grumbled.

"Your mouth tastes like roses." He kissed me on the lips while he tucked in his shirt.

"Blech."

Antonio peeked out the kitchen window then opened the door. Otto stood there with a bag in each hand: one paper, one white plastic.

"Good morning," he said.

"Boun giorno."

"Hi." I took the paper bag from him. It was warm. "Is this food?"

"I got a little breakfast from the place around the corner."

He and Antonio shook hands, and I open tore the bag. I didn't have time for staples and tape. There was hot food to be had. I set out the containers while Antonio looked in the plastic bag. Eggs. Pancakes. Potatoes. Exactly what we needed.

"Otto, I think I love you." I hugged him hard. He patted my back noncommittally, and when I looked at Antonio, I knew why. "Give me a break, Capo. Sit down and eat."

Properly chastened by the woman of the house, they sat down. Antonio peeled open a coffee and drank it black.

"My daughter got the information about Valentina," Otto said, opening Styrofoam boxes. "She's at Sequoia. They kept her overnight, and they'll probably keep her again. She hasn't said she's a captive or nothing. Hasn't asked for the law. Nothing."

"She understands *omertà.* That'll work in our favor."

Otto pushed away his food. I stayed quiet, but his position and attitude didn't bode well.

"Lorenzo," he said. "I don't want to be the one to tell you, but I'm the last one with a mouth to open."

"Zo? Zo what?"

"When you was gone those days, he was on top of the crew. He was good. But he knew you was alive, right?"

"Yes." Antonio's voice, in one syllable, was all right angles and hard surfaces.

"He barely breathed. Said we could mourn you for a week, then we were back to business." Otto took out his cigarettes and turned to me. "You mind?"

"No, go ahead."

Otto lit up and tossed Antonio the pack. "He put the lid on any ideas about vengeance. He was ready. Took control. Laid out a plan to continue business with no interruptions."

"Make your point." Antonio lit his cigarette, tilting his head a little.

"He likes things organized. He…" Otto dragged on his smoke. "He left.

Promised himself to the Carlonis in exchange for peace. I'm sorry, boss. He sends his apologies."

Antonio pushed his chair out with a hard squeak and stood. "Ten minutes."

He stormed out the back door.

Chapter Thirty-Eight

ANTONIO

Those motherfucking sons of whores. Each of them. Fuck all of them. Even Otto. Fuck him too. Fuck all of the little cowardly bastards. If I had the time, I'd stomp them from the face of the earth. Right under my shoe.

I scraped my sole against the pavement. Tomorrow. Once I did what needed doing—retrieving Valentina and sending her home, solidifying my position—they were all going under my shoe. Simone. Enzo. I would save Lorenzo for last. He would cry for his life, that son of a motherfucker. And he had no wife. No kids. No one would miss the little bastard.

And fuck him. He had been too ambitious from the beginning. Ready to jump in my motherfucking grave as soon as I was gone. No wonder he had a sourpuss on the minute we turned up again. He wanted to be boss? Well, he could be boss between now and when I killed his crew.

My crew.

I scraped again and slipped a little on a stone. The sidewalk was troubled with cracks and upended pieces. I heard the water at the end of the block, crashing constantly. I found myself at a railing overlooking the beach, the sky turning bluer, the goddamn ocean in and out same as always. Maybe I'd drown them.

I had a pack of cigarettes that had travelled with me all the way from Tijuana. They stank, but I pulled one out and lit it, then picked a piece of tobacco from the tip of my tongue. An inadequate distraction.

My father would never have tolerated this nonsense. If he let them live, they'd be doing it with one or two limbs less. A crew was a marriage. Worse. Better. It was a blood bond, and they were breaking it.

The thought of it.

I realized my fists were tight when I started pounding the railing and the vibrations rattled my knuckles. I'd lost half my crew after nearly killing Bruno Uvoli. I never knew if I'd lost them because I went off half cocked over Theresa, or because I was too soft to wipe him from the earth. Maybe neither. Maybe both. But I'd been blinded by two things: the fact that my vendetta for my sister's rapists was satisfied, and desire for Theresa filling the place where the desire for revenge had resided.

That moment, looking at Bruno with blood running down his face. He'd tried not to cry. I remembered that, because that was what changed me. I had no need for revenge, only a need for her. And his efforts to be tough and not cry or beg? I'd felt myself feeling pity for him, and if I hadn't known it that night, I knew it standing by the water. She'd been chipping away at my command from day one.

I didn't want to kill my crew, but I felt obligated to. The weight was my anger, yes, but the need to do something about it was the burden. What if I didn't do anything about it? What if I got angry without turning the anger into physical action? What if my anger didn't have consequences?

I'd be killed, for sure. I'd be weak, then dead, because a boss never forgets and only forgives for a price.

I walked back to the house lighter but no wiser. I'd decided nothing but what not to do. The last of my crew was safe from me until I got Valentina.

Theresa and Otto were in the front. He had his phone out, and they watched the screen. Her brow was knotted, and he was rubbing his pinkie space with his thumb. Theresa saw me when I was halfway down the block, and she ran to me, siren hair flying behind her.

"Contessa?"

"They're saying you shot Paulie," she said. "Your face is all over the news."

"Daniel?" I spit the name. "That motherfucker."

I looked at my watch but didn't see the time. How foolish would it be to survive all this and end up in prison? I put my hands to my mouth, imagining being separated from her when we'd worked so hard to be together.

She took my wrists. "Let me see if I can take care of it."

"You? Just you?"

"You can't go anywhere in daylight right now."

"Then neither can you. I never told you, there's a quarter million out for your life."

"That's it? I'm insulted."

"It's not something joke about."

"They don't want me. They have Valentina. It's probably safer for me away from you."

She was wrong. Nothing about this world was safe whenever she was out of my sight.

"She's right," Otto interjected. "They got Tina, and they're all holed up in Sequoia watching her."

"Fuck you, Otto," I said.

He shrugged. Somehow I'd been overruled.

I took her in my arms and held her. My damnation and salvation. My spark of change, dragging me into the light, kicking and screaming. She took my sins and made them her own. If only I could save her before she consigned herself to hell.

"Don't worry," I said. "We'll make it out."

I buried my nose in her hair and breathed her in. I didn't have a plan or a crew. I had nothing. Yet I sat on a throne before a kingdom of possibilities.

Chapter Thirty-Nine

THERESA

I called Dan from Antonio's burner and got him to meet me in a corner booth at the Nickel. At eleven in the morning, most of the red vinyl booths were empty and the tabletop jukeboxes were silent. I slid in next to Daniel, who regarded the menu as if he didn't know he was getting the same thing he always got. BLT. Lightly toasted. Extra mayo.

"Theresa, where have you been?"

I propped the big plastic menu in front of me as if I didn't know what I was ordering. Nothing. I didn't have an appetite. "How did you get the duct tape glue off your face?"

"Nail polish remover. Did you find Valentina?"

"Yes."

"Is she safe?"

"No." I put down the menu. I saw the TV behind the bar, and Antonio's face on it. "We located her. We don't have her."

"Where is she?"

"Why do I see Antonio's face on television?"

"We'd pressured his doctors to declare him dead under the Determination of Death Act, and to be honest, your family pushed it."

"What? Why?"

"He's got a functioning heart and the same rare blood type as your brother. This turned into homicide this morning, and my staff pushed through the indictment while I was busy hanging from a ceiling."

I flipped the songs on the little jukebox, trying to separate my feelings from my strategy. The pink tabs flipped. I knew all the songs yet couldn't place them. "Do you have change? I'm out."

"What's with you?"

I held out my hand. "Ambient noise."

He stretched, reached into his pocket, and came out with a handful of change. I plucked out four quarters.

"You're a wild card, Daniel." I put fifty cents in the jukebox and played some random ballad from the seventies. I rubbed the other two coins together. I liked the way they scraped and slipped at the same time. "One minute I think you're going to do right by me—"

"I told you I'd keep LAPD off you yesterday so you could find Valentina. And I did, but you didn't get her."

"We found her, but no. We didn't get her. Not yet."

"I can only go so far. I have a job and a department full of people with their own minds."

"Right now, he's stuck. If he can't move, he can't get Valentina. And if you think you can get her, forget it. She won't tell you crap, and you know it. She'll swear whoever's holding her are her cousins. You know it's true. He's the best chance she has and the only chance I have. So make it go away."

He leaned forward to make his point and to keep his voice low. "I can't hold back my entire staff. I actually kind of like the guy, but the entire Los Angeles justice system knows Antonio Spinelli shot Paulie Patalano."

"He didn't."

"Well, who did?"

I didn't say a word. I didn't breathe. I just looked the district attorney in the eye until he leaned back.

"Jesus Christ, Theresa." He knew. I didn't have to say it, and he knew. "Jesus, Jesus… why?"

"You understand what'll happen if you allow this to continue. All roads lead to Rome. If you're all right with that, then I have to be."

I didn't wait for an answer. I just slid out of the booth. It wasn't until I reached for the keys to the Porsche that I realized I still had those two quarters between my fingers. I slipped them into my front pocket and drove back to Antonio.

I was a killer. For real and for sure. I couldn't hang on Paulie's working lungs and heart anymore. It was homicide because his death was inevitable. And still, I didn't feel as bad as I thought I would.

Maybe I had been born for this. Maybe it was in my blood. Which gave me an idea. A disturbing idea, but one that might work. I pulled up to the safe house convinced it was our only option.

Antonio met me on the porch.

"You're supposed to stay inside," I said as I stepped up.

"It's too nice a day," he lied. It was clammy and cold.

"Do we know if Valentina's still at the hospital?"

"She is."

"I thought of something," I said. "Remember what you told me about my family? Our history? Who we are?"

"Yes?"

"I think I can get us in. But I don't know if it'll come with a way out."

Chapter Forty

THERESA

"No radio," Antonio said, snapping it off. I'd heard his name and turned up the car stereo. It had started pouring on the way to Sequoia, and the *pat pat pat* on the roof and *puh puh puh* on the windows was going to drive me nuts. It was dusk already.

"They might be saying something we can use," I objected but didn't try to turn the radio back on.

What was it like to have your name all over the media in connection with something as evil as murder? I didn't know. I only knew what it was like to be the actual murderer. I put my back to the passenger door and slipped out of my shoes. Antonio had driven, even though it was Otto's car. We'd parked in the outdoor lot across the street from Sequoia and were waiting for Antonio's only loyal friend to appear with the one person who could help us get in.

"Trust me," he said, "I've done this before. Those reports aren't doing anything but worrying you. Half of what they're saying is lies, and the other half are things we already know."

He was right. I'd been intimate with the media and what they fed to the public.

He took out his pack of cigarettes and shook out the last one. I reached for it, slipping it out before his lips got on it. He raised an eyebrow at me.

"Light me up, Capo."

He clacked open his lighter and I dragged on it until it was lit. I handed the cigarette back to him while blew out the smoke. I hadn't smoked since high school, when I wanted to impress Rachel, who was so cool she seemed other worldly.

Antonio took the cigarette, regarding me before putting it in his lips. I liked everything about the way he did it. The placement of the cigarette between his fingers, the shape of his lips as he pulled on it, and the snap as he removed it.

"How can you look so relaxed?" I asked, taking the smoke from him.

"I can ask you the same."

"I'm worried about Otto." I flicked the ashes in the tray.

"He can do more with eight fingers than most men can do with twelve."

I cocked my head at him. He just looked out the window, touching his lower lip before it stretched into a grin. I jabbed his knee with my foot.

"You're better than that joke."

He put his hand on my foot and ran it up as far as my pants would allow. "No, I'm not. Do you think you can live with a man who makes jokes like that for the rest of your life?"

"I think there's a regular comedian in there." I handed him the cigarette, flame side up. "We just have to draw him out."

"I wish I could laugh." He shook his head a little, still smiling slightly. "I met your father a long time ago, while I was consigliere for Donna Maria. He was building something in our territory. There were union issues. He might remember me."

"This should be a fun get-together then." I wasn't surprised my father had worked with the mob. I was pretty sure that wasn't his first business deal with them, or his last.

"I'm wondering, should I ask him for your hand tonight? Or wait until we're both in jail?"

I took the cigarette from him. It had gotten short and hot, like my temper.

"I don't think you can ask while you're legally married to someone else."

He smiled ruefully and rubbed his eyes. "What a mess."

"They're here," I said. I rolled down the window a crack, as if I was still in high school getting caught being a bad girl.

Antonio looked up, hand reaching for the key. Otto and Declan Drazen, each carrying an umbrella, walked out the sliding doors. Dad looked no worse for the wear in a sport jacket and sweater. He barely looked both ways when crossing, as if a car wouldn't dare try to occupy the same space as him because he was entitled to the world at large.

Or at least that was how I saw it. We all saw him differently, and we were all correct. He was an exacting judge, a paymaster, evil incarnate, a master controller, a father whose only concern was the ten people in his family and their legacy. Only Jonathan had failed to disappoint him, and he was the child who hated him the most.

The back door clicked open, and my father slipped in. Otto closed the door behind him, staying outside to watch.

"Hi, Dad," I said.

"Theresa. Mister Spinelli. Good to see you again."

Antonio reached over the front seat, and they shook hands. "Sorry about the circumstances."

"My daughter explained it." He was talking about Margie, who I'd called first. "Quite involved, this whole situation." In the window behind my father, Otto's cigarette smoke drifted by, unaffected by the rain. "Theresa was always the one who caused no trouble at all." He looked at me. "Guess you were saving it up."

"How's Jonathan?" I asked.

"Near death. You might want to stop by."

"I wish I could."

"Indeed. Now." He jerked his head toward where Otto stood outside. "The gentleman tells me you wanted something?"

"There's a woman inside this hospital," I said. "She's probably being discharged right now. She's being watched by a group of people—"

"The Carloni family?" Dad said.

Antonio twisted around to face my father a little more. Was he regarding him more seriously? That was wise.

"How many?" Antonio asked.

"I haven't had cause to count, but if you put them together with the family of Paulie Patalano, it's like an underworld reunion."

"Dad, this is important. I know you have some pull in this hospital. If you could just put her in a room alone for ten minutes, Antonio and I could go in and walk her out. No problem."

"How is it you can do that?"

"She and I have the same name," Antonio said.

I tensed up. We would have to explain.

Antonio, as if sensing that I needed to get it over with, finished the thought. "I'm her husband. They'll let me take her."

Why had that felt like a knife in my heart? As if I didn't know it already. Was it because my father was sitting right there, and my shame was so great, the pain became fresh and raw all over again? Dad seemed to consider all the implications, letting the pause hang.

"They're going to kill her," I said.

"So they brought her to the hospital? Please, Theresa, you've never been one for dramatics. This is disconcerting. Disheartening, even. Mister Spinelli, I am sure you're a man of values, but they're not my family's. And it seems like in addition to losing my son in the next few days, I've already lost my daughter. My goal in life has been keeping this family together, and it's blown apart."

"It hasn't," I said. "I'm here, and this is a bump in the road."

I didn't even believe it, and neither did he.

"Prove it," he said. "If this is a bump, when it's done, you stay. You don't do a Carrie and move away."

I glanced at Antonio, whose eyes stayed on my father.

"I can't promise that," I said.

"Then I can't promise anything either."

"I promise it," Antonio said. "We'll stay within reach."

I wanted to kick him. Was he giving up his dream of going back home, or his dream of being with me? Or was he failing to take my father seriously?

"Hardly something you can promise, Mister Spinelli, seeing as you're already married."

That should have hurt. Should have cut me to the bone, but it didn't. The initial shock of my father knowing I was sleeping with a married man was bad, but once that was done, I felt nothing either way about it. Antonio had promised. That was good enough for me.

"You told me to make one good choice," I said. "One good choice, and you'd release the funds to keep Zia's afloat when Antonio was gone. Well, I made a good choice—I came back to LA to see Jonathan. Here I am. And I don't need the money anymore. So this is the trade I want."

"You're pushing it."

"I could still be gone."

He leaned forward in his seat. I turned.

"You will never leave," he said. "Not for any man. Not for any money. Not for any reason. You belong here. Your blood runs beach water and backwash." He opened the back door. "If there's a woman being held against her will, you need to call the police."

He was out the door before I could formulate an answer. We watched in silence as he strode across the street.

"It's okay," I said. "We'll figure something out. He was a long shot anyway."

Antonio was too quiet, tapping the steering wheel and watching my father cross the street, his umbrella straight. Not a drop got on him.

"We'll go in the hard way." Did I sound desperate?

"We shouldn't go in. I'll take care of it. I'll do the trade. I'll let them take me and figure it out, or not. I'm not afraid to die."

"If they hurt you, Capo, I'll kill them."

He turned to the windshield and took a deep breath, like a man falling under the weight of his burdens.

I took his hand. I hadn't meant to worry him, but I'd said the wrong thing. The same words that made me feel confident when they came from his lips ripped the world out from under him when they came from mine. I was about to take it back, lie and say I'd do nothing. But he gave my hand a quick squeeze and ran out into the night, dodging a car. The car door slammed behind him, and I lost him in the wash of rain on the window. I rolled it down. Antonio caught up to my father on the other side of the street. Otto watched, smoke rising from under his umbrella.

They were talking, and I couldn't hear a word. I saw Antonio's gyrating hands and the bend of his back. He wasn't flinching from the rain; he was imploring my father for something, arm stretched toward the car, where I was. Jesus. What was he saying? What was he trading? Discomfort spiraled from my gut to my throat. Dad wasn't even talking, just Antonio, out in the cold and wet. Supplicating. Begging for what? I didn't even know. But I couldn't take it anymore. I got out and was pelted with rain. Otto tried to cross around the car to give me his umbrella, but I pushed it away and started across the street.

My father nodded.

They shook hands.

No.

No no no.

"Antonio!"

He came to me, hair flattened and face studded with raindrops, lips dripping before he even spoke.

"What did you say to him?"

"Get in the car." His clothes stuck to him, leaving veiny ridges up his arms. I saw the flex in his forearms when he grabbed my biceps and tried to turn me around.

"Capo."

"Get in the fucking car."

"We're in this together. *Together*. Did you forget?"

He shook his head, eyes dark in the night, with only a glint from the streetlights to tell me confusion and pain swirled in them. He put his lips to mine so hard it hurt, and it wasn't until I yielded to his arms and his mouth that they softened on me.

"Trust me," he said between kisses, cradling my head. "Just trust me."

And I did. Through the raindrops and thunder, the groans building in my throat, the warmed space between our bodies, I trusted him, his judgment, his intentions, his actions.

But I didn't.

Chapter Forty-One

THERESA

We passed Margie's car on the way to the elevator. It was still parked in the spot reserved for the neurology guy she'd helped with a "thing." When this was over, I was going to sit Margie down and ask her what she really did for a living.

Otto stayed in the car while Antonio and I stepped into the elevator.

"What's the plan?" I asked, watching the numbers change. The secure lot was four levels down.

"Cardiac wing is on four." He didn't look at me. He looked at the numbers. "There'll be a distraction in fifteen minutes. We will be on two."

"This sounds pretty vague."

"I'm using what I have."

The elevator dinged, and the doors slid open into a back hallway painted a particularly diarrhea shade of mustard.

Antonio walked out, and I followed. He was closed to me, and I didn't know why. No. Forget that. I did know why. The price for whatever this distraction was must have been sky-high if he would rather shut me out than talk to me.

I'd mastered my impulses long ago, covering them with implacable smiles and social maneuvering, but I almost grabbed Antonio and yanked him back to demand an answer because he'd stripped away all my practiced refinement. But did we even have time for that? Did he have a moment to tell me what we were doing? Or were there too many components to explain as we walked down a hall lined with laundry bins and broken gurneys?

I had to trust him, and when he turned to an open door, stopped himself midway, and looked at me with full engagement, I was glad I'd waited. He gestured at the empty staff lunch room. Two vending machines. A wall of lockers. A coffee maker with a crust of sludge. A round tabletop on a single center pedestal and three red chairs with chrome legs.

I stepped inside, and he pushed me through to the "Pump Room," which was no bigger than the smallest of my mother's closets. Meaning, it had room enough for a glider and footrest, a cabinet, and a little table with a half-full paper coffee cup.

He snapped the door closed behind him.

"What's the problem?" I asked. "What's happening?"

He crashed his lips onto mine.

I pushed him away with force. "There couldn't possibly be a worse time for this."

He took my hands, holding them between us. "Please, just do this for me. Don't ask questions." He turned my hands over and kissed my palms. "Don't ask to be hurt. Don't fight. Just love me."

His voice was soft enough to turn stone to putty, and all desire to defy him left me.

"Okay," I said, "but I—"

He pressed his fingers to my lips. "Hush. Trust me. I've worked it out. All you have to do is follow along."

"The bouncing ball."

"Follow the ball." He picked up my shirt and ran his hands over my nipples until they were as hard as stones. "That's it. I need you by my side, and right now, I need you to love me. No more."

"You're scaring me."

He unbuttoned my pants and slid them down my legs. "You wouldn't be scared if you loved me."

"That's not true."

It was hard to concentrate on everything that was happening when he stroked my thighs, kissing them as I stepped out of my clothes.

"It is. There's no fear if there's love."

He guided me to the wooden slider and sat me in it.

"Open your legs," he whispered, gently parting my knees until I was exposed to him. His eyes alone sent shockwaves through me, and he kept them on me when he kissed inside my thigh slowly, from knee up. He brushed his lips against my folds, flicking his tongue.

"Oh!" I cried. I couldn't help it.

"Shh. Quietly."

He opened me with his thumbs, exposing my clit to his tongue. He was good, so good. Skilled, yes, but he loved it. Loved every inch of my body. Loved every place we joined and touched. No one could do what he did without love.

I dug my fingers into his hair and put my legs on the armrests. I pressed my hips into him, whispering, "Yes, yes, yes."

The closer I got, the slower his tongue got. I was engorged, soaked, gasping for breath, and the tip of his tongue barely touched the very edge of my clit.

"Please, Capo, I'm so close."

He said nothing, answering by keeping his movements slow and light. The build, drop by drop, filling an ocean of tension, felt impossibly taut.

But still… he was slow and steady.

"Please, please. Oh, God let me go."

I looked at him. He moved his face from me, smiling. The air touching my clit was going to bring me right to orgasm.

"Stay there," he said, getting his pants down. "Don't move."

He sat on the footrest, his cock a waiting rod. He pulled me up, and I maneuvered myself to straddle him and brought myself onto him. I was so close already, so full of blood, tight as a drum, that when I slid my body onto his length, my body crackled to life. I moved back up and slowly, slowly back down again. The pace left me time to feel every inch, every trickle of pleasure, building at the next perfectly timed stroke.

I exploded, curving against him, biting back a howl. He held me still while he pounded me from below, and I came in a torrent, wiped clean of worry, stress gone, just a flood of love. When I looked at him, his lips were parted and his breath had become ragged. He held my face and pulled me close. I moved along him, still feeling shots of pleasure where we joined. He put his face to mine, his short breaths against my mouth.

"Ti voglio bene, Theresa. Ti amerò sempre. Fino alla fine dei miei giorni."

His eyes closed in utter surrender, and he came inside me, giving me everything.

We panted together for a few minutes, clutching each other, his dick still inside me. We had ten or fewer short breaths together before he pulled back.

"You ready?" he said, looking at his watch.

I got up, dripping. "I could be if I knew what we were doing."

He yanked up his pants. "We're trusting me. We're not being afraid." He tucked in his shirt.

"We're staying together."

He held out his hand. When I took it, he kissed it. "Let me check outside first."

He took me back out into the lunch room.

I let him, because he asked me to. I slid a paper cone from the sleeve and rested my hand on the watercooler lever. I let him walk to the door because I didn't think anything of it. He'd asked me to trust him, which was redundant, because I trusted him already. He'd tried to leave me to protect me four times, and all four times he'd come back to me.

So why would I expect a fifth time?

That would be crazy.

Right?

I released the water lever when the cone was full, watching him in admiration of his grace. He looked out the door, the angle of his body as desirable in my satisfaction as it had been ten minutes earlier in my ache.

He looked back at me, fingers sliding along the edge of the door. "You should never doubt that I love you."

"Neither should you."

"I'm not trying to protect you," he said.

"Thank you for that." I brought the cone to my mouth. The water numbed my upper lip with an icy shock.

He clicked a button on the door's edge. "This is something else."

He stepped outside and closed the door with a resounding click, and I dropped the paper cone, splashing cold water on my feet.

Then the fire alarm started.

What had he promised in exchange for the blaring klaxon alarm that went off? I didn't wonder about that until after I'd tried the knob and found he'd locked it from the outside. I pounded on the door, screaming his name for all of fifteen seconds, calculating what he'd traded with my father.

Our life together. That could be the only thing my father would want. And I knew Antonio's calculations, because we were of one mind. He hadn't lied in saying that he wasn't trying to protect me. He was doing something else entirely. If his plan was to give me up, take Valentina home… then what?

Then something. Maybe he intended to figure it out once Valentina was safe and he'd made peace. Maybe I already knew the answer.

I trusted him. Even as I screamed for him to open the goddamned door, I trusted him.

Then I caught the stink of smoke.

My eyes burned. Was it in here? Would he leave me if the room was on fire?

I turned around. The room was dark but for the illumination from the chai-colored sky and a tiny pinprick of hot orange.

"So," an Italian-lilted voice said. I heard her clearly between the honks of the alarm. "I can finally see you."

Chapter Forty-Two

ANTONIO

Amor regge senza legge.

Loosely translated… love rules without laws.

Romanticized. A completely painted-pink version of truth. When love swells and all the world seems small in the face of it, the heart feels like the most powerful thing on Earth. Above all worldly things. Money. Laws. Common sense.

One follows the heart to paradise or destruction, but it rules, and it doesn't tell you where you're going. You just go. Laws be damned. Laws of family and country can go to hell, and you can follow.

I'd had no business marrying Valentina, but I loved her. After the first few months, I became dissatisfied in bed, but I stayed faithful. Nothing I did was good enough for her, so I tried to do better. She became an emotional burden, yet I committed myself to her.

Valentina had had no business marrying me, but she did. She was from the north and hated the southern part of the boot. Yet she loved me. She hated the camorra as much as she embraced my family. *Omertà* burned her alive and set her apart from her friends. But she kept silent for me.

As time passed, maybe one of us would have changed enough to make us happy together. Maybe we would have bent toward each other and met. The day I left with the taste of her risotto sliding against my tongue, disappearing behind the growing bite of bitterness, I realized how far we were from each other. She'd become vicious and moody, and no matter what I did, the only thing she wanted to talk about was my walking away from being my father's consigliere.

She was pregnant. She didn't want to bring children into the fold. Saddle them with a father who could be dead or imprisoned. She'd never told me any of that, but I knew it was true. It was obvious.

I didn't owe her anything. We'd failed each other. I was no more responsible for the failures of our marriage up to the point she disappeared than she was. But after that, I blamed her for everything. For keeping my son from me. For letting me grieve for her. For showing up only when she thought I was dead.

I trotted down the hall, running with the *whoop* of the siren. I'd grabbed a white coat and headed against traffic to the cardiac floor. I had a room number. Theresa was locked away. That had been my promise. Declan Drazen would manufacture a way for me to get Valentina if I left Theresa behind. I had to go alone. He was protecting his daughter. I was grateful. At least if I wasn't seeing sense, he was.

I was going to get Valentina and send her home by plane or slow boat. Arrange something with my son she'd agree to. I would apologize to Theresa with the most profound and honest apology I could muster. Then I would end my marriage somehow. I'd do something that was against every tradition in my family and get a divorce. Or get an annulment and make sure my son was taken care of in some other meaningful way. Something more, and something less, than my father had done after my mother annulled their marriage.

I was elated. Walking on air. Everything I wanted was about to come to me. I could settle down and let Zo take the reins of the business without fighting for my crew. Theresa and I had enough money, time, love.

My god, I loved her.

I didn't think it could happen. She and I, together almost normally. But it was going to happen. In the short trip down the hall, I remembered the scent of olive blossoms on the way up the 5 freeway. I would buy a small orchard between Los Angeles and San Diego, and we would live on it together. Close to her family. Close to Zia, who I forgave in my heart for keeping my wife and child from me. I would run the business legitimately, completely above board, and Theresa would keep the books and numbers. She'd pressure me to be more efficient, and I'd teach her why I couldn't be. We'd fight and make up and fight and make up and make children and make up and—

I got to room 498 mid-smile. The door was closed, probably because Valentina was supposed to have checked out already. I had a moment of concern that she might have tried to escape when the alarms went off two floors below, but I was propelled by my plan, thoughtless in my fantasy of a life with Theresa, and naïve in my belief in her father.

They wore white coats, and I felt a prick in my hip. It was too late to say or do anything. Too late to apologize or to ask where Valentina was. Too late to run, too late to fight. The room went sideways, and the smile left my face.

Chapter Forty-Three

THERESA

My eyes adjusted. A woman smoking. Thin as a rail. She sounded old, but I couldn't see her well enough to confirm. She blew a stream of smoke, leaving the last huff for two rings that drifted up in a breaking halo.

"Donna Maria," I said, remembering her from the wedding. The alarm was muffled through the door, but it was a constant that made me raise my voice. "How long have you been here?"

"I've heard people fucking before. Don't worry your pretty head about it."

I let that hang like the layer of smoke collecting at the ceiling. It had been a separate room and a closed door, but still. She stepped forward into the window light. It cast her in blue, revealing her age. I stepped back.

"I wanted to see you," she said. "To get a good look at you. I wanted to see if you have vengeance in you."

"And what if I do?"

"We can't have that."

We regarded each other for too long. I didn't know what I was looking at, but I knew it frightened me. She looked like solid evil. Sin made flesh. As old as she was and as small as she was, she had murder on her hands.

I stepped back again. "How did you know we were here?"

"Why? Are you afraid my consigliere set you up?"

"He didn't." I hadn't considered it because there was no way Antonio or my father would put me in a room with this woman. Lorenzo? Otto? One of them. They would pay.

Donna Maria pointed at my eyes. "And there it is." She shook her head slowly.

"What?"

"Some people are born with a need to make things even. Imbalance is like a stone in their shoe. They need to shake it out. This never changes. It's not even a choice. It's who they are. This is you. I saw it on you just now. For you, there will be an imbalance, and you'll need to correct it, unless I correct you first."

Imbalance?

Vengeance.

Then there must be something to avenge. Oh God.

"Don't." I said one word as a full sentence, begging for Antonio's life as an answer to what was in my head, not what had come from her lips.

She looked at her wrist then at me. "It's probably already done."

I had an excess of physical reactions to quell. My hands got hot. My thighs tingled. My rib cage shrank until all the air was squeezed from my lungs. There might have been more, but I hadn't time to catalog them.

She was on me so fast, she became invisible in the space between us. My feet were lifted from under me, and the floor thwacked the back of my head.

She was so fast. I'd never seen anything like it, even in Antonio. The knife was a streak of blue light against the darkness, and my instincts acted where my mind was too slow, turning my head to avoid the blade. I jerked my hips and threw her off me just as the door opened. A solid wedge of light poured in, and the decibel level of the alarm doubled.

I was alone on the floor, sprawled like a drunk.

"Miss, there's a fire alarm on this floor," said the orderly, turning on the light. "Let's go."

I spun to look for Donna Maria Carloni, scanning every last place she could hide, but she was nowhere to be seen. The door to the pump room was closed. I pointed, but the orderly dragged me out.

Chapter Forty-Four

THERESA

Donna Maria had terrified me, but she'd propelled me into action. If she hadn't tried to kill me, I might have poked around for Antonio, trusting that he'd planned our reconnection.

How long did I have? I followed the orderly and the crowd down the hall until he checked the next doorway, then I slipped away.

Donna Maria had to kill Antonio herself, despite what she'd said to freak me out.

Right?

Unless someone else was supposed to inherit Antonio's territory?

I had a moment of doubt when I worried that he'd intended this. That he'd given himself to death to save both of the women in his life, and Donna Maria had come to me to make sure I wouldn't avenge a death he chose.

I couldn't believe that. I trusted him.

I opened the emergency door just as a throng of staff and patients headed toward me. Jesus, a lot of people worked the late shift.

"Turn around," said a ponytailed woman my age, wearing dark blue scrubs and pulling a gurney.

She took my arm, still guiding her supine patient. We were followed by a crowd of professionals acting calm and bored with a sense of urgency to their motions. The doctor let go of my arm, and as the crowd pushed down the hall, I took one step back into the lunch room. She was gone.

Hoping another staffer wouldn't detain me, I got back out into the hall.

I acted official, as if I was heading back into the burning hospital for official life-saving business that couldn't wait.

My father was a piece of work. A fire. Did he make sure there was a real fire? Or did he just pay someone five figures to pull the wrong lever somewhere in the guts of the building?

Once in the hall, I grabbed a clipboard and trotted against traffic as if I belonged there. I had to get to the cardiac unit. If I could find Valentina, maybe I could retrace his steps. My family was on that floor with Jonathan.

The hall was mostly empty when I passed a room with the door open. It was the third I passed, but for some reason, I stopped. Inside was a man lying down, eyes taped shut, head in a kind of plastic box. I stepped in. The lights flashed against the patient's skin. Fat tubes came out of his mouth, his bow lips gauzed against friction.

"Paulie," I said, my voice drowned out by the klaxon.

He didn't answer. He never would.

I backed out. I wasn't there to make my soul right. I was there to find Antonio. In the reflection in a chrome tray, I saw a dark-haired woman come from around the corner. I dodged and ran to the stairwell.

I clutched my clipboard and fought the traffic to go to the stairs to find the cardiac unit on the fourth floor. Once I got to the third floor, the mad dash stopped. The alarm stopped.

Up on four, nothing had changed. Had the drill only been on the second floor?

As I approached the waiting room my family was in, a cheer went up from them and my blood rushed with the tingle of adrenaline. There stood a version of my family I'd never seen, because the Drazens didn't huddle in a group hug so tight you couldn't identify every participant. They didn't jump up and down together at this time of night. Not my mother. Not Sheila. My father wasn't inside the hug's circle but stood with his hands pressed together, head bowed over them, eyes closed as if in prayer. A part of my brain became electrified when I saw my father in that pose.

"Dad!" I ran to him.

He didn't move. I knew he'd seen me before he closed his eyes over his hands. "Daddy, what have you done?" I asked.

I smelled Antonio, and a forest, and saw my father with the sounds of a thousand birds behind him.

The memory had been activated by an algorithm of input.

The memory of the boy in the forest. The one who came all over my shirt and slapped me. The one who had been found at the bottom of a ravine with a broken neck. The first boy who kissed me like a man. The first one who got his fingers inside me and shocked me by making me come. That boy. I'd laid his death in my father's lap, because all the facts clicked together, but when Dad folded his hands in prayer because Jonathan was obviously going to live, the whole memory came to me. I'd blamed my father not because he was capable of murder, but because I hadn't been able to deal with the fact that I was.

The ravine, and the boy twisted at the bottom, and Dad next to me with his hands folded and saying, "What have I done?"

Me, looking at my own hands and feeling their power. A brown button sat in the center of my right palm. I'd pulled it off when I'd yanked the boy by the shirt and thrown him over a cliff. It was so clear now. Dad had arranged a meeting to simply threaten him, and I'd shown up. I'd swung him by the shirt, using his weight and surprise against him, and let go. Just let go and watched.

"What have I done?" he'd said. Dad had wanted to know what kind of animal he'd raised.

I'd killed that boy. I'd killed him for leaving a swirl of prematurely released semen on my shirt and slapping me. I'd killed him for our shame. I'd been a murderer way before I met Paulie Patalano.

Antonio hadn't made me a killer. Violence was in my blood, my skin, the sinews of my heart.

Dad put his hands down, and the memory shattered, like a painted window broken to reveal an entire landscape beyond.

He opened his eyes. "They found a heart. He's going to be fine."

I pressed my hand to my chest as if checking for my own heart. "I need to know," I said while no one was listening. "Antonio. Where is he? What deal did you make?"

"Two of my children are saved tonight," he said. "That was the deal I made."

If I stayed to grill him further, I would get sucked into my family's joy, and I didn't have time. Antonio didn't have time.

Chapter Forty-Five

THERESA

I didn't know where I was running to with my stolen clipboard and nothing but forward momentum. He had to be alive. Had to be. The life would be sucked from my world if he was removed from it. I had hope, and I clung to it like the last dollar to my name. He had to be alive. He had to be. I trusted him to live.

Jonathan would be okay, and my family would be all right. Antonio had to be fine. I was so mad at him for leaving me in that break room, but I would forgive him and let him fuck me like a rag doll.

I hurled myself down the steps and into the waiting room next to the vending machine Antonio had fed a twenty-dollar bill an eternity ago. My face was bathed in sweat and tears. I couldn't breathe from running toward then away from the make-believe fire, and my ears rang from the alarm. I passed the colorful box of shiny plastic food, all screaming for attention. Something about it made me stop in my tracks. All the crinkly packages held upright by black coils were the same. Or not. I didn't remember the food, because Antonio had been so beautiful with two-day scruff on his cheeks and his sparkling eyes. And his hands, breaking open the granola package… the way the fingers had articulated, the sheer power and dignity of them. Later, I'd learned to love the grace with which those hands managed small things because I knew how rough they could be.

The vending machine wasn't interesting. The memory of my resistance to Antonio was, as was the sobbing of the woman next to it as she crumpled a bunch of papers in her hand. That was why I was attracted to the machine. It wasn't the memory of Antonio or the brightly packaged non-food. It was the woman. It was Valentina.

My ribs took on a life of their own, squeezing the air from my lungs as if I couldn't breathe without the help.

She wasn't supposed to be sitting on a blue plastic chair by herself, crying. Antonio wouldn't leave her like that. Not for a minute. Not for as long as it took me to stare at a bunch of snacks.

That only meant one thing.

Donna Maria had been telling the truth. She had him.

"Valentina?" I sat and said her name at the same time, putting my arm around her. "Where's Antonio?"

She looked up and saw me, her eyes at the bottom of deep, salty puddles. She rattled something off in Italian, hands waving, mouth wet with tears and spit. I looked around the room. Sick grandmothers. Wailing babies. One woman so pale I thought she was wearing a mask. No one cared that a beautiful woman was crying her eyes out.

"Valentina, English, please. Antonio? He was coming to get you. Have you seen him?"

She shook her head. Spit out more Italian. All I understood was the name "Tonio" and the emotion, which read something between regret and resignation.

She wasn't functioning, and more than anything, I needed her to function, at least well enough to tell me that Antonio had left us both for a life on the run, or a third woman, or some other attempt at vengeance. I didn't even care what it was. Didn't even worry about "us" but about the worst-case scenario, which I refused to even tell her.

I set her papers aside and took her hands. I tried to remember his voice, his tone, how he broke through her walls of panic and despair.

"Shh, Tina, tesoro. Shhh. Cinque secondi. Non dire nulla. Respira."

She heard me. She must have. She took a breath through her mouth. It hitched, choked, but I saw the concentration in her face. She looked right at me, as if trying to seek out strength in me she didn't have for herself. I tried to project Antonio-like confidence as I made a show of taking another deep breath. She followed, her second breath hitching that much less.

"Bene," I said. "Another."

We breathed together three more times. She swallowed. Breathed. Sniffed. Dug an overused tissue out of her sweater sleeve and wiped her nose. When she looked at me again and sucked her lips between her teeth as if there was something she wanted to say but was now calm enough to be ashamed of, I panicked.

"Okay. Tell me. Do you know where Antonio is?" In my heart, I still hoped she was crying because he'd broken her heart, not because I liked seeing her hurt but because the other option was terrifying.

"I don't know." Her face started melting again.

I squeezed her hands so hard it must have hurt. At least, that was the intention. "Have you seen him?"

"No."

I needed an open-ended question that went away from Antonio and back to what Valentina knew.

"Why are you crying?" I asked.

"I'm scared."

"Of what?"

"First Daniel. Did they kill Daniel?"

Who? Daniel? That had been years ago. I had to shake myself from thoughts of Antonio to remind myself of the last time she'd seen Daniel. He had been hanging upside down from a beam in his ceiling. Then I pictured on the floor, face red, grey strips of duct tape glue on his cheek.

"He's all right. We got to him."

She broke down in fresh tears that didn't have sorrow or desperation in them, only relief. She put her head in her hands, and I stroked her back. I didn't have a second to let her release, but I didn't have a choice but to let her feel it.

"He's fine," I said softly. "He has a headache."

"They took me away. And my heart gave out. It does when I have stress. They didn't know whether to bother letting me live. They had me in the room." Her arm went straight, pointing at the place she was describing, which may or may not have been in that direction. "They didn't know I have some English. So I just listened. I tried not to give away my face. And they were saying…"

She was going to break down again.

"Stay with me," I said.

"They had him go to the wrong room. They were going to take him away and…" She tilted her head and pivoted her hand around her wrist as if trying to think of a word. "*Sbudellarlo*."

"I don't know what that means."

She made her fingers into a plane and pointed the edge of it toward herself, moving her hand up and down. "Cut him open. My sweet husband."

She broke apart again, and no amount of breathing was going to get her back. She fell into my arms even though I was in no condition to comfort or soothe her. I just stared at the side of the vending machine, eyes wide and blank. The personality I'd cultivated for thirty years poured out of me, and I was empty. Nothing but a vessel for that other self I'd just discovered. The animal. The huntress. The savage. Though I thought that primitive woman would rend everything in her sight to achieve her ends, she surprised me. A cold calm took the place where panic and uncertainty would have been.

I was a stone. In part, I had to be or I'd break, thinking of Antonio dying. But also, if I was to avenge him, I had no time to turn into Valentina.

I took Valentina by the chin and forced her to look at me. "I'm putting you in a cab to Zia's. You stay with her."

Her head shook as much as my fingers allowed.

I let go of her chin. "You can go somewhere else beside Zia's, but—"

"Where are you going?" she interrupted.

"To find him."

"Where?"

If I said "Wilshire and Western" or "under Santa Monica pier," she wouldn't know what I was talking about. I could have made up anything and at least answered the question to her satisfaction, but she was illuminating a point. I didn't know where I was looking.

And she knew it. The bitch. She looked at me with a smug little face I wanted to crack open.

"You know," I said.

"I want to tell the men. This is not the place for us. You're going to get him killed."

"The men?" I set my voice to a sotto growl. "They abandoned him. They sold him. Every one of them."

Except Otto. Maybe. He was I-didn't-even-know-where at that point.

"They said it though?" I asked. "They said where they were taking him? They said the whole plan?"

"All of them?" she asked by way of an answer. "There isn't one of his men to talk to?"

"No. Did they say it in front of you? Just tell me what they said without the particulars."

"We should call his father then."

Was she serious? She wanted to call a man across the world who may or may not have approved his son's assassination? She needed to go back to the fabric factory.

"I don't have a cell," I said, and the ridiculousness of her idea seemed to hit her.

She looked helpless again, trying to twist her mind around matters that were beyond her scope. She was an innocent. A nag and a righteous poseur, but not evil. And not particularly direct or approachable when sober. She was a traditional girl with traditional ideas about what she could do by herself.

"How far away is Whittier?" she asked.

I didn't react. I didn't let blood flow to my face or shift my posture. Instead, I shrugged.

"We're on the west side of LA, more or less," I said casually. "Whittier's on the east side, over the river. But not too far over."

"Are there trees?"

"The preserve has trees."

"They were arguing about whether to hang him from a tree or do it at the compound? I pretended to be asleep. What they were saying? It was sick. My heart was sick. Even thinking of it now. I want to throw up."

She wasn't alone.

"Whose compound?"

"If I tell you, I want to be sick again. I want to tell someone who can stop it from happening."

"Whose compound?" I repeated, throat dry, ears pounding, adrenaline making it nearlu impossible to stay still.

"The old woman."

That was enough. I had it.

Breathe.

Touch St. Christopher.

Run. Run for the phone like a long-limbed animal on the Serengeti. Run like everything you love is on fire. Break the ground beneath your feet with the power of your steps. Stretch your gait past the length of your entire body. Fold space with your speed. Breath fire. Eat air. Take off. Fly.

I was going so fast, I slammed into a bank of phones on the back side of the Sequoia parking lot. First one broken. Second dead. The third had gum in the change slot. I picked it out. It wasn't quite hard yet. I spit on it. Pulled it off.

I had Daniel's two jukebox quarters. I jammed one in the slot. Pushed it past the sticky residue with the second quarter. They both fell in.

I stopped myself before I touched the keys. I had to dial right because I didn't have more quarters.

Twoonethreesevenfourtwothreethreeohnine.

Ring.

Ring.

"Daniel?"

The sheets rustled. "Theresa. What time is it? Where are you?"

"Late. Early. I need your help. Like, now."

He took a deep, waking-up type breath. "Yes. Okay. I was worried about you."

"Valentina's here."

"You found her?" He jumped at the chance to ask, "Is she all right?"

I caught sight of Antonio's wife scuttling toward me. "She's fine. She asked about you." I didn't know why I felt the need to soothe Daniel's ego. Maybe I needed to feel something positive in the middle of a shit storm, or maybe I needed a coin of goodwill in a pocketful of resentment.

"What do you need?" he asked.

"It's… I mean it's so bad. There are so many moving parts. You just have to trust me. They have Antonio at Donna Maria's. They're going to kill him, or they've killed him already."

A breath. More sheets rustling. "Theresa, I can't do much. My credibility is shot."

"I can't get there. I don't even know where it is."

More sheets. A crisper voice. "She lives in the preserve, past the federal parkland. It's a point of contention, but slow down. How do you know?"

"Valentina overheard them. Please, please, I'll tell you everything. I'll tell you how I know. I'll tell you about Paulie. Just get someone over there."

"That's the problem. It's not accessible to local authorities. It's three miles into Turner Canyon."

"You can't call federal marshals? Are you serious?" Desperation forced my voice a few octaves higher.

"If I send them, anything they find could land him in a courtroom."

"Save his life, Daniel. Please."

"How did it all end up like this?"

"Will you or won't you?" I needed confirmation. I needed it nailed to the wall so I could stare at it and make sure it was real.

"I'll try. I'll make the calls. I'll throw my weight around. What little I have left. Just… she overheard them? What did she overhear? I can't send them without a reason."

"*Sbudellarlo,*" I said. The phone clicked. I didn't know why. I'd used a payphone twice in my life.

"Ah, I heard of that when I prosecuted the Taorminas. I'm sorry. I kind of liked him after the other day."

"Don't you ever speak about him in the past tense," I growled, but he said nothing. "Daniel? Daniel?"

The phone was dead. My money had run out.

Chapter Forty-Six

THERESA

"I need your car keys," I said.

I had to get somewhere quickly in Los Angeles, and I had no car.

Margie wasn't taking the urgency seriously, arms folded, sensible shoe tapping the hospital linoleum. "Why?"

"Because."

"That car is registered to me. If it's going to be used in the commission of a crime, I could get disbarred."

"Give me the keys and report it stolen. But give me half an hour to get across town."

"You just admitted you're committing a crime."

"I did not. I was trying to make you feel better. I'm going home. I'm going to bed. I'll be back in the morning to visit Jonathan."

She twisted her bag around so she could reach inside and yanked out a string of keys. She popped off a black key fob and put it in my outstretched hand.

"Thank you," I said.

"Leave me some gas."

I walked away.

"Theresa," she called, and I turned. "Your jacket. In the back."

I reached behind me and felt cold metal. My jacket had slipped behind the gun, exposing it. I didn't thank her. I just got into the elevator.

She got in front of the doors. "Theresa."

"It's all right. I'm just tired."

"Be good. As good as you can be. Okay?"

I was about to promise her I'd be good, but the doors closed before I could lie.

Chapter Forty-Seven

THERESA

Valentina had been waiting in the lobby like a lost puppy I couldn't get rid of. She'd gotten in step behind me and followed me to Margie's car.

I thought of shaking her but decided against it. She was a grown woman, and I didn't have time. She got in the car as if I'd said it was all right, her sense of entitlement as unshakeable as a holy sacrament.

"He could be already dead," she said from the passenger seat.

I got hot everywhere. My hands. My back. My face must have been a searing shade of purple. I'd never felt so angry in the face of the sheer emptiness of the world.

I was supposed to do something when I felt like that. Breathe. *Respira.* Touch the St. Christopher medal.

Of course, touching the medal did nothing. It did not fix the situation. It did not change the danger Antonio was in or transmit his whereabouts into my head. It only reminded me that I was capable of anything, and that even in my savagery, I was a child of the universe and loved by God.

That's all.

I tapped the GPS on the dash, getting a satellite picture of the slice of wilderness between Whittier and Hacienda Heights. Take the 10 east to the 605 South. Off on Beverly. Left. Right. Left onto a dirt road, along a drive into a nondescript house with no address. That had to be the one. It was the only structure in the area large enough to be a house and small enough to be hidden.

"What will you do if he is?" she asked. "Dead, that is."

"Kill all of them." I didn't check for her reaction. If she got to ask off-the-cuff questions about what I'd do with my life, then I got to answer in the immediate.

The 10 was empty, but I stayed a little over the speed limit. Getting pulled over wouldn't get me there any quicker, and I had a loaded gun in the glove compartment.

"Do you know how many men he's killed?" she asked. "Would you like to count? How many wives he left crying? How many children he left without fathers? This isn't something we have to like, but maybe it's justice."

"You left your own son without a father. Where's justice for you?"

"Antonin is better off."

I didn't know how to get through to her. I didn't know what to say, because she was right. Antonio had been damned before he ever set eyes on me. He'd made years' worth of choices that were beyond deplorable. He'd let his rage set his mind to murder again and again, trying to set the scales straight and only making the weight of his crimes greater and greater. There would be no forgiveness for him, not in this world or the next.

"You said he was sweet when you met," I said.

"He was so nice," she said wistfully. Had she been like this when they met? Or had he destroyed her too?

"He said you were gentle. He said you were innocent and beautiful. I think he thought you could save him," I said.

"I kept trying."

"And he kept getting worse."

She nodded.

"He's done everything wrong," I said. "I know he has. He was in the life, and he killed… I don't even know how many men inside his organization. Too many. One is too many. I'm not excusing it. But I think he can be saved. I think we can get that man back. The one you married. Maybe not totally. He'll never forget these years. But that man who brought you strawberries and was gentle and kind? He's still in there, and I think he's ready to be free."

"I'm so confused."

"You're right to be."

"Do you think he can come back?"

"I do." I didn't warn her that he wasn't coming back to *her,* and if he did, then she and I would have a deep, long-standing problem. "He was trying to get out of the life. There's nothing he wants more than an end to it."

"I wish he really was dead," she said, staring at the edge of the morning skyline. It wasn't even close to sunrise, and the city was as quiet as it ever was.

"Yeah, I get that."

I did truly understand. She'd come to Los Angeles to pay respects to a husband she hadn't seen in ten years and wound up at the center of a mob war over a bride he'd abandoned for another woman. If he'd been dead, she'd have closure. If he'd been dead, she could grieve and let go. He'd never change. He would be the subject of her prayers for years to come. I saw her so clearly, and I felt nothing but compassion.

"If you want to leave and go home to your son, I think you'll be forgiven. At least by me. Whatever happens will happen without you."

"Everything already happened without me," she said as I turned off the freeway.

More would happen without her, because whatever I was stepping into, she would be a liability if she came along.

I remembered the map and turned down the dark routes and ways without much trouble until I hit a high fence with barbed wire on top. I parked the car to the side of the road and shut off the lights. The moon was diffused by the rainclouds, which had closed the sky to a slight drizzle.

I should have left Valentina at the hospital, or the freeway entrance, or anywhere but in the middle of nowhere.

"You should stay here," I said.

"Yes," she replied with a sharp nod. "I will."

"I'll be back with Antonio."

"Yes, you will."

"If one of us isn't back by the time the sun is up, can you drive?"

"Of course I can drive. I'm not stupid."

"I'll leave the keys in the ignition."

"Go. Please." She pushed my shoulder with one hand and pointed out the door with the other. "Save him."

"Thank you, Valentina. You're all right."

"You may call me Tina." She shook her hand at the door again.

I took a deep breath and got out.

Chapter Forty-Eight

THERESA

The fence was high enough to be a real obstacle. I'd never climbed a fence, but what I lacked in skill, I made up for in not giving a shit. I was careful, because the chain link was wet from the rain. I got through a gap in the barbed wire right over the entrance hinge while staring into the camera because honestly, I wouldn't trick myself into thinking I knew how to get in without anyone knowing.

I dropped onto the mud and took the gun out of my back waistband. I had no idea how many bullets I had in it. It was heavy, so I knew it wasn't empty, but beyond that, I was at a loss. Yet another place where my instincts highlighted the gaps in my knowledge. If we lived, we were going to laugh about this.

Respira.

The rain had stopped, leaving clear air and good visibility, as little as there was. I took a deep breath and ran. It was dark as hell, and I lifted my feet to clear the mud and tree roots. I was sure I was running in the right direction. I had no cause to be sure, but I was. So I ran faster, and when I saw a dim light ahead, I knew I had been right.

Run. Run like this is the last hour of your life. Run as if there will be nothing left to run to tomorrow. Crush the ground. Pull it off its moorings. Make your mark in this world because it is your last chance. You are about to die. Take off. Fly.

My forward momentum came to an abrupt halt and my thoughts spun on their axis as I hit an obstacle full-on. A yielding obstacle that grunted. A man. I scrambled to a crouch and turned around. Unmoored, I had no idea which direction he was in. I held out my gun as if I could aim at anything but the world at large with my senses scrambled.

My legs went out from under me again, and light and dark went upside down, or right side up, and the ground hit me hard enough to push the air from my lungs.

On my back, I pointed the gun at the cloud-diffused light of the moon.

A form blocked out the light, and I heard a hammer cock.

I squeaked because it was too soon, because I had things I still had to do and I had a tiny bit of air left in my lungs with which to do them. My vocal cords engaged that last breath, and my squeak was audible.

That saved my life.

The form shifted a little, and I kept my gun on him. His face was in shadow, but I didn't need to see the details to shoot him.

He moved his gun away from me, putting up his hands.

"Don't shoot," he croaked. "They'll hear it."

I breathed. It was a hitched inhale made with the very tops of my lungs, but I lived to breathe again. "Antonio?" I kept the gun on him, because I wasn't sure, and the feeling of peril saturated my consciousness.

"Breathe," he said, still struggling to speak.

I scrabbled to my feet without using my gun hand, because I didn't trust that it was him. I didn't trust that the sky was up and the mud was down. My finger was outside the trigger guide. I wouldn't accidentally shoot him, but my brain had short-circuited and I wasn't convinced I shouldn't.

"Prove it," I said.

I expected whoever he was to either kill me or start talking, but he didn't. He pushed my hand out of the way and laid his lips on mine. I tasted him, the sting of burned pine and blood. The arm with the gun went around his shoulders as he owned me with his kiss. Alive. He was alive. In my arms. If we died in the next ten minutes, we would be together. My chest expanded and contracted with relief, and my breaths became short and deep while my eyes fogged with tears.

"Stop," he said.

"How?" I took him in. No shirt. Wet skin against freezing cold. The side of his face was too dark. "What did they do to you?"

"They had no idea how fast I could run. Come on."

He pulled me toward the gate. Behind him, voices. Yelling. Whistling.

"We're going to run?" I said.

"We have to."

I yanked him toward me. "Again?"

"They'll kill you."

"How many bullets are in this gun?"

He let the pressure on my hand go. "You can't—"

"We can end this," I said. "We need to. You can't protect me. I know it's your instinct, but you can't. Face it. The more you try to protect me, the worse it gets."

With everything crashing down on us, time froze. Antonio froze. The kiss he'd left on my mouth tasted like years with him. I'd die with it on me.

The pressure to move toward the gate disappeared as he considered. The line of shouting men from the house got closer. Louder. More intense.

Antonio let me go.

He turned and aimed at them, and I followed suit. I doubted there were enough bullets between us to make any kind of difference. Maybe if every one found a home. Maybe in the event they were all unarmed. Maybe if God was with us, which was unlikely.

Suddenly, they were all cast in bright light. Drowned in shadowless white. Antonio knocked me out of the way a second after I heard the roar of an engine and the creak and scrape of something being dragged.

A car roared past us, pushing a nice length of barbed-wire-topped gate. The men chasing us had to jump over the wire. A couple didn't make it and sprawled away with injuries.

"Margie's going to kill me," I said, getting my feet under me. "That's Valentina. I don't know what she's thinking, but we can't run now."

I stood over Antonio. With his face and chest to the light of the night sky, I saw what they'd done to him, and they were all going to die. I was going to leave a swath of blood across Los Angeles. The decision was calculated. I couldn't detect any emotions in it. Just facts.

He was on his feet like a cat. "With you, I can do anything."

Chapter Forty-Nine

ANTONIO

I'd plucked the gun from Carlo's hand. He'd made the mistake of letting his attention wander while he was alone in the room with me. I'd been ready to die, but there was no reason not to avoid it if I could.

They were clearly interested in my territory and readying to make sure my death at the hands of an old woman was recorded. I would have given every penny to them if there were rules to achieve such a thing. But there weren't, because too many had changed their minds later and brought war.

Kill. Die. Run. Those were the only ways out, and I'd already tried two of the three.

So as much as I'd been running for my life before I crashed into Theresa, I was ready to attack. I had been running because I had no choice. I was attacking because with her, it was possible.

She attacked with me, running in the shadows alongside the car while we could, because they'd assume I was still headed to the gate and they had no idea she was even there.

Get to the house. Attack. Assault. Confront. That much was understood between us. We didn't have a plan any more detailed than that.

The trees opened into the small clearing in front of Donna Maria's house. The light of the car changed behind us, and I turned to look. Valentina had shaken the gate and was making a U-turn. I stopped.

"Jesus," Theresa said.

Valentina headed in the opposite direction. The two men that were left jumped out of her way. They shot at the car, but it kept moving. If she made it out, she'd just keep driving. Theresa and I had no way out of the miles of preserve. I was in no worse position than I had been when I'd crashed into her.

I glanced at her as she watched the car, then she turned back to me.

"No turning back," she said.

She was a cat. A beautiful devil. I feared and admired her. I wished I could fuck her one last time, but I would have to do without. "Let's go."

Chapter Fifty

THERESA

Even with the crazy circumstances, I had expectations. I thought the head of a mafia family would have a house made of dark wood and fat moldings with crystal and doilies. What I got was a squeaky wooden gate leading to a house with worn furniture and the smell of food deep in the fabrics. I touched Antonio's arm and pointed at a corner piled full of bright plastic and googly eyes. He nodded. There were kids around. I didn't have to say a word.

He leaned down and spoke in my ear. "House in the back. I'm going to take her out."

I didn't know who the men were outside. I only knew they shouted, and their voices got closer. The sound waves bounced off the wetness left in the air, making them seem to be everywhere all at once.

Antonio and I, as if pulled by the same strings, looked back through the open door to see them coming. They were going to follow us to the back and pick us off. We'd be dead before we started.

We didn't have to speak. I didn't have time to process the feeling of connection between us, only to react, skipping the niceties.

"I'll go upstairs." I was already leaning toward the stairway.

He grabbed my arm. "No."

"Let me draw the fire. Split them up."

"No!"

"We're together. I swear it. Dead or alive, you're with me. But we, both of us, won't get out unless I draw fire and you take care of business."

Time compressed again, and he spent minutes, hours even, considering.

He grabbed the back of my head and smashed his lips to mine, then jerked away. "Go, before I change my mind."

I stepped back with the sound of approaching hell through the squeaky gate, getting one last look at Antonio in his shirtless wonder. A warrior. A king. My capo, always always always.

I turned and ran up the stairs to a long dark hallway lined with open doors. I got my bearings. I needed to go left in order to face the back. I went through a door halfway down the hall.

It was a nursery. A girl's. Fluffy things. White crib. Soft colors made grey in the darkness. Across from the hall door, French doors to a balcony overlooking the back. I went out and leaned on the railing. The sky turned blueish with morning, and I saw a field lined with animal hutches. They scratched and wailed in nocturnal frustration.

To the left, a house with the lights on. That must be where Donna Maria was. I had to make sure he got in there.

Antonio ran out. I was ready. I held up the gun, waiting for whoever followed him. I was to distract them and draw fire to myself so Antonio could end this by killing an old woman. I was all right with that. We were both going to hell anyway.

I heard them clamor. Antonio looked back into the house before continuing into the yard.

"You're going to hurt yourself with that thing."

I spun back toward the nursery, gun out. Donna Maria stood there holding a baby. It was sleeping. I lowered my weapon when I saw the child.

Donna Maria Carloni smiled.

Chapter Fifty-One

ANTONIO

There were no shots from above. Either she was dead or she'd changed her mind, and there was no way she'd changed her mind. I glanced up along a veranda and saw her with her back to the railing. Someone was with her. I couldn't make them out, but in the moment before Domenico ran out into the yard and I had to react, I regretted leaving her alone. Deeply regretted it.

But regret was a luxury for later. Domenico was followed closely by Zo, who had Enzo and Simone huffing and puffing at his heels. It had been a tough night for those guys, and it was about to get tougher. They were my crew, and to prove their new loyalty, they'd beaten the hell out of me.

I didn't blame them, and I didn't hold it against them. It was business.

I shot Domenico. He fell like a bag of rice.

Then I took aim at Zo, who I'd loved and trusted and who had sold me out at every turn. He stopped long enough to get a clean shot at me.

Chapter Fifty-Two

THERESA

I was confused. I had to clear the way for Antonio to get to Donna Maria, but she was here, right before me, with a baby. I couldn't shoot her, even at close range, with a child in her arms.

The first shot came from below. I spun to look over the railing before the sound was done echoing. A man dropped.

"I'm just an old woman," Donna Maria said, coming up next to me with the baby. "This breaks my heart."

Another man came. And another. The only one I could identify was Antonio. The rest weren't even men but shadows.

"It wasn't supposed to be like this," she continued. "It was supposed to be a business."

There was a dead pause below. A weighted moment when everyone froze.

I had a job. Donna Maria had made me forget it, and if she wanted to kill me for doing it, that was okay. I just had to clear the way for Antonio until he was safe. I could figure out what to do with the misplaced mob boss in a minute.

I held out the gun and took a shot at the last man who came out. It was dark, and the angle was impossible. I think I killed one of the animals, or a dandelion. But the last guy out looked up at us and took aim. I shot at him to draw fire, stepping back when he took aim. I popped off another one, with the *clack clack* of Antonio's shots in the background, and Donna Maria buckled next to me.

Fuck.

The baby dropped headfirst, and some biological instinct made me reach for it, even with the gun still in my hand. I couldn't fight evolution. I got close to Donna Maria as she fell to get my hands under the baby, feeling badly for forgetting to drop the gun, realizing how light the baby was, how smooth its face, how oddly peach.

It was a doll.

And I was close to her. Close enough for a blade to land inside me, releasing pain that shot outward as every cell in my body screamed. Close enough to see the pleasure on her face when she jerked the blade upward so hard my feet came off the floor.

I dropped the doll.

Donna Maria relieved me of my gun. "Thank you, *troia*."

How long would it take to die from a stab wound? Long enough to see Antonio's face below, his mouth a circle of terror as I bent over and blood fell from me.

I'm sorry.

I didn't actually say that. I wanted to. I felt my failure deeply. Antonio put his hands out, and I think he cried out. I think something came from him, but I was suddenly deaf from the rushing in my ears.

Lorenzo turned away from Donna Maria and me and faced Antonio, pointing his gun at him for his territory and his crew. His kingship.

Antonio! Watch out!

I didn't actually have the strength to say that either.

A flash of light and a pop came from Zo's weapon. Antonio spun.

And fell.

And stayed fallen for a millisecond too long.

In the rising light, with his knees bent and his gun two feet from his hand, he stayed down, the ground under his head gelling with mud-pattered blood.

I screamed *Antonio!*

But nothing came out. The scream was sucked back into my gut in the form of pain.

The light in my life had been taken from me, and I wanted only one thing in the world. To die. And to kill. Because inside the pain and the furious rush in my head was a cold place that needed to be taken care of.

I was on all fours. Breathing hurt. Living hurt. My legs shook uncontrollably, and I coughed a stream of blood, heaving air and moisture back in.

I looked up. Donna Maria stood over me. She didn't look old. She looked twenty. Forty tops. She looked like a woman untouched by her own mortality. I grabbed at her, my hand slipping down her corduroy pants. I was pathetic. But I grabbed for her again, and she stepped back.

I had her by the ankle when she stepped back, but I didn't have enough strength to keep my grip. My hands weren't doing what they were supposed to. They were dying, and the life flowing from them did so in waves. I'd caught her on a fisted wave when my hands were grasping and flattening, rigid and slack, completely out of my control. She fell.

My crawl slowed, and my body came closer to the ground. Something scraped.

Donna Maria grumbled and got up on her elbows as if she were lying on the beach, getting the sun. "This is over, my girl. All this foolish nonsense."

The scraping under me. The knife. She'd left it in me. I swiped at it. Missed. My hand had gone flat.

"You don't belong here," she said. "Coulda told you that. Coulda told that *stupido* downstairs with his face in the mud. You till your own soil. What are you going to do with that knife? Anything?"

She had my gun in her hand. She put it against my head. It didn't feel cold. I must have been freezing. I got a grip on the knife and jerked it out.

Pain engulfed me for a second. Stuff started swimming, and I stopped having coherent thoughts. I was going to black out.

Get it together, Theresa.

People came onto the veranda. Men. I didn't know who. I couldn't look at them and finish this job. My fist clamped around the hilt of the knife.

Donna Maria pulled the trigger.

Click.

There were no bullets left.

With my last breath of life, in the interval between milliseconds, where atoms play and thoughts happen so quickly they're lost before they're remembered, I lunged for her throat, knife in front of me. Because I was a killer in my heart, the knife understood what I wanted and lodged itself right below her jaw, where life pulsed.

She didn't even yell. She just sprang forward, blood spurting, mouth open in a soundless scream. I did the impossible and got on my feet. Zo stood in the doorway, meek and boring. Harmless, except when he wasn't. He'd shot Antonio, and I couldn't touch him. His world would continue, and Antonio and I had died together, as promised. I felt a profound loss as my last real emotion, and I understood what drove vengeance all of a sudden.

Envy.

That a wrongdoer would continue with their life while you could not.

That they took something and walked away unscathed.

That they had everything and you had nothing.

Envy. So insidious it could disguise itself as anger or righteousness and travel over seas and mountains to see itself satisfied.

Not having the strength or balance to support myself, I spun around. The edge of the railing bit my side, then nothing nothing nothing as I fell.

The ground.

Hard.

Harder than anything I'd ever felt.

Stuff crunched.

A bag of chips.

The bag was fine.

The chips.

Crushed.

But my name.

Contessa.

The mud hadn't made the ground any softer.

At the bottom of a ravine, a stupid boy twisted.

I'd felt nothing.

Oh my God, Theresa.

Oddly empty.

I'd killed him.

That hard earth under him.

Broken like a bag of chips.

I will kill them.

What had I done?

Wrong.

I'd done wrong.

And Paulie.

Who loved.

Who hurt.

And I felt.

All of them. I will God oh god oh

Regret.

Theresa. Theresatheresatheresa

My family would have to grieve again.

Margie would hate herself for giving me the car.

And Antonio would blame himself forever.

He would kill someone for this.

And that was hell enough.

To be loved so well.

That your death inspires regret.

And envy.

And you die swimming in it.

I opened my eyes. Everything was hard to do. Especially this. Opening my eyes. Breathing. Swallowing blood. But I knew the voice, and I had to see the sweet brown eyes and the lips curved for love one last time.

"Capo," I said. I think.

He had blood over one side of his face, under a gash where the bullet had swiped the side of his head. His mouth was twisted in a rictus of anger and sadness. I wanted to kiss it happy.

"Contessa."

"You're not dead."

"No, no. A scratch."

It was still bleeding. I couldn't see much, but I thought I saw bone.

"Please," I said, guts twisted so tight I could barely get the word out. "Do something for me."

"Anything."

I realized when I heard the sincerity in his voice that the rush of white noise in my ears was gone. I didn't know if it was the fall or if hearing Antonio's voice was God's last gift to me for something I couldn't give words. Not yet. Not until he promised.

"No revenge," I said. "Do not avenge me."

"Theresa—"

"Say it."

"I can't."

"You have to see past all that."

He moved my hair from my face. "I can't see in front of me. You are my life. I have nothing to hope for without you."

"Promise me."

He didn't answer. My lungs weren't holding air, and he was holding himself together with thread. Even in my state, I could see it. I could catch him now. I could get him to promise, then I could remember the thing and I could rest and—

"Promise." I barely breathed it.

He waited forever to answer, as if he couldn't lie to a dead woman so he had to make sure he'd only speak the truth. I kept mouthing the word, waiting for a response, but it got harder with every repetition. Because. The thing.

Promise promise promise

"Yes," he said. "I promise."

"No vengeance?"

"*Come vuoi tu.*"

The thing was the flood of memories of my years on earth. The adult years between the boy and his fingers and the man with the espresso eyes. All those years I was good. All those years I'd chosen happiness. I remembered my sisters and school, and pretty dresses and stupid kindnesses. Katrina. My brother. Rachel. The assistants I'd trained and the good, honest, ethical years of work I gave. None of it made up for what I'd become, but my life hadn't been a waste. Hadn't been a lie.

"Thank you."

I started falling before I even pronounced the first syllable, the gratitude catching my fall into a blackness that grew into the darkness of a truck that smelled like gunpowder and pine, rumbling from Tijuana to Los Angeles. I remembered olive orchards and a life not lived. The wheels under us *hup-shh hup* like a heartbeat. Antonio above me, stroking my eyelids closed and whispering, *This is the day they went to live in the olive orchards. When you close your eyes for the last time, this will be this day you remember as the first day of the long happiness of your life. You will smile your whole journey to heaven.*

Chapter Fifty-Three

DANIEL

There's an old Italian saying. I can't pronounce it, and I'm probably misquoting it entirely, but it goes, "When the snake is dead, the venom is dead."

I don't think that's true. Not in every case. For me, the venom died when I thought Theresa was dead after the wedding. For Antonio, when he was leaning over Theresa on Donna Maria Carloni's compound, I knew his venom was dead. He was broken. Utterly broken.

It was a fucking mess, the whole thing. I'd rushed to the compound as soon as I realized the sheriff's office wasn't going to call the feds and no one gave a shit because the snake had paid all of them to leave her alone on her land.

I knew that because I'd gotten my share.

I'd seen Valentina chewing her nails on the side of the road. She stood near a silver Mercedes that had been having a make-out session with a chain-link fence and barbed wire. She couldn't explain a word in English, so I put her in the car and took her into the compound, following the divots she'd made with the gate.

I took her hand. I hadn't touched her before, but I had a feeling her husband was dead. She broke down crying. I didn't love her then, but I thought I could, maybe. If I got out of that compound in one piece. They'd already trussed me up and hung me from the ceiling. These families weren't known for lowering the stakes from encounter to encounter. I was unarmed, unskilled, and I'd be unaccounted for for a long time if they decided to bury me here.

In retrospect, I was either really brave or really stupid. At the time, I'd felt as though I didn't have any choice but to, at the very least, witness what was happening. Jesus, what a way to get myself killed.

But I kept going. I told Valentina to stay in the car, and she drew the tops of her fingers under her chin and flung them at me. I think she was telling me to go fuck myself. Must have been, because she got out with me.

I'd never seen the actual compound. It was more modest than I thought it would be, and it was a wreck. In the front yard, two women and four children, from twelve to a few months, huddled in the morning light.

"Are you all right?" I asked one of the women. I recognized her as Irene Carloni.

They didn't answer.

"*Stai bene?*" Valentina asked.

Irene, who I knew spoke English, made the same motion Valentina had, a drawing of the fingers under the chin.

"*Omertà,*" Valentina said as I headed into the house. "They will never say."

I smelled gunpowder, heard the batshit squeal of small animals, and ran out to the back. I saw a man's body, his face in the mud. Simone Fiore and Lorenzo Desano stooped together. Hutches of animals. A bloody grate. My eyes fell on Antonio Spinelli, on his knees next to Theresa.

Blood, everywhere. I mean… everywhere and—

Valentina fell apart, but I couldn't—

So I went to them. Antonio looked up and said—

I didn't know what Lorenzo and Simone were up to. Enzo Priole appeared. There was some conflict. Some questions that hadn't been answered.

Jesus Christ, she'd been gutted. I just—

"Can you kill me?" Antonio's question was absolutely sincere.

He was losing his mind, and I couldn't blame him. I couldn't even process a story around what I was seeing. He had blood pouring from his head, and his bruised and welted torso was bare to the winter air.

"I'm not killing you."

I knelt by her. I thought I looked calm. I pushed back the creeping emotions, but I'd feel them later. I knew that. I was a heartless asshole, except when I wasn't.

"How did this happen?" I asked. Even in death, she was beautiful. I touched her face. I didn't care if I got blood on my hands.

Antonio just shook his head. He was in shock.

"Spin." Lorenzo stood over us.

"Get the fuck away from me," Antonio shouted. "You're so fucking lucky you're not dead."

"The Sicilians. Their boss is dead. She—"

Antonio sprang up, took Lorenzo by the collar, and slammed him against a wall. "This is on you, Zo. On you. You got ambition and no brains."

"If you're gonna kill me, just do it!"

"I can't!" Antonio let him go, and Lorenzo dropped.

"Her people are coming. Donna's dead." Lorenzo pointed at Theresa. "She did it, and she's dead. What the—"

"Fuck you!" Antonio was beyond reason.

Lorenzo had a point. If Theresa had killed Donna, a crazy thought I had to just accept at face value, and Donna killed Theresa, the Carloni family had no leader.

"There's a power vacuum," I mumbled, leaning close to Theresa's face.

"Say you done her," Lorenzo said. "Say it, or they'll crush us. Take charge."

"No! No more. I'm done!"

Their fight fell into the background as I bent over Theresa. I'd seen so many dead people, and the one thing I could say about them was that they looked like statues of themselves. Glass blue eyes and hard lips. I put my thumbs on Theresa's eyelids and closed them, and I felt something I shouldn't have.

Warmth.

"You stupid motherfucker," I said, standing. "There is no power vacuum." I had only a second to see Antonio's red eyes on me before I stared at my phone, trying to figure out who to call.

"What?" Antonio said.

"She's alive."

Chapter Fifty-Four

ANTONIO

I didn't realize how crazy I was until I came out of it. It was like being on a descending airplane with compressed ears that whooshed until I yawned or swallowed. Then everything cleared up. I didn't even think I was foggy and deaf until the pressure equalized.

Daniel saying she was alive was that pop. I didn't know what I'd been feeling or doing. I only knew what I couldn't do, which was kill Lorenzo. I'd promised her I wouldn't. Not being able to take him out meant I didn't have a distraction. A little shiny violent thing to experience or a problem to solve. I had to lose her and feel it without diversion. I didn't think I could live through actually feeling that level of pain.

I was a child. I'd been naïve and inexperienced. I thought I'd grieved before, but no—I hadn't allowed it. In the seven or so minutes that I lost Theresa, all I saw was a long descent into oblivion. I despaired for myself as much as I did for her. I couldn't handle it. I didn't have the tools to comprehend a part of myself getting ripped away. I couldn't even finish a sentence in my head. I was half a man. Half a human. Immobilized by a promise and sucked dry by the only death that mattered.

That all came to me after the pop.

She was alive and broken. She could still die, but what I'd been missing in those minutes filled me. Hope. It was the nature of clarity. It set off everything against it. In that tension between what I hoped for and everything else, the world was in focus. I came to myself. I had something to *do.*

I put my hand over Daniel's phone.

"Who are you calling?" I asked.

"Nine one one. We can't move her."

"Trust me."

I made the call crouched over her, noticing the signs of life I'd missed in my despair. The team from Marymount who had taken shrapnel out of Bruno's hand were coming. They were discreet and expensive. I prayed while I told them where we were. I prayed they'd be quick, that I hadn't delayed too long.

Enzo came to me when I got off the phone. "Zo wants—"

"Keep him out of my sight."

"Are you taking charge? Is it you?"

I pulled Enzo away from Daniel. "Did I kill Donna Maria?"

"How should I answer that?" he asked.

"The truth. Who killed her?"

He pointed at Theresa timidly, as if afraid to say.

"There's your capo. Now back up. I said I wouldn't kill anyone. I made no promises about shooting your legs out from under you."

IN THE MINUTES before the ambulance arrived, Zo, Simone, and Enzo whispered. Two of Donna Maria's men showed up. I heard a car in the driveway, and my three crew, the three betrayers who now officially worked for Theresa, subdued Donna Maria's men. Daniel fidgeted. We were both holding back a panic that Theresa's life was pouring out of her and we couldn't do anything.

"You should go," I said, bending over her, afraid to touch her for fear of something broken inside her.

"Fuck you."

"No, fuck you. Get Valentina out of here."

He nodded. "This won't stay under the radar. Too big. It's too big."

The sound of the siren reached us.

"Go," I said.

He took one last glance at Theresa then jogged into the house, passing a cluster of mob soldiers as if we were all commuters on the same train.

Chapter Fifty-Five

THERESA

Pain. I remember pain. My insides. My bones. The place where the needles were. And the itching. The itching was so intense, I thought I'd go mad. But I couldn't move, or talk, or even control my own breathing. I was half conscious, immobilized, in a fog as thick as peanut butter.

I knew I was moved. I knew I was cut open and sewn up. I smelled alcohol and latex, so I knew I was in some kind of hospital. But none of that was important. My body became the responsibility of other people, and my job was to stay still and endure it.

I knew I wasn't alone. That was what was important. That kept me from a confined madness. Margie was there. And my mother. Deirdre. Even Daniel.

But Antonio wasn't. I loved my family. I wanted them, craved them. But I had a creeping concern in my half consciousness that my demand that he not take vengeance wasn't the end of the story of that day.

I prayed for him a lot. Every day that passed with the light coming in, diffused by my eyelids and warming my face, my worry grew. He wouldn't just leave me. Something had to have happened. Something terrible.

"Sit." Margie's voice came through. I didn't think she was talking to me.

"I'm on my ass all day." Jonathan. This was his second visit.

"You had a heart transplant three weeks ago. Your ass isn't half finished."

A chair scraped. "I hate this."

"I'll be an old woman one day, and you can make me sit down when I need to."

I listened for a third person, but no one came. Not one of the hundred doctors. Not a nurse. Not Antonio.

Where's Antonio? I tried to say it and failed.

"You're never getting old, Margaret. Not if you can fix it."

"There are some things a fixer can't even fix."

Every time they came and went, I forgot then remembered. They bickered and joked. They did it out of rote. All of them except Deirdre, who'd prayed out her sense of humor. Even Mom could cut deep with a single word, and just that day, I couldn't bear it.

Antonio.

"You need to put that as an exclusion in the contract," Jonathan quipped.

"Once I can get some blood out of you to sign it in."

Antonio. Please.

"Did she just say something?" Margie asked.

A chair creaked.

"Sit down," Margie snapped.

I opened my eyes. The light felt like knives in my head and my tear ducts went into production mode, fogging everything. I blinked. I felt the drops rush down the side of my head. When I opened my eyes again, Margie's face blocked the light.

"Well, hello."

Antonio.

"Eyes open," she said to Jonathan then looked back at me. "How are you?"

"Antonio." I couldn't believe I got the word out. Every syllable was exhausting.

"He's fine."

"Swear?"

She held up her hand. "Pledge open." She pulled two of my fingers off the sheets.

"Open," I whispered.

"Antonio is alive and healthy. He walks, he talks, he is very, very worried about you. I'll tell him you asked about him. He's going to shit a brick with joy, but he can't visit. Don't be mad at him."

"I'm not."

"All right. I'm going to call a doctor to look at you."

"Tell him…" I swallowed. I didn't know what to say. Everything. "Tell him he's my capo."

"Funny you should say that. He says the same about you. Pledge closed."

I had more to say. More questions. More statements. More more more.

But I didn't even have the energy to close the pledge. Consciousness left and was replaced by a worry-free sleep.

Chapter Fifty-Six

THERESA

I would only ever ask Margie about Antonio, and she constantly reassured me that he was fine. She promised she'd tell me everything. She changed the subject. She told me not to say more because I couldn't see who was in the room.

"Talk to me, or I'll scream." I couldn't have screamed if I wanted to, but the threat was enough to get her to lean over and look at my face.

"Oh, someone's feeling better," Margie said.

"I can feel my body."

"You're so lucky you're not paralyzed. Have I mentioned that?" She pulled her chair close.

"Can you tell me where he is? Did he go home? To Italy?" I swallowed. I couldn't do much more than swallow and blink.

"No. He's in California. And by California, I mean… the state of."

California. Huge state. In the geography of love, it was a nanostate. In the geography of need—it was massive.

"Just tell me."

"It can wait," she said.

"Tell me. Please."

She leaned over me, deep in thought, then sat down. I had a view of the grey ceiling again.

"I want you to remember, as I tell you this, that he's fine."

My chest constricted. Had he run off with Valentina? A machine beeped somewhere.

"Easy, kid. If you make the doctors come in, this conversation ends."

I breathed. I felt the ends and edges of my body, calming them. I'd done that when reporters asked me about my cheating fiancé. I'd done it when talking to Donna Maria for the first time. I'd done it my whole life, and I did it on that bed.

"Okay," I said when I was ready.

"Okay."

"Go, Margie. You're stalling."

She sighed then continued. "There wasn't a mob doctor in California who could help you. He made a choice. He turned himself in. He and Daniel hammered out his story. He said he stabbed you in a lover's quarrel and you fell off the veranda. Everyone in the house corroborated. Valentina said she ran the fence in a jealous rage. No grand jury. No indictment. No nothing."

"Wait… I… there were—"

Bodies.

Blood.

Bullets.

"A wall of silence," Margie said. "Donna Maria Carloni and Domenico Uvoli disappeared. Poof. No one's seen them."

There were holes, but I couldn't get my head around them while one question remained. "He turned himself in? What does that mean?"

"We made the indictment over Paulie go away. There was enough evidence to claim self defense for that, but for what happened to you… look…he skipped everything and copped a plea. I shouldn't tell you since I'm not even supposed to know the details, but I arranged his lawyer, and I'm yours, so there's that."

"Where is he?" I couldn't bear saying it, because the answer—

"He's in prison, Theresa." Her hand was on mine. She squeezed it.

"But—"

"Listen to me. You fought over Valentina. He stabbed you. He threw you off a second-story veranda. That's the end of it. If anyone asks you anything, you say you don't remember. Your memory is fucked beyond repair."

"How long, Margie?"

"If you decide to go honest, a lot of people you love are going away for a long time."

"How long is he in? Tell me!"

She breathed hard then spit it out. "Ten."

"Ten years?" I squeaked my last breath, because my god, my god, a decade?

"Listen…"

I was crying before she finished the word. I heard something about parole. I heard something about good behavior and not making it worse. But I was wrecked.

I had to know if I was allowed to forgive the fake stabbing. I had to know who knew what because I'd been holding on to this string of hope and it was about to break. But I couldn't, because I was crying so hard I couldn't speak. Then the doctors came, and I pretended to know nothing about anything.

Chapter Fifty-Seven

THERESA

I found it easier to just not talk. When the cops came, I claimed to remember nothing of the incident. So sorry. Shrug. Daniel didn't let the interviewer press too long.

"Dan," I asked when it was over, "the election? It's March, almost."

He smiled at me. "I got out in time. And you're my last case I'm overseeing as DA."

He wasn't actually the prosecutor. He couldn't be. But he seemed to be around all the time.

"Then what?"

"I can do commercial litigation, I think? Private sector stuff. I'm still a good lawyer."

"No public advocacy?" I asked.

"My public life is over. Too many proverbial skeletons in the proverbial closet."

"I'm sorry, Dan. It was all my fault."

"No. It was my fault, and it's better this way." He held up his hands. The nails were unbitten. "Less stress. I swear, I get up in the morning feeling… what's the opposite of overwhelmed?"

"Underwhelmed?"

"Not that."

"I know what you mean."

"It'll all be all right. I promise." He squeezed my hand.

But I wanted to die. I missed Antonio every minute of every day. I wanted his company so much I couldn't go to physical therapy some days, and when they took the nylon cast off with a loud *kkkkt* of Velcro, I wanted his touch on my body so badly, I wished they'd put the damned thing back on me.

"Where do you want to go?" Margie asked on my last day at Sequoia.

"Do I still have my loft?" I sat on the edge of the bed, considering the fact that I'd never see those walls again, and I had to face a world without Antonio.

"Yeah. I had it cleaned."

"Okay." I got on my shoes. I could walk, if slowly.

"There are some guys who want to talk to you before you go."

"I don't remember anything."

"Other guys. Names ending in vowels."

I just looked at her. I knew who she meant, more or less. I had no idea why they'd want anything to do with me though.

"You're safe. I have my guy on them. Sit in the chair, would you?"

I turned slowly and sat. I was in a wide skirt because it was easy to get on and a blouse that hid the hunch in my left shoulder. It would take years to fix me completely, and even then, I'd be at ninety percent.

Ninety percent was a miracle. I had to remember that.

Antonio was alive. That was a miracle as well.

And when Lorenzo, Enzo, and Simone shuffled in with Otto trailing behind them, I discovered another miracle.

"Boss," Lorenzo said handing me a fat manila envelope, "I want to offer you an apology and a tribute. I was trying to help us in the organization, and I done wrong. I can't ever make it up to you, but you have my service if you want it."

The envelope flopped back and forth where he held it.

"I'm not Italian," I said, snapping it from him.

"Yeah. It's gonna be a problem."

He obviously didn't even want to talk to me. Otto dropped his envelope on top.

"This is my month, Otto said. "Been great, gotta say, with the Sicilians off our backs."

I peeked into the envelopes. They were stuffed with twenties and hundreds. I thought I should just step down, but there was a reason that was impossible. Killing a boss didn't come without consequences.

"As far as I'm concerned, Antonio runs this operation," I said. "If you have a question or you need something, you go to him and you ask him. This is done, right? When the boss is put away? You visit?"

"Yes," Lorenzo said.

"You bring me the tributes. I'll take care of it. The rest goes through him. I need you guys to keep the peace. I know you want that." I looked at them each individually, stopping at Zo. "You tried to kill Antonio, and you turned everyone against him. It was for peace. I understand that, so there won't be retribution, but we can never trust you again."

He nodded like a shamefaced dog. I didn't feel sorry for him or envy him.

"Go. Visit Antonio."

They scuttled out. Only Otto made eye contact, and I winked at him.

I had this. Eventually, after enough torment, we'd give it all back to them. Even Lorenzo. He'd been loyal to his men and worked for peace instead of war. He'd do fine.

But first, I would rule.

EIGHTEEN MONTHS LATER

Chapter Fifty-Eight

THERESA

I hadn't visited. He didn't want me to. He didn't want the parole board to think he would get out and stab me again. That was what he said, but I thought he just didn't want me to see him behind bulletproof glass. I wrote him letters four times a week, keeping it all above board with newsy news and short declarations of love, and he wrote back with little in the way of prison happenings. It was obvious he didn't want me to know.

The only thing I insisted on telling him over the phone was the only thing that might keep him from returning to me.

"What is it?" he'd said. "It's nothing. I know already. It won't keep me from you."

I'd started crying almost immediately. I missed his voice. I craved his hands. I wasted thirty seconds of a two-minute phone call trying to put myself back into a staid little box.

"Don't tell me," he said. "Whatever it is—"

"I can't…" My breath hitched. Got it together. "Because of the injuries. I can't have children."

"Contessa—"

"I understand if that's a deal-breaker for you."

"I saw what happened, my love. This isn't a surprise."

It was exactly that response that soothed me. If he hadn't already known, I might have thought he was just gathering strength to leave me, or that he hadn't digested what it meant. But he wasn't caught off guard. He'd already dealt with it, and he still wanted me. For months, I didn't know what that meant. Us wanting each other. Us "being with" each other. One year of separation or ten. Anything in between.

Over the course of his time in prison, I continued to insist I didn't remember anything from that night, and Margie pushed for parole from behind the person who actually claimed to be his lawyer.

"For you," she'd insisted. "I'm doing it for you. But if he hurts you, I'm coming down like a hammer."

I'd agree to anything. To get him out, I forked over everything the guys sent in tribute. Cash. Untraceable and convenient as hell for doing stuff like greasing wheels and buying an olive orchard in Temecula. I got a place with multiple buildings for my family and promised the children pony rides.

I thought of him every day. I slept on one side of the bed. I left his dresser drawers empty. I set him up with a desk and a space in the office before I even knew what it meant to run an orchard.

"You have pains," Valentina said as she wiped down a big ceramic bowl in my new kitchen. When she visited the orchard, she acted as if she owned the joint. "You should lie down."

"I'm fine."

She'd arrived that morning and taken on the chores as if she enjoyed them. She'd served Antonio with divorce papers soon after he was sentenced, and there hadn't been much fuss. He was a felon. The Church didn't like it, but the Church didn't have to. She handed him to me on a platter and announced that she didn't expect me to get in the way of her and Daniel.

I wouldn't, but I explained what my ex-fiancé had done and what she could expect from him. Apparently, she expected exactly what he had to give. That day, Daniel had illustrated exactly that by plopping himself on the couch when they arrived and watching a game with the men. He was still an irritating douchebag, but what could I do? He was family now.

"You look a little bent," Sheila said.

"I'm fine. Don't make me say it again."

"Yes, boss," Sheila and Valentina said in unison.

I snapped the dishtowel at both of them.

Zia nudged me to the side. "You're in the way."

"Sorry."

"You want to stand in front of the stove? You can cook." She took the lid off something brown and stewey and stirred it with a wooden spoon.

"No, no, I'm good! You cook."

She held up the sauce-smeared spoon. "Taste."

I blew on it and put my lips to the wood. "Oh my god, what is it?"

She flapped her hand at me. She was always impatient with what I didn't know.

"He's late," Jonathan said, strolling into the kitchen. "Maybe they decided to keep him." He plucked two glasses from the cabinet and filled them with water.

"That's not even funny."

"I'm not laughing," he said.

The children were though. And shouting. They tracked mud all over the kitchen. Bonnie opened the fridge and nearly dropped a gallon of milk.

"You left your wife on the patio to come in here and give me a heart attack?" I said to Jonathan.

He kissed my cheek. "She loves it here. We're buying the place next door."

I couldn't tell if he was serious or not, but I played the odds. "Knock before you visit."

He leaned on the counter. The kids had run back out, and I heard Sheila yelling at them from half a house away. Valentina and Zia had gone to prepare the buffet. Jonathan and I were alone.

He put up his right hand. "Open pledge."

I held up my hand. "Open."

"Swear he didn't stab you and throw you off a balcony."

"It was more of a second-story veranda."

"You're making me nervous."

I held my hand up as if taking the oath of office. "I swear, in pledge, that he didn't stab me and throw me off anything in the architectural lexicon. He has never laid a finger on me in anger or jealousy, and if he did, I'd kill him. Outside pledge, I'm sticking to my story."

I'd made the same pledge to just about every other sibling, in addition to swearing to my mother that it wasn't what it looked like. I tried not to speak to Dad alone, because I didn't have enough forgiveness in my heart for him.

I heard the crunch of dirt and rock and peered out the kitchen window. A black car came through the gate. I put my hand on my chest.

Jonathan flicked my ear. "Close pledge, sister."

"Closed."

I was ready. More than ready. I slapped my towel down and ran to the front door, whipping it open and nearly tripping over Antonin, who stood at the edge of the porch. I took a moment to look at him. He was a serious boy generally, but his sullen face was more thoughtful today than usual.

I stopped and leaned in to him. He was almost my height already.

"It's okay. He won't bite you. We talked about this. He's just a man," I said.

He nodded. I hugged him. He was a good kid, whip smart and acing every single class at Harvard-Westlake. He was a genius under pressure. Valentina said he was more like his father than her, but his sense of humor belonged to his mother. At least he didn't need half a glass of wine to bring it out.

Behind me, a car door slammed. And another as he was let out of the back of the limo.

I didn't think I could turn around, because once I did, the waiting was officially over. My life would begin and preparation would become action. I stood with our families on the porch, waiting.

"Capo," he said.

His voice. Music. An opera in two syllables.

I turned and nearly died, my gasp was so strong.

He was… Antonio.

Everything I remembered and imagined, but in three dimensions. In a white shirt and grey jacket, his thumb hooked on the shoulder strap of his bag, his face shaven, his brown hair falling into a parenthesis on his forehead. When he smiled, the sky opened and God himself showed his favor.

"You lost weight." My bottom lip trembled so hard I could barely get the last word out.

"The second worst part was the food."

I didn't say anything. I was too overwhelmed. I took in every detail. His ebony lashes. His lips, drawn across his face in a grin. I was supposed to ask him the worst part, but the breeze shifted and I was swept away in the scent of campfires and quiet pine forests.

"I missed you," I said. God, would I ever again get a word out without crying? I didn't know how to catalog the relief, the joy, and the feeling of utter liberation, because I'd been in prison with him.

He dropped his bag and engulfed me in his arms.

"I missed you I missed you…" I kept repeating, because I hadn't uttered it in a year and a half and it needed saying.

I felt a hand on my shoulder, and a pair of arms around my legs. I felt the breath and tears of our families as they gathered around us, shielding us with their bodies. I rested my cheek on his shoulder. This was my heaven, with him.

He rocked back and forth, holding me as if I were the last woman in the world. I hadn't been held like that since before the fall. I'd been broken in so many places, I was afraid to embrace anyone, but with Antonio, I wasn't scared to be held. I'd forgotten how safe he made me feel, how loved, how trusted. He could hold me and nothing inside me would break. I was fine.

Better than fine. I was whole.

Chapter Fifty-Nine

THERESA

The food was gone. The dishes were put away. The children were bathed and kissed. A few stragglers stayed up for late night TV.

All was dark.

Except the bathroom. It was white, and the light was on. I'd loved its brightness. I'd designed it so I could see everything, but now I wanted the light dimmed. Or off. Or warmer. I leaned into the mirror. I'd just gotten out of the shower. Hair stuck to my forehead, and droplets hung under my eyes. I hadn't given myself a good look-see in a long time, and tonight, the first night of Antonio's return, was probably way too late.

I was nervous.

The side of the bed I kept for him was about to be filled, but so much had changed in the meantime, I didn't know if it made sense anymore. I didn't know what he'd been through, done, experienced while he was away. He hadn't spoken about it during dinner or the card game after. He seemed reserved. Standoffish, even. I knew he loved me. I knew from the way he put his hand over mine at dinner and the way he looked at me.

"Hello," he said, leaning against the doorframe.

I jumped. "You scared me."

He crossed his arms, and the way he looked at me made me close the neck of my robe tight. "I'm sorry."

"It's all right."

I tried to get past him, but he didn't budge. His cheeks were darkened with late-day growth, and his eyelids drooped a little with exhaustion. He was still the most beautiful man I'd ever seen.

"Do you like our room?" I asked.

"I like the room."

"You can pick a different one, but this one had the nicest patio onto the orchard."

"Theresa. I—"

"I'm sorry, it's just…" I had constructed a hundred ways to talk to him when he hadn't been in front of me. He pressed his hand to my cheek, and without thinking or intending it, I leaned into him, letting his palm cup me.

"Do you want to wait?" he asked. "I won't force you."

"No, I… this… what happened? I'm not the same. I'm ninety percent. Ninety five, actually but not the same."

I'd forgotten how powerful he was in a room. How the energy surrounding him seemed to squeeze out everything else.

"You aren't the same. I could have told you that."

"I just—" I stopped myself. This was stupid. "Oh, fuck it." I stepped into the bedroom and faced him.

"I want to kiss you," he said. "I haven't thought about anything but kissing you for a year and a half. If you don't want to do anything else until you get used to me again, I accept that. But I'm kissing you before I go to sleep."

"I want you to kiss me. You have no idea how badly I want that kiss, but first I have to show you." I opened the robe. It was the hardest thing I'd ever did, not because I thought there was something wrong with me, but because I didn't know how he'd react.

The scar drew his eyes first, but then they drifted all over me, the way they had that first day, and the second, and the time I swore I felt him touching me.

"I see," he said, touching the scar on my abdomen. "Does it hurt?"

"Itches sometimes. But also, my left shoulder. I told you in the letters, but see, I can't really do this anymore." I shifted my shoulder back as far as it would go. Not very far. It had taken the brunt of the fall.

"You need me to be gentle," he said.

My anxiety fell away and was replaced by irrational joy. He knew it was just as simple as that. I only needed him to know that I felt fragile, even if I wasn't.

"I do."

He pushed the robe off my shoulders. It fell at my feet like a snowdrift. I was naked, and he was there. Right there. My body was on fire for him.

"I want my kiss," he breathed into my cheek, his lips grazing me.

"Come and get it." I barely made a sound saying it, then I thought he hadn't heard me, because he didn't do it.

"Do you know why I haven't kissed you all day?" he asked.

"No."

"If I kissed you, I was going to take you. And I didn't want a rush job in a closet."

"If you can take me like this, you can take me."

His lips were so soft on mine, his mouth so supple, his tongue gentle and sweet. He was slow, savoring every turn and twist of our mouths together. His hands landed on my cheeks and traveled down my neck, over my breasts. I groaned as a shudder went through me.

"I want you like this." He leaned forward, guiding me onto the bed until I was on my back and he was on all fours over me. "And like this." He kissed my chin and moved down to my breasts. "And this." He put his lips on my scar. "Just like this." He kissed my navel and below it. "God, I missed you."

He parted my legs so tenderly yet so firmly that I knew he was still in charge, even if he wasn't rough or demanding. He kissed between my legs, flicking his tongue over me. I hadn't been touched in so long that my back arched, and I knew if he flicked it again—

"Stop," I gasped. "Wait."

He looked up from below, his hand on my knee. "Why?"

"I want to see you. I thought about your first night home all the time. And I always imagined looking at you."

He pecked the inside of my thigh and stood at the foot of the bed. His eyes grazed over me. I thought I'd feel more self-conscious about my scar and my little crookedness. I thought I'd have to apologize for being imperfect and overcome my physical inadequacy in his sight. But I didn't feel the need for that at all. I felt warm and loved, whole and perfect before him.

He unbuttoned his shirt.

"Was it terrible in prison?" I asked.

"It wasn't too bad. Boring mostly. And lonely." He undid the cuffs, shrugged the shirt off, and tossed it over a chair.

"Is it true about the showers?"

He laughed.

"I'm serious!"

"You want to know if I took a bitch in the showers?"

Then I laughed. Of course he'd never imagined anyone would top him. Santa Claus would land on the roof first.

He got out of his pants and crawled over me. His erection pressed on my thigh, and I felt two completely separate longings. One for a deep, slow connection, and the other to be torn apart until I couldn't speak.

"Well?" I said, running my hand over his chest. "I'd forgive you as long as he was ugly."

"They're all ugly. It's in the food or something."

"Except you."

"I wasn't really there. I was always here with you." He ran his lips over mine. It wasn't a kiss but a wakening of skin.

"Capo," I said.

"Yes, Capo?" He kissed my cheek softly.

How did I go so long without feeling his breath in my ear? It was the most exciting and distracting thing ever.

I put my hands on his jaw and pushed his face to the front of mine so we were nose to nose. "I'm sorry."

"For what?"

"That you went to prison for me. I wouldn't have let you, but you did. And I'm grateful to you and mad at myself at the same time."

"I would do it again."

"I hope you don't have to. I want to give the whole thing away. I've set it up so it runs itself. Just let it go. I think I can divide it up nicely," I said.

"Come vuoi tu."

"We can talk about it."

"No talking. Just do it."

I hitched myself and wrapped my legs around him. *"Come vuoi tu."*

He laughed softly. "Your accent, my God."

"No more talking." I rotated my hips, getting myself against his length.

He shifted, getting the head of his dick against me. He pushed forward, and I pushed against him. I'd forgotten about his size, and I laughed.

"What?" he asked.

"I love you. Now, fuck me already."

He smiled, pulled my legs apart, and got on his knees. He entered me in three short bursts, each one making me gasp with pain then pleasure. Then pleasure again. And well, it was all good after that.

That night he came home, he bent over me, pressing our bodies together. I looked in his face while we made love so slowly, it was almost torture. I memorized the lines and curves of him all over again. I touched his cheeks and ran my fingers through his hair. And even when I closed my eyes because I couldn't take the rising tide of my orgasm anymore, I kept his face in my hands and let the scent of burned pine and sweet olive blossoms meld and linger until they became a unique harmony of their own, never to be separated again.

I PUT my head on his chest and listened to him breathe.

"It's a good room," he said.

"It's ours. Just ours. Let me show you the best part."

I rolled away and opened the French doors onto the orchard. The breeze caressed his hair, flicking the ends. I sat on his side of the bed, stroking his forehead. A scar so straight it looked as if it had been drawn with a ruler shot across his temple and past his hairline. I drew my finger along it. No hair grew along its length, even past his ear, where it tapered and disappeared.

"Thank you for waiting for me," he said.

"Tomorrow, I'll show you your orchard. We can walk the rows."

"How's business?"

"Breaking even."

"Good. Very good." He rolled onto his side, draping his arm over my thighs. The moonlight fell on his cheek, and the mating calls of crickets filled the air. "I'm so tired. I didn't realize until now."

"Go to sleep, Antonio. I'm here. You can sleep now."

The last word had barely left my lips before his eyes closed and his breathing turned even and slow. I didn't think I'd ever seen him sleep without a care as to how he woke up. I curled up behind him, putting my lips to the back of his neck, and I thanked God for him, for our life, for the love between us that hadn't died even when we almost did.

I was sure we would pay for our sins in either this life or the next. But maybe there was a little in us that could be saved. In this little room with a half-empty closet and a full bed, maybe salvation would come in the form of love.

FIN

WANT MORE DRAZENS?

Check out Fiona's story—

Fiona Drazen has 72 hours to prove she isn't insane, just submissive. Her therapist has to get through three days without falling for her.

DOWNLOAD FORBIDDEN

FOLLOW ME ON FACEBOOK, Twitter, Instagram, Tumblr or Pinterest.

Join my fan groups on Facebook and Goodreads.

Get on the mailing list for deals, sales, new releases and bonus content - JOIN HERE

My website is cdreiss.com

Also In Kindle Unlimited

The *New York Times* bestselling Games Duet

Adam Steinbeck will give his wife a divorce on one condition. She join him in a remote cabin for 30 days, submitting to his sexual dominance.

HIS DARK GAME

Monica insists she's not submissive. Jonathan Drazen is going to prove otherwise, but he might fall in love doing it.

COMPLETE SUBMISSION

Fiona Drazen has 72 hours to prove she isn't insane, just submissive. Her therapist has to get through three days without falling for her.

FORBIDDEN

Margie Drazen has a story and it's going to blow your mind.

THE SIN DUET

Her husband came back from the war with a Dominant streak she didn't know he had.

The complete Edge series

EDGE OF DARKNESS

Contemporary Romances

Hollywood and sports romances for the sweet and sexy romantic.

Shuttergirl | *Hardball* | *Bombshell* | *Bodyguard* | *Only Ever You*

Made in the USA
Monee, IL
03 March 2023

29076799R00381